HARLEM RENAISSANCE

FIVE NOVELS OF THE 1920s

HARLEM RENAISSANCE

FIVE NOVELS OF THE 1920s

Cane • Jean Toomer
Home to Harlem • Claude McKay
Quicksand • Nella Larsen
Plum Bun • Jessie Redmon Fauset
The Blacker the Berry • Wallace Thurman

Rafia Zafar, *editor*

THE LIBRARY OF AMERICA

Home to Harlem reprinted courtesy of the Literary Representative
for the Works of Claude McKay, Schomburg Center for Research
in Black Culture, The New York Public Library, Astor, Lenox
and Tilden Foundations. *Plum Bun* reprinted
by arrangement with Beacon Press.

The paper used in this publication meets the
minimum requirements of the American National Standard for
Information Sciences–Permanence of Paper for Printed
Library Materials, ANSI Z39.48–1984.

Distributed to the trade in the United States
by Penguin Group (USA) Inc.
and in Canada by Penguin Books Canada Ltd.

Library of Congress Control Number: 2010942023
ISBN 978-1-59853-099-5

———

First Printing
The Library of America—217

Manufactured in the United States of America

Harlem Renaissance: Five Novels of the 1920s
is published with support from

THE SHELLEY & DONALD RUBIN FOUNDATION

Contents

CANE

Jean Toomer

Oracular.
Redolent of fermenting syrup,
Purple of the dusk,
Deep-rooted cane.

To my grandmother . . .

Contents

Karintha

Her skin is like dusk on the eastern horizon,
O cant you see it, O cant you see it,
Her skin is like dusk on the eastern horizon
. . . When the sun goes down.

MEN had always wanted her, this Karintha, even as a child,
Karintha carrying beauty, perfect as dusk when the sun
goes down. Old men rode her hobby-horse upon their knees.
Young men danced with her at frolics when they should have
been dancing with their grown-up girls. God grant us youth,
secretly prayed the old men. The young fellows counted the
time to pass before she would be old enough to mate with
them. This interest of the male, who wishes to ripen a growing
thing too soon, could mean no good to her.

Karintha, at twelve, was a wild flash that told the other folks
just what it was to live. At sunset, when there was no wind, and
the pine-smoke from over by the sawmill hugged the earth,
and you couldnt see more than a few feet in front, her sudden
darting past you was a bit of vivid color, like a black bird that
flashes in light. With the other children one could hear, some
distance off, their feet flopping in the two-inch dust. Karintha's
running was a whir. It had the sound of the red dust that sometimes makes a spiral in the road. At dusk, during the hush just
after the sawmill had closed down, and before any of the
women had started their supper-getting-ready songs, her voice,
high-pitched, shrill, would put one's ears to itching. But no
one ever thought to make her stop because of it. She stoned
the cows, and beat her dog, and fought the other children. . .
Even the preacher, who caught her at mischief, told himself
that she was as innocently lovely as a November cotton flower.
Already, rumors were out about her. Homes in Georgia are
most often built on the two-room plan. In one, you cook and
eat, in the other you sleep, and there love goes on. Karintha
had seen or heard, perhaps she had felt her parents loving. One

could but imitate one's parents, for to follow them was the way of God. She played "home" with a small boy who was not afraid to do her bidding. That started the whole thing. Old men could no longer ride her hobby-horse upon their knees. But young men counted faster.

> Her skin is like dusk,
> O cant you see it,
> Her skin is like dusk,
> When the sun goes down.

Karintha is a woman. She who carries beauty, perfect as dusk when the sun goes down. She has been married many times. Old men remind her that a few years back they rode her hobby-horse upon their knees. Karintha smiles, and indulges them when she is in the mood for it. She has contempt for them. Karintha is a woman. Young men run stills to make her money. Young men go to the big cities and run on the road. Young men go away to college. They all want to bring her money. These are the young men who thought that all they had to do was to count time. But Karintha is a woman, and she has had a child. A child fell out of her womb onto a bed of pine-needles in the forest. Pine-needles are smooth and sweet. They are elastic to the feet of rabbits. . . A sawmill was nearby. Its pyramidal sawdust pile smouldered. It is a year before one completely burns. Meanwhile, the smoke curls up and hangs in odd wraiths about the trees, curls up, and spreads itself out over the valley. . . Weeks after Karintha returned home the smoke was so heavy you tasted it in water. Some one made a song:

> Smoke is on the hills. Rise up.
> Smoke is on the hills, O rise
> And take my soul to Jesus.

Karintha is a woman. Men do not know that the soul of her was a growing thing ripened too soon. They will bring their money; they will die not having found it out. . . Karintha at twenty, carrying beauty, perfect as dusk when the sun goes down. Karintha. . .

Her skin is like dusk on the eastern horizon,
O cant you see it, O cant you see it,
Her skin is like dusk on the eastern horizon
. . . When the sun goes down.

Goes down. . .

REAPERS

Black reapers with the sound of steel on stones
Are sharpening scythes. I see them place the hones
In their hip-pockets as a thing that's done,
And start their silent swinging, one by one.
Black horses drive a mower through the weeds,
And there, a field rat, startled, squealing bleeds,
His belly close to ground. I see the blade,
Blood-stained, continue cutting weeds and shade.

NOVEMBER COTTON FLOWER

Boll-weevil's coming, and the winter's cold,
Made cotton-stalks look rusty, seasons old,
And cotton, scarce as any southern snow,
Was vanishing; the branch, so pinched and slow,
Failed in its function as the autumn rake;
Drouth fighting soil had caused the soil to take
All water from the streams; dead birds were found
In wells a hundred feet below the ground—
Such was the season when the flower bloomed.
Old folks were startled, and it soon assumed
Significance. Superstition saw
Something it had never seen before:
Brown eyes that loved without a trace of fear,
Beauty so sudden for that time of year.

Becky

Becky was the white woman who had two Negro sons. She's dead; they've gone away. The pines whisper to Jesus. The Bible flaps its leaves with an aimless rustle on her mound.

BECKY had one Negro son. Who gave it to her? Damn buck nigger, said the white folks' mouths. She wouldnt tell. Common, God-forsaken, insane white shameless wench, said the white folks' mouths. Her eyes were sunken, her neck stringy, her breasts fallen, till then. Taking their words, they filled her, like a bubble rising—then she broke. Mouth setting in a twist that held her eyes, harsh, vacant, staring. . . Who gave black folks' mouths. She wouldnt tell. Poor Catholic poor-white crazy woman, said the black folks' mouths. White folks and black folks built her cabin, fed her and her growing baby, prayed secretly to God who'd put His cross upon her and cast her out.

When the first was born, the white folks said they'd have no more to do with her. And black folks, they too joined hands to cast her out. . . The pines whispered to Jesus. . The railroad boss said not to say he said it, but she could live, if she wanted to, on the narrow strip of land between the railroad and the road. John Stone, who owned the lumber and the bricks, would have shot the man who told he gave the stuff to Lonnie Deacon, who stole out there at night and built the cabin. A single room held down to earth. . . O fly away to Jesus . . . by a leaning chimney. . .

Six trains each day rumbled past and shook the ground under her cabin. Fords, and horse- and mule-drawn buggies went back and forth along the road. No one ever saw her. Train-men, and passengers who'd heard about her, threw out papers and food. Threw out little crumpled slips of paper scribbled with prayers, as they passed her eye-shaped piece of sandy ground. Ground islandized between the road and railroad track. Pushed up where a blue-sheen God with listless eyes could look at it.

Folks from the town took turns, unknown, of course, to each other, in bringing corn and meat and sweet potatoes. Even sometimes snuff. . . O thank y Jesus. . . Old David Georgia, grinding cane and boiling syrup, never went her way without some sugar sap. No one ever saw her. The boy grew up and ran around. When he was five years old as folks reckoned it, Hugh Jourdon saw him carrying a baby. "Becky has another son," was what the whole town knew. But nothing was said, for the part of man that says things to the likes of that had told itself that if there was a Becky, that Becky now was dead.

The two boys grew. Sullen and cunning. . . O pines, whisper to Jesus; tell Him to come and press sweet Jesus-lips against their lips and eyes. . . It seemed as though with those two big fellows there, there could be no room for Becky. The part that prayed wondered if perhaps she'd really died, and they had buried her. No one dared ask. They'd beat and cut a man who meant nothing at all in mentioning that they lived along the road. White or colored? No one knew, and least of all themselves. They drifted around from job to job. We, who had cast out their mother because of them, could we take them in? They answered black and white folks by shooting up two men and leaving town. "Godam the white folks; godam the niggers," they shouted as they left town. Becky? Smoke curled up from her chimney; she must be there. Trains passing shook the ground. The ground shook the leaning chimney. Nobody noticed it. A creepy feeling came over all who saw that thin wraith of smoke and felt the trembling of the ground. Folks began to take her food again. They quit it soon because they had a fear. Becky if dead might be a hant, and if alive—it took some nerve even to mention it. . . O pines, whisper to Jesus. . .

It was Sunday. Our congregation had been visiting at Pulverton, and were coming home. There was no wind. The autumn sun, the bell from Ebenezer Church, listless and heavy. Even the pines were stale, sticky, like the smell of food that makes you sick. Before we turned the bend of the road that would show us the Becky cabin, the horses stopped stock-still, pushed back their ears, and nervously whinnied. We urged, then whipped them on. Quarter of a mile away thin smoke

curled up from the leaning chimney. . . O pines, whisper to
Jesus. . . Goose-flesh came on my skin though there still was
neither chill nor wind. Eyes left their sockets for the cabin.
Ears burned and throbbed. Uncanny eclipse! fear closed my
mind. We were just about to pass. . . Pines shout to
Jesus! . . the ground trembled as a ghost train rumbled by.
The chimney fell into the cabin. Its thud was like a hollow report, ages having passed since it went off. Barlo and I were
pulled out of our seats. Dragged to the door that had swung
open. Through the dust we saw the bricks in a mound upon
the floor. Becky, if she was there, lay under them. I thought I
heard a groan. Barlo, mumbling something, threw his Bible on
the pile. (No one has ever touched it.) Somehow we got away.
My buggy was still on the road. The last thing that I remember
was whipping old Dan like fury; I remember nothing after
that—that is, until I reached town and folks crowded round to
get the true word of it.

Becky was the white woman who had two Negro sons.
She's dead; they've gone away. The pines whisper to Jesus.
The Bible flaps its leaves with an aimless rustle on her
mound.

FACE

Hair—
silver-gray,
like streams of stars,
Brows—
recurved canoes
quivered by the ripples blown by pain,
Her eyes—
mist of tears
condensing on the flesh below
And her channeled muscles
are cluster grapes of sorrow
purple in the evening sun
nearly ripe for worms.

COTTON SONG

Come, brother, come. Lets lift it;
Come now, hewit! roll away!
Shackles fall upon the Judgment Day
But lets not wait for it.

God's body's got a soul,
Bodies like to roll the soul,
Cant blame God if we dont roll,
Come, brother, roll, roll!

Cotton bales are the fleecy way
Weary sinner's bare feet trod,
Softly, softly to the throne of God,
"We aint agwine t wait until th Judgment Day!

Nassur; nassur,
Hump.
Eoho, eoho, roll away!
We aint agwine t wait until th Judgment Day!"

God's body's got a soul,
Bodies like to roll the soul,
Cant blame God if we dont roll,
Come, brother, roll, roll!

Carma

Wind is in the cane. Come along.
Cane leaves swaying, rusty with talk,
Scratching choruses above the guinea's squawk,
Wind is in the cane. Come along.

CARMA, in overalls, and strong as any man, stands behind the old brown mule, driving the wagon home. It bumps, and groans, and shakes as it crosses the railroad track. She, riding it easy. I leave the men around the stove to follow her with my eyes down the red dust road. Nigger woman driving a Georgia chariot down an old dust road. Dixie Pike is what they call it. Maybe she feels my gaze, perhaps she expects it. Anyway, she turns. The sun, which has been slanting over her shoulder, shoots primitive rockets into her mangrove-gloomed, yellow flower face. Hi! Yip! God has left the Moses-people for the nigger. "Gedap." Using reins to slap the mule, she disappears in a cloudy rumble at some indefinite point along the road.

(The sun is hammered to a band of gold. Pine-needles, like mazda, are brilliantly aglow. No rain has come to take the rustle from the falling sweet-gum leaves. Over in the forest, across the swamp, a sawmill blows its closing whistle. Smoke curls up. Marvelous web spun by the spider sawdust pile. Curls up and spreads itself pine-high above the branch, a single silver band along the eastern valley. A black boy . . . you are the most sleepiest man I ever seed, Sleeping Beauty . . . cradled on a gray mule, guided by the hollow sound of cowbells, heads for them through a rusty cotton field. From down the railroad track, the chug-chug of a gas engine announces that the repair gang is coming home. A girl in the yard of a whitewashed shack not much larger than the stack of worn ties piled before it, sings. Her voice is loud. Echoes, like rain, sweep the valley. Dusk takes the polish from the rails. Lights twinkle in scattered houses. From far away, a sad strong song. Pungent and composite, the smell of farmyards is the fragrance of the woman. She does not sing; her body is a song. She is in the forest, dancing.

Torches flare . . juju men, greegree, witch-doctors . . torches
go out. . . The Dixie Pike has grown from a goat path in
Africa.

Night.

Foxie, the bitch, slicks back her ears and barks at the rising
moon.)

> Wind is in the corn. Come along.
> Corn leaves swaying, rusty with talk,
> Scratching choruses above the guinea's squawk,
> Wind is in the corn. Come along.

Carma's tale is the crudest melodrama. Her husband's in the
gang. And its her fault he got there. Working with a contrac-
tor, he was away most of the time. She had others. No one
blames her for that. He returned one day and hung around the
town where he picked up week-old boasts and rumors. . . Bane
accused her. She denied. He couldnt see that she was becoming hysterical. He would have liked to take his fists and beat
her. Who was strong as a man. Stronger. Words, like cork-
screws, wormed to her strength. It fizzled out. Grabbing a gun
she rushed from the house and plunged across the road into a
cane-brake. . There, in quarter heaven shone the crescent
moon. . . Bane was afraid to follow till he heard the gun go
off. Then he wasted half an hour gathering the neighbor men.
They met in the road where lamp-light showed tracks dissolv-
ing in the loose earth about the cane. The search began. Moths
flickered the lamps. They put them out. Really, because she
still might be live enough to shoot. Time and space have no
meaning in a canefield. No more than the interminable
stalks. . . Some one stumbled over her. A cry went up. From
the road, one would have thought that they were cornering a
rabbit or a skunk. . . It is difficult carrying dead weight
through cane. They placed her on the sofa. A curious, nosey
somebody looked for the wound. This fussing with her clothes
aroused her. Her eyes were weak and pitiable for so strong a
woman. Slowly, then like a flash, Bane came to know that
the shot she fired, with averted head, was aimed to whistle like
a dying hornet through the cane. Twice deceived, and one

deception proved the other. His head went off. Slashed one of the men who'd helped, the man who'd stumbled over her. Now he's in the gang. Who was her husband. Should she not take others, this Carma, strong as a man, whose tale as I have told it is the crudest melodrama?

> Wind is in the cane. Come along.
> Cane leaves swaying, rusty with talk,
> Scratching choruses above the guinea's squawk,
> Wind is in the time. Come along.

SONG OF THE SON

Pour O pour that parting soul in song,
O pour it in the sawdust glow of night,
Into the velvet pine-smoke air to-night,
And let the valley carry it along.
And let the valley carry it along.

O land and soil, red soil and sweet-gum tree,
So scant of grass, so profligate of pines,
Now just before an epoch's sun declines
Thy son, in time, I have returned to thee,
Thy son, I have in time returned to thee.

In time, for though the sun is setting on
A song-lit race of slaves, it has not set;
Though late, O soil, it is not too late yet
To catch thy plaintive soul, leaving, soon gone,
Leaving, to catch thy plaintive soul soon gone.

O Negro slaves, dark purple ripened plums,
Squeezed, and bursting in the pine-wood air,
Passing, before they stripped the old tree bare
One plum was saved for me, one seed becomes

An everlasting song, a singing tree,
Caroling softly souls of slavery,
What they were, and what they are to me,
Caroling softly souls of slavery.

GEORGIA DUSK

The sky, lazily disdaining to pursue
  The setting sun, too indolent to hold
  A lengthened tournament for flashing gold,
Passively darkens for night's barbecue,

A feast of moon and men and barking hounds,
  An orgy for some genius of the South
  With blood-hot eyes and cane-lipped scented mouth,
Surprised in making folk-songs from soul sounds.

The sawmill blows its whistle, buzz-saws stop,
  And silence breaks the bud of knoll and hill,
  Soft settling pollen where plowed lands fulfill
Their early promise of a bumper crop.

Smoke from the pyramidal sawdust pile
  Curls up, blue ghosts of trees, tarrying low
  Where only chips and stumps are left to show
The solid proof of former domicile.

Meanwhile, the men, with vestiges of pomp,
  Race memories of king and caravan,
  High-priests, an ostrich, and a juju-man,
Go singing through the footpaths of the swamp

Their voices rise . . the pine trees are guitars,
  Strumming, pine-needles fall like sheets of rain . .
  Their voices rise . . the chorus of the cane
Is caroling a vesper to the stars. .

O singers, resinous and soft your songs
  Above the sacred whisper of the pines,
  Give virgin lips to cornfield concubines,
Bring dreams of Christ to dusky cane-lipped throngs.

Fern

Face flowed into her eyes. Flowed in soft cream foam and plaintive ripples, in such a way that wherever your glance may momentarily have rested, it immediately thereafter wavered in the direction of her eyes. The soft suggestion of down slightly darkened, like the shadow of a bird's wing might, the creamy brown color of her upper lip. Why, after noticing it, you sought her eyes, I cannot tell you. Her nose was aquiline, Semitic. If you have heard a Jewish cantor sing, if he has touched you and made your own sorrow seem trivial when compared with his, you will know my feeling when I follow the curves of her profile, like mobile rivers, to their common delta. They were strange eyes. In this, that they sought nothing—that is, nothing that was obvious and tangible and that one could see, and they gave the impression that nothing was to be denied. When a woman seeks, you will have observed, her eyes deny. Fern's eyes desired nothing that you could give her; there was no reason why they should withhold. Men saw her eyes and fooled themselves. Fern's eyes said to them that she was easy. When she was young, a few men took her, but got no joy from it. And then, once done, they felt bound to her (quite unlike their hit and run with other girls), felt as though it would take them a lifetime to fulfill an obligation which they could find no name for. They became attached to her, and hungered after finding the barest trace of what she might desire. As she grew up, new men who came to town felt as almost everyone did who ever saw her: that they would not be denied. Men were everlastingly bringing her their bodies. Something inside of her got tired of them, I guess, for I am certain that for the life of her she could not tell why or how she began to turn them off. A man in fever is no trifling thing to send away. They began to leave her, baffled and ashamed, yet vowing to themselves that some day they would do some fine thing for her: send her candy every week and not let her know whom it came from, watch out for her wedding-day and give her a magnificent something with no name on it, buy a house and deed it to her, rescue her from some unworthy fellow who had

20

tricked her into marrying him. As you know, men are apt to idolize or fear that which they cannot understand, especially if it be a woman. She did not deny them, yet the fact was that they were denied. A sort of superstition crept into their consciousness of her being somehow above them. Being above them meant that she was not to be approached by anyone. She became a virgin. Now a virgin in a small southern town is by no means the usual thing, if you will believe me. That the sexes were made to mate is the practice of the South. Particularly, black folks were made to mate. And it is black folks whom I have been talking about thus far. What white men thought of Fern I can arrive at only by analogy. They let her alone.

Anyone, of course, could see her, could see her eyes. If you walked up the Dixie Pike most any time of day, you'd be most like to see her resting listless-like on the railing of her porch, back propped against a post, head tilted a little forward because there was a nail in the porch post just where her head came which for some reason or other she never took the trouble to pull out. Her eyes, if it were sunset, rested idly where the sun, molten and glorious, was pouring down between the fringe of pines. Or maybe they gazed at the gray cabin on the knoll from which an evening folk-song was coming. Perhaps they followed a cow that had been turned loose to roam and feed on cotton-stalks and corn leaves. Like as not they'd settle on some vague spot above the horizon, though hardly a trace of wistfulness would come to them. If it were dusk, then they'd wait for the search-light of the evening train which you could see miles up the track before it flared across the Dixie Pike, close to her home. Wherever they looked, you'd follow them and then waver back. Like her face, the whole countryside seemed to flow into her eyes. Flowed into them with the soft listless cadence of Georgia's South. A young Negro, once, was looking at her, spellbound, from the road. A white man passing in a buggy had to flick him with his whip if he was to get by without running him over. I first saw her on her porch. I was passing with a fellow whose crusty numbness (I was from the North and suspected of being prejudiced and stuck-up) was melting as he found me warm. I asked him who she was. "That's Fern," was all that I could get from him. Some folks

already thought that I was given to nosing around; I let it go
at that, so far as questions were concerned. But at first sight of
her I felt as if I heard a Jewish cantor sing. As if his singing rose
above the unheard chorus of a folk-song. And I felt bound to
her. I too had my dreams: something I would do for her. I
have knocked about from town to town too much not to know
the futility of mere change of place. Besides, picture if you can,
this cream-colored solitary girl sitting at a tenement window
looking down on the indifferent throngs of Harlem. Better
that she listen to folk-songs at dusk in Georgia, you would say,
and so would I. Or, suppose she came up North and married.
Even a doctor or a lawyer, say, one who would be sure to get
along—that is, make money. You and I know, who have had
experience in such things, that love is not a thing like prejudice
which can be bettered by changes of town. Could men in
Washington, Chicago, or New York, more than the men of
Georgia, bring her something left vacant by the bestowal of
their bodies? You and I who know men in these cities will have
to say, they could not. See her out and out a prostitute along
State Street in Chicago. See her move into a southern town
where white men are more aggressive. See her become a white
man's concubine. . . Something I must do for her. There was
myself. What could I do for her? Talk, of course. Push back the
fringe of pines upon new horizons. To what purpose? and what
for? Her? Myself? Men in her case seem to lose their selfishness. I lost mine before I touched her. I ask you, friend (it
makes no difference if you sit in the Pullman or the Jim Crow
as the train crosses her road), what thoughts would come to
you—that is, after you'd finished with the thoughts that leap
into men's minds at the sight of a pretty woman who will not
deny them; what thoughts would come to you, had you seen
her in a quick flash, keen and intuitively, as she sat there on
her porch when your train thundered by? Would you have got
off at the next station and come back for her to take her
where? Would you have completely forgotten her as soon as
you reached Macon, Atlanta, Augusta, Pasadena, Madison,
Chicago, Boston, or New Orleans? Would you tell your wife or
sweetheart about a girl you saw? Your thoughts can help me,
and I would like to know. Something I would do for her. . .

One evening I walked up the Pike on purpose, and stopped to say hello. Some of her family were about, but they moved away to make room for me. Damn if I knew how to begin. Would you? Mr. and Miss So-and-So, people, the weather, the crops, the new preacher, the frolic, the church benefit, rabbit and possum hunting, the new soft drink they had at old Pap's store, the schedule of the trains, what kind of town Macon was, Negro's migration north, boll-weevils, syrup, the Bible—to all these things she gave a yassur or nassur, without further comment. I began to wonder if perhaps my own emotional sensibility had played one of its tricks on me. "Lets take a walk," I at last ventured. The suggestion, coming after so long an isolation, was novel enough, I guess, to surprise. But it wasnt that. Something told me that men before me had said just that as a prelude to the offering of their bodies. I tried to tell her with my eyes. I think she understood. The thing from her that made my throat catch, vanished. Its passing left her visible in a way I'd thought, but never seen. We walked down the Pike with people on all the porches gaping at us. "Doesnt it make you mad?" She meant the row of petty gossiping people. She meant the world. Through a canebrake that was ripe for cutting, the branch was reached. Under a sweet-gum tree, and where reddish leaves had dammed the creek a little, we sat down. Dusk, suggesting the almost imperceptible procession of giant trees, settled with a purple haze about the cane. I felt strange, as I always do in Georgia, particularly at dusk. I felt that things unseen to men were tangibly immediate. It would not have surprised me had I had vision. People have them in Georgia more often than you would suppose. A black woman once saw the mother of Christ and drew her in charcoal on the courthouse wall. . . When one is on the soil of one's ancestors, most anything can come to one. . . From force of habit, I suppose, I held Fern in my arms—that is, without at first noticing it. Then my mind came back to her. Her eyes, unusually weird and open, held me. Held God. He flowed in as I've seen the countryside flow in. Seen men. I must have done something—what, I dont know, in the confusion of my emotion. She sprang up. Rushed some distance from me. Fell to her knees, and began swaying, swaying. Her body was tortured with something it could not let out. Like boiling sap it flooded arms and fingers till she shook them as if they burned her. It found her throat, and spattered inarticulately in plaintive, convulsive sounds, mingled with calls to Christ Jesus. And then she sang, brokenly. A Jewish cantor singing with a broken voice. A child's voice, uncertain, or an old man's. Dusk hid her; I could hear only her song. It seemed to me as though she were pounding her head in anguish upon the ground. I rushed to her. She fainted in my arms.

There was talk about her fainting with me in the canefield. And I got one or two ugly looks from town men who'd set themselves up to protect her. In fact, there was talk of making me leave town. But they never did. They kept a watch-out for me, though. Shortly after, I came back North. From the train window I saw her as I crossed her road. Saw her on her porch, head tilted a little forward where the nail was, eyes vaguely focused on the sunset. Saw her face flow into them, the countryside and something that I call God, flowing into them. . . Nothing ever really happened. Nothing ever came to Fern, not even I. Something I would do for her. Some fine unnamed thing. . . And, friend, you? She is still living, I have reason to know. Her name, against the chance that you might happen down that way, is Fernie May Rosen.

NULLO

A spray of pine-needles,
Dipped in western horizon gold,
Fell onto a path.
Dry moulds of cow-hoofs.
In the forest.
Rabbits knew not of their falling,
Nor did the forest catch aflame.

EVENING SONG

Full moon rising on the waters of my heart,
Lakes and moon and fires,
Cloine tires,
Holding her lips apart.

Promises of slumber leaving shore to charm the moon,
Miracle made vesper-keeps,
Cloine sleeps,
And I'll be sleeping soon.

Cloine, curled like the sleepy waters where the moon-waves
    start,
Radiant, resplendently she gleams,
Cloine dreams,
Lips pressed against my heart.

Esther

I

Nine.

ESTHER'S hair falls in soft curls about her high-cheek-boned chalk-white face. Esther's hair would be beautiful if there were more gloss to it. And if her face were not prematurely serious, one would call it pretty. Her cheeks are too flat and dead for a girl of nine. Esther looks like a little white child, starched, frilled, as she walks slowly from her home towards her father's grocery store. She is about to turn in Broad from Maple Street. White and black men loafing on the corner hold no interest for her. Then a strange thing happens. A clean-muscled, magnificent, black-skinned Negro, whom she had heard her father mention as King Barlo, suddenly drops to his knees on a spot called the Spittoon. White men, unaware of him, continue squirting tobacco juice in his direction. The saffron fluid splashes on his face. His smooth black face begins to glisten and to shine. Soon, people notice him, and gather round. His eyes are rapturous upon the heavens. Lips and nostrils quiver. Barlo is in a religious trance. Town folks know it. They are not startled. They are not afraid. They gather round. Some beg boxes from the grocery stores. From old McGregor's notion shop. A coffin-case is pressed into use. Folks line the curb-stones. Business men close shop. And Banker Warply parks his car close by. Silently, all await the prophet's voice. The sheriff, a great florid fellow whose leggings never meet around his bulging calves, swears in three deputies. "Wall, y cant never tell what a nigger like King Barlo might be up t." Soda bottles, five fingers full of shine, are passed to those who want them. A couple of stray dogs start a fight. Old Goodlow's cow comes flopping up the street. Barlo, still as an Indian fakir, has not moved. The town bell strikes six. The sun slips in behind a heavy mass of horizon cloud. The crowd is hushed and expectant. Barlo's under jaw relaxes, and his lips begin to move.

"Jesus has been awhisperin strange words deep down, O way down deep, deep in my ears."

Hums of awe and of excitement.

"He called me to His side an said, 'Git down on your knees beside me, son, Ise gwine t whisper in your ears.'"

An old sister cries, "Ah, Lord."

"'Ise agwine t whisper in your ears,' he said, an I replied, 'Thy will be done on earth as it is in heaven.'"

"Ah, Lord. Amen. Amen."

"An Lord Jesus whispered strange good words deep down, O way down deep, deep in my ears. An He said, 'Tell em till you feel your throat on fire.' I saw a vision. I saw a man arise, an he was big an black an powerful—"

Some one yells, "Preach it, preacher, preach it!"

"—but his head was caught up in th clouds. An while he was agazin at th heavens, heart filled up with th Lord, some little white-ant biddies came an tied his feet to chains. They led him t th coast, they led him t th sea, they led him across th ocean an they didnt set him free. The old coast didnt miss him, an th new coast wasnt free, he left the old-coast brothers, t give birth t you an me. O Lord, great God Almighty, t give birth t you an me."

Barlo pauses. Old gray mothers are in tears. Fragments of melodies are being hummed. White folks are touched and curiously awed. Off to themselves, white and black preachers confer as to how best to rid themselves of the vagrant, usurping fellow. Barlo looks as though he is struggling to continue. People are hushed. One can hear weevils work. Dusk is falling rapidly, and the customary store lights fail to throw their feeble glow across the gray dust and flagging of the Georgia town. Barlo rises to his full height. He is immense. To the people he assumes the outlines of his visioned African. In a mighty voice he bellows:

"Brothers an sisters, turn your faces t th sweet face of the Lord, an fill your hearts with glory. Open your eyes an see th dawnin of th mornin light. Open your ears—"

Years afterwards Esther was told that at that very moment a great, heavy, rumbling voice actually was heard. That hosts of angels and of demons paraded up and down the streets all night. That King Barlo rode out of town astride a pitch-black bull that had a glowing gold ring in its nose. And that old

Limp Underwood, who hated niggers, woke up next morning to find that he held a black man in his arms. This much is certain: an inspired Negress, of wide reputation for being sanctified, drew a portrait of a black madonna on the court-house wall. And King Barlo left town. He left his image indelibly upon the mind of Esther. He became the starting point of the only living patterns that her mind was to know.

2

Sixteen.

Esther begins to dream. The low evening sun sets the windows of McGregor's notion shop aflame. Esther makes believe that they really are aflame. The town fire department rushes madly down the road. It ruthlessly shoves black and white idlers to one side. It whoops. It clangs. It rescues from the second-story window a dimpled infant which she claims for her own. How had she come by it? She thinks of it immaculately. It is a sin to think of it immaculately. She must dream no more. She must repent her sin. Another dream comes. There is no fire department. There are no heroic men. The fire starts. The loafers on the corner form a circle, chew their tobacco faster, and squirt juice just as fast as they can chew. Gallons on top of gallons they squirt upon the flames. The air reeks with the stench of scorched tobacco juice. Women, fat chunky Negro women, lean scrawny white women, pull their skirts up above their heads and display the most ludicrous underclothes. The women scoot in all directions from the danger zone. She alone is left to take the baby in her arms. But what a baby! Black, singed, woolly, tobacco-juice baby—ugly as sin. Once held to her breast, miraculous thing: its breath is sweet and its lips can nibble. She loves it frantically. Her joy in it changes the town folks' jeers to harmless jealousy, and she is left alone.

Twenty-two.

Esther's schooling is over. She works behind the counter of her father's grocery store. "To keep the money in the family," so he said. She is learning to make distinctions between the business and the social worlds. "Good business comes from remembering that the white folks dont divide the niggers, Esther. Be just as black as any man who has a silver dollar." Esther listlessly forgets that she is near white, and that her father is the richest colored man in town. Black folk who drift in to buy lard and snuff and flour of her, call her a sweet-natured, accommodating girl. She learns their names. She forgets them. She thinks about men. "I dont appeal to them. I wonder why." She recalls an affair she had with a little fair boy while still in school. It had ended in her shame when he as much as told her that for sweetness he preferred a lollipop. She remembers the salesman from the North who wanted to take her to the movies that first night he was in town. She refused, of course. And he never came back, having found out who she was. She thinks of Barlo. Barlo's image gives her a slightly stale thrill. She spices it by telling herself his glories. Black. Magnetically so. Best cotton picker in the county, in the state, in the whole world for that matter. Best man with his fists, best man with dice, with a razor. Promoter of church benefits. Of colored fairs. Vagrant preacher. Lover of all the women for miles and miles around. Esther decides that she loves him. And with a vague sense of life slipping by, she resolves that she will tell him so, whatever people say, the next time he comes to town. After the making of this resolution which becomes a sort of wedding cake for her to tuck beneath her pillow and go to sleep upon, she sees nothing of Barlo for five years. Her hair thins. It looks like the dull silk on puny corn ears. Her face pales until it is the color of the gray dust that dances with dead cotton leaves. .

3

Esther is twenty-seven.

Esther sells lard and snuff and flour to vague black faces that drift in her store to ask for them. Her eyes hardly see the people to whom she gives change. Her body is lean and beaten. She rests listlessly against the counter, too weary to sit down. From the street some one shouts, "King Barlo has come back to town." He passes her window, driving a large new car. Cut-out open. He veers to the curb, and steps out. Barlo has made money on cotton during the war. He is as rich as anyone. Esther suddenly is animate. She goes to her door. She sees him at a distance, the center of a group of credulous men. She hears the deep-bass rumble of his talk. The sun swings low. McGregor's windows are aflame again. Pale flame. A sharply dressed white girl passes by. For a moment Esther wishes that she might be like her. Not white; she has no need for being that. But sharp, sporty, with get-up about her. Barlo is connected with that wish. She mustnt wish. Wishes only make you restless. Emptiness is a thing that grows by being moved. "I'll not think. Not wish. Just set my mind against it." Then the thought comes to her that those purposeless, easy-going men will possess him, if she doesnt. Purpose is not dead in her, now that she comes to think of it. That loose women will have their arms around him at Nat Bowle's place to-night. As if her veins are full of fired sun-bleached southern shanties, a swift heat sweeps them. Dead dreams, and a forgotten resolution are carried upward by the flames. Pale flames. "They shant have him. Oh, they shall not. Not if it kills me they shant have him." Jerky, aflutter, she closes the store and starts home. Folks lazing on store window-sills wonder what on earth can be the matter with Jim Crane's gal, as she passes them. "Come to remember, she always was a little off, a little crazy, I reckon." Esther seeks her own room, and locks the door. Her mind is a pink mesh-bag filled with baby toes.

Using the noise of the town clock striking twelve to cover the creaks of her departure, Esther slips into the quiet road. The town, her parents, most everyone is sound asleep. This fact is a stable thing that comforts her. After sundown a chill wind came up from the west. It is still blowing, but to her it is a steady, settled thing like the cold. She wants her mind to be like that. Solid, contained, and blank as a sheet of darkened ice. She will not permit herself to notice the peculiar phosphorescent glitter of the sweet-gum leaves. Their movement would excite her. Exciting too, the recession of the dull familiar homes she knows so well. She doesnt know them at all. She closes her eyes, and holds them tightly. Wont do. Her being aware that they are closed recalls her purpose. She does not want to think of it. She opens them. She turns now into the deserted business street. The corrugated iron canopies and mule- and horse-gnawed hitching posts bring her a strange composure. Ghosts of the commonplaces of her daily life take stride with her and become her companions. And the echoes of her heels upon the flagging are rhythmically monotonous and soothing. Crossing the street at the corner of McGregor's notion shop, she thinks that the windows are a dull flame. Only a fancy. She walks faster. Then runs. A turn into a side street brings her abruptly to Nat Bowle's place. The house is squat and dark. It is always dark. Barlo is within. Quietly she opens the outside door and steps in. She passes through a small room. Pauses before a flight of stairs down which people's voices, muffled, come. The air is heavy with fresh tobacco smoke. It makes her sick. She wants to turn back. She goes up the steps. As if she were mounting to some great height, her head spins She is violently dizzy. Blackness rushes to her eyes. And then she finds that she is in a large room. Barlo is before her.

"Well, I'm sholy damned—skuse me, but what, what brought you here, lil milk-white gal?"

"You." Her voice sounds like a frightened child's that calls homeward from some point miles away.

"Me?"

"Yes, you Barlo."

"This aint th place fer y. This aint th place fer y."

"I know. I know. But I've come for you."

"For me for what?"

She manages to look deep and straight into his eyes. He is slow at understanding. Guffaws and giggles break out from all around the room. A coarse woman's voice remarks, "So thats how th dictie niggers does it." Laughs. "Mus give em credit fo their gall."

Esther doesnt hear. Barlo does. His faculties are jogged. She sees a smile, ugly and repulsive to her, working upward through thick licker fumes. Barlo seems hideous. The thought comes suddenly, that conception with a drunken man must be a mighty sin. She draws away, frozen. Like a somnambulist she wheels around and walks stiffly to the stairs. Down them. Jeers and hoots pelter bluntly upon her back. She steps out. There is no air, no street, and the town has completely disappeared.

CONVERSION

African Guardian of Souls,
Drunk with rum,
Feasting on a strange cassava,
Yielding to new words and a weak palabra
Of a white-faced sardonic god—
Grins, cries
Amen,
Shouts hosanna.

PORTRAIT IN GEORGIA

Hair—braided chestnut,
    coiled like a lyncher's rope,
Eyes—fagots,
Lips—old scars, or the first red blisters,
Breath—the last sweet scent of cane,
And her slim body, white as the ash
    of black flesh after flame.

Blood-Burning Moon

U P from the skeleton stone walls, up from the rotting floor boards and the solid hand-hewn beams of oak of the pre-war cotton factory, dusk came. Up from the dusk the full moon came. Glowing like a fired pine-knot, it illumined the great door and soft showered the Negro shanties aligned along the single street of factory town. The full moon in the great door was an omen. Negro women improvised songs against its spell.

Louisa sang as she came over the crest of the hill from the white folks' kitchen. Her skin was the color of oak leaves on young trees in fall. Her breasts, firm and up-pointed like ripe acorns. And her singing had the low murmur of winds in fig trees. Bob Stone, younger son of the people she worked for, loved her. By the way the world reckons things, he had won her. By measure of that warm glow which came into her mind at the thought of him, he had won her. Tom Burwell, whom the whole town called Big Boy, also loved her. But working in the fields all day, and far away from her, gave him no chance to show it. Though often enough of evenings he had tried to. Somehow, he never got along. Strong as he was with hands upon the ax or plow, he found it difficult to hold her. Or so he thought. But the fact was that he held her to factory town more firmly than he thought for. His black balanced, and pulled against, the white of Stone, when she thought of them. And her mind was vaguely upon them as she came over the crest of the hill, coming from the white folks' kitchen. As she sang softly at the evil face of the full moon.

A strange stir was in her. Indolently, she tried to fix upon Bob or Tom as the cause of it. To meet Bob in the canebrake, as she was going to do an hour or so later, was nothing new. And Tom's proposal which she felt on its way to her could be indefinitely put off. Separately, there was no unusual significance to either one. But for some reason, they jumbled when her eyes gazed vacantly at the rising moon. And from the jumble came the stir that was strangely within her. Her lips trembled. The slow rhythm of her song grew agitant and restless. Rusty black and tan spotted hounds, lying in the dark corners of porches or prowling around back yards, put their noses in the air and caught its tremor. They began plaintively to yelp and howl. Chickens woke up and cackled. Intermittently, all over the countryside dogs barked and roosters crowed as if heralding a weird dawn or some ungodly awakening. The women sang lustily. Their songs were cotton-wads to stop their ears. Louisa came down into factory town and sank wearily upon the step before her home. The moon was rising towards a thick cloud-bank which soon would hide it.

> Red nigger moon. Sinner!
> Blood-burning moon. Sinner!
> Come out that fact'ry door.

2

Up from the deep dusk of a cleared spot on the edge of the forest a mellow glow arose and spread fan-wise into the low-hanging heavens. And all around the air was heavy with the scent of boiling cane. A large pile of cane-stalks lay like ribboned shadows upon the ground. A mule, harnessed to a pole, trudged lazily round and round the pivot of the grinder. Beneath a swaying oil lamp, a Negro alternately whipped out at the mule, and fed cane-stalks to the grinder. A fat boy waddled pails of fresh ground juice between the grinder and the boiling stove. Steam came from the copper boiling pan. The scent of cane came from the copper pan and drenched the forest and the hill that sloped to factory town, beneath its fragrance. It drenched the men in circle seated around the stove. Some of them chewed at the white pulp of stalks, but there was no need for them to, if all they wanted was to taste the cane. One tasted it in factory town. And from factory town one could see the soft haze thrown by the glowing stove upon the low-hanging heavens.

Old David Georgia stirred the thickening syrup with a long

ladle, and ever so often drew it off. Old David Georgia tended
his stove and told tales about the white folks, about moon-
shining and cotton picking, and about sweet nigger gals, to
the men who sat there about his stove to listen to him. Tom
Burwell chewed cane-stalk and laughed with the others till
someone mentioned Louisa. Till some one said something
about Louisa and Bob Stone, about the silk stockings she
must have gotten from him. Blood ran up Tom's neck hotter
than the glow that flooded from the stove. He sprang up.
Glared at the men and said, "She's my gal." Will Manning
laughed. Tom strode over to him. Yanked him up and knocked
him to the ground. Several of Manning's friends got up to
fight for him. Tom whipped out a long knife and would have
cut them to shreds if they hadnt ducked into the woods. Tom
had had enough. He nodded to Old David Georgia and
swung down the path to factory town. Just then, the dogs
started barking and the roosters began to crow. Tom felt
funny. Away from the fight, away from the stove, chill got to
him. He shivered. He shuddered when he saw the full moon
rising towards the cloud-bank. He who didnt give a godam
for the fears of old women. He forced his mind to fasten on
Louisa. Bob Stone. Better not be. He turned into the street
and saw Louisa sitting before her home. He went towards her,
ambling, touched the brim of a marvelously shaped, spotted,
felt hat, said he wanted to say something to her, and then
found that he didnt know what he had to say, or if he did, that
he couldnt say it. He shoved his big fists in his overalls,
grinned, and started to move off.

"Youall want me, Tom?"

"Thats what us wants, sho, Louisa."

"Well, here I am—"

"An here I is, but that aint ahelpin none, all th same."

"You wanted to say something? . ."

"I did that, sho. But words is like th spots on dice: no matter
how y fumbles em, there's times when they jes wont come. I
dunno why. Seems like th love I feels fo yo done stole m
tongue. I got it now. Whee! Louisa, honey, I oughtnt tell y, I
feel I oughtnt cause yo is young an goes t church an I has had
other gals, but Louisa I sho do love y. Lil gal, Ise watched y
from them first days when youall sat right here befo yo door

befo th well an sang sometimes in a way that like t broke m heart. Ise carried y with me into the fields, day after day, an after that, an I sho can plow when yo is there, an I can pick cotton. Yassur! Come near beatin Barlo yesterday. I sho did. Yassur! An next year if ole Stone'll trust me, I'll have a farm. My own. My bales will buy yo what y gets from white folks now. Silk stockings an purple dresses—course I dont believe what some folks been whisperin as t how y gets them things now. White folks always did do for niggers what they likes. An they jes cant help alikin yo, Louisa. Bob Stone likes y. Course he does. But not th way folks is awhisperin. Does he, hon?"

"I dont know what you mean, Tom."

"Course y dont. Ise already cut two niggers. Had t hon, t tell em so. Niggers always tryin t make somethin out a nothin. An then besides, white folks aint up t them tricks so much nowadays. Godam better not be. Leastawise not with yo. Cause I wouldnt stand f it. Nassur."

"What would you do, Tom?"

"Cut him jes like I cut a nigger."

"No, Tom—"

"I said I would an there aint no mo to it. But that aint th talk f now. Sing, honey Louisa, an while I'm listenin t y I'll be makin love."

Tom took her hand in his. Against the tough thickness of his own, hers felt soft and small. His huge body slipped down to the step beside her. The full moon sank upward into the deep purple of the cloud-bank. An old woman brought a lighted lamp and hung it on the common well whose bulky shadow squatted in the middle of the road, opposite Tom and Louisa. The old woman lifted the well-lid, took hold the chain, and began drawing up the heavy bucket. As she did so, she sang. Figures shifted, restless-like, between lamp and window in the front rooms of the shanties. Shadows of the figures fought each other on the gray dust of the road. Figures raised the windows and joined the old woman in song. Louisa and Tom, the whole street, singing:

> Red nigger moon. Sinner!
> Blood-burning moon. Sinner!
> Come out that fact'ry door.

3

Bob Stone sauntered from his veranda out into the gloom of fir trees and magnolias. The clear white of his skin paled, and the flush of his cheeks turned purple. As if to balance this outer change, his mind became consciously a white man's. He passed the house with its huge open hearth which, in the days of slavery, was the plantation cookery. He saw Louisa bent over that hearth. He went in as a master should and took her. Direct, honest, bold. None of this sneaking that he had to go through now. The contrast was repulsive to him. His family had lost ground. Hell no, his family still owned the niggers, practically. Damned if they did, or he wouldnt have to duck around so. What would they think if they knew? His mother? His sister? He shouldnt mention them, shouldnt think of them in this connection. There in the dusk he blushed at doing so. Fellows about town were all right, but how about his friends up North? He could see them incredible, repulsed. They didnt know. The thought first made him laugh. Then, with their eyes still upon him, he began to feel embarrassed. He felt the need of explaining things to them. Explain hell. They wouldnt understand, and moreover, who ever heard of a Southerner getting on his knees to any Yankee, or anyone. No sir. He was going to see Louisa to-night, and love her. She was lovely—in her way. Nigger way. What way was that? Damned if he knew. Must know. He'd known her long enough to know. Was there something about niggers that you couldnt know? Listening to them at church didnt tell you anything. Looking at them didnt tell you anything. Talking to them didnt tell you anything—unless it was gossip, unless they wanted to talk. Of course, about farming, and licker, and craps—but those werent nigger. Nigger was something more. How much more? Something to be afraid of, more? Hell no. Who ever heard of being afraid of a nigger? Tom Burwell. Cartwell had told him that Tom went with Louisa after she reached home. No sir. No nigger had ever been with his girl. He'd like to see one try. Some position for him to be in. Him, Bob Stone, of the old Stone family, in a scrap with a nigger over a nigger girl. In the good old days. . . Ha! Those were the days. His family had lost ground. Not so much, though. Enough for him to have to cut through old Lemon's canefield by way of the woods, that he might meet her. She was worth it. Beautiful nigger gal. Why nigger? Why not, just gal? No, it was because she was nigger that he went to her. Sweet. . . The scent of boiling cane came to him. Then he saw the rich glow of the stove. He heard the voices of the men circled around it. He was about to skirt the clearing when he heard his own name mentioned. He stopped. Quivering. Leaning against a tree, he listened.

"Bad nigger. Yassur, he sho is one bad nigger when he gets started."

"Tom Burwell's been on th gang three times fo cuttin men."

"What y think he's agwine t do t Bob Stone?"

"Dunno yet. He aint found out. When he does— Baby!"

"Aint no tellin."

"Young Stone aint no quitter an I ken tell y that. Blood of th old uns in his veins."

"Thats right. He'll scrap, sho."

"Be gettin too hot f niggers round this away."

"Shut up, nigger. Y dont know what y talkin bout."

Bob Stone's ears burned as though he had been holding them over the stove. Sizzling heat welled up within him. His feet felt as if they rested on red-hot coals. They stung him to quick movement. He circled the fringe of the glowing. Not a twig cracked beneath his feet. He reached the path that led to factory town. Plunged furiously down it. Halfway along, a blindness within veered aside. He crashed into the bordering canebrake. Cane leaves cut his face and lips. He tasted blood. He threw himself down and dug his fingers in the ground. The earth was cool. Cane-roots took the fever from his hands. After a long while, or so it seemed to him, the thought came to him that it must be time to see Louisa. He got to his feet and walked calmly to their meeting place. No Louisa. Tom Burwell had her. Veins in his forehead bulged and distended. Saliva moistened the dried blood on his lips. He bit down on his lips. He tasted blood. Not his own blood; Tom Burwell's blood. Bob drove through the cane and out again upon the road. A hound swung down the path before him towards factory town.

Bob couldnt see it. The dog loped aside to let him pass. Bob's blind rushing made him stumble over it. He fell with a thud that dazed him. The hound yelped. Answering yelps came from all over the countryside. Chickens cackled. Roosters crowed, heralding the bloodshot eyes of southern awakening. Singers in the town were silenced. They shut their windows down. Palpitant between the rooster crows, a chill hush settled upon the huddled forms of Tom and Louisa. A figure rushed from the shadow and stood before them. Tom popped to his feet.

"Whats y want?"

"I'm Bob Stone."

"Yassur—an I'm Tom Burwell. Whats y want?"

Bob lunged at him. Tom side-stepped, caught him by the shoulder, and flung him to the ground. Straddled him.

"Let me up."

"Yassur—but watch yo doins, Bob Stone."

A few dark figures, drawn by the sound of scuffle, stood about them. Bob sprang to his feet.

"Fight like a man, Tom Burwell, an I'll lick y."

Again he lunged. Tom side-stepped and flung him to the ground. Straddled him.

"Get off me, you godam nigger you."

"Yo sho has started somethin now. Get up."

Tom yanked him up and began hammering at him. Each blow sounded as if it smashed into a precious, irreplaceable soft something. Beneath them, Bob staggered back. He reached in his pocket and whipped out a knife.

"Thats my game, sho."

Blue flash, a steel blade slashed across Bob Stone's throat. He had a sweetish sick feeling. Blood began to flow. Then he felt a sharp twitch of pain. He let his knife drop. He slapped one hand against his neck. He pressed the other on top of his head as if to hold it down. He groaned. He turned, and staggered towards the crest of the hill in the direction of white town. Negroes who had seen the fight slunk into their homes and blew the lamps out. Louisa, dazed, hysterical, refused to go indoors. She slipped, crumbled, her body loosely propped against the woodwork of the well. Tom Burwell leaned against it. He seemed rooted there.

Bob reached Broad Street. White men rushed up to him. He collapsed in their arms.

"Tom Burwell. . ."

White men like ants upon a forage rushed about. Except for the taut hum of their moving, all was silent. Shotguns, revolvers, rope, kerosene, torches. Two high-powered cars with glaring search-lights. They came together. The taut hum rose to a low roar. Then nothing could be heard but the flop of their feet in the thick dust of the road. The moving body of their silence preceded them over the crest of the hill into factory town. It flattened the Negroes beneath it. It rolled to the wall of the factory, where it stopped. Tom knew that they were coming. He couldnt move. And then he saw the search-lights of the two cars glaring down on him. A quick shock went through him. He stiffened. He started to run. A yell went up from the mob. Tom wheeled about and faced them. They poured down on him. They swarmed. A large man with dead-white face and flabby cheeks came to him and almost jabbed a gun-barrel through his guts.

"Hands behind y, nigger."

Tom's wrist were bound. The big man shoved him to the well. Burn him over it, and when the woodwork caved in, his body would drop to the bottom. Two deaths for a godam nigger. Louisa was driven back. The mob pushed in. Its pressure, its momentum was too great. Drag him to the factory. Wood and stakes already there. Tom moved in the direction indicated. But they had to drag him. They reached the great door. Too many to get in there. The mob divided and flowed around the walls to either side. The big man shoved him through the door. The mob pressed in from the sides. Taut humming. No words. A stake was sunk into the ground. Rotting floor boards piled around it. Kerosene poured on the rotting floor boards. Tom bound to the stake. His breast was bare. Nails scratches let little lines of blood trickle down and mat into the hair. His face, his eyes were set and stony. Except for irregular breathing, one would have thought him already dead. Torches were flung onto the pile. A great flare muffled in black smoke shot upward. The mob yelled. The mob was silent. Now Tom could be seen within the flames. Only his head, erect, lean, like a blackened stone. Stench of burning flesh soaked the air. Tom's eyes popped. His head settled downward. The mob yelled. Its yell echoed against the skeleton stone walls and sounded like a hundred yells. Like a hundred mobs yelling. Its yell thudded against the thick front wall and fell back. Ghost of a yell slipped through the flames and out the great door of the factory. It fluttered like a dying thing down the single street of factory town. Louisa, upon the step before her home, did not hear it, but her eyes opened slowly. They saw the full moon glowing in the great door. The full moon, an evil thing, an omen, soft showering the homes of folks she knew. Where were they, these people? She'd sing, and perhaps they'd come out and join her. Perhaps Tom Burwell would come. At any rate, the full moon in the great door was an omen which she must sing to:

> Red nigger moon. Sinner!
> Blood-burning moon. Sinner!
> Come out that fact'ry door.

Seventh Street

Money burns the pocket, pocket hurts,
Bootleggers in silken shirts,
Ballooned, zooming Cadillacs,
Whizzing, whizzing down the street-car tracks.

S EVENTH STREET is a bastard of Prohibition and the War. A crude-boned, soft-skinned wedge of nigger life breathing its loafer air, jazz songs and love, thrusting unconscious rhythms, black reddish blood into the white and whitewashed wood of Washington. Stale soggy wood of Washington. Wedges rust in soggy wood. . . Split it! In two! Again! Shred it! . . the sun. Wedges are brilliant in the sun; ribbons of wet wood dry and blow away. Black reddish blood. Pouring for crude-boned soft-skinned life, who set you flowing? Blood suckers of the War would spin in a frenzy of dizziness if they drank your blood. Prohibition would put a stop to it. Who set you flowing? White and whitewash disappear in blood. Who set you flowing? Flowing down the smooth asphalt of Seventh Street, in shanties, brick office buildings, theaters, drug stores, restaurants, and cabarets? Eddying on the corners? Swirling like a blood-red smoke up where the buzzards fly in heaven? God would not dare to suck black red blood. A Nigger God! He would duck his head in shame and call for the Judgment Day. Who set you flowing?

Money burns the pocket, pocket hurts,
Bootleggers in silken shirts,
Ballooned, zooming Cadillacs,
Whizzing, whizzing down the street-car tracks.

Rhobert

RHOBERT wears a house, like a monstrous diver's helmet, on his head. His legs are banty-bowed and shaky because as a child he had rickets. He is way down. Rods of the house like antennæ of a dead thing, stuffed, prop up in the air. He is way down. He is sinking. His house is a dead thing that weights him down. He is sinking as a diver would sink in mud should the water be drawn off. Life is a murky, wiggling, microscopic water that compresses him. Compresses his helmet and would crush it the minute that he pulled his head out. He has to keep it in. Life is water that is being drawn off.

> Brother, life is water that is being drawn off.
> Brother, life is water that is being drawn off.

The dead house is stuffed. The stuffing is alive. It is sinful to draw one's head out of live stuffing in a dead house. The propped-up antennæ would cave in and the stuffing be strewn . . shredded life-pulp . . in the water. It is sinful to have one's own head crushed. Rhobert is an upright man whose legs are banty-bowed and shaky because as a child he had rickets. The earth is round. Heaven is a sphere that surrounds it. Sink where you will. God is a Red Cross man with a dredge and a respiration-pump who's waiting for you at the opposite periphery. God built the house. He blew His breath into its stuffing. It is good to to die obeying Him who can do these things.

A futile something like the dead house wraps the live stuffing of the question: how long before the water will be drawn off? Rhobert does not care. Like most men who wear monstrous helmets, the pressure it exerts is enough to convince him of its practical infinity. And he cares not two straws as to whether or not he will ever see his wife and children again. Many a time he's seen them drown in his dreams and has kicked about joyously in the mud for days after. One thing about him goes straight to the heart. He has an Adam's-apple which strains sometimes as if he were painfully gulping great globules of air . . air floating shredded life-pulp. It is a sad

48

thing to see a banty-bowed, shaky, ricket-legged man straining the raw insides of his throat against smooth air. Holding furtive thoughts about the glory of pulp-heads strewn in water. . He is way down. Down. Mud, coming to his banty knees, almost hides them. Soon people will be looking at him and calling him a strong man. No doubt he is for one who has had rickets. Lets give it to him. Lets call him great when the water shall have been all drawn off. Lets build a monument and set it in the ooze where he goes down. A monument of hewn oak, carved in nigger-heads. Lets open our throats, brother, and sing "Deep River" when he goes down.

> Brother, Rhobert is sinking.
> Lets open our throats, brother,
> Lets sing Deep River when he goes down.

Avey

For a long while she was nothing more to me than one of those skirted beings whom boys at a certain age disdain to play with. Just how I came to love her, timidly, and with secret blushes, I do not know. But that I did was brought home to me one night, the first night that Ned wore his long pants. Us fellers were seated on the curb before an apartment house where she had gone in. The young trees had not outgrown their boxes then. V Street was lined with them. When our legs grew cramped and stiff from the cold of the stone, we'd stand around a box and whittle it. I like to think now that there was a hidden purpose in the way we hacked them with our knives. I like to feel that something deep in me responded to the trees, the young trees that whinnied like colts impatient to be let free. . . On the particular night I have in mind, we were waiting for the top-floor light to go out. We wanted to see Avey leave the flat. This night she stayed longer than usual and gave us a chance to complete the plans of how we were going to stone and beat that feller on the top floor out of town. Ned especially had it in for him. He was about to throw a brick up at the window when at last the room went dark. Some minutes passed. Then Avey, as unconcerned as if she had been paying an old-maid aunt a visit, came out. I don't remember what she had on, and all that sort of thing. But I do know that I turned hot as bare pavements in the summertime at Ned's boast: "Hell, bet I could get her too if you little niggers weren't always spying and crabbing everything." I didnt say a word to him. It wasnt my way then. I just stood there like the others, and something like a fuse burned up inside of me. She never noticed us, but swung along lazy and easy as anything. We sauntered to the corner and watched her till her door banged to. Ned repeated what he'd said. I didnt seem to care. Sitting around old Mush-Head's bread box, the discussion began. "Hang if I can see how she gets away with it," Doc started. Ned knew, of course. There was nothing he didnt know when it came to women. He dilated on the emotional needs of girls. Said they werent much different from men in that respect. And

concluded with the solemn avowal: "It does em good." None
of us liked Ned much. We all talked dirt; but it was the way he
said it. And then too, a couple of the fellers had sisters and had
caught Ned playing with them. But there was no disputing the
superiority of his smutty wisdom. Bubs Sanborn, whose mother
was friendly with Avey's, had overheard the old ladies talking.
"Avey's mother's ont her," he said. We thought that only natural and began to guess at what would happen. Some one said
she'd marry that feller on the top floor. Ned called that a lie
because Avey was going to marry nobody but him. We had
our doubts about that, but we did agree that she'd soon leave
school and marry some one. The gang broke up, and I went
home, picturing myself as married.

Nothing I did seemed able to change Avey's indifference to
me. I played basket-ball, and when I'd make a long clean shot
she'd clap with the others, louder than they, I thought. I'd
meet her on the street, and there'd be no difference in the way
she said hello. She never took the trouble to call me by my
name. On the days for drill, I'd let my voice down a tone and
call for a complicated maneuver when I saw her coming. She'd
smile appreciation, but it was an impersonal smile, never for
me. It was on a summer excursion down to Riverview that she
first seemed to take me into account. The day had been spent
riding merry-go-rounds, scenic-railways, and shoot-the-chutes.
We had been in swimming and we had danced. I was a crack
swimmer then. She didnt know how. I held her up and showed
her how to kick her legs and draw her arms. Of course she
didnt learn in one day, but she thanked me for bothering with
her. I was also somewhat of a dancer. And I had already noticed
that love can start on a dance floor. We danced. But though I
held her tightly in my arms, she was way away. That college
feller who lived on the top floor was somewhere making money
for the next year. I imagined that she was thinking, wishing for
him. Ned was along. He treated her until his money gave out.
She went with another feller. Ned got sore. One by one the
boys' money gave out. She left them. And they got sore. Every
one of them but me got sore. This is the reason, I guess, why I
had her to myself on the top deck of the *Jane Mosely* that night
as we puffed up the Potomac, coming home. The moon was

brilliant. The air was sweet like clover. And every now and then, a salt tang, a stale drift of sea-weed. It was not my mind's fault if it went romancing. I should have taken her in my arms the minute we were stowed in that old lifeboat. I dallied, dreaming. She took me in hers. And I could feel by the touch of it that it wasnt a man-to-woman love. It made me restless. I felt chagrined. I didnt know what it was, but I did know that I couldnt handle it. She ran her fingers through my hair and kissed my forehead. I itched to break through her tenderness to passion. I wanted her to take me in her arms as I knew she had that college feller. I wanted her to love me passionately as she did him. I gave her one burning kiss. Then she laid me in her lap as if I were a child. Helpless. I got sore when she started to hum a lullaby. She wouldnt let me go. I talked. I knew damned well that I could beat her at that. Her eyes were soft and misty, the curves of her lips were wistful, and her smile seemed indulgent of the irrelevance of my remarks. I gave up last and let her love me, silently, in her own way. The moon was brilliant. The air was sweet like clover, and every now and then, a salt tang, a stale drift of sea-weed. . .

The next time I came close to her was the following summer at Harpers Ferry. We were sitting on a flat projecting rock they give the name of Lover's Leap. Some one is supposed to have jumped off it. The river is about six hundred feet beneath. A railroad track runs up the valley and curves out of sight where part of the mountain rock had to be blasted away to make room for it. The engines of this valley have a whistle, the echoes of which sound like iterated gasps and sobs. I always think of them as crude music from the soul of Avey. We sat there holding hands. Our palms were soft and warm against each other. Our fingers were not tight. She would not let them be. She would not let me twist them. I wanted to talk. To explain what I meant to her. Avey was as silent as those great trees whose tops we looked down upon. She has always been like that. At least, to me. I had the notion that if I really wanted to, I could do with her just what I pleased. Like one can strip a tree. I did kiss her. I even let my hands cup her breasts. When I was through, she'd seek my hand and hold it till my pulse cooled down. Evening after evening we sat there. I tried to get her to talk about that college feller. She never would. There was no set time to go home. None of my family had come down. And as for hers, she didnt give a hang about them. The general gossips could hardly say more than they had. The boarding-house porch was always deserted when we returned. No one saw us enter, so the time was set conveniently for scandal. This worried me a little, for I thought it might keep Avey from getting an appointment in the schools. She didnt care. She had finished normal school. They could give her a job if they wanted to. As time went on, her indifference to things began to pique me; I was ambitious. I left the Ferry earlier than she did. I was going off to college. The more I thought of it, the more I resented, yes, hell, thats what it was, her downright laziness. Sloppy indolence. There was no excuse for a healthy girl taking life so easy. Hell! she was no better than a cow. I was certain that she was a cow when I felt an udder in a Wisconsin stock-judging class. Among those energetic Swedes, or whatever they are, I decided to forget her. For two years I thought I did. When I'd come home for the summer she'd be away. And before she returned, I'd be gone. We never wrote; she was too damned lazy for that. But what a bluff I put up about forgetting her. The girls up that way, at least the ones I knew, havent got the stuff: they dont know how to love. Giving themselves completely was tame beside just the holding of Avey's hand. One day I received a note from her. The writing, I decided, was slovenly. She wrote on a torn bit of note-book paper. The envelope had a faint perfume that I remembered. A single line told me she had lost her school and was going away. I comforted myself with the reflection that shame held no pain for one so indolent as she. Nevertheless, I left Wisconsin that year for good. Washington had seemingly forgotten her. I hunted Ned. Between curses, I caught his opinion of her. She was no better than a whore. I saw her mother on the street. The same old pinch-beck, jerky-gaited creature that I'd always known.

Perhaps five years passed. The business of hunting a job or something or other had bruised my vanity so that I could recognize it. I felt old. Avey and my real relation to her, I thought I came to know. I wanted to see her. I had been told that she was in New York. As I had no money, I hiked and bummed my way there. I got work in a ship-yard and walked the streets at night, hoping to meet her. Failing in this, I saved enough to pay my fare back home. One evening in early June, just at the time when dusk is most lovely on the eastern horizon, I saw Avey, indolent as ever, leaning on the arm of a man, strolling under the recently lit arc-lights of U Street. She had almost passed before she recognized me. She showed no surprise. The puff over her eyes had grown heavier. The eyes themselves were still sleepy-large, and beautiful. I had almost concluded— indifferent. "You look older," was what she said. I wanted to convince her that I was, so I asked her to walk with me. The man whom she was with, and whom she never took the trouble to introduce, at a nod from her, hailed a taxi, and drove away. That gave me a notion of what she had been used to. Her dress was of some fine, costly stuff. I suggested the park, and then added that the grass might stain her skirt. Let it get stained, she said, for where it came from there are others.

I have a spot in Soldier's Home to which I always go when I want the simple beauty of another's soul. Robins spring about the lawn all day. They leave their footprints in the grass. I imagine that the grass at night smells sweet and fresh because of them. The ground is high. Washington lies below. Its light spreads like a blush against the darkened sky. Against the soft dusk sky of Washington. And when the wind is from the South, soil of my homeland falls like a fertile shower upon the lean streets of the city. Upon my hill in Soldier's Home. I know the policeman who watches the place of nights. When I go there alone, I talk to him. I tell him I come there to find the truth that people bury in their hearts. I tell him that I do not come there with a girl to do the thing he's paid to watch out for. I look deep in his eyes when I say these things, and he believes me. He comes over to see who it is on the grass. I say hello to him. He greets me in the same way and goes off searching for other black splotches upon the lawn. Avey and I went there. A band in one of the buildings a fair distance off was playing a march. I wished they would stop. Their playing was like a tin spoon in one's mouth. I wanted the Howard Glee Club to sing "Deep River," from the road. To sing "Deep River, Deep

River," from the road. . . Other than the first comments, Avey had been silent. I started to hum a folk-tune. She slipped her hand in mine. Pillowed her head as best she could upon my arm. Kissed the hand that she was holding and listened, or so I thought, to what I had to say. I traced my development from the early days up to the present time, the phase in which I could understand her. I described her own nature and temperament. Told how they needed a larger life for their expression. How incapable Washington was of understanding that need. How it could not meet it. I pointed out that in lieu of proper channels, her emotions had overflowed into paths that dissipated them. I talked, beautifully I thought, about an art that would be born, an art that would open the way for women the likes of her. I asked her to hope, and build up an inner life against the coming of that day. I recited some of my own things to her. I sang, with a strange quiver in my voice, a promise-song. And then I began to wonder why her hand had not once returned a single pressure. My old-time feeling about her laziness came back. I spoke sharply. My policeman friend passed by. I said hello to him. As he went away, I began to visualize certain possibilities. An immediate and urgent passion swept over me. Then I looked at Avey. Her heavy eyes were closed. Her breathing was as faint and regular as a child's in slumber. My passion died. I was afraid to move lest I disturb her. Hours and hours, I guess it was, she lay there. My body grew numb. I shivered. I coughed. I wanted to get up and whittle at the boxes of young trees. I withdrew my hand. I raised her head to waken her. She did not stir. I got up and walked around. I found my policeman friend and talked to him. We both came up, and bent over her. He said it would be all right for her to stay there just so long as she got away before the workmen came at dawn. A blanket was borrowed from a neighbor house. I sat beside her through the night. I saw the dawn steal over Washington. The Capitol dome looked like a gray ghost ship drifting in from sea. Avey's face was pale, and her eyes were heavy. She did not have the gray crimson-splashed beauty of the dawn. I hated to wake her. Orphan-woman. . .

BEEHIVE

Within this black hive to-night
There swarm a million bees;
Bees passing in and out the moon,
Bees escaping out the moon,
Bees returning through the moon,
Silver bees intently buzzing,
Silver honey dripping from the swarm of bees
Earth is a waxen cell of the world comb,
And I, a drone,
Lying on my back,
Lipping honey,
Getting drunk with silver honey,
Wish that I might fly out past the moon
And curl forever in some far-off farmyard flower.

STORM ENDING

Thunder blossoms gorgeously above our heads,
Great, hollow, bell-like flowers,
Rumbling in the wind,
Stretching clappers to strike our ears . .
Full-lipped flowers
Bitten by the sun
Bleeding rain
Dripping rain like golden honey—
And the sweet earth flying from the thunder.

Theater

LIFE of nigger alleys, of pool rooms and restaurants and near-beer saloons soaks into the walls of Howard Theater and sets them throbbing jazz songs. Black-skinned, they dance and shout above the tick and trill of white-walled buildings. At night, they open doors to people who come in to stamp their feet and shout. At night, road-shows volley songs into the mass-heart of black people. Songs soak the walls and seep out to the nigger life of alleys and near-beer saloons, of the Poodle Dog and Black Bear cabarets. Afternoons, the house is dark, and the walls are sleeping singers until rehearsal begins. Or until John comes within them. Then they start throbbing to a subtle syncopation. And the space-dark air grows softly luminous.

John is the manager's brother. He is seated at the center of the theater, just before rehearsal. Light streaks down upon him from a window high above. One half his face is orange in it. One half his face is in shadow. The soft glow of the house rushes to, and compacts about, the shaft of light. John's mind coincides with the shaft of light. Thoughts rush to, and compact about it. Life of the house and of the slowly awakening stage swirls to the body of John, and thrills it. John's body is separate from the thoughts that pack his mind.

Stage-lights, soft, as if they shine through clear pink fingers. Beneath them, hid by the shadow of a set, Dorris. Other chorus girls drift in. John feels them in the mass. And as if his own body were the mass-heart of a black audience listening to them singing, he wants to stamp his feet and shout. His mind, contained above desires of his body, singles the girls out, and tries to trace origins and plot destinies.

A pianist slips into the pit and improvises jazz. The walls awake. Arms of the girls, and their limbs, which . . jazz, jazz . . by lifting up their tight street skirts they set free, jab the air and clog the floor in rhythm to the music. (Lift your skirts, Baby, and talk t papa!) Crude, individualized, and yet . . monotonous. . .

John: Soon the director will herd you, my full-lipped,

58

distant beauties, and tame you, and blunt your sharp thrusts in loosely suggestive movements, appropriate to Broadway. (O dance!) Soon the audience will paint your dusk faces white, and call you beautiful. (O dance!) Soon I. . . (O dance!) I'd like. . .

Girls laugh and shout. Sing discordant snatches of other jazz songs. Whirl with loose passion into the arms of passing show-men.

John: Too thick. Too easy. Too monotonous. Her whom I'd love I'd leave before she knew that I was with her. Her? Which? (O dance!) I'd like to. . .

Girls dance and sing. Men clap. The walls sing and press inward. They press the men and girls, they press John towards a center of physical ecstasy. Go to it, Baby! Fan yourself, and feed your papa! Put . . nobody lied . . and take . . when they said I cried over you. No lie! The glitter and color of stacked scenes, the gilt and brass and crimson of the house, converge towards a center of physical ecstasy. John's feet and torso and his blood press in. He wills thought to rid his mind of passion.

"All right, girls. Alaska. Miss Reynolds, please."

The director wants to get the rehearsal through with.

The girls line up. John sees the front row: dancing ponies. The rest are in shadow. The leading lady fits loosely in the front. Lack-life, monotonous. "One, two, three—" Music starts. The song is somewhere where it will not strain the leading lady's throat. The dance is somewhere where it will not strain the girls. Above the staleness, one dancer throws herself into it. Dorris. John sees her. Her hair, crisp-curled, is bobbed. Bushy, black hair bobbing about her lemon-colored face. Her lips are curiously full, and very red. Her limbs in silk purple stockings are lovely. John feels them. Desires her. Holds off.

John: Stage-door johnny; chorus-girl. No, that would be all right. Dictie, educated, stuck-up; show-girl. Yep. Her suspicion would be stronger than her passion. It wouldnt work. Keep her loveliness. Let her go.

Dorris sees John and knows that he is looking at her. Her own glowing is too rich a thing to let her feel the slimness of his diluted passion.

"Who's that?" she asks her dancing partner.

"Th manager's brother. Dictie. Nothin doin, hon."

Dorris tosses her head and dances for him until she feels she has him. Then, withdrawing disdainfully, she flirts with the director.

Dorris: Nothin doin? How come? Aint I as good as him? Couldnt I have got an education if I'd wanted one? Dont I know respectable folks, lots of em, in Philadelphia and New York and Chicago? Aint I had men as good as him? Better. Doctors an lawyers. Whats a manager's brother, anyhow?

Two steps back, and two steps front.

"Say, Mame, where do you get that stuff?"

"Whatshmean, Dorris?"

"If you two girls cant listen to what I'm telling you, I know where I can get some who can. Now listen."

Mame: Go to hell, you black bastard.

Dorris: Whats eatin at him, anyway?

"Now follow me in this, you girls. Its three counts to the right, three counts to the left, and then you shimmy—"

John: —and then you shimmy. I'll bet she can. Some good cabaret, with rooms upstairs. And what in hell do you think you'd get from it? Youre going wrong. Here's right: get her to herself—(Christ, but how she'd bore you after the first five minutes)—not if you get her right she wouldnt. Touch her, I mean. To herself—in some room perhaps. Some cheap, dingy bedroom. Hell no. Cant be done. But the point is, brother John, it can be done. Get her to herself somewhere, anywhere. Go down in yourself—and she'd be calling you all sorts of asses while you were in the process of going down. Hold em, bud. Cant be done. Let her go. (Dance and I'll love you!) And keep her loveliness.

"All right now, Chicken Chaser. Dorris and girls. Where's Dorris? I told you to stay on the stage, didnt I? Well? Now thats enough. All right. All right there, Professor? All right. One, two, three—"

Dorris swings to the front. The line of girls, four deep, blurs within the shadow of suspended scenes. Dorris wants to dance. The director feels that and steps to one side. He smiles, and picks her for a leading lady, one of these days. Odd ends of stage-men emerge from the wings, and stare and clap. A crap game in the alley suddenly ends. Black faces crowd the rear stage doors. The girls, catching joy from Dorris, whip up within the footlights' glow. They forget set steps; they find their own. The director forgets to bawl them out. Dorris dances.

John: Her head bobs to Broadway. Dance from yourself. Dance! O just a little more.

Dorris' eyes burn across the space of seats to him.

Dorris: I bet he can love. Hell, he cant love. He's too skinny. His lips are too skinny. He wouldnt love me anyway, only for that. But I'd get a pair of silk stockings out of it. Red silk. I got purple. Cut it, kid. You cant win him to respect you that away. He wouldnt anyway. Maybe he would. Maybe he'd love. I've heard em say that men who look like him (what does he look like?) will marry if they love. O will you love me? And give me kids, and a home, and everything? (I'd like to make your nest, and honest, hon, I wouldnt run out on you.) You will if I make you. Just watch me.

Dorris dances. She forgets her tricks. She dances.

Glorious songs are the muscles of her limbs.

And her singing is of canebrake loves and mangrove feastings

The walls press in, singing. Flesh of a throbbing body, they press close to John and Dorris. They close them in. John's heart beats tensely against her dancing body. Walls press his mind within his heart. And then, the shaft of light goes out the window high above him. John's mind sweeps up to follow it. Mind pulls him upward into dream. Dorris dances. . . John dreams:

Dorris is dressed in a loose black gown splashed with lemon ribbons. Her feet taper long and slim from trim ankles. She waits for him just inside the stage door. John, collar and tie colorful and flaring, walks towards the stage door. There are no trees in the alley. But his feet feel as though they step on autumn leaves whose rustle has been pressed out of them by the passing of a million satin slippers. The air is sweet with roasting chestnuts, sweet with bonfires of old leaves. John's melancholy is a deep thing that seals all senses but his eyes, and makes him whole.

Dorris knows that he is coming. Just at the right moment she steps from the door, as if there were no door. Her face is tinted like the autumn alley. Of old flowers, or of a southern canefield, her perfume.

"Glorious Dorris." So his eyes speak. And their sadness is too deep for sweet untruth. She barely touches his arm. They glide off with footfalls softened on the leaves, the old leaves powdered by a million satin slippers.

They are in a room. John knows nothing of it. Only, that the flesh and blood of Dorris are its walls. Singing walls. Lights, soft, as if they shine through clear pink fingers. Soft lights, and warm.

John reaches for a manuscript of his, and reads. Dorris, who has no eyes, has eyes to understand him. He comes to a dancing scene. The scene is Dorris. She dances. Dorris dances. Glorious Dorris. Dorris whirls, whirls, dances. . .

Dorris dances.
The pianist crashes a bumper chord. The whole stage claps. Dorris, flushed, looks quick at John. His whole face is in shadow. She seeks for her dance in it. She finds it a dead thing in the shadow which is his dream. She rushes from the stage. Falls down the steps into her dressing-room. Pulls her hair. Her eyes, over a floor of tears, stare at the whitewashed ceiling. (Smell of dry paste, and paint, and soiled clothing.) Her pal comes in. Dorris flings herself into the old safe arms, and cries bitterly.

"I told you nothin doin," is what Mame says to comfort her.

HER LIPS ARE COPPER WIRE

whisper of yellow globes
gleaming on lamp-posts that sway
like bootleg licker drinkers in the fog

and let your breath be moist against me
like bright beads on yellow globes

telephone the power-house
that the main wires are insulate

(her words play softly up and down
dewy corridors of billboards)

then with your tongue remove the tape
and press your lips to mine
till they are incandescent

Calling Jesus

HER soul is like a little thrust-tailed dog that follows her, whimpering. She is large enough, I know, to find a warm spot for it. But each night when she comes home and closes the big outside storm door, the little dog is left in the vestibule, filled with chills till morning. Some one . . . eoho Jesus . . . soft as a cotton boll brushed against the milk-pod cheek of Christ, will steal in and cover it that it need not shiver, and carry it to her where she sleeps upon clean hay cut in her dreams.

When you meet her in the daytime on the streets, the little dog keeps coming. Nothing happens at first, and then, when she has forgotten the streets and alleys, and the large house where she goes to bed of nights, a soft thing like fur begins to rub your limbs, and you hear a low, scared voice, lonely, calling, and you know that a cool something nozzles moisture in your palms. Sensitive things like nostrils, quiver. Her breath comes sweet as honeysuckle whose pistils bear the life of coming song. And her eyes carry to where builders find no need for vestibules, for swinging on iron hinges, storm doors.

Her soul is like a little thrust-tailed dog, that follows her, whimpering. I've seen it tagging on behind her, up streets where chestnut trees flowered, where dusty asphalt had been freshly sprinkled with clean water. Up alleys where niggers sat on low door-steps before tumbled shanties and sang and loved. At night, when she comes home, the little dog is left in the vestibule, nosing the crack beneath the big storm door, filled with chills till morning. Some one . . . eoho Jesus . . . soft as the bare feet of Christ moving across bales of southern cotton, will steal in and cover it that it need not shiver, and carry it to her where she sleeps: cradled in dream-fluted cane.

Box Seat

HOUSES are shy girls whose eyes shine reticently upon the dusk body of the street. Upon the gleaming limbs and asphalt torso of a dreaming nigger. Shake your curled wool-blossoms, nigger. Open your liver lips to the lean, white spring. Stir the root-life of a withered people. Call them from their houses, and teach them to dream.

Dark swaying forms of Negroes are street songs that woo virginal houses.

Dan Moore walks southward on Thirteenth Street. The low limbs of budding chestnut trees recede above his head. Chestnut buds and blossoms are wool he walks upon. The eyes of houses faintly touch as he passes them. Soft girl-eyes, they set him singing. Girl-eyes within him widen upward to promised faces. Floating away, they dally wistfully over the dusk body of the street. Come on, Dan Moore, come on. Dan sings. His voice is a little hoarse. It cracks. He strains to produce tones in keeping with the houses' loveliness. Cant be done. He whistles. His notes are shrill. They hurt him. Negroes open gates, and go indoors, perfectly. Dan thinks of the house he's going to. Of the girl. Lips, flesh-notes of a forgotten song, plead with him. . .

Dan turns into a side-street, opens an iron gate, bangs it to. Mounts the steps, and searches for the bell. Funny, he cant find it. He fumbles around. The thought comes to him that some one passing by might see him and not understand. Might think that he is trying to sneak, to break in.

Dan: Break in. Get an ax and smash in. Smash in their faces. I'll show em. Break into an engine-house, steal a thousand horse-power fire truck. Smash in with the truck. I'll show em. Grab an ax and brain em. Cut em up. Jack the Ripper. Baboon from the zoo. And then the cops come. "No, I aint a baboon. I aint Jack the Ripper. I'm a poor man out of work. Take your hands off me, you bull-necked bears. Look into my eyes. I am

Dan Moore. I was born in a canefield. The hands of Jesus touched me. I am come to a sick world to heal it. Only the other day, a dope fiend brushed against me— Dont laugh, you mighty, juicy, meat-hook men. Give me your fingers and I will peel them as if they were ripe bananas."

Some one might think he is trying to break in. He'd better knock. His knuckles are raw bone against the thick glass door. He waits. No one comes. Perhaps they havent heard him. He raps again. This time, harder. He waits. No one comes. Some one is surely in. He fancies that he sees their shadows on the glass. Shadows of gorillas. Perhaps they saw him coming and dont want to let him in. He knocks. The tension of his arms makes the glass rattle. Hurried steps come towards him. The door opens.

"Please, you might break the glass—the bell—oh, Mr. Moore! I thought it must be some stranger. How do you do? Come in, wont you? Muriel? Yes. I'll call her. Take your things off, wont you? And have a seat in the parlor. Muriel will be right down. Muriel! Oh Muriel! Mr. Moore to see you. She'll be right down. You'll pardon me, wont you? So glad to see you."

Her eyes are weak. They are bluish and watery from reading newspapers. The blue is steel. It gimlets Dan while her mouth flaps amiably to him.

Dan: Nothing for you to see, old mussel-head. Dare I show you? If I did, delirium would furnish you headlines for a month. Now look here. Thats enough. Go long, woman. Say some nasty thing and I'll kill you. Huh. Better damned sight not. Ta-ta, Mrs. Pribby.

Mrs. Pribby retreats to the rear of the house. She takes up a newspaper. There is a sharp click as she fits into her chair and draws it to the table. The click is metallic like the sound of a bolt being shot into place. Dan's eyes sting. Sinking into a soft couch, he closes them. The house contracts about him. It is a sharp-edged, massed, metallic house. Bolted. About Mrs. Pribby. Bolted to the endless rows of metal houses. Mrs. Pribby's house. The rows of houses belong to other Mrs. Pribbys. No wonder he couldn't sing to them.

Dan: What's Muriel doing here? God, what a place for her. Whats she doing? Putting her stockings on? In the bathroom.

Come out of there, Dan Moore. People must have their privacy. Peeping-toms. I'll never peep. I'll listen. I like to listen.

Dan goes to the wall and places his ear against it. A passing street car and something vibrant from the earth sends a rumble to him. That rumble comes from the earth's deep core. It is the mutter of powerful underground races. Dan has a picture of all the people rushing to put their ears against walls, to listen to it. The next world-savior is coming up that way. Coming up. A continent sinks down. The new-world Christ will need consummate skill to walk upon the waters where huge bubbles burst. . . Thuds of Muriel coming down. Dan turns to the piano and glances through a stack of jazz music sheets. Ji-ji-bo, JI-JI-BO!" . .

"Hello, Dan, stranger, what brought you here?"

Muriel comes in, shakes hands, and then clicks into a high-armed seat under the orange glow of a floor-lamp. Her face is fleshy. It would tend to coarseness but for the fresh fragrant something which is the life of it. Her hair like an Indian's. But more curly and bushed and vagrant. Her nostrils flare. The flushed ginger of her cheeks is touched orange by the shower of color from the lamp.

"Well, you havent told me, you havent answered my question, stranger. What brought you here?"

Dan feels the pressure of the house, of the rear room, of the rows of houses, shift to Muriel. He is light. He loves her. He is doubly heavy.

"Dont know, Muriel—wanted to see you—wanted to talk to you—to see you and tell you that I know what you've been through—what pain the last few months must have been—"

"Lets dont mention that."

"But why not, Muriel? I—"

"Please."

"But Muriel, life is full of things like that. One grows strong and beautiful in facing them. What else is life?"

"I dont know, Dan. And I dont believe I care. Whats the use? Lets talk about something else. I hear there's a good show at the Lincoln this week."

"Yes, so Harry was telling me. Going?"

"To-night."

Dan starts to rise.

"I didnt know. I dont want to keep you."

"Its all right. You dont have to go till Bernice comes. And she wont be here till eight. I'm all dressed. I'll let you know."

"Thanks."

Silence. The rustle of a newspaper being turned comes from the rear room.

Muriel: Shame about Dan. Something awfully good and fine about him. But he don't fit in. In where? Me? Dan, I could love you if I tried. I dont have to try. I do. O Dan, dont you know I do? Timid lover, brave talker that you are. Whats the good of all you know if you dont know that? I wont let myself. I? Mrs. Pribby who reads newspapers all night wont. What has she got to do with me? She *is* me, somehow. No she's not. Yes she is. She is the town, and the town wont let me love you, Dan. Dont you know? You could make it let me if you would. Why wont you? Youre selfish. I'm not strong enough to buck it. Youre too selfish to buck it, for me. I wish you'd go. You irritate me. Dan, please go.

"What are you doing now, Dan?"

"Same old thing, Muriel. Nothing, as the world would have it. Living, as I look at things. Living as much as I can without—"

"But you cant live without money, Dan. Why dont you get a good job and settle down?"

Dan: Same old line. Shoot it at me, sister. Hell of a note, this loving business. For ten minutes of it youve got to stand the torture of an intolerable heaviness and a hundred platitudes. Well, damit, shoot on.

"To what? my dear. Rustling newspapers?"

"You mustnt say that, Dan. It isnt right. Mrs. Pribby has been awfully good to me."

"Dare say she has. Whats that got to do with it?"

"Oh, Dan, youre so unconsiderate and selfish. All you think of is yourself."

"I think of you."

"Too much—I mean, you ought to work more and think less. Thats the best way to get along."

"Mussel-heads get along, Muriel. There is more to you than that—"

"Sometimes I think there is, Dan. But I dont know. I've tried. I've tried to do something with myself. Something real and beautiful, I mean. But whats the good of trying? I've tried to make people, every one I come in contact with, happy—"

Dan looks at her, directly. Her animalism, still unconquered by zoo-restrictions and keeper-taboos, stirs him. Passion tilts upward, bringing with it the elements of an old desire. Muriel's lips become the flesh-notes of a futile, plaintive longing. Dan's impulse to direct her is its fresh life.

"Happy, Muriel? No, not happy. Your aim is wrong. There is no such thing as happiness. Life bends joy and pain, beauty and ugliness, in such a way that no one may isolate them. No one should want to. Perfect joy, or perfect pain, with no contrasting element to define them, would mean a monotony of consciousness, would mean death. Not happy, Muriel. Say that you have tried to make them create. Say that you have used your own capacity for life to cradle them. To start them upward-flowing. Or if you cant say that you have, then say that you will. My talking to you will make you aware of your power to do so. Say that you will love, that you will give yourself in love—"

"To you, Dan?"

Dan's consciousness crudely swerves into his passions. They flare up in his eyes. They set up quivers in his abdomen. He is suddenly over-tense and nervous.

"Muriel—"

The newspaper rustles in the rear room.

"Muriel—"

Dan rises. His arms stretch towards her. His fingers and his palms, pink in the lamplight, are glowing irons. Muriel's chair is close and stiff about her. The house, the rows of houses locked about her chair. Dan's fingers and arms are fire to melt and bars to wrench and force and pry. Her arms hang loose. Her hands are hot and moist. Dan takes them. He slips to his knees before her.

"Dan, you mustnt."

"Muriel—"

"Dan, really you mustnt. No, Dan. No."

"Oh, come, Muriel. Must I—"

"Shhh. Dan, please get up. Please. Mrs. Pribby is right in the next room. She'll hear you. She may come in. Dont, Dan. She'll see you—"

"Well then, lets go out."

"I cant. Let go, Dan. Oh, wont you please let go."

Muriel tries to pull her hands away. Dan tightens his grip. He feels the strength of his fingers. His muscles are tight and strong. He stands up. Thrusts out his chest. Muriel shrinks from him. Dan becomes aware of his crude absurdity. His lips curl. His passion chills. He has an obstinate desire to possess her.

"Muriel, I love you. I want you, whatever the world of Pribby says. Damn your Pribby. Who is she to dictate my love? I've stood enough of her. Enough of you. Come here."

Muriel's mouth works in and out. Her eyes flash and waggle. She wrenches her hands loose and forces them against his breast to keep him off. Dan grabs her wrists. Wedges in between her arms. Her face is close to him. It is hot and blue and moist. Ugly.

"Come here now."

"Dont, Dan. Oh, dont. What are you killing?"

"Whats weak in both of us and a whole litter of Pribbys. For once in your life youre going to face whats real, by God—"

A sharp rap on the newspaper in the rear room cuts between them. The rap is like cool thick glass between them. Dan is hot on one side. Muriel, hot on the other. They straighten. Gaze fearfully at one another. Neither moves. A clock in the rear room, in the rear room, the rear room, strikes eight. Eight slow, cool sounds. Bernice. Muriel fastens on her image. She smooths her dress. She adjusts her skirt. She becomes prim and cool. Rising, she skirts Dan as if to keep the glass between them. Dan, gyrating nervously above the easy swing of his limbs, follows her to the parlor door. Muriel retreats before him till she reaches the landing of the steps that lead upstairs. She smiles at him. Dan sees his face in the hall mirror. He runs his fingers through his hair. Reaches for his hat and coat and puts them on. He moves towards Muriel. Muriel steps backward up one step. Dan's jaw shoots out. Muriel jerks her arm in warning of Mrs. Pribby. She gasps and turns and starts to run. Noise of a chair scraping as Mrs. Pribby rises from it, ratchets down the hall. Dan stops. He makes a wry face, wheels round, goes out, and slams the door.

2

People come in slowly . . . mutter, laughs, flutter, whish-adwash, "I've changed my work-clothes—" . . . and fill vacant seats of Lincoln Theater. Muriel, leading Bernice who is a cross between a washerwoman and a blue-blood lady, a washer-blue, a washer-lady, wanders down the right aisle to the lower front box. Muriel has on an orange dress. Its color would clash with the crimson box-draperies, its color would contradict the sweet rose smile her face is bathed in, should she take her coat off. She'll keep it on. Pale purple shadows rest on the planes of her cheeks. Deep purple comes from her thick-shocked hair. Orange of the dress goes well with these. Muriel presses her coat down from around her shoulders. Teachers are not supposed to have bobbed hair. She'll keep her hat on. She takes the first chair, and indicates that Bernice is to take the one directly behind her. Seated thus, her eyes are level with, and near to, the face of an imaginary man upon the stage. To speak to Berny she must turn. When she does, the audience is square upon her.

People come in slowly . . . "—for my Sunday-go-to-meeting dress. O glory God! O shout Amen!" . . . and fill vacant seats of Lincoln Theater. Each one is a bolt that shoots into a slot, and is locked there. Suppose the Lord should ask, where was Moses when the light went out? Suppose Gabriel should blow his trumpet! The seats are slots. The seats are bolted houses. The mass grows denser. Its weight at first is impalpable upon the box. Then Muriel begins to feel it. She props her arm against the brass box-rail, to ward it off. Silly. These people are friends of hers: a parent of a child she teaches, an old school friend. She smiles at them. They return her courtesy, and she is free to chat with Berny. Berny's tongue, started, runs on, and on. O washer-blue! O washer-lady!

Muriel: Never see Dan again. He makes me feel queer. Starts things he doesnt finish. Upsets me. I am not upset. I am perfectly calm. I am going to enjoy the show. Good show. I've had some show! This damn tame thing. O Dan. Wont see Dan again. Not alone. Have Mrs. Pribby come in. She *was* in. Keep Dan out. If I love him, can I keep him out? Well then, I dont love him. Now he's out. Who is that coming in? Blind as a bat. Ding-bat. Looks like Dan. He mustnt see me. Silly. He cant reach me. He wont dare come in here. He'd put his head down like a goring bull and charge me. He'd trample them. He'd gore. He'd rape! Berny! He won't dare come in here.

"Berny, who was that who just came in? I havent my glasses."

"A friend of yours, a *good* friend so I hear. Mr. Daniel Moore, Lord."

"Oh. He's no friend of mine."

"No? I hear he is."

"Well, he isnt."

Dan is ushered down the aisle. He has to squeeze past the knees of seated people to reach his own seat. He treads on a man's corns. The man grumbles, and shoves him off. He shrivels close beside a portly Negress whose huge rolls of flesh meet about the bones of seat-arms. A soil-soaked fragrance comes from her. Through the cement floor her strong roots sink down. They spread under the asphalt streets. Dreaming, the streets roll over on their bellies, and suck their glossy health from them. Her strong roots sink down and spread under the river and disappear in blood-lines that waver south. Her roots shoot down. Dan's hands follow them. Roots throb. Dan's heart beats violently. He places his palms upon the earth to cool them. Earth throbs. Dan's heart beats violently. He sees all the people in the house rush to the walls to listen to the rumble. A new-world Christ is coming up. Dan comes up. He is startled. The eyes of the woman dont belong to her. They look at him unpleasantly. From either aisle, bolted masses press in. He doesnt fit. The mass grows agitant. For an instant, Dan's and Muriel's eyes meet. His weight there slides the weight on her. She braces an arm against the brass rail, and turns her head away.

Muriel: Damn fool; dear Dan, what did you want to follow me here for? Oh cant you ever do anything right? Must you always pain me, and make me hate you? I do hate you. I wish some one would come in with a horse-whip and lash you out.

I wish some one would drag you up a back alley and brain you with the whip-butt.

Muriel glances at her wrist-watch.

"Quarter of nine. Berny, what time have you?"

"Eight-forty. Time to begin. Oh, look Muriel, that woman with the plume; doesnt she look good! They say she's going with, oh, whats his name. You know. Too much powder. I can see it from here. Here's the orchestra now. O fine! Jim Clem at the piano!"

The men fill the pit. Instruments run the scale and tune. The saxophone moans and throws a fit. Jim Clem, poised over the piano, is ready to begin. His head nods forward. Opening crash. The house snaps dark. The curtain recedes upward from the blush of the footlights. Jazz overture is over. The first act is on.

Dan: Old stuff. Muriel—bored. Must be. But she'll smile and she'll clap. Do what youre bid, you she-slave. Look at her. Sweet, tame woman in a brass box seat. Clap, smile, fawn, clap. Do what youre bid. Drag me in with you. Dirty me. Prop me in your brass box seat. I'm there, am I not? because of you. He-slave. Slave of a woman who is a slave. I'm a damned sight worse than you are. I sing your praises, Beauty! I exalt thee, O Muriel! A slave, thou art greater than all Freedom because I love thee.

Dan fidgets, and disturbs his neighbors. His neighbors glare at him. He glares back without seeing them. The man whose corns have been trod upon speaks to him.

"Keep quiet, cant you, mister. Other people have paid their money besides yourself to see the show."

The man's face is a blur about two sullen liquid things that are his eyes. The eyes dissolve in the surrounding vagueness. Dan suddenly feels that the man is an enemy whom he has long been looking for.

Dan bristles. Glares furiously at the man.

"All right. All right then. Look at the show. I'm not stopping you."

"Shhh," from some one in the rear.

Dan turns around.

"Its that man there who started everything. I didnt say a thing to him until he tried to start something. What have I got to do with whether he has paid his money or not? Thats the manager's business. Do I look like the manager?"

"Shhhh. Youre right. Shhhh."

"Dont tell me to shhh. Tell him. That man there. He started everything. If what he wanted was to start a fight, why didnt he say so?"

The man leans forward.

"Better be quiet, sonny. I aint said a thing about fight, yet."

"Its a good thing you havent."

"Shhhh."

Dan grips himself. Another act is on. Dwarfs, dressed like prize-fighters, foreheads bulging like boxing gloves, are led upon the stage. They are going to fight for the heavyweight championship. Gruesome. Dan glances at Muriel. He imagines that she shudders. His mind curves back into himself, and picks up tail-ends of experiences. His eyes are open, mechanically. The dwarfs pound and bruise and bleed each other, on his eyeballs.

Dan: Ah, but she was some baby! And not vulgar either. Funny how some women can do those things. Muriel dancing like that! Hell. She rolled and wabbled. Her buttocks rocked. She pulled up her dress and showed her pink drawers. Baby! And then she caught my eyes. Dont know what my eyes had in them. Yes I do. God, dont I though! Sometimes I think, Dan Moore, that your eyes could burn clean . . . burn clean . . . BURN CLEAN! . .

The gong rings. The dwarfs set to. They spar grotesquely, playfully, until one lands a stiff blow. This makes the other sore. He commences slugging. A real scrap is on. Time! The dwarfs go to their corners and are sponged and fanned off. Gloves bulge from their wrists. Their wrists are necks for the tight-faced gloves. The fellow to the right lets his eyes roam over the audience. He sights Muriel. He grins.

Dan: Those silly women arguing feminism. Here's what I should have said to them. "It should be clear to you women, that the proposition must be stated thus:

> Me, horizontally above her.
> Action: perfect strokes downward oblique.
> Hence, man dominates because of limitation.
> Or, so it shall be until women learn their stuff.

So framed, the proposition is a mental-filler, Dentist, I want gold teeth. It should become cherished of the technical intellect. I hereby offer it to posterity as one of the important machine-age designs. P. S. It should be noted, that because it *is* an achievement of this age, its growth and hence its causes, up to the point of maturity, antedate machinery. Ery . . ."

The gong rings. No fooling this time. The dwarfs set to. They clinch. The referee parts them. One swings a cruel upper-cut and knocks the other down. A huge head hits the floor. Pop! The house roars. The fighter, groggy, scrambles up. The referee whispers to the contenders not to fight so hard. They ignore him. They charge. Their heads jab like boxing-gloves. They kick and spit and bite. They pound each other furiously. Muriel pounds. The house pounds. Cut lips. Bloody noses. The referee asks for the gong. Time! The house roars. The dwarfs bow, are made to bow. The house wants more. The dwarfs are led from the stage.

Dan: Strange I never really noticed him before. Been sitting there for years. Born a slave. Slavery not so long ago. He'll die in his chair. Swing low, sweet chariot. Jesus will come and roll him down the river Jordan. Oh, come along, Moses, you'll get lost;, stretch out your rod and come across. LET MY PEOPLE GO! Old man. Knows everyone who passes the corners. Saw the first horse-cars. The first Oldsmobile. And he was born in slavery. I did see his eyes. Never miss eyes. But they were bloodshot and watery. It hurt to look at them. It hurts to look in most people's eyes. He saw Grant and Lincoln. He saw Walt—old man, did you see Walt Whitman? Did you see Walt Whitman! Strange force that drew me to him. And I went up to see. The woman thought I saw crazy. I told him to look into the heavens. He did, and smiled. I asked him if he knew what that rumbling is that comes up from the ground. Christ, what a stroke that was. And the jabberin idiots crowding around. And the crossing-cop leaving his job to come over and wheel him away . . .

The house applauds. The house wants more. The dwarfs are led back. But no encore. Must give the house something. The attendant comes out and announces that Mr. Barry, the champion, will sing one of his own songs, "for your approval." Mr. Barry grins at Muriel as he wabbles from the wing. He holds a

fresh white rose, and a small mirror. He wipes blood from his
nose. He signals Jim Clem. The orchestra starts. A sentimental
love song, Mr. Barry sings, first to one girl, and then another
in the audience. He holds the mirror in such a way that it
flashes in the face of each one he sings to. The light swings
around.

Dan: I am going to reach up and grab the girders of this
building and pull them down. The crash will be a signal. Hid
by the smoke and dust Dan Moore will arise. In his right hand
will be a dynamo. In his left, a god's face that will flash white
light from ebony. I'll grab a girder and swing it like a walking-
stick. Lightning will flash. I'll grab its black knob and swing it
like a crippled cane. Lightning . . . Some one's flashing . . .
some one's flashing . . . Who in hell is flashing that mirror?
Take it off me, godam you.

Dan's eyes are half blinded. He moves his head. The light
follows. He hears the audience laugh. He hears the orchestra.
A man with a high-pitched, sentimental voice is singing. Dan
sees the dwarf. Along the mirror flash the song comes. Dan
ducks his head. The audience roars. The light swings around
to Muriel. Dan looks. Muriel is too close. Mr. Barry covers his
mirror. He sings to her. She shrinks away. Nausea. She clutches
the brass box-rail. She moves to face away. The audience is
square upon her. Its eyes smile. Its hands itch to clap. Muriel
turns to the dwarf and forces a smile at him. With a showy
blare of orchestration, the song comes to its close. Mr. Barry
bows. He offers Muriel the rose, first having kissed it. Blood of
his battered lips is a vivid stain upon its petals. Mr. Barry offers
Muriel the rose. The house applauds. Muriel flinches back.
The dwarf steps forward, diffident; threatening. Hate pops
from his eyes and crackles like a brittle heat about the box. The
thick hide of his face is drawn in tortured wrinkles. Above his
eyes, the bulging, tight-skinned brow. Dan looks at it. It grows
calm and massive. It grows profound. It is a thing of wisdom
and tenderness, of suffering and beauty. Dan looks down. The
eyes are calm and luminous. Words come from them . . . Arms
of the audience reach out, grab Muriel, and hold her there.
Claps are steel fingers that manacle her wrists and move them
forward to acceptance. Berny leans forward and whispers:

"Its all right. Go on—take it."

Words form in the eyes of the dwarf:

> Do not shrink. Do not be afraid of me.
> *Jesus*
> See how my eyes look at you.
> *the Son of God*
> I too was made in His image.
> *was once—*
> I give you the rose.

Muriel, tight in her revulsion, sees black, and daintily reaches for the offering. As her hand touches it, Dan springs up in his seat and shouts:

"JESUS WAS ONCE A LEPER!"

Dan steps down.

He is as cool as a green stem that has just shed its flower.

Rows of gaping faces strain towards him. They are distant, beneath him, impalpable. Squeezing out, Dan again treads upon the corn-foot man. The man shoves him.

"Watch where youre going, mister. Crazy or no, you aint going to walk over me. Watch where youre going there."

Dan turns, and serenely tweaks the fellow's nose. The man jumps up. Dan is jammed against a seat-back. A slight swift anger flicks him. His fist hooks the other's jaw.

"Now you have started something. Aint no man living can hit me and get away with it. Come on on the outside."

The house, tumultuously stirring, grabs its wraps and follows the men.

The man leads Dan up a black alley. The alley-air is thick and moist with smells of garbage and wet trash. In the morning, singing niggers will drive by and ring their gongs. . . Heavy with the scent of rancid flowers and with the scent of fight. The crowd, pressing forward, is a hollow roar. Eyes of houses, soft girl-eyes, glow reticently upon the hubbub and blink out. The man stops. Takes off his hat and coat. Dan, having forgotten him, keeps going on.

PRAYER

My body is opaque to the soul.
Driven of the spirit, long have I sought to temper it unto the
    spirit's longing,
But my mind, too, is opaque to the soul.
A closed lid is my soul's flesh-eye.
O Spirits of whom my soul is but a little finger,
Direct it to the lid of its flesh-eye.
I am weak with much giving.
I am weak with the desire to give more.
(How strong a thing is the little finger!)
So weak that I have confused the body with the soul,
And the body with its little finger.
(How frail is the little finger.)
My voice could not carry to you did you dwell in stars,
O Spirits of whom my soul is but a little finger . .

HARVEST SONG

I am a reaper whose muscles set at sundown. All my oats are
    cradled.
But I am too chilled, and too fatigued to bind them. And I
    hunger.

I crack a grain between my teeth. I do not taste it.
I have been in the fields all day. My throat is dry. I hunger.

My eyes are caked with dust of oatfields at harvest-time.
I am a blind man who stares across the hills, seeking stack'd
    fields of other harvesters.

It would be good to see them . . crook'd, split, and iron-
    ring'd handles of the scythes. It would be good to see
    them, dust-caked and blind. I hunger.

(Dusk is a strange fear'd sheath their blades are dull'd in.)
My throat is dry. And should I call, a cracked grain like the
    oats . . . eoho—

I fear to call. What should they hear me, and offer me their
    grain, oats, or wheat, or corn? I have been in the fields
    all day. I fear I could not taste it. I fear knowledge of my
    hunger.

My ears are caked with dust of oatfields at harvest-time.
I am a deaf man who strains to hear the calls of other harvest-
    ers whose throats are also dry.

It would be good to hear their songs . . reapers of the sweet-
    stalk'd cane, cutters of the corn . . even though their
    throats cracked and the strangeness of their voices deaf-
    ened me.

I hunger. My throat is dry. Now that the sun has set and I am
    chilled, I fear to call. (Eoho, my brothers!)

I am a reaper. (Eoho!) All my oats are cradled. But I am too
    fatigued to bind them. And I hunger. I crack a grain. It
    has no taste to it. My throat is dry. . .

O my brothers, I beat my palms, still soft, against the stubble
of my harvesting. (You beat your soft palms, too.) My
pain is sweet. Sweeter than the oats or wheat or corn. It
will not bring me knowledge of my hunger.

Bona and Paul

O N the school gymnasium floor, young men and women are drilling. They are going to be teachers, and go out into the world . . thud, thud . . and give precision to the movements of sick people who all their lives have been drilling. One man is out of step. In step. The teacher glares at him. A girl in bloomers, seated on a mat in the corner because she has told the director that she is sick, sees that the footfalls of the men are rhythmical and syncopated. The dance of his blue-trousered limbs thrills her.

Bona: He is a candle that dances in a grove swung with pale balloons.

Columns of the drillers thud towards her. He is in the front row. He is in no row at all. Bona can look close at him. His red-brown face—

Bona: He is a harvest moon. He is an autumn leaf. He is a nigger. Bona! But dont all the dorm girls say so? And dont you, when you are sane, say so? Thats why I love— Oh, nonsense. You have never loved a man who didnt first love you. Besides—

Columns thud away from her. Come to a halt in line formation. Rigid. The period bell rings, and the teacher dismisses them.

A group collects around Paul. They are choosing sides for basket-ball. Girls against boys. Paul has his. He is limbering up beneath the basket. Bona runs to the girl captain and asks to be chosen. The girls fuss. The director comes to quiet them. He hears what Bona wants.

"But, Miss Hale, you were excused—"

"So I was, Mr. Boynton, but—"

"—you can play basket-ball, but you are too sick to drill."

"If you wish to put it that way."

She swings away from him to the girl captain.

"Helen, I want to play, and you must let me. This is the first time I've asked and I dont see why—"

"Thats just it, Bona. We have our team."

"Well, team or no team, I want to play and thats all there is to it."

She snatches the ball from Helen's hands, and charges down the floor.

Helen shrugs. One of the weaker girls says that she'll drop out. Helen accepts this. The team is formed. The whistle blows. The game starts. Bona, in center, is jumping against Paul. He plays with her. Out-jumps her, makes a quick pass, gets a quick return, and shoots a goal from the middle of the floor. Bona burns crimson. She fights, and tries to guard him. One of her team-mates advises her not to play so hard. Paul shoots his second goal.

Bona begins to feel a little dizzy and all in. She drives on. Almost hugs Paul to guard him. Near the basket, he attempts to shoot, and Bona lunges into his body and tries to beat his arms. His elbow, going up, gives her a sharp crack on the jaw. She whirls. He catches her. Her body stiffens. Then becomes strangely vibrant, and bursts to a swift life within her anger. He is about to give way before her hatred when a new passion flares at him and makes his stomach fall. Bona squeezes him. He suddenly feels stifled, and wonders why in hell the ring of silly gaping faces that's caked about him doesnt make way and give him air. He has a swift illusion that it is himself who has been struck. He looks at Bona. Whir. Whir. They seem to be human distortions spinning tensely in a fog. Spinning . . dizzy . . spinning. . . Bona jerks herself free, flushes a startling crimson, breaks through the bewildered teams, and rushes from the hall.

2

Paul is in his room of two windows.

Outside, the South-Side L track cuts them in two.

Bona is one window. One window, Paul.

Hurtling Loop-jammed L trains throw them in swift shadow.

Paul goes to his. Gray slanting roofs of houses are tinted

lavender in the setting sun. Paul follows the sun, over the stock-yards where a fresh stench is just arising, across wheat lands that are still waving above their stubble, into the sun. Paul follows the sun to a pine-matted hillock in Georgia. He sees the slanting roofs of gray unpainted cabins tinted lavender. A Negress chants a lullaby beneath the mate-eyes of a southern planter. Her breasts are ample for the suckling of a song. She weans it, and sends it, curiously weaving, among lush melodies of cane and corn. Paul follows the sun into himself in Chicago.

He is at Bona's window.

With his own glow he looks through a dark pane.

Paul's room-mate comes in.

"Say, Paul, I've got a date for you. Come on. Shake a leg, will you?"

His blonde hair is combed slick. His vest is snug about him.

He is like the electric light which he snaps on.

"Whatdoysay, Paul? Get a wiggle on. Come on. We havent got much time by the time we eat and dress and everything."

His bustling concentrates on the brushing of his hair.

Art: What in hell's getting into Paul of late, anyway? Christ, but he's getting moony. Its his blood. Dark blood: moony. Doesnt get anywhere unless you boost it. You've got to keep it going—

"Say, Paul!"

—or it'll go to sleep on you. Dark blood; nigger? Thats what those jealous she-hens say. Not Bona though, or she . . from the South . . wouldnt want me to fix a date for him and her. Hell of a thing, that Paul's dark: you've got to always be answering questions

"Say, Paul, for Christ's sake leave that window, cant you?"

"Whats it, Art?"

"Hell, I've told you about fifty times. Got a date for you. Come on."

"With who?"

Art: He didnt use to ask; now he does. Getting up in the air. Getting funny.

"Heres your hat. Want a smoke? Paul! Here. I've got a match. Now come on and I'll tell you all about it on the way to supper."

Paul: He's going to Life this time. No doubt of that. Quit your kidding. Some day, dear Art, I'm going to kick the living slats out of you, and you wont know what I've done it for. And your slats will bring forth Life . . beautiful woman. . .

Pure Food Restaurant.

"Bring me some soup with a lot of crackers, understand? And then a roast-beef dinner. Same for you, eh, Paul? Now as I was saying, you've got a swell chance with her. And she's game. Best proof: she dont give a damn what the dorm girls say about you and her in the gym, or about the funny looks that Boynton gives her, or about what they say about, well, hell, you know, Paul. And say, Paul, she's a sweetheart. Tall, not puffy and pretty, more serious and deep—the kind you like these days. And they say she's got a car. And say, she's on fire. But you know all about that. She got Helen to fix it up with me. The four of us—remember the last party? Crimson Gardens! Boy!"

Paul's eyes take on a light that Art can settle in.

3

Art has on his patent-leather pumps and fancy vest. A loose fall coat is swung across his arm. His face has been massaged, and over a close shave, powdered. It is a healthy pink the blue of evening tints a purple pallor. Art is happy and confident in the good looks that his mirror gave him. Bubbling over with a joy he must spend now if the night is to contain it all. His bubbles, too, are curiously tinted purple as Paul watches them. Paul, contrary to what he had thought he would be like, is cool like the dusk, and like the dusk, detached. His dark face is a floating shade in evening's shadow. He sees Art, curiously. Art is a purple fluid, carbon-charged, that effervesces besides him. He loves Art. But is it not queer, this pale purple facsimile of a red-blooded Norwegian friend of his? Perhaps for some

reason, white skins are not supposed to live at night. Surely,
enough nights would transform them fantastically, or kill them.
And their red passion? Night paled that too, and made it
moony. Moony. Thats what Art thought of him. Bona didnt,
even in the daytime. Bona, would she be pale? Impossible. Not
that red glow. But the conviction did not set his emotion
flowing.

"Come right in, wont you? The young ladies will be right
down. Oh, Mr. Carlstrom, do play something for us while you
are waiting. We just love to listen to your music. You play so
well."

Houses, and dorm sitting-rooms are places where white
faces seclude themselves at night. There is a reason. . .

Art sat on the piano and simply tore it down. Jazz. The picture of Our Poets hung perilously.

Paul: I've got to get the kid to play that stuff for me in
the daytime. Might be different. More himself. More nigger.
Different? There is. Curious, though.

The girls come in. Art stops playing, and almost immediately
takes up a petty quarrel, where he had last left it, with Helen.

Bona, black-hair curled staccato, sharply contrasting with
Helen's puffy yellow, holds Paul's hand. She squeezes it. Her
own emotion supplements the return pressure. And then, for
no tangible reason, her spirits drop. Without them, she is nervous, and slightly afraid. She resents this. Paul's eyes are critical.
She resents Paul. She flares at him. She flares to poise and
security.

"Shall we be on our way?"

"Yes, Bona, certainly."

The Boulevard is sleek in asphalt, and, with arc-lights and
limousines, aglow. Dry leaves scamper behind the whir of cars.
The scent of exploded gasoline that mingles with them is
faintly sweet. Mellow stone mansions overshadow clapboard
homes which now resemble Negro shanties in some southern
alley. Bona and Paul, and Art and Helen, move along an island-
like, far-stretching strip of leaf-soft ground. Above them,
worlds of shadow-planes and solids, silently moving. As if on
one of these, Paul looks down on Bona. No doubt of it: her
face is pale. She is talking. Her words have no feel to them.

One sees them. They are pink petals that fall upon velvet cloth. Bona is soft, and pale, and beautiful.

"Paul, tell me something about yourself—or would you rather wait?"

"I'll tell you anything you'd like to know."

"Not what I want to know, Paul; what you want to tell me."

"You have the beauty of a gem fathoms under sea."

"I feel that, but I dont want to be. I want to be near you. Perhaps I will be if I tell you something. Paul, I love you."

The sea casts up its jewel into his hands, and burns them furiously. To tuck her arm under his and hold her hand will ease the burn.

"What can I say to you, brave dear woman—I cant talk love. Love is a dry grain in my mouth unless it is wet with kisses."

"You would dare? right here on the Boulevard? before Arthur and Helen?"

"Before myself? I dare."

"Here then."

Bona, in the slim shadow of a tree trunk, pulls Paul to her. Suddenly she stiffens. Stops.

"But you have not said you love me."

"I cant—yet—Bona."

"Ach, you never will. Youre cold. Cold."

Bona: Colored; cold. Wrong somewhere. She hurries and catches up with Art and Helen.

4

Crimson Gardens. Hurrah! So one feels. People . . . University of Chicago students, members of the stock exchange, a large Negro in crimson uniform who guards the door . . had watched them enter. Had leaned towards each other over ash-smeared tablecloths and highballs and whispered: What is he, a Spaniard, an Indian, an Italian, a Mexican, a Hindu, or a Japanese? Art had at first fidgeted under their stares . . what are *you* looking at, you godam pack of owl-eyed hyenas? . . but soon settled into his fuss with Helen, and forgot them. A strange thing happened to Paul. Suddenly he knew that he was apart from the people around him. Apart from the pain which they had unconsciously caused. Suddenly he knew that people saw, not attractiveness in his dark skin, but difference. Their stares, giving him to himself, filled something long empty within him, and were like green blades sprouting in his consciousness. There was fullness, and strength and peace about it all. He saw himself, cloudy, but real. He saw the faces of the people at the tables round him. White lights, or as now, the pink lights of the Crimson Gardens gave a glow and immediacy to white faces. The pleasure of it, equal to that of love or dream, of seeing this. Art and Bona and Helen? He'd look. They were wonderfully flushed and beautiful. Not for himself; because they were. Distantly. Who were they, anyway? God, if he knew them. He'd come in with them. Of that he was sure. Come where? Into life? Yes. No. Into the Crimson Gardens. A part of life. A carbon bubble. Would it look purple if he went out into the night and looked at it? His sudden starting to rise almost upset the table.

"What in hell—pardon—whats the matter, Paul?"

"I forgot my cigarettes—"

"Youre smoking one."

"So I am. Pardon me."

The waiter straightens them out. Takes their order.

Art: What in hell's eating Paul? Moony aint the word for it. From bad to worse. And those godam people staring so. Paul's a queer fish. Doesnt seem to mind. . . He's my pal, let me tell you, you horn-rimmed owl-eyed hyena at that table, and a lot better than you whoever you are. . . Queer about him. I could stick up for if he'd only come out, one way or the other, and tell a feller. Besides, a room-mate has a right to know. Thinks I wont understand. Said so. He's got a swell head when it comes to brains, all right. God, he's a good straight feller, though. Only, moony. Nut. Nuttish. Nuttery. Nutmeg. . . "What'd you say, Helen?"

"I was talking to Bona, thank you."

"Well, its nothing to get spiffy about."

"What? Oh, of course not. Please lets dont start some silly argument all over again."

"Well."

"Well."

"Now thats enough. Say, waiter, whats the matter with our order? Make it snappy, will you?"

Crimson Gardens. Hurrah! So one feels. The drinks come. Four highballs. Art passes cigarettes. A girl dressed like a bare-back rider in flaming pink, makes her way through tables to the dance floor. All lights are dimmed till they seem a lush afterglow of crimson. Spotlights the girl. She sings. "Liza, Little Liza Jane."

Paul is rosy before his window.

He moves, slightly, towards Bona.

With his own glow, he seeks to penetrate a dark pane.

Paul: From the South. What does that mean, precisely, except that you'll love or hate a nigger? Thats a lot. What does it mean except that in Chicago you'll have the courage to neither love or hate. A priori. But it would seem that you have. Queer words, arent these, for a man who wears blue pants on a gym floor in the daytime. Well, never matter. You matter. I'd like to know you whom I look at. Know, not love. Not that knowing is a greater pleasure; but that I have just found the joy of it. You came just a month too late. Even this afternoon I dreamed. To-night, along the Boulevard, you found me cold. Paul Johnson, cold! Thats a good one, eh, Art, you fine old stupid fellow, you! But I feel good! The color and the music and the song. . . A Negress chants a lullaby beneath the mate-eyes of a southern planter. O song! . . And those flushed faces. Eager brilliant eyes. Hard to imagine them as awakened. Your own. Oh, they're awake all right. "And you know it too, dont you Bona?"

"What, Paul?"

"The truth of what I was thinking."

"I'd like to know I know—something of you."

"You will—before the evening's over. I promise it."

Crimson Gardens. Hurrah! So one feels. The bare-back rider balances agilely on the applause which is the tail of her song. Orchestral instruments warm up for jazz. The flute is a cat that ripples its fur against the deep-purring saxophone. The drum throws sticks. The cat jumps on the piano keyboard. Hi diddle, hi diddle, the cat and the fiddle. Crimson Gardens . . hurrah! . . jumps over the moon. Crimson Gardens! Helen . . O

Eliza . . rabbit-eyes sparkling, plays up to, and tries to placate what she considers to be Paul's contempt. She always does that . . Little Liza Jane. . . Once home, she burns with the thought of what she's done. She says all manner of snidy things about him, and swears that she'll never go out again when he is along. She tries to get Art to break with him, saying, that if Paul, whom the whole dormitory calls a nigger, is more to him than she is, well, she's through. She does not break with Art. She goes out as often as she can with Art and Paul. She explains this to herself by a piece of information which a friend of hers had given her: men like him (Paul) can fascinate. One is not responsible for fascination. Not one girl had really loved Paul; he fascinated them. Bona didnt; only thought she did. Time would tell. And of course, *she* didnt. Liza. . . She plays up to, and tries to placate, Paul.

"Paul is so deep these days, and I'm so glad he's found some one to interest him."

"I dont believe I do."

The thought escapes from Bona just a moment before her anger at having said it.

Bona: You little puffy cat, I do. I do!

Dont I, Paul? her eyes ask.

Her answer is a crash of jazz from the palm-hidden orchestra. Crimson Gardens is a body whose blood flows to a clot upon the dance floor. Art and Helen clot. Soon, Bona and Paul. Paul finds her a little stiff, and his mind, wandering to Helen (silly little kid who wants every highball spoon her hands touch, for a souvenir), supple, perfect little dancer, wishes for the next dance when he and Art will exchange.

Bona knows that she must win him to herself.

"Since when have men like you grown cold?"

"The first philosopher."

"I thought you were a poet—or a gym director."

"Hence, your failure to make love."

Bona's eyes flare. Water. Grow red about the rims. She would like to tear away from him and dash across the clotted floor.

"What do you mean?"

"Mental concepts rule you. If they were flush with mine— good. I dont believe they are."

"How do you know, Mr. Philosopher?"

"Mostly a priori."

"You talk well for a gym director."

"And you—"

"I hate you. Ou!"

She presses away. Paul, conscious of the convention in it, pulls her to him. Her body close. Her head still strains away. He nearly crushes her. She tries to pinch him. Then sees people staring, and lets her arms fall. Their eyes meet. Both, contemptuous. The dance takes blood from their minds and packs it, tingling, in the torsos of their swaying bodies. Passionate blood leaps back into their eyes. They are a dizzy blood clot on a gyrating floor. They know that the pink-faced people have no part in what they feel. Their instinct leads them away from Art and Helen, and towards the big uniformed black man who opens and closes the gilded exit door. The cloak-room girl is tolerant of their impatience over such trivial things as wraps. And slightly superior. As the black man swings the door for them, his eyes are knowing. Too many couples have passed out, flushed and fidgety, for him not to know. The chill air is a shock to Paul. A strange thing happens. He sees the Gardens purple, as if he were way off. And a spot is in the purple. The spot comes furiously towards him. Face of the black man. It leers. It smiles sweetly like a child's. Paul leaves Bona and darts back so quickly that he doesnt give the door-man a chance to open. He swings in. Stops. Before the huge bulk of the Negro.

"Youre wrong."

"Yassur."

"Brother, youre wrong.

"I came back to tell you, to shake your hand, and tell you that you are wrong. That something beautiful is going to happen. That the Gardens are purple like a bed of roses would be at dusk. That I came into the Gardens, into life in the Gardens with one whom I did not know. That I danced with her, and did not know her. That I felt passion, contempt and passion for her whom I did not know. That I thought of her. That my thoughts were matches thrown into a dark window. And all the while the Gardens were purple like a bed of roses would be at dusk. I came back to tell you, brother, that white faces are petals of roses. That dark faces are petals of dusk. That I am going out and gather petals. That I am going out and know her whom I brought here with me to these Gardens which are purple like a bed of roses would be at dusk."

Paul and the black man shook hands.

When he reached the spot where they had been standing, Bona was gone.

to Waldo Frank.

Kabnis

I

RALPH KABNIS, propped in his bed, tries to read. To read himself to sleep. An oil lamp on a chair near his elbow burns unsteadily. The cabin room is spaced fantastically about it. Whitewashed hearth and chimney, black with sooty saw-teeth. Ceiling, patterned by the fringed globe of the lamp. The walls, unpainted, are seasoned a rosin yellow. And cracks between the boards are black. These cracks are the lips the night winds use for whispering. Night winds in Georgia are vagrant poets, whispering. Kabnis, against his will, lets his book slip down, and listens to them. The warm whiteness of his bed, the lamp-light, do not protect him from the weird chill of their song:

> White-man's land.
> Niggers, sing.
> Burn, bear black children
> Till poor rivers bring
> Rest, and sweet glory
> In Camp Ground.

Kabnis' thin hair is streaked on the pillow. His hand strokes the slim silk of his mustache. His thumb, pressed under his chin, seems to be trying to give squareness and projection to it. Brown eyes stare from a lemon face. Moisture gathers beneath his arm-pits. He slides down beneath the cover, seeking release.

Kabnis: Near me. Now. Whoever you are, my warm glowing sweetheart, do not think that the face that rests beside you is the real Kabnis. Ralph Kabnis is a dream. And dreams are faces with large eyes and weak chins and broad brows that get smashed by the fists of square faces. The body of the world is bull-necked. A dream is a soft face that fits uncertainly upon it. . . God, if I could develop that in words. Give what I know a bull-neck and a heaving body, all would go well with me,

93

wouldnt it, sweetheart? If I could feel that I came to the South to face it. If I, the dream (not what is weak and afraid in me) could become the face of the South. How my lips would sing for it, my songs being the lips of its soul. Soul. Soul hell. There aint no such thing. What in hell was that?

A rat had run across the thin boards of the ceiling. Kabnis thrusts his head out from the covers. Through the cracks, a powdery faded red dust sprays down on him. Dust of slave-fields, dried, scattered. . . No use to read. Christ, if he only could drink himself to sleep. Something as sure as fate was going to happen. He couldnt stand this thing much longer. A hen, perched on a shelf in the adjoining room begins to tread. Her nails scrape the soft wood. Her feathers ruffle.

"Get out of that, you egg-laying bitch."

Kabnis hurls a slipper against the wall. The hen flies from her perch and cackles as if a skunk were after her.

"Now cut out that racket or I'll wring your neck for you."

Answering cackles arise in the chicken yard.

"Why in Christ's hell cant you leave me alone? Damn it, I wish your cackle would choke you. Choke every mother's son of them in this God-forsaken hole. Go away. By God I'll wring your neck for you if you dont. Hell of a mess I've got in: even the poultry is hostile. Go way. Go way. By God, I'll . . ."

Kabnis jumps from his bed. His eyes are wild. He makes for the door. Bursts through it. The hen, driving blindly at the windowpane, screams. Then flies and flops around trying to elude him. Kabnis catches her.

"Got you now, you she-bitch."

With his fingers about her neck, he thrusts open the outside door and steps out into the serene loveliness of Georgian autumn moonlight. Some distance off, down in the valley, a band of pine-smoke, silvered gauze, drifts steadily. The half-moon is a white child that sleeps upon the tree-tops of the forest. White winds croon its sleep-song:

rock a-by baby . .
Black mother sways, holding a white child on her bosom.
when the bough bends . .
Her breath hums through pine-cones.
cradle will fall . .

Teat moon-children at your breasts,
down will come baby . .
Black mother.

Kabnis whirls the chicken by its neck, and throws the head away. Picks up the hopping body, warm, sticky, and hides it in a clump of bushes. He wipes blood from his hands onto the coarse scant grass.

Kabnis: Thats done. Old Chromo in the big house there will wonder whats become of her pet hen. Well, it'll teach her a lesson: not to make a hen-coop of my quarters. Quarters. Hell of a fine quarters, I've got. Five years ago; look at me now. Earth's child. The earth my mother. God is a profligate red-nosed man about town. Bastardy; me. A bastard son has got a right to curse his maker. God. . .

Kabnis is about to shake his fists heavenward. He looks up, and the night's beauty strikes him dumb. He falls to his knees. Sharp stones cut through his thin pajamas. The shock sends a shiver over him. He quivers. Tears mist his eyes. He writhes.

"God Almighty, dear God, dear Jesus, do not torture me with beauty. Take it away. Give me an ugly world. Ha, ugly. Stinking like unwashed niggers. Dear Jesus, do not chain me to myself and set these hills and valleys, heaving with folk-songs, so close to me that I cannot reach them. There is a radiant beauty in the night that touches and . . . tortures me. Ugh. Hell. Get up, you damn fool. Look around. Whats beautiful there? Hog pens and chicken yards. Dirty red mud. Stinking outhouse. Whats beauty anyway but ugliness if it hurts you? God, he doesnt exist, but nevertheless He is ugly. Hence, what comes from Him is ugly. Lynchers and business men, and that cockroach Hanby, especially. How come that he gets to be principal of a school? Of the school I'm driven to teach in? God's handiwork, doubtless. God and Hanby, they belong together. Two godam moral-spouters. Oh, no, I wont let that emotion come up in me. Stay down. Stay down, I tell you. O Jesus, Thou art beautiful. . . Come, Ralph, pull yourself together. Curses and adoration dont come from what is sane. This loneliness, dumbness, awful, intangible oppression is enough to drive a man insane. Miles from nowhere. A speck on a Georgia hillside. Jesus, can you imagine it—an atom of dust in agony on a hillside? Thats a spectacle for you. Come, Ralph, old man, pull yourself together."

Kabnis has stiffened. He is conscious now of the night wind, and of how it chills him. He rises. He totters as a man would who for the first time uses artificial limbs. As a completely artificial man would. The large frame house, squatting on brick pillars, where the principal of the school, his wife, and the boarding girls sleep, seems a curious shadow of his mind. He tries, but cannot convince himself of its reality. His gaze drifts down into the vale, across the swamp, up over the solid dusk bank of pines, and rests, bewildered-like, on the court-house tower. It is dull silver in the moonlight. White child that sleeps upon the top of pines. Kabnis' mind clears. He sees himself yanked beneath that tower. He sees white minds, with indolent assumption, juggle justice and a nigger. . . Somewhere, far off in the straight line of his sight, is Augusta. Christ, how cut off from everything he is. And hours, hours north, why not say a lifetime north? Washington sleeps. Its still, peaceful streets, how desirable they are. Its people whom he had always halfway despised. New York? Impossible. It was a fiction. He had dreamed it. An impotent nostalgia grips him. It becomes intolerable. He forces himself to narrow to a cabin silhouetted on a knoll about a mile away. Peace. Negroes within it are content. They farm. They sing. They love. They sleep. Kabnis wonders if perhaps they can feel him. If perhaps he gives them bad dreams. Things are so immediate in Georgia.

Thinking that now he can go to sleep, he reenters his room. He builds a fire in the open hearth. The room dances to the tongues of flames, and sings to the crackling and spurting of the logs. Wind comes up between the floor boards, through the black cracks of the walls.

Kabnis: Cant sleep. Light a cigarette. If that old bastard comes over here and smells smoke, I'm done for. Hell of a note, cant even smoke. The stillness of it: where they burn and hang men, you cant smoke. Cant take a swig of licker. What do they think this is, anyway, some sort of temperance school? How did I ever land in such a hole? Ugh. One might just as well be in his grave. Still as a grave. Jesus, how still everything is. Does the world know how still it is? People make noise.

They are afraid of silence. Of what lives, and God, of what dies in silence. There must be many dead things moving in silence. They come here to touch me. I swear I feel their fingers. . . Come, Ralph, pull yourself together. What in hell was that? Only the rustle of leaves, I guess. You know, Ralph, old man, it wouldnt surprise me at all to see a ghost. People dont think there are such things. They rationalize their fear, and call their cowardice science. Fine bunch, they are. Damit, that was a noise. And not the wind either. A chicken maybe. Hell, chickens dont wander around this time of night. What in hell is it?

A scraping sound, like a piece of wood dragging over the ground, is coming near.

"Ha, ha. The ghosts down this way havent got any chains to rattle, so they drag trees along with them. Thats a good one. But no joke, something is outside this house, as sure as hell. Whatever it is, it can get a good look at me and I cant see it. Jesus Christ!"

Kabnis pours water on the flames and blows his lamp out. He picks up a poker and stealthily approaches the outside door. Swings it open, and lurches into the night. A calf, carrying a yoke of wood, bolts away from him and scampers down the road.

"Well, I'm damned. This godam place is sure getting the best of me. Come, Ralph, old man, pull yourself together. Nights cant last forever. Thank God for that. Its Sunday already. First time in my life I've ever wanted Sunday to come. Hell of a day. And down here there's no such thing as ducking church. Well, I'll see Halsey and Layman, and get a good square meal. Thats something. And Halsey's a damn good feller. Cant talk to him though. Who in Christ's world can I talk to? A hen. God. Myself. . . I'm going bats, no doubt of that. Come now, Ralph, go in and make yourself go to sleep. Come now . . in the door . . thats right. Put the poker down. There. All right. Slip under the sheets. Close your eyes. Think nothing . . a long time . . nothing, nothing. Dont even think nothing. Blank. Not even blank. Count. No, mustnt count. Nothing . . blank . . nothing . . blank . . space without stars in it. No, nothing . . nothing . .

Kabnis sleeps. The winds, like soft-voiced vagrant poets sing:

White-man's land.
Niggers, sing.
Burn, bear black children
Till poor rivers bring
Rest, and sweet glory
In Camp Ground.

2

The parlor of Fred Halsey's home. There is a seediness about it. It seems as though the fittings have given a frugal service to at least seven generations of middle-class shop-owners. An open grate burns cheerily in contrast to the gray cold changed autumn weather. An old-fashioned mantelpiece supports a family clock (not running), a figure or two in imitation bronze, and two small group pictures. Directly above it, in a heavy oak frame, the portrait of a bearded man. Black hair, thick and curly, intensifies the pallor of the high forehead. The eyes are daring. The nose, sharp and regular. The poise suggests a tendency to adventure checked by the necessities of absolute command. The portrait is that of an English gentleman who has retained much of his culture, in that money has enabled him to escape being drawn through a land-grubbing pioneer life. His nature and features, modified by marriage and circumstances, have been transmitted to his great-grandson, Fred. To the left of this picture, spaced on the wall, is a smaller portrait of the great-grandmother. That here there is a Negro strain, no one would doubt. But it is difficult to say in precisely what feature it lies. On close inspection, her mouth is seen to be wistfully twisted. The expression of her face seems to shift before one's gaze—now ugly, repulsive; now sad, and somehow beautiful in its pain. A tin wood-box rests on the floor below. To the right of the great-grandfather's portrait hangs a family group: the father, mother, two brothers, and one sister of Fred. It includes himself some thirty years ago when his face was an olive white, and his hair luxuriant and dark and wavy. The father is a rich brown. The mother, practically white. Of the children, the girl, quite young, is like Fred; the two brothers, darker. The walls of the room are plastered and painted green. An old upright piano is tucked into the corner near the window. The window looks out on a forlorn, box-like, whitewashed frame church. Negroes are gathering, on foot, driving questionable gray and brown mules, and in an occasional Ford, for afternoon service. Beyond, Georgia hills roll off into the distance, their dreary aspect heightened by the gray spots of unpainted one- and two-room shanties. Clumps of pine trees here and there are the dark points the whole landscape is approaching. The church bell tolls. Above its squat tower, a great spiral of buzzards reaches far into the heavens. An ironic comment upon the path that leads into the Christian land. . . Three rocking chairs are grouped around the grate. Sunday papers scattered on the floor indicate a recent usage. Halsey, a well-built, stocky fellow, hair cropped close, enters the room. His Sunday clothes smell of wood and glue, for it is his habit to potter around his wagon-shop even on the Lord's day. He is followed by Professor Layman, tall, heavy, loose-jointed Georgia Negro, by turns teacher and preacher, who has traveled in almost every nook and corner of the state and hence knows more than would be good for anyone other than a silent man. Kabnis, trying to force through a gathering heaviness, trails in behind them. They slip into chairs before the fire.

Layman: Sholy fine, Mr. Halsey, sholy fine. This town's right good at feedin folks, better'n most towns in th state, even for preachers, but I ken say this beats um all. Yassur. Now aint that right, Professor Kabnis?

Kabnis: Yes sir, this beats them all, all right—best I've had, and thats a fact, though my comparison doesnt carry far, y'know.

Layman: Hows that, Professor?

Kabnis: Well, this is my first time out—

Layman: For a fact. Aint seed you round so much. Whats th trouble? Dont like our folks down this away?

Halsey: Aint that, Layman. He aint like most northern niggers that way. Aint a thing stuck up about him. He likes us, you an me, maybe all—its that red mud over yonder—gets stuck in it an cant get out. (Laughs.) An then he loves th fire so, warm as its been. Coldest Yankee I've ever seen. But I'm goin t get him out now it a jiffy, eh, Kabnis?

Kabnis: Sure, I should say so, sure. Dont think its because I dont like folks down this way. Just the opposite, in fact. Theres more hospitality and everything. Its diff—that is, theres lots of northern exaggeration about the South. Its not half the terror they picture it. Things are not half bad, as one could easily figure out for himself without ever crossing the Mason and Dixie line: all these people wouldnt stay down here, especially the rich, the ones that could easily leave, if conditions were so mighty bad. And then too, sometime back, my family were southerners y'know. From Georgia, in fact—

Layman: Nothin t feel proud about, Professor. Neither your folks nor mine.

Halsey (in a mock religious tone):   Amen t that, brother Layman. Amen (turning to Kabnis, half playful, yet somehow dead in earnest). An Mr. Kabnis, kindly remember youre in th land of cotton—hell of a land. Th white folks get th boll; th niggers get th stalk. An dont you dare touch th boll, or even look at it. They'll swing y sho. (Laughs.)

Kabnis: But they wouldnt touch a gentleman—fellows, men like us three here—

Layman: Nigger's a nigger down this away, Professor. An only two dividins: good an bad. An even they aint permanent categories. They sometimes mixes um up when it comes t lynchin. I've seen um do it.

Halsey: Dont let th fear int y, though, Kabnis. This county's a good un. Aint been a stringin up I can remember. (Laughs.)

Layman: This is a good town an a good county. But theres some that makes up fer it.

Kabnis: Things are better now though since that stir about those peonage cases, arent they?

Layman: Ever hear tell of a single shot killin moren one rabbit, Professor?

Kabnis: No, of course not, that is, but then—

Halsey: Now I know you werent born yesterday, sprung up so rapid like you aint heard of th brick thrown in th hornets' nest. (Laughs.)

Kabnis: Hardly, hardly, I know—

Halsey: Course y do. (To Layman) See, northern niggers aint as dumb as they make out t be.

Kabnis (overlooking the remark): Just stirs them up to sting.

Halsey: T perfection. An put just like a professor should put it.

Kabnis: Thats what actually did happen?

Layman: Well, if it aint sos only because th stingers already movin jes as fast as they ken go. An been goin ever since I ken remember, an then some mo. Though I dont usually make mention of it.

Halsey: Damn sight better not. Say, Layman, you come from where theyre always swarmin, dont y?

Layman: Yassur. I do that, sho. Dont want t mention it, but its a fact. I've seed th time when there werent no use t even stretch out flat upon th ground. Seen um shoot an cut a man t pieces who had died th night befo. Yassur. An they didnt stop when they found out he was dead—jes went on ahackin at him anyway.

Kabnis: What did you do? What did you say to them, Professor?

Layman: Thems th things you neither does a thing or talks about if y want t stay around this away, Professor.

Halsey: Listen t what he's tellin y, Kabnis. May come in handy some day.

Kabnis: Cant something be done? But of course not. This preacher-ridden race. Pray and shout. Theyre in the preacher's hands. Thats what it is. And the preacher's hands are in the white man's pockets.

Halsey: Present company always excepted.

Kabnis: The Professor knows I wasnt referring to him.

Layman: Preacher's a preacher anywheres you turn. No use exceptin.

Kabnis: Well, of course, if you look at it that way. I didnt mean— But cant something be done?

Layman: Sho. Yassur. An done first rate an well. Jes like Sam Raymon done it.

Kabnis: Hows that? What did he do?

Layman: Th white folks (reckon I oughtnt tell it) had jes knocked two others like you kill a cow—brained um with an ax, when they caught Sam Raymon by a stream. They was about t do fer him when he up an says, "White folks, I gotter die, I knows that. But wont y let me die in my own way?" Some was fer gettin after him, but th boss held um back an says, "Jes so longs th nigger dies—" An Sam fell down ont his knees an prayed, "O Lord, Ise comin to y," an he up an jumps int th stream.

Singing from the church becomes audible. Above it, rising and falling in a plaintive moan, a woman's voice swells to shouting. Kabnis hears it. His face gives way to an expression of mingled fear, contempt, and pity. Layman takes no notice of it. Halsey grins at Kabnis. He feels like having a little sport with him.

Halsey: Lets go t church, eh, Kabnis?

Kabnis (seeking control):   All right—no sir, not by a damn sight. Once a days enough for me. Christ, but that stuff gets to me. Meaning no reflection on you, Professor.

Halsey: Course not. Say, Kabnis, noticed y this morning. What'd y get up for an go out?

Kabnis: Couldnt stand the shouting, and thats a fact. We dont have that sort of thing up North. We do, but, that is, some one should see to it that they are stopped or put out when they get so bad the preacher has to stop his sermon for them.

Halsey: Is that th way youall sit on sisters up North?

Kabnis: In the church I used to go to no one ever shouted—

Halsey: Lungs weak?

Kabnis: Hardly, that is—

Halsey: Yankees are right up t th minute in tellin folk how t turn a trick. They always were good at talkin.

Kabnis: Well, anyway, they should be stopped.

Layman: Thats right. Thats true. An its th worst ones in th community that comes int th church t shout. I've sort a made a study of it. You take a man what drinks, th biggest licker-head around will come int th church an yell th loudest. An th sister whats done wrong, an is always doin wrong, will sit down in th Amen corner an swing her arms an shout her head off. Seems as if they cant control themselves out in th world; they cant control themselves in church. Now dont that sound logical, Professor?

Halsey: Reckon its as good as any. But I heard that queer

cuss over yonder—y know him, dont y, Kabnis? Well, y ought t. He had a run-in with your boss th other day—same as you'll have if you dont walk th chalk-line. An th quicker th better. I hate that Hanby. Ornery bastard. I'll mash his mouth in one of these days. Well, as I was sayin, that feller, Lewis's name, I heard him sayin somethin about a stream whats dammed has got t cut loose somewheres. An that sounds good. I know th feelin myself. He strikes me as knowin a bucketful bout most things, that feller does. Seems like he doesnt want t talk, an does, sometimes, like Layman here. Damn queer feller, him.

Layman: Cant make heads or tails of him an I've seen lots o queer possums in my day. Everybody's wonderin about him. White folks too. He'll have t leave here soon, thats sho. Always askin questions. An I aint seed his lips move once. Pokin round an notin somethin. Noted what I said th other day, an that werent fer notin down.

Kabnis: What was that?

Layman: Oh, a lynchin that took place bout a year ago. Th worst I know of round these parts.

Halsey: Bill Burnam?

Layman: Na. Mame Lamkins

Halsey grunts, but says nothing.

The preacher's voice rolls from the church in an insistent chanting monotone. At regular intervals it rises to a crescendo note. The sister begins to shout. Her voice, high-pitched and hysterical, is almost perfectly attuned to the nervous key of Kabnis. Halsey notices his distress, and is amused by it. Layman's face is expressionless. Kabnis wants to hear the story of Mame Lamkins. He does not want to hear it. It can be no worse than the shouting.

Kabnis (his chair rocking faster): What about Mame Lamkins?

Halsey: Tell him, Layman.

The preacher momentarily stops. The choir, together with the entire congregation, sings an old spiritual. The music seems to quiet the shouter. Her heavy breathing has the sound of evening winds that blow through pinecones. Layman's voice is uniformly low and soothing. A canebrake, murmuring the tale to its neighbor-road would be more passionate.

Layman: White folks know that niggers talk, an they dont

mind jes so long as nothing comes of it, so here goes. She was in th family-way, Mame Lamkills was. They killed her in th street, an some white man seein th risin in her stomach as she lay there soppy in her blood like any cow, took an ripped her belly open, an th kid fell out. It was living; but a nigger baby aint supposed t live. So he jabbed his knife in it an stuck it t a tree. An then they all went away.

Kabnis:　Christ no! What had she done?

Layman:　Tried t hide her husband when they was after him.

A shriek pierces the room. The bronze pieces on the mantel hum. The sister cries frantically: "Jesus, Jesus, I've found Jesus. O Lord, glory t God, one mo sinner is acomin home." At the height of this, a stone, wrapped round with paper, crashes through the window. Kabnis springs to his feet, terror-stricken. Layman is worried. Halsey picks up the stone. Takes off the wrapper, smooths it out, and reads: "You northern nigger, its time fer y t leave. Git along now." Kabnis knows that the command is meant for him. Fear squeezes him. Caves him in. As a violent external pressure would. Fear flows inside him. It fills him up. He bloats. He saves himself from bursting by dashing wildly from the room. Halsey and Layman stare stupidly at each other. The stone, the crumpled paper are things, huge things that weight them. Their thoughts are vaguely concerned with the texture of the stone, with the color of the paper. Then they remember the words, and begin to shift them about in sentences. Layman even construes them grammatically. Suddenly the sense of them comes back to Halsey. He grips Layman by the arm and they both follow after Kabnis.

A false dusk has come early. The countryside is ashen, chill. Cabins and roads and canebrakes whisper. The church choir, dipping into a long silence, sings:

> My Lord, what a mourning,
> My Lord, what a mourning,
> My Lord, what a mourning,
> When the stars begin to fall.

Softly luminous over the hills and valleys, the faint spray of a scattered star. . .

3

A splotchy figure drives forward along the cane- and corn-stalk hemmed-in road. A scarecrow replica of Kabnis, awkwardly animate. Fantastically plastered with red Georgia mud. It skirts the big house whose windows shine like mellow lanterns in the dusk. Its shoulder jogs against a sweet-gum tree. The figure caroms off against the cabin door, and lunges in. It slams the door as if to prevent some one entering after it.

"God Almighty, theyre here. After me. On me. All along the road I saw their eyes flaring from the cane. Hounds. Shouts. What in God's name did I run here for? A mud-hole trap. I stumbled on a rope. O God, a rope. Their clammy hands were like the love of death playing up and down my spine. Trying to trip my legs. To trip my spine. Up and down my spine. My spine. . . My legs. . . why in hell didn't they catch me?"

Kabnis wheels around, half defiant, half numbed with a more immediate fear.

"Wanted to trap me here. Get out o there. I see you."

He grabs a broom from beside the chimney and violently pokes it under the bed. The broom strikes a tin wash-tub. The noise bewilders. He recovers.

"Not there. In the closet."

He throws the broom aside and grips the poker. Starts towards the closet door, towards somewhere in the perfect blackness behind the chimney.

"I'll brain you."

He stops short. The barks of hounds, evidently in pursuit, reach him. A voice, liquid in distance, yells, "Hi! Hi!"

"O God, theyre after me. Holy Father, Mother of Christ—hell, this aint no time for prayer—"

Voices, just outside the door:

"Reckon he's here."

"Dont see no light though."

The door is flung open.

Kabnis: Get back or I'll kill you.

He braces himself, brandishing the poker.

Halsey (coming in): Aint as bad as all that. Put that thing down.

Layman: Its only us, Professor. Nobody else after y.

Kabnis: Halsey. Layman. Close that door. Dont light that light. For godsake get away from there.

Halsey: Nobody's after y, Kabnis, I'm tellin y. Put that thing down an get yourself together.

Kabnis: I tell you they are. I saw them. I heard the hounds.

Halsey: These aint th days of hounds an Uncle Tom's Cabin, feller. White folks aint in fer all them theatrics these days. Theys more direct than that. If what they wanted was t get y, theyd have just marched right in an took y where y sat. Somebodys down by th branch chasin rabbits an atreein possums.

A shot is heard.

Halsey: Got him, I reckon. Saw Tom goin out with his gun. Tom's pretty lucky most times.

He goes to the bureau and lights the lamp. The circular fringe is patterned on the ceiling. The moving shadows of the men are huge against the bare wall boards. Halsey walks up to Kabnis, takes the poker from his grip, and without more ado pushes him into a chair before the dark hearth.

Halsey: Youre a mess. Here, Layman. Get some trash an start a fire.

Layman fumbles around, finds some newspapers and old bags, puts them in the hearth, arranges the wood, and kindles the fire. Halsey sets a black iron kettle where it soon will be boiling. Then takes from his hip-pocket a bottle of corn licker which he passes to Kabnis.

Halsey: Here. This'll straighten y out a bit.

Kabnis nervously draws the cork and gulps the licker down.

Kabnis: Ha. Good stuff. Thanks. Thank y, Halsey.

Halsey: Good stuff! Youre damn right. Hanby there dont think so. Wonder he doesnt come over t find out whos burnin his oil. Miserly bastard, him. Th boys what made this stuff—are y listenin t me, Kabnis? th boys what made this stuff have got th art down like I heard you say youd like t be with words. Eh? Have some, Layman?

Layman: Dont think I care for none, thank y jes th same, Mr. Halsey.

Halsey: Care hell. Course y care. Everybody cares around these parts. Preachers an school teachers an everybody. Here. Here, take it. Dont try that line on me.

Layman limbers up a little, but he cannot quite forget that he is on school ground.

Layman: Thats right. Thats true, sho. Shinin is th only business what pays in these hard times.

He takes a nip, and passes the bottle to Kabnis. Kabnis is in the middle of a long swig when a rap sounds on the door. He almost spills the bottle, but manages to pass it to Halsey just as the door swings open and Hanby enters. He is a well-dressed, smooth, rich, black-skinned Negro who thinks there is no one quite so suave and polished as himself. To members of his own race, he affects the manners of a wealthy white planter. Or, when he is up North, he lets it be known that his ideas are those of the best New England tradition. To white men he bows, without ever completely humbling himself. Tradesmen in the town tolerate him because he spends his money with them. He delivers his words with a full consciousness of his moral superiority.

Hanby: Hum. Erer, Professor Kabnis, to come straight to the point: the progress of the Negro race is jeopardized whenever the personal habits and examples set by its guides and mentors fall below the acknowledged and hard-won standard of its average member. This institution, of which I am the humble president, was founded, and has been maintained at a cost of great labor and untold sacrifice. Its purpose is to teach our youth to live better, cleaner, more noble lives. To prove to the world that the Negro race can be just like any other race. It hopes to attain this aim partly by the salutary examples set by its instructors. I cannot hinder the progress of a race simply to indulge a single member. I have thought the matter out beforehand, I can assure you. Therefore, if I find your resignation on my desk by to-morrow morning, Mr. Kabnis, I shall not feel obliged to call in the sheriff. Otherwise. . .

Kabnis: A fellow can take a drink in his own room if he wants to, in the privacy of his own room.

Hanby: His room, but not the institution's room, Mr. Kabnis.

Kabnis: This is my room while I'm in it.

Hanby: Mr. Clayborn (the sheriff) can inform you as to that.

Kabnis: Oh, well, what do I care—glad to get out of this mud-hole.

Hanby: I should think so from your looks.

Kabnis: You neednt get sarcastic about it.

Hanby: No, that is true. And I neednt wait for your resignation either, Mr. Kabnis.

Kabnis: Oh, you'll get that all right. Dont worry.

Hanby: And I should like to have the room thoroughly aired and cleaned and ready for your successor by to-morrow noon, Professor.

Kabnis (trying to rise):   You can have your godam room right away. I dont want it.

Hanby: But I wont have your cursing.

Halsey pushes Kabnis back into his chair.

Halsey: Sit down, Kabnis, till I wash y.

Hanby (to Halsey):   I would rather not have drinking men on the premises, Mr. Halsey. You will oblige me—

Halsey: I'll oblige you by stayin right on this spot, this spot, get me? till I get damned ready t leave.

He approaches Hanby. Hanby retreats, but manages to hold his dignity.

Halsey: Let me get you told right now, Mr. Samuel Hanby. Now listen t me. I aint no slick an span slave youve hired, an dont y think it for a minute. Youve bullied enough about this town. An besides, wheres that bill youve been owin me? Listen t me. If I dont get it paid in by tmorrer noon, Mr. Hanby (he mockingly assumes Hanby's tone and manner), I shall feel obliged t call th sheriff. An that sheriff'll be myself who'll catch y in th road an pull y out your buggy an rightly attend t y. You heard me. Now leave him alone. I'm takin him home with me. I got it fixed. Before you came in. He's goin t work with me. Shapin shafts and buildin wagons'll make a man of him what nobody, y get me? what nobody can take advantage of. Thats all. . .

Halsey burrs off into vague and incoherent comment.

Pause. Disagreeable.

Layman's eyes are glazed on the spurting fire.

Kabnis wants to rise and put both Halsey and Hanby in their places. He vaguely knows that he must do this, else the power of direction will completely slip from him to those outside. The conviction is just strong enough to torture him. To bring a feverish, quick-passing flare into his eyes. To mutter words soggy in hot saliva. To jerk his arms upward in futile protest. Halsey, noticing his gestures, thinks it is water that he desires. He brings a glass to him. Kabnis slings it to the floor. Heat of the conviction dies. His arms crumple. His upper lip, his mustache, quiver. Rap! rap, on the door. The sounds slap Kabnis. They bring a hectic color to his cheeks. Like huge cold finger tips they touch his skin and goose-flesh it. Hanby strikes a commanding pose. He moves toward Layman. Layman's face is innocently immobile.

Halsey: Whos there?

Voice: Lewis.

Halsey: Come in, Lewis. Come on in.

Lewis enters. He is the queer fellow who has been referred to. A tall wiry copper-colored man, thirty perhaps. His mouth and eyes suggest purpose guided by an adequate intelligence. He is what a stronger Kabnis might have been, and in an odd faint way resembles him. As he steps towards the others, he seems to be issuing sharply from a vivid dream. Lewis shakes hands with Halsey. Nods perfunctorily to Hanby, who has stiffened to meet him. Smiles rapidly at Layman, and settles with real interest on Kabnis.

Lewis: Kabnis passed me on the road. Had a piece of business of my own, and couldnt get here any sooner. Thought I might be able to help in some way or other.

Halsey: A good baths bout all he needs now. An somethin t put his mind t rest.

Lewis: I think I can give that. That note was meant for me. Some Negroes have grown uncomfortable at my being here—

Kabnis: You mean, Mr. Lewis, some colored folks threw it? Christ Almighty!

Halsey: Thats what he means. An just as I told y. White folks more direct than that.

Kabnis: What are they after you for?

Lewis: Its a long story, Kabnis. Too long for now. And it might involve present company. (He laughs pleasantly and gestures vaguely in the direction of Hanby.) Tell you about it later on perhaps.

Kabnis: Youre not going?

Lewis: Not till my month's up.

Halsey: Hows that?

Lewis: I'm on a sort of contract with myself. (Is about to leave.) Well, glad its nothing serious—

Halsey: Come round t th shop sometime why dont y, Lewis? I've asked y enough. I'd like t have a talk with y. I aint as dumb as I look. Kabnis an me'll be in most any time. Not much work these days. Wish t hell there was. This burg gets to me when there aint. (In answer to Lewis' question.) He's goin t work with me. Ya. Night air this side th branch aint good fer him. (Looks at Hanby. Laughs.)

Lewis: I see. . .

His eyes turn to Kabnis. In the instant of their shifting, a vision of the life they are to meet. Kabnis, a promise of a soil-soaked beauty; uprooted, thinning out. Suspended a few feet above the soil whose touch would resurrect him. Arm's length removed from him whose will to help. . . There is a swift intuitive interchange of consciousness. Kabnis has a sudden need to rush into the arms of this man. His eyes call, "Brother." And then a savage, cynical twist-about within him mocks his impulse and strengthens him to repulse Lewis. His lips curl cruelly. His eyes laugh. They are glittering needles, stitching. With a throbbing ache they draw Lewis to. Lewis brusquely wheels on Hanby.

Lewis: I'd like to see you, sir, a moment, if you dont mind.

Hanby's tight collar and vest effectively preserve him.

Hanby: Yes, erer, Mr. Lewis. Right away.

Lewis: See you later, Halsey.

Halsey: So long—thanks—sho hope so, Lewis.

As he opens the door and Hanby passes out, a woman, miles down the valley, begins to sing. Her song is a spark that travels swiftly to the near-by cabins. Like purple tallow flames, songs jet up. They spread a ruddy haze over the heavens. The haze swings low. Now the whole countryside is a soft chorus. Lord. O Lord. . . Lewis closes the door behind him. A flame jets out. . .

The kettle is boiling. Halsey notices it. He pulls the wash-tub from beneath the bed. He arranges for the bath before the fire.

Halsey: Told y them theatrics didnt fit a white man. Th niggers, just like I told y. An after him. Aint surprisin though. He aint bowed t none of them. Nassur. T nairy a one of them nairy an inch nairy a time. An only mixed when he was good an ready—

Kabnis: That song, Halsey, do you hear it?

Halsey: Thats a man. Hear me, Kabnis? A man—

Kabnis: Jesus, do you hear it.

Halsey: Hear it? Hear what? Course I hear it. Listen t what I'm tellin y. A man, get me? They'll get him yet if he dont watch out.

Kabnis is jolted into his fear.

Kabnis: Get him? What do you mean? How? Not lynch him?

Halsey: Na. Take a shotgun an shoot his eyes clear out. Well, anyway, it wasnt fer you, just like I told y. You'll stay over at th house an work with me, eh, boy? Good t get away from his nobs, eh? Damn big stiff though, him. An youre not th first an I can tell y. (Laughs.)

He bustles and fusses about Kabnis as if he were a child. Kabnis submits, wearily. He has no will to resist him.

Layman (his voice is like a deep hollow echo): Thats right. Thats true, sho. Everybody's been expectin that th bust up was comin. Surprised um all y held on as long as y did. Teachin in th South aint th thing fer y. Nassur. You ought t be way back up North where sometimes I wish I was. But I've hung on down this away so long—

Halsey: An there'll never be no leavin so fer y.

4

A month has passed.

Halsey's workshop. It is an old building just off the main street of Sempter. The walls to within a few feet of the ground are of an age-worn cement mixture. On the outside they are considerably crumbled and peppered with what looks like musket-shot. Inside, the plaster has fallen away in great chunks, leaving the laths, grayed and cobwebbed, exposed. A sort of loft above the shop proper serves as a break-water for the rain and sunshine which otherwise would have free entry to the main floor. The shop is filled with old wheels and parts of wheels, broken shafts, and wooden litter. A double door, midway the street wall. To the left of this, a work-bench that holds a vise and a variety of wood-work tools. A window with as many panes broken as whole, throws light on the bench. Opposite, in the rear wall, a second window looks out upon the back yard. In the left wall, a rickety smoke-blackened chimney, and hearth with fire blazing. Smooth-worn chairs grouped about the hearth suggest the village meeting-place. Several large wooden blocks, chipped and cut and sawed on their upper surfaces are in the middle of the floor. They are the supports used in almost any sort of wagon-work. Their idleness means that Halsey has no worth-while job on foot. To the right of the central door is a junk heap, and directly behind this, stairs that lead down into the cellar. The cellar is known as "The Hole." Besides being the home of a very old man, it is used by Halsey on those occasions when he spices up the life of the small town.

Halsey, wonderfully himself in his work overalls, stands in the doorway and gazes up the street, expectantly. Then his eyes grow listless. He slouches against the smooth-rubbed frame. He lights a cigarette. Shifts his position. Braces an arm against the door. Kabnis passes the window and stoops to get in under Halsey's arm. He is awkward and ludicrous, like a schoolboy in his big brother's new overalls. He skirts the large blocks on the floor, and drops into a chair before the fire. Halsey saunters towards him.

Kabnis: Time f lunch.

Halsey: Ya.

He stands by the hearth, rocking backward and forward. He stretches his hands out to the fire. He washes them in the warm glow of the flames. They never get cold, but he warms them.

Kabnis: Saw Lewis up th street. Said he'd be down.

Halsey's eyes brighten. He looks at Kabnis. Turns away. Says nothing. Kabnis fidgets. Twists his thin blue cloth-covered limbs. Pulls closer to the fire till the heat stings his shins. Pushes back.

Pokes the burned logs. Puts on several fresh ones. Fidgets. The town bell strikes twelve.

Kabnis: Fix it up f tnight?

Halsey: Leave it t me.

Kabnis: Get Lewis in?

Halsey: Tryin t.

The air is heavy with the smell of pine and resin. Green logs spurt and sizzle. Sap trickles from an old pine-knot into the flames. Layman enters. He carries a lunch-pail. Kabnis, for the moment, thinks that he is a day laborer.

Layman: Evenin, gen'lemun.

Both: Whats say, Layman.

Layman squares a chair to the fire and droops into it. Several town fellows, silent unfathomable men for the most part, saunter in. Overalls. Thick tan shoes. Felt hats marvelously shaped and twisted. One asks Halsey for a cigarette. He gets it. The blacksmith, a tremendous black man, comes in from the forge. Not even a nod from him. He picks up an axle and goes out. Lewis enters. The town men look curiously at him. Suspicion and an open liking contest for possession of their faces. They are uncomfortable. One by one they drift into the street.

Layman: Heard y was leavin, Mr. Lewis.

Kabnis: Months up, eh? Hell of a month I've got.

Halsey: Sorry y goin, Lewis. Just getting acquainted like.

Lewis: Sorry myself, Halscy, in a way—

Layman: Gettin t like our town, Mr. Lewis?

Lewis: I'm afraid its on a different basis, Professor.

Halsey: An I've yet t hear about that basis. Been waitin long enough, God knows. Seems t me like youd take pity on a feller if nothin more.

Kabnis: Somethin that old black cockroach over yonder doesnt like, whatever it is.

Layman: Thats right. Thats right, sho.

Halsey: A feller dropped in here tother day an said he knew what you was about. Said you had queer opinions. Well, I could have told him you was a queer one, myself. But not th way he was driftin. Didnt mean anything by it, but just let drop he thought you was a little wrong up here—crazy, y'know. (Laughs.)

Kabnis: Y mean old Blodson? Hell, he's bats himself.

Lewis: I remember him. We had a talk. But what he found queer, I think, was not my opinions, but my lack of them. In half an hour he had settled everything: boll weevils, God, the World War. Weevils and wars are the pests that God sends against the sinful. People are too weak to correct themselves: the Redeemer is coming back. Get ready, ye sinners, for the advent of Our Lord. Interesting, eh, Kabnis? but not exactly what we want.

Halsey: Y could have come t me. I've sho been after y enough. Most every time I've seen y.

Kabnis (sarcastically):   Hows it y never came t us professors?

Lewis: I did—to one.

Kabnis: Y mean t say y got somethin from that celluloid-collar-eraser-cleaned old codger over in th mud hole?

Halsey: Rough on th old boy, aint he? (Laughs.)

Lewis: Something, yes. Layman here could have given me quite a deal, but the incentive to his keeping quiet is so much greater than anything I could have offered to open up, that I crossed him off my mind. And you—

Kabnis: What about me?

Halsey: Tell him, Lewis, for godsake tell him. I've told him. But its somethin else he wants so bad I've heard him downstairs mumblin with th old man.

Lewis: The old man?

Kabnis: What about me? Come on now, you know so much.

Halsey: Tell him, Lewis. Tell it t him.

Lewis: Life has already told him more than he is capable of knowing. It has given him in excess of what he can receive. I have been offered. Stuff in his stomach curdled, and he vomited me.

Kabnis' face twitches. His body writhes.

Kabnis: You know a lot, you do. How about Halsey?

Lewis: Yes. . . Halsey? Fits here. Belongs here. An artist in your way, arent you, Halsey?

Halsey: Reckon I am, Lewis. Give me th work and fair pay an I aint askin nothin better. Went over-seas an saw France; an I come back. Been up North; an I come back. Went t school;

but there aint no books whats got th feel t them of them there tools. Nassur. An I'm atellin y.

A shriveled, bony white man passes the window and enters the shop. He carries a broken hatchet-handle and the severed head. He speaks with a flat, drawn voice to Halsey, who comes forward to meet him.

Mr. Ramsay: Can y fix this fer me, Halsey?

Halsey (looking it over):   Reckon so, Mr. Ramsay. Here, Kabnis. A little practice fer y.

Halsey directs Kabnis, showing him how to place the handle in the vise, and cut it down. The knife hangs. Kabnis thinks that it must be dull. He jerks it hard. The tool goes deep and shaves too much off. Mr. Ramsay smiles brokenly at him.

Mr. Ramsay (to Halsey):   Still breakin in the new hand, eh, Halsey? Seems like a likely enough faller once he gets th hang of it.

He gives a tight laugh at his own good humor. Kabnis burns red. The back of his neck stings beneath his collar. He feels stifled. Through Ramsay, the whole white South weighs down upon him. The pressure is terrific. He sweats under the arms. Chill beads run down his body. His brows concentrate upon the handle as though his own life was staked upon the perfect shaving of it. He begins to out and out botch the job. Halsey smiles.

Halsey: He'll make a good un some of these days, Mr. Ramsay.

Mr. Ramsay: Y ought t know. Yer daddy was a good un before y. Runs in th family, seems like t me.

Halsey: Thats right, Mr. Ramsay.

Kabnis is hopeless. Halsey takes the handle from him. With a few deft strokes he shaves it. Fits it. Gives it to Ramsay.

Mr. Ramsay: How much on this?

Halsey: No charge, Mr. Ramsay.

Mr. Ramsay (going out):   All right, Halsey. Come down an take it out in trade. Shoe-strings or something.

Halsey: Yassur, Mr. Ramsay.

Halsey rejoins Lewis and Layman. Kabnis, hangdog-fashion, follows him.

Halsey: They like y if y work fer them.

Layman: Thats right, Mr. Halsey. Thats right, sho.

The group is about to resume its talk when Hanby enters. He is all energy, bustle, and business. He goes direct to Kabnis.

Hanby: An axle is out in the buggy which I would like to have shaped into a crow-bar. You will see that it is fixed for me.

Without waiting for an answer, and knowing that Kabnis will follow, he passes out. Kabnis, scowling, silent, trudges after him.

Hanby (from the outside):   Have that ready for me by three o'clock, young man. I shall call for it.

Kabnis (under his breath as he comes in):   Th hell you say, you old black swamp-gut.

He slings the axle on the floor.

Halsey: Wheeee!

Layman, lunch finished long ago, rises, heavily. He shakes hands with Lewis.

Layman: Might not see y again befo y leave, Mr. Lewis. I enjoys t hear y talk. Y might have been a preacher. Maybe a bishop some day. Sho do hope t see y back this away again sometime, Mr. Lewis.

Lewis: Thanks, Professor. Hope I'll see you.

Layman waves a long arm loosely to the others, and leaves. Kabnis goes to the door. His eyes, sullen, gaze up the street.

Kabnis: Carrie K.'s comin with th lunch. Bout time.

She passes the window. Her red girl's-cap, catching the sun, flashes vividly. With a stiff, awkward little movement she crosses the doorsill and gives Kabnis one of the two baskets which she is carrying. There is a slight stoop to her shoulders. The curves of her body blend with this to a soft rounded charm. Her gestures are stiffly variant. Black bangs curl over the forehead of her oval-olive face. Her expression is dazed, but on provocation it can melt into a wistful smile. Adolescent. She is easily the sister of Fred Halsey.

Carrie K.:   Mother says excuse her, brother Fred an Ralph, fer bein late.

Kabnis: Everythings all right an O.K., Carrie Kate. O.K. an all right.

The two men settle on their lunch. Carrie, with hardly a glance in the direction of the hearth, as is her habit, is about to take the second basket down to the old man, when Lewis rises. In doing so he draws her unwitting attention. Their meeting is a swift sun-burst. Lewis impulsively moves towards her. His mind flashes images of her life in the southern town. He sees the nascent woman, her flesh already stiffening to cartilage, drying to bone. Her spirit-bloom, even now touched sullen, bitter. Her rich beauty fading. . . He wants to— He stretches forth his hands to hers. He takes them. They feel like warm cheeks against his palms. The sun-burst from her eyes floods up and haloes him. Christ-eyes, his eyes look to her. Fearlessly she loves into them. And then something happens. Her face blanches. Awkwardly she draws away. The sin-bogies of respectable southern colored folks clamor at her: "Look out! Be a *good* girl. A *good* girl. Look out!" She gropes for her basket that has fallen to the floor. Finds it, and marches with a rigid gravity to her task of feeding the old man. Like the glowing white ash of burned paper, Lewis' eyelids, wavering, settle down. He stirs in the direction of rear window. From the back yard, mules tethered to odd trees and posts blink dumbly at him. They too seem burdened with an impotent pain. Kabnis and Halsey are still busy with their lunch. They havent noticed him. After a while he turns to them.

Lewis: Your sister, Halsey, whats to become of her? What are you going to do for her?

Halsey: Who? What? What am I goin t do? . .

Lewis: What I mean is, what does she do down there?

Halsey: Oh. Feeds th old man. Had lunch, Lewis?

Lewis: Thanks, yes. You have never felt her, have you, Halsey? Well, no, I guess not. I dont suppose you can. Nor can she. . . Old man? Halsey, some one lives down there? I've never heard of him. Tell me—

Kabnis takes time from his meal to answer with some emphasis:

Kabnis: Theres lots of things you aint heard of.

Lewis: Dare say. I'd like to see him.

Kabnis: You'll get all th chance you want tnight.

Halsey: Fixin a little somethin up fer tnight, Lewis. Th three of us an some girls. Come round bout ten-thirty.

Lewis: Glad to. But what under the sun does he do down there?

Halsey: Ask Kabnis. He blows off t him every chance he gets.

Kabnis gives a grunting laugh. His mouth twists. Carrie returns from the cellar. Avoiding Lewis, she speaks to her brother.

Carrie K.:   Brother Fred, father hasnt eaten now goin on th second week, but mumbles an talks funny, or tries t talk when I put his hands ont th food. He frightens me, an I dunno what t do. An oh, I came near fergettin, brother, but Mr. Marmon—he was eatin lunch when I saw him—told me t tell y that th lumber wagon busted down an he wanted y t fix it fer him. Said he reckoned he could get it t y after he ate.

Halsey chucks a half-eaten sandwich in the fire. Gets up. Arranges his blocks. Goes to the door and looks anxiously up the street. The wind whirls a small spiral in the gray dust road.

Halsey: Why didnt y tell me sooner, little sister?

Carrie K.:   I fergot t, an just remembered it now, brother.

Her soft rolled words are fresh pain to Lewis. He wants to take her North with him What for? He wonders what Kabnis could do for her. What she could do for him. Mother him. Carrie gathers the lunch things, silently, and in her pinched manner, curtsies, and departs. Kabnis lights his after-lunch cigarette. Lewis, who has sensed a change, becomes aware that he is not included in it. He starts to ask again about the old man. Decides not to. Rises to go.

Lewis: Think I'll run along, Halsey.

Halsey: Sure. Glad t see y any time.

Kabnis: Dont forget tnight.

Lewis: Dont worry. I wont. So long.

Kabnis: So long. We'll be expectin y.

Lewis passes Halsey at the door. Halsey's cheeks form a vacant smile. His eyes are wide awake, watching for the wagon to turn from Broad Street into his road.

Halsey: So long.

His words reach Lewis halfway to the corner.

5

Night, soft belly of a pregnant Negress, throbs evenly against the torso of the South. Night throbs a womb-song to the South. Cane- and cotton-fields, pine forests, cypress swamps, sawmills, and factories are fecund at her touch. Night's womb-song sets them singing. Night winds are the breathing of the unborn child whose calm throbbing in the belly of a Negress sets them somnolently singing. Hear their song.

> White-man's land.
> Niggers, sing.
> Burn, bear black children
> Till poor rivers bring
> Rest, and sweet glory
> In Camp Ground.

Sempter's streets are vacant and still. White paint on the wealthier houses has the chill blue glitter of distant stars. Negro cabins are a purple blur. Broad Street is deserted. Winds stir beneath the corrugated iron canopies and dangle odd bits of rope tied to horse- and mule-gnawed hitching-posts. One store window has a light in it. Chesterfield cigarette and Chero-Cola cardboard advertisements are stacked in it. From a side door two men come out. Pause, for a last word and then say good night. Soon they melt in shadows thicker than they. Way off down the street four figures sway beneath iron awnings which form a sort of corridor that imperfectly echoes and jumbles what they say. A fifth form joins them. They turn into the road that leads to Halsey's workshop. The old building is phosphorescent above deep shade. The figures pass through the double door. Night winds whisper in the eaves. Sing weirdly in the ceiling cracks. Stir curls of shavings on the floor. Halsey lights a candle. A good-sized lumber wagon, wheels off, rests upon the blocks. Kabnis makes a face at it. An un-earthly hush is upon the place. No one seems to want to talk. To move, lest the scraping of their feet . .

Halsey: Come on down this way, folks.

He leads the way. Stella follows. And close after her, Cora,

Lewis, and Kabnis. They descend into the Hole. It seems huge, limitless in the candle light. The walls are of stone, wonderfully fitted. They have no openings save a small iron-barred window toward the top of each. They are dry and warm. The ground slopes away to the rear of the building and thus leaves the south wall exposed to the sun. The blacksmith's shop is plumb against the right wall. The floor is clay. Shavings have at odd times been matted into it. In the right-hand corner, under the stairs, two good-sized pine mattresses, resting on cardboard, are on either side of a wooden table. On this are several half-burned candles and an oil lamp. Behind the table, an irregular piece of mirror hangs on the wall. A loose something that looks to be a gaudy ball costume dangles from a near-by hook. To the front, a second table holds a lamp and several whiskey glasses. Six rickety chairs are near this table. Two old wagon wheels rest on the floor. To the left, sitting in a high-backed chair which stands upon a low platform, the old man. He is like a bust in black walnut. Gray-bearded. Gray-haired. Prophetic. Immobile. Lewis' eyes are sunk in him. The others, unconcerned, are about to pass on to the front table when Lewis grips Halsey and so turns him that the candle flame shines obliquely on the old man's features.

Lewis: And he rules over—

Kabnis: Th smoke an fire of th forge.

Lewis: Black Vulcan? I wouldnt say so. That forehead. Great woolly beard. Those eyes. A mute John the Baptist of a new religion—or a tongue-tied shadow of an old.

Kabnis: His tongue is tied all right, an I can vouch f that.

Lewis: Has he never talked to you?

Halsey: Kabnis wont give him a chance. He laughs. The girls laugh. Kabnis winces.

Lewis: What do you call him?

Halsey: Father.

Lewis: Good. Father what?

Kabnis: Father of hell.

Halsey: Father's th only name we have fer him. Come on. Lets sit down an get t th pleasure of the evenin.

Lewis: Father John it is from now on. . .

Slave boy whom some Christian mistress taught to read the

Bible. Black man who saw Jesus in the ricefields, and began preaching to his people. Moses- and Christ-words used for songs. Dead blind father of a muted folk who feel their way upward to a life that crushes or absorbs them. (Speak, Father!) Suppose your eyes could see, old man. (The years hold hands. O Sing!) Suppose your lips. . .

Halsey, does he never talk?

Halsey: Na. But sometimes. Only seldom. Mumbles. Sis says he talks—

Kabnis: I've heard him talk.

Halsey: First I've ever heard of it. You dont give him a chance. Sis says she's made out several words, mostly one—an like as not cause it was "sin."

Kabnis: All those old fogies stutter about sin.

Cora laughs in a loose sort of way. She is a tall, thin, mulatto woman. Her eyes are deep-set behind a pointed nose. Her hair is coarse and bushy. Seeing that Stella also is restless, she takes her arm and the two women move towards the table. They slip into chairs. Halsey follows and lights the lamp. He lays out a pack of cards. Stella sorts them as if telling fortunes. She is a beautifully proportioned, large-eyed, brown-skin girl. Except for the twisted line of her mouth when she smiles or laughs, there is about her no suggestion of the life she's been through. Kabnis, with great mock-solemnity, goes to the corner, takes down the robe, and dons it. He is a curious spectacle, acting a part, yet very real. He joins the others at the table. They are used to him. Lewis is surprised. He laughs. Kabnis shrinks and then glares at him with a furtive hatred. Halsey, bringing out a bottle of corn licker, pours drinks.

Halsey: Come on, Lewis. Come on, you fellers. Heres lookin at y.

Then, as if suddenly recalling something, he jerks away from the table and starts towards the steps.

Kabnis: Where y goin, Halsey?

Halsey: Where? Where y think? That oak beam in th wagon—

Kabnis: Come ere. Come ere. Sit down. What in hell's wrong with you fellers? You with your wagon. Lewis with his Father John. This aint th time fer foolin with wagons. Daytime's bad enough f that. Ere, sit down. Ere, Lewis, you too sit down. Have a drink. Thats right. Drink corn licker, love th girls, an listen t th old man mumblin sin.

There seems to be no good-time spirit to the party. Something in the air is too tense and deep for that. Lewis, seated now so that his eyes rest upon the old man, merges with his source and lets the pain and beauty of the South meet there. White faces, pain-pollen, settle downward through a cane-sweet mist and touch the ovaries of yellow flowers. Cotton-bolls bloom, droop. Black roots twist in a parched red soil beneath a blazing sky. Magnolias, fragrant, a trifle futile, lovely, far off. . . His eyelids close. A force begins to heave and rise. . . Stella is serious, reminiscent.

Stella: Usall is brought up t hate sin worse than death—

Kabnis: An then before you have y eyes half open, youre made t love it if y want t live.

Stella: Us never—

Kabnis: Oh, I know your story: that old prim bastard over yonder, an then old Calvert's office—

Stella: It wasnt them—

Kabnis: I know. They put y out of church, an then I guess th preacher came around an asked f some. But thats your body. Now me—

Halsey (passing the bottle): All right, kid, we believe y. Here, take another. Wheres Clover, Stel?

Stella: You know how Jim is when he's just out th swamp. Done up in shine an wouldnt let her come. Said he'd bust her head open if she went out.

Kabnis: Dont see why he doesnt stay over with Laura, where he belongs.

Stella: Ask him, an I reckon he'll tell y. More than you want.

Halsey: Th nigger hates th sight of a black woman worse than death. Sorry t mix y up this way, Lewis. But y see how tis.

Lewis' skin is tight and glowing over the fine bones of his face. His lips tremble. His nostrils quiver. The others notice this and smile knowingly at each other. Drinks and smokes are passed around. They pay no neverminds to him. A real party is being worked up. Then Lewis opens his eyes and looks at them. Their smiles disperse in hot-cold tremors. Kabnis chokes his laugh. It sputters, gurgles. His eyes flicker and turn away. He tries to pass the thing off by taking a long drink which he makes considerable fuss over. He is drawn back to Lewis. Seeing Lewis' gaze still upon him, he scowls.

Kabnis: Whatsha lookin at me for? Y want t know who I am? Well, I'm Ralph Kabnis—lot of good its goin t do y. Well? Whatsha keep lookin for? I'm Ralph Kabnis. Aint that enough f y? Want th whole family history? Its none of your godam business, anyway. Keep off me. Do y hear? Keep off me. Look at Cora. Aint she pretty enough t look at? Look at Halsey, or Stella. Clover ought t be here an you could look at her. An love her. Thats what you need. I know—

Lewis: Ralph Kabnis gets satisfied that way?

Kabnis: Satisfied? Say, quit your kiddin. Here, look at that old man there. See him? He's satisfied. Do I look like him? When I'm dead I dont expect t be satisfied. Is that enough f y, with your godam nosin, or do you want more? Well, y wont get it, understand?

Lewis: The old man as symbol, flesh, and spirit of the past, what do you think he would say if he could see you? You look at him, Kabnis.

Kabnis: Just like any done-up preacher is what he looks t me. Jam some false teeth in his mouth and crank him, an youd have God Almighty spit in torrents all around th floor. Oh, hell, an he reminds me of that black cockroach over yonder. An besides, he aint my past. My ancestors were Southern blue-bloods—

Lewis: And black.

Kabnis: Aint much difference between blue an black.

Lewis: Enough to draw a denial from you. Cant hold them, can you? Master; slave. Soil; and the overarching heavens. Dusk; dawn. They fight and bastardize you. The sun tint of your cheeks, flame of the great season's multicolored leaves, tarnished, burned. Split, shredded: easily burned. No use . . .

His gaze shifts to Stella. Stella's face draws back, her breasts come towards him.

Stella: I aint got nothin f y, mister. Taint no use t look at me.

Halsey: Youre a queer feller, Lewis, I swear y are. Told y so, didnt I, girls? Just take him easy though, an he'll be ridin just th same as any Georgia mule, eh, Lewis? (Laughs.)

Stella: I'm goin t tell y somethin, mister. It aint t you, t th Mister Lewis what noses about. Its t somethin different, I dunno what. That old man there—maybe its him—is like m father used t look. He used t sing. An when he could sing no mo, they'd allus come f him an carry him t church an there he'd sit, befo th pulpit, aswayin an aleadin every song. A white man took m mother an it broke th old man's heart. He died; an then I didnt care what become of me, an I dont now. I dont care now. Dont get it in y head I'm some sentimental Susie askin for yo sop. Nassur. But theres somethin t yo th others aint got. Boars an kids an fools—thats all I've known. Boars when their fever's up. When their fever's up they come t me. Halsey asks me over when he's off th job. Kabnis—it ud be a sin t play with him. He takes it out in talk.

Halsey knows that he has trifled with her. At odd things he has been inwardly penitent before her tasking him. But now he wants to hurt her. He turns to Lewis.

Halsey: Lewis, I got a little licker in me, an thats true. True's what I said. True. But th stuff just seems t wake me up an make my mind a man of me. Listen. You know a lot, queer as hell as y are, an I want t ask y some questions. Theyre too high fer them, Stella an Cora an Kabnis, so we'll just excuse em. A chat between ourselves. (Turns to the others.) You-all cant listen in on this. Twont interest y. So just leave th table t this gen'lemun an myself. Go long now.

Kabnis gets up, pompous in his robe, grotesquely so, and makes as if to go through a grand march with Stella. She shoves him off, roughly, and in a mood swings her body to the steps. Kabnis grabs Cora and parades around, passing the old man, to whom he bows in mock-curtsy. He sweeps by the table, snatches the licker bottle, and then he and Cora sprawl on the mattresses. She meets his weak approaches after the manner she thinks Stella would use.

Halsey contemptuously watches them until he is sure that they are settled.

Halsey: This aint th sort o thing f me, Lewis, when I got work upstairs. Nassur. You an me has got things t do. Wastin time on common low-down women—say, Lewis, look at her now—Stella—aint she a picture? Common wench—na she aint, Lewis. You know she aint. I'm only tryin t fool y. I used t love that girl. Yassur. An sometimes when th moon is thick an I hear dogs up th valley barkin an some old woman fetches out her song, an th winds seem like th Lord made them fer t fetch an carry th smell o pine an cane, an there aint no big job on foot, I sometimes get t thinkin that I still do. But I want t talk t y, Lewis, queer as y are. Y know, Lewis, I went t school once. Ya. In Augusta. But it wasnt a regular school. Na. It was a pussy Sunday-school masqueradin under a regular name. Some goody-goody teachers from th North had come down t teach th niggers. If you was nearly white, they liked y. If you was black, they didnt. But it wasnt that—I was all right, y see. I couldnt stand em messin an pawin over m business like I was a child. So I cussed em out an left. Kabnis there ought t have cussed out th old duck over yonder an left. He'd a been a better man tday. But as I was sayin, I couldnt stand their ways. So I left an came here an worked with my father. An been here ever since. He died. I set in f myself. An its always been; give me a good job an sure pay an I aint far from being satisfied, so far as satisfaction goes. Prejudice is everywheres about this country. An a nigger aint in much standin anywheres. But when it comes t pottin round an doin nothing, with nothin bigger'n an ax-handle t hold a feller down, like it was a while back befo I got this job—that bcam ought t be—but tmorrow mornin early's time enough f that. As I was sayin, I gets t thinkin. Play dumb naturally t white folks. I gets t thinkin. I used to subscribe t th *Literary Digest* an that helped along a bit. But there werent nothing I could sink m teeth int. Theres lots I want t ask y, Lewis. Been askin y t come around. Couldnt get y. Cant get in much tnight. (He glances at the others. His mind fastens on Kabnis.) Say, tell me this, whats on your mind t say on that feller there? Kabnis' name. One queer bird ought t know another, seems like t me.

Licker has released conflicts in Kabnis and set them flowing. He pricks his ears, intuitively feels that the talk is about him, leaves Cora, and approaches the table. His eyes are watery, heavy with passion. He stoops. He is a ridiculous pathetic figure in his showy robe.

Kabnis: Talkin bout me. I know. I'm th topic of conversation everywhere theres talk about this town. Girls an fellers. White folks as well. An if its me youre talkin bout, guess I got a right t listen in. Whats sayin? Whats sayin bout his royal guts, the Duke? Whats sayin, eh?

Halsey (to Lewis):   We'll take it up another time.

Kabnis: No nother time bout it. Now. I'm here now an talkin's just begun. I was born an bred in a family of orators, thats what I was.

Halsey: Preachers.

Kabnis: Na. Preachers hell. I didnt say wind-busters. Y misapprehended me. Y understand what that means, dont y? All right then, y misapprehended me. I didnt say preachers. I said orators. ORATORS. Born one an I'll die one. You understand me, Lewis. (He turns to Halsey and begins shaking his finger in his face.) An as f you, youre all right f choppin things from blocks of wood. I was good at that th day I ducked th cradle. An since then, I've been shapin words after a design that branded here. Know whats here? M soul. Ever heard o that? Th hell y have. Been shapin words t fit m soul. Never told y that before, did I? Thought I couldnt talk. I'll tell y. I've been shapin words; ah, but sometimes theyre beautiful an golden an have a taste that makes them fine t roll over with y tongue. Your tongue aint fit f nothin but t roll an lick hog-meat.

Stella and Cora come up to the table.

Halsey: Give him a shove there, will y, Stel?

Stella jams Kabnis in a chair. Kabnis springs up.

Kabnis: Cant keep a good man down. Those words I was tellin y about, they wont fit int th mold thats branded on m soul. Rhyme, y see? Poet, too. Bad rhyme. Bad poet. Somethin else youve learned tnight. Lewis dont know it all, an I'm atellin y. Ugh. Th form thats burned int my soul is some twisted awful thing that crept in from a dream, a godam nightmare, an wont stay still unless I feed it. An it lives on words. Not beautiful words. God Almighty no. Misshapen, split-gut, tortured, twisted words. Layman was feedin it back there that day you thought I ran out fearin things. White folks feed it cause their looks are words. Niggers, black niggers feed it cause theyre evil an their looks are words. Yallar niggers feed it. This whole

damn bloated purple country feeds it cause its goin down t
hell in a holy avalanche of words. I want t feed th soul—I know
what that is; th preachers dont—but I've got t feed it. I wish t
God some lynchin white man ud stick his knife through it an
pin it to a tree. An pin it to a tree. You hear me? Thats a wish f
y, you little snot-nosed pups who've been makin fun of me, an
fakin that I'm weak. Me, Ralph Kabnis weak. Ha.

Halsey: Thats right, old man. There, there. Here, so much
exertion merits a fittin reward. Help him t be seated, Cora.

Halsey gives him a swig of shine. Cora glides up, seats him,
and then plumps herself down on his lap, squeezing his head
into her breasts. Kabnis mutters. Tries to break loose. Curses.
Cora almost stifles him. He goes limp and gives up. Cora toys
with him. Ruffles his hair. Braids it. Parts it in the middle. Stella
smiles contemptuously. And then a sudden anger sweeps her.
She would like to lash Cora from the place. She'd like to take
Kabnis to some distant pine grove and nurse and mother him.
Her eyes flash. A quick tensioning throws her breasts and neck
into a poised strain. She starts towards them. Halsey grabs her
arms and pulls her to him. She struggles. Halsey pins her arms
and kisses her. She settles, spurting like a pine-knot afire.

Lewis finds himself completely cut out. The glowing within
him subsides. It is followed by a dead chill. Kabnis, Carrie,
Stella, Halsey, Cora, the old man, the cellar, and the work-
shop, the southern town descend upon him. Their pain is too
intense. He cannot stand it. He bolts from the table. Leaps up
the stairs. Plunges through the work-shop and out into the
night.

6

The cellar swims in a pale phosphorescence. The table, the
chairs, the figure of the old man are amœba-like shadows
which move about and float in it. In the corner under the
steps, close to the floor, a solid blackness. A sound comes from
it. A forcible yawn. Part of the blackness detaches itself so that
it may be seen against the grayness of the wall. It moves forward and then seems to be clothing itself in odd dangling bits
of shadow. The voice of Halsey, vibrant and deepened, calls.

Halsey: Kabnis. Cora. Stella.

He gets no response. He wants to get them up, to get on the job. He is intolerant of their sleepiness.

Halsey: Kabnis! Stella! Cora!

Gutturals, jerky and impeded, tell that he is shaking them.

Halsey: Come now, up with you.

Kabnis (sleepily and still more or less intoxicated):   Whats th big idea? What in hell—

Halsey: Work. But never you mind about that. Up with you.

Cora: Oooooo! Look here, mister, I aint used t bein thrown int th street befo day.

Stella: Any bunk whats worked is worth in wages moren this. But come on. Taint no use t arger.

Kabnis: I'll arger. Its preposterous—

The girls interrupt him with none too pleasant laughs.

Kabnis: Thats what I said. Know what it means, dont y? All right, then. I said its preposterous t root an artist out o bed at this ungodly hour, when there aint no use t it. You can start your damned old work. Nobody's stoppin y. But what we got t get up for? Fraid somebody'll see th girls leavin? Some sport, you are. I hand it t y.

Halsey: Up you get, all th same.

Kabnis: Oh, th hell you say.

Halsey: Well, son, seeing that I'm th kind-hearted father, I'll give y chance t open your eyes. But up y get when I come down.

He mounts the steps to the work-shop and starts a fire in the hearth. In the yard he finds some chunks of coal which he brings in and throws on the fire. He puts a kettle on to boil. The wagon draws him. He lifts an oak-beam, fingers it, and becomes abstracted. Then comes to himself and places the beam upon the work-bench. He looks over some newly cut wooden spokes. He goes to the fire and pokes it. The coals are red-hot. With a pair of long prongs he picks them up and places them in a thick iron bucket. This he carries downstairs. Outside, darkness has given way to the impalpable grayness of dawn. This early morning light, seeping through the four barred cellar windows, is the color of the stony walls. It seems to be an emanation from them. Halsey's coals throw out a rich warm glow. He sets them on the floor, a safe distance from the beds.

Halsey: No foolin now. Come. Up with you.

Other than a soft rustling, there is no sound as the girls slip into their clothes. Kabnis still lies in bed.

Stella (to Halsey):   Reckon y could spare us a light?

Halsey strikes a match, lights a cigarette, and then bends over and touches flame to the two candles on the table between the beds. Kabnis asks for a cigarette. Halsey hands him his and takes a fresh one for himself. The girls, before the mirror, are doing up their hair. It is bushy hair that has gone through some straightening process. Character, however, has not all been ironed out. As they kneel there, heavy-eyed and dusky, and throwing grotesque moving shadows on the wall, they are two princesses in Africa going through the early-morning ablutions of their pagan prayers. Finished, they come forward to stretch their hands and warm them over the glowing coals. Red dusk of a Georgia sunset, their heavy, coal-lit faces. . . Kabnis suddenly recalls something.

Kabnis: Th old man talked last night.

Stella: An so did you.

Halsey: In your dreams.

Kabnis: I tell y, he did. I know what I'm talkin about. I'll tell y what he said. Wait now, lemme see.

Halsey: Look out, brother, th old man'll be getting int you by way o dreams. Come, Stel, ready? Cora? Coffee an eggs f both of you.

Halsey goes upstairs.

Stella: Gettin generous, aint he?

She blows the candles out. Says nothing to Kabnis. Then she and Cora follow after Halsey. Kabnis, left to himself, tries to rise. He has slept in his robe. His robe trips him. Finally, he manages to stand up. He starts across the floor. Half-way to the old man, he falls and lies quite still. Perhaps an hour passes. Light of a new sun is about to filter through the windows. Kabnis slowly rises to support upon his elbows. He looks hard, and internally gathers himself together. The side face of Father John is in the direct line of his eyes. He scowls at him. No one is around. Words gush from Kabnis.

Kabnis: You sit there like a black hound spiked to an ivory pedestal. An all night long I heard you murmurin that devilish word. They thought I didnt hear y, but I did. Mumblin, feedin that ornery thing thats livin on my insides. Father John. Father of Satan, more likely. What does it mean t you? Youre dead already. Death. What does it mean t you? To you who died way back there in th 'sixties. What are y throwin it in my throat for? Whats it goin t get y? A good smashin in th mouth, thats what. My fist'll sink int y black mush face clear t y guts—if y got any. Dont believe y have. Never seen signs of none. Death. Death. Sin an Death. All night long y mumbled death. (He forgets the old man as his mind begins to play with the word and its associations.) Death . . . these clammy floors . . . just like th place they used t stow away th worn-out, no-count niggers in th days of slavery . . . that was long ago; not so long ago . . . no windows (he rises higher on his elbows to verify this assertion. He looks around, and, seeing no one but the old man, calls.) Halsey! Halsey! Gone an left me. Just like a nigger. I thought he was a nigger all th time. Now I know it. Ditch y when it comes right down t it. Damn anyway. Godam him. (He looks and re-sees the old man.) Eh, you? T hell with you too. What do I care whether you can see or hear? You know what hell is cause youve been there. Its a feelin an its ragin in my soul in a way that'll pop out of me an run you through, an scorch y, an burn an rip your soul. Your soul. Ha. Nigger soul. A gin soul that gets drunk on a preacher's words. An screams. An shouts. God Almighty, how I hate that shoutin. Where's th beauty in that? Gives a buzzard a windpipe an I'll bet a dollar t a dime th buzzard ud beat y to it. Aint surprisin th white folks hate y so. When you had eyes, did you ever see th beauty of th world? Tell me that. Th hell y did. Now dont tell me. I know y didnt. You couldnt have. Oh, I'm drunk an just as good as dead, but no eyes that have seen beauty ever lose their sight. You aint got no sight. If you had, drunk as I am, I hope Christ will kill me if I couldnt see it. Your eyes are dull and watery, like fish eyes. Fish eyes are dead eyes. Youre an old man, a dead fish man, an black at that. Theyve put y here t die, damn fool y are not t know it. Do y know how many feet youre under ground? I'll tell y. Twenty. An do y think you'll ever see th light of day again, even if you wasnt blind? Do y think youre out of slavery? Huh? Youre where they used t throw th worked-out, no-count slaves. On a damp clammy floor of a dark scum-hole. An they called that an infimary. Th sons-a . . . . Why I can already see you toppled off that stool an stretched out on th floor beside me—not beside me, damn you, by yourself, with th flies buzzin an lickin God knows what they'd find on a dirty, black, foul-breathed mouth like yours . . .

Some one is coming down the stairs. Carrie, bringing food for the old man. She is lovely in her fresh energy of the morning, in the calm untested confidence and nascent maternity which rise from the purpose of her present mission. She walks to within a few paces of Kabnis.

Carrie K.:   Brother says come up now, brother Ralph.

Kabnis: Brother doesnt know what he's talkin bout.

Carrie K.:   Yes he does, Ralph. He needs you on th wagon.

Kabnis: He wants me on th wagon, eh? Does he think some wooden thing can lift me up? Ask him that.

Carrie K.:   He told me t help y.

Kabnis: An how would you help me, child, dear sweet little sister?

She moves forward as if to aid him.

Carrie K.:   I'm not a child, as I've more than once told you, brother Ralph, an as I'll show you now.

Kabnis: Wait, Carrie. No, thats right. Youre not a child. But twont do t lift me bodily. You dont understand. But its th soul of me that needs th risin.

Carrie K: Youre a bad brother an just wont listen t me when I'm tellin y t go t church.

Kabnis doesnt hear her. He breaks down and talks to himself.

Kabnis: Great God Almighty, a soul like mine cant pin itself onto a wagon wheel an satisfy itself in spinnin round. Iron prongs an hickory sticks, an God knows what all . . all right for Halsey . . . use him. Me? I get my life down in this scum-hole. Th old man an me—

Carrie K.:   Has he been talkin?

Kabnis: Huh? Who? Him? No. Dont need to. I talk. An when I really talk, it pays th best of them t listen. Th old man is a good listener. He's deaf; but he's a good listener. An I can talk t him. Tell him anything.

Carrie K.:   He's deaf an blind, but I reckon he hears, an sees too, from th things I've heard.

Kabnis: No. Cant. Cant I tell you. How's he do it?

Carrie K.:   Dunno, except I've heard that th souls of old folks have a way of seein things.

Kabnis: An I've heard them call that superstition.

The old man begins to shake his head slowly. Carrie and Kabnis watch him, anxiously. He mumbles. With a grave motion his head nods up and down. And then, on one of the down-swings—

Father John (remarkably clear and with great conviction): Sin.

He repeats this word several times, always on the downward nodding. Surprised, indignant, Kabnis forgets that Carrie is with him.

Kabnis: Sin! Shut up. What do you know about sin, you old black bastard. Shut up, an stop that swayin an noddin your head.

Father John: Sin.

Kabnis tries to get up.

Kabnis: Didnt I tell y t shut up?

Carrie steps forward to help him. Kabnis is violently shocked at her touch. He springs back.

Kabnis: Carrie! What . . how . . Baby, you shouldnt be down here. Ralph says things. Doesnt mean to. But Carrie, he doesnt know what he's talkin about. Couldnt know. It was only a preacher's sin they knew in those old days, an that wasnt sin at all. Mind me, th only sin is whats done against th soul. Th whole world is a conspiracy t sin, especially in America, an against me. I'm th victim of their sin. I'm what sin is. Does he look like me? Have you ever heard him say th things youve heard me say? He couldn't if he had th Holy Ghost t help him. Dont look shocked, little sweetheart, you hurt me.

Father John: Sin.

Kabnis: Aw, shut up, old man.

Carrie K.:   Leave him be. He wants t say somethin. (She turns to the old man.) What is it, Father?

Kabnis: Whatsha talkin t that old deaf man for? Come away from him.

Carrie K.:   What is it, Father?

The old man's lips begin to work. Words are formed incoherently. Finally, he manages to articulate—

Father John: Th sin whats fixed . . . (Hesitates.)

Carrie K. (restraining a comment from Kabnis):   Go on, Father.

Father John: . . . upon th white folks—

Kabnis: Suppose youre talkin about that bastard race thats roamin round th country. It looks like sin, if thats what y mean. Give us somethin new an up t date.

Father John: —f tellin Jesus—lies. O th sin th white folks 'mitted when they made th Bible lie.

Boom. Boom. BOOM! Thuds on the floor above. The old man sinks back into his stony silence. Carrie is wet-eyed. Kabnis, contemptuous.

Kabnis: So thats your sin. All these years t tell us that th white folks made th Bible lie. Well, I'll be damned. Lewis ought t have been here. You old black fakir—

Carrie K.:   Brother Ralph, is that your best Amen?

She turns him to her and takes his hot cheeks in her firm cool hands. Her palms draw the fever out. With its passing, Kabnis crumples. He sinks to his knees before her, ashamed, exhausted. His eyes squeeze tight. Carrie presses his face tenderly against her. The suffocation of her fresh starched dress feels good to him. Carrie is about to lift her hands in prayer, when Halsey, at the head of the stairs, calls down.

Halsey: Well, well. Whats up? Aint you ever comin? Come on. Whats up down there? Take you all mornin t sleep off a pint? Youre weakenin, man, youre weakenin. Th axle an th beam's all ready waitin f y. Come on.

Kabnis rises and is going doggedly towards the steps. Carrie notices his robe. She catches up to him, points to it, and helps him take it off. He hangs it, with an exaggerated ceremony, on its nail in the corner. He looks down on the tousled beds. His lips curl bitterly. Turning, he stumbles over the bucket of dead coals. He savagely jerks it from the floor. And then, seeing Carrie's eyes upon him, he swings the pail carelessly and with eyes downcast and swollen, trudges upstairs to the work-shop. Carrie's gaze follows him till he is gone. Then she goes to the old man and slips to her knees before him. Her lips murmur, "Jesus, come."

Light streaks through the iron-barred cellar window. Within its soft circle, the figures of Carrie and Father John.

Outside, the sun arises from its cradle in the tree-tops of the forest. Shadows of pines are dreams the sun shakes from its eyes. The sun arises. Gold-glowing child, it steps into the sky and sends a birth-song slanting down gray dust streets and sleepy windows of the southern town.

HOME TO HARLEM

Claude McKay

To My Friend
Louise Bryant

CONTENTS

I
Going Back Home

ALL that Jake knew about the freighter on which he stoked was that it stank between sea and sky. He was working with a dirty Arab crew. The captain signed him on at Cardiff because one of the Arabs had quit the ship. Jake was used to all sorts of rough jobs, but he had never before worked in such a filthy dinghy.

The white sailors who washed the ship would not wash the stokers' water-closet, because they despised the Arabs. And the Arabs themselves made no effort to keep the place clean, although it adjoined their sleeping berth.

The cooks hated the Arabs because they did not eat pork. Whenever there was pork for dinner, something else had to be prepared for the Arabs. The cooks put the stokers' meat, cut in unappetizing chunks, in a broad pan, and the two kinds of vegetables in two other pans. The stoker who carried the food back to the bunks always put one pan inside of the other, and sometimes the bottoms were dirty and bits of potato peelings or egg shells were mixed in with the meat and the vegetables.

The Arabs took up a chunk of meat with their coal-powdered fingers, bit or tore off a piece, and tossed the chunk back into the pan. It was strange to Jake that these Arabs washed themselves after eating and not before. They ate with their clothes stiff-starched to their bodies with coal and sweat. And when they were finished, they stripped and washed and went to sleep in the stinking-dirty bunks. Jake was used to the lowest and hardest sort of life, but even his leather-lined stomach could not endure the Arabs' way of eating. Jake also began to despise the Arabs. He complained to the cooks about the food. He gave the chef a ten-shilling note, and the chef gave him his eats separately.

One of the sailors flattered Jake. "You're the same like us chaps. You ain't like them dirty jabbering coolies."

But Jake smiled and shook his head in a non-committal way.

He knew that if he was just like the white sailors, he might have signed on as a deckhand and not as a stoker. He didn't care about the dirty old boat, anyhow. It was taking him back home—that was all he cared about. He made his shift all right, stoking four hours and resting eight. He didn't sleep well. The stokers' bunks were lousy, and fetid with the mingled smell of stale food and water-closet. Jake had attempted to keep the place clean, but to do that was impossible. Apparently the Arabs thought that a sleeping quarters could also serve as a garbage can.

"Nip me all you wanta, Mister Louse," said Jake. "Roll on, Mister Ship, and stinks all the way as you rolls. Jest take me 'long to Harlem is all I pray. I'm crazy to see again the brown-skin chippies 'long Lenox Avenue. Oh boy!"

Jake was tall, brawny, and black. When America declared war upon Germany in 1917 he was a longshoreman. He was working on a Brooklyn pier, with a score of men under him. He was a little boss and a very good friend of his big boss, who was Irish. Jake thought he would like to have a crack at the Germans. . . . And he enlisted.

In the winter he sailed for Brest with a happy chocolate company. Jake had his own daydreams of going over the top. But his company was held at Brest. Jake toted lumber—boards, planks, posts, rafters—for the hundreds of huts that were built around the walls of Brest and along the coast between Brest and Saint-Pierre, to house the United States soldiers.

Jake was disappointed. He had enlisted to fight. For what else had he been sticking a bayonet into the guts of a stuffed man and aiming bullets straight into a bull's-eye? Toting planks and getting into rows with his white comrades at the Bal Musette were not adventure.

Jake obtained leave. He put on civilian clothes and lit out for Havre. He liquored himself up and hung round a low-down café in Havre for a week.

One day an English sailor from a Channel sloop made up to Jake. "Darky," he said, "you 'arvin' a good time 'round 'ere."

Jake thought how strange it was to hear the Englishman say "darky" without being offended. Back home he would have been spoiling for a fight. There he would rather hear "nigger" than "darky," for he knew that when a Yankee said "nigger" he meant hatred for Negroes, whereas when he said "darky" he meant friendly contempt. He preferred white folks' hatred to their friendly contempt. To feel their hatred made him strong and aggressive, while their friendly contempt made him ridiculously angry, even against his own will.

"Sure Ise having a good time, all right," said Jake. He was making a cigarette and growling cusses at French tobacco. "But Ise got to get a move on 'fore very long."

"Where to?" his new companion asked.

"Any place, Buddy. I'm always ready for something new," announced Jake.

"Been in Havre a long time?"

"Week or two," said Jake. "I tooks care of some mules over heah. Twenty, God damn them, days across the pond. And then the boat plows round and run off and leaves me behind. Kain you beat that, Buddy?"

"It wasn't the best o' luck," replied the other. "Ever been to London?"

"Nope, Buddy," said Jake. "France is the only country I've struck yet this side the water."

The Englishman told Jake that there was a sailor wanted on his tug.

"We never 'ave a full crew—since the war," he said.

Jake crossed over to London. He found plenty of work there as a docker. He liked the West India Docks. He liked Limehouse. In the pubs men gave him their friendly paws and called him "darky." He liked how they called him "darky." He made friends. He found a woman. He was happy in the East End.

The Armistice found him there. On New-Year's Eve, 1919, Jake went to a monster dance with his woman, and his docker friends and their women, in the Mile End Road.

The Armistice had brought many more black men to the East End of London. Hundreds of them. Some of them found work. Some did not. Many were getting a little pension from the government. The price of sex went up in the East End, and the dignity of it also. And that summer Jake saw a big battle staged between the colored and white men of London's East End. Fisticuffs, razor and knife and gun play. For three days his woman would not let him out-of-doors. And when it was all over he was seized with the awful fever of lonesomeness. He felt all alone in the world. He wanted to run away from the kind-heartedness of his lady of the East End.

"Why did I ever enlist and come over here?" he asked himself. "Why did I want to mix mahself up in a white folks' war? It ain't ever was any of black folks' affair. Niggers am evah always such fools, anyhow. Always thinking they've got something to do with white folks' business."

Jake's woman could do nothing to please him now. She tried hard to get down into his thoughts and share them with him. But for Jake this woman was now only a creature of another race—of another world. He brooded day and night.

It was two years since he had left Harlem. Fifth Avenue, Lenox Avenue, and One Hundred and Thirty-fifth Street, with their chocolate-brown and walnut-brown girls, were calling him.

"Oh, them legs!" Jake thought. "Them tantalizing brown legs! . . . Barron's Cabaret! . . . Leroy's Cabaret! . . . Oh, boy!"

Brown girls rouged and painted like dark pansies. Brown flesh draped in soft colorful clothes. Brown lips full and pouted for sweet kissing. Brown breasts throbbing with love.

"Harlem for mine!" cried Jake. "I was crazy thinkin' I was happy over heah. I wasn't mahself. I was like a man charged up with dope every day. That's what it was. Oh, boy! Harlem for mine!

"Take me home to Harlem, Mister Ship! Take me home to the brown gals waiting for the brown boys that done show their mettle over there. Take me home, Mister Ship. Put your beak right into that water and jest move along." . . .

II
Arrival

JAKE was paid off. He changed a pound note he had brought with him. He had fifty-nine dollars. From South Ferry he took an express subway train for Harlem.

Jake drank three Martini cocktails with cherries in them. The price, he noticed, had gone up from ten to twenty-five cents. He went to Bank's and had a Maryland fried-chicken feed—a big one with candied sweet potatoes.

He left his suitcase behind the counter of a saloon on Lenox Avenue. He went for a promenade on Seventh Avenue between One Hundred and Thirty-fifth and One Hundred and Fortieth Streets. He thrilled to Harlem. His blood was hot. His eyes were alert as he sniffed the street like a hound. Seventh Avenue was nice, a little too nice that night.

Jake turned off on Lenox Avenue. He stopped before an ice-cream parlor to admire girls sipping ice-cream soda through straws. He went into a cabaret. . . .

A little brown girl aimed the arrow of her eye at him as he entered. Jake was wearing a steel-gray English suit. It fitted him loosely and well, perfectly suited his presence. She knew at once that Jake must have just landed. She rested her chin on the back of her hands and smiled at him. There was something in his attitude, in his hungry wolf's eyes, that went warmly to her. She was brown, but she had tinted her leaf-like face to a ravishing chestnut. She had on an orange scarf over a green frock, which was way above her knees, giving an adequate view of legs lovely in fine champagne-colored stockings. . . .

Her shaft hit home. . . . Jake crossed over to her table. He ordered Scotch and soda.

"Scotch is better with soda or even water," he said. "English folks don't take whisky straight, as we do."

But she preferred ginger ale in place of soda. The cabaret singer, seeing that they were making up to each other, came expressly over to their table and sang. Jake gave the singer fifty cents. . . .

Her left hand was on the table. Jake covered it with his right.

"Is it clear sailing between us, sweetie?" he asked.

"Sure thing. . . . You just landed from over there?"

"Just today!"

"But there wasn't no boat in with soldiers today, daddy."

"I made it in a special one."

"Why, you lucky baby! . . . I'd like to go to another place, though. What about you?"

"Anything you say, I'm game," responded Jake.

They walked along Lenox Avenue. He held her arm. His flesh tingled. He felt as if his whole body was a flaming wave. She was intoxicated, blinded under the overwhelming force.

But nevertheless she did not forget her business.

"How much is it going to be, daddy?" she demanded.

"How much? *How* much? Five?"

"Aw no, daddy. . . ."

"Ten?"

She shook her head.

"Twenty, sweetie!" he said, gallantly.

"Daddy," she answered, "I wants fifty."

"Good," he agreed. He was satisfied. She was responsive. She was beautiful. He loved the curious color on her cheek.

They went to a buffet flat on One Hundred and Thirty-seventh Street. The proprietress opened the door without removing the chain and peeked out. She was a matronly mulatto woman. She recognized the girl, who had put herself in front of Jake, and she slid back the chain and said, "Come right in."

The windows were heavily and carefully shaded. There was beer and wine, and there was plenty of hard liquor. Black and brown men sat at two tables in one room, playing poker. In the other room a phonograph was grinding out a "blues," and some couples were dancing, thick as maggots in a vat of sweet liquor, and as wriggling.

Jake danced with the girl. They shuffled warmly, gloriously about the room. He encircled her waist with both hands, and she put both of hers up to his shoulders and laid her head against his breast. And they shuffled around.

"Harlem! Harlem!" thought Jake. "Where else could I have

all this life but Harlem? Good old Harlem! Chocolate Harlem!
Sweet Harlem! Harlem, I've got you' number down. Lenox
Avenue, you're a bear, I know it. And, baby honey, sure enough
youse a pippin for your pappy. Oh, boy!" . . .

After Jake had paid for his drinks, that fifty-dollar note was all
he had left in the world. He gave it to the girl. . . .
    "Is we going now, honey?" he asked her.
    "Sure, daddy. Let's beat it." . . .
    Oh, to be in Harlem again after two years away. The deep-
dyed color, the thickness, the closeness of it. The noises of
Harlem. The sugared laughter. The honey-talk on its streets.
And all night long, ragtime and "blues" playing somewhere,
. . . singing somewhere, dancing somewhere! Oh, the contagious fever of Harlem. Burning everywhere in dark-eyed
Harlem. . . . Burning now in Jake's sweet blood. . . .

He woke up in the morning in a state of perfect peace. She
brought him hot coffee and cream and doughnuts. He yawned.
He sighed. He was satisfied. He breakfasted. He washed. He
dressed. The sun was shining. He sniffed the fine dry air.
Happy, familiar Harlem.
    "I ain't got a cent to my name," mused Jake, "but ahm as
happy as a prince, all the same. Yes, I is."
    He loitered down Lenox Avenue. He shoved his hand in his
pocket—pulled out the fifty-dollar note. A piece of paper was
pinned to it on which was scrawled in pencil:
    "Just a little gift from a baby girl to a honey boy!"

III
Zeddy

"GREAT balls of fire! Looka here! See mah luck!" Jake stopped in his tracks . . . went on . . . stopped again . . . retraced his steps . . . checked himself. "Guess I won't go back right now. Never let a woman think you're too crazy about her. But she's a particularly sweet piece a business. . . . Me and her again tonight. . . . Handful o' luck shot straight outa heaven. Oh, boy! Harlem is mine!"

Jake went rolling along Fifth Avenue. He crossed over to Lenox Avenue and went into Uncle Doc's saloon, where he had left his bag. Called for a glass of Scotch. "Gimme the siphon, Doc. I'm off the straight stuff."

"Iszh you? Counta what?"

"Hits the belly better this way. I l'arned it over the other side."

A slap on the shoulder brought him sharply round. "Zeddy Plummer! What grave is you arisen from?" he cried.

"Buddy, you looks so good to me, I could kish you," Zeddy said.

"Where?"

"Everywhere. . . . French style."

"One on one cheek and one on the other."

"Savee-vous?"

"Parlee-vous?"

Uncle Doc set another glass on the counter and poured out pure Bourbon. Zeddy reached a little above Jake's shoulders. He was stocky, thick-shouldered, flat-footed, and walked like a bear. Some more customers came in and the buddies eased round to the short side of the bar.

"What part of the earth done belch you out?" demanded Zeddy. "Nevah heared no God's tidings a you sence we missed you from Brest."

"And how about you?" Jake countered. "Didn't them Germans git you scrambling over the top?"

"Nevah see'd them, buddy. None a them showed the goose-

146

step around Brest. Have a shot on me. . . . Well, dawg bite me, but—say, Jake, we've got some more stuff to booze over."

Zeddy slapped Jake on his breast and looked him over again. "Tha's some stuff you're strutting in, boh. 'Tain't 'Merican and it ain't French." . . .

"English." Jake showed his clean white teeth.

"Mah granny an' me! You been in that theah white folks' country, too?"

"And don't I look as if Ise been? Where else could a fellow git such good and cheap man clothes to cover his skin?"

"Buddy, I know it's the trute. What you doing today?"

"No, when you make me think ovit, particular thing. And you?"

"I'm alongshore but—I ain't agwine to work thisaday."

"I guess I've got to be heaving along right back to it, too, in pretty short time. I got to get me a room but——"

Uncle Doc reminded Jake that his suit-case was there.

"I ain't nevah fohgitting all mah worldly goods," responded Jake.

Zeddy took Jake to a pool-room where they played. Jake was the better man. From the pool-room they went to Aunt Hattie's chitterling joint in One Hundred and Thirty-second Street, where they fed. Fricassee chicken and rice. Green peas. Stewed corn.

Aunt Hattie's was renowned among the lowly of Harlem's Black Belt. It was a little basement joint, smoke-colored. And Aunt Hattie was weather-beaten dark-brown, cheery-faced, with two rusty-red front teeth sticking together conspicuously out of her twisted, spread-away mouth. She cooked delicious food—home-cooked food they called it. None of the boys loafing round that section of Fifth Avenue would dream of going to any other place for their "poke chops."

Aunt Hattie admired her new customer from the kitchen door and he quite filled her sight. And when she went with the dish rag to wipe the oil-cloth before setting down the cocoanut pie, she rubbed her breast against Jake's shoulder and a sensual light gleamed in her aged smoke-red eyes.

The buddies talked about the days of Brest. Zeddy recalled the everlasting unloading and unloading of ships and the toting of lumber. The house of the Young Men's Christian

Association, overlooking the harbor, where colored soldiers were not wanted. . . . The central Rue de Siam and the point near the Prefecture of Marine, from which you could look down on the red lights of the Quartier Réservé. The fatal fights between black men and white in the *maisons closes*. The encounters between apaches and white Americans. The French sailors that couldn't get the Yankee idea of amour and men. And the cemetery, just beyond the old mediæval gate of the town, where he left his second-best buddy.

"Poor boh. Was always belly-aching for a chance over the top. Nevah got it nor nothing. Not even a baid in the hospital. Strong like a bull, yet just knocked off in the dark through raw cracker cussedness. . . . Some life it was, buddy, in them days. We was always on the defensive as if the boches, as the froggies called them, was right down on us."

"Yet you stuck t'rough it toting lumber. Got back to Harlem all right, though."

"You bet I did, boh. You kain trust Zeddy Plummer to look out for his own black hide. . . . But you, buddy. How come you just vanished thataway like a spook? How did you take your tail out ovit?"

Jake told Zeddy how he walked out of it straight to the station in Brest. Le Havre. London. The West India Docks. And back home to Harlem.

"But you must keep it dark, buddy," Zeddy cautioned. "Don't go shooting off your mouth too free. Gov'mant still smoking out deserters and draft dodgers."

"I ain't told no nigger but you, boh. Nor ofay, neither. Ahm in your confidence, chappie."

"That's all right, buddy." Zeddy put his hand on Jake's knee. "It's better to keep your business close all the time. But I'll tell you this for your perticular information. Niggers am awful close-mouthed in some things. There is fellows here in Harlem that just telled the draft to mount upstairs. Pohlice and soldiers were hunting ev'where foh them. And they was right here in Harlem. Fifty dollars apiece foh them. All their friends knowed it and not a one gived them in. I tell you, niggers am amazing sometimes. Yet other times, without any natural reason, they will just go vomiting out their guts to the ofays about one another."

"God; but it's good to get back home again!" said Jake.

"I should think you was hungry foh a li'l' brown honey. I tell you trute, buddy. I made mine ovah there, spitin' ov ev'thing. I l'arned her a little z'inglise and she l'arned me beaucoup plus the French stuff. . . . The real stuff, buddy. But I was tearin' mad and glad to get back all the same. Take it from me, buddy, there ain't no honey lak to that theah comes out of our own belonging-to-us honeycomb."

"Man, what you telling me?" cried Jake. "Don't I knows it? What else you think made me leave over the other side? And dog mah doggone ef I didn't find it just as I landed."

"K-hhhhhhh! K-hhhhhhhh!" Zeddy laughed. "Dog mah cats! You done tasted the real life a'ready?"

"Last night was the end of the world, buddy, and tonight ahm going back there," chanted Jake as he rose and began kicking up his heels round the joint.

Zeddy also got up and put on his gray cap. They went back to the pool-room. Jake met two more fellows that he knew and got into a ring of Zeddy's pals. . . . Most of them were longshoremen. There was plenty of work, Jake learned. Before he left the pool-room he and Zeddy agreed to meet the next evening at Uncle Doc's.

"Got to work tomorrow, boh," Zeddy informed Jake.

"Good old New York! The same old wench of a city. Elevated racketing over you' head. Subway bellowing under you' feet. Me foh wrastling round them piers again. Scratching down to the bottom of them ships and scrambling out. All alongshore for me now. No more fooling with the sea. Same old New York. Everybody dashing round like crazy. . . . Same old New York. But the ofay faces am different from those ovah across the pond. Sure they is. Stiffer. Tighter. Yes, they is that. . . . But the sun does better here than over there. And the sky's so high and dry and blue. And the air it—O Gawd it works in you' flesh and blood like Scotch. O Lawdy, Lawdy! I wants to live to a hundred and finish mah days in New York."

Jake threw himself up as if to catch the air pouring down from the blue sky. . . .

"Harlem! Harlem! Little thicker, little darker and noisier and smellier, but Harlem just the same. The niggers done plowed

through Hundred and Thirtieth Street. Heading straight foh
One Hundred and Twenty-fifth. Spades beyond Eighth Avenue. Going, going, going Harlem! Going up! Nevah befoh I
seed so many dickty shines in sich swell motor-cars. Plenty moh
nigger shops. Seventh Avenue done gone high-brown. O Lawdy!
Harlem bigger, Harlem better . . . and sweeter."

"Street and streets! One Hundred and Thirty-second, Thirty-
third, Thirty-fourth. It wasn't One Hundred and Thirty-fifth
and it wasn't beyond theah. . . . O Lawd! how did I fohgit to
remember the street and number. I reeled outa there like a
drunken man. I been so happy. . . .

"Thirty-fourth, Thirty-second, Thirty-third. . . . Only difference in the name. All the streets am just the same and all the
houses 'like as peas. I could try this one heah or that one there
but—— Rabbit foot! I didn't even git her name. Oh, Jakie,
Jake! What a big Ah-Ah you is.

"I was a fool not to go back right then when I felt like it.
What did I want to tighten up mahself and crow and strut like
a crazy cat for? A grand Ah-Ah I is. Feet in mah hands! Take
me back to the Baltimore tonight. I ain't gwine to know no
peace till I lay these here hands on mah tantalizing brown
again."

IV
Congo Rose

ALL the old cabarets were going still. Connor's was losing ground. The bed of red roses that used to glow in the ceiling was almost dim now. The big handsome black girl that always sang in a red frock was no longer there. What a place Connor's was from 1914 to 1916 when that girl was singing and kicking and showing her bright green panties there! And the little ebony drummer, beloved of every cabaret lover in Harlem, was a fiend for rattling the drum!

Barron's was still Barron's, depending on its downtown white trade. Leroy's, the big common rendezvous shop for everybody. Edmond's still in the running. A fine new place that was opened in Brooklyn was freezing to death. Brooklyn never could support anything.

Goldgraben's on Lenox Avenue was leading all the Negro cabarets in a cruel dance. The big-spirited Jew had brought his cabaret up from the basement and established it in a hall blazing with lights, overlooking Lenox Avenue. He made a popular Harlem Negro manager. There the joy-loving ladies and gentlemen of the Belt collected to show their striking clothes and beautiful skin. Oh, it was some wonderful sight to watch them from the pavement! No wonder the lights of Connor's were dim. And Barron's had plunged deeper for the ofay trade. Goldgraben was grabbing all the golden-browns that had any spendable dough.

But the Congo remained in spite of formidable opposition and foreign exploitation. The Congo was a real throbbing little Africa in New York. It was an amusement place entirely for the unwashed of the Black Belt. Or, if they were washed, smells lingered telling the nature of their occupation. Pot-wrestlers, third cooks, W.C. attendants, scrub maids, dish-washers, stevedores.

Girls coming from the South to try their future in New York always reached the Congo first. The Congo was African in spirit and color. No white persons were admitted there. The

151

proprietor knew his market. He did not cater to the fast trade. "High yallers" were scarce there. Except for such sweetmen that lived off the low-down dark trade.

When you were fed up with the veneer of Seventh Avenue, and Goldgraben's Afro-Oriental garishness, you would go to the Congo and turn rioting loose in all the tenacious odors of service and the warm indigenous smells of Harlem, fooping or jig-jagging the night away. You would if you were a black kid hunting for joy in New York.

Jake went down to the Baltimore. No sign of his honey girl anywhere. He drank Scotch after Scotch. His disappointment mounted to anger against himself—turned to anger against his honey girl. His eyes roved round the room, but saw nobody.

"Oh what a big Ah-Ah I was!"

All round the den, luxuriating under the little colored lights, the dark dandies were loving up their pansies. Feet tickling feet under tables, tantalizing liquor-rich giggling, hands busy above.

"Honey gal! Honey gal! What other sweet boy is loving you now? Don't you know your last night's daddy am waiting for you?"

The cabaret singer, a shiny coffee-colored girl in a green frock and Indian-waved hair, went singing from table to table in a man's bass voice.

> "You wanta know how I do it,
>   How I look so good, how I am so happy,
>   All night on the blessed job—
>   How I slide along making things go snappy?
>   It is easy to tell,
>   I ain't got no plan—
>   But I'm crazy, plumb crazy
>   About a man, mah man.
>
> "It ain't no secret as you think,
>   The glad heart is a state o' mind—
>   Throw a stone in the river and it will sink;
>   But a feather goes whirling on the wind.
>   It is easy to tell. . . ."

She stopped more than usual at Jake's table. He gave her a half dollar. She danced a jagging jig before him that made the giggles rise like a wave in the room. The pansies stared and tightened their grip on their dandies. The dandies tightened their hold on themselves. They looked the favored Jake up and down. All those perfection struts for him. Yet he didn't seem aroused at all.

"I'm crazy, plumb crazy
 About a man, mah man. . . ."

The girl went humming back to her seat. She had poured every drop of her feeling into the song.

"Crazy, plumb crazy about a man, mah man. . . ."

Dandies and pansies, chocolate, chestnut, coffee, ebony, cream, yellow, everybody was teased up to the high point of excitement. . . .

"Crazy, plumb crazy about a man, mah man. . . ."

The saxophone was moaning it. And feet and hands and mouths were acting it. Dancing. Some jigged, some shuffled, some walked, and some were glued together swaying on the dance floor.

Jake was going crazy. A hot fever was burning him up. . . . Where was the singing gal that had danced to him? That dancing was for him all right. . . .

A crash cut through the music. A table went jazzing into the drum. The cabaret singer lay sprawling on the floor. A raging putty-skinned mulattress stamped on her ribs and spat in her face! "That'll teach you to leave mah man be every time." A black waiter rushed the mulattress. "Git off'n her. 'Causen she's down."

A potato-yellow man and a dull-black were locked. The proprietor, a heavy brown man, worked his elbow like a hatchet between them.

The antagonists glowered at each other.

"What you want to knock the gal down like that for, I acks you?"

"Better acks her why she done spits on mah woman."

"*Woman!* White man's wench, you mean. You low-down tripe. . . ."

The black man heaved toward the yellow, but the waiters

hooked and hustled him off. . . . Sitting at a table, the cabaret singer was soothing her eye.

"Git out on the sidewalk, all you trouble-makers," cried the proprietor. "And you, Bess," he cried to the cabaret singer, "nevah you show your face in mah place again."

The cabaret was closed for the rest of the night. Like dogs flicked apart by a whipcord, the jazzers stood and talked resentfully in the street.

"Hi, Jake"—Zeddy, rocking into the group with a nosy air, spotted his buddy—"was you in on the li'l' fun?"

"Yes, buddy, but I wasn't mixed up in it. Sometimes they turn mah stomach, the womens. The same in France, the same in England, the same in Harlem. White against white and black against white and yellow against black and brown. We's all just crazy-dog mad. Ain't no peace on earth with the womens and there ain't no life anywhere without them."

"You said it, boh. It's a be-be itching life"—Zeddy scratched his flank—"and we're all sons of it. . . . But what is you hitting round this joint? I thought you would be feeding off milk and honey tonight?"

"Hard luck, buddy. Done lose out counta mah own indiligence. I fohgit the street and the house. Thought I'd find her heah but. . . ."

"What you thinking 'bout, boh?"

"That gal got beat up in the Baltimore. She done sings me into a tantalizing mood. Ahm feeling like."

"Let's take a look in on the Congo, boh. It's the best pick-me-up place in Harlem."

"I'm with you, buddy."

"Always packed with the best pickings. When the chippies come up from down home, tha's where they hangs out first. You kain always find something that New York ain't done made a fool of yet. Theah's a high-yaller entertainer there that I'se got a crush on, but she ain't nevah gived me a encouraging eye."

"I ain't much for the high-yallers after having been so much fed-up on the ofays," said Jake. "They's so doggone much alike."

"Ah no, boh. A sweet-lovin' high-yaller queen's got something different. K-hhhhhhh, K-hhhhhhh. Something nigger."

The Congo was thick, dark-colorful, and fascinating. Drum and saxophone were fighting out the wonderful drag "blues" that was the favorite of all the low-down dance halls. In all the better places it was banned. Rumor said it was a police ban. It was an old tune, so far as popular tunes go. But at the Congo it lived fresh and green as grass. Everybody there was giggling and wriggling to it.

> And it is ashes to ashes and dust to dust,
> Can you show me a woman that a man can trust?

>> Oh, baby, how are you?
>> Oh, baby, what are you?
>> Oh, can I have you now,
>> Or have I got to wait?
>> Oh, let me have a date,
>> Why do you hesitate?

> And there is two things in Harlem I don't understan'
> It is a bulldycking woman and a faggotty man.

>> Oh, baby how are you?
>> Oh, baby, what are you? . . .

Jake and Zeddy picked two girls from a green bench and waded into the hot soup. The saxophone and drum fought over the punctuated notes. The cymbals clashed. The excitement mounted. Couples breasted each other in rhythmical abandon, grinned back at their friends and chanted:

>> "Oh, baby, how are you?
>> Oh, baby, what are you? . . ."

Clash! The cymbal snuffed out saxophone and drum, the dancers fell apart,—reeled, strutted, drifted back to their green places. . . .

Zeddy tossed down the third glass of Gordon gin and became aware of Rose, the Congo entertainer, singing at the table. Happy for the moment, he gave her fifty cents. She sang some more, but Zeddy saw that it was all for Jake. Finished, she sat down, uninvited, at their table.

How many nights, hungry nights, Zeddy had wished that Rose would sit down voluntarily at his table. He had asked her sometimes. She would sit, take a drink and leave. Nothing doing. If he was a "big nigger," perhaps—but she was too high-priced for him. Now she was falling for Jake. Perhaps it was Jake's nifty suit. . . .

"Gin for mine," Rose said. Jake ordered two gins and a Scotch. "Scotch! That's an ofay drink," Rose remarked. "And I've seen the monkey-chasers order it when they want to put on style."

"It's good," Jake said. "Taste it."

She shook her head. "I have befoh. I don't like the taste. Gimme gin every time or good old red Kentucky."

"I got used to it over the other side," Jake said.

"Oh! You're an over-yonder baby! Sure enough!" She fondled his suit in admiration.

Zeddy, like a good understanding buddy, had slipped away. Another Scotch and Gordon Dry. The glasses kissed. Like a lean lazy leopard the mulattress reclined against Jake.

The milk cans were sounding on the pavements and a few pale stars were still visible in the sky when Rose left the Congo with both hands entwined in Jake's arm.

"You gwina stay with me, mah brown?"

"I ain't got me a room yet," he said.

"Come stay with me always. Got any stuff to bring along?"

"Mah suitcase at Uncle Doc's."

They went to her room in One Hundred and Thirty-third street. Locking the door, she said: "You remember the song they used to sing before you all went over there, mah brown?"

Softly she chanted:

"If I had some one like you at home
    I wouldn't wanta go out, I wouldn't wanta go out. . . .
    If I had some one like you at home,
    I'd put a padlock on the door. . . ."

She hugged him to her.

"I love you. I ain't got no man."

"Gwan, tell that to the marines," he panted.

"Honest to God. Lemme kiss you nice."

It was now eating-time in Harlem. They were hungry. They washed and dressed.

"If you'll be mah man always, you won't have to work," she said.

"Me?" responded Jake. "I've never been a sweetman yet. Never lived off no womens and never will. I always works."

"I don't care what you do whilst you is mah man. But hard work's no good for a sweet-loving papa."

V

On the Job Again

JAKE stayed on in Rose's room. He could not feel about her as he did for his little lost maroon-brown of the Baltimore. He went frequently to the Baltimore, but he never saw her again. Then he grew to hate that cabaret and stopped going there.

The mulattress was charged with tireless activity and Jake was her big, good slave. But her spirit lacked the charm and verve, the infectious joy, of his little lost brown. He sometimes felt that she had no spirit at all—that strange, elusive something that he felt in himself, sometimes here, sometimes there, roaming away from him, going back to London, to Brest, Le Havre, wandering to some unknown new port, caught a moment by some romantic rhythm, color, face, passing through cabarets, saloons, speakeasies, and returning to him. . . . The little brown had something of that in her, too. That night he had felt a reaching out and marriage of spirits. . . . But the mulattress was all a wonderful tissue of throbbing flesh. He had never once felt in her any tenderness or timidity or aloofness. . . .

Jake was working longshore. Hooking barrels and boxes, wrestling with chains and cranes. He didn't have a little-boss job this time. But that didn't worry him. He was one blacka-moor that nourished a perfect contempt for place. There were times when he divided his days between Rose and Uncle Doc's saloon and Dixie Red's pool-room.

He never took money from her. If he gambled away his own and was short, he borrowed from Nije Gridley, the longshore-man broker. Nije Gridley was a tall, thin, shiny black man. His long eyelashes gave his sharp eyes a sleepy appearance, but he was always wide awake. Before Jake was shipped to France, Nije had a rooming-house in Harlem's Fifth Avenue, worked a little at longshoring himself, and lent money on the checks of the hard-gambling boys. Now he had three rooming-houses, one of which, free of mortgage, he owned. His lean belly bore a heavy gold chain and he strutted Fifth and Lenox in a minis-terial crow-black suit. With the war boom of wages, the boys had gambled heavily and borrowed recklessly.

Ordinarily, Nije lent money at the rate of a dollar on four and two on eight per week. He complained bitterly of losses. Twenty-five dollars loaned on a check which, presented, brought only a day's pay. There were tough fellows that played him that game sometimes. They went and never returned to borrow again. But Nije's interest covered up such gaps. And sometimes he gave ten dollars on a forty-dollar check, drew the wages, and never saw his customer again, who had vanished entirely out of that phase of Harlem life.

One week when they were not working, Zeddy came to Jake with wonderful news. Men were wanted at a certain pier to unload pineapples at eight dollars a day. Eight dollars was ex-ceptional wages, but the fruit was spoiling.

Jake went with Zeddy and worked the first day with a group of Negroes and a few white men. The white men were not reg-ular dock workers. The only thing that seemed strange to Jake was that all the men ate inside and were not allowed outside the gates for lunch. But, on the second day, his primitive pas-sion for going against regulation urged him to go out in the street after lunch.

Heaving casually along West Street, he was hailed by a white man. "Hello, fellow-worker!"

"Hello, there! What's up?" Jake asked.

"You working in there?"

"Sure I is. Since yestidday."

The man told Jake that there was a strike on and he was scabbing. Jake asked him why there were no pickets if there was a strike. The man replied that there were no pickets be-cause the union leaders were against the strike, and had con-nived with the police to beat up and jail the pickets.

"Well, pardner," Jake said, "I've done worked through a tur'ble assortments o' jobs in mah lifetime, but I ain't nevah yet scabbed it on any man. I done work in this heah country, and I works good and hard over there in France. I works in London and I nevah was a blackleg, although I been the only black man in mah gang."

"Fine, fellow-worker; that's a real man's talk," said the white man. He took a little red book out of his pocket and asked Jake to let him sign him up in his union.

"It's the only one in the country for a red-blooded worker, no matter what race or nation he belongs to."

"Nope, I won't scab, but I ain't a joiner kind of a fellah," said Jake. "I ain't no white folks' nigger and I ain't no poah white's fool. When I longshored in Philly I was a good union man. But when I made New York I done finds out that they gived the colored mens the worser piers and holds the bes'n a' them foh the Irishmen. No, pardner, keep you' card. I take the best I k'n get as I goes mah way. But I tells you, things ain't none at all lovely between white and black in this heah Gawd's own country."

"We take all men in our union regardless——" But Jake was haunching along out of hearing down West Street. . . . Suddenly he heard sharp, deep, distressful grunts, and saw behind some barrels a black man down and being kicked perilously in the rear end by two white men. Jake drew his hook from his belt and, waving it in the air, he rushed them. The white men shot like rats to cover. The down man scrambled to his feet. One of Zeddy's pals, Jake recognized him.

"What's the matter, buddy, the peckawoods them was doing you in?"

"Becaz they said there was a strike in theah. And I said I didn't give a doughnut, I was going to work foh mah money all the same. I got one o' them bif! in the eye, though. . . ."

"Don't go back, buddy. Let the boss-men stick them jobs up. They are a bunch of rotten aigs. Just using us to do their dirty work. Come on, let's haul bottom away from here to Harlem."

At Dixie Red's pool-room that evening there were some fellows with bandaged arms and heads. One iron-heavy, blue-black lad (he was called Liver-lip behind his back, because of the plankiness of his lips) carried his arm in a sling, and told Jake how he happened to be like that.

"They done jumped on me soon as I turned mah black moon on that li'l saloon tha's catering to us niggers. Heabenly God! But if the stars them didn't twinkle way down in mah eyes. But easy, easy, old man, I got out mah shaving steel and draws it down the goosey flesh o' one o' them, and, buddy, you shoulda heah him squeal. . . . The pohlice?" His massive mouth molded the words to its own form. "They tooks me, yes, but tunned me loose by'n'by. They's with us this time, boh, but, Lawdy! if they hadn't did entervention I woulda gutted gizzard and kidney outa that white tripe."

Jake was angry with Zeddy and asked him, when he came in, why he had not told him at first that the job was a scab job.

"I won't scab on nobody, not even the orneriest crackers," he said.

"Bull Durham!" cried Zeddy. "What was I going to let on about anything for? The boss-man done paid me to git him mens, and I got them. Ain't I working there mahself? I'll take any job in this heah Gawd's country that the white boss make it worf mah while to work at."

"But it ain't decent to scab," said Jake.

"Decent mah black moon!" shouted Zeddy. "I'll scab through hell to make mah living. Scab job or open shop or union am all the same jobs to me. White mens don't want niggers in them unions, nohow. Ain't you a good carpenter? And ain't I a good blacksmith? But kain we get a look-in on our trade heah in this white man's city? Ain't white mens done scabbed niggers outa all the jobs they useter hold down heah in this city? Waiter, bootblack, and barber shop?"

"With all a that scabbing is a low-down deal," Jake maintained.

"Me eye! Seems lak youse gittin' religion, boh. Youse talking death, tha's what you sure is. One thing I know is niggers am made foh life. And I want to live, boh, and feel plenty o' the juice o' life in mah blood. I wanta live and I wanta love. And niggers am got to work hard foh that. Buddy, I'll tell you this and I'll tell it to the wo'l'—all the crackers, all them poah white trash, all the nigger-hitting and nigger-breaking white folks—I loves life and I got to live and I'll scab through hell to live."

Jake did not work again that week. By Saturday morning he didn't have a nickel, so he went to Nije Gridley to borrow money. Nije asked him if he was going that evening to Billy Biasse's railroad flat, the longshoremen gaming rendezvous. Jake said no, he was going with Zeddy to a buffet flat in One Hundred and Fortieth Street. The buffet flat was the rendezvous of a group of railroad porters and club waiters who gambled for big stakes. Jake did not go there often because he had to dress up as if he were going to a cabaret. Also, he was not a big-stake gambler. . . . He preferred Billy Biasse's, where he could go whenever he liked with hook and overalls.

"Oh, that's whar Zeddy's hanging out now," Nije commented, casually.

For some time before Jake's return from Europe Zeddy had stopped going to Billy Biasse's. He told Jake he was fed up with it. Jake did not know that Zeddy owed Nije money and that he did not go to Billy Biasse's because Nije often went there. . . .

Later in the evening Nije went to Billy Biasse's and found a longshoreman who was known at the buffet flat, to take him there.

Gambling was a bigger game than sex at this buffet flat. The copper-hued lady who owned it was herself a very good poker-player. There were only two cocoa-brown girls there. Not young or attractive. They made a show of doing something, serving drinks and trying hard to make jokes. In dining- and sitting-room, five tables were occupied by card-players. Railroad porters, longshoremen, waiters; tight-faced, anxious-eyed. Zeddy sat at the same table with the lady of the flat. He had just eliminated two cards and asked for two when Nije and his escort were let into the flat. Zeddy smelled his man and knew it was Nije without looking up.

Nije swaggered past Zeddy and joined a group at another table. The gaming went on with intermittent calls for drinks. Nije sat where he could watch Zeddy's face. Zeddy also, although apparently intent on the cards, kept a wary eye on Nije. Sometimes their eyes met. No one was aware of the challenge that was developing between the two men.

There was a little slackening in the games, a general call for drinks, and a shifting of chairs. Nije got nearer to Zeddy. . . . Half-smiling and careless-like, he planted his bootheel upon Zeddy's toes.

"Git off mah feets," Zeddy barked. The answer was a hard blow in the face. Zeddy tasted blood in his mouth. He threw his muscular gorilla body upon the tall Nije and hugged him down to the floor.

"You blasted black Jew, say you' prayers!" cried Zeddy.

"Ain't scared o' none o' you barefaced robber niggers." Nije was breathing hard under Zeddy and trying to get the better of him by the help of the wall.

"Black man," growled Zeddy, "I'se gwineta cut your throat just so sure as God is white."

With his knee upon Nije's chest and his left hand on his windpipe, Zeddy flashed the deadly-gleaming blade out of his back pocket. The proprietress let loose a blood-curdling scream, but before Zeddy's hand could achieve its purpose, Jake aimed a swift kick at his elbow. The razor flew spinning upward and fell chopping through a glass of gin on the pianola.

The proprietress fell upon Zeddy and clawed at him. "Wha's the matter all you bums trying to ruin mah place?" she cried. "Ain't I been a good spoht with you all, making everything here nice and respectable?"

Jake took charge of Zeddy. Two men hustled Nije off away out of the flat.

"Who was it put the krimp on me?" asked Zeddy.

"You ought to praise the Lawd you was saved from Sing Sing and don't ask no questions," the woman replied.

Everybody was talking.

"How did that long, tall, blood-suckin' nigger get in heah?"

"Soon as this heah kind a business stahts, the dicks will sartain sure git on to us."

"It ain't no moh than last week they done raided Madame Jerkin's, the niftiest buffet flat in Harlem. O Lawdy!"

"That ole black cock," growled Zeddy, "he wouldn'a' crowed round Harlem no moh after I'd done made that theah fine blade talk in his throat."

"Shut up you," the proprietress said, "or I'll throw you out." And Zeddy, the ape, who was scared of no man in the place, became humble before the woman. She began setting the room to order, helped by the two cocoa-brown girls. A man shuffling a pack of cards called to Zeddy and Jake.

But the woman held up her hand. "No more card-playing tonight. I feel too nervous."

"Let's dance, then," suggested the smaller cocoa-brown girl.

A "blues" came trotting out of the pianola. The proprietress bounced into Jake's arms. The men sprang at the two girls. The unlucky ones paired off with each other.

Oh, "blues," "blues," "blues." Black-framed white grinning. Finger-snapping. Undertone singing. The three men with women teasing the stags. Zeddy's gorilla feet dancing down the dark death lurking in his heart. Zeddy dancing with a pal. "Blues," "blues," "blues." Red moods, black moods, golden moods. Curious, syncopated slipping-over into one mood, back-sliding back to the first mood. Humming in harmony, barbaric harmony, joy-drunk, chasing out the shadow of the moment before.

VI
Myrtle Avenue

ZEDDY was excited over Jake's success in love. He thought how often he had tried to make up to Rose, without succeeding. He was crazy about finding a woman to love him for himself.

He had been married when he was quite a lad to a crust-yellow girl in Petersburg. Zeddy's wife, after deceiving him with white men, had run away from him to live an easier life. That was before Zeddy came North. Since then he had had many other alliances. But none had been successful.

It was true that no Black Belt beauty would ever call Zeddy "mah han'some brown." But there were sweetmen of the Belt more repulsive than he, that women would fight and murder each other for. Zeddy did not seem to possess any of that magic that charms and holds women for a long time. All his attempts at home-making had failed. The women left him when he could not furnish the cash to meet the bills. They never saw his wages. For it was gobbled up by his voracious passion for poker and crap games. Zeddy gambled in Harlem. He gambled with white men down by the piers. And he was always losing.

"If only I could get those kinda gals that falls foh Jake," Zeddy mused. "And Jake is such a fool spade. Don't know how to handle the womens."

Zeddy's chance came at last. One Saturday a yellow-skinned youth, whose days and nights were wholly spent between pool-rooms and Negro speakeasies, invited Zeddy to a sociable at a grass-widow's who lived in Brooklyn and worked as a cook downtown in New York. She was called Gin-head Susy. She had a little apartment in Myrtle Avenue near Prince Street.

Susy was wonderfully created. She was of the complexion known among Negroes as spade or chocolate-to-the-bone. Her eyes shone like big white stars. Her chest was majestic and the general effect like a mountain. And that mountain was overgrand because Susy never wore any other but extremely

French-heeled shoes. Even over the range she always stood poised in them and blazing in bright-hued clothes.

The burning passion of Susy's life was the yellow youth of her race. Susy came from South Carolina. A yellow youngster married her when she was fifteen and left her before she was eighteen. Since then she had lived with a yellow complex at the core of her heart.

Civilization had brought strikingly exotic types into Susy's race. And like many, many Negroes, she was a victim to that. . . . Ancient black life rooted upon its base with all its fascinating new layers of brown, low-brown, high-brown, nut-brown, lemon, maroon, olive, mauve, gold. Yellow balancing between black and white. Black reaching out beyond yellow. Almost-white on the brink of a change. Sucked back down into the current of black by the terribly sweet rhythm of black blood. . . .

Susy's life of yellow complexity was surcharged with gin. There were whisky and beer also at her sociable evenings, but gin was the drink of drinks. Except for herself, her parties were all-male. Like so many of her sex, she had a congenital contempt for women. All-male were her parties and as yellow as she could make them. A lemon-colored or paper-brown poolroom youngster from Harlem's Fifth Avenue or from Prince Street. A bellboy or railroad waiter or porter. Sometimes a chocolate who was a quick, nondiscriminating lover and not remote of attitude like the pampered high-browns. But chocolates were always a rarity among Susy's front-roomful of gin-lovers.

Yet for all of her wages drowned in gin, Susy carried a hive of discontents in her majestic breast. She desired a lover, something like her undutiful husband, but she desired in vain. Her guests consumed her gin and listened to the phonograph, exchanged rakish stories, and when they felt fruit-ripe to dropping, left her place in pursuit of pleasures elsewhere.

Sometimes Susy managed to lay hold of a yellow one for some time. Something all a piece of dirty rags and stench picked up in the street. Cleansed, clothed, and booted it. But so soon as he got his curly hair straightened by the process of Harlem's Ambrozine Palace of Beauty, and started in strutting the pavement of Lenox Avenue, feeling smart as a moving-picture dandy, he would leave Susy.

Apart from Susy's repellent person, no youthful sweetman attempting to love her could hold out under the ridicule of his pals. Over their games of pool and craps the boys had their cracks at Susy.

"What about Gin-head Susy tonight?"

"Sure, let's go and look the crazy old broad over."

"I'll go anywhere foh swilling of good booze."

"She's sho one ugly spade, but she's right there with her Gordon Dry."

"She ain't got 'em from creeps to crown and her trotters is B flat, but her gin is regal."

But now, after all the years of gin sociables and unsatisfactory lemons, Susy was changing just a little. She was changing under the influence of her newly-acquired friend, Lavinia Curdy, the only woman whom she tolerated at her parties. That was not so difficult, as Miss Curdy was less attractive than Susy. Miss Curdy was a putty-skinned mulattress with purple streaks on her face. Two of her upper front teeth had been knocked out and her lower lip slanted pathetically leftward. She was skinny and when she laughed she resembled an old braying jenny.

When Susy came to know Miss Curdy, she unloaded a quantity of the stuff of her breast upon her. Her drab childhood in a South Carolina town. Her early marriage. No girlhood. Her husband leaving her. And all the yellow men that had beaten her, stolen from her, and pawned her things.

Miss Curdy had been very emphatic to Susy about "yaller men." "I know them from long experience. They never want to work. They're a lazy and shiftless lot. Want to be kept like women. I found that out a long, long time ago. And that's why when I wanted a man foh keeps I took me a black plug-ugly one, mah dear."

It wouldn't have supported the plausibility of Miss Curdy's advice if she had mentioned that more than one black plug-ugly had ruthlessly cut loose from her. As the black woman had had her entanglements in yellow, so had the mulattress hers of black. But, perhaps, Miss Curdy did not realize that she could not help desiring black. In her salad days as a business girl her purse was controlled by many a black man. Now, however, her old problems did not arise in exactly the same way, —her purse was old and worn and flat and attracted no attention.

"A black man is as good to me as a yaller when I finds a real one." Susy lied a little to Miss Curdy from a feeling that she ought to show some pride in her own complexion.

"But all these sociables—and you spend so much coin on gin," Miss Curdy had said.

"Well, that's the trute, but we all of us drinks it. And I loves to have company in mah house, plenty of company."

But when Susy came home from work one evening and found that her latest "yaller" sweetie had stolen her suitcase and best dresses and pawned even her gas range, she resolved never to keep another of his kind as a "steady." At least she made that resolve to Miss Curdy. But the sociables went on and the same types came to drink the Saturday evenings away, leaving the two women at the finish to their empty bottles and glasses. Once Susy did make a show of a black lover. He was the house man at the boarding-house where she cooked. But the arrangement did not hold any time, for Susy demanded of the chocolate extremely more than she ever got from her yellows.

"Well, boh, we's Brooklyn bound tonight," said Zeddy to Jake.

"You got to show me that Brooklyn's got any life to it," replied Jake.

"Theah's life anywheres theah's booze and jazz, and theah's cases o' gin and a gramophone whar we's going."

"Has we got to pay foh it, buddy?"

"No, boh, eve'ything is f.o.c. ef the lady likes you."

"Blimey!" A cockney phrase stole Jake's tongue. "Don't bull me."

"I ain't. Honest-to-Gawd Gordon Dry, and moh—ef you're the goods, all f.o.c."

"Well, I'll be browned!" exclaimed Jake.

Zeddy also took along Strawberry Lips, a new pal, burnt-cork black, who was thus nicknamed from the peculiar stage-red color of his mouth. Strawberry Lips was typically the stage Negro. He was proof that a generalization has some foundation in truth. . . . You might live your life in many black belts and arrive at the conclusion that there is no such thing as a typical Negro—no minstrel coon off the stage, no Thomas Nelson Page's nigger, no Octavus Roy Cohen's porter, no lineal descendant of Uncle Tom. Then one day your theory may be upset through meeting with a type by far more perfect than any created counterpart.

"Myrtle Avenue used to be a be-be itching of a place," said Strawberry Lips, "when Doc Giles had his gambling house on there and Elijah Bowers was running his cabaret. H'm. But Bowers was some big guy. He knew swell white folks in politics, and had a grand automobile and a high-yaller wife that hadn't no need of painting to pass. His cabaret was running neck and neck with Marshall's in Fifty-third Street. Then one night he killed a man in his cabaret, and that finished him. The lawyers got him off. But they cleaned him out dry. Done broke him, that case did. And today he's plumb down and out."

Jake, Zeddy, and Strawberry Lips had left the subway train at Borough Hall and were walking down Myrtle Avenue.

"Bowers' cabaret was some place for the teasing-brown pick-me-up then, brother—and the snow. The stuff was cheap then. You sniff, boh?" Strawberry Lips asked Jake and Zeddy.

"I wouldn't know befoh I sees it," Jake laughed.

"I ain't no habitual prisoner," said Zeddy, "but I does any little thing for a change. Keep going and active with anything, says I."

The phonograph was discharging its brassy jazz notes when they entered the apartment. Susy was jerking herself from one side to the other with a potato-skinned boy. Miss Curdy was half-hopping up and down with the only chocolate that was there. Five lads, ranging from brown to yellow in complexion, sat drinking with jaded sneering expressions on their faces. The one that had invited Zeddy was among them. He waved to him to come over with his friends.

"Sit down and try some gin," he said. . . .

Zeddy dipped his hand in his pocket and sent two bones rolling on the table.

"Ise with you, chappie," his yellow friend said. The others

crowded around. The gramophone stopped and Susy, hugging
a bottle, came jerking on her French heels over to the group.
She filled the glasses and everybody guzzled gin.

Miss Curdy looked the newcomers over, paying particular
attention to Jake. A sure-enough eye-filling chocolate, she
thought. I would like to make a steady thing of him.

Over by the door two light-brown lads began arguing about
an actress of the leading theater of the Black Belt.

"I tell you I knows Gertie Kendall. I know her more'n I
know you."

"Know her mah granny. You knows her just like I do, from
the balcony of the Lafayette. Don't hand me none o' that fairy
stuff, for I ain't gwine to swallow it."

"Youse an aching pain. I knows her, I tell you. I even danced
with her at Madame Mulberry's apartment. You thinks I only
hangs out with low-down trash becassin Ise in a place like this,
eh? I done met mos'n all our big niggers: Jack Johnson, James
Reese Europe, Adah Walker, Buddy, who used to play that
theah drum for them Castle Walkers, and Madame Walker."

"Yaller, it 'pears to me that youse jest a nacherally-born
story-teller. You really spec's me to believe youse been associating with the mucty-mucks of the race? Gwan with you. You'll
be telling me next you done speaks with Charlie Chaplin and
John D. Rockefeller——"

Miss Curdy had tuned her ears to the conversation and
broke in: "Why, what is that to make so much fuss about? Sure
he can dance with Gertie Kendall and know the dickty niggers.
In my sporting days I knew Bert Williams and Walker and
Adah Overton and Editor Tukslack and all that upstage race
gang that wouldn't touch Jack Johnson with a ten-foot pole. I
lived in Washington and had Congressmen for my friends—
foop! Why you can get in with the top-crust crowd at any swell
ball in Harlem. All you need is clothes and the coin. I know
them all, yet I don't feel a bit haughty mixing here with Susy
and you all."

"I guess you don't now," somebody said.

Gin went round . . . and round . . . and round. . . .
Desultory dancing. . . . Dice. . . . Blackjack. . . . Poker.
. . . The room became a close, live, intense place. Tight-faced,

the men seemed interested only in drinking and gaming, while Susy and Miss Curdy, guzzling hard, grew uglier. A jungle atmosphere pervaded the room, and, like shameless wild animals hungry for raw meat, the females savagely searched the eyes of the males. Susy's eyes always came back to settle upon the lad that had invited Zeddy. He was her real object. And Miss Curdy was ginned up with high hopes of Jake.

Jake threw up the dice and Miss Curdy seized her chance to get him alone for a little while.

"The cards do get so tiresome," she said. "I wonder how you men can go on and on all night long poking around with poker."

"Better than worser things," retorted Jake. Disgusted by the purple streaks, he averted his eyes from the face of the mulattress.

"I don't know about that," Miss Curdy bridled. "There's many nice ways of spending a sociable evening between ladies and gentlemen."

"Got to show me," said Jake, simply because the popular phrase intrigued his tongue.

"And that I can."

Irritated, Jake turned to move away.

"Where you going? Scared of a lady?"

Jake recoiled from the challenge, and shuffled away from the hideous mulattress. From experience in seaport towns in America, in France, in England, he had concluded that a woman could always go farther than a man in coarseness, depravity, and sheer cupidity. Men were ugly and brutal. But beside women they were merely vicious children. Ignorant about the aim and meaning and fulfillment of life; uncertain and indeterminate; weak. Rude children who loved excelling in spectacular acts to win the applause of women.

But women were so realistic and straight-going. *They* were the real controlling force of life. Jake remembered the balmusette fights between colored and white soldiers in France. Blacks, browns, yellows, whites. . . . He remembered the interracial sex skirmishes in England. Men fought, hurt, wounded, killed each other. Women, like blazing torches, egged them on or denounced them. Victims of sex, the men seemed foolish, apelike blunderers in their pools of blood. Didn't know what they were fighting for, except it was to gratify some vague feeling about women. . . .

Jake's thoughts went roaming after his little lost brown of the Baltimore. The difference! She, in one night, had revealed a fine different world to him. Mystery again. A little stray girl. Finer than the finest!

Some of the fellows were going. In a vexed spirit, Susy had turned away from her unresponsive mulatto toward Zeddy. Relieved, the mulatto yawned, threw his hands backwards and said: "I guess mah broad is home from Broadway by now. Got to final on home to her. Harlem, lemme see you."

Miss Curdy was sitting against the mantelpiece, charming Strawberry Lips. Marvellous lips. Salmon-pink and planky. She had hoisted herself upon his knees, her arm around his thick neck.

Jake went over to the mantelpiece to pour a large chaser of beer and Miss Curdy leered at him. She disgusted him. His life was a free coarse thing, but he detested nastiness and ugliness. Guess I'll haul bottom to Harlem, he thought. Congo Rose was a rearing wild animal, all right, but these women, these boys. . . . Skunks, tame skunks, all of them!

He was just going out when a chocolate lad pointed at a light-brown and said: "The pot calls foh four bits, chappie. Come across or stay out."

"Lemme a quarter!"

"Ain't got it. Staying out?"

Biff! Square on the mouth. The chocolate leaped up like a tiger-cat at his assailant, carrying over card table, little pile of money, and half-filled gin glasses with a crash. Like an enraged ram goat, he held and butted the light-brown boy twice, straight on the forehead. The victim crumpled with a thud to the floor. Susy jerked over to the felled boy and hauled him, his body leaving a liquid trail, to the door. She flung him out in the corridor and slammed the door.

"Sarves him right, pulling off that crap in mah place. And you, Mis'er Jack Johnson," she said to the chocolate youth, "lemme miss you quick."

"He done hits me first," the chocolate said.

"I knows it, but I ain't gwina stand foh no rough-house in

mah place. Ise got a dawg heah wif me all ready foh bawking."

"K-hhhhh, K-hhhhh," laughed Strawberry Lips. "Oh, boh,
I know it's the trute, but——"

The chocolate lad slunk out of the flat.

"Lavinia," said Susy to Miss Curdy, "put on that theah
'Tickling Blues' on the victroly."

The phonograph began its scraping and Miss Curdy started
jig-jagging with Strawberry Lips. Jake gloomed with disgust
against the door.

"Getting outa this, buddy?" he asked Zeddy.

"Nobody's chasing *us*, boh." Zeddy commenced stepping
with Susy to the "Tickling Blues."

Outside, Jake found the light-brown boy still half-stunned
against the wall.

"Ain't you gwine at home?" Jake asked him.

"I can't find a nickel foh car fare," said the boy.

Jake took him into a saloon and bought him a lemon squash.
"Drink that to clear you' haid," he said. "And heah's car fare."
He gave the boy a dollar. "Whar you living at?"

"San Juan Hill."

"Come on, le's git the subway, then."

The Myrtle Avenue Elevated train passed with a high raucous rumble over their heads.

"Myrtle Avenue," murmured Jake. "Pretty name, all right,
but it stinks like a sewer. Legs and feets! Come take me outa it
back home to Harlem."

VII
Zeddy's Rise and Fall

ZEDDY was scarce in Harlem. And Strawberry Lips was also scarce. It was fully a week after the Myrtle Avenue gin-fest before Jake saw Zeddy again. They met on the pavement in front of Uncle Doc's saloon.

"Why, where in the sweet name of niggers in Harlem, buddy, you been keeping you'self?"

"Whar you think?"

"Think? I been very much thinking that Nije Gridley done git you."

"How come you git thataway, boh? Nije Gridley him ain't got a chawnst on the carve or the draw ag'inst Zeddy Plummer so long as Ise got me a black moon."

"Well, what's it done git you, then?"

"Myrtle Avenue."

"Come outa that; you ain't talking. . . ."

"The trute as I knows it, buddy."

"Crazy dog bite mah laig!" cried Jake. "You ain't telling me that you done gone. . . ."

"Transfer mah suitcase and all mah pohsitions to Susy."

"Gin-head Susy!"

"Egsactly; that crechur is mah ma-ma now. I done express mahself ovah theah on that very mahv'lously hang-ovah afternoon of that ginnity mawnin' that you left me theah. And Ise been right theah evah since."

"Well, Ise got to wish you good luck, buddy, although youse been keeping it so dark."

"It's the darkness of new loving, boh. But the honeymoon is good and well ovah, and I'll be li'l moh in Harlem as usual, looking the chippies and chappies ovah. I ain't none at all stuck on Brooklyn."

"It's a swah hole all right," said Jake.

"But theah's sweet stuff in it." Zeddy tongue-wiped his fleshy lips with a salacious laugh.

"It's all right, believe me, boh," he informed Jake. "Susy

ain't nothing to look at like you' fair-brown queen, but she's tur'bly sweet loving. You know when a ma-ma ain't the goods in looks and figure, she's got to make up foh it some. And that Susy does. And she treats me right. Gimme all I wants to drink and brings home the goodest poke chops and fried chicken foh me to put away under mah shirt. . . . Youse got to come and feed with us all one o' these heah evenings."

It was a party of five when Jake went again to Myrtle Avenue for the magnificent free-love feast that Susy had prepared. It was Susy's free Sunday. Miss Curdy and Strawberry Lips were also celebrating. Susy had concocted a pitcherful of knock-out gin cocktails. And such food! Susy could cook. Perhaps it was her splendid style that made her sink all her wages in gin and sweetmen. For she belonged to the ancient aristocracy of black cooks, and knew that she was always sure of a good place, so long as the palates of rich Southerners retained their discriminating taste.

Cream tomato soup. Ragout of chicken giblets. Southern fried chicken. Candied sweet potatoes. Stewed corn. Rum-flavored fruit salad waiting in the ice-box. . . . The stars rolling in Susy's shining face showed how pleased she was with her art.

She may be fat and ugly as a turkey, thought Jake, but her eats am sure beautiful.

"Heah! Pass me you' plate," Susy gave Jake a leg. Zeddy held out his plate again and got a wing. Strawberry Lips received a bit of breast. . . .

"No more chicken for me, Susy," Miss Curdy mumbled, "but I *will* have another helping of that there stewed corn. I don't know what ingredients yo-all puts in it, but, Lawdy! I never tasted anything near so good."

Susy beamed and dipped up three spoonfuls of corn. "Plenty, thank you," Miss Curdy stopped her from filling up her saucer. . . . Susy drank off a tumbler of cocktail at a draught, and wiped her lips with the white serviette that was stuck into the low neck of her vermillion crepe-de-chine blouse. . . .

When Jake was ready to leave, Zeddy announced that he would take a little jaunt with him to Harlem.

"You ain'ta gwine to do no sich thing as that," Susy said.

"Yes I is," responded Zeddy. "Wha' there is to stop me?"

"I is," said Susy.

"And what foh?"

" 'Causen I don't wanchu to go to Harlem. What makes you niggers love Harlem so much? Because it's a bloody ungodly place where niggers nevah go to bed. All night running around speakeasies and cabarets, where bad, hell-bent nigger womens am giving up themselves to open sin."

Susy stood broad and aggressive against the window overlooking Myrtle Avenue.

"Harlem is all right," said Zeddy. "I ain't knocking round no cabarets and speakeasies. Ahm just gwine ovah wif Jake to see somathem boys."

"Can that boy business!" cried Susy. "I've had anuff hell scrapping wif the women ovah mah mens. I ain't agwine to have no Harlem boys seducin' mah man away fwom me. The boy business is a fine excuse indeedy foh sich womens as ain't wise. I always heah the boss say to the missus, 'I gwine out foh a little time wif the boys, dearie,' when him wants an excuse foh a night off. I ain't born yestiday, honey. If you wants the boys foh a li'l' game o' poky, you bring 'em ovah heah. I ain't got the teeeniest bit of objection, and Ise got plenty o' good Gordon Dry foh eve'body."

"Ise got to go scares them up to bring them heah," said Zeddy.

"But not tonight or no night," declared Susy. "You kain do that in the daytime, foh you ain't got nothing to do."

Zeddy moved toward the mantelpiece to get his cap, but Susy blocked his way and held the cap behind her.

Zeddy looked savagely in her eyes and growled: "Come outa that, sistah, and gimme mah cap. It ain't no use stahting trouble."

Susy looked steadily in his eyes and chucked the cap at him. "Theah's you cap, but ef you stahts leaving me nights you . . ."

"What will you do?" asked Zeddy.

"I'll put you' block in the street."

Zeddy's countenance fell flat from its high aggressiveness.

"Well s'long, eve'body," said Jake.

Zeddy put on his cap and rocked out of the apartment after him. In the street he asked Jake, "Think I ought to take a crack at Harlem with you tonight, boh?"

"Not ef you loves you' new home, buddy," Jake replied.

"Bull! That plug-ugly black women is ornery like hell. I ain't gwineta let her bridle and ride me. . . . You ain't in no pickle like that with Rose, is you?"

"Lawd, no! I do as I wanta. But I'm one independent cuss, buddy. We ain't sitchuate the same. I works."

"Black womens when theyse ugly am all sistahs of Satan," declared Zeddy.

"It ain't the black ones only," said Jake.

"I wish I could hit things off like you, boh," said Zeddy. . . . "Well, I'll see you all some night at Billy Biasse's joint. . . . S'long. Don't pick up no bad change."

From that evening Zeddy began to discover that it wasn't all fine and lovely to live sweet. Formerly he had always been envious when any of his pals pointed out an extravagantly-dressed dark dandy and remarked, "He was living sweet." There was something so romantic about the sweet life. To be the adored of a Negro lady of means, or of a pseudo grass-widow whose husband worked on the railroad, or of a hard-working laundress or cook. It was much more respectable and enviable to be sweet—to belong to the exotic aristocracy of sweetmen than to be just a common tout.

But there were strings to Susy's largesse. The enjoyment of Harlem's low night life was prohibited to Zeddy. Susy was jealous of him in the proprietary sense. She believed in free love all right, but not for the man she possessed and supported. She warned him against the ornery hussies of her race.

"Nigger hussies nevah wanta git next to a man 'cep'n' when he's a-looking good to another woman," Susy declared. "I done gived you fair warning to jest keep away from the buffet-flat widdahs and thim Harlem street floaters; foh ef I ketch you making a fool woman of me, I'll throw you' pants in the street."

"Hi, but youse talking sistah. Why don't you wait till you see something before you staht in chewing the rag?"

"I done give you the straight stuff in time so you kain watch you'self when I kain't watch you. I ain't bohding and lodging no black man foh'm to be any other nigger woman's daddy."

So, in a few pointed phrases, Susy let Zeddy understand precisely what she would stand for. Zeddy was well kept like a prince of his type. He could not complain about food . . . and bed. Susy was splendid in her matriarchal way, rolling her eyes with love or disapproval at him, according to the exigencies of the moment.

The Saturday-night gin parties went on as usual. The brown and high-brown boys came and swilled. Miss Curdy was a constant visitor, frequently toting Strawberry Lips along. About her general way of handling things Susy brooked no criticism from Zeddy. She had bargained with him in the interest of necessity and of rivalry and she paid and paid fully, but grimly. She was proud to have a man to boss about in an intimate, casual way.

"Git out another bottle of gin, Zeddy. . . ."

"Bring along that packet o' saltines. . . ."

"Put on that theah 'Tickling Blues' that we's all just crazy about."

To have an aggressive type like Zeddy at her beck and call considerably increased Susy's prestige and clucking pride. She noticed, with carefully-concealed delight, that the interest of the yellow gin-swillers was piqued. She became flirtatious and coy by turns. And she was rewarded by fresh attentions. Even Miss Curdy was now meeting with new adventures, and she was prompted to expatiate upon men and love to Susy.

"Men's got a whole lot of women in their nature, I tell you. Just as women never really see a man until he's looking good to another woman and the hussies want to steal him, it's the same thing with men, mah dear. So soon as a woman is all sugar and candy for another man, you find a lot of them heartbreakers all trying to get next to her. Like a set of strutting game cocks all priming themselves to crow over a li'l' piece o' nothing."

"That's the gospel trute indeed," agreed Susy. "I done have a mess of knowledge 'bout men tucked away heah." Susy tapped her head of tight-rolled kinks knotted with scraps of ribbon of different colors. "I pays foh what I know and I've nevah been sorry, either. Yes, mam, I done larned about mah own self fust. Had no allusions about mahself. I knowed that I was black and ugly and no-class and unejucated. And I knowed that I was bohn foh love. . . . Mah mammy did useter warn

me about love. All what the white folks call white slavery these-
adays. I dunno ef theah's another name foh the nigger-an'-
white side ovit down home in Dixie. Well, I soon found out it
wasn't womens alone in the business, sposing thimselves like
vigitables foh sale in the market. No, mam! I done soon l'arned
that the mens was most buyable thimselves. Mah heart-
breaking high-yaller done left me sence—how miny wintahs I
been counting this heah Nothan snow? All thim and some
moh—dawggone ef I remimber. But evah since I been paying
sistah, paying good and hard foh mah loving feelings."

"Life ain't no country picnic with sweet flute and fiddle,"
Miss Curdy sighed.

"Indeed not," Susy was emphatic. "It ain't got nothing to
do with the rubbish we l'arn at Sunday school and the sweet
snooziness I used to lap up in thim blue-cover story books. My
God! the things I've seen! Working with white folks, so dickty
and high-and-mighty, you think theyse nevah oncet naked and
thim feets nevah touch ground. Yet all the silks and furs and
shining diamonds can't hide the misery a them lives. . . . Servants and heartbreakers from outside stealing the husband's
stuff. And all the men them that can't find no sweet-loving life
at home. Lavinia, I done seen life."

"Me, too, I have seen the real life, mixing as I used to in *real*
society," said Miss Curdy.

"I know society, too, honey, even though I only knows it
watching from the servant window. And I know it ain't no different from *us*. It's the same life even ef they drink champagne
and we drink gin."

"You said it and said it right," responded Miss Curdy.

Zeddy discovered that in his own circles in Harlem he had become something of a joke. It was known that he was living
sweet. But his buddies talked about his lady riding him with a
cruel bit.

"He was kept, all right," they said, "kept under 'Gin-head'
Susy's skirt."

He had had to fight a fellow in Dixie Red's pool-room, for
calling him a "skirt-man."

He was even teased by Billy Biasse or Billy, the Wolf, as he was nicknamed. Billy boasted frankly that he had no time for women. Black women, or the whole diversified world of the sex were all the same to him.

"So Harlem, after the sun done set, has no fun at all foh you, eh, boh?" Billy asked Zeddy.

Zeddy growled something indistinct.

"Sweet with the bit in you' mouf. Black woman riding her nigger. Great life, boh, ef you don't weaken."

"Bull! Wha's the matter with you niggers, anyhow?" Zeddy said in a sort of general way. "Ain't it better than being a wolf?"

"Ise a wolf, all right, but I ain't a lone one," Billy grinned. "I guess Ise the happiest, well-feddest wolf in Harlem. Oh, boy!"

Zeddy spent that evening in Harlem drinking with Jake and two more longshoremen at Uncle Doc's saloon. Late in the night they went to the Congo. Zeddy returned to Myrtle Avenue, an hour before it was time for Susy to rise, fully ginned up.

To Susy's "Whar you been?" he answered, "Shut up or I'll choke you," staggered, swayed, and swept from the dresser a vase of chrysanthemums that broke on the floor.

"Goddam fool flowers," he growled. "Why in hell didn't you put them out of the way, hey, you Suze?"

"Oh, keep quiet and come along to bed," said Susy.

A week later he repeated the performance, coming home with alarming symptoms of gin hiccough. Susy said nothing. After that Zeddy began to prance, as much as a short, heavy-made human could, with the bit out of his mouth. . . .

One Saturday night Susy's gin party was a sad failure. Nobody came beside Miss Curdy with Strawberry Lips. (Zeddy had left for Harlem in the afternoon.) They drank to themselves and played coon-can. Near midnight, when Miss Curdy was going, she said offhandedly, "I wouldn't mind sampling one of those Harlem cabarets now." Susy at once seized upon the idea.

"Sure. Let's go to Harlem for a change."

They caught the subway train for Harlem. Arrived there they gravitated to the Congo.

Before Susy left Myrtle Avenue, Zeddy was already at the Congo with a sweet, timid, satin-faced brown just from down home, that he had found at Aunt Hattie's and induced to go with him to the cabaret. Jake sat at Zeddy's table. Zeddy was determined to go the limit of independence, to show the boys that he was a cocky sweetman and no skirt-man. Plenty of money. He was treating. He wore an elegant nigger-brown sports suit and patent-leather shoes with cream-light spats such as all the sweet swells love to strut in. If Zeddy had only been taller, trimmer, and well-arched he would have been one of Harlem's dandiest sports.

His new-found brown had a glass of Virginia Dare before her; he was drinking gin. Jake, Scotch-and-soda; and Rose, who sat with them when she was not entertaining, had ordered White Rock. The night before, or rather the early morning after her job was done, she had gone on a champagne party and now she was sobering up.

Billy Biasse was there at a neighboring table with a long-shoreman and a straw-colored boy who was a striking advertisement of the Ambrozine Palace of Beauty. The boy was made up with high-brown powder, his eyebrows were elongated and blackened up, his lips streaked with the dark rouge so popular in Harlem, and his carefully-straightened hair lay plastered and glossy under Madame Walker's absinthe-colored salve "for milady of fashion and color."

"Who's the doll baby at the Wolf's table?" Zeddy asked.

"Tha's mah dancing pardner," Rose answered.

"Another entertainer? The Congo is gwine along fast enough."

"You bet you," said Jake. "And the ofays will soon be nosing it out. Then we'll have to take a back seat."

"Who's the Wolf?" Timidly Zeddy's girl asked.

Zeddy pointed out Billy.

"But why Wolf?"

"Khhhhhhh—Khhhhhhhh . . ." Zeddy laughed. " 'Causen he eats his own kind."

It was time for Rose to dance. Her partner had preceded her to the open space and was standing, arm akimbo against the piano, talking to the pianist. The pianist was a slight-built, long-headed fellow. His face shone like anthracite, his eyes were arresting, intense, deep-yellow slits. He seemed in a continual state of swaying excitement, whether or not he was playing.

They were ready, Rose and the dancer-boy. The pianist began, his eyes toward the ceiling in a sort of savage ecstatic
dream. Fiddler, saxophonist, drummer, and cymbalist seemed
to catch their inspiration from him. . . .

> When Luty dances, everything
>   Is dancing in the cabaret.
> The second fiddle asks the first:
>   What makes you sound that funny way?
> The drum talks in so sweet a voice,
>   The cymbal answers in surprise,
> The lights put on a brighter glow
>   To match the shine of Luty's eyes.
>
> For he's a foot-manipulating fool
>   When he hears that crazy moan
>   Come rolling, rolling outa that saxophone. . . .
> Watch that strut; there's no keeping him cool
>   When he's a-rearing with that saxophone. . . .
>   Oh, the tearing, tantalizing tone!
>   Of that moaning saxophone. . . .
>   That saxophone. . . .
>   That saxophone. . . .

They danced, Rose and the boy. Oh, they danced! An exercise of rhythmical exactness for two. There was no motion she
made that he did not imitate. They reared and pranced together, smacking palm against palm, working knee between
knee, grinning with real joy. They shimmied, breast to breast,
bent themselves far back and shimmied again. Lifting high her
short skirt and showing her green bloomers, Rose kicked. And
in his tight nigger-brown suit, the boy kicked even with her.
They were right there together, neither going beyond the
other. . . .

And the pianist! At intervals his yellow eyes, almost bloodshot, swept the cabaret with a triumphant glow, gave the
dancers a caressing look, and returned to the ceiling. Lean,
smart fingers beating barbaric beauty out of a white frame.
Brown bodies, caught up in the wild rhythm, wiggling and
swaying in their seats.

For he's a foot-manipulating fool
When he hears that crazy moan
Come rolling, rolling outa that saxophone. . . .
    That saxophone. . . .
    That saxophone. . . .

Rose was sipping her White Rock. Her partner, at Billy's table, sucked his iced creme-de-menthe through a straw. The high wave of joyful excitement had subsided and the customers sat casually drinking and gossiping as if they had not been soaring a minute before in a realm of pure joy.

From his place, giving a good view of the staircase, Zeddy saw two apparently familiar long legs swinging down the steps. Sure enough, he knew those big, thick-soled red boots.

"Them feets look jest laka Strawberry Lips' own," he said to Jake. Jake looked and saw first Strawberry Lips enter the cabaret, with Susy behind balancing upon her French heels, and Miss Curdy. Susy was gorgeous in a fur coat of rich shiny black, like her complexion. Opened, it showed a cérise blouse and a yellow-and-mauve check skirt. Her head of thoroughly-straightened hair flaunted a green hat with a decoration of red ostrich plumes.

"Great balls of fire! Here's you doom, buddy," said Jake.

"Doom, mah granny," retorted Zeddy. "Ef that theah black ole cow come fooling near me tonight, I'll show her who's wearing the pants."

Susy did not see Zeddy until her party was seated. It was Miss Curdy who saw him first. She dug into Susy's side with her elbow and cried:

"For the love of Gawd, looka there!"

Susy's star eyes followed Miss Curdy's. She glared at Zeddy and fixed her eyes on the girl with him for a moment. Then she looked away and grunted: "He thinks he's acting smart, eh? Him and I will wrastle that out to a salution, but I ain't agwine to raise no stink in heah."

"He's got some more nerve pulling off that low-down stuff, and on your money, too," said Miss Curdy.

"Who that?" asked Strawberry Lips.

"Ain't you seen your best friends over there?" retorted Miss Curdy.

Strawberry Lips waved at Zeddy and Jake, but they were deliberately keeping their eyes away from Susy's table. He got up to go to them.

"Where you going?" Miss Curdy asked.

"To chin wif——"

A yell startled the cabaret. A girl had slapped another's face and replied to her victim's cry of pain with, "If you no like it you can lump it!"

"You low an' dutty bobbin-bitch!"

"Bitch is bobbin in you' sistah's coffin."

They were West Indian girls.

"I'll mek mah breddah beat you' bottom foh you."

"Gash it and stop you' jawing."

They were interrupted by another West Indian girl, who wore a pink-flowered muslin frock and a wide jippi-jappa hat from which charmingly hung two long ends of broad pea-green ribbon.

"It's a shame. Can't you act like decent English people?" she said. Gently she began pushing away the assaulted girl, who burst into tears.

"She come boxing me up ovah a dutty-black 'Merican coon."

"Mek a quick move or I'll box you bumbole ovah de moon," her assailant cried after her. . . .

"The monkey-chasers am scrapping," Zeddy commented.

"In a language all their own," said Jake.

"They are wild womens, buddy, and it's a wild language they're using, too," remarked a young West Indian behind Jake.

"Hmm! but theyse got the excitement fever," a lemon-colored girl at a near table made her contribution and rocked and twisted herself coquettishly at Jake. . . .

Susy had already reached the pavement with Miss Curdy and Strawberry Lips. Susy breathed heavily.

"Lesh git furthest away from this low-down vice hole," she said. "Leave that plug-ugly nigger theah. I ain't got no more use foh him nohow."

"I never did have any time for Harlem," said Miss Curdy. "When I was high up in society all respectable colored people lived in Washington. There was no Harlem full a niggers then. I declare——"

"I should think the nigger heaven of a theater downtown is better than anything in this heah Harlem," said Susy. "When we feels like going out, it's better we enjoy ourse'f in the li'l' corner the white folks 'low us, and then shuffle along back home. It's good and quiet ovah in Brooklyn."

"And we can have all the inside fun we need," said Miss Curdy.

"Brooklyn ain't no better than Harlem," said Strawberry Lips, running the words rolling off his tongue. "Theah's as much shooting-up and cut-up in Prince Street and——"

"There ain't no compahrison atall," stoutly maintained Susy. "This here Harlem is a stinking sink of iniquity. Nigger hell! That's what it is. Looka that theah ugly black nigger loving up a scrimpy brown gal right befoh mah eyes. Jest daring me to turn raw and loose lak them monkey-chasing womens thisanight. But that I wouldn't do. I ain't a woman abandoned to sich publicity stunts. Not even though mah craw was full to bursting. Lemme see'm tonight. . . . Yessam, this heah Harlem is sure nigger hell. Take me way away from it."

When Zeddy at last said good night to his new-found brown, he went straight to an all-night barrel-house and bought a half a pint of whisky. He guzzled the liquor and smashed the flask on the pavement. Drew up his pants, tightened his belt and growled, "Now I'm ready for Susy."

He caught the subway train for Brooklyn. Only local trains were running and it was quite an hour and a half before he got home. He staggered down Myrtle Avenue well primed with the powerful stimulation of gin-and-whisky.

At the door of Susy's apartment he was met by his suitcase. He recoiled as from a blow struck at his face. Immediately he became sober. His eyes caught a little white tag attached to the handle. Examining it by the faint gaslight he read, in Susy's handwriting: "Kip owt that meen you."

Susy had put all Zeddy's belongings into the suitcase, keeping back what she had given him: two fancy-colored silk shirts, silk handkerchiefs, a mauve dressing-gown, and a box of silk socks.

"What he's got on that black back of his'n he can have," she had said while throwing the things in the bag.

Zeddy beat on the door with his fists.

"Wha moh you want?" Susy's voice bawled from within. "Ain'tchu got all you stuff theah? Gwan back where youse coming from."

"Lemme in and quit you joking," cried Zeddy.

"You ugly flat-footed zigaboo," shouted Susy, "may I ketch the 'lectric chair without conversion ef I 'low you dirty black pusson in mah place again. And you better git quick foh I staht mah dawg bawking at you."

Zeddy picked up his suitcase. "Come on, Mistah Bag. Le's tail along back to Harlem. Leave black woman 'lone wif her gin and ugly mug. Black woman is hard luck."

VIII
The Raid of the Baltimore

THE blazing lights of the Baltimore were put out and the entrance was padlocked. Fifth Avenue and Lenox talked about nothing else. Buddy meeting buddy and chippie greeting chippie, asked: "Did you hear the news?" . . . "Well, what do you know about that?"

Yet nothing sensational had happened in the Baltimore. The police had not, on a certain night, swept into it and closed it up because of indecent doings. No. It was an indirect raid. Oh, and that made the gossip toothier! For the Baltimore was not just an ordinary cabaret. It had mortgages and policies in the best of the speakeasy places of the Belt. And the mass of Harlem held the Baltimore in high respect because (it was rumored and believed) it was protected by Tammany Hall.

Jake, since he had given up hoping about his lost brown, had stopped haunting the Baltimore, yet he had happened to be very much in on the affair that cost the Baltimore its license. Jake's living with Rose had, in spite of himself, projected him into a more elegant atmosphere of worldliness. Through Rose and her associates he had gained access to buffet flats and private rendezvous apartments that were called "nifty."

And Jake was a high favorite wherever he went. There was something so naturally beautiful about his presence that everybody liked and desired him. Buddies, on the slightest provocation, were ready to fight for him, and the girls liked to make an argument around him.

Jake had gained admission to Madame Adeline Suarez's buffet flat, which was indeed a great feat. He was the first longshoreman, colored or white, to tread that magnificent red carpet. Madame Suarez catered to sporty colored persons of consequence only and certain groups of downtown whites that used to frequent Harlem in the good old pre-prohibition days.

"Ain't got no time for cheap- no-'count niggers," Madame Suarez often said. "Gimme their room to their company any time, even if they've got money to spend." Madame Suarez came from Florida and she claimed Cuban descent through her father. By her claim to that exotic blood she moved like a queen among the blue-veins of the colored sporting world.

But Jake's rough charm could conquer anything.

"Ofay's mixing in!" he exclaimed to himself the first night he penetrated into Madame Suarez's. "But ofay or ofay not, this here is the real stuff," he reflected. And so many nights he absented himself from the Congo (he had no interest in Rose's art of flirting money out of hypnotized newcomers) to luxuriate with charmingly painted pansies among the colored cushions and under the soft, shaded lights of Madame Suarez's speakeasy. It was a new world for Jake and he took it easily. That was his natural way, wherever he went, whatever new people he met. It had helped him over many a bad crossing at Brest at Havre and in London. . . . Take it easy . . . take life easy. Sometimes he was disgusted with life, but he was never frightened of it.

Jake had never seen colored women so carefully elegant as these rich-browns and yellow-creams at Madame Suarez's. They were fascinating in soft bright draperies and pretty pumps and they drank liquor with a fetching graceful abandon. Gin and whisky seemed to lose their barbaric punch in that atmosphere and take on a romantic color. The women's coiffure was arranged in different striking styles and their arms and necks and breasts tinted to emphasize the peculiar richness of each skin. One girl, who was the favorite of Madame Suarez, and the darkest in the group, looked like a breathing statue of burnished bronze. With their arresting poses and gestures, their deep shining painted eyes, they resembled the wonderfully beautiful pictures of women of ancient Egypt.

Here Jake brushed against big men of the colored sporting world and their white friends. That strange un-American world where colored meets and mingles freely and naturally with white in amusement basements, buffet flats, poker establishments. Sometimes there were two or three white women, who attracted attention because they were white and strange to Harlem, but they appeared like faded carnations among those burning orchids of a tropical race.

One night Jake noticed three young white men, clean-shaven, flashily-dressed, who paid for champagne for everybody in the flat. They were introduced by a perfectly groomed dark-brown man, a close friend of the boss of the Baltimore. Money seemed worthless to them except as a means of getting fun out of it. Madame Suarez made special efforts to please them. Showed them all of the buffet flat, even her own bedroom. One of them, very freckled and red-haired, sat down to the piano and jazzed out popular songs. The trio radiated friendliness all around them. Danced with the colored beauties and made lively conversation with the men. They were gay and recklessly spendthrift. . . .

They returned on a Saturday night, between midnight and morning, when the atmosphere of Madame Suarez's was fairly bacchic and jazz music was snake-wriggling in and out and around everything and forcing everybody into amatory states and attitudes. The three young white men had two others with them. At the piano a girl curiously made up in mauve was rendering the greatest ragtime song of the day. Broadway was wild about it and Harlem was crazy. All America jazzed to it, and it was already world-famous. Already being jazzed perhaps in Paris and Cairo, Shanghai, Honolulu, and Java. It was a song about cocktails and cherries. Like this in some ways:

> Take a juicy cocktail cherry,
>   Take a dainty little bite,
> And we'll all be very merry
>   On a cherry drunk tonight.

> We'll all be merry when you have a cherry,
>   And we'll twine and twine like a fruitful vine,
> Grape vine, red wine, babe mine, bite a berry,
>   You taste a cherry and twine, rose vine, sweet wine.
>   Cherry-ee-ee-ee-ee, cherry-ee-ee-ee-ee-ee, ee-ee-ee
>   Cherry-ee-ee-ee-ee, cherry-ee-ee-ee-ee-ee, ee-ee-ee
>   Grape vine, rose vine, sweet wine. . . .

> Love is like a cocktail cherry,
>   Just a fruity little bit,
> And you've never yet been merry,
>   If you've not been drunk on it.

> We'll all be merry when you have. . . .

The women, carried away by the sheer rhythm of delight, had risen above their commercial instincts (a common trait of Negroes in emotional states) and abandoned themselves to pure voluptuous jazzing. They were gorgeous animals swaying there through the dance, punctuating it with marks of warm physical excitement. The atmosphere was charged with intensity and over-charged with currents of personal reaction. . . .

Then the five young white men unmasked as the Vice Squad and killed the thing.

Dicks! They had wooed and lured and solicited for their trade. For two weeks they had spilled money like water at the Baltimore. Sometimes they were accompanied by white girls who swilled enormous quantities of champagne and outshrieked the little ginned-up Negresses and mulattresses of the cabaret. They had posed as good fellows, regular guys, looking for a good time only in the Black Belt. They were wearied of the pleasures of the big white world, wanted something new—the primitive joy of Harlem.

So at last, with their spendthrift and charming ways, they had convinced the wary boss of the Baltimore that they were fine fellows. The boss was a fine fellow himself, who loved life and various forms of fun and had no morals about them. And so one night when the trio had left their hired white ladies behind, he was persuaded to give his youthful white guests an introduction to Madame Adeline Suarez's buffet flat. . . .

The uniformed police were summoned. Madame Suarez and her clients were ordered to get ready to go down to the Night Court. The women asked permission to veil themselves. Many windows were raked up in the block and heads craned forth to watch the prisoners bundled into waiting taxicabs. The women were afraid. Some of them were false grass-widows whose husbands were working somewhere. Some of them were church members. Perhaps one could claim a place in local society!

They were all fined. But Madame Suarez, besides being fined, was sent to Blackwell's Island for six months.

To the two white girls that were also taken in the raid the judge remarked that it was a pity he had no power to order them whipped. For whipping was the only punishment he considered suitable for white women who dishonored their race by associating with colored persons.

The high point of the case was the indictment of the boss of the Baltimore as accessory to the speakeasy crime. The boss was not convicted, but the Baltimore was ordered to be padlocked. That decision was appealed. But the cabaret remained padlocked. A black member of Tammany had no chances against the Moral Arm of the city.

The Belt's cabaret sets licked their lips over the sensation for weeks. For a long time Negro proprietors would not admit white customers into their cabarets and near-white members of the black race, whose features were unfamiliar in Harlem, had a difficult time proving their identity.

IX
Jake Makes a Move

COMING home from work one afternoon, Jake remarked a taxicab just driving away from his house. He was quite a block off, but he thought it was his number. When he entered Rose's room he immediately detected an unfamiliar smell. He had an uncanny sharp nose for strange smells. Rose always had visitors, of course. Girls, and fellows, too, of her circle. But Jake had a feeling that his nose had scented something foreign to Harlem. The room was close with tobacco smoke; there were many Melachrino butts in a tray, and a half-used box of the same cigarettes on a little table drawn up against the scarlet-covered couch. Also, there was a half-filled bottle of Jake's Scotch whisky on the table and glasses for two. Rose was standing before the dresser, arranging her hair.

"Been having company?" Jake asked, carelessly.

"Yep. It was only Gertie Blake."

Jake knew that Rose was lying. Her visitor had not been Gertie Blake. It had been a man, a strange man, doubtless a white man. Yet he hadn't the slightest feeling of jealousy or anger, whatever the visitor was. Rose had her friends of both sexes and was quite free in her ways. At the Congo she sat and drank and flirted with many fellows. That was a part of her business. She got more tips that way, and the extra personal bargains that gave her the means to maintain her style of living. All her lovers had always accepted her living entirely free. For that made it possible for her to keep them living carefree and sweet.

Rose was disappointed in Jake. She had wanted him to live in the usual sweet way, to be brutal and beat her up a little, and take away her money from her. Once she had a rough leather-brown man who used to beat her up regularly. Sometimes she was beaten so badly she had to stay indoors for days, and to her visiting girl pals she exhibited her bruises and blackened eyes with pride.

As Jake was not brutally domineering, she cooled off from

him perceptibly. But she could not make him change. She confided to her friends that he was "good loving but" (making use of a contraction that common people employ) "a big Ah-Ah all the same." She felt no thrill about the business when her lover was not interested in her earnings.

Jake did not care. He did not love her, had never felt any deep desire for her. He had gone to live with her simply because she had asked him when he was in a fever mood for a steady mate. There was nothing about Rose that touched and roused him as his vivid recollection of his charming little brown-skin of the Baltimore. Rose's room to him was like any ordinary lodging in Harlem. While the room of his little lost brown lived in his mind a highly magnified affair: a bed of gold, fresh, white linen, a magic carpet, all bathed in the rarest perfume. . . . Rose's perfume made his nose itch. It was rank.

He came home another afternoon and found her with a bright batik kimono carelessly wrapped around her and stretched full-length on the couch. There were Melachrino stubs lying about and his bottle of Scotch was on the mantelpiece. Evidently the strange visitor of the week before had been there again.

"Hello!" She yawned and flicked off her cigarette ash and continued smoking. A chic veneer over a hard, restless, insensitive body. Fascinating, nevertheless. . . . For the moment, just as she was, she was desirable and provoked responses in him. He shuffled up to the couch and caressed her.

"Leave me alone, I'm tired," she snarled.

The rebuff hurt Jake. "You slut!" he cried. He went over to the mantelpiece and added, "Youse just everybody's teaser."

"You got a nearve talking to me that way," said Rose. "Since when you staht riding the high horse?"

"It don't take no nearve foh me to tell you what you is. Fact is I'm right now sure tiahd to death of living with you."

"You poor black stiff!" Rose cried. And she leaped over at Jake and scratched at his face.

Jake gave her two savage slaps full in her face and she dropped moaning at his feet.

"There! You done begged foh it," he said. He stepped over her and went out.

Walking down the street, he looked at his palms. "Ahm shame o' you, hands," he murmured. "Mah mother useter tell me, 'Nevah hit no woman,' but that hussy jest made me do it . . . jest *made* me. . . . Well, I'd better pull outa that there mud-hole. . . . It wasn't what I come back to Gawd's own country foh. No, sirree! You bet it wasn't. . . ."

When he returned to the house he heard laughter in the room. Gertie Blake was there and Rose was telling a happy tale. He stood by the closed door and listened for a while.

"Have another drink, Gertie. Don't ever get a wee bit delicate when youse with me. . . . My, mah dear, but he did slap the daylights outa me. When I comed to I wanted to kiss his feet, but he was gone."

"Rose! You're the limit. But didn't it hurt awful?"

"Didn't hurt enough. Honey, it's the first time I ever felt his real strength. A hefty-looking one like him, always acting so nice and proper. I almost thought he was getting sissy. But he's a *ma-an* all right. . . ."

A nasty smile stole into Jake's features. He could not face those women. He left the house again. He strolled down to Dixie Red's pool-room and played awhile. From there he went with Zeddy to Uncle Doc's saloon.

He went home again and found Rose stunning in a new cloth-of-gold frock shining with brilliants. She was refixing a large artificial yellow rose to the side of a pearl-beaded green turban. Jake, without saying a word, went to the closet and took down his suitcase. Then he began tossing shirts, underwear, collars, and ties on to the couch.

"What the devil you're doing?" Rose wheeled round and stared at him in amazement, both hands gripping the dresser behind her.

"Kain't you see?" Jake replied.

She moved down on him like a panther, swinging her hips in a wonderful, rhythmical motion. She sprang upon his neck and brought him down.

"Oh, honey, you ain't mad at me 'counta the little fuss tonight?"

"I don't like hitting no womens," returned Jake's hard-breathing muffled voice.

"Daddy! I love you the more for that."

"You'll spile you' new clothes," Jake said, desperately.

"Hell with them! I love mah daddy moh'n anything. And mah daddy loves me, don't he? Daddy!"

Rose switched on the light and looked at her watch.

"My stars, daddy! We been honey-dreaming some! I am two hours late."

She jumped up and jig-stepped. "I should worry if the Congo . . . I should worry mumbo-jumbo."

She smoothed out her frock, arranged her hair, and put the turban on. "Come along to the Congo a little later," she said to Jake. "Let's celebrate on champagne."

The door closed on him. . . .

"O Lawdy!" he yawned, stretched himself, and got up. He took the rest of his clothes out of the closet, picked up the crumpled things from the couch, packed, and walked out with his suitcase.

SECOND PART

X
The Railroad

Over the heart of the vast gray Pennsylvania country the huge black animal snorted and roared, with sounding rods and couplings, pulling a long chain of dull-brown boxes packed with people and things, trailing on the blue-cold air its white masses of breath.

Hell was playing in the hot square hole of a pantry and the coffin-shaped kitchen of the dining-car. The short, stout, hard-and-horny chef was terrible as a rhinoceros. Against the second, third, and fourth cooks he bellied his way up to the little serving door and glared at the waiters. His tough, aproned front was a challenge to them. In his oily, shining face his big white eyes danced with meanness. All the waiters had squeezed into the pantry at once, excitedly snatching, dropping and breaking things.

"Hey, you there! You mule!"* The chef shouted at the fourth waiter. "Who told you to snitch that theah lamb chops outa the hole?"

"I done think they was the one I ordered——"

"Done think some hell, you down-home black fool. Ain't no thinking to be done on here——"

"Chef, ain't them chops ready yet?" a waiter asked.

"Don't rush me, nigger," the chef bellowed back. "Wha' yu'all trying to do? Run me up a tree? Kain't run this here chef up no tree. Jump off ef you kain't ride him." His eyes gleamed with grim humor. "Jump off or lay down. This heah white man's train service ain't no nigger picnic."

The second cook passed up a platter of chops. The chef rushed it through the hole and licked his fingers.

"There you is, yaller. Take it away. Why ain't you gone yet? Show me some service, yaller, show me some service." He

---

*The fourth waiter on the railroad is nick-named "mule" because he works under the orders of the pantry-man.

rocked his thick, tough body sideways in a sort of dance, licked the sweat from his brow with his forefinger and grunted with aggressive self-satisfaction. Then he bellied his way back to the range and sent the third cook up to the serving window.

"Tha's the stuff to hand them niggers," he told the third cook. "Keep 'em up a tree all the time, but don't let 'em get you up there."

Jake, for he was the third cook, took his place by the window and handed out the orders. It was his first job on the railroad, but from the first day he managed his part perfectly. He rubbed smoothly along with the waiters by remaining himself and not trying to imitate the chef nor taking his malicious advice.

Jake had taken the job on the railroad just to break the hold that Harlem had upon him. When he quitted Rose he felt that he ought to get right out of the atmosphere of Harlem. If I don't git away from it for a while, it'll sure git me, he mused. But not ship-and-port-town life again. I done had enough a that here and ovah there. . . . So he had picked the railroad. One or two nights a week in Harlem. And all the days on the road. He would go on like that until he grew tired of that rhythm. . . .

The rush was over. Everything was quiet. The corridors of the dining-car were emptied of their jam of hungry, impatient guests. The "mule" had scrubbed the slats of the pantry and set them up to dry. The other waiters had put away silver and glasses and soiled linen. The steward at his end of the car was going over the checks. Even the kitchen work was finished and the four cooks had left their coffin for the good air of the dining-room. They sat apart from the dining-room boys. The two grades, cooks and waiters, never chummed together, except for gambling. Some of the waiters were very haughty. There were certain light-skinned ones who went walking with pals of their complexion only in the stopover cities. Others, among the older men, were always dignified. They were fathers of families, their wives moved in some sphere of Harlem society, and their movements were sometimes chronicled in the local Negro newspapers.

Sitting at one of the large tables, four of the waiters were playing poker. Jake wanted to join them, but he had no money. One waiter sat alone at a small table. He was reading. He was of average size, slim, a smooth pure ebony with straight features and a suggestion of whiskers. Jake shuffled up to him and asked him for the loan of two dollars. He got it and went to play. . . .

Jake finished playing with five dollars. He repaid the waiter and said: "Youse a good sport. I'll always look out for you in that theah hole."

The waiter smiled. He was very friendly. Jake half-sprawled over the table. "Wha's this here stuff you reading? Looks lak Greek to me." He spelled the title, "S-A-P-H-O, Sapho."

"What's it all about?" Jake demanded, flattening down the book on the table with his friendly paw. The waiter was reading the scene between Fanny and Jean when the lover discovers the letters of his mistress's former woman friend and exclaims: "Ah *Oui . . . Sapho . . . toute la lyre. . . .*"

"It's a story," he told Jake, "by a French writer named Alphonse Daudet. It's about a sporting woman who was beautiful like a rose and had the soul of a wandering cat. Her lovers called her Sapho. I like the story, but I hate the use of Sapho for its title."

"Why does you?" Jake asked.

"Because Sappho was a real person. A wonderful woman, a great Greek poet——"

"So theah *is* some Greek in the book!" said Jake.

The waiter smiled. "In a sense, yes."

And he told Jake the story of Sappho, of her poetry, of her loves and her passion for the beautiful boy, Phaon. And of her leaping into the sea from the Leucadian cliff because of her love for him.

"Her story gave two lovely words to modern language," said the waiter.

"Which one them?" asked Jake.

"Sapphic and Lesbian . . . beautiful words."

"What is that there Leshbian?"

". . . Lovely word, eh?"

"Tha's what we calls bulldyker in Harlem," drawled Jake. "Them's all ugly womens."

"Not *all*. And that's a damned ugly name," the waiter said.

"Harlem is too savage about some things. *Bulldyker*," the waiter stressed with a sneer.

Jake grinned. "But tha's what they is, ain't it?"

He began humming:

> "And there is two things in Harlem I don't understan'
> It is a bulldyking woman and a faggoty man. . . ."

Charmingly, like a child that does not know its letters, Jake turned the pages of the novel. . . .

"Bumbole! This heah language is most different from how they talk it."

"Bumbole" was now a popular expletive for Jake, replacing such expressions as "Bull," "bawls," "walnuts," and "blimey." Ever since the night at the Congo when he heard the fighting West Indian girl cry, "I'll slap you bumbole," he had always used the word. When his friends asked him what it meant, he grinned and said, "Ask the monks."

"You know French?" the waiter asked.

"*Parlee-vous? Mademoiselle, un baiser, s'il vous plait. Voilà!* I larned that much offn the froggies."

"So you were over there?"

"*Au oui, camarade*," Jake beamed. "I was way, way ovah there after Democracy and them boches, and when I couldn't find one or the other, I jest turned mah black moon from the A.E.F. . . . But you! How come you jest plowing through this here stuff lak that? I could nevah see no light at all in them print, chappie. *Eh bien. Mais vous compris beaucoup.*"

"*C'est ma langue maternelle.*"

"Hm!" Jake made a face and scratched his head. "*Comprendre pas*, chappie. Tell me in straight United States."

"French is my native language. I——"

"Don't crap me," Jake interrupted. "Ain'tchu—ain'tchu one of us, too?"

"Of course I'm Negro," the waiter said, "but I was born in Hayti and the language down there is French."

"Hayti . . . Hayti," repeated Jake. "Tha's where now? Tha's——"

"An island in the Caribbean—near the Panama Canal."

Jake sat like a big eager boy and learned many facts about

Hayti before the train reached Pittsburgh. He learned that the universal spirit of the French Revolution had reached and lifted up the slaves far away in that remote island; that Black Hayti's independence was more dramatic and picturesque than the United States' independence and that it was a strange, almost unimaginable eruption of the beautiful ideas of the "Liberté, Egalité, Fraternité" of Mankind, that shook the foundations of that romantic era.

For the first time he heard the name Toussaint L'Ouverture, the black slave and leader of the Haytian slaves. Heard how he fought and conquered the slave-owners and then protected them; decreed laws for Hayti that held more of human wisdom and nobility than the Code Napoleon; defended his baby revolution against the Spanish and the English vultures; defeated Napoleon's punitive expedition; and how tragically he was captured by a civilized trick, taken to France, and sent by Napoleon to die broken-hearted in a cold dungeon.

"A black man! A black man! Oh, I wish I'd been a soldier under sich a man!" Jake said, simply.

He plied his instructor with questions. Heard of Dessalines, who carried on the fight begun by Toussaint L'Ouverture and kept Hayti independent. But it was incredible to Jake that a little island of freed slaves had withstood the three leading European powers. The waiter told him that Europe was in a complex state of transition then, and that that wonderful age had been electrified with universal ideas—ideas so big that they had lifted up ignorant people, even black, to the stature of gods.

"The world doesn't know," he continued, "how great Toussaint L'Ouverture really was. He was not merely great. He was lofty. He was good. The history of Hayti today might have been different if he had been allowed to finish his work. He was honored by a great enigmatic poet of that period. And I honor both Toussaint and the poet by keeping in my memory the wonderful, passionate lines."

He quoted Wordsworth's sonnet.

> "Toussaint, the most unhappy Man of Men!
>   Whether the whistling Rustic tend his plough
>   Within thy hearing, or thy head be now
> Pillowed in some deep dungeon's earless den;—

Oh miserable Chieftain! Where and when
   Wilt thou find patience? Yet die not; do thou
   Wear rather in thy bonds a cheerful brow:
Though fallen Thyself never to rise again,
Live, and take comfort. Thou hast left behind
   Powers that will work for thee, air, earth, and skies;
There's not a breathing of the common wind
   That will forget thee; thou hast great allies;
   Thy friends are exultations, agonies,
And love, and Man's unconquerable Mind."

Jake felt like one passing through a dream, vivid in rich, varied colors. It was revelation beautiful in his mind. That brief account of an island of savage black people, who fought for collective liberty and were struggling to create a culture of their own. A romance of his race, just down there by Panama. How strange!

Jake was very American in spirit and shared a little of that comfortable Yankee contempt for poor foreigners. And as an American Negro he looked askew at foreign niggers. Africa was jungle, and Africans bush niggers, cannibals. And West Indians were monkey-chasers. But now he felt like a boy who stands with the map of the world in colors before him, and feels the wonder of the world.

The waiter told him that Africa was not jungle as he dreamed of it, nor slavery the peculiar rôle of black folk. The Jews were the slaves of the Egyptians, the Greeks made slaves of their conquered, the Gauls and Saxons were slaves of the Romans. He told Jake of the old destroyed cultures of West Africa and of their vestiges, of black kings who struggled stoutly for the independence of their kingdoms: Prempreh of Ashanti, Tofa of Dahomey, Gbehanzin of Benin, Cetawayo of Zulu-Land, Menelik of Abyssinia. . . .

Had Jake ever heard of the little Republic of Liberia, founded by American Negroes? And Abyssinia, deep-set in the shoulder of Africa, besieged by the hungry wolves of Europe? The only nation that has existed free and independent from the earliest records of history until today! Abyssinia, oldest unconquered nation, ancient-strange as Egypt, persistent as Palestine, legendary as Greece, magical as Persia.

There was the lovely legend of her queen who visited the court of the Royal Rake of Jerusalem, and how he fell in love with her. And her beautiful black body made the Sage so lyrical, he immortalized her in those wonderful pagan verses that are sacred to the hearts of all lovers—even the heart of the Church. . . . The catty ladies of the court of Jerusalem were jealous of her. And Sheba reminded them that she was black but beautiful. . . . And after a happy period she left Jerusalem and returned to her country with the son that came of the royal affair. And that son subsequently became King of Abyssinia. And to this day the rulers of Abyssinia carry the title, Lion of Judah, and trace their descent direct from the liaison of the Queen of Sheba with King Solomon.

First of Christian nations also is the claim of this little kingdom! Christian since the time when Philip, the disciple of Jesus, met and baptized the minister of the Queen of Abyssinia and he returned to his country and converted the court and people to Christianity.

Jake listened, rapt, without a word of interruption.

"All the ancient countries have been yielding up the buried secrets of their civilizations," the waiter said. "I wonder what Abyssinia will yield in her time? Next to the romance of Hayti, because it is my native country, I should love to write the romance of Abyssinia . . . Ethiopia."

"Is that theah country the same Ethiopia that we done l'arned about in the Bible?" asked Jake.

"The same. The Latin peoples still call it Ethiopia."

"Is you a professor?"

"No, I'm a student."

"Whereat? Where did you l'arn English?"

"Well, I learned English home in Port-au-Prince. And I was at Howard. You know the Negro university at Washington. Haven't even finished there yet."

"Then what in the name of mah holy rabbit foot youse doing on this heah white man's chuh-chuh? It ain't no place foh no student. It seems to me you' place down there sounds a whole lot better."

"Uncle Sam put me here."

"Whadye mean Uncle Sam?" cried Jake. "Don't hand me that bull."

"Let me tell you about it," the waiter said. "Maybe you don't know that during the World War Uncle Sam grabbed Hayti. My father was an official down there. He didn't want Uncle Sam in Hayti and he said so and said it loud. They told him to shut up and he wouldn't, so they shut him up in jail. My brother also made a noise and American marines killed him in the street. I had nobody to pay for me at the university, so I had to get out and work. *Voilà!*"

"And you ain't gwine to study no moh?"

"Never going to stop. I study now all the same when I get a little time. Every free day I have in New York I spend at the library downtown. I read there and I write."

Jake shook his head. "This heah work is all right for me, but for a chappie like you. . . . Do you like waiting on them ofays? 'Sall right working longshore or in a kitchen as I does it, but to be rubbing up against them and bowing so nice and all a that. . . ."

"It isn't so bad," the waiter said. "Most of them are pretty nice. Last trip I waited on a big Southern Senator. He was perfectly gentlemanly and tipped me half a dollar. When I have the blues I read Dr. Frank Crane."

Jake didn't understand, but he spat and said a stinking word. The chef called him to do something in the kitchen.

"Leave that theah professor and his nonsense," the chef said. . . .

The great black animal whistled sharply and puff-puffed slowly into the station of Pittsburgh.

XI
Snowstorm in Pittsburgh

In the middle of the little bridge built over the railroad crossing he was suddenly enveloped in a thick mass of smoke spouted out by an in-rushing train. That was Jake's first impression of Pittsburgh. He stepped off the bridge into a saloon. From there along a dull-gray street of grocery and fruit shops and piddling South-European children. Then he was on Wiley Avenue, the long, gray, uphill street.

Brawny bronze men in coal-blackened and oil-spotted blue overalls shadowed the doorways of saloons, pool-rooms, and little basement restaurants. The street was animated with dark figures going up, going down. Houses and men, women, and squinting cats and slinking dogs, everything seemed touched with soot and steel dust.

"So this heah is the niggers' run," said Jake. "I don't like its 'pearance, nohow." He walked down the street and remarked a bouncing little chestnut-brown standing smartly in the entrance of a basement eating-joint. She wore a knee-length yellow-patterned muslin frock and a white-dotted blue apron. The apron was a little longer than the frock. Her sleeves were rolled up. Her arms were beautiful, like smooth burnished bars of copper.

Jake stopped and said, "Howdy!"

"Howdy again!" the girl flashed a row of perfect teeth at him.

"Got a bite of anything good?"

"I should say so, Mister Ma-an."

She rolled her eyes and worked her hips into delightful free-and-easy motions. Jake went in. He was not hungry for food. He looked at a large dish half filled with tapioca pudding. He turned to the pie-case on the counter.

"The peach pie is the best," said the girl, her bare elbow on the counter; "it's fresh." She looked straight in his eyes. "All right, I'll try peach," he said, and, magnetically, his long, shining fingers touched her hand. . . .

*

In the evening he found the Haytian waiter at the big Wiley Avenue pool-room. Quite different from the pool-rooms in Harlem, it was a sort of social center for the railroad men and the more intelligent black workmen of the quarter. Tobacco, stationery, and odds and ends were sold in the front part of the store. There was a table where customers sat and wrote letters. And there were pretty chocolate dolls and pictures of Negroid types on sale. Curious, pathetic pictures; black Madonna and child; a kinky-haired mulatto angel with African lips and Nordic nose, soaring on a white cloud up to heaven; Jesus blessing a black child and a white one; a black shepherd carrying a white lamb—all queerly reminiscent of the crude prints of the great Christian paintings that are so common in poor religious homes.

"Here he is!" Jake greeted the waiter. "What's the new?"

"Nothing new in Soot-hill; always the same."

The railroad men hated the Pittsburgh run. They hated the town, they hated Wiley Avenue and their wretched free quarters that were in it. . . .

"What're you going to do?"

"Ahm gwine to the colored show with a li'l' brown piece," said Jake.

"You find something already? My me! You're a fast-working one."

"Always the same whenever I hits a new town. Always in cock-tail luck, chappie."

"Which one? Manhattan or Bronx?"

"It's Harlem-Pittsburgh thisanight," Jake grinned. "Wachyu gwine make?"

"Don't know. There's nothing ever in Pittsburgh for me. I'm in no mood for the leg-show tonight, and the colored show is bum. Guess I'll go sleep if I can."

"Awright, I'll see you li'l' later, chappie." Jake gripped his hand. "Say—whyn't you tell a fellow you' name? Youse sure more'n second waiter as Ise more'n third cook. Ev'body calls me Jake. And you?"

"Raymond, but everybody calls me Ray."

Jake heaved off. Ray bought some weekly Negro newspapers: *The Pittsburgh Courier*, *The Baltimore American*, *The Negro*

World, The Chicago Defender. Here he found a big assortment
of all the Negro publications that he never could find in
Harlem. In a next-door saloon he drank a glass of sherry and
started off for the waiters' and cooks' quarters.

It was long after midnight when Jake returned to quarters.
He had to pass through the Western men's section to get to
the Eastern crews. Nobody was asleep in the Western men's
section. No early-morning train was chalked up on their board.
The men were grouped off in poker and dice games. Jake
hesitated a little by one group, fascinated by a wiry little long-
headed finger-snapping black, who with strenuous h'h, h'h,
h'h, h'h, was zestfully throwing the bones. Jake almost joined
the game but he admonished himself: "You winned five dollars
thisaday and you made a nice li'l' brown piece. Wha'more you
want?" . . .

He found the beds assigned to the members of his crew.
They were double beds, like Pullman berths. Three of the
waiters had not come in yet. The second and the fourth cooks
were snoring, each a deep frothy bass and a high tenor, and
scratching themselves in their sleep. The chef sprawled like
the carcass of a rhinoceros, half-naked, mouth wide open.
Tormented by bedbugs, he had scratched and tossed in his
sleep and hoofed the covers off the bed. Ray was sitting on a
lower berth on his Negro newspapers spread out to form a
sheet. He had thrown the sheets on the floor, they were so
filthy from other men's sleeping. By the thin flame of gaslight
he was killing bugs.

"Where is I gwine to sleep?" asked Jake.

"Over me, if you can. I saved the bunk for you," said Ray.

"Some music the niggers am making," remarked Jake, nodding in the direction of the snoring cooks. "But whasmat,
chappie, you ain't sleeping?"

"Can't you see?"

"Bugs. Bumbole! This is a hell of a dump for a man to
sleep in."

"The place is rocking crazy with them," said Ray. "I hauled
the cot away from the wall, but the mattress is just swarming."

Hungry and bold, the bugs crept out of their chinks and
hunted for food. They stopped dead-still when disturbed

by the slightest shadow, and flattened their bellies against the wall.

"Le's get outa this stinking dump and chase a drink, chappie."

Ray jumped out of his berth, shoved himself into his clothes and went with Jake. The saloon near by the pool-room was still open. They went there. Ray asked for sherry.

"You had better sample some hard liquor if youse gwine back to wrastle with them bugs tonight," Jake suggested.

Ray took his advice. A light-yellow fellow chummed up with the boys and invited them to drink with him. He was as tall as Jake and very thin. There was a vacant, wandering look in his kindly-weak eyes. He was a waiter on another dining-car of the New York–Pittsburg run. Ray mentioned that he had to quit his bed because he couldn't sleep.

"This here town is the rottenest lay-over in the whole railroad field," declared the light-yellow. "I don't never sleep in the quarters here."

"Where do you sleep, then?" asked Ray.

"Oh, I got a sweet baby way up yonder the other side of the hill."

"Oh, ma-ma!" Jake licked his lips. "So youse all fixed up in this heah town?"

"Not going there tonight, though," the light-yellow said in a careless, almost bored tone. "Too far for mine."

He asked Jake and Ray if they would like to go to a little open-all-night place. They were glad to hear of that.

"Any old thing, boh," Jake said, "to get away from that theah Pennsy bug house."

The little place was something of a barrel-house speak-easy, crowded with black steel-workers in overalls and railroad men, and foggy with smoke. They were all drinking hard liquor and playing cards. The boss was a stocky, genial brown man. He knew the light-yellow waiter and shook hands with him and his friends. He moved away some boxes in a corner and squeezed a little table in it, specially for them. They sat down, jammed into the corner, and drank whisky.

"Better here than the Pennsy pigpen," said the light-yellow.

He was slapped on the back by a short, compact young black.

"Hello, you! What you think youse doing theah?"

"Ain't figuring," retorted the light-yellow, "is you?"

"On the red moon gwine around mah haid, yes. How about a li'l' good snow?"

"Now you got mah number down, Happy."

The black lad vanished again through a mysterious back door.

The light-yellow said: "He's the biggest hophead I ever seen. Nobody can sniff like him. Yet he's always the same happy nigger, stout and strong like a bull."

He took another whisky and went like a lean hound after Happy. Jake looked mischievously at the little brown door, remarking: "It's a great life ef youse in on it." . . .

The light-yellow came back with a cold gleam in his eyes, like arsenic shining in the dark. His features were accentuated by a rigid, disturbing tone and he resembled a smiling wax figure.

"Have a li'l' stuff with the bunch?" he asked Jake.

"I ain't got the habit, boh, but I'll try anything once again."

"And you?" The light-yellow turned to Ray.

"No, chief, thank you, but I don't want to."

The waiter went out again with Jake on his heels. Beyond the door, five fellows, kneeling in the sawdust, were rolling the square bones. Others sat together around two tables with a bottle of red liquor and thimble-like glasses before them.

"Oh, boy!" one said. "When I get home tonight it will be some more royal stuff. I ain'ta gwine to work none 'tall tomorrow."

"Shucks!" Another spread away his big mouth. "This heah ain't nothing foh a fellow to turn royal loose on. I remimber when I was gwine with a money gang that hed no use foh nothing but the pipe. That theah time was life, buddy."

"Wha' sorta pipe was that there?" asked Jake.

"The Chinese stuff, old boy."

Instead of deliberately fisting his, like the others, Jake took it up carelessly between his thumb and forefinger and inhaled.

"Say what you wanta about Chinee or any other stuff," said Happy, "but theah ain't nothing can work wicked like snow and whisky. It'll flip you up from hell into heaven befoh you knows it."

Ray looked into the room.

"Who's you li'l' mascot?" Happy asked the light-yellow.

"Tha's mah best pal," Jake answered. "He's got some moh stuff up here," Jake tapped his head.

"Better let's go on back to quarters," said Ray.

"To them bugs?" demanded Jake.

"Yes, I think we'd better."

"Awright, anything you say, chappie. I kain sleep through worser things." Jake took a few of the little white packets from Happy and gave him some money. "Guess I might need them some day. You never know."

Jake fell asleep as soon as his head touched the dirty pillow. Below him, Ray lay in his bunk, tormented by bugs and the snoring cooks. The low-burning gaslight flickered and flared upon the shadows. The young man lay under the untellable horror of a dead-tired man who wills to sleep and cannot.

In other sections of the big barn building the faint chink of coins touched his ears. Those men gambling the hopeless Pittsburg night away did not disturb him. They were so quiet. It would have been better, perhaps, if they were noisy. He closed his eyes and tried to hypnotize himself to sleep. Sleep . . . sleep . . . sleep . . . sleep . . . sleep. . . . He began counting slowly. His vigil might break and vanish somnolently upon some magic number. He counted a million. Perhaps love would appease this unwavering angel of wakefulness. Oh, but he could not pick up love easily on the street as Jake. . . .

He flung himself, across void and water, back home. Home thoughts, if you can make them soft and sweet and misty-beautiful enough, can sometimes snare sleep. There was the quiet, chalky-dusty street and, jutting out over it, the front of the house that he had lived in. The high staircase built on the outside, and pots of begonias and ferns on the landing. . . .

All the flowering things he loved, red and white and pink hibiscus, mimosas, rhododendrons, a thousand glowing creepers, climbing and spilling their vivid petals everywhere, and bright-buzzing humming-birds and butterflies. All the tropic-warm lilies and roses. Giddy-high erect thatch palms, slender, tall, fur-fronded ferns, majestic cotton trees, stately bamboos creating a green grandeur in the heart of space. . . .

Sleep remained cold and distant. Intermittently the cooks broke their snoring with masticating noises of their fat lips, like animals eating. Ray fixed his eyes on the offensive bug-bitten bulk of the chef. These men claimed kinship with him. They were black like him. Man and nature had put them in the same race. He ought to love them and feel them (if they felt anything). He ought to if he had a shred of social morality in him. They were all chain-ganged together and he was counted as one link. Yet he loathed every soul in that great barrack-room, except Jake. Race. . . . Why should he have and love a race?

Races and nations were things like skunks, whose smells poisoned the air of life. Yet civilized mankind reposed its faith and future in their ancient, silted channels. Great races and big nations! There must be something mighty inspiriting in being the citizen of a great strong nation. To be the white citizen of a nation that can say bold, challenging things like a strong man. Something very different from the keen ecstatic joy a man feels in the romance of being black. Something the black man could never feel nor quite understand.

Ray felt that as he was conscious of being black and impotent, so, correspondingly, each marine down in Hayti must be conscious of being white and powerful. What a unique feeling of confidence about life the typical white youth of his age must have! Knowing that his skin-color was a passport to glory, making him one with ten thousands like himself. All perfect Occidentals and investors in that grand business called civilization. That grand business in whose pits sweated and snored, like the cooks, all the black and brown hybrids and mongrels, simple earth-loving animals, without aspirations toward national unity and racial arrogance.

He remembered when little Hayti was floundering uncontrolled, how proud he was to be the son of a free nation. He used to feel condescendingly sorry for those poor African natives; superior to ten millions of suppressed Yankee "coons." Now he was just one of them and he hated them for being one of them. . . .

But he was not entirely of them, he reflected. He possessed another language and literature that they knew not of. And some day Uncle Sam might let go of his island and he would escape from the clutches of that magnificent monster of civilization and retire behind the natural defenses of his island, where the steam-roller of progress could not reach him. Escape he would. He had faith. He had hope. But, oh, what would become of that great mass of black swine, hunted and cornered by slavering white canaille! Sleep! oh, sleep! Down Thought!

But all his senses were burning wide awake. Thought was not a beautiful and reassuring angel, a thing of soothing music and light laughter and winged images glowing with the rare colors of life. No. It was suffering, horribly real. It seized and worried him from every angle. Pushed him toward the sheer precipice of imagination. It was awful. He was afraid. For thought was a terrible tiger clawing at his small portion of gray substance, throttling, tearing, and tormenting him with pitiless ferocity. Oh, a thousand ideas of life were shrieking at him in a wild orgy of mockery! . . .

He was in the middle of a world suspended in space. A familiar line lit up, like a flame, the vast, crowded, immensity of his vision.

Et l'âme du monde est dans l'air.

A moment's respite. . . .

A loud snore from the half-naked chef brought him back to the filthy fact of the quarters that the richest railroad in the world had provided for its black servitors. Ray looked up at Jake, stretched at full length on his side, his cheek in his right hand, sleeping peacefully, like a tired boy after hard playing, so happy and sweet and handsome. He remembered the neatly-folded white papers in Jake's pocket. Maybe that was the cause of his sleeping so soundly. He reached his hand up to the coat hanging on the nail above his head. It was such an innocent little thing—like a headache powder the paper of which you wipe with your tongue, so that none should be wasted. Apparently the first one had no effect and Ray took the rest.

Sleep capitulated.

Immediately he was back home again. His father's house was a vast forest full of blooming hibiscus and mimosas and giant evergreen trees. And he was a gay humming-bird, fluttering and darting his long needle beak into the heart of a bell-flower. Suddenly he changed into an owl flying by day. . . . Howard University was a prison with white warders. . . . Now he was a young shining chief in a marble palace; slim, naked negresses dancing for his pleasure; courtiers reclining on cushions soft like passionate kisses; gleaming-skinned black boys bearing goblets of wine and obedient eunuchs waiting in the offing. . . .

And the world was a blue paradise. Everything was in gorgeous blue of heaven. Woods and streams were blue, and men and women and animals, and beautiful to see and love. And he was a blue bird in flight and a blue lizard in love. And life was all blue happiness. Taboos and terrors and penalties were transformed into new pagan delights, orgies of Orient-blue carnival, of rare flowers and red fruits, cherubs and seraphs and fetishes and phalli and all the most-high gods. . . .

A thousand pins were pricking Ray's flesh and he was shouting for Jake, but his voice was so faint he could not hear himself. Jake had him in his arms and tried to stand him upon his feet. He crumpled up against the bunk. All his muscles were loose, his cells were cold, and the rhythm of being arrested.

It was high morning and time to go to the train. Jake had picked up the empty little folds of paper from the floor and restored them to his pocket. He knew what had happened to them, and guessed why. He went and called the first and fourth waiters.

The chef bulked big in the room, dressed and ready to go to the railroad yards. He gave a contemptuous glance at Jake looking after Ray and said: "Better leave that theah nigger professor alone and come on 'long to the dining-car with us. That theah nigger is dopey from them books o' hisn. I done told befoh them books would git him yet."

The chef went off with the second and fourth cooks. Jake stayed with Ray. They got his shoes and coat on. The first waiter telephoned the steward, and Ray was taken to the hospital.

"We may all be niggers aw'right, but we ain't nonetall all the same," Jake said as he hurried along to the dining-car, thinking of Ray.

XII
The Treeing of the Chef

Perhaps the chef of Jake's dining-car was the most hated chef in the service. He was repulsive in every aspect. From the elevated bulk of his gross person to the matted burrs of his head and the fat cigar, the constant companion of his sloppy mouth, that he chewed and smoked at the same time. The chef deliberately increased his repulsiveness of form by the meannesses of his spirit.

"I know Ise a mean black nigger," he often said, "and I'll let you all know it on this heah white man's car, too."

The chef was a great black bundle of consciously suppressed desires. That was doubtless why he was so ornery. He was one of the model chefs of the service. His kitchen was well-ordered. The checking up of his provisions always showed a praiseworthy balance. He always had his food ready on time, feeding the heaviest rush of customers as rapidly as the lightest. He fed the steward excellently. He fed the crew well. In a word, he did his duty as only a martinet can.

A chef who is "right-there" at every call is the first asset of importance on an *à la carte* restaurant-car. The chef lived rigidly up to that fact and above it. He was also painfully honest. He had a mulatto wife and a brown boy-child in New York and he never slipped away any of the company's goods to them. Other dining-car men had devised a system of getting by the company's detectives with choice brands of the company's foodstuffs. The chef kept away from that. It was long since the yard detectives had stopped searching any parcel that *he* carried off with him.

"I don't want none o' the white-boss stuff foh mine," he declared. "Ise making enough o' mah own to suppoht mah wife and kid."

And more, the chef had a violent distaste for all the stock things that "coons" are supposed to like to the point of stealing them. He would not eat watermelon, because white people called it "the niggers' ice-cream." Pork chops he fancied not.

Nor corn pone. And the idea of eating chicken gave him a spasm. Of the odds and ends of chicken gizzard, feet, head, rump, heart, wing points, and liver—the chef would make the most delicious stew for the crew, which he never touched himself. The Irish steward never missed his share of it. But for his meal the chef would grill a steak or mutton chop or fry a fish. Oh, chef was big and haughty about not being "no regular darky"! And although he came from the Alabama country, he pretended not to know a coon tail from a rabbit foot.

"All this heah talk about chicken-loving niggers," he growled chuckingly to the second cook. "The way them white passengers clean up on mah fried chicken I wouldn't trust one o' them anywheres near mah hen-coop."

Broiling tender corn-fed chicken without biting a leg. Thus, grimly, the chef existed. Humored and tolerated by the steward and hated by the waiters and undercooks. Jake found himself on the side of the waiters. He did not hate the chef (Jake could not hate anybody). But he could not be obscenely sycophantic to him as the second cook, who was just waiting for the chance to get the chef's job. Jake stood his corner in the coffin, doing his bit in diplomatic silence. Let the chef bawl the waiters out. He would not, like the second cook, join him in that game.

Ray, perhaps, was the chief cause of Jake's silent indignation. Jake had said to him: "I don't know how all you fellows can stand that theah God-damn black bull. I feels like falling down mahself." But Ray had begged Jake to stay on, telling him that he was the only decent man in the kitchen. Jake stayed because he liked Ray. A big friendship had sprung up between them and Jake hated to hear the chef abusing his friend along with the other waiters. The other cooks and waiters called Ray "Professor." Jake had never called him that. Nor did he call him "buddy," as he did Zeddy and his longshoremen friends. He called him "chappie" in a genial, semi-paternal way.

Jake's life had never before touched any of the educated of the ten dark millions. He had, however, a vague idea of who they were. He knew that the "big niggers" that were gossiped about in the saloons and the types he had met at Madame Adelina Suarez's were not *the* educated ones. The educated "dick-tees," in Jake's circles were often subjects for raw and funny sallies. He had once heard Miss Curdy putting them in their place while Susy's star eyes gleamed warm approval.

"Honey, I lived in Washington and I knowed inside and naked out the stuck-up bush-whackers of the race. They all talks and act as if loving was a sin, but I tell you straight, I wouldn't trust any of them after dark with a preacher. . . . Don't ask me, honey. I seen and I knows them all."

"I guess you does, sistah," Susy had agreed. "Nobody kaint hand *me* no fairy tales about niggers. Wese all much of a muchness when you git down to the real stuff."

Difficulties on the dining-car were worsened by a feud between the pantry and the kitchen. The first waiter, who was pantryman by regulation, had a grievance against the chef and was just waiting to "get" him. But, the chef being such a paragon, the "getting" was not easy.

Nothing can be worse on a dining-car than trouble between the pantry and the kitchen, for one is as necessary to the other as oil is to salad. But the war was covertly on and the chef was prepared to throw his whole rhinoceros weight against the pantry. The first waiter had to fight cautiously. He was quite aware that a first-class chef was of greater value than a first-class pantryman.

The trouble had begun through the "mule." The fourth man—a coffee-skinned Georgia village boy, timid like a country girl just come to town—hated the nickname, but the chef would call him nothing else.

"Call him 'Rhinoceros' when he calls you 'Mule,'" Ray told the fourth waiter, but he was too timid to do it. . . .

The dining-car was resting on the tracks in the Altoona yards, waiting for a Western train. The first, third, and fifth waiters were playing poker. Ray was reading Dostoievski's *Crime and Punishment*. The fourth waiter was working in the pantry. Suddenly the restaurant-car was shocked by a terrible roar.

"Gwan I say! Take that theah ice and beat it, you black sissy." . . .

"This ice ain't good for the pantry. You ought to gimme the cleaner one," the timid fourth man stood his ground.

The cigar of the chef stood up like a tusk. Fury was dancing in his enraged face and he would have stamped the guts out of the poor, timid boy if he was not restrained by the fear of losing his job. For on the dining-car, he who strikes the first blow catches the punishment.

"Quit jawing with me, nigger waiter, or I'll jab this heah ice-pick in you' mouf."

"Come and do it," the fourth waiter said, quietly.

"God dam' you' soul!" the chef bellowed. "Ef you don't quit chewing the rag—ef you git fresh with me, I'll throw you off this bloody car. S'elp mah Gawd, I will. You disnificant down-home mule."

The fourth waiter glanced behind him down the corridor and saw Ray, book in hand, and the other waiters, who had left their cards to see the cause of the tumult. Ray winked at the fourth waiter. He screwed up his courage and said to the chef: "I ain't no mule, and youse a dirty rhinoceros."

The chef seemed paralyzed with surprise. "Wha's that name you done call me? Wha's rhinasras?"

All the waiters laughed. The chef looked ridiculous and Ray said: "Why, chef, don't you know? That's the ugliest animal in all Africa."

The chef looked apoplectic. . . . "I don't care a dime foh all you nigger waiters and I ain't joking wif any of you. Cause you manicuring you' finger nails and rubbing up you' stinking black hide against white folks in that theah diner, you all think youse something. But lemme tell you straight, you ain't nothing atall."

"But, chef," cried the pantryman, "why don't you stop riding the fourth man? Youse always riding him."

"Riding who? I nevah rode a man in all mah life. I jest tell that black skunk what to do and him stahts jawing with me. I don't care about any of you niggers, nohow."

"Wese all tiahd of you cussin' and bawking," said the pantry-man. "Why didn't you give the boy a clean piece of ice and finish? You know we need it for the water."

"Yaller nigger, you'd better gwan away from here."

"Don't call me no yaller nigger, you black and ugly cotton-field coon."

"Who dat? You bastard-begotten dime-snatcher, you'd

better gwan back to you' dining-room or I'll throw this heah garbage in you' crap-yaller face. . . . I'd better git long far away from you all 'foh I lose mah haid." The chef bounced into the kitchen and slammed the door.

That "bastard-begotten dime-snatcher" grew a cancer in the heart of the pantryman. It rooted deep because he *was* an "illegitimate" and he bitterly hated the whites he served ("crackers," he called them all) and the tips he picked up. He knew that his father was some red-necked white man who had despised his mother's race and had done nothing for him.

The sight of the chef grew more and more unbearable each day to the pantryman. He thought of knifing or plugging him with a gun some night. He had nursed his resentment to the point of madness and was capable of any act. But getting the chef in the dark would not have been revenge enough. The pantryman wanted the paragon to live, so that he might invent a way of bringing him down humiliatingly from his perch.

But the chef was hard to "get." He had made and kept his place by being a perfect brutal machine, with that advantage that all mechanical creatures have over sensitive human beings. One day the pantryman thought he almost had his man. The chef had fed the steward, but kept the boys waiting for their luncheon. The waiters thought that he had one of his ornery spells on and was intentionally punishing them. They were all standing in the pantry, except Ray.

The fifth said to the first: "Ask him why he don't put the grub in the hole, partner. I'm horse-ways hungry."

"Ask him you'self. I ain't got nothing to do with that black hog moh'n giving him what b'longs to him in this heah pantry."

"Mah belly's making a most beautiful commotion. Jest lak a bleating lamb," drawled the third.

The fifth waiter pushed up the little glass door and stuck his head in the kitchen: "Chef, when are we gwine to go away from here?"

"Keep you' shirt on, nigger," flashed back from the kitchen. "Youall'll soon be stuffing you'self full o' the white man's poke chops. Better than you evah smell in Harlem."

"Wese werking foh't same like you is," the fifth man retorted.

"I don't eat no poke chops, nigger. I cooks the stuff, but I don't eat it, nevah."

"P'raps youse chewing a worser kind o' meat."

"Don't gimme no back talk, nigger waiter. Looka heah ——"

The steward came into the pantry and said: "Chef, it's time to feed the boys. They're hungry. We had a hard day, today."

The chef's cigar drooped upon his slavering lip and almost fell. He turned to the steward with an injured air. "Ain't I doing mah best? Ain't I been working most hard mahself? I done get yourn lunch ready and am getting the crew's own and fixing foh dinner at the same time. I ain't tuk a mouful mahse'f——"

The steward had turned his heels on the pantry. The chef was enraged that he had intervened on behalf of the waiters.

"Ef you dime-chasing niggers keep fooling with me on this car," he said, "I'll make you eat mah spittle. I done do it a'ready and I'll do it again. I'll spit in you' eats——"

"Wha's that? The boss sure gwine to settle this." The pantry-man dashed out of the pantry and called the steward. . . . "Ain't any of us waiters gwine to stay on heah Mis'r Farrel, with a chef like this."

"What's that, now?" The steward was in the pantry again. "What's this fine story, chef?"

"Nothing at all, Sah Farrel. I done pull a good bull on them fellars, tha's all. Cause theyse all trying to get mah goat. L'em quit fooling with the kitchen, Sah Farrel. I does mah wuk and I don't want no fooling fwom them nigger waiters, nohow."

"I guess you spit in it as you said, all right," cried the pantryman. . . . "Yes, you! You'd wallow in a pigpen and eat the filth, youse so doggone low-down."

"Now cut all o' that out," said the steward. "How could he do anything like that, when he eats the food, and I do meself?"

"In the hole!" shouted Jake.

The third and fifth waiters hurried into the pantry and brought out the waiters' food. . . . First a great platter of fish and tomatoes, then pork chops and mashed potatoes, steaming Java and best Borden's cream. The chef had made home-made bread baked in the form of little round caps. Nice and hot,

they quickly melted the butter that the boys sandwiched between them. He was a splendid cook, an artist in creating
palatable stuff. He came out of the kitchen himself, to eat in
the dining-room and, diplomatically, he helped himself from
the waiters' platter of fish. . . . Delicious food. The waiters
fell to it with keen relish. Obliterated from their memory the
sewer-incident of the moment before. . . . Feeding, feeding,
feeding.

But Ray remembered and visualized, and his stomach
turned. He left the food and went outside, where he found
Jake taking the air. He told Jake how he felt.

"Oh, the food is all right," said Jake. "I watch him close
anough in that there kitchen, and he knows I ain't standing in
with him in no low-down stuff."

"But do you think he would ever do such a thing?" asked
Ray.

Jake laughed. "What won't a bad nigger do when he's good
and mean way down in his heart? I ain't 'lowing mahself careless with none o' that kind, chappie."

Two Pullman porters came into the dining-car in the middle
of the waiters' meal.

"Here is the chambermaids," grinned the second cook.

"H'm, but how you all loves to call people names, though,"
commented the fourth waiter.

The waiters invited the porters to eat with them. The pantryman went to get them coffee and cream. The chef offered
to scramble some eggs. He went back to the kitchen and, after
a few minutes, the fourth cook brought out a platter of scrambled eggs for the two porters. The chef came rocking impor-
tantly behind the fourth cook. A clean white cap was poised on
his head and fondly he chewed his cigar. A perfect menial of
the great railroad company. He felt a wave of goodness sweeping over him, as if he had been patted on the head by the
Angel Gabriel for his good works. He asked the porters if they
had enough to eat and they thanked him and said they had
more than enough and that the food was wonderful. The chef
smiled broadly. He beamed upon steward, waiters, and porters,
and his eyes said: See what a really fine fellow I am in spite of
all the worries that go with the duties of a chef?

*

One day Ray saw the chef and the pantryman jesting while the pantryman was lighting his cigarette from the chef's stump of cigar. When Ray found the pantryman alone, he laughingly asked him if he and the chef had smoked the tobacco of peace.

"Fat chance!" retorted the first waiter. "I gotta talk to him, for we get the stores together and check up together with the steward, and I gotta hand him the stuff tha's coming to him outa the pantry, but I ain't settle mah debt with him yet. I ain't got no time for no nigger that done calls me 'bastard-begotten' and means it."

"Oh, forget it!" said Ray. "Christ was one, too, and we all worship him."

"Wha' you mean?" the pantryman demanded.

"What I said," Ray replied. . . .

"Oh! . . . Ain't you got no religion in you none 'tall?"

"My parents were Catholic, but I ain't nothing. God is white and has no more time for niggers than you've got for the chef."

"Well, I'll be browned but once!" cried the pantryman. "Is that theah what youse l'arning in them books? Don't you believe in getting religion?"

Ray laughed.

"You kain laugh, all right, but watch you' step Gawd don't get you yet. Youse sure trifling."

The coldness between the kitchen and the pantry continued, unpleasantly nasty, like the wearing of wet clothes, after the fall of a heavy shower, when the sun is shining again. The chef was uncomfortable. A waiter had never yet opposed open hostility to his personality like that. He was accustomed to the crew's surrendering to his ways with even a little sycophancy. It was always his policy to be amicable with the pantryman, playing him against the other waiters, for it was very disagreeable to keep up a feud when the kitchen and the pantry had so many unavoidable close contacts.

So the chef made overtures to the pantryman with special toothsome tidbits, such as he always prepared for the only steward and himself. But the pantryman refused to have any specially-prepared-for-his-Irishness-the-Steward's stuff that the other waiters could not share. Thereupon the chef gave up trying to placate him and started in hating back with profound African hate. African hate is deep down and hard to stir up, but there is no hate more realistic when it is stirred up.

One morning in Washington the iceman forgot to supply ice to the dining-car. One of the men had brought a little brass top on the diner and the waiters were excited over an easy new game called "put-and-take." The pantryman forgot his business. The chef went to another dining-car and obtained ice for the kitchen. The pantryman did not remember anything about ice until the train was well on its way to New York. He remembered it because the ice-cream was turning soft. He put his head through the hole and asked Jake for a piece of ice. The chef said no, he had enough for the kitchen only.

With a terrible contented expression the chef looked with malicious hate into the pantryman's yellow face. The pantryman glared back at the villainous black face and jerked his head in rage. The ice-cream turned softer. . . .

Luncheon was over, all the work was done, everything in order, and the entire crew was ready to go home when the train reached New York. The steward wanted to go directly home. But he had to wait and go over to the yards with the keys, so that the pantryman could ice up. And the pantryman was severely reprimanded for his laxity in Washington. . . .

The pantryman bided his time, waiting on the chef. He was cordial. He even laughed at the jokes the chef made at the other waiters' expense. The chef swelled bigger in his hide, feeling that everything had bent to his will. The pantryman waited, ignoring little moments for the big moment. It came.

One morning both the second and the fourth cook "fell down on the job," neither of them reporting for duty. The steward placed an order with the commissary superintendent for two cooks. Jake stayed in the kitchen, working, while the chef and the pantryman went to the store for the stock. . . .

The chef and the pantryman returned together with the large baskets of provisions for the trip. The eggs were carried by the chef himself in a neat box. Remembering that he had forgotten coffee, he sent Jake back to the store for it. Then he

began putting away the kitchen stuff. The pantryman was putting away the pantry stuff. . . .

A yellow girl passed by and waved a smile at the chef. He
grinned, his teeth champing his cigar. The chef hated yellow
men with "cracker" hatred, but he loved yellow women with
"cracker" love. His other love was gin. But he never carried a
liquor flask on the diner, because it was against regulations.
And he never drank with any of the crew. He drank alone. And
he did other things alone. In Philadelphia or Washington he
never went to a buffet flat with any of the men.

The girls working in the yards were always flirting with him.
He fascinated them, perhaps because he was so Congo mask-
like in aspect and so duty-strict. They could often wheedle
something nice out of other chefs, but nothing out of *the* chef.
He would rather give them his money than a piece of the company's raw meat. The chef was generous in his way; Richmond
Pete, who owned the saloon near the yards in Queensborough,
could attest to that. He had often gossiped about the chef.
How he "blowed them gals that he had a crush on in the family room and danced an elephant jig while the gals were pulling
his leg."

The yellow girl that waved at the chef through the window
was pretty. Her gesture transformed his face into a foolish
broad-smiling thing. He stepped outside the kitchen for a moment to have a tickling word with her.

In that moment the pantryman made a lightning-bolt move;
and shut down the little glass door between the pantry and the
kitchen. . . .

The train was speeding its way west. The first call for dinner
had been made and the dining-room was already full. Over
half a dozen calls for eggs of different kinds had been bawled
out before the chef discovered that the basket of eggs was
missing. The chef asked the pantryman to call the steward. The
pantryman, curiously preoccupied, forgot. Pandemonium was
loose in the pantry and kitchen when the steward, radish-red,
stuck his head in.

The chef's lower lip had flopped low down, dripping, and
the cigar had fallen somewhere. "Cut them aiggs off o' the bill,
Sah Farrel. O Lawd!" he moaned, "Ise sartain sure I brought

them aiggs on the car mahself, and now I don't know where they is."

"What kind o' blah is that?" cried the steward. "The eggs must be there in the kitchen. I saw them with the stock meself."

"And I brought them here hugging them, Boss, ef I ain't been made fool of by something." The rhinoceros had changed into a meek black lamb. "O Lawd! and I ain't been outa the kitchen sence. Ain't no mortal hand could tuk them. Some evil hand. O Lawd!——"

"Hell!" The steward dashed out of the pantry to cut all the egg dishes off the bill. The passengers were getting clamorous. The waiters were asking those who had ordered eggs to change to something else. . . .

The steward suggested searching the pantry. The pantry was ransacked. "Them ain't there, cep'n' they had feets to walk. O Lawd of Heaben!" the chef groaned. "It's something deep and evil, I knows, for I ain't been outa this heah kitchen." His little flirtation with the yellow girl was completely wiped off his memory.

Only Jake was keeping his head in the kitchen. He was acting second cook, for the steward had not succeeded in getting one. The fourth cook he had gotten was new to the service and he was standing, conspicuously long-headed, with gaping mouth.

"Why'n the debbil's name don't you do some'n, nigger?" bellowed the chef, frothy at the corners of his mouth.

"The chef is up a tree, all right," said Ray to the pantryman.

"And he'll break his black hide getting down," the pantryman replied, bitterly.

"Chef!" The yellow pantryman's face carried a royal African grin. "What's the matter with you and them aiggs?"

"I done gived them to you mammy."

"And fohget you wife, ole timer? Ef you ain't a chicken-roost nigger, as you boast, you surely loves the nest."

Gash! The chef, at last losing control of himself, shied a huge ham bone at the pantryman. The pantryman sprang back as the ham bone flew through the aperture and smashed a bottle of milk in the pantry.

"What's all this bloody business today?" cried the steward,

who was just entering the pantry. . . . "What nonsense is this, chef? You've made a mess of things already and now you start fighting with the waiters. You can't do like that. You losing your head?"

"Lookahere, Sah Farrel, I jes' want ev'body to leave me 'lone."

"But we must all team together on the dining-car. That's the only way. You can't start fighting the waiters because you've lost the eggs."

"Sah Farrel, leave me alone, I say," half roared, half moaned the chef, "or I'll jump off right now and let you run you' kitchen you'self."

"What's that?" The steward started.

"I say I'll jump off, and I mean it as Gawd's mah maker."

The steward slipped out of the pantry without another word.

The steward obtained a supply of eggs in Harrisburg the next morning. The rest of the trip was made with the most dignified formalities between him and the chef. Between the pantry and the chef the atmosphere was tenser, but there were no more explosions.

The dining-car went out on its next trip with a new chef. And the old chef, after standing a little of the superintendent's notoriously sharp tongue, was sent to another car as second cook.

"Hit those fellahs in the pocket-book is the only way," the pantryman overheard the steward talking to one of his colleagues. "Imagine an old experienced chef threatening to jump off when I was short of a second cook."

They were getting the stock for the next trip in the commissary. Jake turned to the pantryman: "But it was sure peculiar, though, how them aiggs just fly outa that kitchen lak that way."

"Maybe they all hatched and growed wings when ole black bull was playing with that sweet yaller piece," the pantryman laughed.

"Honest, though, how do you think it happened?" persisted Jake. "Did you hoodoo them aiggs, or what did you do?"

"I wouldn't know atall. Better ask them rats in the yards ef they sucked the shells dry. What you' right hand does don't tell it to the left, says I."

"You done said a mou'ful, but how did you get away with it so quiet?"

"I ain't said nothing discrimination and I ain't nevah."

"Don't figure against me. Ise with you, buddy," said Jake, "and now that wese good and rid of him, I hope all we niggers will pull together like civilization folks."

"Sure we will. There ain't another down-home nigger like him in this white man's service. He was riding too high and fly, brother. I knew he would tumble and bust something nasty. But I ain't said I knowed a thing about it, all the same."

XIII
One Night in Philly

ONE night in Philadelphia Jake breezed into the waiters' quarters in Market Street, looking for Ray. It was late. Ray was in bed. Jake pulled him up.

"Come on outa that, you slacker. Let's go over to North Philly."

"What for?"

"A li'l' fun. I knows a swell outfit I wanta show you."

"Anything new?"

"Don't know about anything *new*, chappie, but I know there's something *good* right there in Fifteenth Street."

"Oh, I know all about that. I don't want to go."

"Come on. Don't be so particular about you' person. You gotta go with me."

"I have a girl in New York."

"Tha's awright. This is Philly."

"I tell you, Jake, there's no fun in those kinds for me. They'll bore me just like that night in Baltimore."

"Oh, these here am different chippies, I tell you. Come on, le's spend the night away from this damn dump. Wese laying ovah all day tomorrow."

"And some of them will say such rotten things. Pretty enough, all right, but their mouths are loaded with filth, and that's what gets me."

"Them's different ovah there, chappie. I'll kiss the Bible on it. Come on, now. It's no fun me going alone."

They went to a house in Fifteenth Street. As they entered Jake was greeted by a mulatto woman in the full vigor of middle life.

"Why, *you* heart-breaker! It's ages and ages since I saw you. You and me sure going to have a bust-up tonight."

Jake grinned, prancing a little, as if he were going to do the old cake-walk.

226

"Here, Laura, this is mah friend," he introduced Ray casually.

"Bring him over here and sit down," Madame Laura commanded.

She was a big-boned woman, but very agile. A long, irregular, rich-brown face, roving black eyes, deep-set, and shiny black hair heaped upon her head. She wore black velvet, a square-cut blouse low down on her breasts, and a string of large coral beads. The young girls of that house envied her finely-preserved form and her carriage and wondered if they would be anything like that when they reached her age.

The interior of this house gave Ray a shock. It looked so much like a comfortable boarding-house where everybody was cheerful and nice coquettish girls in colorful frocks were doing the waiting. . . . There were a few flirting couples, two groups of men playing cards, and girls hovering around. An attractive black woman was serving sandwiches, gin and bottled beer. At the piano, a slim yellow youth was playing a "blues." . . . A pleasant house party, similar to any other among colored people of that class in Baltimore, New Orleans, Charleston, Richmond, or even Washington, D.C. Different, naturally, from New York, which molds all peoples into a hectic rhythm of its own. Yet even New York, passing its strange thousands through its great metropolitan mill, cannot rob Negroes of their native color and laughter.

"Mah friend's just keeping me company," Jake said to the woman. "He ain't regular—you get me? And I want him treated right."

"He'll be treated better here than he would in church." She laughed and touched Ray's calf with the point of her slipper.

"What kind o' bust-up youse gwine to have with me?" demanded Jake.

"I'll show you just what I'm going to do with you for forgetting me so long."

She got up and went into an adjoining room. When she returned an attractively made-up brown girl followed her carrying a tray with glasses and a bottle of champagne. . . . The cork hit the ceiling, bang! And deftly the woman herself poured the foaming liquor without a wasted drop.

"There! That's our bust-up," she said. "Me and you and your friend. Even if he's a virgin he's all right. I know you ain't never going around with no sap-head."

"Give me some, too," a boy of dull-gold complexion materialized by the side of Madame Laura and demanded a drink. He was about eleven years old.

Affectionately she put her arm around him and poured out a small glass of champagne. The frailness of the boy was pathetic; his eyes were sleepy-sad. He resembled a reed fading in a morass.

"Who is he?" Ray asked.

"He's my son," responded Madame Laura. "Clever kid, too. He loves books."

"Ray will like him, then," said Jake. "Books is his middle name."

Ray suddenly felt a violent dislike for the atmosphere. At first he had liked the general friendliness and warmth and naturalness of it. All so different from what he had expected. But something about the presence of the little boy there and his being the woman's son disgusted him. He could not analyse his aversion. It was just an instinctive, intolerant feeling that the boy did not belong to that environment and should not be there.

He went from Madame Laura and Jake over to the piano and conversed with the pianist. When he glanced again at the table he had left, Madame Laura had her arm around Jake's neck and his eyes were strangely shining.

Madame Laura had set the pace. There were four other couples making love. At one table a big-built, very black man was amusing himself with two attractive girls, one brown-skinned and the other yellow. The girls' complexion was heightened by High-Brown Talc powder and rouge. A bottle of Muscatel stood on the table. The man was well dressed in nigger-brown and he wore an expensive diamond ring on his little finger.

The stags were still playing cards, with girls hovering over them. The happy-faced black woman was doing the managing, as Madame Laura was otherwise engaged. The pianist began banging another blues.

Ray felt alone and a little sorry for himself. Now that he was there, he would like to be touched by the spirit of that atmosphere and, like Jake, fall naturally into its rhythm. He also envied Jake. Just for this night only he would like to be like him. . . .

They were dancing. The little yellow girl, her legs kicked out at oblique angles, appeared as if she were going to fall through the big-built black man.

> We'll all be merry when you taste a cherry,
> And we'll twine and twine like a fruitful vine.

In the middle of the floor, a young railroad porter had his hand flattened straight down the slim, cérise-chiffoned back of a brown girl. Her head was thrown back and her eyes held his gleaming eyes. Her lips were parted with pleasure and they stood and rocked in an ecstasy. Their feet were not moving. Only their bodies rocked, rocked to the "blues." . . .

Ray remarked that Jake was not in the room, nor was Madame Laura in evidence. A girl came to him. "Why is you so all by you'self, baby? Don't you wanta dance some? That there is some more temptation 'blues.'"

Tickling, enticing syncopation. Ray felt that he ought to dance to it. But some strange thing seemed to hold him back from taking the girl in his arms.

"Will you drink something, instead?" he found a way out.

"Awwww-right," disappointed, she drawled.

She beckoned to the happy-faced woman.

"Virginia Dare."

"I'll have some, too," Ray said.

Another brown girl joined them.

"Buy mah pal a drink, too?" the first girl asked.

"Why, certainly," he answered.

The woman brought two glasses of Virginia Dare and Ray ordered a third.

Such a striking exotic appearance the rouge gave these brown girls. Rouge that is so cheap in its general use had here an uncommon quality. Rare as the red flower of the hibiscus would be in a florist's window on Fifth Avenue. Rouge on brown, a warm, insidious chestnut color. But so much more subtle than chestnut. The round face of the first girl, the carnal sympathy of her full, tinted mouth, touched Ray. But something was between them. . . .

The piano-player had wandered off into some dim, far-away, ancestral source of music. Far, far away from music-hall syncopation and jazz, he was lost in some sensual dream of his own. No tortures, banal shrieks and agonies. Tum-tum . . . tum-tum . . . tum-tum . . . tum-tum. . . . The notes were naked acute alert. Like black youth burning naked in the bush. Love in the deep heart of the jungle. . . . The sharp spring of a leopard from a leafy limb, the snarl of a jackal, green lizards in amorous play, the flight of a plumed bird, and the sudden laughter of mischievous monkeys in their green homes. Tum-tum . . . tum-tum . . . tum-tum . . . tum-tum. . . . Simple-clear and quivering. Like a primitive dance of war or of love . . . the marshaling of spears or the sacred frenzy of a phallic celebration.

Black lovers of life caught up in their own free native rhythm, threaded to a remote scarce-remembered past, celebrating the midnight hours in themselves, for themselves, of themselves, in a house in Fifteenth Street, Philadelphia. . . .

"Raided!" A voice screamed. Standing in the rear door, a policeman, white, in full uniform, smilingly contemplated the spectacle. There was a wild scramble for hats and wraps. The old-timers giggled, shrugged, and kept their seats. Madame Laura pushed aside the policeman.

"Keep you' pants on, all of you and carry on with you' fun. What's matter? Scared of a uniform? Pat"—she turned to the policeman—"what you want to throw a scare in the company for? Come on here with you."

The policeman, twirling his baton, marched to a table and sat down with Madame Laura.

"Geewizard!" Jake sat down, too. "Tell 'em next time not to ring the fire alarm so loud."

"You said it, honey-stick. There are no cops in Philly going to mess with this girl. Ain't it the truth, Pat?" Madame Laura twisted the policeman's ear and bridled.

"I know it's the Bible trute," the happy-faced black lady chanted in a sugary voice, setting a bottle of champagne and glasses upon the table and seating herself familiarly beside the policeman.

The champagne foamed in the four glasses.

"Whar's mah li'l' chappie?" Jake asked.

"Gone, maybe. Don't worry," said Madame Laura. "Drink!"

Four brown hands and one white. Chink!

"Here's to you, Pat," cried Madame Laura. "There's Irish in me from the male line." She toasted:

> "Flixy, flaxy, fleasy,
>   Make it good and easy,
>   Flix for start and flax for snappy,
>   Niggers and Irish will always be happy."

The policeman swallowed his champagne at a gulp and got up. "Gotta go now. Time for duty."

"You treat him nice. Is it for love or protection?" asked Jake.

"He's loving *her*"—Madame Laura indicated the now coy lady who helped her manage—"but he's protecting *me*. It's a long time since I ain't got no loving inclination for any skin but chocolate. Get me?"

When Jake returned to the quarters he found Ray sleeping quietly. He did not disturb him. The next morning they walked together to the yards.

"Did the policeman scare you, too, last night?" asked Jake.

"What policeman?"

"Oh, didn't you see him? There was a policeman theah and somebody hollered 'Raid!' scaring everybody. I thought you'd done tuk you'self away from there in quick time becasn a that."

"No, I left before that, I guess. Didn't even smell one walking all the way to the quarters in Market Street."

"Why'd you beat it? One o' the li'l' chippies had a crush on you. Oh, boy! and she was some piece to look at."

"I know it. She was kind of nice. But she had some nasty perfume on her that turned mah stomach."

"Youse awful queer, chappie," Jake commented.

"Why, don't you ever feel those sensations that just turn you back in on yourself and make you isolated and helpless?"

"Wha'd y'u mean?"

"I mean if sometimes you don't feel as I felt last night?"

"Lawdy no. Young and pretty is all I feel."

They stopped in a saloon. Jake had a small whisky and Ray an egg-nogg.

"But Madame Laura isn't young," resumed Ray.

"Ain't she?" Jake showed his teeth. "I'd back her against some of the youngest. She's a wonder, chappie. Her blood's like good liquor. She gave me a present, too. Looka here." Jake took from his pocket a lovely slate-colored necktie sprinkled with red dots. Ray felt the fineness of it.

"Ef I had the sweetman disinclination I wouldn't have to work, chappie," Jake rocked proudly in his walk. "But tha's the life of a pee-wee cutter, says I. Kain't see it for mine."

"She was certainly nice to you last night. And the girls were nice, too. It was just like a jolly parlor social."

"Oh, sure! Them gals not all in the straight business, you know. Some o' them works and just go there for a good time, a li'l' extra stuff. . . . It ain't like that nonetall ovah in Europe, chappie. They wouldn't 'a' treated you so nice. Them places I sampled ovah there was all straight raw business and no camouflage."

"Did you prefer them?"

"Hell, no! I prefer the niggers' way every time. They does it better. . . ."

"Wish I could feel the difference as you do, Jakie. I lump all those ladies together, without difference of race."

"Youse crazy, chappie. You ain't got no experience about it. There's all kinds a difference in that theah life. Sometimes it's the people make the difference and sometimes it's the place. And as foh them sweet marchants, there's as much difference between them as you find in any other class a people. There is them slap-up private-apartmant ones, and there is them of the dickty buffet flats; then the low-down speakeasy customers; the cabaret babies, the family-entrance clients, and the street fliers."

They stopped on a board-walk. The dining-car stood before them, resting on one of the hundred tracks of the great Philadelphia yards.

"I got a free permit to a nifty apartmant in New York, chappie, and the next Saturday night we lay over together in the big city Ise gwine to show you some real queens. It's like everything else in life. Depends on you' luck."

"And you are one lucky dog," Ray laughed.

Jake grinned: "I'd tell you about a li'l' piece o' sweetness I picked up in a cabaret the first day I landed from ovah the other side. But it's too late now. We gotta start work."

"Next time, then," said Ray.

Jake swung himself up by the rear platform and entered the kitchen. Ray passed round by the other side into the dining-room.

XIV
Interlude

Dusk gathered in blue patches over the Black Belt. Lenox Avenue was vivid. The saloons were bright, crowded with drinking men jammed tight around the bars, treating one another and telling the incidents of the day. Longshoremen in overalls with hooks, Pullman porters holding their bags, waiters, elevator boys. Liquor-rich laughter, banana-ripe laughter. . . .

The pavement was a dim warm bustle. Women hurrying home from day's work to get dinner ready for husbands who worked at night. On their arms brown bags and black containing a bit of meat, a head of lettuce, butter. Young men who were stagging through life, passing along with brown-paper packages, containing a small steak, a pork chop, to do their own frying.

From out of saloons came the savory smell of corned beef and cabbage, spare-ribs, Hamburger steaks. Out of little cook-joints wedged in side streets, tripe, pigs' feet, hogs' ears and snouts. Out of apartments, steak smothered with onions, liver and bacon, fried chicken.

The composite smell of cooked stuff assaulted Jake's nostrils. He was hungry. His landlady was late bringing his food. Maybe she was out on Lenox Avenue chewing the rag with some other Ebenezer soul, thought Jake.

Jake was ill. The doctor told him that he would get well very quickly if he remained quietly in bed for a few days.

"And you mustn't drink till you are better. It's bad for you," the doctor warned him.

But Jake had his landlady bring him from two to four pails of beer every day. "I must drink some'n," he reasoned, "and beer can't make me no harm. It's light."

When Ray went to see him, Jake laughed at his serious mien.

"Tha's life, chappie. I goes way ovah yonder and wander and fools around and I hed no mind about nothing. Then I come back to mah own home town and, oh, you snakebite! When I was in the army, chappie, they useter give us all sorts o' lechers about canshankerous nights and prophet-lactic days, but I nevah pay them no mind. Them things foh edjucated guys like you who lives in you' head."

"They are for you, too," Ray said. "This is a new age with new methods of living. You can't just go on like a crazy ram goat as if you were living in the Middle Ages."

"Middle Ages! I ain't seen them yet and don't nevah wanta. All them things you talk about am kill-joy things, chappie. The trute is they make me feel shame."

Ray laughed until tears trickled down his cheeks. . . . He visualized Jake being ashamed and laughed again.

"Sure," said Jake. "I'd feel ashame' ef a chippie—No, chappie, them stuff is foh you book fellahs. I runs around all right, but Ise lak a sailor that don't know nothing about using a compass, but him always hits a safe port."

"You didn't this time, though, Jakie. Those devices that you despise are really for you rather than for me or people like me, who don't live your kind of free life. If you, and the whole strong race of workingman who live freely like you, don't pay some attention to them, then you'll all wither away and rot like weeds."

"Let us pray!" said Jake.

"*That* I don't believe in."

"Awright, then, chappie."

On the next trip, the dining-car was shifted off its scheduled run and returned to New York on the second day, late at night. It was ordered out again early the next day. Ray could not get round to see Jake, so he telephoned his girl and asked her to go.

Agatha had heard much of Ray's best friend, but she had never met him. Men working on a train have something of the spirit of men working on a ship. They are, perforce, bound together in comradeship of a sort in that close atmosphere. In the stopover cities they go about in pairs or groups. But the camaraderie breaks up on the platform in New York as soon as the dining-car returns there. Every man goes his own way unknown to his comrades. Wife or sweetheart or some other magnet of the great magic city draws each off separately.

Agatha was a rich-brown girl, with soft amorous eyes. She worked as assistant in a beauty parlor of the Belt. She was a Baltimore girl and had been living in New York for two years. Ray had met her the year before at a basket-ball match and dance.

She went to see Jake in the afternoon. He was sitting in a Morris chair, reading the Negro newspaper, *The Amsterdam News*, with a pail of beer beside him, when Agatha rapped on the door.

Jake thought it was the landlady. He was thrown off his balance by the straight, beautiful girl who entered the room and quietly closed the door behind her.

"Oh, keep your seat, please," she begged him. "I'll sit there," she indicated a brown chair by the cherrywood chiffonier.

"Ray asked me to come. He was doubled out this morning and couldn't get around to see you. I brought these for you."

She put a paper bag of oranges on the table. "Where shall I put these?" She showed him a charming little bouquet of violets. Jake's drinking-glass was on the floor, half full, beside the pail of beer.

"It's all right, here!" On the chipped, mildew-white washstand there was another glass with a tooth-brush. She took the tooth-brush out, poured some water in the glass, put the violets in, and set it on the chiffonier.

"There!" she said.

Jake thanked her. He was diffident. She was so different a girl from the many he had known. She was certainly one of those that Miss Curdy would have sneered at. She was so full of simple self-assurance and charm. Mah little sister down home in Petersburg, he thought, might have turned out something lak this ef she'd 'a' had a chance to talk English like in books and wear class-top clothes. Nine years sence I quite home. She must be quite a li'l' woman now herself.

Jake loved women's pretty clothes. The plain nigger-brown coat Agatha wore, unbuttoned, showed a fresh peach-colored frock. He asked after Ray.

"I didn't see him myself this trip," she said. "He telephoned me about you."

Jake praised Ray as his best pal.

"He's a good boy," she agreed. She asked Jake about the

railroad. "It must be lots of fun to ride from one town to the other like that. I'd love it, for I love to travel. But Ray hates it."

"It ain't so much fun when youse working," replied Jake.

"I guess you're right. But there's something marvelous about meeting people for a little while and serving them and never seeing them again. It's romantic. You don't have that awful personal everyday contact that domestic workers have to get along with. If I was a man and had to be in service, I wouldn't want better than the railroad."

"Some'n to that, yes," agreed Jake. . . . "But it ain't all peaches, neither, when all them passengers rush you like a herd of hungry swine."

Agatha stayed twenty minutes.

"I wish you better soon," she said, bidding Jake good-by. "It was nice to know you. Ray will surely come to see you when he gets back this time."

Jake drank a glass of beer and eased his back, full length on the little bed.

"She is sure some wonderful brown," he mused. "Now I sure does understand why Ray is so scornful of them easy ones." He gazed at the gray door. It seemed a shining panel of gold through which a radiant vision had passed.

"She sure does like that theah Ray an unconscionable lot. I could see the love stuff shining in them mahvelous eyes of hers when I talked about him. I s'pose it's killing sweet to have some'n loving you up thataway. Some'n real fond o' you for you own self lak, lak—jest lak how mah mammy useter love pa and do everything foh him bafore he done took and died off without giving no notice. . . ."

His thoughts wandered away back to his mysterious little brown of the Baltimore. She was not elegant and educated, but she was nice. Maybe if he found her again—it would be better than just running wild around like that! Thinking honestly about it, after all, he was never satisfied, flopping here and sleeping there. It gave him a little cocky pleasure to brag of his conquests to the fellows around the bar. But after all the swilling and boasting, it would be a thousand times nicer to have a little brown woman of his own to whom he could go home and be his simple self with. Lay his curly head between her brown breasts and be fondled and be the spoiled child that every man loves sometimes to be when he is all alone with a woman. *That* he could never be with the Madame Lauras. They expected him always to be the prancing he-man. Maybe it was the lack of a steady girl that kept him running crazy around. Boozing and poking and rooting around, jolly enough all right, but not altogether contented.

The landlady did not appear with Jake's dinner.

"Guess she is somewhere rocking soft with gin," he thought. "Ise feeling all right enough to go out, anyhow. Guess I'll drop in at Uncle Doc's and have a good feed of spare-ribs. Hm! but the stuff coming out of these heah Harlem kitchens is enough to knock me down. They smell so good."

He dressed and went out. "Oh, Lenox Avenue, but you look good to me, now. Lawdy! though, how the brown-skin babies am humping it along! Strutting the joy-stuff! Invitation for a shimmy. O Lawdy! Pills and pisen, you gotta turn me loose, quick."

Billy Biasse was drinking at the bar of Uncle Doc's when Jake entered.

"Come on, you, and have a drink," Billy cried. "Which hole in Harlem youse been burying you'self in all this time?"

"Which you figure? There is holes outside of Harlem too, boh." Jake ordered a beer.

"Beer!" exclaimed Billy. "Quit you fooling and take some real liquor, nigger. Ise paying foh it. Order that theah ovah-water liquor you useter be so dippy about. That theah Scotch."

"I ain't quite all right, Billy. Gotta go slow on the booze."

"Whasmat? . . . Oh, foh Gawd's sake! Don't let the li'l' beauty break you' heart. Fix her up with gin."

"Might as well, and then a royal feed o' spare-ribs," agreed Jake.

He asked for Zeddy.

"Missing since all the new moon done bless mah luck that you is, too. Last news I heard 'bout him, the gen'man was Yonkers anchored."

"And Strawberry Lips?"

"That nigger's back home in Harlem where he belongs. He done long ago quit that ugly yaller razor-back. And you, boh.

Who's providing foh you' wants sence you done turn Congo
Rose down?"

"Been running wild in the paddock of the Pennsy."

"Oh, boh, you sure did breaks the sweet-loving haht of Congo
Rose. One night she stahted to sing 'You broke mah haht and
went away' and she jest bust out crying theah in the cabaret and
couldn't sing no moh. She hauled harself whimpering out there,
and she laid off o' the Congo foh moh than a week. That li'l'
goosey boy had to do the strutting all by himse'f."

"She was hot stuff all right." Jake laughed richly. "But I had
to quit her or she would have made me either a no-'count or a
bad nigger."

Warmed up by meeting an old pal and hearing all the intimate news of the dives, Jake tossed off he knew not how many
gins. He told Billy Biasse of the places he had nosed out in
Baltimore and Philadelphia. The gossip was good. Jake changed
to Scotch and asked for the siphon.

He had finished the first Scotch and asked for another, when
a pain gripped his belly with a wrench that almost tore him
apart. Jake groaned and doubled over, staggered into a corner,
and crumpled up on the floor. Perspiration stood in beads on
his forehead, trickled down his rigid, chiseled features. He
heard the word "ambulance" repeated several times. He
thought first of his mother. His sister. The little frame house in
Petersburg. The backyard of bleached clothes on the line, the
large lilac tree and the little forked lot that yielded red tomatoes and green peas in spring.

"No hospital foh me," he muttered. "Mah room is jest next
doh. Take me theah."

Uncle Doc told his bar man to help Billy Biasse lift Jake.

"Kain you move you' laigs any at all, boh?" Billy asked.

Jake groaned: "I kain try."

The men took him home. . . .

Jake's landlady had been invited to a fried-chicken feed in
the basement lodging of an Ebenezer sister and friend on Fifth
Avenue. The sister friend had rented the basement of the old-
fashioned house and appropriated the large backyard for her
laundry work. She went out and collected soiled linen every
Monday. Her wealthiest patrons sent their chauffeurs round

with their linen. And the laundress was very proud of white chauffeurs standing their automobiles in front of her humble basement. She noticed with heaving chest that the female residents of the block rubber-necked. Her vocation was very profitable. And it was her pleasure sometimes to invite a sister of her church to dinner. . . .

The fried chicken, with sweet potatoes, was excellent. Over it the sisters chinned and ginned, recounting all the contemporary scandals of the Negro churches. . . .

At last Jake's landlady remembered him and staggered home to prepare his beef broth. But when she took it up to him she found that Jake was out. Returning to the kitchen, she stumbled and broke the white bowl, made a sign with her rabbit foot, and murmured, foggily: "Theah's sure a cross coming to thisa house. I wonder it's foh who?"

The bell rang and rang again and again in spite of the notice: Ring once. And when the landlady opened the door and saw Jake supported between two men, she knew that the broken white bowl was for him and that his time was come.

XV
Relapse

BILLY BIASSE telephoned to the doctor, a young chocolate-complexioned man. He was graduate of a Negro medical college in Tennessee and of Columbia University. He was struggling to overcome the prejudices of the black populace against Negro doctors and wedge himself in among the Jewish doctors that prescribed for the Harlem clientele. A clever man, he was trying, through Democratic influence, to get an appointment in one of the New York hospitals. Such an achievement would put him all over the Negro press and get him all the practice and more than he could handle in the Belt.

Ray had sent Jake to him. . . .

The landlady brought Jake a rum punch. He shook his head. With a premonition of tragedy, she waited for the doctor, standing against the chiffonier, a blue cloth carelessly knotted round her head. . . .

In the corridor she questioned Billy Biasse about Jake's seizure.

"All you younger generation in Harlem don't know no God," she accused Billy and indicted Young Harlem. "All you know is cabarets and movies and the young gals them exposing them legs a theirs in them jumper frocks."

"I wouldn't know 'bout that," said Billy.

"You all ought to know, though, and think of God Almighty before the trumpet sound and it's too late foh black sinners. I nevah seen so many trifling and ungodly niggers as there is in this heah Harlem." She thought of the broken white bowl. "And I done had a warning from heaben."

The doctor arrived. Ordered a hot-water bottle for Jake's belly and a hot lemon drink. There was no other remedy to help him but what he had been taking.

"You've been drinking," the doctor said.

"Jest a li'l' beer," Jake murmured.

"O Lawdy! though, listen at him!" cried the landlady.

"Mister, if he done had a glass, he had a barrel a day. Ain't I been getting it foh him?"

"Beer is the worst form of alcohol you could ever take in your state," said the doctor. "Couldn't be anything worse. Better you had taken wine."

Jake growled that he didn't like wine.

"It's up to you to get well," said the doctor. "You have been ill like that before. It's a simple affair if you will be careful and quiet for a little while. But it's very dangerous if you are foolish. I know you chaps take those things lightly. But you shouldn't, for the consequences are very dangerous."

Two days later Ray's diner returned to New York. It was early afternoon and the crew went over to the yards to get the stock for the next trip. And after stocking up Ray went directly to see Jake.

Jake was getting along all right again. But Ray was alarmed when he heard of his relapse. Indeed, Ray was too easily moved for the world he lived in. The delicate-fibered mechanism of his being responded to sensations that were entirely beyond Jake's comprehension.

"The doctor done hand me his. The landlady stahted warning me against sin with her mouth stinking with gin. And now mah chappie's gwina join the gang." Jake laughed heartily.

"But you must be careful, Jake. You're too sensible not to know good advice from bad."

"Oh, sure, chappie, I'll take care. I don't wanta be crippled up as the doctor says I might. Mah laigs got many moh miles to run yet, chasing after the sweet stuff o' life, chappie."

"Good oh Jake! I know you love life too much to make a fool of yourself like so many of those other fellows. I've never knew that this thing was so common until I started working on the railroad. You know the fourth had to lay off this trip."

"You don't say!"

"Yes, he's got a mean one. And the second cook on Bowman's diner he's been in a chronic way for about three months."

"But how does he get by the doctor? All them crews is examined every week."

"Hm! . . ." Ray glanced carelessly through *The Amsterdam*

News. "I saw Madame Laura in Fairmount Park and I told her you were sick. I gave her your address, too."

"Bumbole! What for?"

"Because she asked me for it. She was sympathetic."

"I never give mah address to them womens, chappie. Bad system that."

"Why?"

"Because you nevah know when they might bust in on you and staht a rough-house. Them's all right, them womens . . . in their own parlors."

"I guess you ought to know. I don't," said Ray. "Say, why don't you move out of this dump up to the Forties? There's a room in the same house I stay in. Cheap. Two flights up, right on the court. Steam heat and everything."

"I guess I could stand a new place to lay mah carcass in, all right," Jake drawled. "Steam heats you say? I'm sure sick o' this here praying-ma-ma hot air. And the trute is it ain't nevah much hotter than mah breath."

"All right. When do you want me to speak to the landlady about the room?"

"This heah very beautiful night, chappie. Mah rent is up to-morrow and I moves. But you got to do me a li'l' favor. Go by Billy Biasse this night and tell him to come and git his ole buddy's suitcase and see him into his new home tomorrow morning."

Jake was as happy as a kid. He would be frisking if he could. But Ray was not happy. The sudden upset of affairs in his home country had landed him into the quivering heart of a naked world whose reality was hitherto unimaginable. It was what they called in print and polite conversation "the underworld." The compound word baffled him, as some English words did sometimes. Why *under*-world he could never understand. It was very much upon the surface as were the others divisions of human life. Having its heights and middle and depths and se-cret places even as they. And the people of this world, waiters, cooks, chauffeurs, sailors, porters, guides, ushers, hod-carriers, factory hands—all touched in a thousand ways the people of the other divisions. They worked over there and slept over here, divided by a street.

Ray had always dreamed of writing words some day. Weaving words to make romance, ah! There were the great books that dominated the bright dreaming and dark brooding days when he was a boy. *Les Misérables*, *Nana*, *Uncle Tom's Cabin*, *David Copperfield*, *Nicholas Nickleby*, *Oliver Twist*.

From them, by way of free-thought pamphlets, it was only a stride to the great scintillating satirists of the age—Bernard Shaw, Ibsen, Anatole France, and the popular problemist, H. G. Wells. He had lived on that brilliant manna that fell like a flame-fall from those burning stars. Then came the great mass carnage in Europe and the great mass revolution in Russia.

Ray was not prophetic-minded enough to define the total evil that the one had wrought nor the ultimate splendor of the other. But, in spite of the general tumults and threats, the perfectly-organized national rages, the ineffectual patching of broken, and hectic rebuilding of shattered, things, he had perception enough to realize that he had lived over the end of an era.

And also he realized that his spiritual masters had not crossed with him into the new. He felt alone, hurt, neglected, cheated, almost naked. But he was a savage, even though he was a sensitive one, and did not mind nakedness. What had happened? Had they refused to come or had he left them behind? Something had happened. But it was not desertion nor young insurgency. It was death. Even as the last scion of a famous line prances out this day and dies and is set aside with his ancestors in their cold whited sepulcher, so had his masters marched with flags and banners flying all their wonderful, trenchant, critical, satirical, mind-sharpening, pity-evoking, constructive ideas of ultimate social righteousness, into the vast international cemetery of this century.

Dreams of patterns of words achieving form. What would he ever do with the words he had acquired? Were they adequate to tell the thoughts he felt, describe the impressions that reached him vividly? What were men making of words now? During the war he had been startled by James Joyce in *The Little Review*. Sherwood Anderson had reached him with *Winesburg, Ohio*. He had read, fascinated, all that D. H. Lawrence published. And wondered if there was not a great Lawrence reservoir of words too terrible and too terrifying for nice printing. Henri Barbusse's *Le Feu* burnt like a flame in his memory. Ray loved the book because it was such a grand anti-romantic presentation of mind and behavior in that hell-pit of life. And literature, story-telling, had little interest for him now if thought and feeling did not wrestle and sprawl with appetite and dark desire all over the pages.

Dreams of making something with words. What could he make . . . and fashion? Could he ever create Art? Art, around which vague, incomprehensible words and phrases stormed? What was art, anyway? Was it more than a clear-cut presenta-tion of a vivid impression of life? Only the Russians of the late era seemed to stand up like giants in the new. Gogol, Dostoi-evski, Tolstoy, Chekhov, Turgeniev. When he read them now he thought: Here were elements that the grand carnage swept over and touched not. The soil of life saved their roots from the fire. They were so saturated, so deep-down rooted in it.

Thank God and Uncle Sam that the old dreams were shat-tered. Nevertheless, he still felt more than ever the utter blind-ing nakedness and violent coloring of life. But what of it? Could he create out of the fertile reality around him? Of Jake nosing through life, a handsome hound, quick to snap up any tempting morsel of poisoned meat thrown carelessly on the pavement? Of a work pal he had visited in the venereal ward of Bellevue, where youths lolled sadly about? And the misery that overwhelmed him there, until life appeared like one big disease and the world a vast hospital?

XVI
A Practical Prank

My Dear Honey-Stick

"I was riding in Fairmount Park one afternoon, just taking the air as usual, when I saw your proper-speaking friend with a mess of books. He told me you were sick and I was so mortified for I am giving a big evening soon and was all set on fixing it on a night when you would certain sure be laying over in Philadelphia. Because you are such good company I may as well say how much you are appreciated here. I guess I'll put it off till you are okay again, for as I am putting my hand in my own pocket to give all of my friends and wellwishers a dandy time it won't be no fun for *me* if I leave out the *principal* one. Guess who!

"I am expecting to come to New York soon on a shopping bent. You know all us weak women who can afford it have got the Fifth Avenue fever, my dear. If I come I'll sure look you up, you can bank on it.

"Bye, bye, honeystick and be good and quiet and better yourself soon. Philadelphia is lonesome without you.

"Lovingly, Laura."

Billy Biasse, calling by Jake's former lodging, found this letter for him, lying there among a pile of others, on the little black round table in the hall. . . .

"Here you is, boh. Whether youse well or sick, them's after you."

"Is they? Lemme see. Hm . . . Philly." . . .

"Who is you' pen-pusher?" asked Billy.

"A queen in Philly. Says she might pay me a visit here. I ain't send out no invitation foh no womens yet."

"Is she the goods?"

"She's a wang, boh. Queen o' Philly, I tell you. And foh me, everything with her is f.o.c. But I don't want that yaller piece o' business come nosing after me here in Harlem."

246

"She ain't got to find you, boh. Jest throws her a bad lead."

"Tha's the stuff to give 'm. Ain't you a buddy with a haid on, though?"

" 'Deed I is. And all you niggers knows it who done frequent mah place."

And so Jake, in a prankish mood, replied to Madame Laura on a picture post-card saying he would be well and up soon and be back on the road and on the job again, and he gave Congo Rose's address.

Madame Laura made her expected trip to New York, traveling "Chair," as was her custom when she traveled. She wore a mauve dress, vermilion-shot at the throat, and short enough to show the curved plumpness of her legs encased in fine un-rumpled rose-tinted stockings. Her modish overcoat was lilac-gray lined with green and a large marine-blue rosette was bunched at the side of her neat gray hat.

In the Fifth Avenue shops she was waited upon as if she were a dark foreign lady of title visiting New York. In the afternoon she took a taxi-cab to Harlem.

Now all the fashionable people who called at Rose's house were generally her friends. And so Rose always went herself to let them in. She could look out from her window, one flight up, and ho-ho down to them.

When Madame Laura rang the bell, Rose popped her head out. Nobody I know, she thought, but the attractive woman in expensive clothes piqued her curiosity. Hastily she dabbed her face with a powder pad, patted her hair into shape, and descended.

"Is Mr. Jacob Brown living here?" Madame Laura asked.

"Well, he was—I mean——" This luxurious woman de-manding Jake tantalized Rose. She still referred to him as her man since his disappearance. No reports of his living with an-other woman having come to her, she had told her friends that Jake's mother had come between them.

"He always had a little some'n' of a mamma's boy about him, you know."

Poor Jake. Since he left home, his mother had become for him a loving memory only. When you saw him, talked to him, he stood forth as one of those unique types of humanity who

lived alone and were never lonely. You would hardly wonder
who were his father and mother and what they were like. He,
in his frame and atmosphere, was the Alpha and Omega himself.

"I mean—— Can you tell me what you want?" asked Rose.

"Must I? I didn't know he—— Why, he wrote to me. Said
he was ill. And sent his friend to tell me he was ill. Can't I see
him?"

"Did he write to you from this here address?"

"Why, certainly. I have his card here." Madame Laura was
fumbling in her handbag.

A triumphant smile stole into Rose's face. Jake had no real
home and had to use her address.

"Is you his sister or what?"

"I'm a friend," Madame Laura said, sharply.

"Well, he's got a nearve." Rose jerked herself angrily. "He's
mah man."

"I didn't come all the way here to hear that," said Madame
Laura. "I thought he was sick and wanting attention."

"Ain't I good enough to give him all the attention required
without another woman come chasing after him?"

"Disgusting!" cried Madame Laura. "I would think this was
a spohting house."

"Gwan with you before I spit in you' eye," cried Rose. "You
look like some'n just outa one you'self."

"You're no lady," retorted Madame Laura, and she hurried
down the steps.

Rose amplified the story exceedingly in telling it to her
friends. "I slapped her face for insulting me," she said.

Billy Biasse heard of it from the boy dancer of the Congo.
When Billy went again to see Jake, one of the patrons of his
gaming joint went with him. It was that yellow youth, the
same one that had first invited Zeddy over to Gin-head Susy's
place. He was a prince of all the day joints and night holes of
the Belt. All the shark players of Dixie Red's pool-room were
proud of losing a game to him, and at the Congo the waiters
danced around to catch his orders. For Yaller Prince, so they
affectionately called him, was living easy and sweet. Three girls,
they said, were engaged in the business of keeping him princely
—one chocolate-to-the-bone, one teasing-brown, and one

yellow. He was always well dressed in a fine nigger-brown or bottle-green suit, excessively creased, and spats. Also he was happy-going and very generous. But there was something slimy about him.

Yaller Prince had always admired Jake, in the way a common-bred admires a thoroughbred, and hearing from Billy that he was ill, he had brought him fruit, cake, and ice cream and six packets of Camels. Yaller Prince was more intimate with Jake's world than Billy, who swerved off at a different angle and was always absorbed in the games and winnings of men.

Jake and Yaller had many loose threads to pick up again and follow for a while. Were the gin parties going on still at Susy's? What had become of Miss Curdy? Yaller didn't know. He had dropped Myrtle Avenue before Zeddy did.

"Susy was free with the gin all right, but, gee whizzard! She was sure black and ugly, buddy," remarked Yaller.

"You said it, boh," agreed Jake. "They was some pair all right, them two womens. Black and ugly is exactly Susy, and that there other Curdy creachur all streaky yaller and ugly. I couldn't love them theah kind."

Yaller uttered a little goat laugh. "I kain't stand them ugly grannies, either. But sometimes they does pay high, buddy, and when the paying is good, I can always transfer mah mind."

"I couldn't foh no price, boh," said Jake. "Gimme a nice sweet-skin brown. I ain't got no time foh none o' you' ugly hard-hided dames."

Jake asked for Strawberry Lips. He was living in Harlem again and working longshore. Up in Yonkers Zeddy was endeavoring to overcome his passion for gambling and start housekeeping with a steady home-loving woman. He was beginning to realize that he was not big enough to carry two strong passions, each pulling him in opposite directions. Some day a grandson of his born in Harlem might easily cope with both passions, might even come to sacrifice woman to gambling. But Zeddy himself was too close to the savage swell of life.

Ray entered with a friend whom he introduced as James Grant. He was also a student working his way through college. But lacking funds to continue, he had left college to find a job. He was fourth waiter on Ray's diner, succeeding the timid boy from Georgia. As both chairs were in use, Grant sat on the edge of the bed and Ray tipped up Jake's suitcase. . . .

Conversation veered off to the railroad.

"I am getting sick of it," Ray said. "It's a crazy, clattering, nerve-shattering life. I think I'll fall down for good."

"Why, ef you quit, chappie, I'll nevah go back on that there white man's sweet chariot," said Jake.

"Whasmat?" asked Billy Biasse. "Kain't you git along on theah without him?"

"It's a whole lot the matter you can't understand, Billy. The white folks' railroad ain't like Lenox Avenue. You can tell on theah when a pal's a real pal."

"I got a pal, I got a gal," chanted Billy, "heah in mah pocket-book." He patted his breast pocket.

"Go long from here with you' lonesome haht, you wolf," cried Jake.

"Wolf is mah middle name, but . . . I ain't bad as I hear, and ain't you mah buddy, too?" Billy said to Jake. "Git you'self going quick and come on down to mah place, son. The bones am lonesome foh you."

Billy and Yaller Prince left.

"Who is the swell strutter?" Ray's friend asked.

"Hm! . . . I knowed him long time in Harlem," said Jake. "He's a good guy. Just brought me all them eats and cigarettes."

"What does he work at?" asked Ray.

"Nothing menial. He's a p-i." . . .

"Low-down yaller swine," said Ray's friend. "Harlem is stinking with them."

"Oh, Yaller is all right, though," said Jake. "A real good-hearted scout."

"Good-hearted!" Grant sneered. "A man's heart is cold dead when he has women doing that for him. How can a man live that way and strut in public, instead of hiding himself underground like a worm?" He turned indignantly to Ray.

"Search me!" Ray laughed a little. "You might as well ask why all mulattoes have unpleasant voices."

Grant was slightly embarrassed. He was yellow-skinned and his voice was hard and grainy. Jake he-hawed.

"Not all, chappie, I know some with sweet voice."

"Mulat*tress, mon ami.*" Ray lifted a finger. "That's an exception. And now, James, let us forget Jake's kind friend."

"Oh, I don't mind him talking," said Jake. "I don't approve of Yaller's trade mahself, but ef he can do it, well— It's because you don't know how many womens am running after the fellahs jest begging them to do that. They been after me moh time I can remember. There's lots o' folks living easy and living sweet, but . . ."

"There are as many forms of parasitism as there are ways of earning a living," said Ray.

"But to live the life of carrion," sneered Grant, "fatten on rotting human flesh. It's the last ditch, where dogs go to die. When you drop down in that you cease being human."

"You done said it straight out, brother," said Jake. "It's a stinking life and I don't like stinks."

"Your feeling against that sort of thing is fine, James," said Ray. "But that's the most I could say for it. It's all right to start out with nice theories from an advantageous point in life. But when you get a chance to learn life for yourself, it's quite another thing. The things you call fine human traits don't belong to any special class, nation or race of people. Nobody can pull that kind of talk now and get away with it, least of all a Negro."

"Why not?" asked Grant. "Can't a Negro have fine feelings about life?"

"Yes, but not the old false-fine feelings that used to be monopolized by educated and cultivated people. You should educate yourself away from that sort of thing."

"But education is something to make you fine!"

"No, modern education is planned to make you a sharp, snouty, rooting hog. A Negro getting it is an anachronism. We ought to get something new, we Negroes. But we get our education like—like our houses. When the whites move out, we move in and take possession of the old dead stuff. Dead stuff that this age has no use for."

"How's that?"

"Can you ask? You and I were born in the midst of the illness of this age and have lived through its agony. . . . Keep your fine feelings, indeed, but don't try to make a virtue of them. You'll lose them, then. They'll become all hollow inside, false and dry as civilization itself. And civilization is rotten. We are all rotten who are touched by it."

"I am not rotten," retorted Grant, "and I couldn't bring myself and my ideas down to the level of such filthy parasites."

"All men have the disease of pimps in their hearts," said Ray. "We can't be civilized and not. I have seen your high and mighty civilized people do things that some pimps would be ashamed of——"

"You said it, then, and most truly," cried Jake, who, lying on the bed, was intently following the dialogue.

"Do it in the name of civilization," continued Ray. "And I have been forced down to the level of pimps and found some of them more than human. One of them was so strange. . . . I never thought he could feel anything. Never thought he could do what he did. Something so strange and wonderful and awful, it just lifted me up out of my little straight thoughts into a big whirl where all of life seemed hopelessly tangled and colored without point or purpose."

"Tell us about it," said Grant.

"All right," said Ray. "I'll tell it."

XVII
He Also Loved

IT was in the winter of 1916 when I first came to New York to hunt for a job. I was broke. I was afraid I would have to pawn my clothes, and it was dreadfully cold. I didn't even know the right way to go about looking for a job. I was always timid about that. For five weeks I had not paid my rent. I was worried, and Ma Lawton, my landlady, was also worried. She had her bills to meet. She was a good-hearted old woman from South Carolina. Her face was all wrinkled and sensitive like finely-carved mahogany.

Every bed-space in the flat was rented. I was living in the small hall bedroom. Ma Lawton asked me to give it up. There were four men sleeping in the front room; two in an old, chipped-enameled brass bed, one on a davenport, and the other in a folding chair. The old lady put a little canvas cot in that same room, gave me a pillow and a heavy quilt, and said I should try and make myself comfortable there until I got work.

The cot was all right for me. Although I hate to share a room with another person and the fellows snoring disturbed my rest. Ma Lawton moved into the little room that I had had, and rented out hers—it was next to the front room—to a man and a woman.

The woman was above ordinary height, chocolate-colored. Her skin was smooth, too smooth, as if it had been pressed and fashioned out for ready sale like chocolate candy. Her hair was straightened out into an Indian Straight after the present style among Negro ladies. She had a mongoose sort of a mouth, with two top front teeth showing. She wore a long mink coat.

The man was darker than the woman. His face was longish, with the right cheek somewhat caved in. It was an interesting face, an attractive, salacious mouth, with the lower lip protruding. He wore a bottle-green peg-top suit, baggy at the hips. His coat hung loose from his shoulders and it was much longer

253

than the prevailing style. He wore also a Mexican hat, and in his breast pocket he carried an Ingersoll watch attached to a heavy gold chain. His name was Jericho Jones, and they called him Jerco for short. And she was Miss Whicher—Rosalind Whicher.

Ma Lawton introduced me to them and said I was broke, and they were both awfully nice to me. They took me to a big feed of corned beef and cabbage at Burrell's on Fifth Avenue. They gave me a good appetizing drink of gin to commence with. And we had beer with the eats; not ordinary beer, either, but real Budweiser, right off the ice.

And as good luck sometimes comes pouring down like a shower, the next day Ma Lawton got me a job in the little free-lunch saloon right under her flat. It wasn't a paying job as far as money goes in New York, but I was glad to have it. I had charge of the free-lunch counter. You know the little dry crackers that go so well with beer, and the cheese and fish and the potato salad. And I served, besides, spare-ribs and whole boiled potatoes and corned beef and cabbage for those customers who could afford to pay for a lunch. I got no wages at all, but I got my eats twice a day. And I made a few tips, also. For there were about six big black men with plenty of money who used to eat lunch with us, specially for our spare-ribs and sweet potatoes. Each one of them gave me a quarter. I made enough to pay Ma Lawton for my canvas cot.

Strange enough, too, Jerco and Rosalind took a liking to me. And sometimes they came and ate lunch perched up there at the counter, with Rosalind the only woman there, all made up and rubbing her mink coat against the men. And when they got through eating, Jerco would toss a dollar bill at me.

We got very friendly, we three. Rosalind would bring up squabs and canned stuff from the German delicatessen in One Hundred and Twenty-fifth Street, and sometimes they asked me to dinner in their room and gave me good liquor.

I thought I was pretty well fixed for such a hard winter. All I had to do as extra work was keeping the saloon clean. . . .

One afternoon Jerco came into the saloon with a man who looked pretty near white. Of course, you never can tell for sure about a person's race in Harlem, nowadays, when there are so many high-yallers floating round—colored folks that would make Italian and Spanish people look like Negroes beside them. But I figured out from his way of talking and acting that the man with Jerco belonged to the white race. They went in through the family entrance into the back room, which was unusual, for the family room of a saloon, as you know, is only for women in the business and the men they bring in there with them. Real men don't sit in a saloon here as they do at home. I suppose it would be sissified. There's a bar for them to lean on and drink and joke as long as they feel like.

The boss of the saloon was a little fidgety about Jerco and his friend sitting there in the back. The boss was a short pumpkin-bellied brown man, a little bald off the forehead. Twice he found something to attend to in the back room, although there was nothing at all there that wanted attending to. . . . I felt better, and the boss, too, I guess, when Rosalind came along and gave the family room its respectable American character. I served Rosalind a Martini cocktail extra dry, and afterward all three of them, Rosalind, Jerco, and their friend, went up to Ma Lawton's.

The two fellows that slept together were elevator operators in a department store, so they had their Sundays free. On the afternoon of the Sunday of the same week that the white-looking man had been in the saloon with Jerco, I went upstairs to change my old shoes—they'd got soaking wet behind the counter—and I found Ma Lawton talking to the two elevator fellows.

The boys had given Ma Lawton notice to quit. They said they couldn't sleep there comfortably together on account of the goings-on in Rosalind's room. The fellows were members of the Colored Y.M.C.A. and were queerly quiet and pious. One of them was studying to be a preacher. They were the sort of fellows that thought going to cabarets a sin, and that parlor socials were leading Harlem straight down to hell. They only went to church affairs themselves. They had been rooming with Ma Lawton for over a year. She called them her gentle-men lodgers.

Ma Lawton said to me: "Have you heard anything phony outa the next room, dear?"

"Why, no, Ma," I said, "nothing more unusual than you can hear all over Harlem. Besides, I work so late, I am dead tired when I turn in to bed, so I sleep heavy."

"Well, it's the truth I do like that there Jerco an' Rosaline," said Ma Lawton. "They did seem quiet as lambs, although they was always havin' company. But Ise got to speak to them, 'cause I doana wanta lose ma young mens. . . . But theyse a real nice-acting couple. Jerco him treats me like him was mah son. It's true that they doan work like all poah niggers, but they pays that rent down good and prompt ehvery week."

Jerco was always bringing in ice-cream and cake or some-thing for Ma Lawton. He had a way about him, and everybody liked him. He was a sympathetic type. He helped Ma Lawton move beds and commodes and he fixed her clothes lines. I had heard somebody talking about Jerco in the saloon, however, saying that he could swing a mean fist when he got his dander up, and that he had been mixed up in more than one razor cut-up. He did have a nasty long razor scar on the back of his right hand.

The elevator fellows had never liked Rosalind and Jerco. The one who was studying to preach Jesus said he felt pretty sure that they were an ungodly-living couple. He said that late one night he had pointed out their room to a woman that looked white. He said the woman looked suspicious. She was perfumed and all powdered up and it appeared as if she didn't belong among colored people.

"There's no sure telling white from high-yaller these days," I said. "There are so many swell-looking quadroons and octo-roons of the race."

But the other elevator fellow said that one day in the tender-loin section he had run up against Rosalind and Jerco together with a petty officer of marines. And that just put the lid on anything favorable that could be said about them.

But Ma Lawton said: "Well, Ise got to run mah flat right an' try mah utmost to please youall, but I ain't wanta dip mah nose too deep in a lodger's affairs."

Late that night, toward one o'clock, Jerco dropped in at the saloon and told me that Rosalind was feeling badly. She hadn't eaten a bite all day and he had come to get a pail of beer, because she had asked specially for draught beer. Jerco was worried, too.

"I hopes she don't get bad," he said. "For we ain't got a cent o' money. Wese just in on a streak o' bad luck."

"I guess she'll soon be all right," I said.

The next day after lunch I stole a little time and went up to see Rosalind. Ma Lawton was just going to attend to her when I let myself in, and she said to me: "Now the poor woman is sick, poor chile, ahm so glad mah conscience is free and that I hadn't a said nothing evil t' her."

Rosalind was pretty sick. Ma Lawton said it was the grippe. She gave Rosalind hot whisky drinks and hot milk, and she kept her feet warm with a hot-water bottle. Rosalind's legs were lead-heavy. She had a pain that pinched her side like a pair of pincers. And she cried out for thirst and begged for draught beer.

Ma Lawton said Rosalind ought to have a doctor. "You'd better go an' scares up a white one," she said to Jerco. "Ise nevah had no faith in these heah nigger doctors."

"I don't know how we'll make out without money," Jerco whined. He was sitting in the old Morris chair with his head heavy on his left hand.

"You kain pawn my coat," said Rosalind. "Old man Greenbaum will give you two hundred down without looking at it."

"I won't put a handk'chief o' yourn in the hock shop," said Jerco. "You'll need you' stuff soon as you get better. Specially you' coat. You kain't go anywheres without it."

"S'posin' I don't get up again," Rosalind smiled. But her countenance changed suddenly as she held her side and moaned. Ma Lawton bent over and adjusted the pillows.

Jerco pawned his watch chain and his own overcoat, and called in a Jewish doctor from the upper Eighth Avenue fringe of the Belt. But Rosalind did not improve under medical treatment. She lay there with a sad, tired look, as if she didn't really care what happened to her. Her lower limbs were apparently paralyzed. Jerco told the doctor that she had been sick unto death like that before. The doctor shot a lot of stuff into her system. But Rosalind lay there heavy and fading like a felled tree.

The elevator operators looked in on her. The student one gave her a Bible with a little red ribbon marking the chapter in St. John's Gospel about the woman taken in adultery. He also wanted to pray for her recovery. Jerco wanted the prayer, but Rosalind said no. Her refusal shocked Ma Lawton, who believed in God's word.

The doctor stopped Rosalind from drinking beer. But Jerco slipped it in to her when Ma Lawton was not around. He said he couldn't refuse it to her when beer was the only thing she cared for. He had an expensive sweater. He pawned it. He also pawned their large suitcase. It was real leather and worth a bit of money.

One afternoon Jerco sat alone in the back room of the saloon and began to cry.

"I'd do anything. There ain't anything too low I wouldn't do to raise a little money," he said.

"Why don't you hock Rosalind's fur coat?" I suggested. "That'll give you enough money for a while."

"Gawd, no! I wouldn't touch none o' Rosalind's clothes. I jest kain't," he said. "She'll need them as soon as she's better."

"Well, you might try and find some sort of a job, then," I said.

"Me find a job? What kain I do? I ain't no good foh no job. I kain't work. I don't know how to ask for no job. I wouldn't know how. I wish I was a woman."

"Good God! Jerco," I said, "I don't see any way out for you but some sort of a job."

"What kain I do? What kain I do?" he whined. "I kain't do nothing. That's why I don't wanta hock Rosalind's fur coat. She'll need it soon as she's better. Rosalind's so wise about picking up good money. Just like that!" He snapped his fingers.

I left Jerco sitting there and went into the saloon to serve a customer a plate of corned beef and cabbage.

After lunch I thought I'd go up to see how Rosalind was making out. The door was slightly open, so I slipped in without knocking. I saw Jerco kneeling down by the open wardrobe and kissing the toe of one of her brown shoes. He started as he saw me, and looked queer kneeling there. It was a high old-fashioned wardrobe that Ma Lawton must have picked up at some sale. Rosalind's coat was hanging there, and it gave me a spooky feeling, for it looked so much more like the real Rosalind than the woman that was dozing there on the bed.

Her other clothes were hanging there, too. There were three gowns—a black silk, a glossy green satin, and a flimsy chiffon-like yellow thing. In a corner of the lowest shelf was a bundle of soiled champagne-colored silk stockings and in the other four pairs of shoes—one black velvet, one white kid, and an-other gold-finished. Jerco regarded the lot with dog-like affection.

"I wouldn't touch not one of her things until she's better," he said. "I'd sooner hock the shirt off mah back."

Which he was preparing to do. He had three expensive striped silk shirts, presents from Rosalind. He had just taken two out of the wardrobe and the other off his back, and made a parcel of them for old Greenbaum. . . . Rosalind woke up and murmured that she wanted some beer. . . .

A little later Jerco came to the saloon with the pail. He was shivering. His coat collar was turned up and fastened with a safety pin, for he only had an undershirt on.

"I don't know what I'd do if anything happens to Rosalind," he said. "I kain't live without her."

"Oh yes, you can," I said in a not very sympathetic tone. Jerco gave me such a reproachful pathetic look that I was sorry I said it.

The tall big fellow had turned into a scared, trembling baby. "You ought to buck up and hold yourself together," I told him. "Why, you ought to be game if you like Rosalind, and don't let her know you're down in the dumps."

"I'll try," he said. "She don't know how miserable I am. When I hooks up with a woman I treat her right, but I never let her know everything about me. Rosalind is an awful good woman. The straightest woman I ever had, honest."

I gave him a big glass of strong whisky.

Ma Lawton came in the saloon about nine o'clock that eve-ning and said that Rosalind was dead. "I told Jerco we'd have to sell that theah coat to give the poah woman a decent fun'ral, an' he jest brokes down crying like a baby."

That night Ma Lawton slept in the kitchen and put Jerco in

her little hall bedroom. He was all broken up. I took him up a pint of whisky.

"I'll nevah find another one like Rosalind," he said, "nevah!" He sat on an old black-framed chair in which a new yellow-varnished bottom had just been put. I put my hand on his shoulder and tried to cheer him up: "Buck up, old man. Never mind, you'll find somebody else." He shook his head. "Perhaps you didn't like the way me and Rosalind was living. But she was one naturally good woman, all good inside her."

I felt foolish and uncomfortable. "I always liked Rosalind, Jerco," I said, "and you, too. You were both awfully good scouts to me. I have nothing against her. I am nothing myself."

Jerco held my hand and whimpered: "Thank you, old top. Youse all right. Youse always been a regular fellar."

It was late, after two a. m. I went to bed. And, as usual, I slept soundly.

Ma Lawton was an early riser. She made excellent coffee and she gave the two elevator runners and another lodger, a porter who worked on Ellis Island, coffee and hot homemade biscuits every morning. The next morning she shook me abruptly out of my sleep.

"Ahm scared to death. Thar's moah tur'ble trouble. I kain't git in the barfroom and the hallway's all messy."

I jumped up, hauled on my pants, and went to the bathroom. A sickening purplish liquid coming from under the door had trickled down the hall toward the kitchen. I took Ma Lawton's rolling-pin and broke through the door.

Jerco had cut his throat and was lying against the bowl of the water-closet. Some empty coke papers were on the floor. And he sprawled there like a great black boar in a mess of blood.

XVIII
A Farewell Feed

RAY and Grant had found jobs on a freighter that was going down across the Pacific to Australia and from there to Europe. Ray had reached the point where going any further on the railroad was impossible. He had had enough to vomit up of Philadelphia and Baltimore, Pittsburgh and Washington. More than enough of the bar-to-bar camaraderie of railroad life.

And Agatha was acting wistfully. He knew what would be the inevitable outcome of meeting that subtle wistful yearning halfway. Soon he would become one of the contented hogs in the pigpen of Harlem, getting ready to litter little black piggies. If he could have felt about things as Jake, how different his life might have been! Just to hitch up for a short while and be irresponsible! But he and Agatha were slaves of the civilized tradition. . . . Harlem nigger strutting his stuff. . . Harlem niggers! How often he had listened to those phrases, like jets of saliva, spewing from the lips of his work pals. They pursued, scared, and haunted him. He was afraid that some day the urge of the flesh and the mind's hankering after the pattern of respectable comfort might chase his high dreams out of him and deflate him to the contented animal that was a Harlem nigger strutting his stuff. "No happy-nigger strut for me," he would mutter, when the feeling for Agatha worked like a fever in his flesh. He saw destiny working in her large, dream-sad eyes, filling them with the passive softness of resignation to life, and seeking to encompass and yoke him down as just one of the thousand niggers of Harlem. And he hated Agatha and, for escape, wrapped himself darkly in self-love.

Oh, he was scared of that long red steel cage whose rumbling rollers were eternally heavy-lipped upon shining, continent-circling rods. If he forced himself to stay longer he would bang right off his head. Once upon a time he used to wonder at that great body of people who worked in nice cages: bank clerks in steel-wire cages, others in wooden cages, salespeople

261

behind counters, neat, dutiful, respectful, all of them. God! how could they carry it on from day to day and remain quietly obliging and sane? If the railroad had not been cacophonous and riotous enough to balance the dynamo roaring within him, he would have jumped it long ago.

Life burned in Ray perhaps more intensely than in Jake. Ray felt more and his range was wider and he could not be satisfied with the easy, simple things that sufficed for Jake. Sometimes he felt like a tree with roots in the soil and sap flowing out and whispering leaves drinking in the air. But he drank in more of life than he could distill into active animal living. Maybe that was why he felt he had to write.

He was a reservoir of that intense emotional energy so peculiar to his race. Life touched him emotionally in a thousand vivid ways. Maybe his own being was something of a touchstone of the general emotions of his race. Any upset—a terror-breathing, Negro-baiting headline in a metropolitan newspaper or the news of a human bonfire in Dixie—could make him miserable and despairingly despondent like an injured child. While any flash of beauty or wonder might lift him happier than a god. It was the simple, lovely touch of life that charmed and stirred him most. . . . The warm, rich-brown face of a Harlem girl seeking romance . . . a late wet night on Lenox Avenue, when all forms are soft-shadowy and the street gleams softly like a still, dim stream under the misted yellow lights. He remembered once the melancholy-comic notes of a "Blues" rising out of a Harlem basement before dawn. He was going to catch an early train and all that trip he was sweetly, deliciously happy humming the refrain and imagining what the interior of the little dark den he heard it in was like. "Blues" . . . melancholy-comic. That was the key to himself and to his race. That strange, child-like capacity for wistfulness-and-laughter. . . .

No wonder the whites, after five centuries of contact, could not understand his race. How could they when the instinct of comprehension had been cultivated out of them? No wonder they hated them, when out of their melancholy environment the blacks could create mad, contagious music and high laughter. . . .

Going away from Harlem. . . . Harlem! How terribly Ray

could hate it sometimes. Its brutality, gang rowdyism, promiscuous thickness. Its hot desires. But, oh, the rich blood-red color of it! The warm accent of its composite voice, the fruitiness of its laughter, the trailing rhythm of its "blues" and the improvised surprises of its jazz. He had known happiness, too, in Harlem, joy that glowed gloriously upon him like the high-noon sunlight of his tropic island home.

How long would he be able to endure the life of a cabin boy or mess boy on a freighter? Jake had tried to dissuade him. "A seaman's life is no good, chappie, and it's easier to jump off a train in the field than offn a ship gwine across the pond."

"Maybe it's not so bad in the mess," suggested Ray.

" 'Deed it's worse foh mine, chappie. Stoking and A.B.S. is cleaner work than messing with raw meat and garbage. I never was in love with no kitchen job. And tha's why I ain't none crazy about the white man's chu-chuing buggy."

Going away from Harlem. . . .

Jake invited Ray and Grant to a farewell feed, for which Billy Biasse was paying. Billy was a better pal for Jake than Zeddy. Jake was the only patron of his gambling house that Billy really chummed with. They made a good team. Their intimate interests never clashed. And it never once entered Jake's head that there was anything ugly about Billy's way of earning a living. Tales often came roundabout to Billy of patrons grumbling that "he was swindling poah hardworking niggers outa their wages." But he had never heard of Jake backbiting.

"The niggers am swindling themselves," Billy always retorted. "I runs a gambling place foh the gang and they pays becas they love to gamble. I plays even with them mahself. I ain't no miser hog like Nije Gridley."

Billy liked Jake because Jake played for the fun of the game and then quit. Gambling did not have a strangle hold upon him any more than dope or desire did. Jake took what he wanted of whatever he fancied and . . . kept going.

The feed was spread at Aunt Hattie's cook-shop. Jake maintained that Aunt Hattie's was the best place for good eats in Harlem. A bottle of Scotch whisky was on the table and a bottle of gin.

While the boys sampled the fine cream tomato soup, Aunt Hattie bustled in and out of the kitchen, with a senile-fond

look for Jake and an affectionate phrase, accompanied by a salacious lick of her tongue.

"Why, it's good and long sence you ain't been in reg'lar to
see me, chile. Whar's you been keeping you'self?"

"Ain't been no reg'lar chile of Harlem sence I done jump on
the white man's chu-chu," said Jake.

"And is you still on that theah business?" Aunt Hattie
asked.

"I don't know ef I is and I don't know ef I ain't. Ise been laid
off sick."

"Sick! Poah chile, and I nevah knowed so I could come
off'ring you a li'l' chicken broth. You jest come heah and eats
any time you wanta, whether youse got money or not."

Aunt Hattie shuffled back to the kitchen to pick the nicest
piece of fried chicken for Jake.

"Always in luck, Jakey," said Billy. "It's no wonder you nevah
see niggers in the bread line. And you'll nevah so long as
theah's good black womens like Aunt Hattie in Harlem."

Jake poured Scotch for three.

"Gimme gin," said Billy.

Jake called to Aunt Hattie to bring her glass. "What you
gwine to have, Auntie?"

"Same thing youse having, chile," replied Aunt Hattie.

"This heah stuff is from across the pond."

"Lemme taste it, then. Ef youse always so eye-filling drinking it, it might ginger up mah bones some."

"Well, here's to us, fellahs," cried Billy. "Let's hope that hard
luck nevah turn our glasses down or shet the door of a saloon
in our face."

Glasses clinked and Aunt Hattie touched Jake's twice and
closed her eyes as with trembling hand she guzzled.

"You had better said, 'Le's hope that this heah Gawd's own
don't shut the pub in our face'," replied Jake. "Prohibition is
right under our tail."

Everybody laughed. . . . Ray bit into the tender leg of his
fried chicken. The candied sweet potatoes were sweeter than
honey to his palate.

"Drink up, fellahs," said Billy.

"Got to leave you, Harlem," Ray sang lightly. "Got to turn
our backs on you."

"And our black moon on the Pennsy," added Jake.

"Tomorrow the big blue beautiful ocean," said Ray.

"You'll puke in it," Jake grinned devilishly. "Why not can the idea, chappie? The sea is hell and when you hits shore it's the same life all ovah."

"I guess you are right," replied Ray. "Goethe said the same thing in *Werther*."

"Who is that?" Jake asked.

"A German——"

"A boche?"

"Yes, a great one who made books instead of war. He was mighty and contented like a huge tame elephant. Genteel lovers of literature call that Olympian."

Jake gripped Ray's shoulder: "Chappie, I wish I was edjucated mahself."

"Christ! What for?" demanded Ray.

"Becaz I likes you." Like a black Pan out of the woods Jake looked into Ray's eyes with frank savage affection and Billy Biasse exclaimed:

"Lawdy in heaben! A li'l' foreign booze gwine turn you all soft?"

"Can't you like me just as well as you are?" asked Ray. "I can't feel any difference at all. If I was famous as Jack Johnson and rich as Madame Walker I'd prefer to have you as my friend than—President Wilson."

"Like bumbole you would!" retorted Jake. "Ef I was edjucated, I could understand things better and be proper-speaking like you is. . . . And I mighta helped mah li'l sister to get edjucated, too (she must be a li'l' woman, now), and she would be nice-speaking like you' sweet brown, good enough foh you to hitch up with. Then we could all settle down and make money like edjucated people do, instead a you gwine off to throw you'self away on some lousy dinghy and me chasing around all the time lak a hungry dawg."

"Oh, you heart-breaking, slobbering nigger!" cried Billy Biasse. "That's the stuff youse got tuck away there under your tough black hide."

"Muzzle you' mouf," retorted Jake. "Sure Ise human. I ain't no lonesome wolf lak you is."

"A wolf is all right ef he knows the jungle."

"The fact is, Jake," Ray said, "I don't know what I'll do with my little education. I wonder sometimes if I could get rid of it and go and lose myself in some savage culture in the jungles of Africa. I am a misfit—as the doctors who dole out newspaper advice to the well-fit might say—a misfit with my little education and constant dreaming, when I should be getting the nightmare habit to hog in a whole lot of dough like everybody else in this country. Would you like to be educated to be like me?"

"If I had your edjucation I wouldn't be slinging no hash on the white man's chu-chu," Jake responded.

"Nobody knows, Jake. Anyway, you're happier than I as you are. The more I learn the less I understand and love life. All the learning in this world can't answer this little question, Why are we living?"

"Why, becaz Gawd wants us to, chappie," said Billy Biasse.

"Come on le's all go to Uncle Doc's," said Jake, "and finish the night with a li'l' sweet jazzing. This is you last night, chappie. Make the most of it, foh there ain't no jazzing like Harlem jazzing over the other side."

They went to Uncle Doc's, where they drank many ceremonious rounds. Later they went to Leroy's Cabaret. . . .

The next afternoon the freighter left with Ray signed on as a mess boy.

THIRD PART

XIX
Spring in Harlem

THE lovely trees of Seventh Avenue were a vivid flame-green. Children, lightly clad, skipped on the pavement. Light open coats prevailed and the smooth bare throats of brown girls were a token as charming as the first pussy-willows. Far and high over all, the sky was a grand blue benediction, and beneath it the wonderful air of New York tasted like fine dry champagne.

Jake loitered along Seventh Avenue. Crossing to Lenox, he lazied northward and over the One Hundred and Forty-ninth Street bridge into the near neighborhood of the Bronx. Here, just a step from compactly-built, teeming Harlem, were frame houses and open lots and people digging. A colored couple dawdled by, their arms fondly caressing each other's hips. A white man forking a bit of ground stopped and stared expressively after them.

Jake sat down upon a mound thick-covered with dandelions. They glittered in the sun away down to the rear of a rusty-gray shack. They filled all the green spaces. Oh, the common little things were glorious there under the sun in the tender spring grass. Oh, sweet to be alive in that sun beneath that sky! And to be in love—even for one hour of such rare hours! One day! One night! Somebody with spring charm, like a dandelion, seasonal and haunting like a lovely dream that never repeats itself. . . . There are hours, there are days, and nights whose sheer beauty overwhelm us with happiness, that we seek to make even more beautiful by comparing them with rare human contacts. . . . It was a day like this we romped in the grass . . . a night as soft and intimate as this on which we forgot the world and ourselves. . . . Hours of pagan abandon, celebrating ourselves. . . .

And Jake felt as all men who love love for love's sake can feel. He thought of the surging of desire in his boy's body and of his curious pure nectarine beginnings, without pain, without disgust, down home in Virginia. Of his adolescent breaking-through when the fever-and-pain of passion gave him a wonderful strange-sweet taste of love that he had never known again. Of rude contacts and swift satisfactions in Norfolk, Baltimore, and other coast ports. . . . Havre. . . . The West India Dock districts of London. . . .

"Only that cute heart-breaking brown of the Baltimore," he mused. "A day like this sure feels like her. Didn't even get her name. O Lawdy! what a night that theah night was. Her and I could sure make a hallelujah picnic outa a day like this." . . .

Jake and Billy Biasse, leaving Dixie Red's pool-room together, shuffled into a big excited ring of people at the angle of Fifth Avenue and One Hundred and Thirty-third Street. In the ring three bad actors were staging a rough play—a yellow youth, a chocolate youth, and a brown girl.

The girl had worked herself up to the highest pitch of obscene frenzy and was sicking the dark strutter on to the yellow with all the filthiest phrases at her command. The two fellows pranced round, menacing each other with comic gestures.

"Why, ef it ain't Yaller Prince!" said Jake.

"Him sure enough," responded Billy Biasse. "Guess him done laid off from that black gal why she's shooting her stinking mouth off at him."

"Is she one of his producing goods?"

"She was. But I heard she done beat up anether gal of hisn—a fair-brown that useta hand over moh change than her and Yaller turn' her loose foh it." . . .

"You lowest-down face-artist!" the girl shrieked at Yaller Prince. "I'll bawl it out so all a Harlem kain know what you is." And ravished by the fact that she was humiliating her one-time lover, she gesticulated wildly.

"Hit him, Obadiah!" she yelled to the chocolate chap. "Hit him I tell you. Beat his mug up foh him, beat his mug and bleed his mouf." Over and over again she yelled: "Bleed his mouf!" As if that was the thing in Yaller Prince she had desired most. For it she had given herself up to the most unthinkable acts of degradation. Nothing had been impossible to do. And now she would cut and bruise and bleed that mouth that had once loved her so well so that he should not smile upon her rivals for many a day.

"Two-faced yaller nigger, you does ebery low-down thing, but you nevah done a lick of work in you lifetime. Show him, Obadiah. Beat his face and bleed his mouf."

"Yaller nigger," cried the extremely bandy-legged and grim-faced Obadiah, "Ise gwine kick you pants."

"I ain't scared a you, black buzzard," Yaller Prince replied in a thin, breathless voice, and down he went on his back, no one knowing whether he fell or was tripped up. Obadiah lifted a bottle and swung it down upon his opponent. Yaller Prince moaned and blood bubbled from his nose and his mouth.

"He's a sweet-back, all right, but he ain't a strong one," said some one in the crowd. The police had been conspicuously absent during the fracas, but now a baton tap-tapped upon the pavement and two of them hurried up. The crowd melted away.

Jake had pulled Yaller Prince against the wall and squatted to rest the bleeding head against his knee.

"What's matter here now? What's matter?" the first policeman, with revolver drawn, asked harshly.

"Nigger done beat this one up and gone away from heah, tha's whatsmat," said Billy Biasse.

They carried Yaller Prince into a drugstore for first aid, and the policeman telephoned for an ambulance. . . .

"We gotta look out foh him in hospital. He was a pretty good skate for a sweetman," Billy Biasse said.

"Poor Yaller!" Jake, shaking his head, commented; "it's a bad business."

"He's plumb crazy gwine around without a gun when he's a-playing that theah game," said Billy, "with all these cut-thwoat niggers in Harlem ready to carve up one another foh a li'l' insisnificant humpy."

"It's the same ole life everywhere," responded Jake. "In white man's town or nigger town. Same bloody-sweet life across the pond. I done lived through the same blood-battling foh womens ovah theah in London. Between white and white and between white and black. Done see it in the froggies' country, too. A mess o' fat-headed white soldiers them was

knocked off by apaches. Don't tell *me* about cut-thwoat niggers in Harlem. The whole wul' is boody-crazy——"

"But Harlem is the craziest place foh that, I bet you, boh,"
Billy laughed richly. "The stuff it gives the niggers brain-fevah,
so far as I see, and this heah wolf has got a big-long horeezon.
Wese too thick together in Harlem. Wese all just lumped together without a chanst to choose and so we nacherally hate
one another. It's nothing to wonder that you' buddy Ray done
runned away from it. Why, jest the other night I witnessed a
nasty stroke. You know that spade prof that's always there on
the Avenue handing out the big stuff about niggers and their
rights and the wul' and bolschism. . . . He was passing by
the pool-room with a bunch o' books when a bad nigger jest
lunges out and socks him bif! in the jaw. The poah frightened
prof. started picking up his books without a word said, so I ups
and asks the boxer what was the meaning o' that pass. He
laughed and asked me ef I really wanted to know, and before
he could squint I landed him one in the eye and pulled mah
gun on him. I chased him off that corner all right. I tell you,
boh, Harlem is lousy with crazy-bad niggers, as tough as Hell's
Kitchen, and I always travel with mah gun ready."

"And ef all the niggers did as you does," said Jake, "theah'd
be a regular gun-toting army of us up here in the haht of the
white man's city. . . . Guess ef a man stahts gunning after you
and means to git you he will someways——"

"But you might git him fierst, too, boh, ef youse in luck."

"I mean ef you don't know he's gunning after you," said Jake.
"I don't carry no weapons nonetall, but mah two long hands."

"Youse a punk customer, then, I tell you," declared Billy
Biasse, "and no real buddy o' mine. Ise got a A number one
little barker I'll give it to you. You kain't lay you'self wide open
lak thataways in this heah burg. No boh!"

Jake went home alone in a mood different from the lyrical
feelings that had fevered his blood among the dandelions.
"Niggers fixing to slice one another's throats. Always fighting.
Got to fight if youse a man. It ain't because Yaller was a p-i.
. . . It coulda been me or anybody else. Wese too close and
thick in Harlem. Need some moh fresh air between us. . . .
Hitting out at a edjucated nigger minding his own business
and without a word said. . . . Guess Billy is right toting his

silent dawg around with him. He's gotta, though, when he's running a gambling joint. All the same, I gambles mahself and you nevah know when niggers am gwineta git crazy-mad. Guess I'll take the li'l' dawg offn Billy, all right. It ain't costing me nothing." . . .

In the late afternoon he lingered along Seventh Avenue in a new nigger-brown suit. The fine gray English suit was no longer serviceable for parade. The American suit did not fit him so well. Jake saw and felt it. . . . The only thing he liked better about the American suit was the pantaloons made to wear with a belt. And the two hip pockets. If you have the American habit of carrying your face-cloth on the hip instead of sticking it up in your breast pocket like a funny decoration, and if, like Billy Biasse, you're accustomed to toting some steely thing, what is handier than two hip pockets?

Except for that, Jake had learned to prefer the English cut of clothes. Such first-rate tweed stuff, and so cheap and durable compared with American clothes! Jake knew nothing of tariff laws and naïvely wondered why the English did not spread their fine cloth all over the American clothes market. . . . He worked up his shoulders in his nigger-brown coat. It didn't feel right, didn't hang so well. There was something a little too chic in American clothes. Not nearly as awful as French, though, Jake horse-laughed, vividly remembering the popular French styles. Broad-pleated, long-waisted, tight-bottomed pants and close-waisted coats whose breast pockets stick out their little comic signs of color. . . . Better color as a savage wears it, or none at all, instead of the Frenchman's peeking bit. The French must consider the average bantam male killing handsome, and so they make clothes to emphasize all the angular elevated rounded and pendulated parts of the anatomy. . . .

The broad pavements of Seventh Avenue were colorful with promenaders. Brown babies in white carriages pushed by little black brothers wearing nice sailor suits. All the various and varying pigmentation of the human race were assembled there: dim brown, clear brown, rich brown, chestnut, copper, yellow, near-white, mahogany, and gleaming anthracite. Charming brown matrons, proud yellow matrons, dark nursemaids pulled a zigzag course by their restive little charges. . . .

And the elegant strutters in faultless spats; West Indians, carrying canes and wearing trousers of a different pattern from their coats and vests, drawing sharp comments from their Afro-Yank rivals.

Jake mentally noted: "A dickty gang sure as Harlem is black, but——"

The girls passed by in bright batches of color, according to station and calling. High class, menial class, and the big trading class, flaunting a front of chiffon-soft colors framed in light coats, seizing the fashion of the day to stage a lovely leg show and spilling along the Avenue the perfume of Djer-kiss, Fougère, and Brown Skin.

"These heah New York gals kain most sartainly wear some moh clothes," thought Jake, "jest as nifty as them French gals." . . .

Twilight was enveloping the Belt, merging its life into a soft blue-black symphony. . . . The animation subsided into a moment's pause, a muffled, tremulous soul-stealing note . . . then electric lights flared everywhere, flooding the scene with dazzling gold.

Jake went to Aunt Hattie's to feed. Billy Biasse was there and a gang of longshoremen who had boozed and fed and were boozing again and, touched by the tender spring night, were swapping love stories and singing:

"Back home in Dixie is a brown gal there,
  Back home in Dixie is a brown gal there,
  Back home in Dixie is a brown gal there,
    Back home in Dixie I was bawn in.

"Back home in Dixie is a gal I know,
  Back home in Dixie is a gal I know,
  Back home in Dixie is a gal I know,
    And I wonder what nigger is saying to her a bootiful
      good mawnin'."

A red-brown West Indian among them volunteered to sing a Port-of-Spain song. It immortalized the drowning of a young black sailor. It was made up by the bawdy colored girls of the port, with whom the deceased had been a favorite, and became very popular among the stevedores and sailors of the island.

> "Ring the bell again,
> Ring the bell again,
> Ring the bell again,
> But the sharks won't puke him up.
> Oh, ring the bell again.

> "Empty is you' room,
> Empty is you' room,
> Empty is you' room,
> But you find one in the sea.
> Oh, empty is you' room.

> "Ring the bell again,
> Ring the bell again,
> Ring the bell again,
> But we know who feel the pain.
> Oh, ring the bell again."

The song was curious, like so many Negro songs of its kind, for the strange strengthening of its wistful melody by a happy rhythm that was suitable for dancing.

Aunt Hattie, sitting on a low chair, was swaying to the music and licking her lips, her wrinkled features wearing an expression of ecstatic delight. Billy Biasse offered to stand a bottle of gin. Jake said he would also sing a sailor song he had picked up in Limehouse. And so he sang the chanty of Bullocky Bill who went up to town to see a fair young maiden. But he could not remember most of the words, therefore Bullocky Bill cannot be presented here. But Jake was boisterously applauded for the scraps of it that he rendered.

The singing finished, Jake confided to Billy: "I sure don't feel lak spending a lonesome night this heah mahvelous night."

"Ain't nobody evah lonely in Harlem that don't wanta be," retorted Billy. "Even yours truly lone Wolf ain't nevah lonesome."

"But I want something as mahvelous as mah feelings."

Billy laughed and fingered his kinks: "Harlem has got the right stuff, boh, for all feelings."

"Youse right enough," Jake agreed, and fell into a reverie of full brown mouth and mischievous brown eyes all composing a perfect whole for his dark-brown delight.

"You wanta take a turn down the Congo?" asked Billy.

"Ah no."

"Rose ain't there no moh."

Rose had stepped up a little higher in her profession and had been engaged to tour the West in a Negro company.

"All the same, I don't feel like the Congo tonight," said Jake. "Le's go to Sheba Palace and jazz around a little."

Sheba Palace was an immense hall that was entirely monopolized for the amusements of the common workaday Negroes of the Belt. Longshoremen, kitchen-workers, laundresses, and W.C. tenders—all gravitated to the Sheba Palace, while the upper class of servitors—bell-boys, butlers, some railroad workers and waiters, waitresses and maids of all sorts—patronized the Casino and those dancings that were given under the auspices of the churches.

The walls of Sheba Palace were painted with garish gold, and tables and chairs were screaming green. There were green benches also lined round the vast dancing space. The music stopped with an abrupt clash just as Jake entered. Couples and groups were drinking at tables. Deftly, quickly the waiters slipped a way through the tables to serve and collect the money before the next dance. . . . Little white-filled glasses, little yellow-filled glasses, general guzzling of gin and whisky. Little saucy brown lips, rouged maroon, sucking up iced crème de menthe through straws, and many were sipping the golden Virginia Dare, in those days the favorite wine of the Belt. On the green benches couples lounged, sprawled, and, with the juicy love of spring and the liquid of Bacchus mingled in fascinating white eyes curious in their dark frames, apparently oblivious of everything outside of themselves, were loving in every way but . . .

The orchestra was tuning up. . . . The first notes fell out like a general clapping for merrymaking and chased the dancers running, sliding, shuffling, trotting to the floor. Little girls energetically chewing Spearmint and showing all their teeth dashed out on the floor and started shivering amorously, itching for their partners to come. Some lads were quickly on their feet, grinning gayly and improvising new steps with snapping of fingers while their girls were sucking up the last of their crème de menthe. The floor was large and smooth enough for anything.

They had a new song-and-dance at the Sheba and the black fellows were playing it with *éclat*.

> Brown gal crying on the corner,
> Yaller gal done stole her candy,
> Buy him spats and feed him cream,
> Keep him strutting fine and dandy.

> Tell me, pa-pa, Ise you' ma-ma,
> Yaller gal can't make you fall,
> For Ise got some loving pa-pa
> Yaller gal ain't got atall.

"Tell me, pa-pa, Ise you' ma-ma." The black players grinned and swayed and let the music go with all their might. The yellow in the music must have stood out in their imagination like a challenge, conveying a sense of that primitive, ancient, eternal, inexplicable antagonism in the color taboo of sex and society. The dark dancers picked up the refrain and jazzed and shouted with delirious joy, "Tell me, pa-pa, Ise you' ma-ma." The handful of yellow dancers in the crowd were even more abandoned to the spirit of the song. "White," "green," or "red" in place of "yaller" might have likewise touched the same deep-sounding, primitive chord. . . .

> Yaller gal sure wants mah pa-pa,
> But mah chocolate turns her down,
> 'Cause he knows there ain't no loving
> Sweeter than his loving brown.

> Tell me, pa-pa, Ise you' ma-ma,
> Yaller gal can't make you fall,
> For Ise got some loving pa-pa
> Yaller gal ain't got atall.

Jake was doing his dog with a tall, shapely quadroon girl when, glancing up at the balcony, he spied the little brown that he had entirely given over as lost. She was sitting at a table while "Tell me pa-pa" was tickling everybody to the uncontrollable point—she was sitting with her legs crossed and well exposed, and, with the aid of the mirror attached to her vanity case, was saucily and nonchalantly powdering her nose.

The quadroon girl nearly fell as Jake, without a word of explanation, dropped her in the midst of a long slide and, dashing across the floor, bounded up the stairs.

"Hello, sweetness! What youse doing here?"

The girl started and knocked over a glass of whisky on the floor: "O my Gawd! it's mah heartbreaking daddy! Where was you all this time?"

Jake drew a chair up beside her, but she jumped up: "Lawdy, no! Le's get outa here quick, 'cause Ise got somebody with me and now I don't want see him no moh."

" 'Sawright, I kain take care of mahself," said Jake.

"Oh, honey, no! I don't want no trouble and he's a bad actor, that nigger. See, I done break his glass o' whisky and tha's bad luck. Him's just theah in the lav'try. Come quick. I don't want him to ketch us."

And the flustered little brown heart hustled Jake down the stairs and out of the Sheba Palace.

"Tell me, pa-pa, Ise you' ma-ma . . ."

The black shouting chorus pursued them outside.

"There ain't no yaller gal gwine get mah honey daddy thisanight." She took Jake's arm and cuddled up against his side.

"Aw no, sweetness. I was dogging it with one and jest drops her flat when I seen you."

"And there ain't no nigger in the wul' I wouldn't ditch foh you, daddy. O Lawdy! How Ise been crazy longing to meet you again."

XX
Felice

"WHAR'S we gwine?" Jake asked.

They had walked down Madison Avenue, turned on One Hundred and Thirtieth Street, passing the solid gray-grim mass of the whites' Presbyterian church, and were under the timidly whispering trees of the decorously silent and distinguished Block Beautiful. . . . The whites had not evacuated that block yet. The black invasion was threatening it from One Hundred and Thirty-first Street, from Fifth Avenue, even from behind in One Hundred and Twenty-ninth Street. But desperate, frightened, blanch-faced, the ancient sepulchral Respectability held on. And giving them moral courage, the Presbyterian church frowned on the corner like a fortress against the invasion. The Block Beautiful was worth a struggle. With its charming green lawns and quaint white-fronted houses, it preserved the most Arcadian atmosphere in all New York. When there was a flat to let in that block, you would have to rubberneck terribly before you saw in the corner of a window-pane a neat little sign worded, Vacancy. But groups of loud-laughing-and-acting black swains and their sweethearts had started in using the block for their afternoon promenade. That was the limit: the desecrating of that atmosphere by black love in the very shadow of the gray, gaunt Protestant church! The Ancient Respectability was getting ready to flee. . . .

The beautiful block was fast asleep. Up in the branches the little elfin green things were barely whispering. The Protestant church was softened to a shadow. The atmosphere was perfect, the moment sweet for something sacred.

The burning little brownskin cuddled up against Jake's warm tall person: "Kiss me, daddy," she said. He folded her closely to him and caressed her. . . .

"But whar was you all this tur'bly long time?" demanded Jake.

Light-heartedly, she frisky like a kitten, they sauntered along

Seventh Avenue, far from the rough environment of Sheba Palace.

"Why, daddy, I waited foh you all that day after you went away and all that night! Oh, I had a heart-break on foh you, I was so tur'bly disappointed. I nev' been so crazy yet about no man. Why didn't you come back, honey?"

Jake felt foolish, remembering why. He said that shortly after leaving her he had discovered the money and the note. He had met some of his buddies of his company who had plenty of money, and they all went celebrating until that night, and by then he had forgotten the street.

"Mah poor daddy!"

"Even you' name, sweetness, I didn't know. Ise Jake Brown—Jake for ev'body. What is you', sweetness?"

"They calls me Felice."

"Felice. . . . But I didn't fohget the cabaret nonatall. And I was back theah hunting foh you that very night and many moh after, but I nevah finds you. Where was you?"

"Why, honey, I don't lives in cabarets all mah nights 'cause Ise got to work. Furthermore, I done went away that next week to Palm Beach——"

"Palm Beach! What foh?"

"Work of course. What you think? You done brokes mah heart in one mahvelous night and neveh returns foh moh. And I was jest right down sick and tiahd of Harlem. So I went away to work. I always work. . . . I know what youse thinking, honey, but I ain't in the reg'lar business. 'Cause Ise a funny gal. I kain't go with a fellah ef I don't like him some. And ef he kain make me like him enough I won't take nothing off him and ef he kain make me fall the real way, I guess I'd work like a wop for him."

"Youse the baby I been waiting foh all along," said Jake. "I knowed you was the goods."

"Where is we gwine, daddy?"

"Ise got a swell room, sweetness, up in 'Fortiet' Street whar all them dickty shines live."

"But kain you take me there?"

"Sure thing, baby. Ain't no nigger renting a room in Harlem whar he kain't have his li'l' company."

"Oh, goody, goody, honey-stick!"

Jake took Felice home to his room. She was delighted with it. It was neat and orderly.

"Your landlady must be one of them proper persons," she remarked. "How did you find such a nice place way up here?"

"A chappie named Ray got it foh me when I was sick——"

"O Lawdy! was it serious? Did they all take good care a you?"

"It wasn't nothing much and the fellahs was all awful good spohts, especially Ray."

"Who is this heah Ray?"

Jake told her. She smoothed out the counterpane on the bed, making a mental note that it was just right for two. She admired the geraniums in the window that looked on the large court.

"These heah new homes foh niggers am sure nice," she commented.

She looked behind the curtain where his clothes were hanging and remarked his old English suit. Then she regarded archly his new nigger-brown rig-out.

"You was moh illegant in that other, but I likes you in this all the same."

Jake laughed. "Everything's gotta wear out some day."

Felice hung round his neck, twiddling her pretty legs.

He held her as you might hold a child and she ruffled his thick mat of hair and buried her face in it. She wriggled down with a little scream:

"Oh, I gotta go get mah bag!"

"I'll come along with you," said Jake.

"No, lemme go alone. I kain manage better by mahself."

"But suppose that nigger is waiting theah foh you? You better lemme come along."

"No, honey, I done figure he's waiting still in Sheba Palace, or boozing. Him and some friends was all drinking befoh and he was kinder full. Ise sure he ain't gone home. Anyway, I kain manage by mahself all right, but ef you comes along and we runs into him— No, honey, you stays right here. I don't want messing up in no blood-baff. Theah's too much a that in Harlem."

They compromised, Felice agreeing that Jake should accompany her to the corner of Seventh Avenue and One Hundred and Thirty-fifth Street and wait for her there. She had not the faintest twinge of conscience herself. She had met the male that she preferred and gone with him, leaving the one that she was merely makeshifting with. It was a very simple and natural thing to her. There was nothing mean about it. She was too nice to be mean. However, she was aware that in her world women scratched and bit into each other's flesh and men razored and gunned at each other over such things. . . .

Felice recalled one memorable afternoon when two West Indian women went for each other in the back yard of a house in One Hundred and Thirty-second Street. One was a laundress, a whopping brown woman who had come to New York from Colon, and the other was a country girl, a buxom Negress from Jamaica. They were quarreling over a vain black bantam, one of the breed that delight in women's scratching over them. The laundress had sent for him to come over from the Canal Zone to New York. They had lived together there and she had kept him, making money in all the ways that a gay and easy woman can on the Canal Zone. But now the laundress bemoaned the fact that "sence mah man come to New Yawk, him jest gone back on me in the queerest way you can imagine."

Her man, in turn, blamed the situation upon her, said she was too aggressive and mannish and had harried the energy out of him. But the other girl seemed to endow him again with virility. . . . After keeping him in Panama and bringing him to New York, the laundress hesitated about turning her male loose in Harlem, although he was apparently of no more value to her. But his rejuvenating experience with the younger girl had infuriated the laundress. A sister worker from Alabama, to whom she had confided her secret tragedy, had hinted: "Lawdy! sistah, that sure sounds phony-like. Mebbe you' man is jest playing 'possum with you." And the laundress was crazy with suspicion and jealousy and a feeling for revenge. She challenged her rival to fight the affair out. They were all living in the same house. . . .

Felice also lived in that house. And one afternoon she was startled by another girl from an adjoining room pounding on her door and shrieking: "Open foh the love of Jesus! . . . Theah's sweet hell playing in the back yard."

The girls rushed to the window and saw the two black women squaring off at each other down in the back yard. They were stark naked.

After the challenge, the women had decided to fight with their clothes off. An old custom, perhaps a survival of African tribalism, had been imported from some remote West Indian hillside into a New York back yard. Perhaps, the laundress had thought, that with her heavy and powerful limbs she could easily get her rival down and sit on her, mauling her properly. But the black girl was as nimble as a wild goat. She dodged away from the laundress who was trying to get ahold of her big bush of hair, and suddenly sailing fullfront into her, she seized the laundress, shoulder and neck, and butted her twice on the forehead as only a rough West Indian country girl can butt. The laundress staggered backward, groggy, into a bundle of old carpets. But she rallied and came back at the grinning Negress again. The laundress had never learned the brutal art of butting. The girl bounded up at her forehead with another well-aimed butt and sent her reeling flop on her back among the carpets. The girl planted her knees upon the laundress's high chest and wrung her hair.

"You don't know me, but I'll make you remember me forebber. I'll beat you' mug ugly. There!" Bam! Bam! She slapped the laundress's face.

"Git off mah stomach, nigger gal, and leave me in peace," the laundress panted. The entire lodging-house was in a sweet fever over the event. Those lodgers whose windows gave on the street had crowded into their neighbors' rear rooms and some had descended into the basement for a close-up view. Apprised of the naked exhibition, the landlord hurried in from the corner saloon and threatened the combatants with the police. But there was nothing to do. The affair was settled and the women had already put their shifts on.

The women lodgers cackled gayly over the novel staging of the fight.

"It sure is better to disrobe like that, befoh battling," one declared. "It turn you' hands and laigs loose for action."

"And saves you' clothes being ripped into ribbons," said another.

A hen-fight was more fun than a cock-fight, thought Felice, as she hastily threw her things into her bag. The hens pluck feathers, but they never wring necks like the cocks.

And Jake. Standing on the corner, he waited, restive, nervous. But, unlike Felice, his thought was not touched by the faintest fear of a blood battle. His mind was a circle containing the girl and himself only, making a thousand plans of the joys they would create together. She was a prize to hold. Had slipped through his fingers once, but he wasn't ever going to lose her again. That little model of warm brown flesh. Each human body has its own peculiar rhythm, shallow or deep or profound. Transient rhythms that touch and pass you, unrememberable, and rhythms unforgetable. Imperial rhythms whose vivid splendor blinds your sight and destroys your taste for lesser ones.

Jake possessed a sure instinct for the right rhythm. He was connoisseur enough. But although he had tasted such a varied many, he was not raw animal enough to be undiscriminating, nor civilized enough to be cynical. . . .

Felice came hurrying as much as she could along One Hundred and Thirty-fifth Street, bumping a cumbersome portmanteau on the pavement and holding up one unruly lemon-bright silk stocking with her left hand. Jake took the bag from her. They went into a delicatessen store and bought a small cold chicken, ham, mustard, olives, and bread. They stopped in a sweet shop and bought a box of chocolate-and-vanilla ice-cream and cake. Felice also took a box of chocolate candy. Their last halt was at a United Cigar Store, where Jake stocked his pockets with a half a dozen packets of Camels. . . .

Felice had just slipped out of her charming strawberry frock when her hands flew down to her pretty brown leg. "O Gawd! I done fohget something!" she cried in a tone that intimated something very precious.

"What's it then?" demanded Jake.

"It's mah luck," she said. "It's the fierst thing that was gived to me when I was born. Mah gran'ma gived it and I wears it always foh good luck."

This lucky charm was an old plaited necklace, leathery in appearance, with a large, antique blue bead attached to it, that Felice's grandmother (who had superintended her coming into the world) had given to her immediately after that event. Her grandmother had dipped the necklace into the first water that Felice was washed in. Felice had religiously worn her charm around her neck all during her childhood. But since she was grown to ripe girlhood and low-cut frocks were the fashion and she loved them so much, she had transferred the unsightly necklace from her throat to her leg. But before going to the Sheba Palace she had unhooked the thing. And she had forgotten it there in the closet, hanging by a little nail against the wash-bowl.

"I gotta go get it," she said.

"Aw no, you won't bother," drawled Jake. And he drew the little agitated brown body to him and quieted it. "It was good luck you fohget it, sweetness, for it made us find one another."

"Something to that, daddy," Felice said, and her mouth touched his mouth.

They wove an atmosphere of dreams around them and were lost in it for a week. Felice asked the landlady to let her use the kitchen to cook their meals at home. They loitered over the wide field and lay in the sweet grass of Van Cortlandt Park. They went to the Negro Picture Theater and held each other's hand, gazing in raptures at the crude pictures. It was odd that all these cinematic pictures about the blacks were a broad burlesque of their home and love life. These colored screen actors were all dressed up in expensive evening clothes, with automobiles, and menials, to imitate white society people. They laughed at themselves in such rôles and the laughter was good on the screen. They pranced and grinned like good-nigger servants, who know that "mas'r" and "missus," intent on being amused, are watching their antics from an upper window. It was quite a little funny and the audience enjoyed it. Maybe that was the stuff the Black Belt wanted.

XXI
The Gift That Billy Gave

"WE gotta celebrate to-night," said Felice when Saturday
came round again. Jake agreed to do anything she
wanted. Monday they would have to think of working. He
wanted to dine at Aunt Hattie's, but Felice preferred a "nif-
tier" place. So they dined at the Nile Queen restaurant on Seventh Avenue. After dinner they subwayed down to Broadway.
They bought tickets for the nigger heaven of a theater, whence
they watched high-class people make luxurious love on the
screen. They enjoyed the exhibition. There is no better angle
from which one can look down on a motion picture than that
of the nigger heaven.

They returned to Harlem after the show in a mood to celebrate until morning. Should they go to Sheba Palace where
chance had been so good to them, or to a cabaret? Sentiment
was in favor of Sheba Palace but her love of the chic and novel
inclined Felice toward an attractive new Jewish-owned Negro
cabaret. She had never been there and could not go under
happier circumstances.

The cabaret was a challenge to any other in Harlem. There
were one or two cabarets in the Belt that were distinguished
for their impolite attitude toward the average Negro customer,
who could not afford to swill expensive drinks. He was pushed
off into a corner and neglected, while the best seats and service
were reserved for notorious little gangs of white champagne-
guzzlers from downtown.

The new cabaret specialized in winning the good will of the
average blacks and the approval of the fashionable set of
the Belt. The owner had obtained a college-bred Negro to be
manager, and the cashier was a genteel mulatto girl. On the
opening night the management had sent out special invitations
to the high lights of the Negro theatrical world and free champagne had been served to them. The new cabaret was also
drawing nightly a crowd of white pleasure-seekers from down-

town. The war was just ended and people were hungry for any amusements that were different from the stale stock things.

Besides its spacious floor, ladies' room, gentlemen's room and coat-room, the new cabaret had a bar with stools, where men could get together away from their women for a quick drink and a little stag conversation. The bar was a paying innovation. The old-line cabarets were falling back before their formidable rival. . . .

The fashionable Belt was enjoying itself there on this night. The press, theatrical, and music world were represented. Madame Mulberry was there wearing peacock blue with patches of yellow. Madame Mulberry was a famous black beauty in the days when Fifty-third Street was the hub of fashionable Negro life. They called her then, Brown Glory. She was the wife of Dick Mulberry, a promoter of Negro shows. She had no talent for the stage herself, but she knew all the celebrated stage people of her race. She always gossiped reminiscently of Bert Williams, George Walker and Aida Overton Walker, Anita Patti Brown and Cole and Johnson.

With Madame Mulberry sat Maunie Whitewing with a dapper cocoa-brown youth by her side, who was very much pleased by his own person and the high circle to which it gained him admission. Maunie was married to a nationally-known Negro artist, who lived simply and quietly. But Maunie was notorious among the scandal sets of Brooklyn, New York, and Washington. She was always creating scandals wherever she went, gallivanting around with improper persons at improper places, such as this new cabaret. Maunie's beauty was Egyptian in its exoticism and she dared to do things in the manner of ancient courtesans. Dignified colored matrons frowned upon her ways, but they had to invite her to their homes, nevertheless, when they asked her husband. But Maunie seldom went.

The sports editor of *Colored Life* was also there, with a prominent Negro pianist. It was rumored that Bert Williams might drop in after midnight. Madame Mulberry was certain he would.

James Reese Europe, the famous master of jazz, was among a group of white admirers. He had just returned from France, full of honors, with his celebrated band. New York had acclaimed him and America was ready to applaud. . . . That was his last appearance in a Harlem cabaret before his heart was shot out during a performance in Boston by a savage buck of his race. . . .

Prohibition was on the threshold of the country and drinking was becoming a luxury, but all the joy-pacers of the Belt who adore the novel and the fashionable and had a dollar to burn had come together in a body to fill the new cabaret.

The owner of the cabaret knew that Negro people, like his people, love the pageantry of life, the expensive, the fine, the striking, the showy, the trumpet, the blare—sumptuous settings and luxurious surroundings. And so he had assembled his guests under an enchanting-blue ceiling of brilliant chandeliers and a dome of artificial roses bowered among green leaves. Great mirrors reflected the variegated colors and poses. Shaded, multi-colored sidelights glowed softly along the golden walls.

It was a scene of blazing color. Soft, barbaric, burning, savage, clashing, planless colors—all rioting together in wonderful harmony. There is no human sight so rich as an assembly of Negroes ranging from lacquer black through brown to cream, decked out in their ceremonial finery. Negroes are like trees. They wear all colors naturally. And Felice, rouged to a ravishing maroon, and wearing a close-fitting, chrome-orange frock and cork-brown slippers, just melted into the scene.

They were dancing as Felice entered and she led Jake right along into it.

"Tell me, pa-pa, Ise you ma-ma . . ."

Every cabaret and dancing-hall was playing it. It was the tune for the season. It had carried over from winter into spring and was still the favorite. Oh, ma-ma! Oh, pa-pa!

The dancing stopped. . . . A brief interval and a dwarfish, shiny black man wearing a red-brown suit, with kinks straightened and severely plastered down in the Afro-American manner, walked into the center of the floor and began singing. He had a massive mouth, which he opened wide, and a profoundly big and quite good voice came out of it.

"I'm so doggone fed up, I don't know what to do.
Can't find a pal that's constant, can't find a gal that's true.

But I ain't gwine to worry 'cause mah buddy was a ham;
Ain't gwine to cut mah throat 'cause mah gal ain't worf a
        damn.
Ise got the blues all ovah, the coal-black biting blues,
Like a prowling tom-cat that's got the low-down mews.

"I'm gwine to lay me in a good supply a gin,
Foh gunning is a crime, but drinking ain't no sin.
I won't do a crazy deed 'cause of a two-faced pal,
Ain't gwineta break mah heart ovah a no-'count gal
Ise got the blues all ovah, the coal-black biting blues,
Like a prowling tom-cat that's got the low-down mews."

There was something of the melancholy charm of Tschaikov-
sky in the melody. The black singer made much of the triumphant note of strength that reigned over the sad motif. When
he sang, "I ain't gwine to cut mah throat," "Ain't gwine to
break mah heart," his face became grim and full of will as a
bulldog's.

He conquered his audience and at the finish he was greeted
with warm applause and a shower of silver coins ringing on the
tiled pavement. An enthusiastic white man waved a dollar note
at the singer and, to show that Negroes could do just as good
or better, Maunie Whitewing's sleek escort imitated the gesture
with a two-dollar note. That started off the singer again.

"Ain't gwine to cut mah throat . . .
        Ain't gwine to break mah heart . . ."

"That zigaboo is a singing fool," remarked Jake.

Billy Biasse entered resplendent in a new bottle-green suit,
and joined Jake and Felice at their table.

"What you say, Billy?" Jake's greeting.

"I say Ise gwineta blow. Toss off that theah liquor, you
two. Ise gwineta blow champagne as mah compliments, old
top." . . .

"Heah's good luck t'you, boh, and plenty of joy-stuff and
happiness," continued Billy, when the champagne was poured.
"You sure been hugging it close this week."

Jake smiled and looked foolish. . . . The second cook,
whom he had not seen since he quitted the railroad, entered

the cabaret with a mulatto girl on his arm and looked round for seats. Jake stood up and beckoned him over to his table.

"It's awright, ain't it Billy?" he asked his friend.

"Sure. Any friend a yourn is awright."

The two girls began talking fashion around the most striking dresses in the place. Jake asked about the demoted rhinoceros. He was still on the railroad, the second cook said, taking orders from another chef, "jest as savage and mean as ever, but not so moufy. I hear you friend Ray done quit us for the ocean, Jakey." . . .

There was still champagne to spare, nevertheless the second cook invited the boys to go up to the bar for a stiff drink of real liquor.

Negroes, like all good Americans, love a bar. I should have said, Negroes under Anglo-Saxon civilization. A bar has a charm all of its own that makes drinking there pleasanter. We like to lean up against it, with a foot on the rail. We will leave our women companions and choice wines at the table to snatch a moment of exclusive sex solidarity over a thimble of gin at the bar.

The boys left the girls to the fashions for a little while. Billy Biasse, being a stag as always, had accepted the invitation with alacrity. He loved to indulge in naked man-stuff talk, which would be too raw even for Felice's ears. As they went out Maunie Whitewing (she was a traveled woman of the world and had been abroad several times with and without her husband) smiled upon Jake with a bold stare and remarked to Madame Mulberry: "*Quel beau garçon! J'aimerais beaucoup faire l'amour avec lui.*"

"Superb!" agreed Madame Mulberry, appreciating Jake through her lorgnette.

Felice caught Maunie Whitewing's carnal stare at her man and said to the mulatto girl: "Jest look at that high-class hussy!"

And the dapper escort tried to be obviously unconcerned.

At the bar the three pals had finished one round and the barman was in the act of pouring another when a loud scream tore through music and conversation. Jake knew that voice and dashed down the stairs. What he saw held him rooted at the foot of the stairs for a moment. Zeddy had Felice's wrists in a hard grip and she was trying to wrench herself away.

"Leggo a me, I say," she bawled.

"I ain't gwineta do no sich thing. Youse mah woman."

"You lie! I ain't and you ain't mah man, black nigger."

"We'll see ef I ain't. Youse gwine home wif me right now."

Jake strode up to Zeddy. "Turn that girl loose."

"Whose gwineta make me?" growled Zeddy.

"I is. She's mah woman. I knowed her long before you. For Gawd's sake quit you' fooling and don't let's bust up the man's cabaret."

All the fashionable folk had already fled.

"She's *my* woman and I'll carve any damn-fool nigger for her." Lightning-quick Zeddy released the girl and moved upon Jake like a terrible bear with open razor.

"Don't let him kill him, foh Gawd's sake don't," a woman shrieked, and there was a general stampede for the exit.

But Zeddy had stopped like a cowed brute in his tracks, for leveled straight at his heart was the gift that Billy gave.

"Drop that razor and git you' hands up," Jake commanded, "and don't make a fool move or youse a dead nigger."

Zeddy obeyed. Jake searched him and found nothing. "I gotta good mind fixing you tonight, so you won't evah pull a razor on another man."

Zeddy looked Jake steadily in the face and said: "You kain kill me, nigger, ef you wanta. You come gunning at me, but you didn't go gunning after the Germans. Nosah! You was scared and runned away from the army."

Jake looked bewildered, sick. He was hurt now to his heart and he was dumb. The waiters and a few rough customers that the gun did not frighten away looked strangely at him.

"Yes, mah boy," continued Zeddy, "that's what life is everytime. When youse good to a buddy, he steals you woman and pulls a gun on you. Tha's what I get for prohceeding a slacker. A-llll right, boh, I was a good sucker, but—I ain't got no reason to worry sence youse down in the white folks' books." And he ambled away.

Jake shuffled off by himself. Billy Biasse tried to say a decent word, but he waved him away.

These miserable cock-fights, beastly, tigerish, bloody. They had always sickened, saddened, unmanned him. The wild, shrieking mad woman that is sex seemed jeering at him. Why should love create terror? Love should be joy lifting man out of the humdrum ways of life. He had always managed to delight in love and yet steer clear of the hate and violence that govern it in his world. His love nature was generous and warm without any vestige of the diabolical or sadistic.

Yet here he was caught in the thing that he despised so thoroughly. . . . Brest, London, and his America. Their vivid brutality tortured his imagination. Oh, he was infinitely disgusted with himself to think that he had just been moved by the same savage emotions as those vile, vicious, villainous white men who, like hyenas and rattlers, had fought, murdered, and clawed the entrails out of black men over the common, commercial flesh of women. . . .

He reached home and sat brooding in the shadow upon the stoop.

"Zeddy. My own friend in some ways. Naturally lied about me and the army, though. Playing martyr. How in hell did *he* get hooked up with her? Thought he was up in Yonkers. Would never guess one in a hundred it was he. What a crazy world! He must have passed us drinking at the bar. Wish I'd seen him. Would have had him drinking with us. And maybe we would have avoided that stinking row. Maybe and maybe not. Can't tell about Zeddy. He was always a bad-acting razor-flashing nigger."

A little hand timidly took his arm.

"Honey, you ain't mad at you sweetness, is you?"

"No. . . . I'm jest sick and tiah'd a everything."

"I nevah know you knowed one anether, honey. Oh, I was so scared. . . . But how could I know?"

"No, you couldn't. I ain't blaming nothing on you. I nevah would guess it was him mahself. I ain't blaming nobody at all."

Felice cuddled closer to Jake and fondled his face. "It was a good thing you had you' gun, though, honey, or—— O Lawd! what mighta happened!"

"Oh, I woulda been a dead nigger this time or a helpless one," Jake laughed and hugged her closer to him. "It was Billy gived me that gun and I didn't even wanta take it."

"Didn't you? Billy is a good friend, eh?"

"You bet he is. Nevah gets mixed up with—in scraps like that."

"Honest, honey, I nevah liked Zeddy, but——"

"Oh, you don't have to explain me nothing. I know it's jest connexidence. It coulda been anybody else. That don't worry mah skin."

"I really didn't like him, though, honey. Lemme tell you. I was kinder sorry for him. It was jest when I got back from Palm Beach I seen him one night at a buffet flat. And he was that nice to me. He paid drinks for the whole houseful a people and all because a me. I couldn't act mean, so I had to be nice mahself. And the next day he ups and buys me two pair a shoes and silk stockings and a box a chocolate candy. So I jest stayed on and gived him a li'l' loving, honey, but I nevah did tuk him to mah haht."

"It's awright, sweetness. What do I care so long as wese got one another again?"

She drew down his head and sought his mouth. . . .

"But what is we gwineta do, daddy? Sence they say that youse a slacker or deserter, I don't which is which——"

"He done lied about that, though," Jake said, angrily. "I didn't run away because I was scared a them Germans. But I beat it away from Brest because they wouldn't give us a chance at them, but kept us in that rainy, sloppy, Gawd-forsaken burg working like wops. They didn't seem to want us niggers foh no soldiers. We was jest a bunch a despised hod-carriers, and Zeddy know that."

Now it was Felice's turn. "You ain't telling me a thing, daddy. I'll be slack with you and desert with you. What right have niggers got to shoot down a whole lot a Germans for? Is they worse than Americans or any other nation a white people? You done do the right thing, honey, and Ise with you and I love you the more for that. . . . But all the same, we can't stay in Harlem no longer, for the bulls will sure get you."

"I been thinking a gitting away from the stinking mess and go on off to sea again."

"Ah no, daddy," Felice tightened her hold on his arm. "And what'll become a me? I kain't go 'board a ship with you and I needs you."

Jake said nothing.

"What you wanta go knocking around them foreign countries again for like swallow come and swallow go from year to
year and nevah settling down no place? This heah is you' country, daddy. What you gwine away from it for?"

"And what kain I do?"

"Do? Jest le's beat it away from Harlem, daddy. This heah
country is good and big enough for us to git lost in. You know
Chicago?"

"Haven't made that theah burg yet."

"Why, le's go to Chicago, then. I hear it's a mahvelous place
foh niggers. Chicago, honey."

"When?"

"This heah very night. Ise ready. Ain't nothing in Harlem
holding *me*, honey. Come on. Le's pack."

Zeddy rose like an apparition out of the shadow. Automatically Jake's hand went to his pocket.

"Don't shoot!" Zeddy threw up his hands. "I ain't here foh
no trouble. I jest wanta ast you' pahdon, Jake. Excuse me, boh.
I was crazy-mad and didn't know what I was saying. Ahm
bloody well ashamed a mahself. But you know how it is when
a gal done make a fool outa you. I done think it ovah and said
to mah inner man: Why, you fool fellah, whasmat with you? Ef
Zeddy slit his buddy's thwoat for a gal, that won't give back
the gal to Zeddy. . . . So I jest had to come and tell it to you
and ast you pahdon. You kain stay in Harlem as long as you
wanta. Zeddy ain'ta gwineta open his mouf against you. You was
always a good man-to-man buddy and nevah did wears you
face bahind you. Don't pay no mind to what I done said in that
theah cabaret. Them niggers hanging around was all drunk
and wouldn't shoot their mouf off about you nohow. You ain't
no moh slacker than me. What you done was all right, Jakey,
and I woulda did it mahself ef I'd a had the guts to."

"It's all right, Zeddy," said Jake. "It was jest a crazy mix-up
we all got into. I don't bear you no grudge."

"Will you take the paw on it?"

"Sure!" Jake gripped Zeddy's hand.

"So long, buddy, and fohgit it."

"So long, Zeddy, ole top." And Zeddy bear-walked off,
without a word or a look at Felice, out of Jake's life forever.
Felice was pleased, yet, naturally, just a little piqued. He might

have said good-by to *me*, too, she thought. I would even have kissed him for the last time. She took hold of Jake's hands and swung them meditatively: "It's all right daddy, but——"

"But what?"

"I think we had better let Harlem miss us foh a little while."

"Scared?"

"Yes, daddy, but for you only. Zeddy won't go back on you. I guess not. But news is like a traveling agent, honey, going from person to person. I wouldn't take no chances."

"I guess youse right, sweetness. Come on, le's get our stuff together."

The two leather cases were set together against the wall. Felice sat upon the bed dangling her feet and humming "Tell me, pa-pa, Ise you ma-ma." Jake, in white shirt-sleeves, was arranging in the mirror a pink-yellow-and-blue necktie.

"All set! What you say, sweetness?"

"I say, honey, le's go to the Baltimore and finish the night and ketch the first train in the morning."

"Why, the Baltimore is padlocked!" said Jake.

"It was, daddy, but it's open again and going strong. White folks can't padlock niggers outa joy forever. Let's go, daddy."

She jumped down from the bed and jazzed around.

"Oh, I nearly made a present of these heah things to the landlady!" She swept from the bed a pink coverlet edged with lace, and pillow-slips of the same fantasy (they were her own make), with which she had replaced the flat, rooming-house-white ones, and carefully folded them to fit in the bag that Jake had ready open for her. He slid into his coat, made certain of his pocket-book, and picked up the two bags.

The Baltimore was packed with happy, grinning wrigglers. Many pleasure-seekers who had left the new cabaret, on account of the Jake-Zeddy incident, had gone there. It was brighter than before the raid. The ceiling and walls were kalsomined in white and lilac and the lights glared stronger from new chandeliers.

The same jolly, compact manager was there, grinning a welcome to strange white visitors, who were pleased and never guessed what cautious reserve lurked under that grin.

Tell me, pa-pa, Ise you' ma-ma. . . .

Jake and Felice squeezed a way in among the jazzers. They were all drawn together in one united mass, wriggling around to the same primitive, voluptuous rhythm.

Tell me, pa-pa, Ise you' ma-ma. . . .

Haunting rhythm, mingling of naïve wistfulness and charming gayety, now sheering over into mad riotous joy, now, like a jungle mask, strange, unfamiliar, disturbing, now plunging headlong into the far, dim depths of profundity and rising out as suddenly with a simple, childish grin. And the white visitors laugh. They see the grin only. Here are none of the well-patterned, well-made emotions of the respectable world. A laugh might finish in a sob. A moan end in hilarity. That gorilla type wriggling there with his hands so strangely hugging his mate, may strangle her tonight. But he has no thought of that now. He loves the warm wriggle and is lost in it. Simple, raw emotions and real. They may frighten and repel refined souls, because they are too intensely real, just as a simple savage stands dismayed before nice emotions that he instantly perceives are false.

Tell me, pa-pa, Ise you' ma-ma. . . .

Jake was the only guest left in the Baltimore. The last wriggle was played. The waiters were picking up things and settling accounts.

"Whar's the little hussy?" irritated and perplexed, Jake wondered.

Felice was not in the cabaret nor outside on the pavement. Jake could not understand how she had vanished from his side.

"Maybe she was making a high sign when you was asleep," a waiter laughed.

"Sleep hell!" retorted Jake. He was in no joking mood.

"We gwineta lock up now, big boy," the manager said.

Jake picked up the bags and went out on the sidewalk again. "I kain't believe she'd ditch me like that at the last moment," he said aloud. "Anyhow, I'm bound foh Chicago. I done made up mah mind to go all becausing a her, and I ain'ta gwineta change it whether she throws me down or not. But sure she kain'ta run off and leaves her suitcase. What the hell is I gwine do with it?"

Felice came running up to him, panting, from Lenox Avenue.

"Where in hell you been all this while?" he growled.

"Oh, daddy, don't get mad!"

"Whar you been I say?"

"I done been to look for mah good-luck necklace. I couldn't go to Chicago without it."

Jake grinned. "Whyn't you tell me you was gwine? Weren't you scared a Zeddy?"

"I was and I wasn't. Ef I'd a told you, you woulda said it wasn't worth troubling about. So I jest made up mah mind to slip off and git it. The door wasn't locked and Zeddy wasn't home. It was hanging same place where I left it and I slipped it on mah leg and left the keys on the table. You know I had the keys. Ah, daddy, ef I'd a had mah luck with me, we nevah woulda gotten into a fight at that cabaret."

"You really think so, sweetness?"

They were walking to the subway station along Lenox Avenue.

"I ain't thinking, honey. I knows it. I'll nevah fohgit it again and it'll always give us good luck."

QUICKSAND

Nella Larsen

For E. S. I.

My old man died in a fine big house.
My ma died in a shack.
I wonder where I'm gonna die,
Being neither white nor black?

LANGSTON HUGHES

One

ELGA CRANE sat alone in her room, which at that hour, eight in the evening, was in soft gloom. Only a single reading lamp, dimmed by a great black and red shade, made a pool of light on the blue Chinese carpet, on the bright covers of the books which she had taken down from their long shelves, on the white pages of the opened one selected, on the shining brass bowl crowded with many-colored nasturtiums beside her on the low table, and on the oriental silk which covered the stool at her slim feet. It was a comfortable room, furnished with rare and intensely personal taste, flooded with Southern sun in the day, but shadowy just then with the drawn curtains and single shaded light. Large, too. So large that the spot where Helga sat was a small oasis in a desert of darkness. And eerily quiet. But that was what she liked after her taxing day's work, after the hard classes, in which she gave willingly and unsparingly of herself with no apparent return. She loved this tranquillity, this quiet, following the fret and strain of the long hours spent among fellow members of a carelessly unkind and gossiping faculty, following the strenuous rigidity of conduct required in this huge educational community of which she was an insignificant part. This was her rest, this intentional isolation for a short while in the evening, this little time in her own attractive room with her own books. To the rapping of other teachers, bearing fresh scandals, or seeking information, or other more concrete favors, or merely talk, at that hour Helga Crane never opened her door.

An observer would have thought her well fitted to that framing of light and shade. A slight girl of twenty-two years, with narrow, sloping shoulders and delicate, but well-turned, arms and legs, she had, none the less, an air of radiant, careless health. In vivid green and gold negligee and glistening brocaded mules, deep sunk in the big high-backed chair, against whose dark tapestry her sharply cut face, with skin like yellow satin, was distinctly outlined, she was—to use a hackneyed word—attractive. Black, very broad brows over soft, yet penetrating, dark eyes, and a pretty mouth, whose sensitive and sensuous lips had a slight questioning petulance and a tiny dissatisfied droop, were the features on which the observer's attention would fasten; though her nose was good, her ears delicately chiseled, and her curly blue-black hair plentiful and always straying in a little wayward, delightful way. Just then it was tumbled, falling unrestrained about her face and on to her shoulders.

Helga Crane tried not to think of her work and the school as she sat there. Ever since her arrival in Naxos she had striven to keep these ends of the days from the intrusion of irritating thoughts and worries. Usually she was successful. But not this evening. Of the books which she had taken from their places she had decided on Marmaduke Pickthall's *Saïd the Fisherman*. She wanted forgetfulness, complete mental relaxation, rest from thought of any kind. For the day had been more than usually crowded with distasteful encounters and stupid perversities. The sultry hot Southern spring had left her strangely tired and a little unnerved. And annoying beyond all other happenings had been that affair of the noon period, now again thrusting itself on her already irritated mind.

She had counted on a few spare minutes in which to indulge in the sweet pleasure of a bath and a fresh, cool change of clothing. And instead her luncheon time had been shortened, as had that of everyone else, and immediately after the hurried gulping down of heavy hot meal the hundreds of students and teachers had been herded into the sun-baked chapel to listen to the banal, the patronizing, and even the insulting remarks of one of the renowned white preachers of the state.

Helga shuddered a little as she recalled some of the statements made by that holy white man of God to the black folk sitting so respectfully before him.

This was, he had told them with obvious sectional pride, the finest school for Negroes anywhere in the country, north or south; in fact, it was better even than a great many schools for white children. And he had dared any Northerner to come south and after looking upon this great institution to say that the Southerner mistreated the Negro. And he had said that if all Negroes would only take a leaf out of the book of Naxos and conduct themselves in the manner of the Naxos products, there would be no race problem, because Naxos Negroes knew what was expected of them. They had good sense and they had good taste. They knew enough to stay in their places, and that, said the preacher, showed good taste. He spoke of his great admiration for the Negro race, no other race in so short a time had made so much progress, but he had urgently besought them to know when and where to stop. He hoped, he sincerely hoped, that they wouldn't become avaricious and grasping, thinking only of adding to their earthly goods, for that would be a sin in the sight of Almighty God. And then he had spoken of contentment, embellishing his words with scriptural quotations and pointing out to them that it was their duty to be satisfied in the estate to which they had been called, hewers of wood and drawers of water. And then he had prayed.

Sitting there in her room, long hours after, Helga again felt a surge of hot anger and seething resentment. And again it subsided in amazement at the memory of the considerable applause which had greeted the speaker just before he had asked his God's blessing upon them.

The South. Naxos. Negro education. Suddenly she hated them all. Strange, too, for this was the thing which she had ardently desired to share in, to be a part of this monument to one man's genius and vision. She pinned a scrap of paper about the bulb under the lamp's shade, for, having discarded her book in the certainty that in such a mood even *Saïd* and his audacious villainy could not charm her, she wanted an even more soothing darkness. She wished it were vacation, so that she might get away for a time.

"No, forever!" she said aloud.

The minutes gathered into hours, but still she sat motionless, a disdainful smile or an angry frown passing now and then across her face. Somewhere in the room a little clock ticked time away. Somewhere outside, a whippoorwill wailed. Evening died. A sweet smell of early Southern flowers rushed in on a newly-risen breeze which suddenly parted the thin silk curtains at the opened windows. A slender, frail glass vase fell from the sill with tingling crash, but Helga Crane did not shift her position. And the night grew cooler, and older.

At last she stirred, uncertainly, but with an overpowering desire for action of some sort. A second she hesitated, then rose abruptly and pressed the electric switch with determined firmness, flooding suddenly the shadowy room with a white glare of light. Next she made a quick nervous tour to the end of the long room, paused a moment before the old bow-legged secretary that held with almost articulate protest her school-teacher paraphernalia of drab books and papers. Frantically Helga Crane clutched at the lot and then flung them violently, scornfully toward the wastebasket. It received a part, allowing the rest to spill untidily over the floor. The girl smiled ironically, seeing in the mess a simile of her own earnest endeavor to inculcate knowledge into her indifferent classes.

Yes, it was like that; a few of the ideas which she tried to put into the minds behind those baffling ebony, bronze, and gold faces reached their destination. The others were left scattered about. And, like the gay, indifferent wastebasket, it wasn't their fault. No, it wasn't the fault of those minds back of the diverse colored faces. It was, rather, the fault of the method, the general idea behind the system. Like her own hurried shot at the basket, the aim was bad, the material drab and badly prepared for its purpose.

This great community, she thought, was no longer a school. It had grown into a machine. It was now a show place in the black belt, exemplification of the white man's magnanimity, refutation of the black man's inefficiency. Life had died out of it. It was, Helga decided, now only a big knife with cruelly sharp edges ruthlessly cutting all to a pattern, the white man's pattern. Teachers as well as students were subjected to the paring process, for it tolerated no innovations, no individualisms. Ideas it rejected, and looked with open hostility on one and all who had the temerity to offer a suggestion or ever so mildly express a disapproval. Enthusiasm, spontaneity, if not actually suppressed, were at least openly regretted as unladylike or ungentlemanly qualities. The place was smug and fat with self-satisfaction.

A peculiar characteristic trait, cold, slowly accumulated unreason in which all values were distorted or else ceased to exist, had with surprising ferociousness shaken the bulwarks of that self-restraint which was also, curiously, a part of her nature. And now that it had waned as quickly as it had risen, she smiled again, and this time the smile held a faint amusement, which wiped away the little hardness which had congealed her lovely face. Nevertheless she was soothed by the impetuous discharge of violence, and a sigh of relief came from her.

She said aloud, quietly, dispassionately: "Well, I'm through with that," and, shutting off the hard, bright blaze of the over-head lights, went back to her chair and settled down with an odd gesture of sudden soft collapse, like a person who had been for months fighting the devil and then unexpectedly had turned round and agreed to do his bidding.

Helga Crane had taught in Naxos for almost two years, at first with the keen joy and zest of those immature people who have dreamed dreams of doing good to their fellow men. But gradually this zest was blotted out, giving place to a deep hatred for the trivial hypocrisies and careless cruelties which were, unintentionally perhaps, a part of the Naxos policy of uplift. Yet she had continued to try not only to teach, but to befriend those happy singing children, whose charm and dis-tinctiveness the school was so surely ready to destroy. Instinc-tively Helga was aware that their smiling submissiveness covered many poignant heartaches and perhaps much secret contempt for their instructors. But she was powerless. In Naxos between teacher and student, between condescending author-ity and smoldering resentment, the gulf was too great, and too few had tried to cross it. It couldn't be spanned by one sympa-thetic teacher. It was useless to offer her atom of friendship, which under the existing conditions was neither wanted nor understood.

Nor was the general atmosphere of Naxos, its air of self-rightness and intolerant dislike of difference, the best of medi-ums for a pretty, solitary girl with no family connections. Helga's essentially likable and charming personality was smudged out. She had felt this for a long time. Now she faced with determi-nation that other truth which she had refused to formulate in her thoughts, the fact that she was utterly unfitted for teach-ing, even for mere existence, in Naxos. She was a failure here. She had, she conceded now, been silly, obstinate, to persist for so long. A failure. Therefore, no need, no use, to stay longer. Suddenly she longed for immediate departure. How good, she thought, to go now, tonight!—and frowned to remember how

impossible that would be. "The dignitaries," she said, "are not
in their offices, and there will be yards and yards of red tape to
unwind, gigantic, impressive spools of it."

And there was James Vayle to be told, and much-needed
money to be got. James, she decided, had better be told at
once. She looked at the clock racing indifferently on. No, too
late. It would have to be tomorrow.

She hated to admit that money was the most serious difficulty. Knowing full well that it was important, she nevertheless
rebelled at the unalterable truth that it could influence her actions, block her desires. A sordid necessity to be grappled with.
With Helga it was almost a superstition that to concede to
money its importance magnified its power. Still, in spite of
her reluctance and distaste, her financial situation would have
to be faced, and plans made, if she were to get away from
Naxos with anything like the haste which she now so ardently
desired.

Most of her earnings had gone into clothes, into books, into
the furnishings of the room which held her. All her life Helga
Crane had loved and longed for nice things. Indeed, it was this
craving, this urge for beauty which had helped to bring her
into disfavor in Naxos—"pride" and "vanity" her detractors
called it.

The sum owing to her by the school would just a little more
than buy her ticket back to Chicago. It was too near the end of
the school term to hope to get teaching-work anywhere. If she
couldn't find something else, she would have to ask Uncle
Peter for a loan. Uncle Peter was, she knew, the one relative
who thought kindly, or even calmly, of her. Her step-father,
her step-brothers and sisters, and the numerous cousins, aunts,
and other uncles could not be even remotely considered. She
laughed a little, scornfully, reflecting that the antagonism was
mutual, or, perhaps, just a trifle keener on her side than on
theirs. They feared and hated her. She pitied and despised
them. Uncle Peter was different. In his contemptuous way he
was fond of her. Her beautiful, unhappy mother had been
his favorite sister. Even so, Helga Crane knew that he would
be more likely to help her because her need would strengthen
his oft-repeated conviction that because of her Negro blood
she would never amount to anything, than from motives of

affection or loving memory. This knowledge, in its present aspect of truth, irritated her to an astonishing degree. She regarded Uncle Peter almost vindictively, although always he had been extraordinarily generous with her and she fully intended to ask his assistance. "A beggar," she thought ruefully, "cannot expect to choose."

Returning to James Vayle, her thoughts took on the frigidity of complete determination. Her resolution to end her stay in Naxos would of course inevitably end her engagement to James. She had been engaged to him since her first semester there, when both had been new workers, and both were lonely. Together they had discussed their work and problems in adjustment, and had drifted into a closer relationship. Bitterly she reflected that James had speedily and with entire ease fitted into his niche. He was now completely "naturalized," as they used laughingly to call it. Helga, on the other hand, had never quite achieved the unmistakable Naxos mold, would never achieve it, in spite of much trying. She could neither conform, nor be happy in her unconformity. This she saw clearly now, and with cold anger at all the past futile effort. What a waste! How pathetically she had struggled in those first months and with what small success. A lack somewhere. Always she had considered it a lack of understanding on the part of the community, but in her present new revolt she realized that the fault had been partly hers. A lack of acquiescence. She hadn't really wanted to be made over. This thought bred a sense of shame, a feeling of ironical disillusion. Evidently there were parts of her she couldn't be proud of. The revealing picture of her past striving was too humiliating. It was as if she had deliberately planned to steal an ugly thing, for which she had no desire, and had been found out.

Ironically she visualized the discomfort of James Vayle. How her maladjustment had bothered him! She had a faint notion that it was behind his ready assent to her suggestion anent a longer engagement than, originally, they had planned. He was liked and approved of in Naxos and loathed the idea that the girl he was to marry couldn't manage to win liking and approval also. Instinctively Helga had known that secretly he had placed the blame upon her. How right he had been! Certainly his attitude had gradually changed, though he still gave her his attentions. Naxos pleased him and he had become content with life as it was lived there. No longer lonely, he was now one of the community and so beyond the need or the desire to discuss its affairs and its failings with an outsider. She was, she knew, in a queer indefinite way, a disturbing factor. She knew too that a something held him, a something against which he was powerless. The idea that she was in but one nameless way necessary to him filled her with a sensation amounting almost to shame. And yet his mute helplessness against that ancient appeal by which she held him pleased her and fed her vanity— gave her a feeling of power. At the same time she shrank away from it, subtly aware of possibilities she herself couldn't predict.

Helga's own feelings defeated inquiry, but honestly confronted, all pretense brushed aside, the dominant one, she suspected, was relief. At least, she felt no regret that tomorrow would mark the end of any claim she had upon him. The surety that the meeting would be a clash annoyed her, for she had no talent for quarreling—when possible she preferred to flee. That was all.

The family of James Vayle, in near-by Atlanta, would be glad. They had never liked the engagement, had never liked Helga Crane. Her own lack of family disconcerted them. No family. That was the crux of the whole matter. For Helga, it accounted for everything, her failure here in Naxos, her former loneliness in Nashville. It even accounted for her engagement to James. Negro society, she had learned, was as complicated and as rigid in its ramifications as the highest strata of white society. If you couldn't prove your ancestry and connections, you were tolerated, but you didn't "belong." You could be queer, or even attractive, or bad, or brilliant, or even love beauty and such nonsense if you were a Rankin, or a Leslie, or a Scoville; in other words, if you had a family. But if you were just plain Helga Crane, of whom nobody had ever heard, it was presumptuous of you to be anything but inconspicuous and conformable.

To relinquish James Vayle would most certainly be social suicide, for the Vayles were people of consequence. The fact that they were a "first family" had been one of James's attractions for the obscure Helga. She had wanted social background, but—she had not imagined that it could be so stuffy.

She made a quick movement of impatience and stood up. As she did so, the room whirled about her in an impish, hateful way. Familiar objects seemed suddenly unhappily distant. Faintness closed about her like a vise. She swayed, her small, slender hands gripping the chair arms for support. In a moment the faintness receded, leaving in its wake a sharp resentment at the trick which her strained nerves had played upon her. And after a moment's rest she got hurriedly into bed, leaving her room disorderly for the first time.

Books and papers scattered about the floor, fragile stockings and underthings and the startling green and gold negligee dripping about on chairs and stool, met the encounter of the amazed eyes of the girl who came in the morning to awaken Helga Crane.

Two

S HE woke in the morning unrefreshed and with that feeling of half-terrified apprehension peculiar to Christmas and birthday mornings. A long moment she lay puzzling under the sun streaming in a golden flow through the yellow curtains. Then her mind returned to the night before. She had decided to leave Naxos. That was it.

Sharply she began to probe her decision. Reviewing the situation carefully, frankly, she felt no wish to change her resolution. Except—that it would be inconvenient. Much as she wanted to shake the dust of the place from her feet forever, she realized that there would be difficulties. Red tape. James Vayle. Money. Other work. Regretfully she was forced to acknowledge that it would be vastly better to wait until June, the close of the school year. Not so long, really. Half of March, April, May, some of June. Surely she could endure for that much longer conditions which she had borne for nearly two years. By an effort of will, her will, it could be done.

But this reflection, sensible, expedient, though it was, did not reconcile her. To remain seemed too hard. Could she do it? Was it possible in the present rebellious state of her feelings? The uneasy sense of being engaged with some formidable antagonist, nameless and un-understood, startled her. It wasn't, she was suddenly aware, merely the school and its ways and its decorous stupid people that oppressed her. There was something else, some other more ruthless force, a quality within herself, which was frustrating her, had always frustrated her, kept her from getting the things she had wanted. Still wanted.

But just what did she want? Barring a desire for material security, gracious ways of living, a profusion of lovely clothes, and a goodly share of envious admiration, Helga Crane didn't know, couldn't tell. But there was, she knew, something else. Happiness, she supposed. Whatever that might be. What, exactly, she wondered, was happiness. Very positively she wanted it. Yet her conception of it had no tangibility. She couldn't define it, isolate it, and contemplate it as she could some other abstract things. Hatred, for instance. Or kindness.

The strident ringing of a bell somewhere in the building brought back the fierce resentment of the night. It crystallized her wavering determination.

From long habit her biscuit-coloured feet had slipped mechanically out from under the covers at the bell's first unkind jangle. Leisurely she drew them back and her cold anger vanished as she decided that, now, it didn't at all matter if she failed to appear at the monotonous distasteful breakfast which was provided for her by the school as part of her wages.

In the corridor beyond her door was a medley of noises incident to the rising and preparing for the day at the same hour of many schoolgirls—foolish giggling, indistinguishable snatches of merry conversation, distant gurgle of running water, patter of slippered feet, low-pitched singing, good-natured admonitions to hurry, slamming of doors, clatter of various unnamable articles, and—suddenly—calamitous silence.

Helga ducked her head under the covers in the vain attempt to shut out what she knew would fill the pregnant silence—the sharp sarcastic voice of the dormitory matron. It came.

"Well! Even if every last one of you did come from homes where you weren't taught any manners, you might at least try to pretend that you're capable of learning some here, now that you have the opportunity. Who slammed the shower-baths door?"

Silence.

"Well, you needn't trouble to answer. It's rude, as all of you know. But it's just as well, because none of you can tell the truth. Now hurry up. Don't let me hear of a single one of you being late for breakfast. If I do there'll be extra work for everybody on Saturday. And *please* at least try to act like ladies and not like savages from the backwoods."

On her side of the door, Helga was wondering if it had ever occurred to the lean and desiccated Miss MacGooden that most of her charges had actually come from the backwoods. Quite recently too. Miss MacGooden, humorless, prim, ugly, with a face like dried leather, prided herself on being a "lady" from one of the best families—an uncle had been a congressman in the period of the Reconstruction. She was therefore, Helga Crane reflected, perhaps unable to perceive that the inducement to act like a lady, her own acrimonious example, was slight, if not altogether negative. And thinking on Miss Mac-Gooden's "ladyness," Helga grinned a little as she remembered that one's expressed reason for never having married, or intending to marry. There were, so she had been given to understand, things in the matrimonial state that were of necessity entirely too repulsive for a lady of delicate and sensitive nature to submit to.

Soon the forcibly shut-off noises began to be heard again, as the evidently vanishing image of Miss MacGooden evaporated from the short memories of the ladies-in-making. Preparations for the intake of the day's quota of learning went on again. Almost naturally.

"So much for that!" said Helga, getting herself out of bed.

She walked to the window and stood looking down into the great quadrangle below, at the multitude of students streaming from the six big dormitories which, two each, flanked three of its sides, and assembling into neat phalanxes preparatory to marching in military order to the sorry breakfast in Jones Hall on the fourth side. Here and there a male member of the faculty, important and resplendent in the regalia of an army officer, would pause in his prancing or strutting, to jerk a negligent or offending student into the proper attitude or place. The massed phalanxes increased in size and number, blotting out pavements, bare earth, and grass. And about it all was a depressing silence, a sullenness almost, until with a horrible abruptness the waiting band blared into "The Star Spangled Banner." The goose-step began. Left, right. Left, right. Forward! March! The automatons moved. The squares disintegrated into fours. Into twos. Disappeared into the gaping doors of Jones Hall. After the last pair of marchers had entered, the huge doors were closed. A few unlucky latecomers, apparently already discouraged, tugged half-heartedly at the knobs, and finding, as they had evidently expected, that they were indeed barred out, turned resignedly away.

Helga Crane turned away from the window, a shadow dimming the pale amber loveliness of her face. Seven o'clock it was now. At twelve those children who by some accident had been a little minute or two late would have their first meal after five hours of work and so-called education. Discipline, it was called.

There came a light knocking on her door.

"Come in," invited Helga unenthusiastically. The door opened to admit Margaret Creighton, another teacher in the English department and to Helga the most congenial member of the whole Naxos faculty. Margaret, she felt, appreciated her.

Seeing Helga still in night robe seated on the bedside in a mass of cushions, idly dangling a mule across bare toes like one with all the time in the world before her, she exclaimed in dismay: "Helga Crane, do you know what time it is? Why, it's long after half past seven. The students—"

"Yes, I know," said Helga defiantly, "the students are coming out from breakfast. Well, let them. I, for one, wish that there was some way that they could forever stay out from the poisonous stuff thrown at them, literally thrown at them, Margaret Creighton, for food. Poor things."

Margaret laughed. "That's just ridiculous sentiment, Helga, and you know it. But you haven't had any breakfast, yourself. Jim Vayle asked if you were sick. Of course nobody knew. You never tell anybody anything about yourself. I said I'd look in on you."

"Thanks awfully," Helga responded, indifferently. She was watching the sunlight dissolve from thick orange into pale yellow. Slowly it crept across the room, wiping out in its path the morning shadows. She wasn't interested in what the other was saying.

"If you don't hurry, you'll be late to your first class. Can I help you?" Margaret offered uncertainly. She was a little afraid of Helga. Nearly everyone was.

"No. Thanks all the same." Then quickly in another, warmer tone: "I do mean it. Thanks, a thousand times, Margaret. I'm really awfully grateful, but—you see, it's like this, I'm not going to be late to my class. I'm not going to be there at all."

The visiting girl, standing in relief, like old walnut against the buff-colored wall, darted a quick glance at Helga. Plainly she was curious. But she only said formally: "Oh, then you *are* sick." For something there was about Helga which discouraged questionings.

No, Helga wasn't sick. Not physically. She was merely disgusted. Fed up with Naxos. If that could be called sickness.

The truth was that she had made up her mind to leave. That very day. She could no longer abide being connected with a place of shame, lies, hypocrisy, cruelty, servility, and snobbishness. "It ought," she concluded, "to be shut down by law."

"But, Helga, you can't go now. Not in the middle of the term." The kindly Margaret was distressed.

"But I can. And I am. Today."

"They'll never let you," prophesied Margaret.

"*They* can't stop me. Trains leave here for civilization every day. All that's needed is money," Helga pointed out.

"Yes, of course. Everybody knows that. What I mean is that you'll only hurt yourself in your profession. They won't give you a reference if you jump up and leave like this now. At this time of the year. You'll be put on the black list. And you'll find it hard to get another teaching-job. Naxos has enormous influence in the South. Better wait till school closes."

"Heaven forbid," answered Helga fervently, "that I should ever again want work anywhere in the South! I hate it." And fell silent, wondering for the hundredth time just what form of vanity it was that had induced an intelligent girl like Margaret Creighton to turn what was probably nice live crinkly hair, perfectly suited to her smooth dark skin and agreeable round features, into a dead straight, greasy, ugly mass.

Looking up from her watch, Margaret said: "Well, I've really got to run, or I'll be late myself. And since I'm staying— Better think it over, Helga. There's no place like Naxos, you know. Pretty good salaries, decent rooms, plenty of men, and all that. Ta-ta." The door slid to behind her.

But in another moment it opened. She was back. "I do wish you'd stay. It's nice having you here, Helga. We all think so. Even the dead ones. We need a few decorations to brighten our sad lives." And again she was gone.

Helga was unmoved. She was no longer concerned with what anyone in Naxos might think of her, for she was now in love with the piquancy of leaving. Automatically her fingers adjusted the Chinese-looking pillows on the low couch that served for her bed. Her mind was busy with plans for departure. Packing, money, trains, and—could she get a berth?

Three

O N one side of the long, white, hot sand road that split the flat green, there was a little shade, for it was bordered with trees. Helga Crane walked there so that the sun could not so easily get at her. As she went slowly across the empty campus she was conscious of a vague tenderness for the scene spread out before her. It was so incredibly lovely, so appealing, and so facile. The trees in their spring beauty sent through her restive mind a sharp thrill of pleasure. Seductive, charming, and beckoning as cities were, they had not this easy unhuman loveliness. The trees, she thought, on city avenues and boulevards, in city parks and gardens, were tamed, held prisoners in a surrounding maze of human beings. Here they were free. It was human beings who were prisoners. It was too bad. In the midst of all this radiant life. They weren't, she knew, even conscious of its presence. Perhaps there was too much of it, and therefore it was less than nothing.

In response to her insistent demand she had been told that Dr. Anderson could give her twenty minutes at eleven o'clock. Well, she supposed that she could say all that she had to say in twenty minutes, though she resented being limited. Twenty minutes. In Naxos, she was as unimportant as that.

He was a new man, this principal, for whom Helga remembered feeling unaccountably sorry, when last September he had first been appointed to Naxos as its head. For some reason she had liked him, although she had seen little of him: he was so frequently away on publicity and money-raising tours. And as yet he had made but few and slight changes in the running of the school. Now she was a little irritated at finding herself wondering just how she was going to tell him of her decision. What did it matter to him? Why should she mind if it did? But there returned to her that indistinct sense of sympathy for the remote silent man with the tired gray eyes, and she wondered again by what fluke of fate such a man, apparently a humane and understanding person, had chanced into the command of this cruel educational machine. Suddenly, her own resolve loomed as an almost direct unkindness. This increased her annoyance and discomfort. A sense of defeat, of being cheated of justification, closed down on her. Absurd!

She arrived at the administration building in a mild rage, as unreasonable as it was futile, but once inside she had a sudden attack of nerves at the prospect of traversing that great outer room which was the workplace of some twenty-odd people. This was a disease from which Helga had suffered at intervals all her life, and it was a point of honor, almost, with her never to give way to it. So, instead of turning away, as she felt inclined, she walked on, outwardly indifferent. Half-way down the long aisle which divided the room, the principal's secretary, a huge black man, surged toward her.

"Good-morning, Miss Crane, Dr. Anderson will see you in a few moments. Sit down right here."

She felt the inquiry in the shuttered eyes. For some reason this dissipated her self-consciousness and restored her poise. Thanking him, she seated herself, really careless now of the glances of the stenographers, book-keepers, clerks. Their curiosity and slightly veiled hostility no longer touched her. Her coming departure had released her from the need for conciliation which had irked her for so long. It was pleasant to Helga Crane to be able to sit calmly looking out of the window on to the smooth lawn, where a few leaves quite prematurely fallen dotted the grass, for once uncaring whether the frock which she wore roused disapproval or envy.

Turning from the window, her gaze wandered contemptuously over the dull attire of the women workers. Drab colors, mostly navy blue, black, brown, unrelieved, save for a scrap of white or tan about the hands and necks. Fragments of a speech made by the dean of women floated through her thoughts— "Bright colors are vulgar"—"Black, gray, brown, and navy blue are the most becoming colors for colored people"— "Dark-complected people shouldn't wear yellow, or green or red."—The dean was a woman from one of the "first families" —a great "race" woman; she, Helga Crane, a despised mulatto, but something intuitive, some unanalyzed driving spirit of loyalty to the inherent racial need for gorgeousness told her that bright colours *were* fitting and that dark-complexioned people *should* wear yellow, green, and red. Black, brown, and gray were ruinous to them, actually destroyed the luminous tones lurking in their dusky skins. One of the loveliest sights Helga had ever seen had been a sooty black girl decked out in a flaming orange dress, which a horrified matron had next day consigned to the dyer. Why, she wondered, didn't someone write *A Plea for Color*?

These people yapped loudly of race, of race consciousness, of race pride, and yet suppressed its most delightful manifestations, love of color, joy of rhythmic motion, naïve, spontaneous laughter. Harmony, radiance, and simplicity, all the essentials of spiritual beauty in the race they had marked for destruction.

She came back to her own problems. Clothes had been one of her difficulties in Naxos. Helga Crane loved clothes, elaborate ones. Nevertheless, she had tried not to offend. But with small success, for, although she had affected the deceptively simple variety, the hawk eyes of dean and matrons had detected the subtle difference from their own irreproachably conventional garments. Too, they felt that the colors were queer; dark purples, royal blues, rich greens, deep reds, in soft, luxurious woolens, or heavy, clinging silks. And the trimmings—when Helga used them at all—seemed to them odd. Old laces, strange embroideries, dim brocades. Her faultless, slim shoes made them uncomfortable and her small plain hats seemed to them positively indecent. Helga smiled inwardly at the thought that whenever there was an evening affair for the faculty, the dear ladies probably held their breaths until she had made her appearance. They existed in constant fear that she might turn out in an evening dress. The proper evening wear in Naxos was afternoon attire. And one could, if one wished, garnish the hair with flowers.

Quick, muted footfalls sounded. The secretary had returned.

"Dr. Anderson will see you now, Miss Crane."

She rose, followed, and was ushered into the guarded sanctum, without having decided just what she was to say. For a moment she felt behind her the open doorway and then the gentle impact of its closing. Before her at a great desk her eyes picked out the figure of a man, at first blurred slightly in outline in that dimmer light. At his "Miss Crane?" her lips formed for speech, but no sound came. She was aware of inward confusion. For her the situation seemed charged, unaccountably, with strangeness and something very like hysteria. An almost overpowering desire to laugh seized her. Then, miraculously, a complete ease, such as she had never known in Naxos, possessed her. She smiled, nodded in answer to his questioning salutation, and with a gracious "Thank you" dropped into the chair which he indicated. She looked at him frankly now, this man still young, thirty-five perhaps, and found it easy to go on in the vein of a simple statement.

"Dr. Anderson, I'm sorry to have to confess that I've failed in my job here. I've made up my mind to leave. Today."

A short, almost imperceptible silence, then a deep voice of peculiarly pleasing resonance, asking gently: "You don't like Naxos, Miss Crane?"

She evaded. "Naxos, the place? Yes, I like it. Who wouldn't like it? It's so beautiful. But I—well—I don't seem to fit here."

The man smiled, just a little. "The school? You don't like the school?"

The words burst from her. "No, I don't like it. I hate it!"

"Why?" The question was detached, too detached.

In the girl blazed a desire to wound. There he sat, staring dreamily out of the window, blatantly unconcerned with her or her answer. Well, she'd tell him. She pronounced each word with deliberate slowness.

"Well, for one thing, I hate hypocrisy. I hate cruelty to students, and to teachers who can't fight back. I hate backbiting, and sneaking, and petty jealousy. Naxos? It's hardly a place at all. It's more like some loathsome, venomous disease. Ugh! Everybody spending his time in a malicious hunting for the weaknesses of others, spying, grudging, scratching."

"I see. And you don't think it might help to cure us, to have someone who doesn't approve of these things stay with us? Even just one person, Miss Crane?"

She wondered if this last was irony. She suspected it was humor and so ignored the half-pleading note in his voice.

"No, I don't! It doesn't do the disease any good. Only irritates it. And it makes me unhappy, dissatisfied. It isn't pleasant to be always made to appear in the wrong, even when I know I'm right."

His gaze was on her now, searching. "Queer," she thought,

"how some brown people have gray eyes. Gives them a strange, unexpected appearance. A little frightening."

The man said, kindly: "Ah, you're unhappy. And for the reasons you've stated?"

"Yes, partly. Then, too, the people here don't like me. They don't think I'm in the spirit of the work. And I'm not, not if it means suppression of individuality and beauty."

"And does it?"

"Well, it seems to work out that way."

"How old are you, Miss Crane?"

She resented this, but she told him, speaking with what curtness she could command only the bare figure: "Twenty-three."

"Twenty-three. I see. Some day you'll learn that lies, injustice, and hypocrisy are a part of every ordinary community. Most people achieve a sort of protective immunity, a kind of callousness, toward them. If they didn't, they couldn't endure. I think there's less of these evils here than in most places, but because we're trying to do such a big thing, to aim so high, the ugly things show more, they irk some of us more. Service is like clean white linen, even the tiniest speck shows." He went on, explaining, amplifying, pleading.

Helga Crane was silent, feeling a mystifying yearning which sang and throbbed in her. She felt again the urge for service, not now for her people, but for this man who was talking so earnestly of his work, his plans, his hopes. An insistent need to be a part of them sprang in her. With compunction tweaking at her heart for even having entertained the notion of deserting him, she resolved not only to remain until June, but to return next year. She was shamed, yet stirred. It was not sacrifice she felt now, but actual desire to stay, and to come back next year.

He came, at last, to the end of the long speech, only part of which she had heard. "You see, you understand?" he urged.

"Yes, oh yes, I do."

"What we need is more people like you, people with a sense of values, and proportion, an appreciation of the rarer things of life. You have something to give which we badly need here in Naxos. You mustn't desert us, Miss Crane."

She nodded, silent. He had won her. She knew that she

would stay. "It's an elusive something," he went on. "Perhaps I can best explain it by the use of that trite phrase, 'You're a lady.' You have dignity and breeding."

At these words turmoil rose again in Helga Crane. The intricate pattern of the rug which she had been studying escaped her. The shamed feeling which had been her penance evaporated. Only a lacerated pride remained. She took firm hold of the chair arms to still the trembling of her fingers.

"If you're speaking of family, Dr. Anderson, why, I haven't any. I was born in a Chicago slum."

The man chose his words, carefully he thought. "That doesn't at all matter, Miss Crane. Financial, economic circumstances can't destroy tendencies inherited from good stock. You yourself prove that!"

Concerned with her own angry thoughts, which scurried here and there like trapped rats, Helga missed the import of his words. Her own words, her answer, fell like drops of hail.

"The joke is on you, Dr. Anderson. My father was a gambler who deserted my mother, a white immigrant. It is even uncertain that they were married. As I said at first, I don't belong here. I shall be leaving at once. This afternoon. Good-morning."

Four

LONG, soft white clouds, clouds like shreds of incredibly fine cotton, streaked the blue of the early evening sky. Over the flying landscape hung a very faint mist, disturbed now and then by a languid breeze. But no coolness invaded the heat of the train rushing north. The open windows of the stuffy day coach, where Helga Crane sat with others of her race, seemed only to intensify her discomfort. Her head ached with a steady pounding pain. This, added to her wounds of the spirit, made traveling something little short of a medieval torture. Desperately she was trying to right the confusion in her mind. The temper of the morning's interview rose before her like an ugly mutilated creature crawling horribly over the flying landscape of her thoughts. It was no use. The ugly thing pressed down on her, held her. Leaning back, she tried to doze as others were doing. The futility of her effort exasperated her.

Just what had happened to her there in that cool dim room under the quizzical gaze of those piercing gray eyes? Whatever it was had been so powerful, so compelling, that but for a few chance words she would still be in Naxos. And why had she permitted herself to be jolted into a rage so fierce, so illogical, so disastrous, that now after it was spent she sat despondent, sunk in shameful contrition? As she reviewed the manner of her departure from his presence, it seemed increasingly rude.

She didn't, she told herself, after all, like this Dr. Anderson. He was too controlled, too sure of himself and others. She detested cool, perfectly controlled people. Well, it didn't matter. He didn't matter. But she could not put him from her mind. She set it down to annoyance because of the cold discourtesy of her abrupt action. She disliked rudeness in anyone.

She had outraged her own pride, and she had terribly wronged her mother by her insidious implication. Why? Her thoughts lingered with her mother, long dead. A fair Scandinavian girl in love with life, with love, with passion, dreaming, and risking all in one blind surrender. A cruel sacrifice. In forgetting all but love she had forgotten, or had perhaps never known, that some things the world never forgives. But as Helga knew, she had remembered, or had learned in suffering and longing all the rest of her life. Her daughter hoped she had been happy, happy beyond most human creatures, in the little time it had lasted, the little time before that gay suave scoundrel, Helga's father, had left her. But Helga Crane doubted it. How could she have been? A girl gently bred, fresh from an older, more polished civilization, flung into poverty, sordidness, and dissipation. She visualized her now, sad, cold, and— yes, remote. The tragic cruelties of the years had left her a little pathetic, a little hard, and a little unapproachable.

That second marriage, to a man of her own race, but not of her own kind—so passionately, so instinctively resented by Helga even at the trivial age of six—she now understood as a grievous necessity. Even foolish, despised women must have food and clothing; even unloved little Negro girls must be somehow provided for. Memory, flown back to those years following the marriage, dealt her torturing stabs. Before her rose the pictures of her mother's careful management to avoid those ugly scarifying quarrels which even at this far-off time caused an uncontrollable shudder, her own childish self-effacement, the savage unkindness of her stepbrothers and sisters, and the jealous, malicious hatred of her mother's husband. Summers, winters, years, passing in one long, changeless stretch of aching misery of soul. Her mother's death, when Helga was fifteen. Her rescue by Uncle Peter, who had sent her to school, a school for Negroes, where for the first time she could breathe freely, where she discovered that because one was dark, one was not necessarily loathsome, and could, therefore, consider oneself without repulsion.

Six years. She had been happy there, as happy as a child unused to happiness dared be. There had been always a feeling of strangeness, of outsideness, and one of holding her breath for fear that it wouldn't last. It hadn't. It had dwindled gradually into eclipse of painful isolation. As she grew older, she became gradually aware of a difference between herself and the girls about her. They had mothers, fathers, brothers, and sisters of whom they spoke frequently, and who sometimes visited them. They went home for the vacations which Helga spent in the city where the school was located. They visited each other and knew many of the same people. Discontent for which there was no remedy crept upon her, and she was glad almost when these most peaceful years which she had yet known came to their end. She had been happier, but still horribly lonely.

She had looked forward with pleasant expectancy to working in Naxos when the chance came. And now this! What was it that stood in her way? Helga Crane couldn't explain it, put a name to it. She had tried in the early afternoon in her gentle but staccato talk with James Vayle. Even to herself her explanation had sounded inane and insufficient; no wonder James had been impatient and unbelieving. During their brief and unsatisfactory conversation she had had an odd feeling that he felt somehow cheated. And more than once she had been aware of a suggestion of suspicion in his attitude, a feeling that he was being duped, that he suspected her of some hidden purpose which he was attempting to discover.

Well, that was over. She would never be married to James Vayle now. It flashed upon her that, even had she remained in Naxos, she would never have been married to him. She couldn't have married him. Gradually, too, there stole into her thoughts of him a curious sensation of repugnance, for which she was at a loss to account. It was new, something unfelt before. Certainly she had never loved him overwhelmingly, not, for example, as her mother must have loved her father, but she *had* liked him, and she had expected to love him, after their marriage. People generally did love then, she imagined. No, she had not loved James, but she had wanted to. Acute nausea rose in her as she recalled the slight quivering of his lips sometimes when her hands had unexpectedly touched his; the throbbing vein in his forehead on a gay day when they had wandered off alone across the low hills and she had allowed him frequent kisses under the shelter of some low-hanging willows. Now she shivered a little, even in the hot train, as if she had suddenly come out from a warm scented place into cool, clear air. She must have been mad, she thought; but she couldn't tell why she thought so. This, too, bothered her.

Laughing conversation buzzed about her. Across the aisle a bronze baby, with bright staring eyes, began a fretful whining, which its young mother essayed to silence by a low droning croon. In the seat just beyond, a black and tan young pair were absorbed in the eating of a cold fried chicken, audibly crunching the ends of the crisp, browned bones. A little distance away a tired laborer slept noisily. Near him two children dropped the peelings of oranges and bananas on the already soiled floor. The smell of stale food and ancient tobacco irritated Helga like a physical pain. A man, a white man, strode through the packed car and spat twice, once in the exact centre of the dingy door panel, and once into the receptacle which held the drinking-water. Instantly Helga became aware of stinging thirst. Her eyes sought the small watch at her wrist. Ten hours to Chicago. Would she be lucky enough to prevail upon the conductor to let her occupy a berth, or would she have to remain here all night, without sleep, without food, without drink, and with that disgusting door panel to which her purposely averted eyes were constantly, involuntarily straying?

Her first effort was unsuccessful. An ill-natured "No, you know you can't," was the answer to her inquiry. But farther on along the road, there was a change of men. Her rebuff had made her reluctant to try again, but the entry of a farmer carrying a basket containing live chickens, which he deposited on the seat (the only vacant one) beside her, strengthened her weakened courage. Timidly, she approached the new conductor, an elderly gray-mustached man of pleasant appearance, who subjected her to a keen, appraising look, and then promised to see what could be done. She thanked him, gratefully, and went back to her shared seat, to wait anxiously. After half an hour he returned, saying he could "fix her up," there was a section she could have, adding: "It'll cost you ten dollars." She murmured: "All right. Thank you." It was twice the price and she needed every penny, but she knew she was fortunate to get it even at that, and so was very thankful, as she followed his tall, loping figure out of that car and through seemingly endless others, and at last into one where she could rest a little.

She undressed and lay down, her thoughts still busy with the morning's encounter. Why hadn't she grasped his meaning? Why, if she had said so much, hadn't she said more about herself and her mother? He would, she was sure, have understood, even sympathized. Why had she lost her temper and given way to angry half-truths?— Angry half-truths— Angry half—

Five

GRAY Chicago seethed, surged, and scurried about her. Helga shivered a little, drawing her light coat closer. She had forgotten how cold March could be under the pale skies of the North. But she liked it, this blustering wind. She would even have welcomed snow, for it would more clearly have marked the contrast between this freedom and the cage which Naxos had been to her. Not but what it was marked plainly enough by the noise, the dash, the crowds.

Helga Crane, who had been born in this dirty, mad, hurrying city, had no home here. She had not even any friends here. It would have to be, she decided, the Young Women's Christian Association. "Oh dear! The uplift. Poor, poor colored people. Well, no use stewing about it. I'll get a taxi to take me out, bag and baggage, then I'll have a hot bath and a really good meal, peep into the shops—mustn't buy anything—and then for Uncle Peter. Guess I won't phone. More effective if I surprise him."

It was late, very late, almost evening, when finally Helga turned her steps northward, in the direction of Uncle Peter's home. She had put it off as long as she could, for she detested her errand. The fact that that one day had shown her its acute necessity did not decrease her distaste. As she approached the North Side, the distaste grew. Arrived at last at the familiar door of the old stone house, her confidence in Uncle Peter's welcome deserted her. She gave the bell a timid push and then decided to turn away, to go back to her room and phone, or, better yet, to write. But before she could retreat, the door was opened by a strange red-faced maid, dressed primly in black and white. This increased Helga's mistrust. Where, she wondered, was the ancient Rose, who had, ever since she could remember, served her uncle.

The hostile "Well?" of this new servant forcibly recalled the reason for her presence there. She said firmly: "Mr. Nilssen, please."

"Mr. Nilssen's not in," was the pert retort. "Will you see Mrs. Nilssen?"

Helga was startled. "Mrs. Nilssen! I beg your pardon, did you say Mrs. Nilssen?"

"I did," answered the maid shortly, beginning to close the door.

"What is it, Ida?" A woman's soft voice sounded from within.

"Someone for Mr. Nilssen, m'am." The girl looked embarrassed.

In Helga's face the blood rose in a deep-red stain. She explained: "Helga Crane, his niece."

"She says she's his niece, m'am."

"Well, have her come in."

There was no escape. She stood in the large reception hall, and was annoyed to find herself actually trembling. A woman, tall, exquisitely gowned, with shining gray hair piled high, came forward murmuring in a puzzled voice: "His niece, did you say?"

"Yes, Helga Crane. My mother was his sister, Karen Nilssen. I've been away. I didn't know Uncle Peter had married." Sensitive to atmosphere, Helga had felt at once the latent antagonism in the woman's manner.

"Oh, yes! I remember about you now. I'd forgotten for a moment. *Well*, he isn't exactly your uncle, is he? Your mother wasn't married, was she? I mean, to your father?"

"I—I don't know," stammered the girl, feeling pushed down to the uttermost depths of ignominy.

"Of course she wasn't." The clear, low voice held a positive note. "Mr. Nilssen has been very kind to you, supported you, sent you to school. But you mustn't expect anything else. And you mustn't come here any more. It—well, frankly, it isn't convenient. I'm sure an intelligent girl like yourself can understand that."

"Of course," Helga agreed, coldly, freezingly, but her lips quivered. She wanted to get away as quickly as possible. She reached the door. There was a second of complete silence, then Mrs. Nilssen's voice, a little agitated: "And please remember that my husband is not your uncle. No indeed! Why, that, that would make me your aunt! He's not—"

But at last the knob had turned in Helga's fumbling hand. She gave a little unpremeditated laugh and slipped out. When she was in the street, she ran. Her only impulse was to get as far away from her uncle's house, and this woman, his wife, who so plainly wished to dissociate herself from the outrage of her very existence. She was torn with mad fright, an emotion against which she knew but two weapons: to kick and scream, or to flee.

The day had lengthened. It was evening and much colder, but Helga Crane was unconscious of any change, so shaken she was and burning. The wind cut her like a knife, but she did not feel it. She ceased her frantic running, aware at last of the curious glances of passers-by. At one spot, for a moment less frequented than others, she stopped to give heed to her disordered appearance. Here a man, well groomed and pleasant-spoken, accosted her. On such occasions she was wont to reply scathingly, but, tonight, his pale Caucasian face struck her breaking faculties as too droll. Laughing harshly, she threw at him the words: "You're not my uncle."

He retired in haste, probably thinking her drunk, or possibly a little mad.

Night fell, while Helga Crane in the rushing swiftness of a roaring elevated train sat numb. It was as if all the bogies and goblins that had beset her unloved, unloving, and unhappy childhood had come to life with tenfold power to hurt and frighten. For the wound was deeper in that her long freedom from their presence had rendered her the more vulnerable. Worst of all was the fact that under the stinging hurt she understood and sympathized with Mrs. Nilssen's point of view, as always she had been able to understand her mother's, her step-father's, and his children's points of view. She saw herself for an obscene sore in all their lives, at all costs to be hidden. She understood, even while she resented. It would have been easier if she had not.

Later in the bare silence of her tiny room she remembered the unaccomplished object of her visit. Money. Characteristically, while admitting its necessity, and even its undeniable desirability, she dismissed its importance. Its elusive quality she had as yet never known. She would find work of some kind. Perhaps the library. The idea clung. Yes, certainly the library. She knew books and loved them.

She stood intently looking down into the glimmering street,

far below, swarming with people, merging into little eddies and disengaging themselves to pursue their own in individual ways. A few minutes later she stood in the doorway, drawn by an uncontrollable desire to mingle with the crowd. The purple sky showed tremulous clouds piled up, drifting here and there with a sort of endless lack of purpose. Very like the myriad human beings pressing hurriedly on. Looking at these, Helga caught herself wondering who they were, what they did, and of what they thought. What was passing behind those dark molds of flesh. Did they really think at all? Yet, as she stepped out into the moving multi-colored crowd, there came to her a queer feeling of enthusiasm, as if she were tasting some agreeable, exotic food—sweetbreads, smothered with truffles and mushrooms—perhaps. And, oddly enough, she felt, too, that she had come home. She, Helga Crane, who had no home.

Six

HELGA woke to the sound of rain. The day was leaden gray, and misty black, and dullish white. She was not surprised, the night had promised it. She made a little frown, remembering that it was today that she was to search for work.

She dressed herself carefully, in the plainest garments she possessed, a suit of fine blue twill faultlessly tailored, from whose left pocket peeped a gay kerchief, an unadorned, heavy silk blouse, a small, smart, fawn-colored hat, and slim, brown oxfords, and chose a brown umbrella. In a near-by street she sought out an appealing little restaurant, which she had noted in her last night's ramble through the neighborhood, for the thick cups and the queer dark silver of the Young Women's Christian Association distressed her.

After a slight breakfast she made her way to the library, that ugly gray building, where was housed much knowledge and a little wisdom, on interminable shelves. The friendly person at the desk in the hall bestowed on her a kindly smile when Helga stated her business and asked for directions.

"The corridor to your left, then the second door to your right," she was told.

Outside the indicated door, for half a second she hesitated, then braced herself and went in. In less than a quarter of an hour she came out, in surprised disappointment. "Library training"—"civil service"—"library school"—"classification" —"cataloguing"—"training class"—"examination"—"probation period"—flitted through her mind.

"How erudite they must be!" she remarked sarcastically to herself, and ignored the smiling curiosity of the desk person as she went through the hall to the street. For a long moment she stood on the high stones steps above the avenue, then shrugged her shoulders and stepped down. It *was* a disappointment, but of course there were other things. She would find something else. But what? Teaching, even substitute teaching, was hopeless now, in March. She had no business training, and the shops didn't employ colored clerks or sales-people, not even the smaller ones. She couldn't sew, she couldn't cook. Well, she *could* do housework, or wait on table, for a short time at least. Until she got a little money together. With this thought she remembered that the Young Women's Christian Association maintained an employment agency.

"Of course, the very thing!" she exclaimed, aloud. "I'll go straight back."

But, though the day was still drear, rain had ceased to fall, and Helga, instead of returning, spent hours in aimless strolling about the hustling streets of the Loop district. When at last she did retrace her steps, the business day had ended, and the employment office was closed. This frightened her a little, this and the fact that she had spent money, too much money, for a book and a tapestry purse, things which she wanted, but did not need and certainly could not afford. Regretful and dismayed, she resolved to go without her dinner, as a self-inflicted penance, as well as an economy—and she would be at the employment office the first thing tomorrow morning.

But it was not until three days more had passed that Helga Crane sought the Association, or any other employment office. And then it was sheer necessity that drove her there, for her money had dwindled to a ridiculous sum. She had put off the hated moment, had assured herself that she was tired, needed a bit of vacation, was due one. It had been pleasant, the leisure, the walks, the lake, the shops and streets with their gay colors, their movement, after the great quiet of Naxos. Now she was panicky.

In the office a few nondescript women sat scattered about on the long rows of chairs. Some were plainly uninterested, others wore an air of acute expectancy, which disturbed Helga. Behind a desk two alert young women, both wearing a superior air, were busy writing upon and filing countless white cards. Now and then one stopped to answer the telephone.

"Y.W.C.A. employment. . . . Yes. . . . Spell it, please. . . . Sleep in or out? Thirty dollars? . . . Thank you, I'll send one right over."

Or, "I'm awfully sorry, we haven't anybody right now, but I'll send you the first one that comes in."

Their manners were obtrusively business-like, but they ignored the already embarrassed Helga. Diffidently she approached the desk. The darker of the two looked up and turned on a little smile.

"Yes?" she inquired.

"I wonder if you can help me? I want work," Helga stated simply.

"Maybe. What kind? Have you references?"

Helga explained. She was a teacher. A graduate of Devon. Had been teaching in Naxos.

The girl was not interested. "Our kind of work wouldn't do for you," she kept repeating at the end of each of Helga's statements. "Domestic mostly."

When Helga said that she was willing to accept work of any kind, a slight, almost imperceptible change crept into her manner and her perfunctory smile disappeared. She repeated her question about the references. On learning that Helga had none, she said sharply, finally: "I'm sorry, but we never send out help without references."

With a feeling that she had been slapped, Helga Crane hurried out. After some lunch she sought out an employment agency on State Street. An hour passed in patient sitting. Then came her turn to be interviewed. She said, simply, that she wanted work, work of any kind. A competent young woman, whose eyes stared frog-like from great tortoise-shell-rimmed glasses, regarded her with an appraising look and asked for her history, past and present, not forgetting the "references." Helga told her that she was a graduate of Devon, had taught in Naxos. But even before she arrived at the explanation of the lack of references, the other's interest in her had faded.

"I'm sorry, but we have nothing that you would be interested in," she said and motioned to the next seeker, who immediately came forward, proffering several much worn papers.

"References," thought Helga, resentfully, bitterly, as she went out the door into the crowded garish street in search of another agency, where her visit was equally vain.

Days of this sort of thing. Weeks of it. And of the futile scanning and answering of newspaper advertisements. She traversed acres of streets, but it seemed that in that whole energetic place nobody wanted her services. At least not the kind that she offered. A few men, both white and black, offered her money, but the price of the money was too dear. Helga Crane did not feel inclined to pay it.

She began to feel terrified and lost. And she was a little hungry too, for her small money was dwindling and she felt the need to economize somehow. Food was the easiest.

In the midst of her search for work she felt horribly lonely too. This sense of loneliness increased, it grew to appalling proportions, encompassing her, shutting her off from all of life around her. Devastated she was, and always on the verge of weeping. It made her feel small and insignificant that in all the climbing massed city no one cared one whit about her.

Helga Crane was not religious. She took nothing on trust. Nevertheless on Sundays she attended the very fashionable, very high services in the Negro Episcopal church on Michigan Avenue. She hoped that some good Christian would speak to her, invite her to return, or inquire kindly if she was a stranger in the city. None did, and she became bitter, distrusting religion more than ever. She was herself unconscious of that faint hint of offishness which hung about her and repelled advances, an arrogance that stirred in people a peculiar irritation. They noticed her, admired her clothes, but that was all, for the self-sufficient uninterested manner adopted instinctively as a protective measure for her acute sensitiveness, in her child days, still clung to her.

An agitated feeling of disaster closed in on her, tightened. Then, one afternoon, coming in from the discouraging round of agencies and the vain answering of newspaper wants to the stark neatness of her room, she found between door and sill a small folded note. Spreading it open, she read:

> *Miss Crane:*
> *Please come into the employment office*
> *as soon as you return.*
>
> *Ida Ross*

Helga spent some time in the contemplation of this note. She was afraid to hope. Its possibilities made her feel a little hysterical. Finally, after removing the dirt of the dusty streets, she went down, down to that room where she had first felt the smallness of her commercial value. Subsequent failures had augmented her feeling of incompetence, but she resented the fact that these clerks were evidently aware of her unsuccess. It required all the pride and indifferent hauteur she could summon to support her in their presence. Her additional arrogance passed unnoticed by those for whom it was assumed. They were interested only in the business for which they had summoned her, that of procuring a traveling-companion for a lecturing female on her way to a convention.

"She wants," Miss Ross told Helga, "someone intelligent, someone who can help her get her speeches in order on the train. We thought of you right away. Of course, it isn't permanent. She'll pay your expenses and there'll be twenty-five dollars besides. She leaves tomorrow. Here's her address. You're to go to see her at five o'clock. It's after four now. I'll phone that you're on your way."

The presumptuousness of their certainty that she would snatch at the opportunity galled Helga. She became aware of a desire to be disagreeable. The inclination to fling the address of the lecturing female in their face stirred in her, but she remembered the lone five-dollar bill in the rare old tapestry purse swinging from her arm. She couldn't afford anger. So she thanked them very politely and set out for the home of Mrs. Hayes-Rore on Grand Boulevard, knowing full well that she intended to take the job, if the lecturing one would take her. Twenty-five dollars was not to be looked at with nose in air when one was the owner of but five. And meals—meals for four days at least.

Mrs. Hayes-Rore proved to be a plump lemon-colored woman with badly straightened hair and dirty finger-nails. Her direct, penetrating gaze was somewhat formidable. Notebook in hand, she gave Helga the impression of having risen early for consultation with other harassed authorities on the race problem, and having been in conference on the subject all day. Evidently, she had had little time or thought for the careful donning of the five-years-behind-the-mode garments which covered her, and which even in their youth could hardly have fitted or suited her. She had a tart personality, and prying. She approved of Helga, after asking her endless questions about her education and her opinions on the race problem, none of which she was permitted to answer, for Mrs. Hayes-Rore either went on to the next or answered the question herself by re-marking: "Not that it matters, if you can only do what I want done, and the girls at the 'Y' said that you could. I'm on the Board of Managers, and I know they wouldn't send me any-body who wasn't all right." After this had been repeated twice in a booming, oratorical voice, Helga felt that the Association secretaries had taken an awful chance in sending a person about whom they knew as little as they did about her.

"Yes, I'm sure you'll do. I don't really need ideas, I've plenty of my own. It's just a matter of getting someone to help me get my speeches in order, correct and condense them, you know. I leave at eleven in the morning. Can you be ready by then? . . . That's good. Better be here at nine. Now, don't disappoint me. I'm depending on you."

As she stepped into the street and made her way skillfully through the impassioned human traffic, Helga reviewed the plan which she had formed, while in the lecturing one's pres-ence, to remain in New York. There would be twenty-five dollars, and perhaps the amount of her return ticket. Enough for a start. Surely she could get work there. Everybody did. Anyway, she would have a reference.

With her decision she felt reborn. She began happily to paint the future in vivid colors. The world had changed to silver and life ceased to be a struggle and became a gay adventure. Even the advertisements in the shop windows seemed to shine with radiance.

Curious about Mrs. Hayes-Rore, on her return to the "Y" she went into the employment office, ostensibly to thank the girls and to report that that important woman would take her. Was there, she inquired, anything that she needed to know? Mrs. Hayes-Rore had appeared to put such faith in their recommendation of her that she felt almost obliged to give satisfaction. And she added: "I didn't get much chance to ask questions. She seemed so—er—busy."

Both the girls laughed. Helga laughed with them, surprised that she hadn't perceived before how really likable they were.

"We'll be through here in ten minutes. If you're not busy, come in and have your supper with us and we'll tell you about her," promised Miss Ross.

Seven

HAVING finally turned her attention to Helga Crane, Fortune now seemed determined to smile, to make amends for her shameful neglect. One had, Helga decided, only to touch the right button, to press the right spring, in order to attract the jade's notice.

For Helga that spring had been Mrs. Hayes-Rore. Ever afterwards on recalling that day on which with wellnigh empty purse and apprehensive heart she had made her way from the Young Women's Christian Association to the Grand Boulevard home of Mrs. Hayes-Rore, always she wondered at her own lack of astuteness in not seeing in the woman someone who by a few words was to have a part in the shaping of her life.

The husband of Mrs. Hayes-Rore had at one time been a dark thread in the soiled fabric of Chicago's South Side politics, who, departing this life hurriedly and unexpectedly and a little mysteriously, and somewhat before the whole of his suddenly acquired wealth had had time to vanish, had left his widow comfortably established with money and some of that prestige which in Negro circles had been his. All this Helga had learned from the secretaries at the "Y." And from numerous remarks dropped by Mrs. Hayes-Rore herself she was able to fill in the details more or less adequately.

On the train that carried them to New York, Helga had made short work of correcting and condensing the speeches, which Mrs. Hayes-Rore as a prominent "race" woman and an authority on the problem was to deliver before several meetings of the annual convention of the Negro Women's League of Clubs, convening the next week in New York. These speeches proved to be merely patchworks of others' speeches and opinions. Helga had heard other lecturers say the same things in Devon and again in Naxos. Ideas, phrases, and even whole sentences and paragraphs were lifted bodily from previous orations and published works of Wendell Phillips, Frederick Douglass, Booker T. Washington, and other doctors of the race's ills. For variety Mrs. Hayes-Rore had seasoned hers with a peppery dash of Du Bois and a few vinegary statements of her own. Aside from these it was, Helga reflected, the same old thing.

But Mrs. Hayes-Rore was to her, after the first short, awkward period, interesting. Her dark eyes, bright and investigating, had, Helga noted, a humorous gleam, and something in the way she held her untidy head gave the impression of a cat watching its prey so that when she struck, if she so decided, the blow would be unerringly effective. Helga, looking up from a last reading of the speeches, was aware that she was being studied. Her employer sat leaning back, the tips of her fingers pressed together, her head a bit on one side, her small inquisitive eyes boring into the girl before her. And as the train hurled itself frantically toward smoke-infested Newark, she decided to strike.

"Now tell me," she commanded, "how is it that a nice girl like you can rush off on a wildgoose chase like this at a moment's notice. I should think your people'd object, or'd make inquiries, or something."

At that command Helga Crane could not help sliding down her eyes to hide the anger that had risen in them. Was she to be forever explaining her people—or lack of them? But she said courteously enough, even managing a hard little smile: "Well you see, Mrs. Hayes-Rore, I haven't any people. There's only me, so I can do as I please."

"Ha!" said Mrs. Hayes-Rore.

Terrific, thought Helga Crane, the power of that sound from the lips of this woman. How, she wondered, had she succeeded in investing it with so much incredulity.

"If you didn't have people, you wouldn't be living. Everybody has people, Miss Crane. Everybody."

"*I* haven't, Mrs. Hayes-Rore."

Mrs. Hayes-Rore screwed up her eyes. "Well, that's mighty mysterious, and I detest mysteries." She shrugged, and into those eyes there now came with alarming quickness, an accusing criticism.

"It isn't," Helga said defensively, "a mystery. It's a fact and a mighty unpleasant one. Inconvenient too," and she laughed a little, not wishing to cry.

Her tormentor, in sudden embarrassment, turned her sharp eyes to the window. She seemed intent on the miles of red clay sliding past. After a moment, however, she asked gently: "You wouldn't like to tell me about it, would you? It seems to bother you. And I'm interested in girls."

Annoyed, but still hanging, for the sake of the twenty-five dollars, to her self-control, Helga gave her head a little toss and flung out her hands in a helpless, beaten way. Then she shrugged. What did it matter? "Oh, well, if you really want to know. I assure you, it's nothing interesting. Or nasty," she added maliciously. "It's just plain horrid. For me." And she began mockingly to relate her story.

But as she went on, again she had that sore sensation of revolt, and again the torment which she had gone through loomed before her as something brutal and undeserved. Passionately, tearfully, incoherently, the final words tumbled from her quivering petulant lips.

The other woman still looked out of the window, apparently so interested in the outer aspect of the drab sections of the Jersey manufacturing city through which they were passing that, the better to see, she had now so turned her head that only an ear and a small portion of cheek were visible.

During the little pause that followed Helga's recital, the faces of the two women, which had been bare, seemed to harden. It was almost as if they had slipped on masks. The girl wished to hide her turbulent feelings and to appear indifferent to Mrs. Hayes-Rore's opinion of her story. The woman felt that the story, dealing as it did with race intermingling and possibly adultery, was beyond definite discussion. For among black people, as among white people, it is tacitly understood that these things are not mentioned—and therefore they do not exist.

Sliding adroitly out from under the precarious subject to a safer, more decent one, Mrs. Hayes-Rore asked Helga what she was thinking of doing when she got back to Chicago. Had she anything in mind?

Helga, it appeared, hadn't. The truth was she had been thinking of staying in New York. Maybe she could find something there. Everybody seemed to. At least she could make the attempt.

Mrs. Hayes-Rore sighed, for no obvious reason. "Um, maybe I can help you. I know people in New York. Do you?"

"No."

"New York's the lonesomest place in the world if you don't know anybody."

"It couldn't possibly be worse than Chicago," said Helga savagely, giving the table support a violent kick.

They were running into the shadow of the tunnel. Mrs. Hayes-Rore murmured thoughtfully: "You'd better come uptown and stay with me a few days. I may need you. Something may turn up."

It was one of those vicious mornings, windy and bright. There seemed to Helga, as they emerged from the depths of the vast station, to be a whirling malice in the sharp air of this shining city. Mrs. Hayes-Rore's words about its terrible loneliness shot through her mind. She felt its aggressive unfriendliness. Even the great buildings, the flying cabs, and the swirling crowds seemed manifestations of purposed malevolence. And for that first short minute she was awed and frightened and inclined to turn back to that other city, which, though not kind, was yet not strange. This New York seemed somehow more appalling, more scornful, in some inexplicable way even more terrible and uncaring than Chicago. Threatening almost. Ugly. Yes, perhaps she'd better turn back.

The feeling passed, escaped in the surprise of what Mrs. Hayes-Rore was saying. Her oratorical voice boomed above the city's roar. "I suppose I ought really to have phoned Anne from the station. About you, I mean. Well, it doesn't matter. She's got plenty of room. Lives alone in a big house, which is something Negroes in New York don't do. They fill 'em up with lodgers usually. But Anne's funny. Nice, though. You'll like her, and it will be good for you to know her if you're going to stay in New York. She's a widow, my husband's sister's son's wife. The war, you know."

"Oh," protested Helga Crane, with a feeling of acute misgiving, "but won't she be annoyed and inconvenienced by having me brought in on her like this? I supposed we were going to the 'Y' or a hotel or something like that. Oughtn't we really to stop and phone?"

The woman at her side in the swaying cab smiled, a peculiar invincible, self-reliant smile, but gave Helga Crane's suggestion no other attention. Plainly she was a person accustomed to having things her way. She merely went on talking of other plans. "I think maybe I can get you some work. With a new Negro insurance company. They're after me to put quite a tidy sum into it. Well, I'll just tell them that they may as well take you with the money," and she laughed.

"Thanks awfully," Helga said, "but will they like it? I mean being made to take me because of the money."

"They're not being made," contradicted Mrs. Hayes-Rore. "I intended to let them have the money anyway, and I'll tell Mr. Darling so—after he takes you. They ought to be glad to get you. Colored organizations always need more brains as well as more money. Don't worry. And don't thank me again. You haven't got the job yet, you know."

There was a little silence, during which Helga gave herself up to the distraction of watching the strange city and the strange crowds, trying hard to put out of her mind the vision of an easier future which her companion's words had conjured up; for, as had been pointed out, it was, as yet, only a possibility.

Turning out of the park into the broad thoroughfare of Lenox Avenue, Mr. Hayes-Rore said in a too carefully casual manner: "And, by the way, I wouldn't mention that my people are white, if I were you. Colored people won't understand it, and after all it's your own business. When you've lived as long as I have, you'll know that what others don't know can't hurt you. I'll just tell Anne that you're a friend of mine whose mother's dead. That'll place you well enough and it's all true. I never tell lies. She can fill in the gaps to suit herself and anyone else curious enough to ask."

"Thanks," Helga said again. And so great was her gratitude that she reached out and took her new friend's slightly soiled hand in one of her own fastidious ones, and retained it until their cab turned into a pleasant tree-lined street and came to a halt before one of the dignified houses in the center of the block. Here they got out.

In after years Helga Crane had only to close her eyes to see herself standing apprehensively in the small cream-colored hall, the floor of which was covered with deep silver-hued carpet; to see Mrs. Hayes-Rore pecking the cheek of the tall slim creature beautifully dressed in a cool green tailored frock; to hear herself being introduced to "my niece, Mrs. Grey" as "Miss Crane, a little friend of mine whose mother's died, and I think perhaps a while in New York will be good for her"; to feel her hand grasped in quick sympathy, and to hear Anne Grey's pleasant voice, with its faint note of wistfulness, saying: "I'm so sorry, and I'm glad Aunt Jeanette brought you here. Did you have a good trip? I'm sure you must be worn out. I'll have Lillie take you right up." And to feel like a criminal.

Eight

A YEAR thick with various adventures had sped by since that spring day on which Helga Crane had set out away from Chicago's indifferent unkindness for New York in the company of Mrs. Hayes-Rore. New York she had found not so unkind, not so unfriendly, not so indifferent. There she had been happy, and secured work, had made acquaintances and another friend. Again she had had that strange transforming experience, this time not so fleetingly, that magic sense of having come home. Harlem, teeming black Harlem, had welcomed her and lulled her into something that was, she was certain, peace and contentment.

The request and recommendation of Mrs. Hayes-Rore had been sufficient for her to obtain work with the insurance company in which that energetic woman was interested. And through Anne it had been possible for her to meet and to know people with tastes and ideas similar to her own. Their sophisticated cynical talk, their elaborate parties, the unobtrusive correctness of their clothes and homes, all appealed to her craving for smartness, for enjoyment. Soon she was able to reflect with a flicker of amusement on that constant feeling of humiliation and inferiority which had encompassed her in Naxos. Her New York friends looked with contempt and scorn on Naxos and all its works. This gave Helga a pleasant sense of avengement. Any shreds of self-consciousness or apprehension which at first she may have felt vanished quickly, escaped in the keenness of her joy at seeming at last to belong somewhere. For she considered that she had, as she put it, "found herself."

Between Anne Grey and Helga Crane there had sprung one of those immediate and peculiarly sympathetic friendships. Uneasy at first, Helga had been relieved that Anne had never returned to the uncomfortable subject of her mother's death so intentionally mentioned on their first meeting by Mrs. Hayes-Rore, beyond a tremulous brief: "You won't talk to me about it, will you? I can't bear the thought of death. Nobody ever talks to me about it. My husband, you know." This Helga discovered to be true. Later, when she knew Anne better, she suspected that it was a bit of a pose assumed for the purpose of doing away with the necessity of speaking regretfully of a husband who had been perhaps not too greatly loved.

After the first pleasant weeks, feeling that her obligation to Anne was already too great, Helga began to look about for a permanent place to live. It was, she found, difficult. She eschewed the "Y" as too bare, impersonal, and restrictive. Nor did furnished rooms or the idea of a solitary or a shared apartment appeal to her. So she rejoiced when one day Anne, looking up from her book, said lightly: "Helga, since you're going to be in New York, why don't you stay here with me? I don't usually take people. It's too disrupting. Still, it *is* sort of pleasant having somebody in the house and I don't seem to mind you. You don't bore me, or bother me. If you'd like to stay— Think it over."

Helga didn't, of course, require to think it over, because lodgment in Anne's home was in complete accord with what she designated as her "æsthetic sense." Even Helga Crane approved of Anne's house and the furnishings which so admirably graced the big cream-colored rooms. Beds with long, tapering posts to which tremendous age lent dignity and interest, bonneted old highboys, tables that might be by Duncan Phyfe, rare spindle-legged chairs, and others whose ladder backs gracefully climbed the delicate wall panels. These historic things mingled harmoniously and comfortably with brass-bound Chinese teachests, luxurious deep chairs and davenports, tiny tables of gay color, a lacquered jade-green settee with gleaming black satin cushions, lustrous Eastern rugs, ancient copper, Japanese prints, some fine etchings, a profusion of precious bric-a-brac, and endless shelves filled with books.

Anne Grey herself was, as Helga expressed it, "almost too good to be true." Thirty, maybe, brownly beautiful, she had the face of a golden Madonna, grave and calm and sweet, with shining black hair and eyes. She carried herself as queens are reputed to bear themselves, and probably do not. Her manners were as agreeably gentle as her own soft name. She possessed an impeccably fastidious taste in clothes, knowing what suited her and wearing it with an air of unconscious assurance. The unusual thing, a native New Yorker, she was also a person of distinction, financially independent, well connected and much sought after. And she was interesting, an odd confusion of wit and intense earnestness; a vivid and remarkable person. Yes, undoubtedly, Anne was almost too good to be true. She was almost perfect.

Thus established, secure, comfortable, Helga soon became thoroughly absorbed in the distracting interests of life in New York. Her secretarial work with the Negro insurance company filled her day. Books, the theater, parties, used up the nights. Gradually in the charm of this new and delightful pattern of her life she lost that tantalizing oppression of loneliness and isolation which always, it seemed, had been a part of her existence.

But, while the continuously gorgeous panorama of Harlem fascinated her, thrilled her, the sober mad rush of white New York failed entirely to stir her. Like thousands of other Harlem dwellers, she patronized its shops, its theaters, its art galleries, and its restaurants, and read its papers, without considering herself a part of the monster. And she was satisfied, unenvious. For her this Harlem was enough. Of that white world, so distant, so near, she asked only indifference. No, not at all did she crave, from those pale and powerful people, awareness. Sinister folk, she considered them, who had stolen her birthright. Their past contribution to her life, which had been but shame and grief, she had hidden away from brown folk in a locked closet, "never," she told herself, "to be reopened."

Some day she intended to marry one of those alluring brown or yellow men who danced attendance on her. Already financially successful, any one of them could give to her the things which she had now come to desire, a home like Anne's, cars of expensive makes such as lined the avenue, clothes and furs from Bendel's and Revillon Frères', servants, and leisure.

Always her forehead wrinkled in distaste whenever, involuntarily, which was somehow frequently, her mind turned on the speculative gray eyes and visionary uplifting plans of Dr. Anderson. That other, James Vayle, had slipped absolutely from her consciousness. Of him she never thought. Helga Crane meant, now, to have a home and perhaps laughing, appealing dark-eyed children in Harlem. Her existence was bounded by Central Park, Fifth Avenue, St. Nicholas Park, and One Hundred and Forty-fifth street. Not at all a narrow life, as

Negroes live it, as Helga Crane knew it. Everything was there, vice and goodness, sadness and gayety, ignorance and wisdom, ugliness and beauty, poverty and richness. And it seemed to her that somehow of goodness, gayety, wisdom, and beauty always there was a little more than of vice, sadness, ignorance, and ugliness. It was only riches that did not quite transcend poverty.

"But," said Helga Crane, "what of that? Money isn't everything. It isn't even the half of everything. And here we have so much else—and by ourselves. It's only outside of Harlem among those others that money really counts for everything."

In the actuality of the pleasant present and the delightful vision of an agreeable future she was contented, and happy. She did not analyze this contentment, this happiness, but vaguely, without putting it into words or even so tangible a thing as a thought, she knew it sprang from a sense of freedom, a release from the feeling of smallness which had hedged her in, first during her sorry, unchildlike childhood among hostile white folk in Chicago, and later during her uncomfortable sojourn among snobbish black folk in Naxos.

Nine

B UT it didn't last, this happiness of Helga Crane's.
Little by little the signs of spring appeared, but strangely
the enchantment of the season, so enthusiastically, so lavishly
greeted by the gay dwellers of Harlem, filled her only with
restlessness. Somewhere, within her, in a deep recess, crouched
discontent. She began to lose confidence, in the fullness of her
life, the glow began to fade from her conception of it. As the
days multiplied, her need of something, something vaguely familiar, but which she could not put a name to and hold for
definite examination, became almost intolerable. She went
through moments of overwhelming anguish. She felt shut in,
trapped. "Perhaps I'm tired, need a tonic, or something," she
reflected. So she consulted a physician, who, after a long, solemn examination, said that there was nothing wrong, nothing
at all. "A change of scene, perhaps for a week or so, or a few
days away from work," would put her straight most likely.
Helga tried this, tried them both, but it was no good. All interest had gone out of living. Nothing seemed any good. She became a little frightened, and then shocked to discover that, for
some unknown reason, it was of herself she was afraid.

Spring grew into summer, languidly at first, then flauntingly.
Without awareness on her part, Helga Crane began to draw
away from those contacts which had so delighted her. More
and more she made lonely excursions to places outside of
Harlem. A sensation of estrangement and isolation encompassed her. As the days became hotter and the streets more
swarming, a kind of repulsion came upon her. She recoiled in
aversion from the sight of the grinning faces and from the
sound of the easy laughter of all these people who strolled,
aimlessly now, it seemed, up and down the avenues. Not only
did the crowds of nameless folk on the street annoy her, she
began also actually to dislike her friends.

Even the gentle Anne distressed her. Perhaps because Anne
was obsessed by the race problem and fed her obsession. She
frequented all the meetings of protest, subscribed to all the
complaining magazines, and read all the lurid newspapers

spewed out by the Negro yellow press. She talked, wept, and ground her teeth dramatically about the wrongs and shames of her race. At times she lashed her fury to surprising heights for one by nature so placid and gentle. And, though she would not, even to herself, have admitted it, she reveled in this orgy of protest.

"Social equality," "Equal opportunity for all," were her slogans, often and emphatically repeated. Anne preached these things and honestly thought that she believed them, but she considered it an affront to the race, and to all the vari-colored peoples that made Lenox and Seventh Avenues the rich spectacles which they were, for any Negro to receive on terms of equality any white person.

"To me," asserted Anne Grey, "the most wretched Negro prostitute that walks One Hundred and Thirty-fifth Street is more than any president of these United States, not excepting Abraham Lincoln." But she turned up her finely carved nose at their lusty churches, their picturesque parades, their naïve clowning on the streets. She would not have desired or even have been willing to live in any section outside the black belt, and she would have refused scornfully, had they been tendered, any invitation from white folk. She hated white people with a deep and burning hatred, with the kind of hatred which, finding itself held in sufficiently numerous groups, was capable some day, on some great provocation, of bursting into dangerously malignant flames.

But she aped their clothes, their manners, and their gracious ways of living. While proclaiming loudly the undiluted good of all things Negro, she yet disliked the songs, the dances, and the softly blurred speech of the race. Toward these things she showed only a disdainful contempt, tinged sometimes with a faint amusement. Like the despised people of the white race, she preferred Pavlova to Florence Mills, John McCormack to Taylor Gordon, Walter Hampden to Paul Robeson. Theoretically, however, she stood for the immediate advancement of all things Negroid, and was in revolt against social inequality.

Helga had been entertained by this racial ardor in one so little affected by racial prejudice as Anne, and by her inconsistencies. But suddenly these things irked her with a great irksomeness and she wanted to be free of this constant prattling of the incongruities, the injustices, the stupidities, the viciousness of white people. It stirred memories, probed hidden wounds, whose poignant ache bred in her surprising oppression and corroded the fabric of her quietism. Sometimes it took all her self-control to keep from tossing sarcastically at Anne Ibsen's remark about there being assuredly something very wrong with the drains, but after all there were other parts of the edifice.

It was at this period of restiveness that Helga met again Dr. Anderson. She had gone, unwillingly, to a meeting, a health meeting, held in a large church—as were most of Harlem's uplift activities—as a substitute for her employer, Mr. Darling. Making her tardy arrival during a tedious discourse by a pompous saffron-hued physician, she was led by the irritated usher, whom she had roused from a nap in which he had been pleasantly freed from the intricacies of Negro health statistics, to a very front seat. Complete silence ensued while she subsided into her chair. The offended doctor looked at the ceiling, at the floor, and accusingly at Helga, and finally continued his lengthy discourse. When at last he had ended and Helga had dared to remove her eyes from his sweating face and look about, she saw with a sudden thrill that Robert Anderson was among her nearest neighbors. A peculiar, not wholly disagreeable, quiver ran down her spine. She felt an odd little faintness. The blood rushed to her face. She tried to jeer at herself for being so moved by the encounter.

He, meanwhile, she observed, watched her gravely. And having caught her attention, he smiled a little and nodded.

When all who so desired had spouted to their hearts' content —if to little purpose—and the meeting was finally over, Anderson detached himself from the circle of admiring friends and acquaintances that had gathered around him and caught up with Helga half-way down the long aisle leading out to fresher air.

"I wondered if you were really going to cut me. I see you were," he began, with that half-quizzical smile which she remembered so well.

She laughed. "Oh, I didn't think you'd remember me." Then she added: "Pleasantly, I mean."

The man laughed too. But they couldn't talk yet. People

kept breaking in on them. At last, however, they were at the door, and then he suggested that they share a taxi "for the sake of a little breeze." Helga assented.

Constraint fell upon them when they emerged into the hot street, made seemingly hotter by a low-hanging golden moon and the hundreds of blazing electric lights. For a moment, before hailing a taxi, they stood together looking at the slow moving mass of perspiring human beings. Neither spoke, but Helga was conscious of the man's steady gaze. The prominent gray eyes were fixed upon her, studying her, appraising her. Many times since turning her back on Naxos she had in fancy rehearsed this scene, this re-encounter. Now she found that rehearsal helped not at all. It was so absolutely different from anything that she had imagined.

In the open taxi they talked of impersonal things, books, places, the fascination of New York, of Harlem. But underneath the exchange of small talk lay another conversation of which Helga Crane was sharply aware. She was aware, too, of a strange ill-defined emotion, a vague yearning rising within her. And she experienced a sensation of consternation and keen regret when with a lurching jerk the cab pulled up before the house in One Hundred and Thirty-ninth Street. So soon, she thought.

But she held out her hand calmly, coolly. Cordially she asked him to call some time. "It is," she said, "a pleasure to renew our acquaintance." Was it, she was wondering, merely an acquaintance?

He responded seriously that he too thought it a pleasure, and added: "You haven't changed. You're still seeking for something, I think."

At his speech there dropped from her that vague feeling of yearning, that longing for sympathy and understanding which his presence evoked. She felt a sharp stinging sensation and a recurrence of that anger and defiant desire to hurt which had so seared her on that past morning in Naxos. She searched for a biting remark, but, finding none venomous enough, she merely laughed a little rude and scornful laugh and, throwing up her small head, bade him an impatient good-night and ran quickly up the steps.

Afterwards she lay for long hours without undressing, thinking angry self-accusing thoughts, recalling and reconstructing that other explosive contact. That memory filled her with a sort of aching delirium. A thousand indefinite longings beset her. Eagerly she desired to see him again to right herself in his thoughts. Far into the night she lay planning speeches for their next meeting, so that it was long before drowsiness advanced upon her.

When he did call, Sunday, three days later, she put him off on Anne and went out, pleading an engagement, which until then she had not meant to keep. Until the very moment of his entrance she had had no intention of running away, but something, some imp of contumacy, drove her from his presence, though she longed to stay. Again abruptly had come the uncontrollable wish to wound. Later, with a sense of helplessness and inevitability, she realized that the weapon which she had chosen had been a boomerang, for she herself had felt the keen disappointment of the denial. Better to have stayed and hurled polite sarcasms at him. She might then at least have had the joy of seeing him wince.

In this spirit she made her way to the corner and turned into Seventh Avenue. The warmth of the sun, though gentle on that afternoon, had nevertheless kissed the street into marvelous light and color. Now and then, greeting an acquaintance, or stopping to chat with a friend, Helga was all the time seeing its soft shining brightness on the buildings along its sides or on the gleaming bronze, gold, and copper faces of its promenaders. And another vision, too, came haunting Helga Crane; level gray eyes set down in a brown face which stared out at her, coolly, quizzically, disturbingly. And she was not happy.

The tea to which she had so suddenly made up her mind to go she found boring beyond endurance, insipid drinks, dull conversation, stupid men. The aimless talk glanced from John Wellinger's lawsuit for discrimination because of race against a downtown restaurant and the advantages of living in Europe, especially in France, to the significance, if any, of the Garvey movement. Then it sped to a favorite Negro dancer who had just then secured a foothold on the stage of a current white musical comedy, to other shows, to a new book touching on Negroes. Thence to costumes for a coming masquerade dance, to a new jazz song, to Yvette Dawson's engagement to a Boston lawyer who had seen her one night at a party and proposed to her the next day at noon. Then back again to racial discrimination.

Why, Helga wondered, with unreasoning exasperation, didn't they find something else to talk of? Why must the race problem always creep in? She refused to go on to another gathering. It would, she thought, be simply the same old thing.

On her arrival home she was more disappointed than she cared to admit to find the house in darkness and even Anne gone off somewhere. She would have liked that night to have talked with Anne. Get her opinion of Dr. Anderson.

Anne it was who the next day told her that he had given up his work in Naxos; or rather that Naxos had given him up. He had been too liberal, too lenient, for education as it was inflicted in Naxos. Now he was permanently in New York, employed as a welfare worker by some big manufacturing concern, which gave employment to hundreds of Negro men.

"Uplift," sniffed Helga contemptuously, and fled before the onslaught of Anne's harangue on the needs and ills of the race.

Ten

WITH the waning summer the acute sensitiveness of Helga Crane's frayed nerves grew keener. There were days when the mere sight of the serene tan and brown faces about her stung her like a personal insult. The care-free quality of their laughter roused in her the desire to scream at them: "Fools, fools! Stupid fools!" This passionate and unreasoning protest gained in intensity, swallowing up all else like some dense fog. Life became for her only a hateful place where one lived in intimacy with people one would not have chosen had one been given choice. It was, too, an excruciating agony. She was continually out of temper. Anne, thank the gods! was away, but her nearing return filled Helga with dismay.

Arriving at work one sultry day, hot and dispirited, she found waiting a letter, a letter from Uncle Peter. It had originally been sent to Naxos, and from there it had made the journey back to Chicago to the Young Women's Christian Association, and then to Mrs. Hayes-Rore. That busy woman had at last found time between conventions and lectures to readdress it and had sent it on to New York. Four months, at least, it had been on its travels. Helga felt no curiosity as to its contents, only annoyance at the long delay, as she ripped open the thin edge of the envelope, and for a space sat staring at the peculiar foreign script of her uncle.

> *715 Sheridan Road*
> *Chicago, Ill.*
>
> *Dear Helga:*
>
> *It is now over a year since you made your unfortunate call here. It was unfortunate for us all, you, Mrs. Nilssen, and myself. But of course you couldn't know. I blame myself. I should have written you of my marriage.*
>
> *I have looked for a letter, or some word from you; evidently, with your usual penetration, you understood thoroughly that I must terminate my outward relation with you. You were always a keen one.*
>
> *Of course I am sorry, but it can't be helped. My*

*wife must be considered, and she feels very strongly
about this.*

*You know, of course, that I wish you the best of
luck. But take an old man's advice and don't do as
your mother did. Why don't you run over and visit
your Aunt Katrina? She always wanted you. Maria
Kirkeplads, No. 2, will find her.*

*I enclose what I intended to leave you at my death.
It is better and more convenient that you get it now. I
wish it were more, but even this little may come in
handy for a rainy day.*

Best wishes for your luck.

Peter Nilssen

Beside the brief, friendly, but none the less final, letter there
was a check for five thousand dollars. Helga Crane's first feeling
was one of unreality. This changed almost immediately into one
of relief, of liberation. It was stronger than the mere security
from present financial worry which the check promised. Money
as money was still not very important to Helga. But later, while
on an errand in the big general office of the society, her puzzled
bewilderment fled. Here the inscrutability of the dozen or more
brown faces, all cast from the same indefinite mold, and so like
her own, seemed pressing forward against her. Abruptly it
flashed upon her that the harrowing irritation of the past weeks
was a smoldering hatred. Then, she was overcome by another,
so actual, so sharp, so horribly painful, that forever afterwards
she preferred to forget it. It was as if she were shut up, boxed
up, with hundreds of her race, closed up with that something in
the racial character which had always been, to her, inexplicable,
alien. Why, she demanded in fierce rebellion, should she be
yoked to these despised black folk?

Back in the privacy of her own cubicle, self-loathing came
upon her. "They're my own people, my own people," she kept
repeating over and over to herself. It was no good. The feeling
would not be routed. "I can't go on like this," she said to herself. "I simply can't."

There were footsteps. Panic seized her. She'd have to get out.
She terribly needed to. Snatching hat and purse, she hurried to
the narrow door, saying in a forced, steady voice, as it opened

to reveal her employer: "Mr. Darling, I'm sorry, but I've got to go out. Please, may I be excused?"

At his courteous "Certainly, certainly. And don't hurry. It's much too hot," Helga Crane had the grace to feel ashamed, but there was no softening of her determination. The necessity for being alone was too urgent. She hated him and all the others too much.

Outside, rain had begun to fall. She walked bare-headed, bitter with self-reproach. But she rejoiced too. She didn't, in spite of her racial markings, belong to these dark segregated people. She was different. She felt it. It wasn't merely a matter of color. It was something broader, deeper, that made folk kin.

And now she was free. She would take Uncle Peter's money and advice and revisit her aunt in Copenhagen. Fleeting pleasant memories of her childhood visit there flew through her excited mind. She had been only eight, yet she had enjoyed the interest and the admiration which her unfamiliar color and dark curly hair, strange to those pink, white, and gold people, had evoked. Quite clearly now she recalled that her Aunt Katrina had begged for her to be allowed to remain. Why, she wondered, hadn't her mother consented? To Helga it seemed that it would have been the solution to all their problems, her mother's, her stepfather's, her own.

At home in the cool dimness of the big chintz-hung living-room, clad only in a fluttering thing of green chiffon, she gave herself up to day-dreams of a happy future in Copenhagen, where there were no Negroes, no problems, no prejudice, until she remembered with perturbation that this was the day of Anne's return from her vacation at the sea-shore. Worse. There was a dinner-party in her honor that very night. Helga sighed. She'd have to go. She couldn't possibly get out of a dinner-party for Anne, even though she felt that such an event on a hot night was little short of an outrage. Nothing but a sense of obligation to Anne kept her from pleading a splitting headache as an excuse for remaining quietly at home.

Her mind trailed off to the highly important matter of clothes. What should she wear? White? No, everybody would, because it was hot. Green? She shook her head, Anne would be sure to. The blue thing. Reluctantly she decided against it; she loved it, but she had worn it too often. There was that cobwebby black net touched with orange, which she had bought last spring in a fit of extravagance and never worn, because on getting it home both she and Anne had considered it too *décolleté*, and too *outré*. Anne's words: "There's not enough of it, and what there is gives you the air of something about to fly," came back to her, and she smiled as she decided that she would certainly wear the black net. For her it would be a symbol. She was about to fly.

She busied herself with some absurdly expensive roses which she had ordered sent in, spending an interminable time in their arrangement. At last she was satisfied with their appropriateness in some blue Chinese jars of great age. Anne *did* have such lovely things, she thought, as she began conscientiously to prepare for her return, although there was really little to do; Lillie seemed to have done everything. But Helga dusted the tops of the books, placed the magazines in ordered carelessness, redressed Anne's bed in fresh-smelling sheets of cool linen, and laid out her best pale-yellow pajamas of *crêpe de Chine*. Finally she set out two tall green glasses and made a great pitcher of lemonade, leaving only the ginger-ale and claret to be added on Anne's arrival. She was a little conscience-stricken, so she wanted to be particularly nice to Anne, who had been so kind to her when she first came to New York, a forlorn friendless creature. Yes, she was grateful to Anne; but, just the same, she meant to go. At once.

Her preparations over, she went back to the carved chair from which the thought of Anne's home-coming had drawn her. Characteristically she writhed at the idea of telling Anne of her impending departure and shirked the problem of evolving a plausible and inoffensive excuse for its suddenness. "That," she decided lazily, "will have to look out for itself; I can't be bothered just now. It's too hot."

She began to make plans and to dream delightful dreams of change, of life somewhere else. Some place where at last she would be permanently satisfied. Her anticipatory thoughts waltzed and eddied about to the sweet silent music of change. With rapture almost, she let herself drop into the blissful sensation of visualizing herself in different, strange places, among approving and admiring people, where she would be appreciated, and understood.

Eleven

IT was night. The dinner-party was over, but no one wanted to go home. Half-past eleven was, it seemed, much too early to tumble into bed on a Saturday night. It was a sulky, humid night, a thick furry night, through which the electric torches shone like silver fuzz—an atrocious night for cabareting, Helga insisted, but the others wanted to go, so she went with them, though half unwillingly. After much consultation and chatter they decided upon a place and climbed into two patiently waiting taxis, rattling things which jerked, wiggled, and groaned, and threatened every minute to collide with others of their kind, or with inattentive pedestrians. Soon they pulled up before a tawdry doorway in a narrow crosstown street and stepped out. The night was far from quiet, the streets far from empty. Clanging trolley bells, quarreling cats, cackling phonographs, raucous laughter, complaining motor-horns, low singing, mingled in the familiar medley that is Harlem. Black figures, white figures, little forms, big forms, small groups, large groups, sauntered, or hurried by. It was gay, grotesque, and a little weird. Helga Crane felt singularly apart from it all. Entering the waiting doorway, they descended through a furtive, narrow passage, into a vast subterranean room. Helga smiled, thinking that this was one of those places characterized by the righteous as a hell.

A glare of light struck her eyes, a blare of jazz split her ears. For a moment everything seemed to be spinning round; even she felt that she was circling aimlessly, as she followed with the others the black giant who led them to a small table, where, when they were seated, their knees and elbows touched. Helga wondered that the waiter, indefinitely carved out of ebony, did not smile as he wrote their order—"four bottles of White Rock, four bottles of ginger-ale." Bah! Anne giggled, the others smiled and openly exchanged knowing glances, and under the tables flat glass bottles were extracted from the women's evening scarfs and small silver flasks drawn from the men's hip pockets. In a little moment she grew accustomed to the smoke and din.

They danced, ambling lazily to a crooning melody, or violently twisting their bodies, like whirling leaves, to a sudden streaming rhythm, or shaking themselves ecstatically to a thumping of unseen tomtoms. For the while, Helga was oblivious of the reek of flesh, smoke, and alcohol, oblivious of the oblivion of other gyrating pairs, oblivious of the color, the noise, and the grand distorted childishness of it all. She was drugged, lifted, sustained, by the extraordinary music, blown out, ripped out, beaten out, by the joyous, wild, murky orchestra. The essence of life seemed bodily motion. And when suddenly the music died, she dragged herself back to the present with a conscious effort; and a shameful certainty that not only had she been in the jungle, but that she had enjoyed it, began to taunt her. She hardened her determination to get away. She wasn't, she told herself, a jungle creature. She cloaked herself in a faint disgust as she watched the entertainers throw themselves about to the bursts of syncopated jangle, and when the time came again for the patrons to dance, she declined. Her rejected partner excused himself and sought an acqaintance a few tables removed. Helga sat looking curiously about her as the buzz of conversation ceased, strangled by the savage strains of music, and the crowd became a swirling mass. For the hundredth time she marveled at the gradations within this oppressed race of hers. A dozen shades slid by. There was sooty black, shiny black, taupe, mahogany, bronze, copper, gold, orange, yellow, peach, ivory, pinky white, pastry white. There was yellow hair, brown hair, black hair; straight hair, straightened hair, curly hair, crinkly hair, woolly hair. She saw black eyes in white faces, brown eyes in yellow faces, gray eyes in brown faces, blue eyes in tan faces. Africa, Europe, perhaps with a pinch of Asia, in a fantastic motley of ugliness and beauty, semi-barbaric, sophisticated, exotic, were here. But she was blind to its charm, purposely aloof and a little contemptuous, and soon her interest in the moving mosaic waned.

She had discovered Dr. Anderson sitting at a table on the far side of the room, with a girl in a shivering apricot frock. Seriously he returned her tiny bow. She met his eyes gravely smiling, then blushed, furiously, and averted her own. But they went back immediately to the girl beside him, who sat indifferently sipping a colorless liquid from a high glass, or puffing a precariously hanging cigarette. Across dozens of tables, littered with corks, with ashes, with shriveled sandwiches, through slits in the swaying mob, Helga Crane studied her.

She was pale, with a peculiar, almost deathlike pallor. The brilliantly red, softly curving mouth was somehow sorrowful. Her pitch-black eyes, a little aslant, were veiled by long, drooping lashes and surmounted by broad brows, which seemed like black smears. The short dark hair was brushed severely back from the wide forehead. The extreme *décolleté* of her simple apricot dress showed a skin of unusual color, a delicate, creamy hue, with golden tones. "Almost like an alabaster," thought Helga.

Bang! Again the music died. The moving mass broke, separated. The others returned. Anne had rage in her eyes. Her voice trembled as she took Helga aside to whisper: "There's your Dr. Anderson over there, with Audrey Denney."

"Yes, I saw him. She's lovely. Who is she?"

"She's Audrey Denney, as I said, and she lives downtown. West Twenty-second Street. Hasn't much use for Harlem any more. It's a wonder she hasn't some white man hanging about. The disgusting creature! I wonder how she inveigled Anderson? But that's Audrey! If there is any desirable man about, trust her to attach him. She ought to be ostracized."

"Why?" asked Helga curiously, noting at the same time that three of the men in their own party had deserted and were now congregated about the offending Miss Denney.

"Because she goes about with white people," came Anne's indignant answer, "and they know she's colored."

"I'm afraid I don't quite see, Anne. Would it be all right if they didn't know she was colored?"

"Now, don't be nasty, Helga. You know very well what I mean." Anne's voice was shaking. Helga didn't see, and she was greatly interested, but she decided to let it go. She didn't want to quarrel with Anne, not now, when she had that guilty feeling about leaving her. But Anne was off on her favorite subject, race. And it seemed, too, that Audrey Denney was to her particularly obnoxious.

"Why, she gives parties for white and colored people together. And she goes to white people's parties. It's worse than disgusting, it's positively obscene."

"Oh, come, Anne, you haven't been to any of the parties, I know, so how can you be so positive about the matter?"

"No, but I've heard about them. I know people who've been."

"Friends of yours, Anne?"

Anne admitted that they were, some of them.

"Well, then, they can't be so bad. I mean, if your friends sometimes go, can they? Just what goes on that's so terrible?"

"Why, they drink, for one thing. Quantities, they say."

"So do we, at the parties here in Harlem," Helga responded. An idiotic impulse seized her to leave the place, Anne's presence, then, forever. But of course she couldn't. It would be foolish, and so ugly.

"And the white men dance with the colored women. Now you know, Helga Crane, that can mean only one thing." Anne's voice was trembling with cold hatred. As she ended, she made a little clicking noise with her tongue, indicating an abhorrence too great for words.

"Don't the colored men dance with the white women, or do they sit about, impolitely, while the other men dance with their women?" inquired Helga very softly, and with a slowness approaching almost to insolence. Anne's insinuations were too revolting. She had a slightly sickish feeling, and a flash of anger touched her. She mastered it and ignored Anne's inadequate answer.

"It's the principle of the thing that I object to. You can't get round the fact that her behavior is outrageous, treacherous, in fact. That's what's the matter with the Negro race. They won't stick together. She certainly ought to be ostracized. I've nothing but contempt for her, as has every other self-respecting Negro."

The other women and the lone man left to them—Helga's own escort—all seemingly agreed with Anne. At any rate, they didn't protest. Helga gave it up. She felt that it would be useless to tell them that what she felt for the beautiful, calm, cool girl who had the assurance, the courage, so placidly to ignore racial barriers and give her attention to people, was not contempt, but envious admiration. So she remained silent, watching the girl.

At the next first sound of music Dr. Anderson rose. Languidly the girl followed his movement, a faint smile parting her sorrowful lips at some remark he made. Her long, slender body swayed with an eager pulsing motion. She danced with grace and abandon, gravely, yet with obvious pleasure, her legs, her hips, her back, all swaying gently, swung by that wild music from the heart of the jungle. Helga turned her glance to Dr. Anderson. Her disinterested curiosity passed. While she still felt for the girl envious admiration, that feeling was now augmented by another, a more primitive emotion. She forgot the garish crowded room. She forgot her friends. She saw only two figures, closely clinging. She felt her heart throbbing. She felt the room receding. She went out the door. She climbed endless stairs. At last, panting, confused, but thankful to have escaped, she found herself again out in the dark night alone, a small crumpled thing in a fragile, flying black and gold dress. A taxi drifted toward her, stopped. She stepped into it, feeling cold, unhappy, misunderstood, and forlorn.

Twelve

HELGA CRANE felt no regret as the cliff-like towers faded. The sight thrilled her as beauty, grandeur, of any kind always did, but that was all.

The liner drew out from churning slate-colored waters of the river into the open sea. The small seething ripples on the water's surface became little waves. It was evening. In the western sky was a pink and mauve light, which faded gradually into a soft gray-blue obscurity. Leaning against the railing, Helga stared into the approaching night, glad to be at last alone, free of that great superfluity of human beings, yellow, brown, and black, which, as the torrid summer burnt to its close, had so oppressed her. No, she hadn't belonged there. Of her attempt to emerge from that inherent aloneness which was part of her very being, only dullness had come, dullness and a great aversion.

Almost at once it was time for dinner. Somewhere a bell sounded. She turned and with buoyant steps went down. Already she had begun to feel happier. Just for a moment, outside the dining-salon, she hesitated, assailed with a tiny uneasiness which passed as quickly as it had come. She entered softly, unobtrusively. And, after all, she had had her little fear for nothing. The purser, a man grown old in the service of the Scandinavian-American Line, remembered her as the little dark girl who had crossed with her mother years ago, and so she must sit at his table. Helga liked that. It put her at her ease and made her feel important.

Everyone was kind in the delightful days which followed, and her first shyness under the politely curious glances of turquoise eyes of her fellow travelers soon slid from her. The old forgotten Danish of her childhood began to come, awkwardly at first, from her lips, under their agreeable tutelage. Evidently they were interested, curious, and perhaps a little amused about this Negro girl on her way to Denmark alone.

Helga was a good sailor, and mostly the weather was lovely with the serene calm of the lingering September summer, under whose sky the sea was smooth, like a length of watered silk, unruffled by the stir of any wind. But even the two rough days found her on deck, reveling like a released bird in her returned feeling of happiness and freedom, that blessed sense of belonging to herself alone and not to a race. Again, she had put the past behind her with an ease which astonished even herself. Only the figure of Dr. Anderson obtruded itself with surprising vividness to irk her because she could get no meaning from that keen sensation of covetous exasperation that had so surprisingly risen within her on the night of the cabaret party. This question Helga Crane recognized as not entirely new; it was but a revival of the puzzlement experienced when she had fled so abruptly from Naxos more than a year before. With the recollection of that previous flight and subsequent half-questioning a dim disturbing notion came to her. She wasn't, she couldn't be, in love with the man. It was a thought too humiliating, and so quickly dismissed. Nonsense! Sheer nonsense! When one is in love, one strives to please. Never, she decided, had she made an effort to be pleasing to Dr. Anderson. On the contrary, she had always tried, deliberately, to irritate him. She was, she told herself, a sentimental fool.

Nevertheless, the thought of love stayed with her, not prominent, definite; but shadowy, incoherent. And in a remote corner of her consciousness lurked the memory of Dr. Anderson's serious smile and gravely musical voice.

On the last morning Helga rose at dawn, a dawn outside old Copenhagen. She lay lazily in her long chair watching the feeble sun creeping over the ship's great green funnels with sickly light; watching the purply gray sky change to opal, to gold, to pale blue. A few other passengers, also early risen, excited by the prospect of renewing old attachments, of glad homecomings after long years, paced nervously back and forth. Now, at the last moment, they were impatient, but apprehensive fear, too, had its place in their rushing emotions. Impatient Helga Crane was not. But she *was* apprehensive. Gradually, as the ship drew into the lazier waters of the dock, she became prey to sinister fears and memories. A deep pang of misgiving nauseated her at the thought of her aunt's husband, acquired since Helga's childhood visit. Painfully, vividly, she remembered the frightened anger of Uncle Peter's new wife, and looking back at her precipitate departure from America, she was amazed at her own stupidity. She had not even considered the remote possibility that her aunt's husband might be like Mrs. Nilssen. For the first time in nine days she wished herself back in New York, in America.

The little gulf of water between the ship and the wharf lessened. The engines had long ago ceased their whirring, and now the buzz of conversation, too, died down. There was a sort of silence. Soon the welcoming crowd on the wharf stood under the shadow of the great sea-monster, their faces turned up to the anxious ones of the passengers who hung over the railing. Hats were taken off, handkerchiefs were shaken out and frantically waved. Chatter. Deafening shouts. A little quiet weeping. Sailors and laborers were yelling and rushing about. Cables were thrown. The gangplank was laid.

Silent, unmoving, Helga Crane stood looking intently down into the gesticulating crowd. Was anyone waving to her? She couldn't tell. She didn't in the least remember her aunt, save as a hazy pretty lady. She smiled a little at the thought that her aunt, or anyone waiting there in the crowd below, would have no difficulty in singling her out. But—had she been met? When she descended the gangplank she was still uncertain and was trying to decide on a plan of procedure in the event that she had not. A telegram before she went through the customs? Telephone? A taxi?

But, again, she had all her fears and questionings for nothing. A smart woman in olive-green came toward her at once. And, even in the fervent gladness of her relief, Helga took in the carelessly trailing purple scarf and correct black hat that completed the perfection of her aunt's costume, and had time to feel herself a little shabbily dressed. For it was her aunt; Helga saw that at once, the resemblance to her own mother was unmistakable. There was the same long nose, the same beaming blue eyes, the same straying pale-brown hair so like sparkling beer. And the tall man with the fierce mustache who followed carrying hat and stick must be Herr Dahl, Aunt Katrina's husband. How gracious he was in his welcome, and how anxious to air his faulty English, now that her aunt had finished kissing her and exclaimed in Danish: "Little Helga! Little Helga! Goodness! But how you have grown!"

Laughter from all three.

"Welcome to Denmark, to Copenhagen, to our home," said the new uncle in queer, proud, oratorical English. And to Helga's smiling, grateful "Thank you," he returned: "Your trunks? Your checks?" also in English, and then lapsed into Danish.

"Where in the world are the Fishers? We must hurry the customs."

Almost immediately they were joined by a breathless couple, a young gray-haired man and a fair, tiny, doll-like woman. It developed that they had lived in England for some years and so spoke English, real English, well. They were both breathless, all apologies and explanations.

"So early!" sputtered the man, Herr Fisher. "We inquired last night and they said nine. It was only by accident that we called again this morning to be sure. Well, you can imagine the rush we were in when they said eight! And of course we had trouble in finding a cab. One always does if one is late." All this in Danish. Then to Helga in English: "You see, I was especially asked to come because Fru Dahl didn't know if you remembered your Danish, and your uncle's English—well—"

More laughter.

At last, the customs having been hurried and a cab secured, they were off, with much chatter, through the toy-like streets, weaving perilously in a nd out among the swarms of bicycles.

It had begun, a new life for Helga Crane.

Thirteen

SHE liked it, this new life. For a time it blotted from her mind all else. She took to luxury as the proverbial duck to water. And she took to admiration and attention even more eagerly.

It was pleasant to wake on that first afternoon, after the insisted-upon nap, with that sensation of lavish contentment and well-being enjoyed only by impecunious sybarites waking in the houses of the rich. But there was something more than mere contentment and well-being. To Helga Crane it was the realization of a dream that she had dreamed persistently ever since she was old enough to remember such vague things as day-dreams and longings. Always she had wanted, not money, but the things which money could give, leisure, attention, beautiful surroundings. Things. Things. Things.

So it was more than pleasant, it was important, this awakening in the great high room which held the great high bed on which she lay, small but exalted. It was important because to Helga Crane it was the day, so she decided, to which all the sad forlorn past had led, and from which the whole future was to depend. This, then, was where she belonged. This was her proper setting. She felt consoled at last for the spiritual wounds of the past.

A discreet knocking on the tall paneled door sounded. In response to Helga's "Come in" a respectful rosy-faced maid entered and Helga lay for a long minute watching her adjust the shutters. She was conscious, too, of the girl's sly curious glances at her, although her general attitude was quite correct, willing and disinterestd. In New York, America, Helga would have resented this sly watching. Now, here, she was only amused. Marie, she reflected, had probably never seen a Negro outside the pictured pages of her geography book.

Another knocking. Aunt Katrina entered, smiling at Helga's quick, lithe spring from the bed. They were going out to tea, she informed Helga. What, the girl inquired, did one wear to tea in Copenhagen, meanwhile glancing at her aunt's dark purple dress and bringing forth a severely plain blue *crêpe* frock. But no! It seemed that that wouldn't at all do.

"Too sober," pronounced Fru Dahl. "Haven't you something lively, something bright?" And, noting Helga's puzzled glance at her own subdued costume, she explained laughingly: "Oh, I'm an old married lady, and a Dane. But you, you're young. And you're a foreigner, and different. You must have bright things to set off the color of your lovely brown skin. Striking things, exotic things. You must make an impression."

"I've only these," said Helga Crane, timidly displaying her wardrobe on couch and chairs. "Of course I intend to buy here. I didn't want to bring over too much that might be useless."

"And you were quite right too. Umm. Let's see. That black there, the one with the cerise and purple trimmings. Wear that."

Helga was shocked. "But for tea, Aunt! Isn't it too gay? Too—too—*outré?*"

"Oh dear, no. Not at all, not for you. Just right." Then after a little pause she added: "And we're having people in to dinner tonight, quite a lot. Perhaps we'd better decide on our frocks now." For she was, in spite of all her gentle kindness, a woman who left nothing to chance. In her own mind she had determined the role that Helga was to play in advancing the social fortunes of the Dahls of Copenhagen, and she meant to begin at once.

At last, after much trying on and scrutinizing, it was decided that Marie should cut a favorite emerald-green velvet dress a little lower in the back and add some gold and mauve flowers, "to liven it up a bit," as Fru Dahl put it.

"Now that," she said, pointing to the Chinese red dressing-gown in which Helga had wrapped herself when at last the fitting was over, "suits you. Tomorrow we'll shop. Maybe we can get something that color. That black and orange thing there is good too, but too high. What a prim American maiden you are, Helga, to hide such a fine back and shoulders. Your feet are nice too, but you ought to have higher heels—and buckles."

Left alone, Helga began to wonder. She was dubious, too,

and not a little resentful. Certainly she loved color with a passion that perhaps only Negroes and Gypsies know. But she had a deep faith in the perfection of her own taste, and no mind to be bedecked in flaunting flashy things. Still—she had to admit that Fru Dahl was right about the dressing-gown. It did suit her. Perhaps an evening dress. And she knew that she had lovely shoulders and her feet *were* nice.

When she was dressed in the shining black taffeta with its bizarre trimmings of purple and cerise, Fru Dahl approved her and so did Herr Dahl. Everything in her responded to his "She's beautiful; beautiful!" Helga Crane knew she wasn't that, but it pleased her that he could think so, and say so. Aunt Katrina smiled in her quiet, assured way, taking to herself her husband's compliment to her niece. But a little frown appeared over the fierce mustache, as he said, in his precise, faintly feminine voice: "She ought to have ear-rings, long ones. Is it too late for Garborg's? We could call up."

And call up they did. And Garborg, the jeweler, in Fredericksgaarde waited for them. Not only were ear-rings bought, long ones brightly enameled, but glittering shoe-buckles and two great bracelets. Helga's sleeves being long, she escaped the bracelets for the moment. They were wrapped to be worn that night. The ear-rings, however, and the buckles came into immediate use and Helga felt like a veritable savage as they made their leisurely way across the pavement from the shop to the waiting motor. This feeling was intensified by the many pedestrians who stopped to stare at the queer dark creature, strange to their city. Her cheeks reddened, but both Herr and Fru Dahl seemed oblivious of the stares or the audible whispers in which Helga made out the one frequently recurring word "*sorte*," which she recognized as the Danish word for "black."

Her Aunt Katrina merely remarked: "A high color becomes you, Helga. Perhaps tonight a little rouge—" To which her husband nodded in agreement and stroked his mustache meditatively. Helga Crane said nothing.

They were pleased with the success she was at the tea, or rather the coffee—for no tea was served—and later at dinner. Hegla herself felt like nothing so much as some new and strange species of pet dog being proudly exhibited. Everyone was very polite and very friendly, but she felt the massed curiosity and interest, so discreetly hidden under the polite greetings. The very atmosphere was tense with it. "As if I had horns, or three legs," she thought. She was really nervous and a little terrified, but managed to present an outward smiling composure. This was assisted by the fact that it was taken for granted that she knew nothing or very little of the language. So she had only to bow and look pleasant. Herr and Fru Dahl did the talking, answered the questions. She came away from the coffee feeling that she had acquitted herself well in the first skirmish. And, in spite of the mental strain, she had enjoyed her prominence.

If the afternoon had been a strain, the evening was something more. It was more exciting too. Marie had indeed "cut down" the prized green velvet, until, as Helga put it, it was "practically nothing but a skirt." She was thankful for the barbaric bracelets, for the dangling ear-rings, for the beads about her neck. She was even thankful for the rouge on her burning cheeks and for the very powder on her back. No other woman in the stately pale-blue room was so greatly exposed. But she liked the small murmur of wonder and admiration which rose when Uncle Poul brought her in. She liked the compliments in the men's eyes as they bent over her hand. She liked the subtle half-understood flattery of her dinner partners. The women too were kind, feeling no need for jealousy. To them this girl, this Helga Crane, this mysterious niece of the Dahls, was not to be reckoned seriously in their scheme of things. True, she was attractive, unusual, in an exotic, almost savage way, but she wasn't one of them. She didn't at all count.

Near the end of the evening, as Helga sat effectively posed on a red satin sofa, the center of an admiring group, replying to questions about America and her trip over, in halting, inadequate Danish, there came a shifting of the curious interest away from herself. Following the others' eyes, she saw that there had entered the room a tallish man with a flying mane of reddish blond hair. He was wearing a great black cape, which swung gracefully from his huge shoulders, and in his long, nervous hand he held a wide soft hat. An artist, Helga decided at once, taking in the broad streaming tie. But how affected! How theatrical!

With Fru Dahl he came forward and was presented. "Herr Olsen, Herr Axel Olsen." To Helga Crane that meant nothing.

The man, however, interested her. For an imperceptible second he bent over her hand. After that he looked intently at her for what seemed to her an incredibly rude length of time from under his heavy drooping lids. At last, removing his stare of startled satisfaction, he wagged his leonine head approvingly.

"Yes, you're right. She's amazing. Marvelous," he muttered.

Everyone else in the room was deliberately not staring. About Helga there sputtered a little staccato murmur of manufactured conversation. Meanwhile she could think of no proper word of greeting to the outrageous man before her. She wanted, very badly, to laugh. But the man was as unaware of her omission as of her desire. His words flowed on and on, rising and rising. She tried to follow, but his rapid Danish eluded her. She caught only words, phrases, here and there. "Superb eyes . . . color . . . neck column . . . yellow . . . hair . . . alive . . . wonderful. . . ." His speech was for Fru Dahl. For a bit longer he lingered before the silent girl, whose smile had become a fixed aching mask, still gazing appraisingly, but saying no word to her, and then moved away with Fru Dahl, talking rapidly and excitedly to her and her husband, who joined them for a moment at the far side of the room. Then he was gone as suddenly as he had come.

"Who is he?" Helga put the question timidly to a hovering young army officer, a very smart captain just back from Sweden. Plainly he was surprised.

"Herr Olsen, Herr Axel Olsen, the painter. Portraits, you know."

"Oh," said Helga, still mystified.

"I guess he's going to paint you. You're lucky. He's queer. Won't do everybody."

"Oh, no. I mean, I'm sure you're mistaken. He didn't ask, didn't say anything about it."

The young man laughed. "Ha ha! That's good! He'll arrange that with Herr Dahl. He evidently came just to see you, and it was plain that he was pleased." He smiled, approvingly.

"Oh," said Helga again. Then at last she laughed. It was too funny. The great man hadn't addressed a word to her. Here she was, a curiosity, a stunt, at which people came and gazed. And was she to be treated like a secluded young miss, a Danish *frøkken,* not to be consulted personally even on matters affecting her personally? She, Helga Crane, who almost all her life had looked after herself, was she now to be looked after by Aunt Katrina and her husband? It didn't seem real.

It was late, very late, when finally she climbed into the great bed after having received an aunty kiss. She lay long awake reviewing the events of the crowded day. She was happy again. Happiness covered her like the lovely quilts under which she rested. She was mystified too. Her aunt's words came back to her. "You're young and a foreigner and—and different." Just what did that mean, she wondered. Did it mean that the difference was to be stressed, accented? Helga wasn't so sure that she liked that. Hitherto all her efforts had been toward similarity to those about her.

"How odd," she thought sleepily, "and how different from America!"

Fourteen

THE young officer had been right in his surmise. Axel Olsen was going to paint Helga Crane. Not only was he going to paint her, but he was to accompany her and her aunt on their shopping expedition. Aunt Katrina was frankly elated. Uncle Poul was also visibly pleased. Evidently they were not above kotowing to a lion. Helga's own feelings were mixed; she was amused, grateful, and vexed. It had all been decided and arranged without her, and, also, she was a little afraid of Olsen. His stupendous arrogance awed her.

The day was an exciting, not easily to be forgotten one. Definitely, too, it conveyed to Helga her exact status in her new environment. A decoration. A curio. A peacock. Their progress through the shops was an event; an event for Copenhagen as well as for Helga Crane. Her dark, alien appearance was to most people an astonishment. Some stared surreptitiously, some openly, and some stopped dead in front of her in order more fully to profit by their stares. "*Den Sorte*" dropped freely, audibly, from many lips.

The time came when she grew used to the stares of the population. And the time came when the population of Copenhagen grew used to her outlandish presence and ceased to stare. But at the end of that first day it was with thankfulness that she returned to the sheltering walls of the house on Maria Kirkeplads.

They were followed by numerous packages, whose contents all had been selected or suggested by Olsen and paid for by Aunt Katrina. Helga had only to wear them. When they were opened and the things spread out upon the sedate furnishings of her chamber, they made a rather startling array. It was almost in a mood of rebellion that Helga faced the fantastic collection of garments incongruously laid out in the quaint, stiff, pale old room. There were batik dresses in which mingled indigo, orange, green, vermilion, and black; dresses of velvet and chiffon in screaming colors, blood-red, sulphur-yellow, sea-green; and one black and white thing in striking combination. There was a black Manila shawl strewn with great scarlet and lemon flowers, a leopard-skin coat, a glittering opera-cape. There were turban-like hats of metallic silks, feathers and furs, strange jewelry, enameled or set with odd semi-precious stones, a nauseous Eastern perfume, shoes with dangerously high heels. Gradually Helga's perturbation subsided in the unusual pleasure of having so many new and expensive clothes at one time. She began to feel a little excited, incited.

Incited. That was it, the guiding principle of her life in Copenhagen. She was incited to make an impression, a voluptuous impression. She was incited to inflame attention and admiration. She was dressed for it, subtly schooled for it. And after a little while she gave herself up wholly to the fascinating business of being seen, gaped at, desired. Against the solid background of Herr Dahl's wealth and generosity she submitted to her aunt's arrangement of her life to one end, the amusing one of being noticed and flattered. Intentionally she kept to the slow, faltering Danish. It was, she decided, more attractive than a nearer perfection. She grew used to the extravagant things with which Aunt Katrina chose to dress her. She managed, too, to retain that air of remoteness which had been in America so disastrous to her friendships. Here in Copenhagen it was merely a little mysterious and added another clinging wisp of charm.

Helga Crane's new existence was intensely pleasant to her; it gratified her augmented sense of self-importance. And it suited her. She had to admit that the Danes had the right idea. To each his own milieu. Enhance what was already in one's possession. In America Negroes sometimes talked loudly of this, but in their hearts they repudiated it. In their lives too. They didn't want to be like themselves. What they wanted, asked for, begged for, was to be like their white overlords. They were ashamed to be Negroes, but not ashamed to beg to be something else. Something inferior. Not quite genuine. Too bad!

Helga Crane didn't, however, think often of America, excepting in unfavorable contrast to Denmark. For she had resolved never to return to the existence of ignominy which the New World of opportunity and promise forced upon Negroes. How stupid she had been ever to have thought that she could marry and perhaps have children in a land where every dark child was handicapped at the start by the shroud of color! She saw, suddenly, the giving birth to little, helpless, unprotesting Negro children as a sin, an unforgivable outrage. More black folk to suffer indignities. More dark bodies for mobs to lynch. No, Helga Crane didn't think often of America. It was too humiliating, too disturbing. And she wanted to be left to the peace which had come to her. Her mental difficulties and questionings had become simplified. She now believed sincerely that there was a law of compensation, and that sometimes it worked. For all those early desolate years she now felt recompensed. She recalled a line that had impressed her in her lonely school-days, "The far-off interest of tears."

To her, Helga Crane, it had come at last, and she meant to cling to it. So she turned her back on painful America, resolutely shutting out the griefs, the humiliations, the frustrations, which she had endured there.

Her mind was occupied with other and nearer things.

The charm of the old city itself, with its odd architectural mixture of medievalism and modernity, and the general air of well-being which pervaded it, impressed her. Even in the so-called poor sections there was none of that untidiness and squalor which she remembered as the accompaniment of poverty in Chicago, New York, and the Southern cities of America. Here the door-steps were always white from constant scrubbings, the women neat, and the children washed and provided with whole clothing. Here were no tatters and rags, no beggars. But, then, begging, she learned, was an offense punishable by law. Indeed, it was unnecessary in a country where everyone considered it a duty somehow to support himself and his family by honest work; or, if misfortune and illness came upon one, everyone else, including the State, felt bound to give assistance, a lift on the road to the regaining of independence.

After the initial shyness and consternation at the sensation caused by her strange presence had worn off, Helga spent hours driving or walking about the city, at first in the protecting company of Uncle Poul or Aunt Katrina or both, or sometimes Axel Olsen. But later, when she had become a little familiar with the city, and its inhabitants a little used to her, and when she had learned to cross the streets in safety, dodging successfully the innumerable bicycles like a true Copenhagener, she went often alone, loitering on the long bridge which spanned the placid lakes, and watching the pageant of the blue-clad, sprucely tailored soldiers in the daily parade at Amalienborg Palace, or in the historic vicinity of the long, low-lying Exchange, a picturesque structure in picturesque surroundings, skirting as it did the great canal, which always was alive with many small boats, flying broad white sails and pressing close on the huge ruined pile of the Palace of Christiansborg. There was also the Gammelstrand, the congregating-place of the venders of fish, where daily was enacted a spirited and interesting scene between sellers and buyers, and where Helga's appearance always roused lively and audible, but friendly, interest, long after she became in other parts of the city an accepted curiosity. Here it was that one day an old countrywoman asked her to what manner of mankind she belonged and at Helga's replying: "I'm a Negro," had become indignant, retorting angrily that, just because she was old and a countrywoman she could not be so easily fooled, for she knew as well as everyone else that Negroes were black and had woolly hair.

Against all this walking the Dahls had at first uttered mild protest. "But, Aunt dear, I have to walk, or I'll get fat," Helga asserted. "I've never, never in all my life, eaten so much." For the accepted style of entertainment in Copenhagen seemed to be a round of dinner-parties, at which it was customary for the hostess to tax the full capacity not only of her dining-room, but of her guests as well. Helga enjoyed these dinner-parties, as they were usually spirited affairs, the conversation brilliant and witty, often in several languages. And always she came in for a goodly measure of flattering attention and admiration.

There were, too, those popular afternoon gatherings for the express purpose of drinking coffee together, where between much talk, interesting talk, one sipped the strong and steaming beverage from exquisite cups fashioned of Royal Danish porcelain and partook of an infinite variety of rich cakes and *smørrebrød*. This *smørrebrød*, dainty sandwiches of an endless and tempting array, was distinctly a Danish institution. Often Helga wondered just how many of these delicious sandwiches she had consumed since setting foot on Denmark's soil. Always, wherever food was served, appeared the inevitable *smørrebrød*, in the home of the Dahls, in every other home that she visited, in hotels, in restaurants.

At first she had missed, a little, dancing, for, though excellent dancers, the Danes seemed not to care a great deal for that pastime, which so delightfully combines exercise and pleasure. But in the winter there was skating, solitary, or in gay groups. Helga liked this sport, though she was not very good at it. There were, however, always plenty of efficient and willing men to instruct and to guide her over the glittering ice. One could, too, wear such attractive skating-things.

But mostly it was with Axel Olsen that her thoughts were occupied. Brilliant, bored, elegant, urbane, cynical, worldly, he was a type entirely new to Helga Crane, familiar only, and that but little, with the restricted society of American Negroes. She was aware, too, that this amusing, if conceited, man was interested in her. They were, because he was painting her, much together. Helga spent long mornings in the eccentric studio opposite the Folkemuseum, and Olsen came often to the Dahl home, where, as Helga and the man himself knew, he was something more than welcome. But in spite of his expressed interest and even delight in her exotic appearance, in spite of his constant attendance upon her, he gave no sign of the more personal kind of concern which—encouraged by Aunt Katrina's mild insinuations and Uncle Poul's subtle questionings—she had tried to secure. Was it, she wondered, race that kept him silent, held him back. Helga Crane frowned on this thought, putting it furiously from her, because it disturbed her sense of security and permanence in her new life, pricked her self-assurance.

Nevertheless she was startled when on a pleasant afternoon while drinking coffee in the Hotel Vivili, Aunt Katrina mentioned, almost casually, the desirability of Helga's making a good marriage.

"Marriage, Aunt dear!"

"Marriage," firmly repeated her aunt, helping herself to another anchovy and olive sandwich. "You are," she pointed out, "twenty-five."

"Oh, Aunt, I couldn't! I mean, there's nobody here for me to marry." In spite of herself and her desire not to be, Helga was shocked.

"Nobody?" There was, Fru Dahl asserted, Captain Frederick Skaargaard—and very handsome he was too—and he would have money. And there was Herr Hans Tietgen, not so handsome, of course, but clever and a good business man; he too would be rich, very rich, some day. And there was Herr Karl Pedersen, who had a good berth with the Landmands-bank and considerable shares in a prosperous cement-factory at Aalborg. There was, too, Christian Lende, the young owner of the new Odin Theater. Any of these Helga might marry, was Aunt Katrina's opinion. "And," she added, "others." Or maybe Helga herself had some ideas.

Helga had. She didn't, she responded, believe in mixed marriages, "between races, you know." They brought only trouble —to the children—as she herself knew but too well from bitter experience.

Fru Dahl thoughtfully lit a cigarette. Eventually, after a satisfactory glow had manifested itself, she announced: "Because your mother was a fool. Yes, she was! If she'd come home after she married, or after you were born, or even after your father —er—went off like that, it would have been different. If even she'd left you when she was here. But why in the world she should have married again and a person like that, I can't see. She wanted to keep you, she insisted on it, even over his protest, I think. She loved you so much, she said.—And so she made you unhappy. Mothers, I suppose, are like that. Selfish. And Karen was always stupid. If you've got any brains at all they came from your father."

Into this Helga would not enter. Because of its obvious partial truths she felt the need for disguising caution. With a detachment that amazed herself she asked if Aunt Katrina didn't think, really, that miscegenation was wrong, in fact as well as principle.

"Don't," was her aunt's reply, "be a fool too, Helga. We don't think of those things here. Not in connection with individuals, at least." And almost immediately she inquired: "Did you give Herr Olsen my message about dinner tonight?"

"Yes, Aunt." Helga was cross, and trying not to show it.

"He's coming?"

"Yes, Aunt," with precise politeness.

"What about him?"

"I don't know. *What* about him?"

"He likes you?"

"I don't know. How can I tell that?" Helga asked with irritating reserve, her concentrated attention on the selection of a sandwich. She had a feeling of nakedness. Outrage.

Now Fru Dahl was annoyed and showed it. "What nonsense! Of course you know. Any girl does," and her satin-covered foot tapped, a little impatiently, the old tiled floor.

"Really, I don't know, Aunt," Helga responded in a strange voice, a strange manner, coldly formal, levelly courteous. Then suddenly contrite, she added: "Honestly, I don't. I can't tell a thing about him," and fell into a little silence. "Not a thing," she repeated. But the phrase, though audible, was addressed to no one. To herself.

She looked out into the amazing orderliness of the street. Instinctively she wanted to combat this searching into the one thing which, here, surrounded by all other things which for so long she had so positively wanted, made her a little afraid. Started vague premonitions.

Fru Dahl regarded her intently. It would be, she remarked with a return of her outward casualness, by far the best of all possibilities. Particularly desirable. She touched Helga's hand with her fingers in a little affectionate gesture. Very lightly.

Helga Crane didn't immediately reply. There was, she knew, so much reason—from one viewpoint—in her aunt's statement. She could only acknowledge it. "I know that," she told her finally. Inwardly she was admiring the cool, easy way in which Aunt Katrina had brushed aside the momentary acid note of the conversation and resumed her customary pitch. It took, Helga thought, a great deal of security. Balance.

"Yes," she was saying, while leisurely lighting another of those long, thin, brown cigarettes which Helga knew from distressing experience to be incredibly nasty tasting, "it would be the ideal thing for you, Helga." She gazed penetratingly into the masked face of her niece and nodded, as though satisfied with what she saw there. "And you of course realize that you are a very charming and beautiful girl. Intelligent too. If you put your mind to it, there's no reason in the world why you shouldn't—" Abruptly she stopped, leaving her implication at once suspended and clear. Behind her there were footsteps. A small gloved hand appeared on her shoulder. In the short moment before turning to greet Fru Fischer she said quietly, meaningly: "Or else stop wasting your time, Helga."

Helga Crane said: "Ah, Fru Fischer. It's good to see you." She meant it. Her whole body was tense with suppressed indignation. Burning inside like the confined fire of a hot furnace. She was so harassed that she smiled in self-protection. And suddenly she was oddly cold. An intimation of things distant, but none the less disturbing, oppressed her with a faintly sick feeling. Like a heavy weight, a stone weight, just where, she knew, was her stomach.

Fru Fischer was late. As usual. She apologized profusely. Also as usual. And, yes, she would have some coffee. And some *smørrebrød*. Though she must say that the coffee here at the Vivili was atrocious. Simply atrocious. "I don't see how you stand it." And the place was getting so common, always so many Bolsheviks and Japs and things. And she didn't—"begging your pardon, Helga"—like that hideous American music they were forever playing, even if it was considered very smart. "Give me," she said, "the good old-fashioned Danish melodies of Gade and Heise. Which reminds me, Herr Olsen says that Nielsen's 'Helios' is being performed with great success just now in England. But I suppose you know all about it, Helga. He's already told you. What?" This last was accompanied with an arch and insinuating smile.

A shrug moved Helga Crane's shoulders. Strange she'd never before noticed what a positively disagreeable woman Fru Fischer was. Stupid, too.

Fifteen

WELL into Helga's second year in Denmark, came an indefinite discontent. Not clear, but vague, like a storm gathering far on the horizon. It was long before she would admit that she was less happy than she had been during her first year in Copenhagen, but she knew that it was so. And this subconscious knowledge added to her growing restlessness and little mental insecurity. She desired ardently to combat this wearing down of her satisfaction with her life, with herself. But she didn't know how.

Frankly the question came to this: what was the matter with her? Was there, without her knowing it, some peculiar lack in her? Absurd. But she began to have a feeling of discouragement and hopelessness. Why couldn't she be happy, content, somewhere? Other people managed, somehow, to be. To put it plainly, didn't she know how? Was she incapable of it?

And then on a warm spring day came Anne's letter telling of her coming marriage to Anderson, who retained still his shadowy place in Helga Crane's memory. It added, somehow, to her discontent, and to her growing dissatisfaction with her peacock's life. This, too, annoyed her.

What, she asked herself, was there about that man which had the power always to upset her? She began to think back to her first encounter with him. Perhaps if she hadn't come away— She laughed. Derisively. "Yes, if I hadn't come away, I'd be stuck in Harlem. Working every day of my life. Chattering about the race problem."

Anne, it seemed, wanted her to come back for the wedding. This, Helga had no intention of doing. True, she had liked and admired Anne better than anyone she had ever known, but even for her she wouldn't cross the ocean.

Go back to America, where they hated Negroes! To America, where Negroes were not people. To America, where Negroes were allowed to be beggars only, of life, of happiness, of security. To America, where everything had been taken from those dark ones, liberty, respect, even the labor of their hands. To America, where if one had Negro blood, one mustn't expect money, education, or, sometimes, even work whereby one might earn bread. Perhaps she was wrong to bother about it now that she was so far away. Helga couldn't, however, help it. Never could she recall the shames and often the absolute horrors of the black man's existence in America without the quickening of her heart's beating and a sensation of disturbing nausea. It was too awful. The sense of dread of it was almost a tangible thing in her throat.

And certainly she wouldn't go back for any such idiotic reason as Anne's getting married to that offensive Robert Anderson. Anne was really too amusing. Just why, she wondered, and how had it come about that he was being married to Anne. And why did Anne, who had so much more than so many others—more than enough—want Anderson too? Why couldn't she— "I think," she told herself, "I'd better stop. It's none of my business. I don't care in the least. Besides," she added irrelevantly, "I hate such nonsensical soul-searching."

One night not long after the arrival of Anne's letter with its curious news, Helga went with Olsen and some other young folk to the great Circus, a vaudeville house, in search of amusement on a rare off night. After sitting through several numbers they reluctantly arrived at the conclusion that the whole entertainment was dull, unutterably dull, and apparently without alleviation, and so not to be borne. They were reaching for their wraps when out upon the stage pranced two black men, American Negroes undoubtedly, for as they danced and cavorted, they sang in the English of America an old rag-time song that Helga remembered hearing as a child, "Everybody Gives Me Good Advice." At its conclusion the audience applauded with delight. Only Helga Crane was silent, motionless.

More songs, old, all of them old, but new and strange to that audience. And how the singers danced, pounding their thighs, slapping their hands together, twisting their legs, waving their abnormally long arms, throwing their bodies about with a loose ease! And how the enchanted spectators clapped and howled and shouted for more!

Helga Crane was not amused. Instead she was filled with a fierce hatred for the cavorting Negroes on the stage. She felt shamed, betrayed, as if these pale pink and white people among whom she lived had suddenly been invited to look upon something in her which she had hidden away and wanted to forget. And she was shocked at the avidity at which Olsen beside her drank it in.

But later, when she was alone, it became quite clear to her that all along they had divined its presence, had known that in her was something, some characteristic, different from any that they themselves possessed. Else why had they decked her out as they had? Why subtly indicated that she was different? And they hadn't despised it. No, they had admired it, rated it as a precious thing, a thing to be enhanced, preserved. Why? She, Helga Crane, didn't admire it. She suspected that no Negroes, no Americans, did. Else why their constant slavish imitation of traits not their own? Why their constant begging to be considered as exact copies of other people? Even the enlightened, the intelligent ones demanded nothing more. They were all beggars like the motley crowd in the old nursery rhyme:

> *Hark! Hark!*
> *The dogs do bark.*
> *The beggars are coming to town.*
> *Some in rags,*
> *Some in tags,*
> *And some in velvet gowns.*

The incident left her profoundly disquieted. Her old unhappy questioning mood came again upon her, insidiously stealing away more of the contentment from her transformed existence.

But she returned again and again to the Circus, always alone, gazing intently and solemnly at the gesticulating black figures, an ironical and silently speculative spectator. For she knew that into her plan for her life had thrust itself a suspensive conflict in which were fused doubts, rebellion, expediency, and urgent longings.

It was at this time that Axel Olsen asked her to marry him. And now Helga Crane was surprised. It was a thing that at one time she had much wanted, had tried to bring about, and had at last relinquished as impossible of achievement. Not so much because of its apparent hopelessness as because of a feeling, intangible almost, that, excited and pleased as he was with her, her origin a little repelled him, and that, prompted by some impulse of racial antagonism, he had retreated into the fastness of a protecting habit of self-ridicule. A mordantly personal pride and sensitiveness deterred Helga from further efforts at incitation.

True, he had made, one morning, while holding his brush poised for a last, a very last stroke on the portrait, one admirably draped suggestion, speaking seemingly to the pictured face. Had he insinuated marriage, or something less—and easier? Or had he paid her only a rather florid compliment, in somewhat dubious taste? Helga, who had not at the time been quite sure, had remained silent, striving to appear unhearing.

Later, having thought it over, she flayed herself for a fool. It wasn't, she should have known, in the manner of Axel Olsen to pay florid compliments in questionable taste. And had it been marriage that he had meant, he would, of course, have done the proper thing. He wouldn't have stopped—or, rather, have begun—by making his wishes known to her when there was Uncle Poul to be formally consulted. She had been, she told herself, insulted. And a goodly measure of contempt and wariness was added to her interest in the man. She was able, however, to feel a gratifying sense of elation in the remembrance that she had been silent, ostensibly unaware of his utterance, and therefore, as far as he knew, not affronted.

This simplified things. It did away with the quandary in which the confession to the Dahls of such a happening would have involved her, for she couldn't be sure that they, too, might not put it down to the difference of her ancestry. And she could still go attended by him, and envied by others, to openings in Kongens Nytorv, to showings at the Royal Academy or Charlottenborg's Palace. He could still call for her and Aunt Katrina of an afternoon or go with her to Magasin du Nord to select a scarf or a length of silk, of which Uncle Poul could say casually in the presence of interested acquaintances: "Um, pretty scarf"—or "frock"—"you're wearing, Helga. Is that the new one Olsen helped you with?"

Her outward manner toward him changed not at all, save that gradually she became, perhaps, a little more detached and indifferent. But definitely Helga Crane had ceased, even remotely, to consider him other than as someone amusing, desirable, and convenient to have about—if one was careful.

She intended, presently, to turn her attention to one of the others. The decorative Captain of the Hussars, perhaps. But in the ache of her growing nostalgia, which, try as she might, she could not curb, she no longer thought with any seriousness on either Olsen or Captain Skaargaard. She must, she felt, see America again first. When she returned—

Therefore, where before she would have been pleased and proud at Olsen's proposal, she was now truly surprised. Strangely, she was aware also of a curious feeling of repugnance, as her eyes slid over his face, as smiling, assured, with just the right note of fervor, he made his declaration and request. She was astonished. Was it possible? Was it really this man that she had thought, even wished, she could marry?

He was, it was plain, certain of being accepted, as he was always certain of acceptance, of adulation, in any and every place that he deigned to honor with his presence. Well, Helga was thinking, that wasn't as much his fault as her own, her aunt's, everyone's. He was spoiled, childish almost.

To his words, once she had caught their content and recovered from her surprise, Helga paid not much attention. They would, she knew, be absolutely appropriate ones, and they didn't at all matter. They meant nothing to her—now. She was too amazed to discover suddenly how intensely she disliked him, disliked the shape of his head, the mop of his hair, the line of his nose, the tones of his voice, the nervous grace of his long fingers; disliked even the very look of his irreproachable clothes. And for some inexplicable reason, she was a little frightened and embarrassed, so that when he had finished speaking, for a short space there was only stillness in the small room, into which Aunt Katrina had tactfully had him shown. Even Thor, the enormous Persian, curled on the window ledge in the feeble late afternoon sun, had rested for the moment from his incessant purring under Helga's idly stroking fingers.

Helga, her slight agitation vanished, told him that she was surprised. His offer was, she said, unexpected. Quite.

A little sardonically, Olsen interrupted her. He smiled too. "But of course I expected surprise. It is, is it not, the proper thing? And always you are proper, Frøkken Helga, always."

Helga, who had a stripped, naked feeling under his direct

glance, drew herself up stiffly. Herr Olsen needn't, she told him, be sarcastic. She *was* surprised. He must understand that she was being quite sincere, quite truthful about that. Really, she hadn't expected him to do her so great an honor.

He made a little impatient gesture. Why, then, had she refused, ignored, his other, earlier suggestion?

At that Helga Crane took a deep indignant breath and was again, this time for an almost imperceptible second, silent. She had, then, been correct in her deduction. Her sensuous, petulant mouth hardened. That he should so frankly—so insolently, it seemed to her—admit his outrageous meaning was too much. She said, coldly: "Because, Herr Olsen, in my country the men, of my race, at least, don't make such suggestions to decent girls. And thinking that you were a gentleman, introduced to me by my aunt, I chose to think myself mistaken, to give you the benefit of the doubt."

"Very commendable, my Helga—and wise. Now you have your reward. Now I offer you marriage."

"Thanks," she answered, "thanks, awfully."

"Yes," and he reached for her slim cream hand, now lying quiet on Thor's broad orange and black back. Helga let it lie in his large pink one, noting their contrast. "Yes, because I, poor artist that I am, cannot hold out against the deliberate lure of you. You disturb me. The longing for you does harm to my work. You creep into my brain and madden me," and he kissed the small ivory hand. Quite decorously, Helga thought, for one so maddened that he was driven, against his inclination, to offer her marriage. But immediately, in extenuation, her mind leapt to the admirable casualness of Aunt Katrina's expressed desire for this very thing, and recalled the unruffled calm of Uncle Poul under any and all circumstances. It was, as she had long ago decided, security. Balance.

"But," the man before her was saying, "for me it will be an experience. It may be that with you, Helga, for wife, I will become great. Immortal. Who knows? I didn't want to love you, but I had to. That is the truth. I make of myself a present to you. For love." His voice held a theatrical note. At the same time he moved forward putting out his arms. His hands touched air. For Helga had moved back. Instantly he dropped his arms and took a step away, repelled by something suddenly wild in her face and manner. Sitting down, he passed a hand over his face with a quick, graceful gesture.

Tameness returned to Helga Crane. Her ironic gaze rested on the face of Axel Olsen, his leonine head, his broad nose— "broader than my own"—his bushy eyebrows, surmounting thick, drooping lids, which hid, she knew, sullen blue eyes. He stirred sharply, shaking off his momentary disconcertion.

In his assured, despotic way he went on: "You know, Helga, you are a contradiction. You have been, I suspect, corrupted by the good Fru Dahl, which is perhaps as well. Who knows? You have the warm impulsive nature of the women of Africa, but, my lovely, you have, I fear, the soul of a prostitute. You sell yourself to the highest buyer. I should of course be happy that it is I. And I am." He stopped, contemplating her, lost apparently, for the second, in pleasant thoughts of the future.

To Helga he seemed to be the most distant, the most unreal figure in the world. She suppressed a ridiculous impulse to laugh. The effort sobered her. Abruptly she was aware that in the end, in some way, she would pay for this hour. A quick brief fear ran through her, leaving in its wake a sense of impending calamity. She wondered if for this she would pay all that she'd had.

And, suddenly, she didn't at all care. She said, lightly, but firmly: "But you see, Herr Olsen, I'm not for sale. Not to you. Not to any white man. I don't at all care to be owned. Even by you."

The drooping lids lifted. The look in the blue eyes was, Helga thought, like the surprised stare of a puzzled baby. He hadn't at all grasped her meaning.

She proceeded, deliberately. "I think you don't understand me. What I'm trying to say is this, I don't want you. I wouldn't under any circumstances marry you," and since she was, as she put it, being brutally frank, she added: "*Now.*"

He turned a little away from her, his face white but composed, and looked down into the gathering shadows in the little park before the house. At last he spoke, in a queer frozen voice: "You refuse me?"

"Yes," Helga repeated with intentional carelessness. "I refuse you."

The man's full upper lip trembled. He wiped his forehead, where the gold hair was now lying flat and pale and lusterless. His eyes still avoided the girl in the high-backed chair before him. Helga felt a shiver of compunction. For an instant she regretted that she had not been a little kinder. But wasn't it after all the greatest kindness to be cruel? But more gently, less indifferently, she said: "You see, I couldn't marry a white man. I simply couldn't. It isn't just you, not just personal, you understand. It's deeper, broader than that. It's racial. Some day maybe you'll be glad. We can't tell, you know; if we were married, you might come to be ashamed of me, to hate me, to hate all dark people. My mother did that."

"I have offered you marriage, Helga Crane, and you answer me with some strange talk of race and shame. What nonsense is this?"

Helga let that pass because she couldn't, she felt, explain. It would be too difficult, too mortifying. She had no words which could adequately, and without laceration to her pride, convey to him the pitfalls into which very easily they might step. "I might," she said, "have considered it once—when I first came. But you, hoping for a more informal arrangement, waited too long. You missed the moment. I had time to think. Now I couldn't. Nothing is worth the risk. We might come to hate each other. I've been through it, or something like it. I know. I couldn't do it. And I'm glad."

Rising, she held out her hand, relieved that he was still silent. "Good afternoon," she said formally. "It has been a great honor—"

"A tragedy," he corrected, barely touching her hand with his moist finger-tips.

"Why?" Helga countered, and for an instant felt as if something sinister and internecine flew back and forth between them like poison.

"I mean," he said, and quite solemnly, "that though I don't entirely understand you, yet in a way I do too. And—" He hesitated. Went on. "I think that my picture of you is, after all, the true Helga Crane. Therefore—a tragedy. For someone. For me? Perhaps."

"Oh, the picture!" Helga lifted her shoulders in a little impatient motion.

Ceremoniously Axel Olsen bowed himself out, leaving her grateful for the urbanity which permitted them to part without too much awkwardness. No other man, she thought, of her acquaintance could have managed it so well—except, perhaps, Robert Anderson.

"I'm glad," she declared to herself in another moment, "that I refused him. And," she added honestly, "I'm glad that I had the chance. He took it awfully well, though—for a tragedy." And she made a tiny frown.

The picture—she had never quite, in spite of her deep interest in him, and her desire for his admiration and approval, forgiven Olsen for that portrait. It wasn't, she contended, herself at all, but some disgusting sensual creature with her features. Herr and Fru Dahl had not exactly liked it either, although collectors, artists, and critics had been unanimous in their praise and it had been hung on the line at an annual exhibition, where it had attracted much flattering attention and many tempting offers.

Now Helga went in and stood for a long time before it, with its creator's parting words in mind: ". . . a tragedy . . . my picture is, after all, the true Helga Crane." Vehemently she shook her head. "It isn't, it isn't at all," she said aloud. Bosh! Pure artistic bosh and conceit. Nothing else. Anyone with half an eye could see that it wasn't, at all, like her.

"Marie," she called to the maid passing in the hall, "do you think this is a good picture of me?"

Marie blushed. Hesitated. "Of course, Frøkken, I know Herr Olsen is a great artist, but no, I don't like that picture. It looks bad, wicked. Begging your pardon, Frøkken."

"Thanks, Marie, I don't like it either."

Yes, anyone with half an eye could see that it wasn't she.

Sixteen

Glad though the Dahls may have been that their niece had had the chance of refusing the hand of Axel Olsen, they were anything but glad that she had taken that chance. Very plainly they said so, and quite firmly they pointed out to her the advisability of retrieving the opportunity, if, indeed, such a thing were possible. But it wasn't, even had Helga been so inclined, for, they were to learn from the columns of *Politikken*, Axel Olsen had gone off suddenly to some queer place in the Balkans. To rest, the newspapers said. To get Frøkken Crane out of his mind, the gossips said.

Life in the Dahl ménage went on, smoothly as before, but not so pleasantly. The combined disappointment and sense of guilt of the Dahls and Helga colored everything. Though she had resolved not to think that they felt that she had, as it were, "let them down," Helga knew that they did. They had not so much expected as hoped that she would bring down Olsen, and so secure the link between the merely fashionable set to which they belonged and the artistic one after which they hankered. It was of course true that there were others, plenty of them. But there was only one Olsen. And Helga, for some idiotic reason connected with race, had refused him. Certainly there was no use in thinking, even, of the others. If she had refused him, she would refuse any and all for the same reason. It was, it seemed, all-embracing.

"It isn't," Uncle Poul had tried to point out to her, "as if there were hundreds of mulattoes here. That, I can understand, might make it a little different. But there's only you. You're unique here, don't you see? Besides, Olsen has money and enviable position. Nobody'd dare to say, or even to think anything odd or unkind of you or him. Come now, Helga, it isn't this foolishness about race. Not here in Denmark. You've never spoken of it before. It can't be just that. You're too sensible. It must be something else. I wish you'd try to explain. You don't perhaps like Olsen?"

Helga had been silent, thinking what a severe wrench to Herr Dahl's ideas of decency was this conversation. For he had an almost fanatic regard for reticence, and a peculiar shrinking from what he looked upon as indecent exposure of the emotions.

"Just what is it, Helga?" he asked again, because the pause had grown awkward, for him.

"I can't explain any better than I have," she had begun tremulously, "it's just something—something deep down inside of me," and had turned away to hide a face convulsed by threatening tears.

But that, Uncle Poul had remarked with a reasonableness that was wasted on the miserable girl before him, was nonsense, pure nonsense.

With a shaking sigh and a frantic dab at her eyes, in which had come a despairing look, she had agreed that perhaps it was foolish, but she couldn't help it. "Can't you, won't you understand, Uncle Poul?" she begged, with a pleading look at the kindly worldly man who at that moment had been thinking that this strange exotic niece of his wife's was indeed charming. He didn't blame Olsen for taking it rather hard.

The thought passed. She was weeping. With no effort at restraint. Charming, yes. But insufficiently civilized. Impulsive. Imprudent. Selfish.

"Try, Helga, to control yourself," he had urged gently. He detested tears. "If it distresses you so, we won't talk of it again. You, of course, must do as you yourself wish. Both your aunt and I want only that you should be happy." He had wanted to make an end of this fruitless wet conversation.

Helga had made another little dab at her face with the scrap of lace and raised shining eyes to his face. She had said, with sincere regret: "You've been marvelous to me, you and Aunt Katrina. Angelic. I don't want to seem ungrateful. I'd do anything for you, anything in the world but this."

Herr Dahl had shrugged. A little sardonically he had smiled. He had refrained from pointing out that this was the only thing she could do for them, the only thing that they had asked of her. He had been too glad to be through with the uncomfortable discussion.

So life went on. Dinners, coffees, theaters, pictures, music, clothes. More dinners, coffees, theaters, clothes, music. And that nagging aching for America increased. Augmented by the uncomfortableness of Aunt Katrina's and Uncle Poul's disappointment with her, that tormenting nostalgia grew to an unbearable weight. As spring came on with many gracious tokens of following summer, she found her thoughts straying with increasing frequency to Anne's letter and to Harlem, its dirty streets, swollen now, in the warmer weather, with dark, gay humanity.

Until recently she had had no faintest wish ever to see America again. Now she began to welcome the thought of a return. Only a visit, of course. Just to see, to prove to herself that there was nothing there for her. To demonstrate the absurdity of even thinking that there could be. And to relieve the slight tension here. Maybe when she came back—

Her definite decision to go was arrived at with almost bewildering suddenness. It was after a concert at which Dvořák's "New World Symphony" had been wonderfully rendered. Those wailing undertones of "Swing Low, Sweet Chariot" were too poignantly familiar. They struck into her longing heart and cut away her weakening defenses. She knew at least what it was that had lurked formless and undesignated these many weeks in the back of her troubled mind. Incompleteness.

"I'm homesick, not for America, but for Negroes. That's the trouble."

For the first time Helga Crane felt sympathy rather than contempt and hatred for that father, who so often and so angrily she had blamed for his desertion of her mother. She understood, now, his rejection, his repudiation, of the formal calm her mother had represented. She understood his yearning, his intolerable need for the inexhaustible humor and the incessant hope of his own kind, his need for those things, not material, indigenous to all Negro environments. She understood and could sympathize with his facile surrender to the irresistible ties of race, now that they dragged at her own heart. And as she attended parties, the theater, the opera, and mingled with people on the streets, meeting only pale serious faces when she longed for brown laughing ones, she was able to forgive him. Also, it was as if in this understanding and forgiving she had come upon knowledge of almost sacred importance.

Without demur, opposition, or recrimination Herr and Fru Dahl accepted Helga's decision to go back to America. She had expected that they would be glad and relieved. It was agreeable to discover that she had done them less than justice. They were, in spite of their extreme worldliness, very fond of her, and would, as they declared, miss her greatly. And they did want her to come back to them, as they repeatedly insisted. Secretly they felt as she did, that perhaps when she returned— So it was agreed upon that it was only for a brief visit, "for your friend's wedding," and that she was to return in the early fall.

The last day came. The last good-byes were said. Helga began to regret that she was leaving. Why couldn't she have two lives, or why couldn't she be satisfied in one place? Now that she was actually off, she felt heavy at heart. Already she looked back with infinite regret at the two years in the country which had given her so much, of pride, of happiness, of wealth, and of beauty.

Bells rang. The gangplank was hoisted. The dark strip of water widened. The running figures of friends suddenly grown very dear grew smaller, blurred into a whole, and vanished. Tears rose in Helga Crane's eyes, fear in her heart.

Good-bye Denmark! Good-bye. Good-bye!

Seventeen

A SUMMER had ripened and fall begun. Anne and Dr. Anderson had returned from their short Canadian wedding journey. Helga Crane, lingering still in America, had tactfully removed herself from the house in One Hundred and Thirty-ninth Street to a hotel. It was, as she could point out to curious acquaintances, much better for the newly-married Andersons not to be bothered with a guest, not even with such a close friend as she, Helga, had been to Anne.

Actually, though she herself had truly wanted to get out of the house when they came back, she had been a little surprised and a great deal hurt that Anne had consented so readily to her going. She might at least, thought Helga indignantly, have acted a little bit as if she had wanted her to stay. After writing for her to come, too.

Pleasantly unaware was Helga that Anne, more silently wise than herself, more determined, more selfish, and less inclined to leave anything to chance, understood perfectly that in a large measure it was the voice of Robert Anderson's inexorable conscience that had been the chief factor in bringing about her second marriage—his ascetic protest against the sensuous, the physical. Anne had perceived that the decorous surface of her new husband's mind regarded Helga Crane with that intellectual and æsthetic appreciation which attractive and intelligent women would always draw from him, but that underneath that well-managed section, in a more lawless place where she herself never hoped or desired to enter, was another, a vagrant primitive groping toward something shocking and frightening to the cold asceticism of his reason. Anne knew also that though she herself was lovely—more beautiful than Helga—and interesting, with her he had not to struggle against that nameless and to him shameful impulse, that sheer delight, which ran through his nerves at mere proximity to Helga. And Anne intended that her marriage should be a success. She intended that her husband should be happy. She was sure that it could be managed by tact and a little cleverness on her own part. She was truly fond of Helga, but seeing how she had grown more charming, more aware of her power, Anne wasn't so sure that her sincere and urgent request to come over for her wedding hadn't been a mistake. She was, however, certain of herself. She could look out for her husband. She could carry out what she considered her obligation to him, keep him undisturbed, unhumiliated. It was impossible that she could fail. Unthinkable.

Helga, on her part, had been glad to get back to New York. How glad, or why, she did not truly realize. And though she sincerely meant to keep her promise to Aunt Katrina and Uncle Poul and return to Copenhagen, summer, September, October, slid by and she made no move to go. Her uttermost intention had been a six or eight weeks' visit, but the feverish rush of New York, the comic tragedy of Harlem, still held her. As time went on, she became a little bored, a little restless, but she stayed on. Something of that wild surge of gladness that had swept her on the day when with Anne and Anderson she had again found herself surrounded by hundreds, thousands, of dark-eyed brown folk remained with her. *These* were her people. Nothing, she had come to understand now, could ever change that. Strange that she had never truly valued this kinship until distance had shown her its worth. How absurd she had been to think that another country, other people, could liberate her from the ties which bound her forever to these mysterious, these terrible, these fascinating, these lovable, dark hordes. Ties that were of the spirit. Ties not only superficially entangled with mere outline of features or color of skin. Deeper. Much deeper than either of these.

Thankful for the appeasement of that loneliness which had again tormented her like a fury, she gave herself up to the miraculous joyousness of Harlem. The easement which its heedless abandon brought to her was a real, a very definite thing. She liked the sharp contrast to her pretentious stately life in Copenhagen. It was as if she had passed from the heavy solemnity of a church service to a gorgeous care-free revel.

Not that she intended to remain. No. Helga Crane couldn't, she told herself and others, live in America. In spite of its glamour, existence in America, even Harlem, was for Negroes too cramped, too uncertain, too cruel; something not to be endured for a lifetime if one could escape; something demanding a courage greater than was in her. No. She couldn't stay. Nor, she saw now, could she remain away. Leaving, she would have to come back.

This knowledge, this certainty of the division of her life into two parts in two lands, into physical freedom in Europe and spiritual freedom in America, was unfortunate, inconvenient, expensive. It was, too, as she was uncomfortably aware, even a trifle ridiculous, and mentally she caricatured herself moving shuttle-like from continent to continent. From the prejudiced restrictions of the New World to the easy formality of the Old, from the pale calm of Copenhagen to the colorful lure of Harlem.

Nevertheless she felt a slightly pitying superiority over those Negroes who were apparently so satisfied. And she had a fine contempt for the blatantly patriotic black Americans. Always when she encountered one of those picturesque parades in the Harlem streets, the Stars and Stripes streaming ironically, insolently, at the head of the procession tempered for her, a little, her amusement at the childish seriousness of the spectacle. It was too pathetic.

But when mental doors were deliberately shut on those skeletons that stalked lively and in full health through the consciousness of every person of Negro ancestry in America—conspicuous black, obvious brown, or indistinguishable white—life was intensely amusing, interesting, absorbing, and enjoyable; singularly lacking in that tone of anxiety which the insecurities of existence seemed to ferment in other peoples.

Yet Helga herself had an acute feeling of insecurity, for which she could not account. Sometimes it amounted to fright almost. "I must," she would say then, "get back to Copenhagen." But the resolution gave her not much pleasure. And for this she now blamed Axel Olsen. It was, she insisted, he who had driven her back, made her unhappy in Denmark. Though she knew well that it wasn't. Misgivings, too, rose in her. Why hadn't she married him? Anne was married—she would not say Anderson— Why not she? It would serve Anne right if she married a white man. But she knew in her soul that she wouldn't. "Because I'm a fool," she said bitterly.

Eighteen

ONE November evening, impregnated still with the kindly warmth of the dead Indian summer, Helga Crane was leisurely dressing in pleasant anticipation of the party to which she had been asked for that night. It was always amusing at the Tavernors'. Their house was large and comfortable, the food and music always of the best, and the type of entertainment always unexpected and brilliant. The drinks, too, were sure to be safe.

And Helga, since her return, was more than ever popular at parties. Her courageous clothes attracted attention, and her deliberate lure—as Olsen had called it—held it. Her life in Copenhagen had taught her to expect and accept admiration as her due. This attitude, she found, was as effective in New York as across the sea. It was, in fact, even more so. And it was more amusing too. Perhaps because it was somehow a bit more dangerous.

In the midst of curious speculation as to the possible identity of the other guests, with an indefinite sense of annoyance she wondered if Anne would be there. There was of late something about Anne that was to Helga distinctly disagreeable, a peculiar half-patronizing attitude, mixed faintly with distrust. Helga couldn't define it, couldn't account for it. She had tried. In the end she had decided to dismiss it, to ignore it.

"I suppose," she said aloud, "it's because she's married again. As if anybody couldn't get married. Anybody. That is, if mere marriage is all one wants."

Smoothing away the tiny frown between the broad black brows, she got herself into a little shining, rose-colored slip of a frock knotted with a silver cord. The gratifying result soothed her ruffled feelings. It didn't really matter, this new manner of Anne's. Nor did the fact that Helga knew that Anne disapproved of her. Without words Anne had managed to make that evident. In her opinion, Helga had lived too long among the enemy, the detestable pale faces. She understood them too well, was too tolerant of their ignorant stupidities. If they had been Latins, Anne might conceivably have forgiven the disloyalty.

394

But Nordics! Lynchers! It was too traitorous. Helga smiled a little, understanding Anne's bitterness and hate, and a little of its cause. It was of a piece with that of those she so virulently hated. Fear. And then she sighed a little, for she regretted the waning of Anne's friendship. But, in view of diverging courses of their lives, she felt that even its complete extinction would leave her undevastated. Not that she wasn't still grateful to Anne for many things. It was only that she had other things now. And there would, forever, be Robert Anderson between them. A nuisance. Shutting them off from their previous confident companionship and understanding. "And anyway," she said again, aloud, "he's nobody much to have married. Anybody could have married him. Anybody. If a person wanted only to be married— If it had been somebody like Olsen— That would be different—something to crow over, perhaps."

The party was even more interesting than Helga had expected. Helen, Mrs. Tavenor, had given vent to a malicious glee, and had invited representatives of several opposing Harlem political and social factions, including the West Indian, and abandoned them helplessly to each other. Helga's observing eyes picked out several great and near-great sulking or obviously trying hard not to sulk in widely separated places in the big rooms. There were present, also, a few white people, to the open disapproval or discomfort of Anne and several others. There too, poised, serene, certain, surrounded by masculine black and white, was Audrey Denney.

"Do you know, Helen," Helga confided, "I've never met Miss Denney. I wish you'd introduce me. Not this minute. Later, when you can manage it. Not so—er—apparently by request, you know."

Helen Tavenor laughed. "No, you wouldn't have met her, living as you did with Anne Grey. Anderson, I mean. She's Anne's particular pet aversion. The mere sight of Audrey is enough to send her into a frenzy for a week. It's too bad, too, because Audrey's an awfully interesting person and Anne's said some pretty awful things about her. *You'll* like her, Helga."

Helga nodded. "Yes, I expect to. And I know about Anne. One night—" She stopped, for across the room she saw, with a stab of surprise, James Vayle. "Where, Helen did you get him?"

"Oh, that? That's something the cat brought in. Don't ask which one. He came with somebody, I don't remember who. I think he's shocked to death. Isn't he lovely? The dear baby. I was going to introduce him to Audrey and tell her to do a good job of vamping on him as soon as I could remember the darling's name, or when it got noisy enough so he wouldn't hear what I called him. But you'll do just as well. Don't tell me you know him!" Helga made a little nod. "Well! And I suppose you met him at some shockingly wicked place in Europe. That's always the way with those innocent-looking men."

"Not quite. I met him ages ago in Naxos. We were engaged to be married. Nice, isn't he? His name's Vayle. James Vayle."

"Nice," said Helen throwing out her hands in a characteristic dramatic gesture—she had beautiful hands and arms—"is exactly the word. Mind if I run off? I've got somebody here who's going to sing. *Not* spirituals. And I haven't the faintest notion where he's got to. The cellar, I'll bet."

James Vayle hadn't, Helga decided, changed at all. Someone claimed her for a dance and it was some time before she caught his eyes, half questioning, upon her. When she did, she smiled in a friendly way over her partner's shoulder and was rewarded by a dignified little bow. Inwardly she grinned, flattered. He hadn't forgotten. He was still hurt. The dance over, she deserted her partner and deliberately made her way across the room to James Vayle. He was for the moment embarrassed and uncertain. Helga Crane, however, took care of that, thinking meanwhile that Helen was right. Here he did seem frightfully young and delightfully unsophisticated. He must be, though, every bit of thirty-two or more.

"They say," was her bantering greeting, "that if one stands on the corner of One Hundred and Thirty-fifth Street and Seventh Avenue long enough, one will eventually see all the people one has ever known or met. It's pretty true, I guess. Not literally of course." He was, she saw, getting himself together. "It's only another way of saying that everybody, almost, some time sooner or later comes to Harlem, even you."

He laughed. "Yes, I guess that is true enough. I didn't come to stay, though." And then he was grave, his earnest eyes searchingly upon her.

"Well, anyway, you're here now, so let's find a quiet corner if that's possible, where we can talk. I want to hear all about you."

For a moment he hung back and a glint of mischief shone in Helga's eyes. "I see," she said, "you're just the same. However, you needn't be anxious. This isn't Naxos, you know. Nobody's watching us, or if they are, they don't care a bit what we do."

At that he flushed a little, protested a little, and followed her. And when at last they had found seats in another room, not so crowded, he said: "I didn't expect to see you here. I thought you were still abroad."

"Oh, I've been back some time, ever since Dr. Anderson's marriage. Anne, you know, is a great friend of mine. I used to live with her. I came for the wedding. But, of course, I'm not staying. I didn't think I'd be here this long."

"You don't mean that you're going to live over there? Do you really like it so much better?"

"Yes and no, to both questions. I was awfully glad to get back, but I wouldn't live here always. I couldn't. I don't think that any of us who've lived abroad for any length of time would ever live here altogether again if they could help it."

"Lot of them do, though," James Vayle pointed out.

"Oh, I don't mean tourists who rush over to Europe and rush all over the continent and rush back to America thinking they know Europe. I mean people who've actually lived there, actually lived among the people."

"I still maintain that they nearly all come back here eventually to live."

"That's because they can't help it," Helga Crane said firmly. "Money, you know."

"Perhaps, I'm not so sure. I was in the war. Of course, that's not really living over there, but I saw the country and the difference in treatment. But, I can tell you, I was pretty darn glad to get back. All the fellows were." He shook his head solemnly. "I don't think anything, money or lack of money, keeps us here. If it was only that, if we really wanted to leave, we'd go all right. No, it's something else, something deeper than that."

"And just what do you think it is?"

"I'm afraid it's hard to explain, but I suppose it's just that we like to be together. I simply can't imagine living forever away from colored people."

A suspicion of a frown drew Helga's brows. She threw out rather tartly: "I'm a Negro too, you know."

"Well, Helga, you were always a little different, a little dissatisfied, though I don't pretend to understand you at all. I never did," he said a little wistfully.

And Helga, who was beginning to feel that the conversation had taken an impersonal and disappointing tone, was reassured and gave him her most sympathetic smile and said almost gently: "And now let's talk about you. You're still at Naxos?"

"Yes I'm still there. I'm assistant principal now."

Plainly it was a cause for enthusiastic congratulation, but Helga could only manage a tepid "How nice!" Naxos was to her too remote, too unimportant. She did not even hate it now.

How long, she asked, would James be in New York?

He couldn't say. Business, important business for the school, had brought him. It was, he said, another tone creeping into his voice, another look stealing over his face, awfully good to see her. She was looking tremendously well. He hoped he would have the opportunity of seeing her again.

But of course. He must come to see her. Any time, she was always in, or would be for him. And how did he like New York, Harlem?

He didn't, it seemed, like it. It was nice to visit, but not to live in. Oh, there were so many things he didn't like about it, the rush, the lack of home life, the crowds, the noisy meaninglessness of it all.

On Helga's face there had come that pityingly sneering look peculiar to imported New Yorkers when the city of their adoption is attacked by alien Americans. With polite contempt she inquired: "And is that all you don't like?"

At her tone the man's bronze face went purple. He answered coldly, slowly, with a faint gesture in the direction of Helen Tavenor, who stood conversing gayly with one of her white guests: "And I don't like that sort of thing. In fact I detest it."

"Why?" Helga was striving hard to be casual in her manner.

James Vayle, it was evident, was beginning to be angry. It was also evident that Helga Crane's question had embarrassed him. But he seized the bull by the horns and said: "You know as well as I do, Helga, that it's the colored girls these men come up here to see. They wouldn't think of bringing their wives." And he blushed furiously at his own implication. The blush restored Helga's good temper. James was really too funny.

"That," she said softly, "is Hugh Wentworth, the novelist, you know." And she indicated a tall olive-skinned girl being whirled about to the streaming music in the arms of a towering black man. "And that is his wife. She isn't colored, as you've probably been thinking. And now let's change the subject again."

"All right! And this time let's talk about you. You say you don't intend to live here. Don't you ever intend to marry, Helga?"

"Some day, perhaps. I don't know. Marriage—that means children, to me. And why add more suffering to the world? Why add any more unwanted, tortured Negroes to America? Why *do* Negroes have children? Surely it must be sinful. Think of the awfulness of being responsible for the giving of life to creatures doomed to endure such wounds to the flesh, such wounds to the spirit, as Negroes have to endure."

James was aghast. He forgot to be embarrassed. "But Helga! Good heavens! Don't you see that if we—I mean people like us—don't have children, the others will still have. That's one of the things that's the matter with us. The race is sterile at the top. Few, very few Negroes of the better class have children, and each generation has to wrestle again with the obstacles of the preceding ones, lack of money, education, and background. I feel very strongly about this. We're the ones who must have the children if the race is to get anywhere."

"Well, I for one don't intend to contribute any to the cause. But how serious we are! And I'm afraid that I've really got to leave you. I've already cut two dances for your sake. Do come to see me."

"Oh, I'll come to see you all right. I've got several things that I want to talk to you about and one thing especially."

"Don't," Helga mocked, "tell me you're going to ask me again to marry you."

"That," he said, "is just what I intend to do."

Helga Crane was suddenly deeply ashamed and very sorry for James Vayle, so she told him laughingly that it was shameful of him to joke with her like that, and before he could answer, she had gone tripping off with a handsome coffee-colored youth whom she had beckoned from across the room with a little smile.

Later she had to go upstairs to pin up a place in the hem of her dress which had caught on a sharp chair corner. She finished the temporary repair and stepped out into the hall, and somehow, she never quite knew exactly just how, into the arms of Robert Anderson. She drew back and looked up smiling to offer an apology.

And then it happened. He stooped and kissed her, a long kiss, holding her close. She fought against him with all her might. Then, strangely, all power seemed to ebb away, and a long-hidden, half-understood desire welled up in her with the suddenness of a dream. Helga Crane's own arms went up about the man's neck. When she drew away, consciously confused and embarrassed, everything seemed to have changed in a space of time which she knew to have been only seconds. Sudden anger seized her. She pushed him indignantly aside and with a little pat for her hair and dress went slowly down to the others.

Nineteen

THAT night riotous and colorful dreams invaded Helga Crane's prim hotel bed. She woke in the morning weary and a bit shocked at the uncontrolled fancies which had visited her. Catching up a filmy scarf, she paced back and forth across the narrow room and tried to think. She recalled her flirtations and her mild engagement with James Vayle. She was used to kisses. But none had been like that of last night. She lived over those brief seconds, thinking not so much of the man whose arms had held her as of the ecstasy which had flooded her. Even recollection brought a little onrush of emotion that made her sway a little. She pulled herself together and began to fasten on the solid fact of Anne and experienced a pleasant sense of shock in the realization that Anne was to her exactly what she had been before the incomprehensible experience of last night. She still liked her in the same degree and in the same manner. She still felt slightly annoyed with her. She still did not envy her marriage with Anderson. By some mysterious process the emotional upheaval which had racked her had left all the rocks of her existence unmoved. Outwardly nothing had changed.

Days, weeks, passed; outwardly serene; inwardly tumultuous. Helga met Dr. Anderson at the social affairs to which often they were both asked. Sometimes she danced with him, always in perfect silence. She couldn't, she absolutely couldn't, speak a word to him when they were thus alone together, for at such times lassitude encompassed her; the emotion which had gripped her retreated, leaving a strange tranquillity, troubled only by a soft stir of desire. And shamed by his silence, his apparent forgetting, always after these dances she tried desperately to persuade herself to believe what she wanted to believe: that it had not happened, that she had never had that irrepressible longing. It was of no use.

As the weeks multiplied, she became aware that she must get herself out of the mental quagmire into which that kiss had thrown her. And she should be getting herself back to Copenhagen, but she had now no desire to go.

Abruptly one Sunday in a crowded room, in the midst of teacups and chatter, she knew that she couldn't go, that she hadn't since that kiss intended to go without exploring to the end that unfamiliar path into which she had strayed. Well, it was of no use lagging behind or pulling back. It was of no use trying to persuade herself that she didn't want to go on. A species of fatalism fastened on her. She felt that, ever since that last day in Naxos long ago, somehow she had known that this thing would happen. With this conviction came an odd sense of elation. While making a pleasant assent to some remark of a fellow guest she put down her cup and walked without haste, smiling and nodding to friends and acquaintances on her way to that part of the room where he stood looking at some examples of African carving. Helga Crane faced him squarely. As he took the hand which she held out with elaborate casualness, she noted that his trembled slightly. She was secretly congratulating herself on her own calm when it failed her. Physical weariness descended on her. Her knees wobbled. Gratefully she slid into the chair which he hastily placed for her. Timidity came over her. She was silent. He talked. She did not listen. He came at last to the end of his long dissertation on African sculpture, and Helga Crane felt the intentness of his gaze upon her.

"Well?" she questioned.

"I want very much to see you, Helga. Alone."

She held herself tensely on the edge of her chair, and suggested: "Tomorrow?"

He hesitated a second and then said quickly: "Why, yes, that's all right."

"Eight o'clock?"

"Eight o'clock," he agreed.

Eight o'clock tomorrow came. Helga Crane never forgot it. She had carried away from yesterday's meeting a feeling of increasing elation. It had seemed to her that she hadn't been so happy, so exalted, in years, if ever. All night, all day, she had mentally prepared herself for the coming consummation; physically too, spending hours before the mirror.

Eight o'clock had come at last and with it Dr. Anderson. Only then had uneasiness come upon her and a feeling of fear for possible exposure. For Helga Crane wasn't, after all, a rebel from society, Negro society. It did mean something to her. She had no wish to stand alone. But these late fears were overwhelmed by the hardiness of insistent desire; and she had got herself down to the hotel's small reception room.

It was, he had said, awfully good of her to see him. She instantly protested. No, she had wanted to see him. He looked at her surprised. "You know, Helga," he had begun with an air of desperation, "I can't forgive myself for acting such a swine at the Travenors' party. I don't at all blame you for being angry and not speaking to me except when you had to."

But that, she exclaimed, was simply too ridiculous. "I wasn't angry a bit." And it had seemed to her that things were not exactly going forward as they should. It seemed that he had been very sincere, and very formal. Deliberately. She had looked down at her hands and inspected her bracelets, for she had felt that to look at him would be, under the circumstances, too exposing.

"I was afraid," he went on, "that you might have misunderstood; might have been unhappy about it. I could kick myself. It was, it must have been, Tavenor's rotten cocktails."

Helga Crane's sense of elation had abruptly left her. At the same time she had felt the need to answer carefully. No, she replied, she hadn't thought of it at all. It had meant nothing to her. She had been kissed before. It was really too silly of him to have been at all bothered about it. "For what," she had asked, "is one kiss more or less, these days, between friends?" She had even laughed a little.

Dr. Anderson was relieved. He had been, he told her, no end upset. Rising, he said: "I see you're going out. I won't keep you."

Helga Crane too had risen. Quickly. A sort of madness had swept over her. She felt that he had belittled and ridiculed her. And thinking this, she had suddenly savagely slapped Robert Anderson with all her might, in the face.

For a short moment they had both stood stunned, in the deep silence which had followed that resounding slap. Then, without a word of contrition or apology, Helga Crane had gone out of the room and upstairs.

She had, she told herself, been perfectly justified in slapping

Dr. Anderson, but she was not convinced. So she had tried hard to make herself very drunk in order that sleep might come to her, but had managed only to make herself very sick.

Not even the memory of how all living had left his face, which had gone a taupe gray hue, or the despairing way in which he had lifted his head and let it drop, or the trembling hands which he had pressed into his pockets, brought her any scrap of comfort. She had ruined everything. Ruined it because she had been so silly as to close her eyes to all indications that pointed to the fact that no matter what the intensity of his feelings or desires might be, he was not the sort of man who would for any reason give up one particle of his own good opinion of himself. Not even for her. Not even though he knew that she had wanted so terribly something special from him.

Something special. And now she had forfeited it forever. Forever. Helga had an instantaneous shocking perception of what forever meant. And then, like a flash, it was gone, leaving an endless stretch of dreary years before her appalled vision.

Twenty

THE day was a rainy one. Helga Crane, stretched out on her bed, felt herself so broken physically, mentally, that she had given up thinking. But back and forth in her staggered brain wavering, incoherent thoughts shot shuttle-like. Her pride would have shut out these humiliating thoughts and painful visions of herself. The effort was too great. She felt alone, isolated from all other human beings, separated even from her own anterior existence by the disaster of yesterday. Over and over, she repeated: "There's nothing left but to go now." Her anguish seemed unbearable.

For days, for weeks, voluptuous visions had haunted her. Desire had burned in her flesh with uncontrollable violence. The wish to give herself had been so intense that Dr. Anderson's surprising, trivial apology loomed as a direct refusal of the offering. Whatever outcome she had expected, it had been something else than this, this mortification, this feeling of ridicule and self-loathing, this knowledge that she had deluded herself. It was all, she told herself, as unpleasant as possible.

Almost she wished she could die. Not quite. It wasn't that she was afraid of death, which had, she thought, its picturesque aspects. It was rather that she knew she would not die. And death, after the debacle, would but intensify its absurdity. Also, it would reduce her, Helga Crane, to unimportance, to nothingness. Even in her unhappy present state, that did not appeal to her. Gradually, reluctantly, she began to know that the blow to her self-esteem, the certainty of having proved herself a silly fool, was perhaps the severest hurt which she had suffered. It was her self-assurance that had gone down in the crash. After all, what Dr. Anderson thought didn't matter. She could escape from the discomfort of his knowing gray eyes. But she couldn't escape from sure knowledge that she had made a fool of herself. This angered her further and she struck the wall with her hands and jumped up and began hastily to dress herself. She couldn't go on with the analysis. It was too hard. Why bother when she could add nothing to the obvious fact that she had been a fool?

"I can't stay in this room any longer. I must get out or I'll choke." Her self-knowledge had increased her anguish. Distracted, agitated, incapable of containing herself, she tore open drawers and closets trying desperately to take some interest in the selection of her apparel.

It was evening and still raining. In the streets, unusually deserted, the electric lights cast dull glows. Helga Crane, walking rapidly, aimlessly, could decide on no definite destination. She had not thought to take umbrella or even rubbers. Rain and wind whipped cruelly about her, drenching her garments and chilling her body. Soon the foolish little satin shoes which she wore were sopping wet. Unheeding these physical discomforts, she went on, but at the open corner of One Hundred and Thirty-eighth Street a sudden more ruthless gust of wind ripped the small hat from her head. In the next minute the black clouds opened wider and spilled their water with unusual fury. The streets became swirling rivers. Helga Crane, forgetting her mental torment, looked about anxiously for a sheltering taxi. A few taxis sped by, but inhabited, so she began desperately to struggle through wind and rain toward one of the buildings, where she could take shelter in a store or a doorway. But another whirl of wind lashed her and, scornful of her slight strength, tossed her into the swollen gutter.

Now she knew beyond all doubt that she had no desire to die, and certainly not there nor then. Not in such a messy wet manner. Death had lost all of its picturesque aspects to the girl lying soaked and soiled in the flooded gutter. So, though she was very tired and very weak, she dragged herself up and succeeded finally in making her way to the store whose blurred light she had marked for her destination.

She had opened the door and had entered before she was aware that, inside, people were singing a song which she was conscious of having heard years ago—hundreds of years it seemed. Repeated over and over, she made out the words:

> . . . *Showers of blessings,*
> *Showers of blessings* . . .

She was conscious too of a hundred pairs of eyes upon her as she stood there, drenched and disheveled, at the door of this improvised meeting-house.

. . . Showers of blessings . . .

The appropriateness of the song, with its constant reference to showers, the ridiculousness of herself in such surroundings, was too much for Helga Crane's frayed nerves. She sat down on the floor, a dripping heap, and laughed and laughed and laughed.

It was into a shocked silence that she laughed. For at the first hysterical peal the words of the song had died in the singers' throats, and the wheezy organ had lapsed into stillness. But in a moment there were hushed solicitous voices; she was assisted to her feet and led haltingly to a chair near the low platform at the far end of the room. On one side of her a tall angular black woman under a queer hat sat down, on the other a fattish yellow man with huge outstanding ears and long, nervous hands.

The singing began again, this time a low wailing thing:

> *Oh, the bitter shame and sorrow*
> *That a time could ever be,*
> *When I let the Savior's pity*
> *Plead in vain, and proudly answered:*
> *"All of self and none of Thee,*
> *All of self and none of Thee."*

> *Yet He found me, I beheld Him,*
> *Bleeding on the cursed tree;*
> *Heard Him pray: "Forgive them, Father."*
> *And my wistful heart said faintly,*
> *"Some of self and some of Thee,*
> *Some of self and some of Thee."*

There were, it appeared, endless moaning verses. Behind Helga a woman had begun to cry audibly, and soon, somewhere else, another. Outside, the wind still bellowed. The wailing singing went on:

> *. . . Less of self and more of Thee,*
> *Less of self and more of Thee.*

Helga too began to weep, at first silently, softly; then with great racking sobs. Her nerves were so torn, so aching, her body so wet, so cold! It was a relief to cry unrestrainedly, and she gave herself freely to soothing tears, not noticing that the groaning and sobbing of those about her had increased, unaware that the grotesque ebony figure at her side had begun gently to pat her arm to the rhythm of the singing and to croon softly: "Yes, chile, yes, chile." Nor did she notice the furtive glances that the man on her other side cast at her between his fervent shouts of "Amen!" and "Praise God for a sinner!"

She did notice, though, that the tempo, the atmosphere of the place, had changed, and gradually she ceased to weep and gave her attention to what was happening about her. Now they were singing:

> . . . *Jesus knows all about my troubles* . . .

Men and women were swaying and clapping their hands, shouting and stamping their feet to the frankly irreverent melody of the song. Without warning the woman at her side threw off her hat, leaped to her feet, waved her long arms, and shouted shrilly: "Glory! Hallelujah!" and then, in wild ecstatic fury jumped up and down before Helga clutching at the girl's soaked coat, and screamed: "Come to Jesus, you pore los' sinner!" Alarmed for the fraction of a second, involuntarily Helga had shrunk from her grasp, wriggling out of the wet coat when she could not loosen the crazed creature's hold. At the sight of the bare arms and neck growing out of the clinging red dress, a shudder shook the swaying man at her right. On the face of the dancing woman before her a disapproving frown gathered. She shrieked: "A scarlet 'oman. Come to Jesus, you pore los' Jezebel!"

At this the short brown man on the platform raised a placating hand and sanctimoniously delivered himself of the words: "Remembah de words of our Mastah: 'Let him that is without sin cast de first stone.' Let us pray for our errin' sistah."

Helga Crane was amused, angry, disdainful, as she sat there, listening to the preacher praying for her soul. But though she was contemptuous, she was being too well entertained to leave. And it was, at least, warm and dry. So she stayed, listening to the fervent exhortation to God to save her and to the zealous shoutings and groanings of the congregation. Particularly she was interested in the writhings and weepings of the feminine portion, which seemed to predominate. Little by little the performance took on an almost Bacchic vehemence. Behind her, before her, beside her, frenzied women gesticulated, screamed, wept, and tottered to the praying of the preacher, which had gradually become a cadenced chant. When at last he ended, another took up the plea in the same moaning chant, and then another. It went on and on without pause with the persistence of some unconquerable faith exalted beyond time and reality.

Fascinated, Helga Crane watched until there crept upon her an indistinct horror of an unknown world. She felt herself in the presence of a nameless people, observing rites of a remote obscure origin. The faces of the men and women took on the aspect of a dim vision. "This," she whispered to herself, "is terrible. I must get out of here." But the horror held her. She remained motionless, watching as if she lacked the strength to leave the place—foul, vile, and terrible, with its mixture of breaths, its contact of bodies, its concerted convulsions, all in wild appeal for a single soul. Her soul.

And as Helga watched and listened, gradually a curious influence penetrated her, she felt an echo of the weird orgy resound in her own heart; she felt herself possessed by the same madness; she too felt a brutal desire to shout and to sling herself about. Frightened at the strength of the obsession, she gathered herself for one last effort to escape, but vainly. In rising, weakness and nausea from last night's unsuccessful attempt to make herself drunk overcame her. She had eaten nothing since yesterday. She fell forward against the crude railing which enclosed the little platform. For a single moment she remained there in silent stillness, because she was afraid she was going to be sick. And in that moment she was lost—or saved. The yelling figures about her pressed forward, closing her in on all sides. Maddened, she grasped at the railing, and with no previous intention began to yell like one insane, drowning every other clamor, while torrents of tears streamed down her face. She was unconscious of the words she uttered, or their meaning: "Oh God, mercy, mercy. Have mercy on me!" but she repeated them over and over.

From those about her came a thunderclap of joy. Arms were stretched toward her with savage frenzy. The women dragged themselves upon their knees or crawled over the floor like reptiles, sobbing and pulling their hair and tearing off their clothing. Those who succeeded in getting near to her leaned forward to encourage the unfortunate sister, dropping hot tears and beads of sweat upon her bare arms and neck.

The thing became real. A miraculous calm came upon her. Life seemed to expand, and to become very easy. Helga Crane felt within her a supreme aspiration toward the regaining of simple happiness, a happiness unburdened by the complexities of the lives she had known. About her the tumult and the shouting continued, but in a lesser degree. Some of the more exuberant worshipers had fainted into inert masses, the voices of others were almost spent. Gradually the room grew quiet and almost solemn, and to the kneeling girl time seemed to sink back into the mysterious grandeur and holiness of far-off simpler centuries.

Twenty-One

On leaving the mission Helga Crane had started straight back to her room at the hotel. With her had gone the fattish yellow man who had sat beside her. He had introduced himself as the Reverend Mr. Pleasant Green in proffering his escort for which Helga had been grateful because she had still felt a little dizzy and much exhausted. So great had been this physical weariness that as she had walked beside him, without attention to his verbose information about his own "field," as he called it, she had been seized with a hateful feeling of vertigo and obliged to lay firm hold on his arm to keep herself from falling. The weakness had passed as suddenly as it had come. Silently they had walked on. And gradually Helga had recalled that the man beside her had himself swayed slightly at their close encounter, and that frantically for a fleeting moment he had gripped at a protruding fence railing. That man! Was it possible? As easy as that?

Instantly across her still half-hypnotized consciousness little burning darts of fancy had shot themselves. No. She couldn't. It would be too awful. Just the same, what or who was there to hold her back? Nothing. Simply nothing. Nobody. Nobody at all.

Her searching mind had become in a moment quite clear. She cast at the man a speculative glance, aware that for a tiny space she had looked into his mind, a mind striving to be calm. A mind that was certain that it was secure because it was concerned only with things of the soul, spiritual things, which to him meant religious things. But actually a mind by habit at home amongst the mere material aspect of things, and at that moment consumed by some longing for the ecstasy that might lurk behind the gleam of her cheek, the flying wave of her hair, the pressure of her slim fingers on his heavy arm. An instant's flashing vision it had been and it was gone at once. Escaped in the aching of her own senses and the sudden disturbing fear that she herself had perhaps missed the supreme secret of life.

After all, there was nothing to hold her back. Nobody to

care. She stopped sharply, shocked at what she was on the verge of considering. Appalled at where it might lead her.

The man—what was his name?—thinking that she was almost about to fall again, had reached out his arms to her. Helga Crane had deliberately stopped thinking. She had only smiled, a faint provocative smile, and pressed her fingers deep into his arms until a wild look had come into his slightly bloodshot eyes.

The next morning she lay for a long while, scarcely breathing, while she reviewed the happenings of the night before. Curious. She couldn't be sure that it wasn't religion that had made her feel so utterly different from dreadful yesterday. And gradually she became a little sad, because she realized that with every hour she would get a little farther away from this soothing haziness, this rest from her long trouble of body and of spirit; back into the clear bareness of her own small life and being, from which happiness and serenity always faded just as they had shaped themselves. And slowly bitterness crept into her soul. Because, she thought, all I've ever had in life has been things—except just this one time. At that she closed her eyes, for even remembrance caused her to shiver a little.

Things, she realized, hadn't been, weren't, enough for her. She'd have to have something else besides. It all came back to that old question of happiness. Surely this was it. Just for a fleeting moment Helga Crane, her eyes watching the wind scattering the gray-white clouds and so clearing a speck of blue sky, questioned her ability to retain, to bear, this happiness at such cost as she must pay for it. There was, she knew, no getting round that. The man's agitation and sincere conviction of sin had been too evident, too illuminating. The question returned in a slightly new form. Was it worth the risk? Could she take it? Was she able? Though what did it matter—now?

And all the while she knew in one small corner of her mind that such thinking was useless. She had made her decision. Her resolution. It was a chance at stability, at permanent happiness, that she meant to take. She had let so many other things, other chances, escape her. And anyway there was God, He would perhaps make it come out all right. Still confused and not so sure that it wasn't the fact that she was "saved" that had contributed to this after feeling of well-being, she clutched the

hope, the desire to believe that now at last she had found some
One, some Power, who was interested in her. Would help her.

She meant, however, for once in her life to be practical. So
she would make sure of both things, God and man.

Her glance caught the calendar over the little white desk.
The tenth of November. The steamer *Oscar II* sailed today.
Yesterday she had half thought of sailing with it. Yesterday.
How far away!

With the thought of yesterday came the thought of Robert
Anderson and a feeling of elation, revenge. She had put herself
beyond the need of help from him. She had made it impossible
for herself ever again to appeal to him. Instinctively she had
the knowledge that he would be shocked. Grieved. Horribly
hurt even. Well, let him!

The need to hurry suddenly obsessed her. She must. The
morning was almost gone. And she meant, if she could manage it, to be married today. Rising, she was seized with a fear so
acute that she had to lie down again. For the thought came to
her that she might fail. Might not be able to confront the situation. That would be too dreadful. But she became calm again.
How could he, a naïve creature like that, hold out against her? If
she pretended to distress? To fear? To remorse? He couldn't. It
would be useless for him even to try. She screwed up her face
into a little grin, remembering that even if protestations were
to fail, there were other ways.

And, too, there was God.

Twenty-Two

A ND so in the confusion of seductive repentance Helga Crane was married to the grandiloquent Reverend Mr. Pleasant Green, that rattish yellow man, who had so kindly, so unctuously, proffered his escort to her hotel on the memorable night of her conversion. With him she willingly, even eagerly, left the sins and temptations of New York behind her to, as he put it, "labor in the vineyard of the Lord" in the tiny Alabama town where he was pastor to a scattered and primitive flock. And where, as the wife of the preacher, she was a person of relative importance. Only relative.

Helga did not hate him, the town, or the people. No. Not for a long time.

As always, at first the novelty of the thing, the change, fascinated her. There was a recurrence of the feeling that now, at last, she had found a place for herself, that she was really living. And she had her religion, which in her new status as a preacher's wife had of necessity become real to her. She believed in it. Because in its coming it had brought this other thing, this anæsthetic satisfaction for her senses. Hers was, she declared to herself, a truly spiritual union. This one time in her life, she was convinced, she had not clutched a shadow and missed the actuality. She felt compensated for all previous humiliations and disappointments and was glad. If she remembered that she had had something like this feeling before, she put the unwelcome memory from her with the thought: "This time I know I'm right. This time it will last."

Eagerly she accepted everything, even that bleak air of poverty which, in some curious way, regards itself as virtuous, for no other reason than that it is poor. And in her first hectic enthusiasm she intended and planned to do much good to her husband's parishioners. Her young joy and zest for the uplifting of her fellow men came back to her. She meant to subdue the cleanly scrubbed ugliness of her own surroundings to soft inoffensive beauty, and to help the other women to do likewise. Too, she would help them with their clothes, tactfully point out that sunbonnets, no matter how gay, and aprons, no matter how frilly, were not quite the proper things for Sunday church wear. There would be a sewing circle. She visualized herself instructing the children, who seemed most of the time to run wild, in ways of gentler deportment. She was anxious to be a true helpmate, for in her heart was a feeling of obligation, of humble gratitude.

In her ardor and sincerity Helga even made some small beginnings. True, she was not very successful in this matter of innovations. When she went about to try to interest the women in what she considered more appropriate clothing and in inexpensive ways of improving their homes according to her ideas of beauty, she was met, always, with smiling agreement and good-natured promises. "Yuh all is right, Mis' Green," and "Ah suttinly will, Mis' Green," fell courteously on her ear at each visit.

She was unaware that afterwards they would shake their heads sullenly over their wash-tubs and ironing-boards. And that among themselves they talked with amusement, or with anger, of "dat uppity, meddlin' No'the'nah," and "pore Reve'end," who in their opinion "would 'a done bettah to a ma'ied Clementine Richards." Knowing, as she did, nothing of this, Helga was unperturbed. But even had she known, she would not have been disheartened. The fact that it was difficult but increased her eagerness, and made the doing of it seem only the more worth while. Sometimes she would smile to think how changed she was.

And she was humble too. Even with Clementine Richards, a strapping black beauty of magnificent Amazon proportions and bold shining eyes of jet-like hardness. A person of awesome appearance. All chains, strings of beads, jingling bracelets, flying ribbons, feathery neck-pieces, and flowery hats. Clementine was inclined to treat Helga with an only partially concealed contemptuousness, considering her a poor thing without style, and without proper understanding of the worth and greatness of the man, Clementine's own adored pastor, whom Helga had somehow had the astounding good luck to marry. Clementine's admiration of the Reverend Mr. Pleasant Green was open. Helga was at first astonished. Until she learned that there was really no reason why it should be concealed. Everybody was aware of it. Besides, open adoration was the prerogative, the almost religious duty, of the female portion of the flock. If this unhidden and exaggerated approval contributed to his already oversized pomposity, so much the better. It was what they expected, liked, wanted. The greater his own sense of superiority became, the more flattered they were by his notice and small attentions, the more they cast at him killing glances, the more they hung enraptured on his words.

In the days before her conversion, with its subsequent blurring of her sense of humor, Helga might have amused herself by tracing the relation of this constant ogling and flattering on the proverbially large families of preachers; the often disastrous effect on their wives of this constant stirring of the senses by extraneous women. Now, however, she did not even think of it.

She was too busy. Every minute of the day was full. Necessarily. And to Helga this was a new experience. She was charmed by it. To be mistress in one's own house, to have a garden, and chickens, and a pig; to have a husband—and to be "right with God"—what pleasure did that other world which she had left contain that could surpass these? Here, she had found, she was sure, the intangible thing for which, indefinitely, always she had craved. It had received embodiment.

Everything contributed to her gladness in living. And so for a time she loved everything and everyone. Or thought she did. Even the weather. And it was truly lovely. By day a glittering gold sun was set in an unbelievably bright sky. In the evening silver buds sprouted in a Chinese blue sky, and the warm day was softly soothed by a slight, cool breeze. And night! Night, when a languid moon peeped through the wide-opened windows of her little house, a little mockingly, it may be. Always at night's approach Helga was bewildered by a disturbing medley of feelings. Challenge. Anticipation. And a small fear.

In the morning she was serene again. Peace had returned. And she could go happily, inexpertly, about the humble tasks of her household, cooking, dish-washing, sweeping, dusting, mending, and darning. And there was the garden. When she worked there, she felt that life was utterly filled with the glory and the marvel of God.

Helga did not reason about this feeling, as she did not at that time reason about anything. It was enough that it was there, coloring all her thoughts and acts. It endowed the four rooms of her ugly brown house with a kindly radiance, obliterating the stark bareness of its white plaster walls and the nakedness of its uncovered painted floors. It even softened the choppy lines of the shiny oak furniture and subdued the awesome horribleness of the religious pictures.

And all the other houses and cabins shared in this illumination. And the people. The dark undecorated women unceasingly concerned with the actual business of life, its rounds of births and christenings, of loves and marriages, of deaths and funerals, were to Helga miraculously beautiful. The smallest, dirtiest, brown child, barefooted in the fields or muddy roads, was to her an emblem of the wonder of life, of love, and of God's goodness.

For the preacher, her husband, she had a feeling of gratitude, amounting almost to sin. Beyond that, she thought of him not at all. But she was not conscious that she had shut him out from her mind. Besides, what need to think of him? He was there. She was at peace, and secure. Surely their two lives were one, and the companionship in the Lord's grace so perfect that to think about it would be tempting providence. She had done with soul-searching.

What did it matter that he consumed his food, even the softest varieties, audibly? What did it matter that, though he did no work with his hands, not even in the garden, his finger-nails were always rimmed with black? What did it matter that he failed to wash his fat body, or to shift his clothing, as often as Helga herself did? There were things that more than outweighed these. In the certainty of his goodness, his righteousness, his holiness, Helga somehow overcame her first disgust at the odor of sweat and stale garments. She was even able to be unaware of it. Herself, Helga had come to look upon as a finicky, showy thing of unnecessary prejudices and fripperies. And when she sat in the dreary structure, which had once been a stable belonging to the estate of a wealthy horse-racing man and about which the odor of manure still clung, now the church and social center of the Negroes of the town, and heard him expound with verbal extravagance the gospel of blood and love, of hell and heaven, of fire and gold streets, pounding with clenched fists the frail table before him or shaking those fists in the faces of the congregation like direct personal threats, or pacing wildly back and forth and even sometimes shedding great tears as he besought them to repent, she was, she told herself, proud and gratified that he belonged to her. In some strange way she was able to ignore the atmosphere of self-satisfaction which poured from him like gas from a leaking pipe.

And night came at the end of every day. Emotional, palpitating, amorous, all that was living in her sprang like rank weeds at the tingling thought of night, with a vitality so strong that it devoured all shoots of reason.

Twenty-Three

A FTER the first exciting months Helga was too driven, too occupied, and too sick to carry out any of the things for which she had made such enthusiastic plans, or even to care that she had made only slight progress toward their accomplishment. For she, who had never thought of her body save as something on which to hang lovely fabrics, had now constantly to think of it. It had persistently to be pampered to secure from it even a little service. Always she felt extraordinarily and annoyingly ill, having forever to be sinking into chairs. Or, if she was out, to be pausing by the roadside, clinging desperately to some convenient fence or tree, waiting for the horrible nausea and hateful faintness to pass. The light, care-free days of the past, when she had not felt heavy and reluctant or weak and spent, receded more and more and with increasing vagueness, like a dream passing from a faulty memory.

The children used her up. There were already three of them, all born within the short space of twenty months. Two great healthy twin boys, whose lovely bodies were to Helga like rare figures carved out of amber, and in whose sleepy and mysterious black eyes all that was puzzling, evasive, and aloof in life seemed to find expression. No matter how often or how long she looked at these two small sons of hers, never did she lose a certain delicious feeling in which were mingled pride, tenderness, and exaltation. And there was a girl, sweet, delicate, and flower-like. Not so healthy or so loved as the boys, but still miraculously her own proud and cherished possession.

So there was no time for the pursuit of beauty, or for the uplifting of other harassed and teeming women, or for the instruction of their neglected children.

Her husband was still, as he had always been, deferentially kind and incredulously proud of her—and verbally encouraging. Helga tried not to see that he had rather lost any personal interest in her, except for the short spaces between the times when she was preparing for or recovering from childbirth. She shut her eyes to the fact that his encouragement had become a little platitudinous, limited mostly to "The Lord will look out for you," "We must accept what God sends," or "My mother had nine children and was thankful for every one." If she was inclined to wonder a little just how they were to manage with another child on the way, he would point out to her that her doubt and uncertainty were a stupendous ingratitude. Had not the good God saved her soul from hell-fire and eternal damnation? Had He not in His great kindness given her three small lives to raise up for His glory? Had He not showered her with numerous other mercies (evidently too numerous to be named separately)?

"You must," the Reverend Mr. Pleasant Green would say unctuously, "trust the Lord more fully, Helga."

This pabulum did not irritate her. Perhaps it was the fact that the preacher was, now, not so much at home that even lent to it a measure of real comfort. For the adoring women of his flock, noting how with increasing frequency their pastor's house went unswept and undusted, his children unwashed, and his wife untidy, took pleasant pity on him and invited him often to tasty orderly meals, specially prepared for him, in their own clean houses.

Helga, looking about in helpless dismay and sick disgust at the disorder around her, the permanent assembly of partly emptied medicine bottles on the clock-shelf, the perpetual array of drying baby-clothes on the chair-backs, the constant debris of broken toys on the floor, the unceasing litter of half-dead flowers on the table, dragged in by the toddling twins from the forlorn garden, failed to blame him for the thoughtless selfishness of these absences. And, she was thankful, whenever possible, to be relieved from the ordeal of cooking. There were times when, having had to retreat from the kitchen in lumbering haste with her sensitive nose gripped between tightly squeezing fingers, she had been sure that the greatest kindness that God could ever show to her would be to free her forever from the sight and smell of food.

How, she wondered, did other women, other mothers, manage? Could it be possible that, while presenting such smiling and contented faces, they were all always on the edge of health? All always worn out and apprehensive? Or was it only she, a poor weak city-bred thing, who felt that the strain of what the Reverend Mr. Pleasant Green had so often gently and patiently reminded her was a natural thing, an act of God, was almost unendurable?

One day on her round of visiting—a church duty, to be done no matter how miserable one was—she summoned up sufficient boldness to ask several women how they felt, how they managed. The answers were a resigned shrug, or an amused snort, or an upward rolling of eyeballs with a mention of "de Lawd" looking after us all.

" 'Tain't nothin', nothin' at all, chile," said one, Sary Jones, who, as Helga knew, had had six children in about as many years. "Yuh all takes it too ha'd. Jes' remembah et's natu'al fo' a 'oman to hab chilluns an' don' fret so."

"But," protested Helga, "I'm always so tired and half sick. That can't be natural."

"Laws, chile, we's all ti'ed. An' Ah reckons we's all gwine a be ti'ed till kingdom come. Jes' make de bes' of et, honey. Jes' make de bes' yuh can."

Helga sighed, turning her nose away from the steaming coffee which her hostess had placed for her and against which her squeamish stomach was about to revolt. At the moment the compensations of immortality seemed very shadowy and very far away.

"Jes' remembah," Sary went on, staring sternly into Helga's thin face, "we all gits ouah res' by an' by. In de nex' worl' we's all recompense'. Jes' put yo' trus' in de Sabioah."

Looking at the confident face of the little bronze figure on the opposite side of the immaculately spread table, Helga had a sensation of shame that she should be less than content. Why couldn't she be as trusting and as certain that her troubles would not overwhelm her as Sary Jones was? Sary, who in all likelihood had toiled every day of her life since early childhood except on those days, totalling perhaps sixty, following the birth of her six children. And who by dint of superhuman saving had somehow succeeded in feeding and clothing them and sending them all to school. Before her Helga felt humbled and oppressed by the sense of her own unworthiness and lack of sufficient faith.

"Thanks, Sary," she said, rising in retreat from the coffee, "you've done me a world of good. I'm really going to try to be more patient."

So, though with growing yearning she longed for the great ordinary things of life, hunger, sleep, freedom from pain, she resigned herself to the doing without them. The possibility of alleviating her burdens by a greater faith became lodged in her mind. She gave herself up to it. It *did* help. And the beauty of leaning on the wisdom of God, of trusting, gave to her a queer sort of satisfaction. Faith was really quite easy. One had only to yield. To ask no questions. The more weary, the more weak she became, the easier it was. Her religion was to her a kind of protective coloring, shielding her from the cruel light of an unbearable reality.

This utter yielding in faith to what had been sent her found her favor, too, in the eyes of her neighbors. Her husband's flock began to approve and commend this submission and humility to a superior wisdom. The womenfolk spoke more kindly and more affectionately of the preacher's Northern wife. "Pore Mis' Green, wid all dem small chilluns at once. She suah do hab it ha'd. An' she don' nebah complains an' frets no mo'e. Jes' trus' in de Lawd lak de Good Book say. Mighty sweet lil' 'oman too."

Helga didn't bother much about the preparations for the coming child. Actually and metaphorically she bowed her head before God, trusting in Him to see her through. Secretly she was glad that she had not to worry about herself or anything. It was a relief to be able to put the entire responsibility on someone else.

Twenty-Four

IT began, this next child-bearing, during the morning services of a breathless hot Sunday while the fervent choir soloist was singing: "Ah am freed of mah sorrow," and lasted far into the small hours of Tuesday morning. It seemed, for some reason, not to go off just right. And when, after that long frightfulness, the fourth little dab of amber humanity which Helga had contributed to a despised race was held before her for maternal approval, she failed entirely to respond properly to this sob of consolation for the suffering and horror through which she had passed. There was from her no pleased, proud smile, no loving, possessive gesture, no manifestation of interest in the important matters of sex and weight. Instead she deliberately closed her eyes, mutely shutting out the sickly infant, its smiling father, the soiled midwife, the curious neighbors, and the tousled room.

A week she lay so. Silent and listless. Ignoring food, the clamoring children, the comings and goings of solicitous, kind-hearted women, her hovering husband, and all of life about her. The neighbors were puzzled. The Reverend Mr. Pleasant Green was worried. The midwife was frightened.

On the floor, in and out among the furniture and under her bed, the twins played. Eager to help, the church-women crowded in and, meeting there others on the same laudable errand, stayed to gossip and to wonder. Anxiously the preacher sat, Bible in hand, beside his wife's bed, or in a nervous half-guilty manner invited the congregated parishioners to join him in prayer for the healing of their sister. Then, kneeling, they would beseech God to stretch out His all-powerful hand on behalf of the afflicted one, softly at first, but with rising vehemence, accompanied by moans and tears, until it seemed that the God to whom they prayed must in mercy to the sufferer grant relief. If only so that she might rise up and escape from the tumult, the heat, and the smell.

Helga, however, was unconcerned, undisturbed by the commotion about her. It was all part of the general unreality. Nothing reached her. Nothing penetrated the kind darkness into which her bruised spirit had retreated. Even that red-letter event, the coming to see her of the old white physician from downtown, who had for a long time stayed talking gravely to her husband, drew from her no interest. Nor for days was she aware that a stranger, a nurse from Mobile, had been added to her household, a brusquely efficient woman who produced order out of chaos and quiet out of bedlam. Neither did the absence of the children, removed by good neighbors at Miss Hartley's insistence, impress her. While she had gone down into that appalling blackness of pain, the ballast of her brain had got loose and she hovered for a long time somewhere in that delightful borderland on the edge of unconsciousness, an enchanted and blissful place where peace and incredible quiet encompassed her.

After weeks she grew better, returned to earth, set her reluctant feet to the hard path of life again.

"Well, here you are!" announced Miss Hartley in her slightly harsh voice one afternoon just before the fall of evening. She had for some time been standing at the bedside gazing down at Helga with an intent speculative look.

"Yes," Helga agreed in a thin little voice, "I'm back." The truth was that she had been back for some hours. Purposely she had lain silent and still, wanting to linger forever in that serene haven, that effortless calm where nothing was expected of her. There she could watch the figures of the past drift by. There was her mother, whom she had loved from a distance and finally so scornfully blamed, who appeared as she had always remembered her, unbelievably beautiful, young, and remote. Robert Anderson, questioning, purposely detached, affecting, as she realized now, her life in a remarkably cruel degree; for at last she understood clearly how deeply, how passionately, she must have loved him. Anne, lovely, secure, wise, selfish. Axel Olsen, conceited, worldly, spoiled. Audrey Denney, placid, taking quietly and without fuss the things which she wanted. James Vayle, snobbish, smug, servile. Mrs. Hayes-Rore, important, kind, determined. The Dahls, rich, correct, climbing. Flashingly, fragmentarily, other long-forgotten figures, women in gay fashionable frocks and men in formal black and white glided by in bright rooms to distant, vaguely familiar music.

It was refreshingly delicious, this immersion in the past. But it was finished now. It was over. The words of her husband, the Reverend Mr. Pleasant Green, who had been standing at the window looking mournfully out at the scorched melon-patch, ruined because Helga had been ill so long and unable to tend it, were confirmation of that.

"The Lord be praised," he said, and came forward. It was distinctly disagreeable. It was even more disagreeable to feel his moist hand on hers. A cold shiver brushed over her. She closed her eyes. Obstinately and with all her small strength she drew her hand away from him. Hid it far down under the bed-covering, and turned her face away to hide a grimace of unconquerable aversion. She cared nothing, at that moment, for his hurt surprise. She knew only that, in the hideous agony that for interminable hours—no, centuries—she had borne, the luster of religion had vanished; that revulsion had come upon her; that she hated this man. Between them the vastness of the universe had come.

Miss Hartley, all-seeing and instantly aware of a situation, as she had been quite aware that her patient had been conscious for some time before she herself had announced the fact, intervened, saying firmly: "I think it might be better if you didn't try to talk to her now. She's terribly sick and weak yet. She's still got some fever and we mustn't excite her or she's liable to slip back. And we don't want that, do we?"

No, the man, her husband, responded, they didn't want that. Reluctantly he went from the room with a last look at Helga, who was lying on her back with one frail, pale hand under her small head, her curly black hair scattered loose on the pillow. She regarded him from behind dropped lids. The day was hot, her breasts were covered only by a nightgown of filmy *crêpe*, a relic of prematrimonial days, which had slipped from one carved shoulder. He flinched. Helga's petulant lip curled, for she well knew that this fresh reminder of her desirability was like the flick of a whip.

Miss Hartley carefully closed the door after the retreating husband. "It's time," she said, "for your evening treatment, and then you've got to try to sleep for a while. No more visitors tonight."

Helga nodded and tried unsuccessfully to make a little smile.

She was glad of Miss Hartley's presence. It would, she felt, protect her from so much. She mustn't, she thought to herself, get well too fast. Since it seemed she was going to get well. In bed she could think, could have a certain amount of quiet. Of aloneness.

In that period of racking pain and calamitous fright Helga had learned what passion and credulity could do to one. In her was born angry bitterness and an enormous disgust. The cruel, unrelieved suffering had beaten down her protective wall of artificial faith in the infinite wisdom, in the mercy, of God. For had she not called in her agony on Him? And He had not heard. Why? Because, she knew now, He wasn't there. Didn't exist. Into that yawning gap of unspeakable brutality had gone, too, her belief in the miracle and wonder of life. Only scorn, resentment, and hate remained—and ridicule. Life wasn't a miracle, a wonder. It was, for Negroes at least, only a great disappointment. Something to be got through with as best one could. No one was interested in them or helped them. God! Bah! And they were only a nuisance to other people.

Everything in her mind was hot and cold, beating and swirling about. Within her emaciated body raged disillusion. Chaotic turmoil. With the obscuring curtain of religion rent, she was able to look about her and see with shocked eyes this thing that she had done to herself. She couldn't, she thought ironically, even blame God for it, now that she knew that He didn't exist. No. No more than she could pray to Him for the death of her husband, the Reverend Mr. Pleasant Green. The white man's God. And His great love for all people regardless of race! What idiotic nonsense she had allowed herself to believe. How could she, how could anyone, have been so deluded? How could ten million black folk credit it when daily before their eyes was enacted its contradiction? Not that she at all cared about the ten million. But herself. Her sons. Her daughter. These would grow to manhood, to womanhood, in this vicious, this hypocritical land. The dark eyes filled with tears.

"I wouldn't," the nurse advised, "do that. You've been dreadfully sick, you know. I can't have you worrying. Time enough for that when you're well. Now you must sleep all you possibly can."

Helga did sleep. She found it surprisingly easy to sleep. Aided by Miss Hartley's rather masterful discernment, she took advantage of the ease with which this blessed enchantment stole over her. From her husband's praisings, prayers, and caresses she sought refuge in sleep, and from the neighbors' gifts, advice, and sympathy.

There was that day on which they told her that the last sickly infant, born of such futile torture and lingering torment, had died after a short week of slight living. Just closed his eyes and died. No vitality. On hearing it Helga too had just closed her eyes. Not to die. She was convinced that before her there were years of living. Perhaps of happiness even. For a new idea had come to her. She had closed her eyes to shut in any telltale gleam of the relief which she felt. One less. And she had gone off into sleep.

And there was that Sunday morning on which the Reverend Mr. Pleasant Green had informed her that they were that day to hold a special thanksgiving service for her recovery. There would, he said, be prayers, special testimonies, and songs. Was there anything particular she would like to have said, to have prayed for, to have sung? Helga had smiled from sheer amusement as she replied that there was nothing. Nothing at all. She only hoped that they would enjoy themselves. And, closing her eyes that he might be discouraged from longer tarrying, she had gone off into sleep.

Waking later to the sound of joyous religious abandon floating in through the opened windows, she had asked a little diffidently that she be allowed to read. Miss Hartley's sketchy brows contracted into a dubious frown. After a judicious pause she had answered: "No, I don't think so." Then, seeing the rebellious tears which had sprung into her patient's eyes, she added kindly: "But I'll read to you a little if you like."

That, Helga replied, would be nice. In the next room on a high-up shelf was a book. She'd forgotten the name, but its author was Anatole France. There was a story, "The Procurator of Judea." Would Miss Hartley read that? "Thanks. Thanks awfully."

"'Lælius Lamia, born in Italy of illustrious parents,'" began the nurse in her slightly harsh voice.

Helga drank it in.

" '. . . For to this day the women bring down doves to the altar as their victims. . . .' "

Helga closed her eyes.

" '. . . Africa and Asia have already enriched us with a considerable number of gods. . . .' "

Miss Hartley looked up. Helga had slipped into slumber while the superbly ironic ending which she had so desired to hear was yet a long way off. A dull tale, was Miss Hartley's opinion, as she curiously turned the pages to see how it turned out.

" 'Jesus? . . . Jesus—of Nazareth? I cannot call him to mind.' "

"Huh!" she muttered, puzzled. "Silly." And closed the book.

Twenty-Five

DURING the long process of getting well, between the dreamy intervals when she was beset by the insistent craving for sleep, Helga had had too much time to think. At first she had felt only an astonished anger at the quagmire in which she had engulfed herself. She had ruined her life. Made it impossible ever again to do the things that she wanted, have the things that she loved, mingle with the people she liked. She had, to put it as brutally as anyone could, been a fool. The damnedest kind of a fool. And she had paid for it. Enough. More than enough.

Her mind, swaying back to the protection that religion had afforded her, almost she wished that it had not failed her. An illusion. Yes. But better, far better, than this terrible reality. Religion had, after all, its uses. It blunted the perceptions. Robbed life of its crudest truths. Especially it had its uses for the poor—and the blacks.

For the blacks. The Negroes.

And this, Helga decided, was what ailed the whole Negro race in America, this fatuous belief in the white man's God, this childlike trust in full compensation for all woes and privations in "kingdom come." Sary Jones's absolute conviction, "In de nex' worl' we's all recompense'," came back to her. And ten million souls were as sure of it as was Sary. How the white man's God must laugh at the great joke he had played on them! Bound them to slavery, then to poverty and insult, and made them bear it unresistingly, uncomplainingly, almost, by sweet promises of mansions in the sky by and by.

"Pie in the sky," Helga said aloud derisively, forgetting for the moment Miss Hartley's brisk presence, and so was a little startled at hearing her voice from the adjoining room saying severely: "My goodness! No! I should say you can't have pie. It's too indigestible. Maybe when you're better—"

"That," assented Helga, "is what I said. Pie—by and by. That's the trouble."

The nurse looked concerned. Was this an approaching relapse? Coming to the bedside, she felt at her patient's pulse

429

while giving her a searching look. No. "You'd better," she admonished, a slight edge to her tone, "try to get a little nap. You haven't had any sleep today, and you can't get too much of it. You've got to get strong, you know."

With this Helga was in full agreement. It seemed hundreds of years since she had been strong. And she would need strength. For in some way she was determined to get herself out of this bog into which she had strayed. Or—she would have to die. She couldn't endure it. Her suffocation and shrinking loathing were too great. Not to be borne. Again. For she had to admit that it wasn't new, this feeling of dissatisfaction, of asphyxiation. Something like it she had experienced before. In Naxos. In New York. In Copenhagen. This differed only in degree. And it was of the present and therefore seemingly more reasonable. The other revulsions were of the past, and now less explainable.

The thought of her husband roused in her a deep and contemptuous hatred. At his every approach she had forcibly to subdue a furious inclination to scream out in protest. Shame, too, swept over her at every thought of her marriage. Marriage. This sacred thing of which parsons and other Christian folk ranted so sanctrimoniously, how immoral—according to their own standards—it could be! But Helga felt also a modicum of pity for him, as for one already abandoned. She meant to leave him. And it was, she had to concede, all of her own doing, this marriage. Nevertheless, she hated him.

The neighbors and churchfolk came in for their share of her all-embracing hatred. She hated their raucous laughter, their stupid acceptance of all things, and their unfailing trust in "de Lawd." And more than all the rest she hated the jangling Clementine Richards, with her provocative smirkings, because she had not succeeded in marrying the preacher and thus saving her, Helga, from that crowning idiocy.

Of the children Helga tried not to think. She wanted not to leave them—if that were possible. The recollection of her own childhood, lonely, unloved, rose too poignantly before her for her to consider calmly such a solution. Though she forced herself to believe that this was different. There was not the element of race, of white and black. They were all black together. And they would have their father. But to leave them would be a tearing agony, a rending of deepest fibers. She felt that through all the rest of her lifetime she would be hearing their cry of "Mummy, Mummy, Mummy," through sleepless nights. No. She couldn't desert them.

How, then, was she to escape from the oppression, the degradation, that her life had become? It was so difficult. It was terribly difficult. It was almost hopeless. So for a while—for the immediate present, she told herself—she put aside the making of any plan for her going. "I'm still," she reasoned, "too weak, too sick. By and by, when I'm really strong—"

It was so easy and so pleasant to think about freedom and cities, about clothes and books, about the sweet mingled smell of Houbigant and cigarettes in softly lighted rooms filled with inconsequential chatter and laughter and sophisticated tuneless music. It was so hard to think out a feasible way of retrieving all these agreeable, desired things. Just then. Later. When she got up. By and by. She must rest. Get strong. Sleep. Then, afterwards, she could work out some arrangement. So she dozed and dreamed in snatches of sleeping and waking, letting time run on. Away.

And hardly had she left her bed and become able to walk again without pain, hardly had the children returned from the homes of the neighbors, when she began to have her fifth child.

PLUM BUN

A NOVEL WITHOUT A MORAL

Jessie Redmon Fauset

"To Market, to Market
To buy a Plum Bun;
Home again, Home again,
Market is done."

To
MY FATHER AND MOTHER
REDMOND AND ANNA FAUSET

Contents

HOME

Chapter I

OPAL STREET, as streets go, is no jewel of the first water. It is merely an imitation, and none too good at that. Narrow, unsparkling, uninviting, it stretches meekly off from dull Jefferson Street to the dingy, drab market which forms the north side of Oxford Street. It has no mystery, no allure, either of exclusiveness or of downright depravity; its usages are plainly significant,—an unpretentious little street lined with unpretentious little houses, inhabited for the most part by unpretentious little people.

The dwellings are three stories high, and contain six boxes called by courtesy, rooms—a "parlour", a midget of a dining-room, a larger kitchen and, above, a front bedroom seemingly large only because it extends for the full width of the house, a mere shadow of a bathroom, and another back bedroom with windows whose possibilities are spoiled by their outlook on sad and diminutive back-yards. And above these two, still two others built in similar wise.

In one of these houses dwelt a father, a mother and two daughters. Here, as often happens in a home sheltering two generations, opposite, unevenly matched emotions faced each other. In the houses of the rich the satisfied ambition of the older generation is faced by the overwhelming ambition of the younger. Or the elders may find themselves brought in opposition to the blank indifference and ennui of youth engendered by the realization that there remain no more worlds to conquer; their fathers having already taken all. In houses on Opal Street these niceties of distinction are hardly to be found; there is a more direct and concrete contrast. The satisfied ambition of maturity is a foil for the restless despair of youth.

Affairs in the Murray household were advancing towards this stage; yet not a soul in that family of four could have foretold its coming. To Junius and Mattie Murray, who had known poverty

437

and homelessness, the little house on Opal Street represented the *ne plus ultra* of ambition; to their daughter Angela it seemed the dingiest, drabbest chrysalis that had ever fettered the wings of a brilliant butterfly. The stories which Junius and Mattie told of difficulties overcome, of the arduous learning of trades, of the pitiful scraping together of infinitesimal savings; would have made a latter-day Iliad, but to Angela they were merely a description of a life which she at any cost would avoid living. Somewhere in the world were paths which lead to broad thoroughfares, large, bright houses, delicate niceties of existence. Those paths Angela meant to find and frequent. At a very early age she had observed that the good things of life are unevenly distributed; merit is not always rewarded; hard labour does not necessarily entail adequate recompense. Certain fortuitous endowments, great physical beauty, unusual strength, a certain unswerving singleness of mind,—gifts bestowed quite blindly and disproportionately by the forces which control life,—these were the qualities which contributed toward a glowing and pleasant existence.

Angela had no high purpose in life; unlike her sister Virginia, who meant some day to invent a marvellous method for teaching the pianoforte, Angela felt no impulse to discover, or to perfect. True she thought she might become eventually a distinguished painter, but that was because she felt within herself an ability to depict which as far as it went was correct and promising. Her eye for line and for expression was already good and she had a nice feeling for colour. Moreover she possessed the instinct for self-appraisal which taught her that she had much to learn. And she was sure that the knowledge once gained would flower in her case to perfection. But her gift was not for her the end of existence; rather it was an adjunct to a life which was to know light, pleasure, gaiety and freedom.

Freedom! That was the note which Angela heard oftenest in the melody of living which was to be hers. With a wildness that fell just short of unreasonableness she hated restraint. Her father's earlier days as coachman in a private family, his later successful, independent years as boss carpenter, her mother's youth spent as maid to a famous actress, all this was to Angela a manifestation of the sort of thing which happens to those enchained it might be by duty, by poverty, by weakness or by colour.

Colour or rather the lack of it seemed to the child the one

absolute prerequisite to the life of which she was always dreaming. One might break loose from a too hampering sense of
duty; poverty could be overcome; physicians conquered weakness; but colour, the mere possession of a black or a white skin,
that was clearly one of those fortuitous endowments of the
gods. Gratitude was no strong ingredient in this girl's nature,
yet very often early she began thanking Fate for the chance
which in that household of four had bestowed on her the heritage of her mother's fair skin. She might so easily have been,
like her father, black, or have received the melange which had
resulted in Virginia's rosy bronzeness and her deeply waving
black hair. But Angela had received not only her mother's
creamy complexion and her soft cloudy, chestnut hair, but
she had taken from Junius the aquiline nose, the gift of some
remote Indian ancestor which gave to his face and his eldest
daughter's that touch of chiselled immobility.

It was from her mother that Angela learned the possibilities for
joy and freedom which seemed to her inherent in mere whiteness. No one would have been more amazed than that same
mother if she could have guessed how her daughter interpreted
her actions. Certainly Mrs. Murray did not attribute what she
considered her happy, busy, sheltered life on tiny Opal Street
to the accident of her colour; she attributed it to her black husband whom she had been glad and proud to marry. It is equally
certain that that white skin of hers had not saved her from occasional contumely and insult. The famous actress for whom
she had worked was aware of Mattie's mixed blood and, boasting
temperament rather than refinement, had often dubbed her
"white nigger".

Angela's mother employed her colour very much as she practised certain winning usages of smile and voice to obtain indul-
gences which meant much to her and which took nothing from
anyone else. Then, too, she was possessed of a keener sense
of humour than her daughter; it amused her when by herself
to take lunch at an exclusive restaurant whose patrons would
have been panic-stricken if they had divined the presence of
a "coloured" woman no matter how little her appearance
differed from theirs. It was with no idea of disclaiming her own
that she sat in orchestra seats which Philadelphia denied to

coloured patrons. But when Junius or indeed any other dark friend accompanied her she was the first to announce that she liked to sit in the balcony or gallery, as indeed she did; her infrequent occupation of orchestra seats was due merely to a mischievous determination to flout a silly and unjust law.

Her years with the actress had left their mark, a perfectly harmless and rather charming one. At least so it seemed to Junius, whose weakness was for the qualities known as "essentially feminine". Mrs. Murray loved pretty clothes, she liked shops devoted to the service of women; she enjoyed being even on the fringe of a fashionable gathering. A satisfaction that was almost ecstatic seized her when she drank tea in the midst of modishly gowned women in a stylish tea-room. It pleased her to stand in the foyer of a great hotel or of the Academy of Music and to be part of the whirling, humming, palpitating gaiety. She had no desire to be of these people, but she liked to look on; it amused and thrilled and kept alive some unquenchable instinct for life which thrived within her. To walk through Wanamaker's on Saturday, to stroll from Fifteenth to Ninth Street on Chestnut, to have her tea in the Bellevue Stratford, to stand in the lobby of the St. James' fitting on immaculate gloves; all innocent, childish pleasures pursued without malice or envy contrived to cast a glamour over Monday's washing and Tuesday's ironing, the scrubbing of kitchen and bathroom and the fashioning of children's clothes. She was endowed with a humorous and pungent method of presentation; Junius, who had had the wit not to interfere with these little excursions and the sympathy to take them at their face value, preferred one of his wife's sparkling accounts of a Saturday's adventure in "passing" to all the tall stories told by cronies at his lodge.

Much of this pleasure, harmless and charming though it was, would have been impossible with a dark skin.

In these first years of marriage, Mattie, busied with the house and the two babies had given up those excursions. Later, when the children had grown and Junius had reached the stage where he could afford to give himself a half-holiday on Saturdays, the two parents inaugurated a plan of action which eventually became a fixed programme. Each took a child, and Junius went off to a beloved but long since suspended pastime of exploring old Philadelphia, whereas Mattie embarked once more on her social adventures. It is true that Mattie accompanied by brown Virginia could not move quite as freely as when with Angela. But her maternal instincts were sound; her children, their feelings and their faith in her meant much more than the pleasure which she would have been first to call unnecessary and silly. As it happened the children themselves quite unconsciously solved the dilemma; Virginia found shopping tiring and stupid, Angela returned from her father's adventuring worn and bored. Gradually the rule was formed that Angela accompanied her mother and Virginia her father.

On such fortuities does life depend. Little Angela Murray, hurrying through Saturday morning's scrubbing of steps in order that she might have her bath at one and be with her mother on Chestnut Street at two, never realized that her mother took her pleasure among all these pale people because it was there that she happened to find it. It never occurred to her that the delight which her mother obviously showed in meeting friends on Sunday morning when the whole united Murray family came out of church was the same as she showed on Chestnut Street the previous Saturday, because she was finding the qualities which her heart craved, bustle, excitement and fashion. The daughter could not guess that if the economic status or the racial genius of coloured people had permitted them to run modish hotels or vast and popular department stores her mother would have been there. She drew for herself certain clearly formed conclusions which her subconscious mind thus codified:

First, that the great rewards of life—riches, glamour, pleasure, —are for white-skinned people only. Secondly, that Junius and Virginia were denied these privileges because they were dark; here her reasoning bore at least an element of verisimilitude but she missed the essential fact that her father and sister did not care for this type of pleasure. The effect of her fallaciousness was to cause her to feel a faint pity for her unfortunate relatives and also to feel that coloured people were to be considered fortunate only in the proportion in which they measured up to the physical standards of white people.

One Saturday excursion left a far-reaching impression. Mrs. Murray and Angela had spent a successful and interesting afternoon. They had browsed among the contents of the small exclusive shops in Walnut Street; they had had soda at Adams' on Broad Street and they were standing finally in the portico of the Walton Hotel deciding with fashionable and idle elegance what they should do next. A thin stream of people constantly passing threw an occasional glance at the quietly modish pair, the well-dressed, assured woman and the refined and no less assured daughter. The door-man knew them; it was one of Mrs. Murray's pleasures to proffer him a small tip, much appreciated since it was uncalled for. This was the atmosphere which she loved. Angela had put on her gloves and was waiting for her mother, who was drawing on her own with great care, when she glimpsed in the laughing, hurrying Saturday throng the figures of her father and of Virginia. They were close enough for her mother, who saw them too, to touch them by merely descending a few steps and stretching out her arm. In a second the pair had vanished. Angela saw her mother's face change—with trepidation she thought. She remarked: "It's a good thing Papa didn't see us, you'd have had to speak to him, wouldn't you?" But her mother, giving her a distracted glance, made no reply.

That night, after the girls were in bed, Mattie, perched on the arm of her husband's chair, told him about it. "I was at my old game of playacting again to-day, June, passing you know, and darling, you and Virginia went by within arm's reach and we never spoke to you. I'm so ashamed."

But Junius consoled her. Long before their marriage he had known of his Mattie's weakness and its essential harmlessness. "My dear girl, I told you long ago that where no principle was involved, your passing means nothing to me. It's just a little joke; I don't think you'd be ashamed to acknowledge your old husband anywhere if it were necessary."

"I'd do that if people were mistaking me for a queen," she assured him fondly. But she was silent, not quite satisfied. "After all," she said with her charming frankness, "it isn't you, dear, who make me feel guilty. I really am ashamed to think that I let Virginia pass by without a word. I think I should feel very badly if she were to know it. I don't believe I'll ever let myself be quite as silly as that again."

But of this determination Angela, dreaming excitedly of Saturdays spent in turning her small olive face firmly away from peering black countenances was, unhappily, unaware.

Chapter II

SATURDAY came to be the day of the week for Angela, but her sister Virginia preferred Sundays. She loved the atmosphere of golden sanctity which seemed to hover with a sweet glory about the stodgy, shabby little dwelling. Usually she came downstairs first so as to enjoy by herself the blessed "Sunday feeling" which, she used to declare, would have made it possible for her to recognize the day if she had awakened to it even in China. She was only twelve at this time, yet she had already developed a singular aptitude and liking for the care of the home, and this her mother gratefully fostered. Gradually the custom was formed of turning over to her small hands all the duties of Sunday morning; they were to her a ritual. First the kettle must be started boiling, then the pavement swept. Her father's paper must be carried up and left outside his door. Virginia found a nameless and sweet satisfaction in performing these services.

She prepared the Sunday breakfast which was always the same,—bacon and eggs, strong coffee with good cream for Junius, chocolate for the other three and muffins. After the kettle had boiled and the muffins were mixed it took exactly half an hour to complete preparations. Virginia always went about these matters in the same way. She set the muffins in the oven, pursing her lips and frowning a little just as she had seen her mother do; then she went to the foot of the narrow, enclosed staircase and called "hoo-hoo" with a soft rising inflection,—"last call to dinner," her father termed it. And finally, just for those last few minutes before the family descended she went into the box of a parlour and played hymns, old-fashioned and stately tunes,—"How firm a foundation", "The spacious firmament on high", "Am I a soldier of the Cross". Her father's inflexible bass, booming down the stairs, her mother's faint alto in thirds mingled with her own sweet treble; a shaft of sunlight, faint and watery in winter, strong and golden in summer, shimmering through the room in the morning dusk completed for the little girl a sensation of happiness which lay perilously near tears.

*

After breakfast came the bustle of preparing for church. Junius of course had come down in complete readiness; but the others must change their dresses; Virginia had mislaid her Sunday hair-ribbon again; Angela had discovered a rip in her best gloves and could not be induced to go down until it had been mended. "Wait for me just a minute, Jinny dear, I can't go out looking like this, can I?" She did not like going to church, at least not to their church, but she did care about her appearance and she liked the luxuriousness of being "dressed up" on two sucessive days. At last the little procession filed out, Mattie hoping that they would not be late, she did hate it so; Angela thinking that this was a stupid way to spend Sunday and wondering at just what period of one's life existence began to shape itself as *you* wanted it. Her father's thoughts were inchoate; expressed they would have revealed a patriarchal aspect almost biblical. He had been a poor boy, homeless, a nobody, yet he had contrived in his mid-forties to attain to the status of a respectable citizen, house-owner, a good provider. He possessed a charming wife and two fine daughters, and as was befitting he was accompanying them to the house of the Lord. As for Virginia, no one to see her in her little red hat and her mother's cut-over blue coat could have divined how near she was to bursting with happiness. Father, mother and children, well-dressed, well-fed, united, going to church on a beatiful Sunday morning; there was an immense cosmic rightness about all this which she sensed rather than realized. She envied no one the incident of finer clothes or a larger home; this unity was the core of happiness, all other satisfactions must radiate from this one; greater happiness could be only a matter of degree but never of essence. When she grew up she meant to live the same kind of life; she would marry a man exactly like her father and she would conduct her home exactly as did her mother. Only she would pray very hard every day for five children, two boys and two girls and then a last little one,—it was hard for her to decide whether this should be a boy or a girl,—which should stay small for a long, long time. And on Sundays they would all go to church.

Intent on her dreaming she rarely heard the sermon. It was different with the hymns, for they constituted the main part of the service for her father, and she meant to play them again for him later in the happy, golden afternoon or the grey dusk of early evening. But first there were acquaintances to greet, friends of her parents who called them by their first names and who, in speaking of Virginia and Angela still said: "And these are the babies; my, how they grow! It doesn't seem as though it could be you, Mattie Ford, grown up and with children!"

On Communion Sundays the service was very late, and Angela would grow restless and twist about in her seat, but the younger girl loved the sudden, mystic hush which seemed to descend on the congregation. Her mother's sweetly merry face took on a certain childish solemnity, her father's stern profile softened into beatific expectancy. In the exquisite diction of the sacramental service there were certain words, certain phrases that almost made the child faint; the minister had a faint burr in his voice and somehow this lent a peculiar underlying reso-nance to his intonation; he half spoke, half chanted and when, picking up the wafer he began "For in the night" and then broke it, Virginia could have cried out with the ecstasy which filled her. She felt that those who partook of the bread and wine were somehow transfigured; her mother and father wore an expression of ineffable content as they returned to their seats and there was one woman, a middle-aged, mischief mak-ing person, who returned from taking the sacrament, walking down the aisle, her hands clasped loosely in front of her and her face so absolutely uplifted that Virginia used to hasten to get within earshot of her after the church was dismissed, sure that her first words must savour of something mystic and holy. But her assumption proved always to be ill-founded.

The afternoon and the evening repeated the morning's charm but in a different key. Usually a few acquaintances dropped in; the parlour and dining-room were full for an hour or more of pleasant, harmless chatter. Mr. Henson, the policeman, a tall, yellow man with freckles on his nose and red "bad hair" would clap Mr. Murray on the back and exclaim "I tell you what, June,"—which always seemed to Virginia a remarkably daring way in which to address her tall, dignified father. Matthew Henson, a boy of sixteen, would inevitably be hovering about Angela who found him insufferably boresome and made no

effort to hide her ennui. Mrs. Murray passed around rather
hard cookies and delicious currant wine, talking stitches and
patterns meanwhile with two or three friends of her youth with
a frequent injection of "Mame, do you remember!"

Presently the house, emptied of all but the family, grew still
again, dusk and the lamp light across the street alternately pan-
elling the walls. Mrs. Murray murmured something about fixing a bite to eat, "I'll leave it in the kitchen if anybody wants
it". Angela reflected aloud that she had still to get her Algebra
or History or French as the case may be, but nobody moved.
What they were really waiting for was for Virginia to start to
play and finally she would cross the narrow absurdity of a room
and stretching out her slim, brown hands would begin her version, a glorified one, of the hymns which they had sung in
church that morning, and then the old favourites which she
had played before breakfast. Even Angela, somewhat remote
and difficult at first, fell into this evening mood and asked for a
special tune or a repetition: "I like the way you play that,
Jinny". For an hour or more they were as close and united as it
is possible for a family to be.

At eight o'clock or thereabouts Junius said exactly as though
it had not been in his thoughts all evening: "Play the 'Dying
Christian', daughter". And Virginia, her treble sounding very
childish and shrill against her father's deep, unyielding bass,
began Pope's masterpiece on the death of a true believer. The
magnificently solemn words: "Vital spark of heavenly flame",
strangely appropriate minor music filled the little house with
an awesome beauty which was almost palpable. It affected Angela
so that in sheer self-defence she would go out in the kitchen
and eat her share of the cold supper set by her mother. But
Mattie, although she never sang this piece, remained while her
husband and daughter sang on. Death triumphant and mighty
had no fears for her. It was inevitable, she knew, but she would
never have to face it alone. When her husband died, she
would die too, she was sure of it; and if death came to her first
it would be only a little while before Junius would be there
stretching out his hand and guiding her through all the rough,
strange places just as years ago, when he had been a coachman to
the actress for whom she worked, he had stretched out his good,

honest hand and had saved her from a dangerous and equivocal position. She wiped away happy and grateful tears.

"The world recedes, it disappears," sang Virginia. But it made no difference how far it drifted away as long as the four of them were together; and they would always be together, her father and mother and she and Angela. With her visual mind she saw them proceeding endlessly through space; there were her parents, arm in arm, and she and—but to-night and other nights she could not see Angela; it grieved her to lose sight thus of her sister, she knew she must be there, but grope as she might she could not find her. And then quite suddenly Angela was there again, but a different Angela, not quite the same as in the beginning of the picture.

And suddenly she realized that she was doing four things at once and each of them with all the intentness which she could muster; she was singing, she was playing, she was searching for Angela and she was grieving because Angela as she knew her was lost forever.

"Oh Death, oh Death, where is thy sting!" the hymn ended triumphantly,—she and the piano as usual came out a little ahead of Junius which was always funny. She said, "Where's Angela?" and knew what the answer would be. "I'm tired, mummy! I guess I'll go to bed."

"You ought to, you got up so early and you've been going all day."

Kissing her parents good-night she mounted the stairs languidly, her whole being pervaded with the fervid yet delicate rapture of the day.

Chapter III

MONDAY morning brought the return of the busy, happy week. It meant wash-day for Mattie, for she and Junius had never been able to raise their ménage to the status either of a maid or of putting out the wash. But this lack meant nothing to her,—she had been married fifteen years and still had the ability to enjoy the satisfaction of having a home in which she had full sway instead of being at the beck and call of others. She was old enough to remember a day when poverty for a coloured girl connoted one of three things: going out to service, working as ladies' maid, or taking a genteel but poorly paid position as seamstress with one of the families of the rich and great on Rittenhouse Square, out West Walnut Street or in one of the numerous impeccable, aristocratic suburbs of Philadelphia.

She had tried her hand at all three of these possibilities, had known what it meant to rise at five o'clock, start the laundry work for a patronizing indifferent family of people who spoke of her in her hearing as "the girl" or remarked of her in a slightly lower but still audible tone as being rather better than the usual run of niggers,—"She never steals, I'd trust her with anything and she isn't what you'd call lazy either." For this family she had prepared breakfast, gone back to her washing, served lunch, had taken down the clothes, sprinkled and folded them, had gone upstairs and made three beds, not including her own and then had returned to the kitchen to prepare dinner. At night she nodded over the dishes and finally stumbling up to the third floor fell into her unmade bed, sometimes not even fully undressed. And Tuesday morning she would begin on the long and tedious strain of ironing. For this she received four dollars a week with the privilege of every other Sunday and every Thursday off. But she could have no callers.

As a seamstress, life had been a little more endurable but more precarious. The wages were better while they lasted, she had a small but comfortable room; her meals were brought up to her on a tray and the young girls of the households in which she was employed treated her with a careless kindness which while it still had its element of patronage was not offensive. But such families had a disconcerting habit of closing their households and departing for months at a time, and there was Mattie stranded and perilously trying to make ends meet by taking in sewing. But her clientèle was composed of girls as poor as she, who either did their own dressmaking or could afford to pay only the merest trifle for her really exquisite and meticulous work.

The situation with the actress had really been the best in many, in almost all, respects. But it presented its pitfalls. Mattie was young, pretty and innocent; the actress was young, beautiful and sophisticated. She had been married twice and had been the heroine of many affairs; maidenly modesty, virtue for its own sake, were qualities long since forgotten, high ideals and personal self-respect were too abstract for her slightly coarsened mind to visualize, and at any rate they were incomprehensible and even absurd in a servant, and in a coloured servant to boot. She knew that in spite of Mattie's white skin there was black blood in her veins; in fact she would not have taken the girl on had she not been coloured; all her servants must be coloured, for hers was a carelessly conducted household, and she felt dimly that all coloured people are thickly streaked with immorality. They were naturally loose, she reasoned, when she thought about it at all. "Look at the number of mixed bloods among them; look at Mattie herself for that matter, a perfectly white nigger if ever there was one. I'll bet her mother wasn't any better than she should be."

When the girl had come to her with tears in her eyes and begged her not to send her as messenger to the house of a certain Haynes Brokinaw, politician and well-known man about town, Madame had laughed out loud. "How ridiculous! He'll treat you all right. I should like to know what a girl like you expects. And anyway, if I don't care, why should you? Now run along with the note and don't bother me about this again. I hire you to do what I want, not to do as you want." She was not even jealous,—of a coloured working girl! And anyway, constancy was no virtue in her eyes; she did not possess it herself and she valued it little in others.

Mattie was in despair. She was receiving twenty-five dollars a month, her board, and a comfortable, pleasant room. She was seeing something of the world and learning of its amenities. It was during this period that she learned how very pleasant indeed life could be for a person possessing only a very little extra money and a white skin. But the special attraction which her present position held for her was that every day she had a certain amount of time to call her own, for she was Madame's personal servant; in no wise was she connected with the routine of keeping the house. If Madame elected to spend the whole day away from home, Mattie, once she had arranged for the evening toilette, was free to act and to go where she pleased.

And now here was this impasse looming up with Brokinaw. More than once Mattie had felt his covetous eyes on her; she had dreaded going to his rooms from the very beginning. She had even told his butler, "I'll be back in half an hour for the answer"; and she would wait in the great square hall as he had indicated for there she was sure that danger lurked. But the third time Brokinaw was standing in the hall. "Just come into my study," he told her, "while I read this and write the answer." And he had looked at her with his cold, green eyes and had asked her why she was so out of breath. "There's no need to rush so, child; stay here and rest. I'm in no hurry, I assure you. Are you really coloured? You know, I've seen lots of white girls not as pretty as you. Sit here and tell me all about your mother, —and your father. Do—do you remember him?" His whole bearing reeked with intention.

Within a week Madame was sending her again and she had suggested fearfully the new coachman. "No," said Madame. "It's Wednesday, his night off, and I wouldn't send him anyway; coachmen are too hard to keep nowadays; you're all getting so independent." Mattie had come down from her room and walked slowly, slowly to the corner where the new coachman, tall and black and grave, was just hailing a car. She ran to him and jerked down the arm which he had just lifted to seize the railing. "Oh, Mr. Murray," she stammered. He had been so astonished and so kind. Her halting explanation done, he took the note in silence and delivered it, and the next night and for many nights thereafter they walked through the silent, beautiful square, and Junius had told her haltingly and with fear that he loved her. She threw her arms about his neck: "And I love you too."

"You don't mind my being so dark then? Lots of coloured girls I know wouldn't look at a black man."

But it was partly on account of his colour that she loved him; in her eyes his colour meant safety. "Why should I mind?" she asked with one of her rare outbursts of bitterness, "my own colour has never brought me anything but insult and trouble."

The other servants, it appeared, had told him that sometimes she—he hesitated—"passed".

"Yes, yes, of course I do," she explained it eagerly, "but never to them. And anyway when I am alone what can I do? I can't label myself. And if I'm hungry or tired and I'm near a place where they don't want coloured people, why should I observe their silly old rules, rules that are unnatural and unjust,—because the world was made for everybody, wasn't it, Junius?"

She had told him then how hard and joyless her girlhood life had been,—she had known such dreadful poverty and she had been hard put to it to keep herself together. But since she had come to live with Madame Sylvio she had glimpsed, thanks to her mistress's careless kindness, something of the life of comparative ease and beauty and refinement which one could easily taste if he possessed just a modicum of extra money and the prerequisite of a white skin.

"I've only done it for fun but I won't do it any more if it displeases you. I'd much rather live in the smallest house in the world with you, Junius, than be wandering around as I have so often, lonely and unknown in hotels and restaurants." Her sweetness disarmed him. There was no reason in the world why she should give up her harmless pleasure unless, he added rather sternly, some genuine principle were involved.

It was the happiest moment of her life when Junius had gone to Madame and told her that both he and Mattie were leaving. "We are going to be married," he announced proudly. The actress had been sorry to lose her, and wanted to give her a hundred dollars, but the tall, black coachman would not let his wife accept it. "She is to have only what she earned," he said in stern refusal. He hated Madame Sylvio for having thrown the girl in the way of Haynes Brokinaw.

They had married and gone straight into the little house on Opal Street which later was to become their own. Mattie her husband considered a perfect woman, sweet, industrious, affectionate and illogical. But to her he was God.

When Angela and Virginia were little children and their mother used to read them fairy tales she would add to the ending, " And so they lived happily ever after, just like your father and me."

All this was passing happily through her mind on this Monday morning. Junius was working somewhere in the neighbourhood; his shop was down on Bainbridge Street, but he tried to devote Mondays and Tuesdays to work up town so that he could run in and help Mattie on these trying days. Before the advent of the washing machine he used to dart in and out two or three times in the course of a morning to lend a hand to the heavy sheets and the bed-spreads. Now those articles were taken care of in the laundry, but Junius still kept up the pleasant fiction.

Virginia attended school just around the corner, and presently she would come in too, not so much to get her own lunch as to prepare it for her mother. She possessed her father's attitude toward Mattie as someone who must be helped, indulged and protected. Moreover she had an unusually keen sense of gratitude toward her father and mother for their kindness and their unselfish ambitions for their children. Jinny never tired of hearing of the difficult childhood of her parents. She knew of no story quite so thrilling as the account of their early trials and difficulties. She thought it wonderfully sweet of them to plan, as they constantly did, better things for their daughters.

"My girls shall never come through my experiences," Mattie would say firmly. They were both to be school-teachers and independent.

It is true that neither of them felt any special leaning toward this calling. Angela frankly despised it, but she supposed she must make her living some way. The salary was fairly good—in fact, very good for a poor girl—and there would be the long summer vacation. At fourteen she knew already how much money she would save during those first two or three years and how she would spend those summer vacations. But although she proffered this much information to her family she kept her plans to herself. Mattie often pondered on this lack of openness in her older daughter. Virginia was absolutely transparent. She did not think she would care for teaching either, that is, not for teaching in the ordinary sense. But she realized that for the present that was the best profession which her parents could have chosen for them. She would spend her summers learning all she could about methods of teaching music.

"And a lot of good it will do you," Angela scoffed. "You know perfectly well that there are no coloured teachers of music in the public schools here in Philadelphia." But Jinny thought it possible that there might be. "When Mamma was coming along there were very few coloured teachers at all, and now it looks as though there'd be plenty of chance for us. And anyway you never know your luck."

By four o'clock the day's work was over and Mattie free to do as she pleased. This was her idle hour. The girls would get dinner, a Monday version of whatever the main course had been the day before. Their mother was on no account to be disturbed or importuned. To-day as usual she sat in the Morris chair in the dining-room, dividing her time between the Sunday paper and the girls' chatter. It was one of her most cherished experiences,—this sense of a day's hard labour far behind her, the happy voices of her girls, her joyous expectation of her husband's home-coming. Usually the children made a game of their preparations, recalling some nonsense of their early child-hood days when it had been their delight to dress up as ladies. Virginia would approach Angela: "Pardon me, is this Mrs. Henrietta Jones?" And Angela, drawing herself up haughtily would reply: "Er,—really you have the advantage of me." Then Virginia: "Oh pardon! I thought you were Mrs. Jones and I had heard my friend Mrs. Smith speak of you so often and since you were in the neighbourhood and passing, I was going to ask you in to have some ice-cream". The game of course being that Angela should immediately drop her haughtiness and proceed for the sake of the goodies to ingratiate herself into her neighbour's esteem. It was a poor joke, long since worn thin, but the two girls still used the greeting and for some reason it had become part of the Monday ritual of preparing the supper.

But to-night Angela's response lacked spontaneity. She was absorbed and reserved, even a little sulky. Deftly and swiftly she moved about her work, however, and no one who had not attended regularly on those Monday evening preparations could have guessed that there was anything on her mind other than complete absorption in the problem of cutting the bread or garnishing the warmed over roast beef. But Mattie was aware of the quality of brooding in her intense concentration. She had seen it before in her daughter but to-night, though to her practised eye it was more apparent than ever, she could not put her hand on it. Angela's response, if asked what was the matter, would be "Oh, nothing". It came to her suddenly that her older daughter was growing up; in a couple of months she would be fifteen. Children were often absorbed and moody when they were in their teens, too engaged in finding themselves to care about their effect on others. She must see to it that the girl had plenty of rest; perhaps school had been too strenuous for her to-day; she thought the high school programme very badly arranged, five hours one right after the other were much too long. "Angela, child, I think you'd better not be long out of bed to-night; you look very tired to me."

Angela nodded. But her father came in then and in the little hubbub that arose about his home-coming and the final preparations for supper her listlessness went without further remark.

Chapter IV

THE third storey front was Angela's bed-room. She was glad of its loneliness and security to-night,—even if her mother had not suggested her going to bed early she would have sought its shelter immediately after supper. Study for its own sake held no attractions for her; she did not care for any of her subjects really except Drawing and French. And when she was drawing she did not consider that she was studying, it was too naturally a means of self-expression. As for French, she did have to study that with great care, for languages did not come to her with any great readiness, but there was an element of fine lady-ism about the beautiful, logical tongue that made her in accordance with some secret subconscious ambition resolve to make it her own.

The other subjects, History, English, and Physical Geography, were not drudgery, for she had a fair enough mind; but then they were not attractive either, and she was lacking in Virginia's dogged resignation to unwelcome duties. Even when Jinny was a little girl she had been know to say manfully in the face of an uncongenial task: "Well I dotta det it done". Angela was not like that. But to-night she was concentrating with all her power on her work. During the day she had been badly hurt; she had received a wound whose depth and violence she would not reveal even to her parents,—because, and this only increased the pain, young as she was she knew that there was nothing they could do about it. There was nothing to be done but to get over it. Only she was not developed enough to state this stoicism to herself. She was like a little pet cat that had once formed part of their household; its leg had been badly torn by a passing dog, and the poor thing had dragged itself into the house and lain on its cushion patiently, waiting stolidly for this unfamiliar agony to subside. So Angela waited for the hurt in her mind to cease.

But across the history dates on the printed page and through stately lines of Lycidas she kept seeing Mary Hastings' accusing face, hearing Mary Hastings' accusing voice:

"Coloured! Angela, you never told me that you were coloured!"

And then her own voice in tragic but proud bewilderment. "Tell you that I was coloured! Why of course I never told you that I was coloured. Why should I?"

She had been so proud of Mary Hastings' friendship. In the dark and tortured spaces of her difficult life it had been a lovely, hidden refuge. It had been an experience so rarely sweet that she had hardly spoken of it even to Virginia. The other girls in her class had meant nothing to her. At least she had schooled herself to have them mean nothing. Some of them she had known since early childhood; they had lived in her neighbourhood and had gone to the graded schools with her. They had known that she was coloured, for they had seen her with Virginia, and sometimes her tall, black father had come to fetch her home on a rainy day. There had been pleasant enough contacts and intimacies; in the quiet of Jefferson Street they had played "The Farmer in the Dell", and "Here come three jolly, jolly sailor-boys"; dark retreats of the old market had afforded endless satisfaction for "Hide and Go Seek". She and those other children had gone shopping arm in arm for school supplies, threading their way in and out of the bustle and confusion that were Columbia Avenue.

As she grew older many of these intimacies lessened, in some cases ceased altogether. But she was never conscious of being left completely alone; there was always some one with whom to eat lunch or who was going her way after school. It was not until she reached the high school that she began to realize how solitary her life was becoming. There were no other coloured girls in her class but there had been only two or three during her school-life, and if there had been any she would not necessarily have confined herself to them; that this might be a good thing to do in sheer self-defence would hardly have occurred to her. But this problem did not confront her; what did confront her was that the very girls with whom she had grown up were evading her; when she went to the Assembly none of them sat next to her unless no other seat were vacant; little groups toward which she drifted during lunch, inexplicably dissolved to re-form in another portion of the room. Sometimes a girl in this new group threw her a backward glance charged either with a mean amusement or with annoyance.

Angela was proud; she did not need such a hint more than once, but she was bewildered and hurt. She took stories to school to read at recess, or wandered into the drawing laboratory and touched up her designs. Miss Barrington thought her an unusually industrious student.

And then in the middle of the term Mary Hastings had come, a slender, well-bred girl of fifteen. She was rather stupid in her work, in fact she shone in nothing but French and good manners. Undeniably she had an air, and her accent was remarkable. The other pupils, giggling, produced certain uncouth and unheard of sounds, but Mary said in French: "No, I have lent my knife to the brother-in-law of the gardener but here is my cane," quite as though the idiotic phrase were part of an imaginary conversation which she was conducting and appreciating. "She really knows what she's talking about," little Esther Bayliss commented, and added that Mary's family had lost some money and they had had to send her to public school. But it was some time before this knowledge, dispensed by Esther with mysterious yet absolute authenticity, became generally known. Meanwhile Mary was left to her own devices while the class with complete but tacit unanimity "tried her out". Mary, unaware of this, looked with her near-sighted, slightly supercilious gaze about the room at recess and seeing only one girl, and that girl Angela, who approached in dress, manner and deportment her own rather set ideas, had taken her lunch over to the other pupil's desk and said: "Come on, let's eat together while you tell me who everybody is."

Angela took the invitation as simply as the other had offered. "That little girl in the purplish dress is Esther Bayliss and the tall one in the thick glasses——"

Mary, sitting with her back to the feeding groups, never troubled to look around. "I don't mean the girls. I expect I'll know them soon enough when I get around to it. I mean the teachers. Do you have to dig for them?" She liked Angela and she showed it plainly and directly. Her home was in some remote fastness of West Philadelphia which she could reach with comparative swiftness by taking the car at Spring Garden Street. Instead she walked half way home with her new friend,

up Seventeenth Street as far as Girard Avenue where, after a final exchange of school matters and farewells, she took the car,
leaving Angela to her happy, satisfied thoughts. And presently
she began to know more than happiness and satisfaction, she
was knowing the extreme gratification of being the chosen
companion of a popular and important girl, for Mary, although
not quick at her studies, was a power in everything else. She
dressed well, she had plenty of pocket money, she could play
the latest marches in the gymnasium, she received a certain indefinable but flattering attention from the teachers, and she
could make things "go". The school paper was moribund and
Mary knew how to resuscitate it; she brought in advertisements from her father's business friends; she made her married
sisters obtain subscriptions. Without being obtrusive or over-
bearing, without condescension and without toadying she was
the leader of her class. And with it all she stuck to Angela. She
accepted popularity because it was thrust upon her, but she
was friendly with Angela because the latter suited her.

Angela was happy. She had a friend and the friendship brought
her unexpected advantages. She was no longer left out of
groups because there could be no class plans without Mary
and Mary would remain nowhere for any length of time without Angela. So to save time and argument, and also to avoid
offending the regent, Angela was always included. Not that
she cared much about this, but she did like Mary; as is the way
of a "fidus Achates", she gave her friendship whole-heartedly.
And it was gratifying to be in the midst of things.

In April the school magazine announced a new departure.
Henceforth the editorial staff was to be composed of two representatives from each class; of these one was to be the chief
representative chosen by vote of the class, the other was to be
assistant, selected by the chief. The chief representative, said
the announcement pompously, would sit in at executive meetings and have a voice in the policy of the paper. The assistant
would solicit and collect subscriptions, collect fees, receive and
report complaints and in brief, said Esther Bayliss, "do all the
dirty work". But she coveted the position and title for all that.

Angela's class held a brief meeting after school and elected
Mary Hastings as representative without a dissenting vote.

"No," said Angela holding up a last rather grimy bit of paper.
"Here is one for Esther Bayliss." Two or three of the girls giggled; everyone knew that she must have voted for herself; indeed it had been she who had insisted on taking a ballot rather
than a vote by acclaim. Mary was already on her feet. She had
been sure of the result of the election, would have been astonished indeed had it turned out any other way. "Well, girls," she
began in her rather high, refined voice, "I wish to thank you
for the—er—confidence you have bestowed, that is, placed in
me and I'm sure you all know I'll do my best to keep the old
paper going. And while I'm about it I might just as well announce that I'm choosing Angela Murray for my assistant."

There was a moment's silence. The girls who had thought
about it at all had known that if Mary were elected, as assuredly she would be, this meant also the election of Angela. And
those who had taken no thought saw no reason to object to
her appointment. And anyway there was nothing to be done.
But Esther Bayliss pushed forward: "I don't know how it is
with the rest of you, but I should have to think twice before
I'd trust my subscription money to a coloured girl."

Mary said in utter astonishment: "Coloured, why what are
you talking about? Who's coloured?"

"Angela, Angela Murray, that's who's coloured. At least she
used to be when we all went to school at Eighteenth and
Oxford."

Mary said again: "Coloured!" And then, "Angela, you never
told me you were coloured!"

Angela's voice was as amazed as her own: "Tell you that I
was coloured! Why of course I never told you that I was coloured! Why should I?"

"There," said Esther, "see she never told Mary that she was
coloured. What wouldn't she have done with our money!"

Angela had picked up her books and strolled out the door. But
she flew down the north staircase and out the Brandywine
Street entrance and so to Sixteenth Street where she would
meet no one she knew, especially at this belated hour. At home
there would be work to do, her lessons to get and the long,
long hours of the night must pass before she would have to
face again the hurt and humiliation of the classroom; before

she would have to steel her heart and her nerves to drop Mary Hastings before Mary Hastings could drop her. No one, no one, Mary least of all, should guess how completely she had been wounded. Mary and her shrinking bewilderment! Mary and her exclamation: "Coloured!" This was a curious business, this colour. It was the one god apparently to whom you could sacrifice everything. On account of it her mother had neglected to greet her own husband on the street. Mary Hastings could let it come between her and her friend.

In the morning she was at school early; the girls should all see her there and their individual attitude should be her attitude. She would remember each one's greetings, would store it away for future guidance. Some of the girls were especially careful to speak to her, one or two gave her a meaning smile, or so she took it, and turned away. Some did not speak at all. When Mary Hastings came in Angela rose and sauntered unseeing and unheeding deliberately past her through the doorway, across the hall to Miss Barrington's laboratory. As she returned she passed Mary's desk, and the girl lifted troubled but not unfriendly eyes to meet her own; Angela met the glance fully but without recognition. She thought to herself: "Coloured! If they had said to me Mary Hastings is a voodoo, I'd have answered, 'What of it? She's my friend.'"

Before June Mary Hastings came up to her and asked her to wait after school. Angela who had been neither avoiding nor seeking her gave a cool nod. They walked out of the French classroom together. When they reached the corner Mary spoke:

"Oh, Angela, let's be friends again. It doesn't really make any difference. See, I don't care any more."

"But that's what I don't understand. Why should it have made any difference in the first place? I'm just the same as I was before you knew I was coloured and just the same afterwards. Why should it ever have made any difference at all?"

"I don't know, I'm sure. I was just surprised. It was all so unexpected."

"What was unexpected?"

"Oh, I don't know. I can't explain it. But let's be friends."

"Well," said Angela slowly, "I'm willing, but I don't think it will ever be the same again."

It wasn't. Some element, spontaneity, trustfulness was lacking. Mary, who had never thought of speaking of colour, was suddenly conscious that here was a subject which she must not discuss. She was less frank, at times even restrained. Angela, too young to define her thoughts, yet felt vaguely: "She failed me once,—I was her friend,—yet she failed me for something with which I had nothing to do. She's just as likely to do it again. It's in her."

Definitely she said to herself, "Mary withdrew herself not because I was coloured but because she didn't know I was coloured. Therefore if she had never known I was coloured she would always have been my friend. We would have kept on having our good times together." And she began to wonder which was the more important, a patent insistence on the fact of colour or an acceptance of the good things of life which could come to you in America if either you were not coloured or the fact of your racial connections was not made known.

During the summer Mary Hastings' family, it appeared, recovered their fallen fortunes. At any rate she did not return to school in the fall and Angela never saw her again.

Chapter V

VIRGINIA came rushing in. "Angela, where's Mummy?"

"Out. What's all the excitement?"

"I've been appointed. Isn't it great? Won't Mother and Dad be delighted! Right at the beginning of the year too, so I won't have to wait. The official notice isn't out yet but I know it's all right. Miss Herren wants me to report tomorrow. Isn't it perfectly marvellous! Here I graduate from the Normal in June and in the second week of school in September I've got my perfectly good job. Darling child, it's very much better, as you may have heard me observe before, to be born lucky than rich. But I am lucky and I'll be rich too. Think of that salary for my very own! With both of us working, Mummy won't have to want for a thing, nor Father either. Mummy won't have to do a lick of work if she doesn't want to. Well, what have you got to say about it, old Rain-in-the-Face? Or perhaps this isn't Mrs. Henrietta Jones whom I'm addressing of?"

Angela giggled, then raised an imaginary lorgnette. "Er,— really I think you have the advantage of me. Well, I was thinking how fortunate you were to get your appointment right off the bat and how you'll hate it now that you have got it."

She herself, appointed two years previously, had had no such luck. Strictly speaking there are no coloured schools as such in Philadelphia. Yet, by an unwritten law, although coloured children may be taught by white teachers, white children must never receive knowledge at the hands of coloured instructors. As the number of coloured Normal School graduates is steadily increasing, the city gets around this difficulty by manning a school in a district thickly populated by Negroes, with a coloured principal and a coloured teaching force. Coloured children living in that district must thereupon attend that school. But no attention is paid to the white children who leave this same district for the next nearest white or "mixed" school.

Angela had been sixth on the list of coloured graduates. Five had been appointed, but there was no vacancy for her, and for several months she was idle with here and there a day, perhaps a week of substituting. She could not be appointed in any but

462

a coloured school, and she was not supposed to substitute in
any but this kind of classroom. Then her father discovered that
a young white woman was teaching in a coloured school. He
made some searching inquiries and was met with the complacent rejoinder that as soon as a vacancy occurred in a white
school, Miss McSweeney would be transferred there and his
daughter could have her place.

Just as she had anticipated, Angela did not want the job after
she received it. She had expected to loathe teaching little
children and her expectation, it turned out, was perfectly well
grounded. Perhaps she might like to teach drawing to grown-
ups; she would certainly like to have a try at it. Meanwhile it
was nice to be independent, to be holding a lady-like, respectable position so different from her mother's early days, to be
able to have pretty clothes and to help with the house, in brief
to be drawing an appreciably adequate and steady salary. For
one thing it made it possible for her to take up work at the
Philadelphia Academy of Fine Arts at Broad and Cherry.

Jinny was in excellent spirits at dinner. "Now, Mummy darling,
you really shall walk in silk attire and siller hae to spare."
Angela's appointment had done away with the drudgery of
washday. "We'll get Hettie Daniels to come in Saturdays and
clean up. I won't have to scrub the front steps any more and
everything will be feasting and fun." Pushing aside her plate
she rushed over to her father, climbed on his knee and flung
her lovely bronze arms around his neck. She still adored him, still
thought him the finest man in the world; she still wanted her
husband to be just exactly like him; he would not be so tall nor
would he be quite as dark. Matthew Henson was of only
medium height and was a sort of reddish yellow and he distinctly was not as handsome as her father. Indeed Virginia
thought, with a pang of shame at her disloyalty, that it would
have been a fine thing if he could exchange his lighter skin for
her father's colour if in so doing he might have gained her
father's thick, coarsely grained but beautifully curling, open
black hair. Matthew had inherited his father's thick, tight,
"bad" hair. Only, thank heaven, it was darker.

Junius tucked his slender daughter back in the hollow of his
arm.

"Well, baby, you want something off my plate?" As a child Virginia had been a notorious beggar.

"Darling! I was thinking that now you could buy Mr. Hallowell's car. He's got his eye on a Cadillac, Kate says, and he'd be willing to let Henry Ford go for a song."

Junius was pleased, but he thought he ought to protest. "Do I look as old as all that? I might be able to buy the actual car, now that my girls are getting so monied, but the upkeep, I understand, is pretty steep."

"Oh, nonsense," said Mattie. "Go on and get it, June. Think how nice it will be riding out North Broad Street in the evenings."

And Angela added kindly: "I think you owe it to yourself to get it, Dad. Jinny and I'll carry the house till you get it paid for."

"Well, there's no reason of course why I——" he corrected himself, "why we shouldn't have a car if we want it." He saw himself spending happy moments digging in the little car's inmost mysteries. He would buy new parts, change the engine perhaps, paint it and overhaul her generally. And he might just as well indulge himself. The little house was long since paid for; he was well insured, and his two daughters were grown up and taking care of themselves. He slid Jinny off his knee.

"I believe I'll run over to the Hallowells now and see what Tom'll take for that car. Catch him before he goes down town in it."

Virginia called after him. "Just think! Maybe this time next week you'll be going down town in it."

She was very happy. Life was turning out just right. She was young, she was twenty, she was about to earn her own living, —"to be about to live"—she said, happily quoting a Latin construction which had always intrigued her. Her mother would never have to work again; her father would have a Henry Ford; she herself would get a new, good music teacher and would also take up the study of methods at the University of Pennsylvania.

Angela could hear her downstairs talking to Matthew Henson whose ring she had just answered. "Only think, Matt, I've been appointed."

"Great!" said Matthew. "Is Angela in? Do you think she'd like to go to the movies with me to-night? She was too tired last time. Run up and ask her, there's a good girl."

Angela sighed. She didn't want to go out with Matthew; he wearied her so. And besides people always looked at her so strangely. She wished he would take it into his head to come and see Jinny.

Sunday was still a happy day. Already an air of prosperity, of having arrived beyond the striving point, had settled over the family. Mr. Murray's negotiations with Tom Hallowell had been most successful. The Ford, a little four-seater coupé, compact and sturdy, had changed hands. Its former owner came around on Sunday to give Junius a lesson. The entire household piled in, for both girls were possessed of the modern slenderness. They rode out Jefferson Street and far, far out Ridge Avenue to the Wissahickon and on to Chestnut Hill. From time to time, when the traffic was thin, Junius took the wheel, anticipating Tom's instructions with the readiness of the born mechanic. They came back laughing and happy and pardonably proud. The dense, tender glow of the late afternoon September sun flooded the little parlour, the dining-room was dusky and the kitchen was redolent of scents of ginger bread and spiced preserves. After supper there were no lessons to get. "It'll be years before I forget all that stuff I learned in practice school," said Jinny gaily.

Later on some boys came in; Matthew Henson inevitably, peering dissatisfied through the autumn gloom for Angela and immediately content when he saw her; Arthur Sawyer, who had just entered the School of Pedagogy and was a little ashamed of it, for he considered teaching work fit only for women. "But I've got to make a living somehow, ain't I? And I won't go into that post-office!"

"What's the matter with the post-office?" Henson asked indignantly. He had just been appointed. In reality he did not fancy the work himself, but he did not want it decried before Angela.

"Tell me what better or surer job is there for a coloured man in Philadelphia?"

"Nothing," said Sawyer promptly, "not a thing in the world

except school teaching. But that's just what I object to. I'm sick of planning my life with regard to being coloured. I'm not a bit ashamed of my race. I don't mind in the least that once we were slaves. Every race in the world has at some time occupied a servile position. But I do mind having to take it into consideration every time I want to eat outside of my home, every time I enter a theatre, every time I think of a profession."

"But you do have to take it into consideration," said Jinny softly. "At present it's one of the facts of our living, just as lameness or near-sightedness might be for a white man."

The inevitable race discussion was on.

"Ah, but there you're all off, Miss Virginia." A tall, lanky, rather supercilious youth spoke up from the corner. He had been known to them all their lives as Franky Porter, but he had taken lately to publishing poems in the Philadelphia *Tribunal* which he signed F. Seymour Porter. "Really you're all off, for you speak as though colour itself were a deformity. Whereas, as Miss Angela being an artist knows, colour may really be a very beautiful thing, mayn't it?"

"Oh don't drag me into your old discussion," Angela answered crossly. "I'm sick of this whole race business if you ask me. And don't call me Miss Angela. Call me Angela as you've all done all our lives or else call me Miss Murray. No, I don't think being coloured in America is a beautiful thing. I think it's nothing short of a curse."

"Well," said Porter slowly, "I think its being or not being a curse rests with you. You've got to decide whether or not you're going to let it interfere with personal development and to that extent it may be harmful or it may be an incentive. I take it that Sawyer here, who even when we were all kids always wanted to be an engineer, will transmute his colour either into a bane or a blessing according to whether he lets it make him hide his natural tendencies under the bushel of school-teaching or become an inspiration toward making him the very best kind of engineer that there ever was so that people will just have to take him for what he is and overlook the fact of colour."

"That's it," said Jinny. "You know, being coloured often does spur you on."

"And that's what I object to," Angela answered perversely. "I'm sick of this business of always being below or above a certain norm. Doesn't anyone think that we have a right to be happy simply, naturally?"

Gradually they drifted into music. Virginia played a few popular songs and presently the old beautiful airs of all time, "Drink to me only with thine eyes" and "Sweet and Low". Arthur Sawyer had a soft, melting tenor and Angela a rather good alto; Virginia and the other boys carried the air while Junius boomed his deep, unyielding bass. The lovely melodies and the peace of the happy, tranquil household crept over them, and presently they exchanged farewells and the young men passed wearied and contented out into the dark confines of Opal Street. Angela and Mattie went upstairs, but Viginia and her father stayed below and sang very softly so as not to disturb the sleeping street; a few hymns and finally the majestic strains of "The Dying Christian" floated up. Mrs. Murray had complained of feeling tired. "I think I'll just lie a moment on your bed, Angela, until your father comes up." But her daughter noticed that she had not relaxed, instead she was straining forward a little and Angela realized that she was trying to catch every note of her husband's virile, hearty voice.

She said, "You heard what we were all talking about before the boys left. You and father don't ever bother to discuss such matters, do you?"

Her mother seemed to strain past the sound of her voice. "Not any more; oh, of course we used to talk about such things, but you get so taken up with the problem of living, just life itself you know, that by and by being coloured or not is just one thing more or less that you have to contend with. But of course there have been times when colour was the starting point of our discussions. I remember how when you and Jinny were little things and she was always running to the piano and you were scribbling all over the walls,—many's the time I've slapped your little fingers for that, Angela,—we used to spend half the night talking about you, your father and I. I wanted you to be great artists but Junius said: 'No, we'll give them a good, plain education and set them in the way of earning a sure and honest living; then if they've got it in them to travel over all the rocks that'll be in their way as coloured girls, they'll manage, never you fear.' And he was right." The music downstairs ceased and she lay back, relaxed and drowsy. "Your father's always right."

Much of this was news to Angela, and she would have liked to learn more about those early nocturnal discussions. But she only said, smiling, "You're still crazy about father, aren't you, darling?"

Her mother was wide awake in an instant. "Crazy! I'd give my life for him!"

The Saturday excursions were long since a thing of the past; Henry Ford had changed that. Also the extra work which the girls had taken upon themselves in addition to their teaching, —Angela at the Academy, Virginia at the University,—made Saturday afternoon a too sorely needed period of relaxation to be spent in the old familiar fashion. Still there were times when Angela in search of a new frock or intent on the exploration of a picture gallery asked her mother to accompany her. And at such times the two indulged in their former custom of having tea and a comfortable hour's chat in the luxurious comfort of some exclusive tearoom or hotel. Mattie, older and not quite so lightly stepping in these days of comparative ease as in those other times when a week's arduous duties lay behind her, still responded joyously to the call of fashion and grooming, the air of "good living" which pervaded these places. Moreover she herself was able to contribute to this atmosphere. Her daughters insisted on presenting her with the graceful and dainty clothes which she loved, and they were equally insistent on her wearing them. "No use hanging them in a closet," said Jinny blithely. All her prophecies had come true—her mother had the services of a maid whenever she needed them, she went clad for the most part "in silk attire", and she had "siller to spare" and to spend.

She was down town spending it now. The Ladies' Auxiliary of her church was to give a reception after Lent, and Mattie meant to hold her own with the best of them. "We're getting to be old ladies," she said a bit wistfully, "but we'll make you young ones look at us once or twice just the same." Angela replied that she was sure of that. "And I know one or two little secrets for the complexion that will make it impossible for you to call yourself old."

But those her mother knew already. However she expressed a willingness to accept Angela's offer. She loved to be fussed over, and of late Angela had shown a tendency to rival even Jinny in this particular. The older girl was beginning to lose some of her restlessness. Life was pretty hum-drum, but it was comfortable and pleasant; her family life was ideal and her time at the art school delightful. The instructor was interested in her progress, and one or two of the girls had shown a desire for real intimacy. These intimations she had not followed up very closely, but she was seeing enough of a larger, freer world to make her chafe less at the restrictions which somehow seemed to bind in her own group. As a result of even this slight satisfaction of her cravings, she was indulging less and less in brooding and introspection, although at no time was she able to adapt herself to living with the complete spontaneity so characteristic of Jinny.

But she was young, and life would somehow twist and shape itself to her subsconscious yearnings, just as it had done for her mother, she thought, following Mattie in and out of shops, delivering opinions and lending herself to all the exigencies which shopping imposed. It was not an occupation which she particularly enjoyed, but, like her mother, she adored the atmosphere and its accompaniment of well-dressed and luxuriously stationed women. No one could tell, no one would have thought for a moment that she and her mother had come from tiny Opal Street; no one could have dreamed of their racial connections. "And if Jinny were here," she thought, slowly selecting another cake, "she really would be just as capable of fitting into all this as mother and I; but they wouldn't let her light." And again she let herself dwell on the fallaciousness of a social system which stretched appearance so far beyond being.

From the tea-room they emerged into the damp greyness of the March afternoon. The streets were slushy and slimy; the sky above sodden and dull. Mattie shivered and thought of the Morris chair in the minute but cosy dining-room of her home. She wanted to go to the "Y" on Catherine Street and there were two calls to make far down Fifteenth. But at last all this was accomplished. "Now we'll get the next car and before you know it you'll be home."

"You look tired, Mother," said Angela.

"I am tired," she acknowledged, and, suddenly sagging against her daughter, lost consciousness. About them a small crowd formed, and a man passing in an automobile kindly drove the two women to a hospital in Broad Street two blocks away. It was a hospital to which no coloured woman would ever have been admitted except to char, but there was no such question to be raised in the case of this patient. "She'll be all right presently," the interne announced, "just a little fainting spell brought on by over-exertion. Was that your car you came in? It would be nice if you could have one to get her home in."

"Oh, but I can," and in a moment Angela had rushed to the telephone forgetting everything except that her father was in his shop to-day and therefore almost within reach and so was the car.

Not long after he came striding into the hospital, tall and black and rather shabby in his working clothes. He was greeted by the clerk with a rather hostile, "Yes, and what do you want?"

Angela, hastening across the lobby to him, halted at the intonation.

Junius was equal to the moment's demands. "I'm Mrs. Murray's chauffeur," he announced, hating the deception, but he would not have his wife bundled out too soon. "Is she very badly off, Miss Angela?"

His daughter hastened to reassure him. "No, she'll be down in a few minutes now."

"And meanwhile you can wait outside," said the attendant icily. She did not believe that black people were exactly human; there was no place for them in the scheme of life so far as she could see.

Junius withdrew, and in a half hour's time the young interne and the nurse came out supporting his wan wife. He sprang to the pavement: "Lean on me, Mrs. Murray."

But sobbing, she threw her arms about his neck. "Oh Junius, Junius!"

He lifted her then, drew back for Angela and mounting himself, drove away. The interne stepped back into the hospital raging about these damn white women and their nigger servants. Such women ought to be placed in a psycho-pathic ward and the niggers burned.

*

The girls got Mrs. Murray into the Morris chair and ran upstairs for pillows and wraps. When they returned Junius was in
the chair and Mrs. Murray in his arms. "Oh, June, dear June,
such a service of love."

"Do you suppose she's going to die?" whispered Jinny, stricken.
What, she wondered, would become of her father.

But in a few days Mattie was fully recovered and more happy
than ever in the reflorescence of love and tenderness which
had sprung up between herself and Junius. Only Junius was
not so well. He had had a slight touch of grippe during the
winter and the half hour's loitering in the treacherous March
weather, before the hospital, had not served to improve it. He
was hoarse and feverish, though this he did not immediately
admit. But a tearing pain in his chest compelled him one
morning to suggest the doctor. In a panic Mattie sent for him.
Junius really ill! She had never seen him in anything but the
pink of condition. The doctor reluctantly admitted pneumonia
—"a severe case but I think we can pull him through."

He suffered terribly—Mattie suffered with him, never leaving his bedside. On the fifth day he was delirious. His wife
thought, "Surely God isn't going to let him die without speaking to me again."

Toward evening he opened his eyes and saw her tender,
stricken face. He smiled. "Dear Mattie," and then, "Jinny, I'd
like to hear some music, 'Vital spark'——"

So his daughter went down to the little parlour and played
and sang "The Dying Christian".

Angela thought, "Oh, isn't this terrible! Oh how can she?"
Presently she called softly, "Jinny, Jinny come up."

Junius' hand was groping for Mattie's. She placed it in his.
"Dear Mattie," he said, " Heaven opens on my eyes,——"

The house was still with the awful stillness that follows a funeral. All the bustle and hurry were over; the end, the fulfilment toward which the family had been striving for the last
three days was accomplished. The baked funeral meats had
been removed; Virginia had seen to that. Angela was up in her
room, staring dry-eyed before her; she loved her father, but

not even for him could she endure this aching, formless pain of bereavement. She kept saying to herself fiercely: "I must get over this, I can't stand this. I'll go away."

Mrs. Murray sat in the old Morris chair in the dining-room. She stroked its arms with her plump, worn fingers; she laid her face again and again on its shabby back. One knew that she was remembering a dark, loved cheek. Jinny said, "Come up-stairs and let me put you to bed, darling. You're going to sleep with me, you know. You're going to comfort your little girl, aren't you, Mummy?" Then as there was no response, "Darling, you'll make yourself ill."

Her mother sat up suddenly. "Yes, that's what I want to do. Oh, Jinny, do you think I can make myself ill enough to follow him soon? My daughter, try to forgive me, but I must go to him. I can't live without him. I don't deserve a daughter like you, but,—don't let them hold me back. I want to die, I must die. Say you forgive me,——"

"Darling," and it was as though her husband rather than her daughter spoke, "whatever you want is what I want." By a supreme effort she held back her tears, but it was years before she forgot the picture of her mother sitting back in the old Morris chair, composing herself for death.

Chapter VI

A T the Academy matters progressed smoothly without the flawing of a ripple. Angela looked forward to the hours which she spent there and honestly regretted their passage. Her fellow students and the instructors were more than cordial, there was an actual sense of camaraderie among them. She had not mentioned the fact of her Negro strain, indeed she had no occasion to, but she did not believe that this fact if known would cause any change in attitude. Artists were noted for their broad-mindedness. They were the first persons in the world to judge a person for his worth rather than by any hallmark. It is true that Miss Henderson, a young lady of undeniable colour, was not received with the same cordiality and attention which Angela was receiving, and this, too, despite the fact that the former's work showed undeniable talent, even originality. Angela thought that something in the young lady's personality precluded an approach to friendship; she seemed to be wary, almost offensively stand-offish. Certainly she never spoke unless spoken to; she had been known to spend a whole session without even glancing at a fellow student.

Angela herself had not arrived at any genuine intimacies. Two of the girls had asked her to their homes but she had always refused; such invitations would have to be returned with similar ones and the presence of Jinny would entail explanations. The invitation of Mr. Shields, the instructor, to have tea at his wife's at home was another matter and of this she gladly availed herself. She could not tell to just what end she was striving. She did not like teaching and longed to give it up. On the other hand she must make her living. Mr. Shields had suggested that she might be able to increase both her earning capacity and her enjoyments through a more practical application of her art. There were directorships of drawing in the public schools, positions in art schools and colleges, or, since Angela frankly acknowledged her unwillingness to instruct, there was such a thing as being buyer for the art section of a department store.

"And anyway," said Mrs. Shields, "you never know what may

be in store for you if you just have preparation." She and her husband were both attracted to the pleasant-spoken, talented girl. Angela possessed an undeniable air, and she dressed well, even superlatively. Her parents' death had meant the possession of half the house and half of three thousand dollars' worth of insurance. Her salary was adequate, her expenses light. Indeed even her present mode of living gave her little cause for complaint except that her racial affiliations narrowed her confines. But she was restlessly conscious of a desire for broader horizons. She confided something like this to her new friends.

"Perfectly natural," they agreed. "There's no telling where your tastes and talents will lead you,—to Europe perhaps and surely to the formation of new and interesting friendships. You'll find artistic folk the broadest, most liberal people in the world."

"There are possibilities of scholarships, too," Mr. Shields concluded more practically. The Academy offered a few in competition. But there were others more liberally endowed and practically without restriction.

Sundays on Opal Street bore still their aspect of something different and special. Jinny sometimes went to church, sometimes packed the car with a group of laughing girls of her age and played at her father's old game of exploring. Angela preferred to stay in the house. She liked to sleep late, get up for a leisurely bath and a meticulous toilet. Afterwards she would turn over her wardrobe, sorting and discarding; read the week's forecast of theatres, concerts and exhibits. And finally she would begin sketching, usually ending up with a new view of Hetty Daniels' head.

Hetty, who lived with them now in the triple capacity, as she saw it, of housekeeper, companion, and chaperone, loved to pose. It satisfied some unquenchable vanity in her unloved, empty existence. She could not conceive of being sketched because she was, in the artistic jargon, "interesting", "paintable", or "difficult". Models, as she understood it, were chosen for their beauty. Square and upright she sat, regaling Angela with tales of the romantic adventures of some remote period which was her youth. She could not be very old, the young girl thought; indeed, from some of her dates she must have been at least twelve years younger than her mother. Yet Mrs. Murray had carried with her to the end some irrefragable quality of girlishness which would keep her memory forever young.

Miss Daniels' great fetish was sex morality. "Them young fellers was always 'round me thick ez bees; wasn't any night they wasn't more fellows in my kitchen then you an' Jinny ever has in yore parlour. But I never listened to none of the' talk, jist held out agin 'em and kept my pearl of great price untarnished. I aimed then and I'm continual to aim to be a verjous woman."

Her unslaked yearnings gleamed suddenly out of her eyes, transforming her usually rather expressionless face into something wild and avid. The dark brown immobile mask of her skin made an excellent foil for the vividness of an emotion which was so apparent, so palpable that it seemed like something superimposed upon the background of her countenance.

"If I could just get that look for Mr. Shields," Angela said half aloud to herself, "I bet I could get any of their old scholarships. . . . So you had lots more beaux than we have, Hetty? Well you wouldn't have to go far to outdo us there."

The same half dozen young men still visited the Murray household on Sundays. None of them except Matthew Henson came as a suitor; the others looked in partly from habit, partly, Jinny used to say, for the sake of Hetty Daniels' good ginger bread, but more than for any other reason for the sake of having a comfortable place in which to argue and someone with whom to conduct the argument.

"They certainly do argue," Angela grumbled a little, but she didn't care. Matthew was usually the leader in their illimitable discussions, but she much preferred him at this than at his clumsy and distasteful love-making. Of course she could go out, but there was no place for her to visit and no companions for her to visit with. If she made calls there would be merely a replica of what she was finding in her own household. It was true that in the ultra-modern set Sunday dancing was being taken up. But she and Virginia did not fit in here any too well. Her fancy envisaged a comfortable drawing-room (there *were* folks who used that term), peopled with distinguished men and women who did things, wrote and painted and acted,— people with a broad, cultural background behind them, or, lacking that, with the originality of thought and speech which comes from failing, deliberately failing, to conform to the pattern. Somewhere, she supposed, there must be coloured people like that. But she didn't know any of them. She knew there were people right in Philadelphia who had left far, far behind them the economic class to which her father and mother had belonged. But their thoughts, their actions were still cramped and confined; they were sitting in their new, even luxurious quarters, still mental parvenus, still discussing the eternal race question even as these boys here.

To-night they were hard at it again with a new phase which Angela, who usually sat only half attentive in their midst, did not remember ever having heard touched before. Seymour Porter had started the ball by forcing their attention to one of his poems. It was not a bad poem; as modern verse goes it possessed a touch distinctly above the mediocre.

"Why don't you stop that stuff and get down to brass tacks, Porter?" Matthew snarled. "You'll be of much more service to your race as a good dentist than as a half-baked poet." Henson happened to know that the amount of study which the young poet did at the University kept him just barely registered in the dental college.

Porter ran his hand over his beautifully groomed hair. He had worn a stocking cap in his room all the early part of the day to enable him to perform this gesture without disaster. "There you go, Henson,—service to the race and all the rest of it. Doesn't it ever occur to you that the race is made up of individuals and you can't conserve the good of the whole unless you establish that of each part? Is it better for me to be a first rate dentist and be a cabined and confined personality or a half-baked poet, as you'd call it, and be myself?"

Henson reasoned that a coloured American must take into account that he is usually living in a hostile community. "If you're only a half-baked poet they'll think that you're a representative of your race and that we're all equally no account. But if you're a fine dentist, they won't think, it's true, that we're all as skilled as you, but they will respect you and concede that probably there're a few more like you. Inconsistent, but that's the way they argue."

Arthur Sawyer objected to this constant yielding to an invisible censorship. "If you're coloured you've just got to straddle a bit; you've got to consider both racial and individual integrity. I've got to be sure of a living right now. So in order not to bring the charge of vagrancy against my family I'm going to teach until I've saved enough money to study engineering in comfort."

"And when you get through?" Matthew asked politely.

"When I get through, if this city has come to its senses, I'll get a big job with Baldwin. If not I'll go to South America and take out naturalization papers."

"But you can't do that," cried Jinny, "we'd need you more than ever if you had all that training. You know what I think? We've all of us got to make up our minds to the sacrifice of something. I mean something more than just the ordinary sacrifices in life, not so much for the sake of the next generation as for the sake of some principle, for the sake of some immaterial quality like pride or intense self-respect or even a saving complacency; a spiritual tonic which the race needs perhaps just as much as the body might need iron or whatever it does need to give the proper kind of resistance. There are some things which an individual might want, but which he'd just have to give up forever for the sake of the more important whole."

"It beats me," said Sawyer indulgently, "how a little thing like you can catch hold of such a big thought. I don't know about a man's giving up his heart's desire forever, though, just because he's coloured. That seems to me a pretty large order."

"Large order or not," Henson caught him up, "she comes mighty near being right. What do you think, Angela?"

"Just the same as I've always thought. I don't see any sense in living unless you're going to be happy."

Angela took the sketch of Hetty Daniels to school. "What an interesting type!" said Gertrude Quale, the girl next to her. "Such cosmic and tragic unhappiness in that face. What is she, not an American?"

"Oh yes she is. She's an old coloured woman who's worked in our family for years and she was born right here in Philadelphia."

"Oh coloured! Well, of course I suppose you would call her

an American though I never think of darkies as Americans. Coloured,—yes that would account for that unhappiness in her face. I suppose they all mind it awfully."

It was the afternoon for the life class. The model came in, a short, rather slender young woman with a faintly pretty, shrewish face full of a certain dark, mean character. Angela glanced at her thoughtfully, full of pleasant anticipation. She liked to work for character, preferred it even to beauty. The model caught her eye; looked away and again turned her full gaze upon her with an insistent, slightly incredulous stare. It was Esther Bayliss who had once been in the High School with Angela. She had left not long after Mary Hastings' return to her boarding school.

Angela saw no reason why she should speak to her and presently, engrossed in the portrayal of the round, yet pointed little face, forgot the girl's identity. But Esther kept her eyes fixed on her former school-mate with a sort of intense, angry brooding so absorbing that she forgot her pose and Mr. Shield spoke to her two or three times. On the third occasion he said not unkindly, "You'll have to hold your pose better than this, Miss Bayliss, or we won't be able to keep you on."

"I don't want you to keep me on." She spoke with an amazing vindictiveness. "I haven't got to the point yet where I'm going to lower myself to pose for a coloured girl."

He looked around the room in amazement; no, Miss Henderson wasn't there, she never came to this class he remembered. "Well after that we couldn't keep you anyway. We're not taking orders from our models. But there's no coloured girl here."

"Oh yes there is, unless she's changed her name." She laughed spitefully. "Isn't that Angela Murray over there next to that Jew girl?" In spite of himself, Shields nodded. "Well, she's coloured though she wouldn't let you know. But I know. I went to school with her in North Philadelphia. And I tell you I wouldn't stay to pose for her not if you were to pay me ten times what I'm getting. Sitting there drawing from me just as though she were as good as a white girl!"

Astonished and disconcerted, he told his wife about it. "But I can't think she's really coloured, Mabel. Why she looks and acts just like a white girl. She dresses in better taste than anybody in the room. But that little wretch of a model insisted that she was coloured."

"Well she just can't be. Do you suppose I don't know a coloured woman when I see one? I can tell 'em a mile off."

It seemed to him a vital and yet such a disgraceful matter. "If she is coloured she should have told me. I'd certainly like to know, but hang it all, I can't ask her, for suppose she should be white in spite of what that little beast of a model said?" He found her address in the registry and overcome one afternoon with shamed curiosity drove up to Opal Street and slowly past her house. Jinny was coming in from school and Hetty Daniels on her way to market greeted her on the lower step. Then Virginia put the key in the lock and passed inside. "She is coloured," he told his wife, "for no white girl in her senses would be rooming with coloured people."

"I should say not! Coloured, is she? Well, she shan't come here again, Henry."

Angela approached him after class on Saturday. "How is Mrs. Shields? I can't get out to see her this week but I'll be sure to run in next."

He blurted out miserably, "But, Miss Murray, you never told me that you were coloured."

She felt as though she were rehearsing a well-known part in a play. "Coloured! Of course I never told you that I was coloured. Why should I?"

But apparently there was some reason why she should tell it; she sat in her room in utter dejection trying to reason it out. Just as in the old days she had not discussed the matter with Jinny, for what could the latter do? She wondered if her mother had ever met with any such experiences. Was there something inherently wrong in "passing"?

Her mother had never seemed to consider it as anything but a lark. And on the one occasion, that terrible day in the hospital when passing or not passing might have meant the difference between good will and unpleasantness, her mother had deliberately given the whole show away. But her mother, she had long since begun to realize, had not considered this business of colour or the lack of it as pertaining intimately to her personal happiness. She was perfectly satisfied, absolutely content whether she was part of that white world with Angela or up on little Opal Street with her dark family and friends. Whereas it seemed to Angela that all the things which she most wanted were wrapped up with white people. All the good things were theirs. Not, some coldly reasoning instinct within was saying, because they were white. But because for the present they had power and the badge of that power was whiteness, very like the colours on the escutcheon of a powerful house. She possessed the badge, and unless there was someone to tell she could possess the power for which it stood.

Hetty Daniels shrilled up: "Mr. Henson's down here to see you."

Tiresome though his presence was, she almost welcomed him to-night, and even accepted his eager invitation to go to see a picture. "It's in a little gem of a theatre, Angela. You'll like the surroundings almost as much as the picture, and that's very good. Sawyer and I saw it about two weeks ago. I thought then that I'd like to take you."

She knew that this was his indirect method of telling her that they would meet with no difficulty in the matter of admission; a comforting assurance, for Philadelphia theatres, as Angela knew, could be very unpleasant to would-be coloured patrons. Henson offered to telephone for a taxi while she was getting on her street clothes, and she permitted the unnecessary extravagance, for she hated the conjectures on the faces of passengers in the street cars; conjectures, she felt in her sensitiveness, which she could only set right by being unusually kind and friendly in her manner to Henson. And this produced undesirable effects on him. She had gone out with him more often in the Ford, which permitted a modicum of privacy. But Jinny was off in the little car to-night.

At Broad and Ridge Avenue the taxi was held up; it was twenty-five minutes after eight when they reached the theatre. Matthew gave Angela a bill. "Do you mind getting the tickets while I settle for the cab?" he asked nervously. He did not want her to miss even the advertisements. This, he almost prayed, would be a perfect night.

Cramming the change into his pocket, he rushed into the lobby and joined Angela who, almost as excited as he, for she liked a good picture, handed the tickets to the attendant. He

returned the stubs. "All right, good seats there to your left."
The theatre was only one storey. He glanced at Matthew.

"Here, here, where do you think you're going?"

Matthew answered unsuspecting: "It's all right. The young
lady gave you the tickets."

"Yes, but not for you; she can go in, but you can't." He
handed him the torn ticket, turned and took one of the stubs
from Angela, and thrust that in the young man's unwilling
hand. "Go over there and get your refund."

"But," said Matthew and Angela could feel his very manhood sickening under the silly humiliation of the moment,
"there must be some mistake. I sat in this same theatre less
than three weeks ago."

"Well, you won't sit in there to-night; the management's
changed hands since then, and we're not selling tickets to
coloured people." He glanced at Angela a little uncertainly.
"The young lady can come in——"

Angela threw her ticket on the floor. "Oh, come Matthew,
come."

Outside he said stiffly, "I'll get a taxi, we'll go somewhere
else."

"No, no! We wouldn't enjoy it. Let's go home and we don't
need a taxi. We can get the Sixteenth Street car right at the
corner."

She was very kind to him in the car; she was so sorry for
him, suddenly conscious of the pain which must be his at being
stripped before the girl he loved of his masculine right to protect, to appear the hero.

She let him open the two doors for her but stopped him in
the box of a hall. "I think I'll say good-night now, Matthew;
I'm more tired than I realized. But,—but it was an adventure,
wasn't it?"

His eyes adored her, his hand caught hers: "Angela, I'd have
given all I hope to possess to have been able to prevent it;
you know I never dreamed of letting you in for such humiliation. Oh how are we ever going to get this thing straight?"

"Well, it wasn't your fault." Unexpectedly she lifted her delicate face to his, so stricken and freckled and woebegone, and
kissed him; lifted her hand and actually stroked his reddish,
stiff, "bad" hair.

Like a man in a dream he walked down the street wondering how long it would be before they married.

Angela, waking in the middle of the night and reviewing to herself the events of the day, said aloud: "This is the end," and fell asleep again.

The little back room was still Jinny's, but Angela, in order to give the third storey front to Hetty Daniels, had moved into the room which had once been her mother's. She and Virginia had placed the respective head-boards of their narrow, virginal beds against the dividing wall so that they could lie in bed and talk to each other through the communicating door-way, their voices making a circuit from speaker to listener in what Jinny called a hairpin curve.

Angela called in as soon as she heard her sister moving, "Jinny, listen. I'm going away."

Her sister, still half asleep, lay intensely quiet for another second, trying to pick up the continuity of this dream. Then her senses came to her.

"What'd you say, Angela?"

"I said I was going away. I'm going to leave Philadelphia, give up school teaching, break away from our loving friends and acquaintances, and bust up the whole shooting match."

"Haven't gone crazy, have you?"

"No, I think I'm just beginning to come to my senses. I'm sick, sick, sick of seeing what I want dangled right before my eyes and then of having it snatched away from me and all of it through no fault of my own."

"Darling, you know I haven't the faintest idea of what you're driving at."

"Well, I'll tell you." Out came the whole story, an accumulation of the slights, real and fancied, which her colour had engendered throughout her lifetime; though even then she did not tell of that first hurt through Mary Hastings. That would always linger in some remote, impenetrable fastness of her mind, for wounded trust was there as well as wounded pride and love. "And these two last happenings with Matthew and Mr. Shields are just too much; besides they've shown me the way."

"Shown you what way?"

Virginia had arisen and thrown an old rose kimono around her. She had inherited her father's thick and rather coarsely waving black hair, enhanced by her mother's softness. She was slender, yet rounded; her cheeks were flushed with sleep and excitement. Her eyes shone. As she sat in the brilliant wrap, cross-legged at the foot of her sister's narrow bed, she made the latter think of a strikingly dainty, colourful robin.

"Well you see as long as the Shields thought I was white they were willing to help me to all the glories of the promised land. And the doorman last night,—he couldn't tell what I was, but he could tell about Matthew, so he put him out; just as the Shields are getting ready in another way to put me out. But as long as they didn't know it didn't matter. Which means it isn't being coloured that makes the difference, it's letting it be known. Do you see?

"So I've thought and thought. I guess really I've had it in my mind for a long time, but last night it seemed to stand right out in my consciousness. Why should I shut myself off from all the things I want most,—clever people, people who do things, Art,—" her voice spelt it with a capital,—"travel and a lot of things which are in the world for everybody really but which only white people, as far as I can see, get their hands on. I mean scholarships and special funds, patronage. Oh Jinny, you don't know, I don't think you can understand the things I want to see and know. You're not like me——".

"I don't know why I'm not," said Jinny looking more like a robin than ever. Her bright eyes dwelt on her sister. "After all, the same blood flows in my veins and in the same proportion. Sure you're not laying too much stress on something only temporarily inconvenient?"

"But it isn't temporarily inconvenient; it's happening to me every day. And it isn't as though it were something that I could help. Look how Mr. Shields stressed the fact that I hadn't told him I was coloured. And see how it changed his attitude toward me; you can't think how different his manner was. Yet as long as he didn't know, there was nothing he wasn't willing and glad, glad to do for me. Now he might be willing but he'll not be glad though I need his assistance more than some white girl who will find a dozen people to help her just because she is white." Some faint disapproval in her sister's face halted her for a moment. "What's the matter? You certainly don't think I ought to say first thing: 'I'm Angela Murray. I know I look white but I'm coloured and expect to be treated accordingly!' Now do you?"

"No," said Jinny, "of course that's absurd. Only I don't think you ought to mind quite so hard when they do find out the facts. It seems sort of an insult to yourself. And then, too, it makes you lose a good chance to do something for—for all of us who can't look like you but who really have the same combination of blood that you have."

"Oh that's some more of your and Matthew Henson's philosophy. Now be practical, Jinny; after all I am both white and Negro and look white. Why shouldn't I declare for the one that will bring me the greatest happiness, prosperity and respect?"

"No reason in the world except that since in this country public opinion is against any infusion of black blood it would seem an awfully decent thing to put yourself, even in the face of appearances, on the side of black blood and say: 'Look here, this is what a mixture of black and white really means!'"

Angela was silent and Virginia, feeling suddenly very young, almost childish in the presence of this issue, took a turn about the room. She halted beside her sister.

"Just what is it you want to do, Angela? Evidently you have some plan."

She had. Her idea was to sell the house and to divide the proceeds. With her share of this and her half of the insurance she would go to New York or to Chicago, certainly to some place where she could by no chance be known, and launch out "into a freer, fuller life".

"And leave me!" said Jinny astonished. Somehow it had not dawned on her that the two would actually separate. She did not know what she had thought, but certainly not that. The tears ran down her cheeks.

Angela, unable to endure either her own pain or the sight of it in others, had all of a man's dislike for tears.

"Don't be absurd, Jinny! How could I live the way I want to if you're with me. We'd keep on loving each other and seeing one another from time to time, but we might just as well face the facts. Some of those girls in the art school used to ask me to their homes; it would have meant opportunity, a broader outlook, but I never dared accept because I knew I couldn't return the invitation."

Under that Jinny winced a little, but she spoke with spirit. "After that, Angela dear, I'm beginning to think that you *have* more white blood in your veins than I, and it was that extra amount which made it possible for you to make that remark." She trailed back to her room and when Hetty Daniels announced breakfast she found that a bad headache required a longer stay in bed.

For many years the memory of those next few weeks lingered in Virginia's mind beside that other tragic memory of her mother's deliberate submission to death. But Angela was almost tremulous with happiness and anticipation. Almost as though by magic her affairs were arranging themselves. She was to have the three thousand dollars and Jinny was to be the sole possessor of the house. Junius had paid far less than this sum for it, but it had undoubtedly increased in value. "It's a fair enough investment for you, Miss Virginia," Mr. Hallowell remarked gruffly. He had disapproved heartily of this summary division, would have disapproved more thoroughly and openly if he had had any idea of the reasons behind it. But the girls had told no one, not even him, of their plans. "Some sisters' quarrel, I suppose," he commented to his wife. "I've never seen any coloured people yet, relatives that is, who could stand the joint possession of a little money."

A late Easter was casting its charm over the city when Angela, trim, even elegant, in her conventional tailored suit, stood in the dining-room of the little house waiting for her taxi. She had burned her bridges behind her, had resigned from school, severed her connection with the Academy, and had permitted an impression to spread that she was going West to visit indefinitely a distant cousin of her mother's. In reality she was going to New York. She had covered her tracks very well, she thought; none of her friends was to see her off; indeed, none of them knew the exact hour of her departure. She was even leaving from the North Philadelphia station so that none of the porters of the main depôt, friends perhaps of the boys who came to her house, and, through some far flung communal instinct familiar to coloured people, acquainted with her by sight, would be able to tell of her going. Jinny, until she heard of this, had meant to accompany her to the station, but Angela's precaution palpably scotched this idea; she made no comment when Virginia announced that it would be impossible for her to see her sister off. An indefinable steeliness was creeping upon them.

Yet when the taxi stood rumbling and snorting outside, Angela, her heart suddenly mounting to her throat, her eyes smarting, put her arm tightly about her sister who clung to her frankly crying. But she only said: "Now, Jinny, there's nothing to cry about. You'll be coming to New York soon. First thing I know you'll be walking up to me: 'Pardon me! Isn't this Mrs. Henrietta Jones?'"

Virginia tried to laugh, "And you'll be saying: 'Really you have the advantage of me.' Oh, Angela, don't leave me!"

The cabby was honking impatiently. "I must, darling. Good-bye, Virginia. You'll hear from me right away."

She ran down the steps, glanced happily back. But her sister had already closed the door.

MARKET

Chapter I

FIFTH AVENUE is a canyon; its towering buildings dwarf the importance of the people hurrying through its narrow confines. But Fourteenth Street is a river, impersonally flowing, broad-bosomed, with strange and devious craft covering its expanse. To Angela the famous avenue seemed but one manifestation of living, but Fourteenth Street was the rendezvous of life itself. Here for those first few weeks after her arrival in New York she wandered, almost prowled, intent upon the jostling shops, the hurrying, pushing people, above all intent upon the faces of those people with their showings of grief, pride, gaiety, greed, joy, ambition, content. There was little enough of this last. These men and women were living at a sharper pitch of intensity than those she had observed in Philadelphia. The few coloured people whom she saw were different too; they possessed an independence of carriage, a purposefulness, an assurance in their manner that pleased her. But she could not see that any of these people, black or white, were any happier than those whom she had observed all her life.

But *she* was happier; she was living on the crest of a wave of excitement and satisfaction which would never wane, never break, never be spent. She was seeing the world, she was getting acquainted with life in her own way without restrictions or restraint; she was young, she was temporarily independent, she was intelligent, she was white. She remembered an expression "free, white and twenty-one",—this was what it meant then, this sense of owning the world, this realization that other things being equal, all things were possible. "If I were a man," she said, "I could be president", and laughed at herself for the "if" itself proclaimed a limitation. But that inconsistency bothered her little; she did not want to be a man. Power, greatness, authority, these were fitting and proper for men; but there were sweeter, more beautiful gifts for women, and power of a

certain kind too. Such a power she would like to exert in this
glittering new world, so full of mysteries and promise. If she
could afford it she would have a salon, a drawing-room where
men and women, not necessarily great, but real, alive, free, and
untrammelled in manner and thought, should come and pour
themselves out to her sympathy and magnetism. To accomplish
this she must have money and influence; indeed since she was so
young she would need even protection; perhaps it would be
better to marry . . . a white man. The thought came to her
suddenly out of the void; she had never thought of this possibility before. If she were to do this, do it suitably, then all that
richness, all that fullness of life which she so ardently craved
would be doubly hers. She knew that men had a better time of
it than women, coloured men than coloured women, white men
than white women. Not that she envied them. Only it would
be fun, great fun to capture power and protection in addition
to the freedom and independence which she had so long coveted and which now lay in her hand.

But, she smiled to herself, she had no way of approaching
these ends. She knew no one in New York; she could conceive
of no manner in which she was likely to form desirable acquaintances; at present her home consisted of the four walls of
the smallest room in Union Square Hotel. She had gone there
the second day after her arrival, having spent an expensive twenty-
four hours at the Astor. Later she came to realize that there
were infinitely cheaper habitations to be had, but she could
not tear herself away from Fourteenth Street. It was Spring,
and the Square was full of rusty specimens of mankind who sat
on the benches, as did Angela herself, for hours at a stretch, as
though they thought the invigorating air and the mellow sun
would work some magical burgeoning on their garments such
as was worked on the trees. But though these latter changed,
the garments changed not nor did their owners. They remained
the same, drooping, discouraged down and outers. "I am seeing life," thought Angela, "this is the way people live," and
never realized that some of these people looking curiously,
speculatively at her wondered what had been her portion to
bring her thus early to this unsavoury company.

"A great picture!" she thought. "I'll make a great picture of
these people some day and call them 'Fourteenth Street types.'"

And suddenly a vast sadness invaded her; she wondered if there were people more alive, more sentient to the joy, the adventure of living, even than she, to whom she would also be a "type". But she could not believe this. She was at once almost irreconcilably too concentrated and too objective. Her living during these days was so intense, so almost solidified, as though her desire to live as she did and she herself were so one and the same thing that it would have been practically impossible for another onlooker like herself to insert the point of his discrimination into her firm panoply of satisfaction. So she continued to browse along her chosen thoroughfare, stopping most often in the Square or before a piano store on the same street. There was in this shop a player-piano which was usually in action, and as the front glass had been removed the increased clearness of the strains brought a steady, patient, apparently insatiable group of listeners to a standstill. They were mostly men, and as they were far less given, Angela observed, to concealing their feelings than women, it was easy to follow their emotional gamut. Jazz made them smile but with a certain wistfulness—if only they had time for dancing now, just now when the mood was on them! The young woman looking at the gathering of shabby pedestrians, worn business men and ruminative errand boys felt for them a pity not untinged with satisfaction. *She* had taken what she wanted while the mood was on her. Love songs, particularly those of the sorrowful ballad variety brought to these unmindful faces a strained regret. But there was one expression which Angela could only half interpret. It drifted on to those listening countenances usually at the playing of old Irish and Scottish tunes. She noticed then an acuter attitude of attention, the eyes took on a look of inwardness of utter remoteness. A passer-by engrossed in thought caught a strain and at once his gait and expression fell under the spell. The listeners might be as varied as fifteen people may be, yet for the moment they would be caught in a common, almost cosmic nostalgia. If the next piece were jazz, that particular crowd would disperse, its members going on their meditative ways, blessed or cursed with heaven knew what memories which must not be disturbed by the strident jangling of the latest popular song.

"Homesick," Angela used to say to herself. And she would feel so, too, though she hardly knew for what,—certainly not for Philadelphia and that other life which now seemed so removed as to have been impossible. And she made notes in her sketch book to enable her some day to make a great picture of these "types" too.

Of course she was being unconscionably idle; but as her days were filled to overflowing with the impact of new impressions, this signified nothing. She could not guess what life would bring her. For the moment it seemed to her both wise and amusing to sit with idle hands and see what would happen. By a not inexplicable turn of mind she took to going very frequently to the cinema where most things did happen. She found herself studying the screen with a strained and ardent intensity, losing the slight patronizing scepticism which had once been hers with regard to the adventures of these shadowy heroes and heroines; so utterly unforeseen a turn had her own experiences taken. This time last year she had never dreamed of, had hardly dared to long for a life as free and as full as hers was now and was promising to be. Yet here she was on the threshhold of a career totally different from anything that a scenario writer could envisage. Oh yes, she knew that hundreds, indeed thousands of white coloured people "went over to the other side", but that was just the point, she knew the fact without knowing hitherto any of the possibilities of the adventure. Already Philadelphia and her trials were receding into the distance. Would these people, she wondered, glancing about her in the soft gloom of the beautiful theatre, begrudge her, if they knew, her cherished freedom and sense of unrestraint? If she were to say to this next woman for instance, "I'm coloured," would she show the occasional dog-in-the-manger attitude of certain white Americans and refuse to sit by her or make a complaint to the usher? But she had no intention of making such an announcement. So she spent many happy, irresponsible, amused hours in the marvellous houses on Broadway or in the dark commonplaceness of her beloved Fourteenth Street. There was a theatre, too, on Seventh Avenue just at the edge of the Village, which she came to frequent, not so much for the sake of the plays, which were the same as elsewhere, as for the sake of the audience, a curiously intimate sort of audience made of numerous still more intimate groups.

Their members seemed both purposeful and leisurely. When she came here her loneliness palled on her, however. All unaware her face took on the wistfulness of the men gazing in the music store. She wished she knew some of these pleasant people.

It came to her that she was neglecting her Art. "And it was for that that I broke away from everything and came to New York. I must hunt up some classes." This she felt was not quite true, then the real cause rushed up to the surface of her mind: "And perhaps I'll meet some people."

She enrolled in one of the art classes in Cooper Union. This, after all, she felt would be the real beginning of her adventure. For here she must make acquaintances and one of them, perhaps several, must produce some effect on her life, perhaps alter its whole tenor. And for the first time she would be seen, would be met against her new background or rather, against no background. No boyish stowaway on a ship had a greater exuberance in going forth to meet the unknown than had Angela as she entered her class that first afternoon. In the room were five people, working steadily and chatting in an extremely desultory way. The instructor, one of the five, motioned her to a seat whose position made her one of the group. He set up her easel and as she arranged her material she glanced shyly but keenly about her. For the first time she realized how lonely she had been. She thought with a joy which surprised herself: "Within a week I'll be chatting with them too; perhaps going to lunch or to tea with one of them." She arranged herself for a better view. The young woman nearest her, the possessor of a great mop of tawny hair and smiling clear, slate-grey eyes glanced up at her and nodded, "Am I in your way?" Except for her hair and eyes she was nondescript. A little beyond sat a coloured girl of medium height and build, very dark, very clean, very reserved. Angela, studying her with inner secret knowledge, could feel her constantly withdrawn from her companions. Her refinement was conspicuous but her reserve more so; when asked she passed and received erasers and other articles but she herself did no borrowing nor did she initiate any conversation. Her squarish head capped with a mass of unnaturally straight and unnaturally burnished hair possessed a kind of ugly beauty. Angela could not tell whether her features were good but blurred and blunted by the soft night of her skin or really ugly with an ugliness lost and plunged in that skin's deep concealment. Two students were still slightly behind her. She wondered how she could best contrive to see them.

Someone said: "Hi, there! Miss New One, have *you* got a decent eraser? all mine are on the blink." Not so sure whether or not the term applied to herself she turned to meet the singularly intent gaze of a slender girl with blue eyes, light chestnut hair and cheeks fairly blazing with some unguessed excitement. Angela smiled and offered her eraser.

"It ought to be decent, it's new."

"Yes, it's a very good one; many thanks. I'll try not to trouble you again. My name's Paulette Lister, what's yours?"

"Angèle Mory." She had changed it thus slightly when she came to New York. Some troubling sense of loyalty to her father and mother had made it impossible for her to do away with it altogether.

"Mory," said a young man who had been working just beyond Paulette; "that's Spanish. Are you by any chance?"

"I don't think so."

"He is," said Paulette. "His name is Anthony Cruz—isn't that a lovely name? But he changed it to Cross because no American would ever pronounce the z right, and he didn't want to be taken for a widow's cruse."

"That's a shameful joke," said Cross, "but since I made it up, I think you might give me a chance to spring it, Miss Lister. A poor thing but mine own. You might have a heart."

"Get even with her, why don't you, by introducing her as Miss Blister?" asked Angela, highly diverted by the foolish talk.

Several people came in then, and she discovered that she had been half an hour too early, the class was just beginning. She glanced about at the newcomers, a beautiful Jewess with a pearly skin and a head positively foaming with curls, a tall Scandinavian, an obvious German, several more Americans. Not one of them made the photograph on her mind equal to those made by the coloured girl whose name, she learned, was Rachel Powell, the slate-eyed Martha Burden, Paulette Lister and Anthony Cross. Her prediction came true. With in a week she was on jestingly intimate terms with every one of them except Miss Powell, who lent her belongings, borrowed nothing, and spoke only when she was spoken to. At the end of ten days Miss Burden asked Angela to come and have lunch "at the same place where I go".

On an exquisite afternoon she went to Harlem. At One Hundred and Thirty-fifth Street she left the 'bus and walked through from Seventh Avenue to Lenox, then up to One Hundred and Forty-seventh Street and back down Seventh Avenue to One Hundred and Thirty-ninth Street, through this to Eighth Avenue and then weaving back and forth between the two Avenues through Thirty-eighth, Thirty-seventh down to One Hundred and Thirty-fifth Street to Eighth Avenue where she took the Elevated and went back to the New York which she knew.

But she was amazed and impressed at this bustling, frolicking, busy, laughing great city within a greater one. She had never seen coloured life so thick, so varied, so complete. Moreover, just as this city reproduced in microcosm all the important features of any metropolis, so undoubtedly life up here was just the same, she thought dimly, as life anywhere else. Not all these people, she realized, glancing keenly at the throngs of black and brown, yellow and white faces about her were servants or underlings or end men. She saw a beautiful woman all brown and red dressed as exquisitely as anyone she had seen on Fifth Avenue. A man's sharp, high-bred face etched itself on her memory,--the face of a professional man perhaps, —it might be an artist. She doubted that; he might of course be a musician, but it was unlikely that he would be her kind of an artist, for how could he exist? Ah, there lay the great difference. In all material, even in all practical things these two worlds were alike, but in the production, the fostering of those ultimate manifestations, this world was lacking, for its people were without the means or the leisure to support them and enjoy. And these were the manifestations which she craved, together with the freedom to enjoy them. No, she was not sorry that she had chosen as she had, even though she could now realize that life viewed from the angle of Opal and Jefferson

Streets in Philadelphia and that same life viewed from One
Hundred and Thirty-fifth Street and Seventh Avenue in New
York might present bewilderingly different facets.

Unquestionably there was something very fascinating, even
terrible, about this stream of life,—it seemed to her to run
thicker, more turgidly than that safe, sublimated existence in
which her new friends had their being. It was deeper, more
mightily moving even than the torrent of Fourteenth Street.
Undoubtedly just as these people,—for she already saw them
objectively, doubly so, once with her natural remoteness and
once with the remoteness of her new estate,—just as these
people could suffer more than others, just so they could enjoy
themselves more. She watched the moiling groups on Lenox
Avenue; the amazingly well-dressed and good-looking throngs
of young men on Seventh Avenue at One Hundred and Thirty-
seventh and Thirty-fifth Streets. They were gossiping, laughing, dickering, chaffing, combining the customs of the small
town with the astonishing cosmopolitanism of their clothes
and manners. Nowhere down town did she see life like this.
Oh, all this was fuller, richer, not finer but richer with the difference in quality that there is between velvet and silk. Harlem
was a great city, but after all it was a city within a city, and she
was glad, as she strained for last glimpses out of the lurching
"L" train, that she had cast in her lot with the dwellers outside
its dark and serried tents.

Chapter II

"WHERE do you live?" asked Paulette, "when you're not here at school?"

Angela blushed as she told her.

"In a hotel? In Union Square? Child, are you a millionaire? Where did you come from? Don't you care anything about the delights of home? Mr. Cross, come closer. Here is this poor child living benightedly in a hotel when she might have two rooms at least in the Village for almost the same price."

Mr. Cross came closer but without saying anything. He was really, Angela thought, a very serious, almost sad young man. He had never continued long the bantering line with which he had first made her acquaintance.

She explained that she had not known where to go. "Often I've thought of moving, and of course I'm spending too much money for what I get out of it,—I've the littlest room."

Paulette opened her eyes very wide which gave an onlooker the effect of seeing suddenly the blue sky very close at hand. Her cheeks took on a flaming tint. She was really a beautiful, even fascinating girl—or woman,—Angela never learned which, for she never knew her age. But her fascination did not rest on her looks, or at least it did not arise from that source; it was more the result of her manner. She was so alive, so intense, so interested, if she were interested, that all her nerves, her emotions even were enlisted to accomplish the end which she might have in view. And withal she possessed the simplicity of a child. There was an unsuspected strength about her also that was oddly at variance with the rather striking fragility of her appearance, the trustingness of her gaze, the limpid unaffectedness of her manner. Mr. Cross, Angela thought negligently, must be in love with her; he was usually at her side when they sketched. But later she came to see that there was nothing at all between these two except a certain friendly appreciation tempered by a wary kindness on the part of Mr. Cross and a negligent generosity on the part of Paulette.

She displayed no negligence of generosity in her desire and

eagerness to find Angela a suitable apartment. She did hold out, however, with amazing frankness for one "not too near me but also not too far away". But this pleased the girl, for she had been afraid that Paulette would insist on offering to share her own apartment and she would not have known how to refuse. She had the complete egoist's desire for solitude.

Paulette lived on Bank Street; she found for her new friend "a duck,—just a duck,—no other word will describe it,—of an apartment" on Jayne Street, two rooms, bath and kitchenette. There was also a tiny balcony giving on a mews. It was more than Angela should have afforded, but the ease with which her affairs were working out gave her an assurance, almost an arrogance of confidence. Besides she planned to save by getting her own meals. The place was already furnished, its former occupant was preparing to go to London for two or more years.

"Two years," Angela said gaily, "everything in the world can happen to me in that time. Oh I wonder what will have happened; what I will be like!" And she prepared to move in her slender store of possessions. Anthony, prompted, she suspected by Paulette, offered rather shyly to help her. It was a rainy day, there were several boxes after all, and taxis were scarce, though finally he captured one for her and came riding back in triumph with the driver. Afterwards a few books had to be arranged, pictures must be hung. She had an inspiration.

"You tend to all this and I'll get you the best dinner you ever tasted in your life." Memories of Monday night dinners on Opal Street flooded her memory. She served homely, filling dishes, "fit for a drayman," she teased him. There were cornbeef hash, roasted sweet potatoes, corn pudding, and, regardless of the hour, muffins. After supper she refused to let him help her with the dishes but had him rest in the big chair in the living-room while she laughed and talked with him from the kitchenette at a distance of two yards. Gradually, as he sat there smoking, the sadness and strain faded out of his thin, dark face, he laughed and jested like any other normal young man. When he bade her good-bye he let his slow dark gaze rest in hers for a long silent moment. She closed the door and stood laughing, arranging her hair before the mirror.

"Of course he's loads better looking, but something about him makes me think of Matthew Henson. But nothing doing, young-fellow-me-lad. Spanish and I suppose terribly proud. I wonder what he'd say if he really knew?"

She was to go to Paulette's to dinner. "Just we two," stipulated Miss Lister. "Of course, I could have a gang of men, but I think it will be fun for us to get acquainted." Angela was pleased; she was very fond of Paulette, she liked for her generous, capable self. And she was not quite ready for meeting men. She must know something more about these people with whom she was spending her life. Anthony Cross had been affable enough, but she was not sure that he, with his curious sadness, his half-proud, half-sensitive tendency to withdrawal, were a fair enough type. However, in spite of Paulette's protestations, there were three young men standing in her large, dark living-room when Angela arrived.

"But you've got to go at once," said Paulette, laughing but firm; "here is my friend,—isn't she beautiful? We've too many things to discuss without being bothered by you."

"Paulette has these fits of cruelty," said one of the three, a short, stocky fellow with an ugly, sensitive face. "She'd have made a good Nero. But anyway I'm glad I stayed long enough to see you. Don't let her hide you from us altogether." Another man made a civil remark; the third one standing back in the gloomy room said nothing, but the girl caught the impression of tallness and blondness and of a pair of blue eyes which stared at her intently. She felt awkward and showed it.

"See, you've made her shy," said Paulette accusingly. "I won't bother introducing them, Angèle, you'll meet them all too soon." Laughing, protesting, the men filed out, and their unwilling hostess closed the door on them with sincere lack of regret. "Men," she mused candidly. "Of course we can't get along without them any more than they can without us, but I get tired of them,—they're nearly all animals. I'd rather have a good woman friend any day." She sighed with genuine sincerity. "Yet my place is always full of men. Would you rather have your chops rare or well done? I like mine cooked to a cinder." Angela preferred hers well done. "Stay here and look around; see if I have anything to amuse you." Catching up an apron she vanished into some smaller and darker retreat which she called her kitchen.

The apartment consisted of the whole floor of a house on Bank Street, dark and constantly within the sound of the opening front door and the noises of the street. "But you don't have the damned stairs when you come in late at night," Paulette explained. The front room was, Angela supposed, the bedroom, though the only reason for this supposition was the appearance of a dressing-table and a wide, flat divan about one foot and a half from the floor, covered with black or purple velvet. The dressing table was a good piece of mahogany, but the chairs were indifferently of the kitchen variety and of the sort which, magazines affirm, may be made out of a large packing box. In the living room, where the little table was set, the same anomaly prevailed; the china was fine, even dainty, but the glasses were thick and the plating had begun to wear off the silver ware. On the other hand the pictures were unusual, none of the stereotyped things; instead Angela remarked a good copy of Breughel's "Peasant Wedding", the head of Bernini and two etchings whose authors she did not know. The bookcase held two paper bound volumes of the poems of Béranger and Villon and a little black worn copy of Heine. But the other books were high-brow to the point of austerity: Ely, Shaw and Strindberg.

"Perhaps you'd like to wash your hands?" called Paulette. "There's a bathroom down the corridor there, you can't miss it. You may have some of my favourite lotion if you want it—up there on the shelf." Angela washed her hands and looked up for the lotion. Her eyes opened wide in amazement. Beside the bottle stood a man's shaving mug and brush and a case of razors.

The meal, "for you can't call it a dinner," the cook remarked candidly, was a success. The chops were tender though smoky; there were spinach, potatoes, tomato and lettuce salad, rolls, coffee and cheese. Its rugged quality surprised Angela not a little; it was more a meal for a working man than for a woman, above all, a woman of the faery quality of Paulette. "I get so tired," she said, lifting a huge mouthful, "if I don't eat heartily; besides it ruins my temper to go hungry." Her whole attitude toward the meal was so masculine and her appearance so daintily feminine that Angela burst out laughing, explaining with much amusement the cause of her merriment. "I hope you don't mind," she ended, "for of course you are conspicuously feminine. There's nothing of the man about you."

To her surprise Paulette resented this last statement. "There is a great deal of the man about me. I've learned that a woman is a fool who lets her femininity stand in the way of what she wants. I've made a philosophy of it. I see what I want; I use my wiles as a woman to get it, and I employ the qualities of men, tenacity and ruthlessness, to keep it. And when I'm through with it, I throw it away just as they do. Consequently I have no regrets and no encumbrances."

A packet of cigarettes lay open on the table and she motioned to her friend to have one. Angela refused, and sat watching her inhale in deep respirations; she had never seen a woman more completely at ease, more assuredly mistress of herself and of her fate. When they had begun eating Paulette had poured out two cocktails, tossing hers off immediately and finishing Angela's, too, when the latter, finding it too much like machine oil for her taste, had set it down scarcely diminished. "You'll get used to them if you go about with these men. You'll be drinking along with the rest of us."

She had practically no curiosity and on the other hand no reticences. And she had met with every conceivable experience, had visited France, Germany and Sweden; she was now contemplating a trip to Italy and might go to Russia; she would go now, in fact, if it were not that a friend of hers, Jack Hudson, was about to go there, too, and as she was on the verge of having an affair with him she thought she'd better wait. She didn't relish the prospect of such an event in a foreign land, it put you too much at the man's mercy. An affair, if you were going to have one, was much better conducted on your own *pied à terre*.

"An affair?" gasped Angela.

"Yes,—why, haven't you ever had a lover?"

"A lover?"

"Goodness me, are you a poll parrot? Why yes, a lover. I've had"—she hesitated before the other's complete amazement, —"I've had more than one, I can tell you."

"And you've no intention of marrying?"

"Oh I don't say that; but what's the use of tying yourself up now while you're young? And then, too, this way you don't always have them around your feet; you can always leave them or they'll leave you. But it's better for you to leave them first. It insures your pride." With her babyish face and her sweet, high voice she was like a child babbling precociously. Yet she seemed bathed in intensity. But later she began to talk of her books and of her pictures, of her work and on all these subjects she spoke with the same subdued excitement; her eyes flashed, her cheeks grew scarlet, all experience meant life to her in various manifestations. She had been on a newspaper, one of the New York dailies; she had done press-agenting. At present she was illustrating for a fashion magazine. There was no end to her versatilities.

Angela said she must go.

"But you'll come again soon, won't you, Angèle?"

A wistfulness crept into her voice. "I do so want a woman friend. When a woman really is your friend she's so dependable and she's not expecting anything in return." She saw her guest to the door. "We could have some wonderful times. Good-night, Angèle." Like a child she lifted her face to be kissed.

Angela's first thought as she walked down the dark street was for the unfamiliar name by which Paulette had called her. For though she had signed herself very often as Angèle, no one as yet used it. Her old familiar formula came to her: "I wonder what she would think if she knew." But of one thing she was sure: if Paulette had been in her place she would have acted in exactly the same way. "She would have seen what she wanted and would have taken it," she murmured and fell to thinking of the various confidences which Paulette had bestowed upon her,—though so frank and unreserved were her remarks that "confidences" was hardly the name to apply to them. Certainly, Angela thought, she was in a new world and with new people. Beyond question some of the coloured people of her acquaintance must have lived in a manner which would not bear inspection, but she could not think of one who would thus have discussed it calmly with either friend or stranger. Wondering what it would be like to conduct oneself absolutely according to one's own laws, she turned into the dark little vestibule on Jayne Street. As usual the Jewish girl who lived above her was standing blurred in the thick blackness of the hall, and as usual Angela did not realize this until, touching the button and turning on the light, she caught sight of Miss Salting straining her face upwards to receive her lover's kiss.

Chapter III

FROM the pinnacle of her satisfaction in her studies, in her new friends and in the joke which she was having upon custom and tradition she looked across the class-room at Miss Powell who preserved her attitude of dignified reserve. Angela thought she would try to break it down; on Wednesday she asked the coloured girl to have lunch with her and was pleased to have the invitation accepted. She had no intention of taking the girl up as a matter either of patronage or of loyalty. But she thought it would be nice to offer her the ordinary amenities which their common student life made natural and possible. Miss Powell it appeared ate generally in an Automat or in a cafeteria, but Angela knew of a nice tea-room. "It's rather arty, but they do serve a good meal and it's cheap." Unfortunately on Wednesday she had to leave before noon; she told Miss Powell to meet her at the little restaurant. "Go in and get a table and wait for me, but I'm sure I'll be there as soon as you will." After all she was late, but, what was worse, she found to her dismay that Miss Powell, instead of entering the tea-room, had been awaiting her across the street. There were no tables and the two had to wait almost fifteen minutes before being served.

"Why on earth didn't you go in?" asked Angela a trifle impatiently, "you could have held the table." Miss Powell answered imperturbably: "Because I didn't know how they would receive me if I went in by myself." Angela could not pretend to misunderstand her. "Oh, I think they would have been all right," she murmured blushing at her stupidity. How quickly she had forgotten those fears and uncertainties. She had never experienced this sort of difficulty herself, but the certainly knew of them from Virginia and others.

The lunch was not a particularly pleasant one. Either Miss Powell was actually dull or she had made a resolve never to let herself go in the presence of white people; perhaps she feared being misunderstood, perhaps she saw in such encounters a lurking attempt at sociological investigations; she would lend herself to no such procedure, that much was plain. Angela could feel her effort to charm, to invite confidence, glance upon and fall back from this impenetrable armour. She had been amazed to find both Paulette and Martha Burden already gaining their living by their sketches. Miss Burden indeed was a caricaturist of no mean local reputation; Anthony Cross was frankly a commercial artist, though he hoped some day to be a recognised painter of portraits. She was curious to learn of Miss Powell's prospects. Inquiry revealed that the young lady had one secret aspiration; to win or earn enough money to go to France and then after that, she said with sudden ardour, "anything could happen". To this end she had worked, saved, scraped, gone without pleasures and clothes. Her work was creditable, indeed above the average, but not sufficiently im-bued, Angela thought, with the divine promise to warrant this sublimation of normal desires.

Miss Powell seemed to read her thought. "And then it gives me a chance to show America that one of us can stick; that we have some idea above the ordinary humdrum of existence."

She made no attempt to return the luncheon but she sent Angela one day a bunch of beautiful jonquils,—and made no further attempt at friendship. To one versed in the psychology of this proud, sensitive people the reason was perfectly plain. "You've been awfully nice to me and I appreciate it but don't think I'm going to thrust myself upon you. Your ways and mine lie along different paths."

Such contacts, such interpretations and investigations were making up her life, a life that for her was interesting and ab-sorbing, but which had its perils and uncertainties. She had no purpose, for it was absurd for her, even with her ability, to con-sider Art an end. She was using it now deliberately, as she had always used it vaguely, to get in touch with interesting people and with a more attractive atmosphere. And she was spending money too fast; she had been in New York eight months, and she had already spent a thousand dollars. At this rate her little fortune which had seemed at first inexhaustible would last her less than two years; at best, eighteen months more. Then she must face,—what? Teaching again? Never, she'd had enough of that. Perhaps she could earn her living with her brush, do-ing menu cards, Christmas and birthday greetings, flowers,

Pierrots and Pierrettes on satin pillow tops. She did not relish that. True there were the specialities of Paulette and of Martha Burden, but she lacked the deft sureness of the one and the slightly mordant philosophy underlying the work of the other. Her own speciality she felt sure lay along the line of reproducing, of interpreting on a face the emotion which lay back of that expression. She thought of her Fourteenth Street "types", —that would be the sort of work which she would really enjoy, that and the depicting of the countenance of a purse-proud but lonely man, of the silken inanity of a society girl, of the smiling despair of a harlot. Even in her own mind she hesitated before the use of that terrible word, but association was teaching her to call a spade a spade.

Yes, she might do worse than follow the example of Mr. Cross and become a portrait painter. But somehow she did not want to have to do this; necessity would, she was sure, spoil her touch; besides, she hated the idea of the position in which she would be placed, fearfully placating and flattering possible patrons, hurrying through with an order because she needed the cheque, accepting patronage and condescension. No, she hoped to be sought after, to have the circumstances which would permit her to pick and choose, to refuse if the whim pleased her. It should mean something to be painted by "Mory". People would say, "I'm going to have my portrait done by 'Mory'". But all this would call for position, power, wealth. And again she said to herself . . . "I might marry—a white man. Marriage is the easiest way for a woman to get those things, and white men have them." But she knew only one white man, Anthony Cross, and he would never have those qualities, at feast not by his deliberate seeking. They might come eventually but only after long years. Long, long years of struggle with realities. There was a simple, genuine steadfastness in him that made her realize that he would seek for the expression of truth and of himself even at the cost of the trimmings of life. And she was ashamed, for she knew that for the vanities and gewgaws of a leisurely and irresponsible existence she would sacrifice her own talent, the integrity of her ability to interpret life, to write down a history with her brush.

*

Martha Burden was as strong and as pronounced a personage as Paulette; even stronger perhaps because she had the great gift of silence. Paulette, as Angela soon realized, lived in a state of constant defiance. "I don't care what people think," was her slogan; men and women appealed to her in proportion to the opposition which they, too, proclaimed for the established thing. Angela was surprised that she clung as persistently as she did to a friendship with a person as conventional and reactionary as herself. But Martha Burden was not like that. One could not tell whether or not she was thinking about other people's opinions. It was probable that the other people and their attitude never entered her mind. She was cool and slightly aloof, with the coolness and aloofness of her slaty eyes and her thick, tawny hair. Neither the slatiness nor the tawniness proclaimed warmth—only depth, depth and again depth. It was impossible to realize what she would be like if impassioned or deeply stirred to anger. There would probably be something implacable, god-like about her; she would be capable of a long, slow, steady burning of passion. Few men would love Martha though many might admire her. But a man once enchanted might easily die for her.

Angela liked her house with its simple elegance, its fine, soft curtains and steady, shaded glow of light that stood somehow for home. She liked her husband, Ladislas Starr, whom Martha produced without a shade of consciousness that this was the first intimation she had given of being married. They were strong individualists, molten and blended in a design which failed to obscure their emphatic personalities. Their apartment in the Village was large and neat and sunny; it bore no trace of palpable wealth, yet nothing conducing to comfort was lacking. Book-cases in the dining-room and living-room spilled over; the *Nation*, the *Mercury*, the *Crisis, a magazine of the darker races*, left on the broad arm of an easy chair, mutely invited; it was late autumn, almost winter, but there were jars of fresh flowers. The bedroom where Angela went to remove her wrap was dainty and restful.

The little gathering to which Martha had invited her was made up of members as strongly individual as the host and hostess. They were all specialists in their way, and specialists for the most part in some offshoot of a calling or movement which was itself already highly specialized. Martha presented a psychiatrist, a war correspondent,—"I'm that only when there is a war of course," he explained to Angela's openly respectful gaze, —a dramatist, a corporation lawyer, a white-faced, conspicuously beautiful poet with a long evasive Russian name, two press agents, a theatrical manager, an actress who played only Shakespeare rôles, a teacher of defective children and a medical student who had been a conscientious objector and had served a long time at Leavenworth. He lapsed constantly into a rapt self-communing from which he only roused himself to utter fiery tirades against the evils of society.

In spite of their highly specialised interests they were all possessed of a common ground of knowledge in which such subjects as Russia, Consumers' Leagues, and the coming presidential election figured most largely. There was much laughter and chaffing but no airiness, no persiflage. One of the press agents, Mrs. Cecil, entered upon a long discussion with the corporation lawyer on a Bill pending before Congress; she knew as much as he about the matter and held her own in a long and almost bitter argument which only the coming of refreshments broke up.

Just before the close of the argument two other young men had come in, but Angela never learned their vocation. Furthermore she was interested in observing the young teacher of defective children. She was coloured; small and well-built, exquisitely dressed, and of a beautiful tint, all bronze and soft red, "like Jinny" thought Angela, a little astonished to observe how the warmth of her appearance overshadowed or rather overshone everyone else in the room. The tawniness even of Miss Burden's hair went dead beside her. The only thing to cope with her richness was the classical beauty of the Russian poet's features. He seemed unable to keep his eyes away from her; was punctiliously attentive to her wants and leaned forward several times during the long political discussion to whisper low spoken and apparently amusing comments. The young woman, perfectly at ease in her deep chair, received his attentions with a slightly detached, amused objectivity; an objectivity which she had for everyone in the room including Angela at whom she had glanced once rather sharply. But the detachment of her manner was totally different from Miss Powell's sensitive dignity. Totally without self-consciousness she let her warm dark eyes travel from one face to another. She might have been saying: "How far you are away from the things that really matter, birth and death and hard, hard work!" The Russian poet must have realized this, for once Angela heard him say, leaning forward, "*You* think all this is futile, don't you?"

Martha motioned for her to wait a moment until most of the other guests had gone, then she came forward with one of the two young men who had come in without introduction. "This is Roger Fielding, he'll see you home."

He was tall and blond with deeply blue eyes which smiled on her as he said: "Would you like to walk or ride? It's raining a little."

Angela said she preferred to walk.

"All right then. Here, Starr, come across with that umbrella I lent you."

They went out into the thin, tingling rain of late Autumn. "I was surprised," said Roger, "to see you there with the high-brows. I didn't think you looked that way when I met you at Paulette's."

"We've met before? I'm—I'm sorry, but I don't seem to re-member you."

"No I don't suppose you would. Well, we didn't exactly meet; I saw you one day at Paulette's. That's why I came this evening, because I heard you'd be here and I'd get a chance to see you again; but I was surprised because you didn't seem like that mouthy bunch. They make me tired taking life so plaguey seriously. Martha and her old high-brows!" he ended ungratefully.

Angela, a little taken back with the frankness of his desire to meet her, said she hadn't thought they were serious.

"Not think them serious? Great Scott! what kind of talk are you used to? You look as though you'd just come out of a Sunday-school! Do you prefer bible texts?"

But she could not explain to him the picture which she saw in her mind of men and women at her father's home in Opal Street,—the men talking painfully of rents, of lynchings, of building and loan associations; the women of child-bearing and the sacrifices which must be made to put Gertie through school, to educate Howard. "I don't mean for any of my children to go through what I did." And in later years in her own first maturity, young Henson and Sawyer and the others in the tiny parlour talking of ideals and inevitable sacrifices for the race; the burnt-offering of individualism for some dimly glimpsed racial whole. This was seriousness, even sombreness, with a great sickening vital upthrust of reality. But these other topics, peaks of civilization superimposed upon peaks, she found, even though interesting, utterly futile.

They had reached the little hall now. "We must talk loud," she whispered.

"Why?" he asked, speaking obediently very loud indeed.

"Wait a minute; no, she's not there. The girl above me meets her young man here at night and just as sure as I forget her and come in quietly there they are in the midst of a kiss. I suspect she hates me."

In his young male sophistication he thought at first that this was a lead, but her air was so gay and so childishly guileless that he changed his opinion. "Though no girl in this day and time could be as simple and innocent as *she* looks."

But aloud he said, "Of course she doesn't hate you, nobody could do that. I assure you I don't."

She thought his gallantries very amusing. "Well, it relieves me to hear you say so; that'll keep me from worrying for one night at least." And withdrawing her hand from his retaining grasp, she ran upstairs.

A letter from Virginia lay inside the door. Getting ready for bed she read it in bits.

"Angela darling, wouldn't it be fun if I were to come to New York too? Of course you'd keep on living in your Village and I'd live in famous Harlem, but we'd both be in the same city, which is where two only sisters ought to be,—dumb I calls it to live apart the way we do. The man out at the U. of P. is crazy to have me take an exam. in music; it would be easy enough and much better pay than I get here. So there are two perfectly good reasons why I should come. He thinks I'll do him credit and I want to get away from this town."

Then between the lines the real reason betrayed itself:

"I do have such awful luck. Edna Brown had a party out in Merion not long ago and Matthew took me. And you know what riding in a train can do for me,—well that night of all nights I had to become car-sick. Matthew had been so nice. He came to see me the next morning, but, child, he's never been near me from that day to this. I suppose a man can't get over a girl's being such a sight as I was that night. Can't things be too hateful!"

Angela couldn't help murmuring: "Imagine anyone wanting old Matthew so badly that she's willing to break up her home to get over him. Now why couldn't he have liked her instead of me?"

And pondering on such mysteries she crept into bed. But she fell to thinking again about the evening she had spent with Martha and the people whom she had met. And again it seemed to her that they represented an almost alarmingly unnecessary class. If any great social cataclysm were to happen they would surely be the first to be swept out of the running. Only the real people could survive. Even Paulette's mode of living, it seemed to her, had something more forthright and vital.

Chapter IV

I N the morning she was awakened by the ringing of the telephone. The instrument was an extravagance, for, save for
Anthony's, she received few calls and made practically none.
But the woman from whom she had taken the apartment had
persuaded her into keeping it. Still, as she had never indicted
the change in ownership, its value was small. She lay there for
a moment blinking drowsily in the thin but intensely gold sunshine of December thinking that her ears were deceiving her.

Finally she reached out a rosy arm, curled it about the edge
of the door jamb and, reaching the little table that stood in the
other room just on the other side of the door, set the instrument
up in her bed. The apartment was so small that almost everything was within arm's reach.

"Hello," she murmured sleepily.

"Oh, I thought you must be there; I said to myself: 'She
couldn't have left home this early'. What time do you go to
that famous drawing class of yours anyway?"

"I beg your pardon! Who is this speaking, please?"

"Why, Roger, of course,—Roger Fielding. Don't say you've
forgotten me already. This is Angèle, isn't it?"

"Yes this is Angèle Mory speaking, Mr. Fielding."

"Did I offend your Highness, Miss Mory? Will you have
lunch with me to-day and let me tell you how sorry I am?"

But she was lunching with Anthony. "I have an engagement."

"Of course you have. Well, will you have tea, dinner, supper
to-day,—breakfast and all the other meals to-morrow and so
on for a week? You might just as well say 'yes' because I'll pes-
ter you till you do."

"I'm engaged for tea, too, but I'm not really as popular as I
sound. That's my last engagement for this week; I'll be glad to
have dinner with you."

"Right-oh! Now don't go back and finish up that beauty
sleep, for if you're any more charming than you were last night
I won't answer for myself. I'll be there at eight."

Inexperienced as she was, she was still able to recognize his
method as a bit florid; she preferred, on the whole, Anthony's

510

manner at lunch when he leaned forward and touching her hand very lightly said: "Isn't it great for us to be here! I'm so content, Angèle. Promise me you'll have lunch with me every day this week. I've had a streak of luck with my drawings."

She promised him, a little thrilled herself with his evident sincerity and with the niceness of the smile which so transfigured his dark, thin face, robbing it of its tenseness and strain.

Still something, some vanity, some vague premonition of adventure, led her to linger over her dressing for the dinner with Roger. There was never very much colour in her cheeks, but her skin was warm and white; there was vitality beneath her pallor; her hair was warm, too, long and thick and yet so fine that it gave her little head the effect of being surrounded by a nimbus of light; rather wayward, glancing, shifting light for there were little tendrils and wisps and curls in front and about the temples which no amount of coaxing could subdue. She touched up her mouth a little, not so much to redden it as to give a hint of the mondaine to her appearance. Her dress was flame-colour—Paulette had induced her to buy it,—of a plain, rather heavy beautiful glowing silk. The neck was high in back and girlishly modest in front. She had a string of good artificial pearls and two heavy silver bracelets. Thus she gave the effect of a flame herself; intense and opaque at the heart where her dress gleamed and shone, transparent and fragile where her white warm neck and face rose into the tenuous shadow of her hair. Her appearance excited herself.

Roger found her delightful. As to women he considered himself a connoisseur. This girl pleased him in many respects. She was young; she was, when lighted from within by some indescribable mechanism, even beautiful; she had charm and, what was for him even more important, she was puzzling. In repose, he noticed, studying her closely, her quiet look took on the resemblance of an arrested movement, a composure on tip-toe so to speak, as though she had been stopped in the swift transition from one mood to another. And back of that momentary cessation of action one could see a mind darting, quick, restless, indefatigable, observing, tabulating, perhaps even mocking. She had for him the quality of the foreigner, but she gave this quality an objectivity as though he were the stranger and she the well-known established personage taking note of his peculiarities and apparently boundlessly diverted by them.

But of all this Angela was absolutely unaware. No wonder she was puzzling to Roger, for, in addition to the excitement which she—a young woman in the high tide of her youth, her health, and her beauty—would be feeling at receiving in the proper setting the devotion and attention which all women crave, she was swimming in the flood of excitement created by her unique position. Stolen waters are the sweetest. And Angela never forgot that they were stolen. She thought: "Here I am having everything that a girl ought to have just because I had sense enough to suit my actions to my appearance." The realization, the secret fun bubbling back in some hidden recess of her heart, brought colour to her cheeks, a certain temerity to her manner. Roger pondered on this quality. If she were reckless!

The dinner was perfect; it was served with elegance and beauty. Indeed she was surprised at the surroundings, the grandeur even of the hotel to which he had brought her. She had no idea of his means, but had supposed that his circumstances were about those of her other new friends; probably he was better off than Anthony, whose poverty she instinctively sensed, and she judged that his income, whatever it might be, was not so perilous as Paulette's. But she would have put him on the same footing as the Starrs. This sort of expenditure, however, meant money, "unless he really does like me and is splurging this time just for me". The idea appealed to her vanity and gave her a sense of power; she looked at Roger with a warm smile. At once his intent, considering gaze filmed; he was already leaning toward her but he bent even farther across the perfect little table and asked in a low, eager tone: "Shall we stay here and dance or go to your house and talk and smoke a bit?"

"Oh we'll stay and dance; it would be so late by the time we get home that we'd only have a few minutes."

Presently the golden evening was over and they were in the vestibule at Jayne Street. Roger said very loudly: "Where's that push button?" Then lower: "Well, your young lovers aren't here to-night either. I'm beginning to think you made that story up, Angèle."

She assured him, laughing, that she had told the truth. "You come here some time and you'll see them for yourself." But she wished she could think of something more ordinary to say. His hands held hers very tightly; they were very strong and for the first time she noticed that the veins stood up on them like cords. She tried to pull her own away and he released them and, taking her key, turned the lock in the inner door, then stood looking down at her.

"Well I'm glad they're not here to-night to take their revenge." And as he handed her back the key he kissed her on the lips. His knowledge of women based on many, many such experiences, told him that her swift retreat was absolutely unfeigned.

As on a former occasion she stood, after she had gained her room, considering herself in the glass. She had been kissed only once before, by Matthew Henson, and that kiss had been neither as casual nor as disturbing as this. She was thrilled, excited, and vaguely displeased. "He is fresh, I'll say that for him." And subsiding into the easy chair she thought for a long time of Anthony Cross and his deep respectful ardour.

In the morning there were flowers.

From the class-room she went with Paulette to deliver the latter's sketches. "Have tea to-day with me; we'll blow ourselves at the Ritz. This is the only time in the month that I have any money, so we'll make the best of it."

Angela looked about the warm, luxurious room at the serene, luxurious women, the super-groomed, super-deferential, tremendously confident men. She sighed. "I love all this, love it."

Paulette, busy blowing smoke-rings, nodded. "I blew sixteen that time. Watch me do it again. There's nothing really to this kind of life, you know."

"Oh don't blow smoke-rings! It's the only thing in the world that can spoil your looks. What do you mean there's nothing to it?"

"Well for a day-in-and-day-out existence, it just doesn't do. It's too boring. It's fun for you and me to drift in here twice a year when we've just had a nice, fat cheque which we've got to spend. But there's nothing to it for every day; it's too much

like reaching the harbour where you would be. The tumult
and the shouting are all over. I'd rather live just above the danger line down on little old Bank Street, and think up a way to
make five hundred dollars so I could go to the French Riviera
second class and bum around those little towns, Villefranche,
Beaulieu, Cagnes,—you must see them, Angèle—and have a
spanking affair with a real man with honest to God blood in
his veins than to sit here and drink tea and listen to the noth-
ings of all these tame tigers, trying you out, seeing how much
it will take to buy you."

Angela was bewildered by this outburst. "I thought you said
you didn't like affairs unless you could conduct them in your
own *pied à terre.*"

"Did I? Well that was another time—not to-day. By the way,
what would you say if I were to tell you that I'm going to
Russia?"

She glanced at her friend with the bright shamelessness of a
child, for she knew that Angela had heard of Jack Hudson's acceptance as newspaper correspondent in Moscow.

"I wouldn't say anything except that I'd much rather be here
in the warmth and cleanliness of the Ritz than be in Moscow
where I'm sure it will be cold and dirty."

"That's because you've never wanted anyone." Her face for
a moment was all desire. Beautiful but terrible too. "She actually looks like Hetty Daniels," thought Angela in astonishment.
Only, alas, there was no longer any beauty in Hetty's face.

"When you've set your heart on anybody or on anything
there'll be no telling what you'll do, Angèle. For all your innocence you're as deep, you'll be as desperate as Martha Burden
once you're started. I know your kind. Well, if you must play
around in the Ritz, etcet., etcet., I'll tell Roger Fielding. He's
a good squire and he can afford it."

"Why? Is he so rich?"

"Rich! If all the wealth that he—no, not he, but his father—if
all the wealth that old man Fielding possesses were to be converted into silver dollars there wouldn't be space enough in
this room, big as it is, to hold it."

Angela tried to envisage it. "And Roger, what does he do?"

"Spend it. What is there for him to do? Nothing except have
a good time and keep in his father's good graces. His father's

some kind of a personage and all that, you know, crazy about his name and his posterity. Roger doesn't dare get drunk and lie in the gutter and he mustn't make a misalliance. Outside of that the world's his oyster and he eats it every day. There's a boy who gets everything he wants."

"What do you mean by a misalliance? He's not royalty."

"Spoken like a good American. No, he's not. But he mustn't marry outside certain limits. No chorus girl romances for his father. The old man wouldn't care a rap about money but he would insist on blue blood and the Mayflower. The funny thing is that Roger, for all his appearing so democratic, is that way too. But of course he's been so run after the marvel is that he's as unspoiled as he is. But it's the one thing I can't stick in him. I don't mind a man's not marrying me; but I can't forgive him if he thinks I'm not good enough to marry him. Any woman is better than the best of men." Her face took on its intense, burning expression; one would have said she was consumed with excitement.

Angela nodded, only half-listening. Roger a multi-millionaire! Roger who only two nights ago had kissed and mumbled her fingers, his eyes avid and yet so humble and beseeching!

"One thing, if you do start playing around with Roger be careful. He's a good bit of a rotter, and he doesn't care what he says or spends to gain his ends." She laughed at the inquiry in her friend's eyes. "No, I've never given Roger five minutes' thought. But I know his kind. They're dangerous. It's wrong for men to have both money and power; they're bound to make some woman suffer. Come on up the Avenue with me and I'll buy a hat. I can't wear this whang any longer. It's too small, looks like a peanut on a barrel."

Angela was visual minded. She saw the days of the week, the months of the year in little narrow divisions of space. She saw the past years of her life falling into separate, uneven compartments whose ensemble made up her existence. Whenever she looked back on this period from Christmas to Easter she saw a bluish haze beginning in a white mist and flaming into something red and terrible; and across the bluish haze stretched the name: Roger.

Roger! She had never seen anyone like him: so gay, so

beautiful, like a blond, glorious god, so overwhelming, so persistent. She had not liked him so much at first except as one likes the sun or the sky or a singing bird, anything jolly and free. There had been no touching points for their minds. He knew nothing of life except what was pleasurable; it is true his idea of the pleasurable did not always coincide with hers. He had no fears, no restraints, no worries. Yes, he had one; he did not want to offend his father. He wanted ardently and unswervingly his father's money. He did not begrudge his senior a day, an hour, a moment of life; about this he had a queer, unselfish sincerity. The old financial war horse had made his fortune by hard labour and pitiless fighting. He had given Roger his being, the *entrée* into a wonderful existence. Already he bestowed upon him an annual sum which would have kept several families in comfort. If Roger had cared to save for two years he need never have asked his father for another cent. With any kind of luck he could have built up for himself a second colossal fortune. But he did not care to do this. He did not wish his father one instant's loss of life or of its enjoyment. But he did want final possession of those millions.

Angela liked him best when he talked about "my dad"; he never mentioned the vastness of his wealth, but by now she could not have helped guessing even without Paulette's aid that he was a wealthy man. She would not take jewellery from him, but there was a steady stream of flowers, fruit, candy, books, fine copies of the old masters. She was afraid and ashamed to express a longing in his presence. And with all this his steady, constant attendance. And an odd watchfulness which she felt but could not explain.

"He must love me," she said to herself, thinking of his caresses. She had been unable to keep him from kissing her. Her uneasiness had amused and charmed him: he laughed at her Puritanism, succeeded in shaming her out of it. "Child, where have you lived? Why there's nothing in a kiss. If I didn't kiss you I couldn't come to see you. And I have to see you, Angèle!" His voice grew deep; the expression in his eyes made her own falter.

Yet he did not ask her to marry him. "But I suppose it's because he can see I don't love him yet." And she wondered what it would be like to love. Even Jinny knew more about this than

she, for she had felt, perhaps still did feel, a strong affection for
Matthew Henson. Well, anyway, if they married she would
probably come to love him; most women learned to love their
husbands. At first after her conversation with Paulette about
Roger she had rather expected a diminution at any time of his
attentions, for after all she was unknown; from Roger's angle
she would be more than outside the pale. But she was sure
now that he loved and would want to marry her, for it never
occurred to her that men bestowed attentions such as these on
a passing fancy. She saw her life rounding out like a fairy tale.
Poor, coloured—coloured in America; unknown, a nobody!
And here at her hand was the forward thrust shadow of love
and of great wealth. She would do lots of good among coloured people; she would see that Miss Powell, for instance,
had her scholarship. Oh she would hunt out girls and men like
Seymour Porter,—she had almost forgotten his name,—or was
it Arthur Sawyer?—and give them a taste of life in its fullness
and beauty such as they had never dreamed of.

To-night she was to go out with Roger. She wore her flame-
coloured dress again; a pretty green one was also hanging up
in her closet, but she wore the flame one because it lighted her
up from within—lighted not only her lovely, fine body but her
mind too. Her satisfaction with her appearance let loose some
inexplicable spring of gaiety and merriment and simplicity so
that she seemed almost daring.

Roger, sitting opposite, tried to probe her mood, tried to
gauge the invitation of her manner and its possibilities. She
touched him once or twice, familiarly; he thought almost possessively. She seemed to be within reach now if along with that
accessibility she had recklessness. It was this attribute which
for the first time to-night he thought to divine within her. If in
addition to her insatiable interest in life—for she was always
asking him about people and places,—she possessed this recklessness, then indeed he might put to her a proposal which had
been hanging on his lips for weeks and months. Something innocent, pathetically untouched about her had hitherto kept
him back. But if she had the requisite daring! They were dining in East Tenth Street in a small *cafè*—small contrasted with
the Park Avenue Hotel to which he had first taken her. But
about them stretched the glitter and perfection of crystal and

silver, of marvellous napery and of obsequious service. Everything, Angela thought, looking about her, was translated. The
slight odour of food was, she told Fielding, really an aroma:
the mineral water which he was drinking because he could not
help it and she because she could not learn to like wine, was
nectar; the bread, the fish, the courses were ambrosia. The
food, too, in general was to be spoken of as viands.

"Vittles, translated," she said laughing.

"And you, you, too, are translated. Angèle, you are wonderful, you are charming," his lips answered but his senses beat
and hammered. Intoxicated with the magic of the moment and
the surroundings, she turned her smiling countenance a little
nearer, and saw his face change, darken. A cloud over the sun.

"Excuse me," he said and walked hastily across the room
back of her. In astonishment she turned and looked after him.
At a table behind her three coloured people (under the direction of a puzzled and troubled waiter,) were about to take a
table. Roger went up and spoke to the headwaiter authorita-
tively, even angrily. The latter glanced about the room, nodded
obsequiously and crossing, addressed the little group. There
was a hasty, slightly acrid discussion. Then the three filed out,
past Angela's table this time, their heads high.

She turned back to her plate, her heart sick. For her the evening was ended. Roger came back, his face flushed, triumphant,
"Well I put a spoke in the wheel of those 'coons'! They forget
themselves so quickly, coming in here spoiling white people's
appetites. I told the manager if they brought one of their
damned suits I'd be responsible. I wasn't going to have them
here with you, Angèle. I could tell that night at Martha Burden's by the way you looked at that girl that you had no time
for darkies. I'll bet you'd never been that near to one before
in your life, had you? Wonder where Martha picked that
one up."

She was silent, lifeless. He went on recounting instances of
how effectively he had "spoked the wheel" of various coloured
people. He had blackballed Negroes in Harvard, aspirants for
small literary or honour societies. "I'd send 'em all back to
Africa if I could. There's been a darkey up in Harlem's got the
right idea, I understand; though he must be a low brute to
cave in on his race that way; of course it's merely a matter of

money with him. He'd betray them all for a few thousands. Gosh, if he could really pull it through I don't know but what I'd be willing to finance it."

To this tirade there were economic reasons to oppose, tenets of justice, high ideals of humanity. But she could think of none of them. Speechless, she listened to him, her appetite fled.

"What's the matter, Angèle? Did it make you sick to see them?"

"No, no not that. I—I don't mind them; you're mistaken about me and that girl at Martha Burden's. It's you, you're so violent. I didn't know you were that way!"

"And I've made you afraid of me? Oh, I don't want to do that." But he was flattered to think that he had affected her. "See here, let's get some air. I'll take you for a spin around the Park and then run you home."

But she did not want to go to the Park; she wanted to go home immediately. His little blue car was outside; in fifteen minutes they were at Jayne Street. She would not permit him to come inside, not even in the vestibule; she barely gave him her hand.

"But Angèle, you can't leave me like this; why what have I done? Did it frighten you because I swore a little? But I'd never swear at you. Don't go like this."

She was gone, leaving him staring and nonplussed on the sidewalk. Lighting a cigarette, he climbed back in his car. "Now what the devil!" He shifted his gears. "But she likes me. I'd have sworn she liked me to-night. Those damn niggers! I bet she's thinking about me this minute."

He would have lost his bet. She was thinking about the coloured people.

She could visualize them all so plainly; she could interpret their changing expressions as completely as though those changes lay before her in a book. There were a girl and two men, one young, the other the father perhaps of either of the other two. The fatherly-looking person, for so her mind docketed him, bore an expression of readiness for any outcome whatever. She knew and understood the type. His experiences of surprises engendered by this thing called prejudice had been too vast for them to appear to him as surprises. If they were served this was a lucky day; if not he would refuse to let the incident shake his stout spirit.

It was to the young man and the girl that her interest went winging. In the mirror behind Roger she had seen them entering the room and she had thought: "Oh, here are some of them fighting it out again. O God! please let them be served, please don't let their evening be spoiled." She was so happy herself and she knew that the reception of fifty other *maîtres d'hotel* could not atone for a rebuff at the beginning of the game. The young fellow was nervous, his face tense,—thus might he have looked going to meet the enemy's charge in the recent Great War; but there the odds were even; here the cards were already stacked against him. Presently his expression would change for one of grimness, determination and despair. Talk of a lawsuit would follow; apparently did follow; still a lawsuit at best is a poor substitute for an evening's fun.

But the girl, the girl in whose shoes she herself might so easily have been! She was so clearly a nice girl, with all that the phrase implies. To Angela watching her intently and yet with the indifference of safety she recalled Virginia, so slender, so appealing she was and so brave. So very brave! Ah, that courage! It affected at first a gay hardihood: "Oh I know it isn't customary for people like us to come into this café, but everything is going to be all right." It met Angela's gaze with a steadiness before which her own quailed, for she thought: "Oh, poor thing! perhaps she thinks that I don't want her either." And when the blow had fallen the courage had had to be translated anew into a comforting assurance. "Don't worry about me, Jimmy," the watching guest could just hear her. "Indeed, indeed it won't spoil the evening, I should say not; there're plenty of places where they'd be all right. We just happened to pick a lemon."

The three had filed out, their heads high, their gaze poised and level. But the net result of the evening's adventure would be an increased cynicism in the elderly man, a growing bitterness for the young fellow, and a new timidity in the girl, who, even after they had passed into the street, could not relieve her feelings, for she must comfort her baffled and goaded escort.

Angela wondered if she had been half as consoling to Matthew Henson,—was it just a short year ago? And suddenly, sitting immobile in her arm-chair, her evening cloak slipping unnoticed to the floor, triumph began to mount in her. Life could never cheat her as it had cheated that coloured girl this evening, as it had once cheated her in Philadephia with Matthew. She was free, free to taste life in all its fullness and sweetness, in all its minutest details. By exercising sufficient courage to employ the unique weapon which an accident of heredity had placed in her grasp she was able to master life. How she blessed her mother for showing her the way! In a country where colour or the lack of it meant the difference between freedom and fetters how lucky she was!

But, she told herself, she was through with Roger Fielding.

Chapter V

Now it was Spring, Spring in New York. Washington Square was a riot of greens that showed up bravely against the great red brick houses on its north side. The Arch viewed from Fifth Avenue seemed a gateway to Paradise. The long deep streets running the length of the city invited an exploration to the ends where pots of gold doubtless gleamed. On the short crosswise streets the April sun streamed in splendid banners of deep golden light.

In two weeks Angela had seen Roger only once. He telephoned every day, pleading, beseeching, entreating. On the one occasion when she did permit him to call there were almost tears in his eyes. "But, darling, what did I do? If you'd only tell me that. Perhaps I could explain away whatever it is that's come between us." But there was nothing to explain she told him gravely, it was just that he was harder, more cruel than she had expected; no, it wasn't the coloured people, she lied and felt her soul blushing, it was that now she knew him when he was angry or displeased, and she could see how ruthless, how determined he was to have things his way. His willingness to pay the costs of the possible lawsuit had filled her with a sharp fear. What could one do against a man, against a group of men such as he and his kind represented who would spend time and money to maintain a prejudice based on a silly, time-worn tradition?

Yet she found she did not want to lose sight of him completely. The care, the attention, the flattery with which he had surrounded her were beginning to produce their effect. In the beautiful but slightly wearying balminess of the Spring she missed the blue car which had been constantly at her call; eating a good but homely meal in her little living room with the cooking odours fairly overwhelming her from the kitchenette, she found herself longing unconsciously for the dainty food, the fresh Spring delicacies which she knew he would be only too glad to procure for her. Shamefacedly she had to acknowledge that the separation which she was so rigidly enforcing meant a difference in her tiny exchequer, for it had now been many months since she had regularly taken her main meal by herself and at her own expense.

To-day she was especially conscious of her dependence upon him, for she was to spend the afternoon in Van Cortlandt Park with Anthony. There had been talk of subways and the Elevated. Roger would have had the blue car at the door and she would have driven out of Jayne Street in state. Now it transpired that Anthony was to deliver some drawings to a man, a tricky customer, whom it was best to waylay if possible on Saturday afternoon. Much as he regretted it he would probably be a little late. Angela, therefore, to save time must meet him at Seventy-second Street. Roger would never have made a request like that; he would have brought his lawyer or his business man along in the car with him and, dismissing him with a curt "Well I'll see if I can finish this to-morrow," would have hastened to her with his best Walter Raleigh manner, and would have produced the cloak, too, if she would but say so. Perhaps she'd have to take him back. Doubtless later on she could manage his prejudices if only he would speak. But how was she to accomplish that?

Still it was lovely being here with Anthony in the park, so green and fresh, so new with the recurring newness of Spring. Anthony touched her hand and said as he had once before, "I'm so content to be with you, Angel. I may call you Angel, mayn't I? You are that to me, you know. Oh if you only knew how happy it makes me to be content, to be satisfied like this. I could get down on my knees and thank God for it like a little boy." He looked like a little boy as he said it. "Happiness is a hard thing to find and harder still to keep."

She asked him idly, "Haven't you always been happy?"

His face underwent a startling change. Not only did the old sadness and strain come back on it, but a great bitterness such as she had never before seen.

"No," he said slowly as though thinking through long years of his life. " I haven't been happy for years, not since I was a little boy. Never once have I been happy nor even at ease until I met you."

But she did not want him to find his happiness in her. That way would only lead to greater unhappiness for him. So she said, to change the subject: "Could you tell me about it?"

But there was nothing to tell, he assured her, his face growing darker, grimmer. "Only my father was killed when I was a
little boy, killed by his enemies. I've hated them ever since; I
never stopped hating them until I met you." But this was just
as dangerous a road as the other plus the possibilities of re-
opening old wounds. So she only shivered and said vaguely,
"Oh, that was terrible! Too terrible to talk about. I'm sorry,
Anthony!" And then as a last desperate topic: "Are you ever
going back to Brazil?" For she knew that he had come to the
United States from Rio de Janeiro. He had spent Christmas at
her house, and had shown her pictures of the great, beautiful
city and of his mother, a slender, dark-eyed woman with a perpetual sadness in her eyes.

The conversation languished, She thought: "It must be terrible to be a man and to have these secret hates and horrors
back of one." Some Spanish feud, a matter of hot blood and
ready knives, a sudden stroke, and then this deadly memory
for him.

"No," he said after a long pause. "I'm never going back to
Brazil. I couldn't." He turned to her suddenly. "Tell me, Angel,
what kind of girl are you, what do you think worth while?
Could you, for the sake of love, for the sake of being loyal to
the purposes and vows of someone you loved, bring yourself
to endure privation and hardship and misunderstanding, hardship that would be none the less hard because it really could be
avoided?"

She thought of her mother who had loved her father so
dearly, and of the wash-days which she had endured for him,
the long years of household routine before she and Jinny had
been old enough to help her first with their hands and then
with their earnings. She thought of the little, dark, shabby house,
of the made-over dresses and turned coats. And then she saw
Roger and his wealth and his golden recklessness, his golden
keys which could open the doors to beauty and ease and—
decency! Oh, it wasn't decent for women to have to scrub and
work and slave and bear children and sacrifice their looks and
their pretty hands,—she saw her mother's hands as they had always looked on wash day, they had a white, boiled appearance.
No, she would not fool herself nor Anthony. She was no senti-
mentalist. It was not likely that she, a girl who had left her little

sister and her home to go out to seek life and happiness, would throw it over for poverty,—hardship. If a man loved a woman how could he ask her that?

So she told him gently: "No, Anthony, I couldn't," and watched the blood drain from his face and the old look of unhappiness drift into his eyes.

He answered inadequately. "No, of course you couldn't." And turning over—he had been sitting on the grass at her feet —he lay face downward on the scented turf. Presently he sat up and giving her a singularly sweet but wistful smile, said: "I almost touched happiness, Angèle. Did you by any chance ever happen to read Browning's 'Two in the Roman Campagna'?"

But she had read very little poetry except what had been required in her High School work, and certainly not Browning.

He began to interpret the fragile, difficult beauty of the poem with its light but sure touch on evanescent, indefinable feeling. He quoted:

> "How is it under our control
> To love or not to love?"

And again:

> "Infinite yearning and the pang
> Of finite hearts that yearn."

They were silent for a long time. And again she wondered how it would feel to love. He watched the sun drop suddenly below some tree tops and rose to his feet shivering a little as though its disappearance had made him immediately cold.

"'So the good moment goes.' Come, Angel, we'll have to hasten. It's getting dark and it's a long walk to the subway."

The memory of the afternoon stayed by her, shrouding her thoughts, clinging to them like a tenuous, adhering mantle. But she said to herself: "There's no use thinking about that. I'm not going to live that kind of life." And she knew she wanted Roger and what he could give her and the light and gladness which he always radiated. She wanted none of Anthony's poverty and privation and secret vows,—he meant, she supposed, some promise to devote himself to REAL ART,—her visual mind saw it in capitals. Well, she was sick of tragedy, she belonged to a tragic race. "God knows it's time for one member of it to be having a little fun."

"Yes," she thought all through her class, painting furiously —for she had taken up her work in earnest since Christmas— "yes, I'll just make up my mind to it. I'll take Roger back and get married and settle down to a pleasant, safe, beautiful life." And useful. It should be very useful. Perhaps she'd win Roger around to helping coloured people. She'd look up all sorts of down-and-outers and give them a hand. And she'd help Anthony, at least she'd offer to help him; she didn't believe he would permit her.

Coming out of the building a thought occurred to her: "Take Roger back, but back to what? To his old status of admiring, familiar, generous friend? Just that and no more?" Here was her old problem again. She stopped short to consider it.

Martha Burden overtook her. "Planning the great masterpiece of the ages, Angèle? Better come along and work it out by my fireside. I can give you some tea. Are you coming?"

"Yes," said Angela, still absorbed.

"Well," said Martha after they had reached the house. "I've never seen any study as deep as that. Come out of it Angèle, you'll drown. You're not by any chance in love, are you?"

"No," she replied, "at least I don't know. But tell me, Martha, suppose—suppose I were in love with one of them, what do you do about it, how do you get them to propose?"

Martha lay back and laughed. "Such candour have I not met, no, not in all Flapperdom. Angèle, if I could answer that I'd be turning women away from my door and handing out my knowledge to the ones I did admit at a hundred dollars a throw."

"But there must be some way. Oh, of course, I know lots of them propose, but how do you get a proposal from the ones you want,—the,—the interesting ones?"

"You really want to know? The only answer I can give you is Humpty Dumpty's dictum to Alice about verbs and adjectives: 'It depends on which is the stronger." She interpreted for her young guest was clearly mystified. "It depends on (A) whether you are strong enough to make him like you more than you like him; (B) whether if you really do like him more than he does you you can conceal it. In other words, so far as liking is concerned you must always be ahead of the game, you must always like or appear to like him a little less than he does you. And you must make him want you. But you mustn't give. Oh yes, I know that men are always wanting women to give, but they don't want the women to want to give. They want to take,—or at any rate to compel the giving."

"It sounds very complicated, like some subtle game."

A deep febrile light came into Martha's eyes. "It is a game, and the hardest game in the world for a woman, but the most fascinating; the hardest in which to strike a happy medium. You see, you have to be careful not to withhold too much and yet to give very little. If we don't give enough we lose them. If we give too much we lose ourselves. Oh, Angèle, God doesn't like women."

"But," said Angela thinking of her own mother, "there are some women who give all and men like them the better for it."

"Oh, yes, that's true. Those are the blessed among women. They ought to get down on their knees every day and thank God for permitting them to be their normal selves and not having to play a game." For a moment her still, proud face broke into deeps of pain. "Oh, Angèle, think of loving and never, never being able to show it until you're asked for it; think of living a game every hour of your life!" Her face quivered back to its normal immobility.

Angela walked home through the purple twilight musing no longer on her own case but on this unexpected revelation. "Well," she said, "I certainly shouldn't like to love like that." She thought of Anthony: "A woman could be her true self with him." But she had given him up.

If the thing to do were to play a game she would play one. Indeed she rather enjoyed the prospect. She was playing a game now, a game against public tradition on the one hand and family instinct on the other; the stakes were happiness and excitement, and almost anyone looking at the tricks which she had already taken would prophesy that she would be the winner. She decided to follow all the rules as laid down by Martha Burden and to add any workable ideas of her own. When Roger called again she was still unable to see him, but her voice was a shade less curt over the telephone; she did not cut him off so abruptly. "I must not withhold too much," she reminded herself. He was quick to note the subtle change in intonation. "But you're going to let me come to see you soon, Angèle," he pleaded. "You wouldn't hold out this way against me forever. Say when I may come."

"Oh, one of these days; I must go now, Roger. Good-bye."

After the third call she let him come to spend Friday evening. She heard the blue car rumbling in the street and a few minutes later he came literally staggering into the living-room so laden was he with packages. Flowers, heaps of spring posies had come earlier in the day, lilacs, jonquils, narcissi. Now this evening there were books and candy, handkerchiefs,—"they were so dainty and they looked just like you," he said fearfully, for she had never taken an article of dress from him,—two pictures, a palette and some fine brushes and last a hamper of all sorts of delicacies. "I thought if you didn't mind we'd have supper here; it would be fun with just us two."

How much he pleased her he could not divine; it was the first time he had ever given a hint of any desire for sheer domesticity. Anthony had sought nothing better than to sit and smoke and watch her flitting about in her absurd red or violet apron. Matthew Henson had been speechless with ecstasy when on a winter night she had allowed him to come into the kitchen while she prepared for him a cup of cocoa. But Roger's palate had been so flattered by the concoctions of chefs famous in London, Paris and New York that he had set no store by her simple cooking. Indeed his inevitable comment had been: "Here, what do you want to get yourself all tired out for? Let's go to a restaurant. It's heaps less bother."

But to-night he, too, watched her with humble, delighted eyes. She realized that he was conscious of her every movement; once he tried to embrace her, but she whirled out of his reach without reproach but with decision. He subsided, too thankful to be once more in her presence to take any risks. And when he left he had kissed her hand.

She began going about with him again, but with condescension, with kindness. And with the new vision gained from her talk with Martha she could see his passion mounting. "Make him want you,"—that was the second rule. It was clear that he did, no man could be as persevering as this otherwise. Still he did not speak. They were to meet that afternoon in front of the school to go "anywhere you want, dear, I'm yours to command". It was the first time that he had called for her at the building, and she came out a little early, for she did not want any of the three, Martha, Paulette, nor Anthony, to see whom she was meeting. It would be better to walk to the corner, she thought, they'd be just that much less likely to recognize him. She heard footsteps hurrying behind her, heard her name and turned to see Miss Powell, pleased and excited. She laid her hand on Angela's arm but the latter shook her off. Roger must not see her on familiar terms like this with a coloured girl for she felt that the afternoon portended something and she wanted no side issues. The coloured girl gave her a penetrating glance; then her habitual reserve settled down blotting out the eagerness, leaving her face blurred and heavy. "I beg your pardon, Miss Mory, I'm sure," she murmured and stepped out into the tempestuous traffic of Fourth Avenue. Angela was sorry; she would make it up to-morrow, she thought, but she had not dismissed her a moment too soon for Roger came rushing up, his car resplendent and resplendent himself in a grey suit, soft grey hat and blue tie. Angela looked at him approvingly. "You look just like the men in the advertising pages of the Saturday *Evening Post*," she said, and the fact that he did not wince under the compliment proved the depth of his devotion, for every one of his outer garments, hat, shoes, and suit, had been made to measure.

They went to Coney Island. "The ocean will be there, but very few people and only a very few amusements," said Roger. They had a delightful time; they were like school children, easily and frankly amused; they entered all the booths that were open, ate pop-corn and hot dogs and other local dainties. And presently they were flying home under the double line of trees on Ocean Parkway and entering the bosky loveliness of Prospect Park. Roger slowed down a little.

"Oh," said Angela. "I love this car."

He bent toward her instantly. "Does it please you? Did you miss it when you made me stay away from you?"

She was afraid she had made a mistake: "Yes, but that's not why I let you come back."

"I know that. But you do like it, don't you, comfort and beauty and dainty surroundings?"

"Yes," she said solemnly, "I love them all."

He was silent then for a long, long time, his face a little set, a worried line on his forehead.

"Well now what's he thinking about?" she asked herself, watching his hands and their clever manipulation of the steering wheel though his thoughts, she knew, were not on that.

He turned to her with an air of having made up his mind. "Angèle, I want you to promise to spend a day out riding with me pretty soon. I—I have something I want to say to you." He was a worldly young man about town but he was actually mopping his brow. "I've got to go south for a week for my father,—he owns some timber down there with which he used to supply saw-mills but since the damned niggers have started running north it's been something of a weight on his hands. He wants me to go down and see whether it's worth his while to hold on to it any longer. It's so rarely that he asks anything of me along a business line that I'd hate to refuse him. But I'll be back the morning of the twenty-sixth. I'll have to spend the afternoon and evening with him out on Long Island but on the twenty-seventh could you go out with me?"

She said as though all this preamble portended nothing: "I couldn't give you the whole day, but I'd go in the afternoon."

"Oh," his face fell a little. "Well, the afternoon then. Only of course we won't be able to go far out. Perhaps you'd like me to arrange a lunch and we'd go to one of the Parks, Central or the Bronx, or Van Cortlandt,——"

"No, not Van Cortlandt," she told him. That park was sacred to Anthony Cross.

"Well, wherever you say. We can settle it even that day. The main thing is that you'll go."

She said to herself. "Aren't men funny! He could have asked me five times over while he was making all these arrangements." But she was immensely relieved, even happy. She felt very kindly toward him; perhaps she was in love after all, only she was not the demonstrative kind. It was too late for him to come in, but they sat in the car in the dark security of Jayne Street and she let him take her in his arms and kiss her again and again. For the first time she returned his kisses.

*

Weary but triumphant she mounted the stairs almost stumbling from a sudden, overwhelming fatigue. She had been under a strain! But it was all over now; she had conquered, she had been the stronger. She had secured not only him but an assured future, wealth, protection, influence, even power. She herself was power,—like the women one reads about, like Cleopatra,—Cleopatra's African origin intrigued her, it was a fitting comparison. Smiling, she took the last steep stairs lightly, springily, suddenly reinvigorated.

As she opened the door a little heap of letters struck her foot. Switching on the light she sat in the easy chair and incuriously turned them over. They were bills for the most part, she had had to dress to keep herself dainty and desirable for Roger. At the bottom of the heap was a letter from Virginia. When she became Mrs. Roger Fielding she would never have to worry about a bill again; how she would laugh when she remembered the small amounts for which these called! Never again would she feel the slight quake of dismay which always overtook her when she saw she words: "Miss Angèle Mory in account with, ——" Outside of the regular monthly statement for gas she had never seen a bill in her father's house. Well, she'd have no difficulty in getting over her squeamish training.

Finally she opened Jinny's letter. Her sister had written:

"Angela I'm coming up for an exam on the twenty-eighth. I'll arrive on the twenty-sixth or I could come the day before. You'll meet me, won't you? I know where I'm going to stay,"— she gave an address on 139th Street—"but I don't know how to get there; I don't know your school hours, write and tell me so I can arrive when you're free. There's no reason why I should put you out."

So Virginia was really coming to try her luck in New York. It would be nice to have her so near. "Though I don't suppose we'll be seeing so much of each other," she thought, absently reaching for her schedule. "Less than ever now, for I suppose Roger and I will live in Long Island; yes, that would be much wiser. I'll wear a veil when I go to meet her, for those coloured porters stare at you so and they never forget you."

The twenty-seventh came on Thursday; she had classes in the morning; well, Jinny would be coming in the afternoon anyway, and after twelve she had,—Oh heavens that was *the* day, the day she was to go out with Roger, the day that he would put the great question. And she wrote to Virginia:

"Come the twenty-sixth, Honey, any time after four. I couldn't possibly meet you on the twenty-seventh. But the twenty-sixth is all right. Let me know when your train comes in and I'll be there. And welcome to our city."

Chapter VI

THE week was one of tumult, almost of agony. After all, matters were not completely settled, you never could tell. She would be glad when the twenty-seventh had come and gone, for then, then she would be rooted, fixed. She and Roger would marry immediately. But now he was so far away, in Georgia; she missed him and evidently he missed her for the first two days brought her long telegrams almost letters. "I can think of nothing but next Thursday, are you thinking of it too?" The third day brought a letter which said practically the same thing, adding, "Oh, Angèle; I wonder what you will say!"

"But he could ask me and find out," she said to herself and suddenly felt assured and triumphant. Every day thereafter brought her a letter reiterating this strain. "And I know how he hates to write!"

The letter on Wednesday read, "Darling, when you get this I'll actually be in New York; if I can I'll call you up but I'll have to rush like mad so as to be free for Thursday, so perhaps I can't manage."

She made up her mind not to answer the telephone even if it did ring, she would strike one last note of indifference though only she herself would be aware of it.

It was the day on which Jinny was to arrive. It would be fun to see her, talk to her, hear all the news about the queer, staid people whom she had left so far behind. Farther now than ever. Matthew Henson was still in the post-office, she knew. Arthur Sawyer was teaching at Sixteenth and Fitzwater; she could imagine the sick distaste that mantled his face every time he looked at the hideous, discoloured building. Porter had taken his degree in dentistry but he was not practising, on the contrary he was editing a small weekly, getting deeper, more and more hopelessly into debt she was sure. . . . It would be fun some day to send him a whopping cheque; after all, he had taken a chance just as she had; she recognized his revolt as akin to her own, only he had not had her luck. She must ask Jinny about all this.

It was too bad that she had to meet her sister,—but she

must. Just as likely as not she'd be car sick and then New York was terrifying for the first time to the stranger,—she had known an instant's sick dread herself that first day when she had stood alone and ignorant in the great rotunda of the station. But she was different from Jinny; nothing about life ever made her really afraid; she might hurt herself, suffer, meet disappointment, but life could not alarm her; she loved to come to grips with it, to force it to a standstill, to yield up its treasures. But Jinny although brave, had secret fears, she was really only a baby. Her little sister! For the first time in months she thought of her with a great surge of sisterly tenderness.

It was time to go. She wore her most unobtrusive clothes, a dark blue suit, a plain white silk shirt, a dark blue, bell-shaped hat—a *cloche*—small and fitting down close over her eyes. She pulled it down even farther and settled her modish veil well over the tip of her nose. It was one thing to walk about the Village with Miss Powell. There were practically no coloured people there. But this was different. Those curious porters should never be able to recognize her. Seymour Porter had worked among them one summer at Broad Street station in Philadelphia. He used to say: "They aren't really curious, you know, but their job makes them sick; so they're always hunting for the romance, for the adventure which for a day at least will take the curse off the monotonous obsequiousness of their lives."

She was sorry for them, but she could not permit them to remedy their existence at her expense.

In her last letter she had explained to Jinny about those two troublesome staircases which lead from the train level of the New York Pennsylvania Railroad station to the street level. "There's no use my trying to tell you which one to take in order to bring you up to the right hand or to the left hand side of the elevator because I never know myself. So all I can say, dear, is when you do get up to the elevator just stick to it and eventually I'll see you or you'll see me as I revolve around it. Don't you move, for it might turn out that we were both going in the same direction."

True to her own instructions, she was stationed between the

two staircases, jerking her neck now toward one staircase, now toward the other, stopping short to look at the elevator itself. She thrust up her veil to see better.

A man sprinted by in desperate haste, brushing so closely by her that the corner of his suit-case struck sharply on the thin inner curve of her knee.

"My goodness!" she exclaimed involuntarily.

For all his haste he was a gentleman, for he pulled of his hat, threw her a quick backward glance and began: "I beg your—why darling, darling, you don't mean to say you came to meet me!"

"Meet you! I thought you came in this morning." It was Roger, Roger and the sight of him made her stupid with fear.

He stooped and kissed her, tenderly, possessively. "I did,—oh Angela you *are* a beauty! Only a beauty can wear plain things like that. I did come in this morning but I'm trying to catch Kirby, my father's lawyer, he ought to be coming in from Newark just now and I thought I'd take him down to Long Island with me for the night. I've got a lot of documents for him here in this suitcase—that Georgia business was most complicated—that way I won't have to hunt him up in the morning and I'll have more time to—to arrange for our trip in the afternoon. What are you doing here?"

What was she doing there? Waiting for her sister Jinny who was coloured and who showed it. And Roger hated Negroes. She was lost, ruined, unless she could get rid of him. She told the first lie that came into her mind.

"I'm waiting for Paulette." All this could be fixed up with Paulette later. Miss Lister would think as little of deceiving a man, any man, as she would of squashing a mosquito. They were fair game and she would ask no questions.

His face clouded. "Can't say I'm so wild about your waiting for Paulette. Well we can wait together—is she coming up from Philadelphia? That train's bringing my man too from Newark." He had the male's terrible clarity of understanding for train connections.

"What time does your train go to Long Island? I thought you wanted to get the next one."

"Well, I'd like to but they're only half an hour apart. I can wait. Better the loss of an hour to-day than all of to-morrow morning. We can wait together; see the people are beginning to come up. I wish I could take you home but the minute he shows up I'll have to sprint with him."

"Now God be on my side," she prayed. Sometimes these trains were very long. If Mr. Kirby were in the first car and Jinny toward the end that would make all of ten minutes' difference. If only she hadn't given those explicit directions!

There was Jinny, her head suddenly emerging into view above the stairs. She saw Angela, waved her hand. In another moment she would be flinging her arms about her sister's neck; she would be kissing her and saying, "Oh, Angela, Angela darling!"

And Roger, who was no fool, would notice the name Angela —Angèle; he would know no coloured girl would make a mistake like this.

She closed her eyes in a momentary faintness, opened them again.

"What's the matter?" said Roger sharply, "are you sick?"

Jinny was beside her. Now, now the bolt would fall. She heard the gay, childish voice saying laughingly, assuredly:

"I beg your pardon, but isn't this Mrs. Henrietta Jones?"

Oh, God was good! Here was one chance if only Jinny would understand! In his astonishment Roger had turned from her to face the speaker. Angela, her eyes beseeching her sister's from under her close hat brim, could only stammer the old formula: "Really you have the advantage of me. No, I'm not Mrs. Jones."

Roger said rudely, "Of course she isn't Mrs. Jones. Come, Angèle." Putting his arm through hers he stooped for the suitcase.

But Jinny, after a second's bewildered but incredulous stare, was quicker even than they. Her slight figure, her head high, preceded them; vanished into a telephone booth.

Roger glared after her. "Well of all the damned cheek!"

For the first time in the pursuit of her chosen ends she began to waver. Surely no ambition, no pinnacle of safety was supposed to call for the sacrifice of a sister. She might be selfish,— oh, undoubtedly she had been selfish all these months to leave Jinny completely to herself—but she had never meant to be cruel. She tried to picture the tumult of emotions in her sister's mind, there must have been amazement,—oh she had seen it all on her face, the utter bewilderment, the incredulity and then the settling down on that face of a veil of dignity and pride—like a baby trying to harden mobile features. She was in her apartment again now, pacing the floor, wondering what to do. Already she had called up the house in 139th Street, it had taken her a half-hour to get the number for she did not know the householder's name and "Information" had been coy,—but Miss Murray had not arrived yet. Were they expecting her? Yes, Miss Murray had written to say that she would be there between six and seven; it was seven-thirty now and she had not appeared. Was there any message? "No, no!" Angela explained she would call again.

But where was Jinny? She couldn't be lost, after all she was grown-up and no fool, she could ask directons. Perhaps she had taken a cab and in the evening traffic had been delayed,—or had met with an accident. This thought sent Angela to the telephone again. There was no Miss Murray as yet. In her wanderings back and forth across the room she caught sight of herself in the mirror. Her face was flushed, her eyes shining with remorse and anxiety. Her vanity reminded her: "If Roger could just see me now". Roger and to-morrow! He would have to speak words of gold to atone for this breach which for his sake she had made in her sister's trust and affecton.

At the end of an hour she called again. Yes, Miss Murray had come in. So great was her relief that her knees sagged under her. Yes of course they would ask her to come to the telephone. After a long silence the voice rang again over the wire. "I didn't see her go out but she must have for she's not in her room."

"Oh all right," said Angela, "the main thing was to know that she was there." But she was astonished. Jinny's first night in New York and she was out already! She could not go to see her Thursday because of the engagement with Roger, but she'd make good the next day; she'd be there the first thing, Friday morning. Snatching up a sheet of note-paper she began a long letter full of apologies and excuses. "And I can't come to-morrow, darling, because as I told you I have a very important engagement, an engagement that means very much to me. Oh you'll understand when I tell you about it." She put a special delivery stamp on the letter.

Her relief at learning that Jinny was safe did not ease her guilty conscience. In a calmer mood she tried now to find excuses for herself, extenuating circumstances. As soon as Jinny understood all that was involved she would overlook it. After all, Jinny would want her to be happy. "And anyway," she thought to herself sulkily, "Mamma didn't speak to Papa that day that we were standing on the steps of the Hotel Walton." But she knew that the cases were not analogous; no principle was involved, her mother's silence had not exposed her husband to insult or contumely, whereas Roger's attitude to Virginia had been distinctly offensive. "And moreover," her thoughts continued with merciless clarity, "when a principle *was* at stake your mother never hesitated a moment to let those hospital attendants know of the true status of affairs. In fact she was not aware that she was taking any particular stand. Her husband was her husband and she was glad to acknowledge that relationship."

A sick distaste for her action, for her daily deception, for Roger and his prejudices arose within her. But with it came a dark anger against a country and a society which could create such an issue. And she thought: "If I had spoken to Jinny, had acknowledged her, what good would it have done me or her either? After it was all over she would have been exactly where she was before and I would have lost everything. And I do so want to be happy, to have a good time. At this very hour to-morrow I'll probably be one of the most envied girls in New York. And afterwards I can atone for it all. I'll be good to all sorts of people; I'll really help humanity, lots of coloured folks will be much better of on account of me. And if I had spoken to Jinny I could never have helped them at all." Once she murmured: "I'll help Jinny too, the darling! She shall have everything in the world she wants." But in her heart she knew already that Jinny would want nothing.

Chapter VII

THURSDAY came and Thursday sped as Thursdays will. For a long time Angela saw it as a little separate entity of time shut away in some hidden compartment of her mind, a compartment whose door she dreaded to open.

On Friday she called up her sister early in the morning. "Is that you, Jinny? Did you get my letter? Is it all right for me to come up?"

"Yes," said Jinny noncommittally, to all questions, then laconically: "But you'd better come right away if you want to catch me. I take the examination to-day and haven't much time."

Something in the matter-of-factness of her reply disconcerted Angela. Yet there certainly was no reason why her sister should show any enthusiasm over seeing her. Only she did want to see her, to talk to some one of her very own to-day. She would like to burrow her head in Virginia's shoulder and cry! But a mood such as Jinny's voice indicated did not invite confidences.

A stout brown-skinned bustling woman suggesting immense assurance and ability opened the door. "Miss Murray told me that she was expecting someone. You're to go right on up. Her's is the room right next to the third storey front."

"She was expecting someone." Evidently Virginia had been discreet. This unexpected, unsought for carefulness carried a sting with it.

"Hello," said Jinny, casually thrusting a dishevelled but picturesque head out of the door. "Can you find your way in? This room's larger than any two we ever had at home, yet already it looks like a ship at sea." She glanced about the disordered place. "I wonder if this is what they mean by 'shipshape'. Here I'll hang up this suit, then you can sit down. Isn't it a sweetie? Got it at Snellenburg's."

She had neither kissed nor offered to shake hands with her sister, yet her manner was friendly enough, even cordial. "See I've bobbed my hair," she went on. "Like it? I'm wild about it even if it does take me forever to fix it." Standing before a mirror she began shaping the ends under with a curling iron.

Angela thought she had never seen any one so pretty and so colourful. Jinny had always shown a preference for high colours; to-day she was revelling in them; her slippers were high heeled small red mules; a deep green dressing-gown hung gracefully from her slim shoulders and from its open collar flamed the rose and gold of her smooth skin. Her eyes were bright and dancing. Her hair, black, alive and curling, ended in a thick velvety straightness like cut plush.

Angela said stiffly, "I hope I didn't get you up, telephoning so early."

Virginia smiled, flushing a little more deeply under the dark gold of her skin. "Oh dear no! I'd already had an earlier call than that this morning."

"You had!" exclaimed Angela, astonished. "I didn't know you knew anyone in New York." She remembered her sister's mysterious disappearance the first night of her arrival. "And see here, Jinny, I'm awfully sorry about what happened the other night. I wouldn't have had it happen for a great deal. I wish I could explain to you about it." How confidently she had counted on having marvellous news to tell Virginia and now how could she drag to the light yesterday's sorry memory? "But I called you up again and again and you hadn't arrived and then when they finally did tell me that you had come, it appeared that you had gone out. Where on earth did you go?"

Jenny began to laugh, to giggle in fact. For a moment she was the Virginia of her school days, rejoicing in some innocent mischief, full of it. "I wasn't out. There's a wash-room down the hall and I went there to wash my face,——" it clouded a moment. "And when I came back I walked as I thought into my room. Instead of that I had walked into the room of another lodger. And there he sat——"

"Oh," said Angela inattentively. "I'm glad you weren't out. I was quite worried. Listen, Virginia," she began desperately, "I know you think that what I did in the station the other day was unspeakable; it seems almost impossible for me to explain it to you. But that man with me was a very special friend,——"

"He must have been indeed," Jinny interrupted drily, "to make you cut your own sister." She was still apparently fooling with her hair, her head perched on one side, her eyes glued to the mirror. But she was not making much progress and her lips were trembling.

Angela proceeded unheeding, afraid to stop. "A special friend, and we had come to a very crucial point in our relationship. It was with him that I had the engagement yesterday."

"Well, what about it? Were you expecting him to ask you to marry him? Did he?"

"No," said Angela very low, "that's just what he didn't do though he,—he asked everything else."

Virginia, dropping the hair-brush, swung about sharply. "And you let him talk like that?"

"I couldn't help it once he had begun,—I was so taken by surprise, and, besides, I think that his ultimate intentions are all right."

"His ultimate intentions! Why, Angela what are you talking about? You know perfectly well what his ultimate intentions are. Isn't he a white man? Well, what kind of intentions would he have toward a coloured woman?"

"Simple! He doesn't know I'm coloured. And besides some of them are decent. You must remember that I know something about these people and you don't, you couldn't, living that humdrum little life of yours at home."

"I know enough about them and about men in general to recognize an insult when I hear one. Some men bear their character stamped right on their faces. Now this man into whose room I walked last night by mistake,——"

"I don't see how you can do very much talking walking into strange men's rooms at ten o'clock at night."

The triviality of the retort left Jinny dumb.

It was their first quarrel.

They sat in silence for a few minutes; for several minutes. Virginia, apparently completely composed, was letting the tendrils of her mind reach far, far out to the ultimate possibilities of this *impasse* in relationship between herself and her sister. She thought: "I really have lost her, she's really gone out of my ken just as I used to lose her years ago when father and I would be singing 'The Dying Christian'. I'm twenty-three years old and I'm really all alone in the world." Up to this time she had always felt she had Angela's greater age and supposedly greater

wisdom to fall back on, but she banished this conjecture forever. "Because if she could cut me when she hadn't seen me for
a year for the sake of a man who she must have known meant
to insult her, she certainly has no intention of openly acknowl-
edging me again. And I don't believe I want to be a sister in
secret. I hate this hole and corner business."

She saw again the scene in the station, herself at first so
serene, so self-assured, Angela's confused coldness, Roger's
insolence. Something hardened, grew cold within her. Even
his arrogance had failed to bring Angela to her senses, and
suddenly she remembered that it had been possible in slavery
times for white men and women to mistreat their mulatto relations, their own flesh and blood, selling them into deeper
slavery in the far South or standing by watching them beaten,
almost, if not completely, to death. Perhaps there was something fundamentally different between white and coloured blood
after all. Aloud she said: "You know before you went away that
Sunday morning you said that you and I were different.
Perhaps you're right, Angela; perhaps there is an extra infusion
of white blood in your veins which lets you see life at another
angle. If that's the case I have no right to judge you. You must
forgive my ignorant comments."

She began slipping into a ratine dress of old blue trimmed
with narrow collars and cuffs and a tiny belt of old rose. Above
the soft shades the bronze and black of her head etched themselves sharply; she might have been a dainty bird of Paradise
cast in a new arrangement of colours but her tender face was
set in strange and implacable lines.

Angela looked at her miserably. She had not known just
what, in her wounded pride and humiliation, she had expected
to gain from her sister, but certainly she had hoped for some
balm. And in any event not this cool aloofness. She had forgotten that her sister might be suffering from a wound as poignant
as her own. The year had made a greater breach than she had
anticipated; she had never been as outspoken, as frank with
Virginia as the latter had been with her, but there had always
been a common ground between them, a meeting place. In
the household Jinny had had something of a reputation for her
willingness to hear all sides of a story, to find an excuse or
make one.

An old aphorism of Hetty Daniels returned to her. "He who would have friends must show himself friendly." And she had done anything but that; she had neglected Jinny, had failed to answer her letters, had even planned,—was it only day before yesterday!—to see very little of her in what she had dreamed would be her new surroundings. Oh she had been shameful! But she would make it up to Jinny now—and then she could come to her at this, this crisis in her life which so frightened and attracted her. She was the more frightened because she felt that attraction. She would make her sister understand the desires and longings which had come to her in this strange, dear, free world, and then together they would map out a plan of action. Jinny might be a baby but she had strength. So much strength, said something within her, that just as likely as not she would say: "Let the whole thing go, Angela, Angela! You don't want to be even on the outskirts of a thing like this."

Before she could begin her overtures Jinny was speaking. "Listen, Angela, I've got to be going. I don't know when we'll be seeing each other again, and after what happened Wednesday you can hardly expect me to be looking you up, and as you doubtless are very busy you'd hardly be coming 'way up here. But there are one or two things I want to talk to you about. First about the house."

"About the house? Why it's yours. I've nothing more to do with it."

"I know, but I'm thinking of selling it. There is such a shortage of houses in Philadelphia just now; Mr. Hallowell says I can get at least twice as much as father paid for it. And in that case you've some more money coming to you."

If only she had known of this,—when?—twenty-four hours earlier, how differently she might have received Roger's proposition. If she had met Virginia Wednesday and had had the talk for which she had planned!

"Well of course it would be awfully nice to have some more money. But what I don't understand is how are you going to live? What are you going to do?"

"If I pass this examination I'm coming over here, my appointment would be only a matter of a few months. I'm sure of that. This is May and I'd only have to wait until September. Well, I wouldn't be working this summer anyway. And there's no way in the world which I could fail to pass. In fact I'm really thinking of taking a chance and coming over here to substitute. Mr. Holloster, the University of Pennsylvania man, has been investigating and he says there's plenty of work. And I guess I'm due to have a change; New York rather appeals to me. And there certainly is something about Harlem!" In spite of her careless manner Angela knew she was thinking about Matthew Henson. She stretched out her hand, pulled Jinny's head down on her shoulder. "Oh darling, don't worry about him. Matthew really wasn't the man for you."

"Well," said Virginia, "as long as I think he was, the fact that he wasn't doesn't make any real difference, does it? At least not at first. But I certainly shan't worry about it."

"No don't,—I,——" It was on the tip of her tongue to say "I know two or three nice young men whom you can play around with. I'll introduce you to them." But could she? Jinny understood her silence; smiled and nodded. "It's all right, honey, you can't do anything; you would if you could. We've just got to face the fact that you and I are two separate people and we've got to live our lives apart, not like the Siamese twins. And each of us will have to go her chosen way. After all each of us is seeking to get all she can out of life! and if you can get more out of it by being white, as you undoubtedly can, why, why shouldn't you? Only it seems to me that there are certain things in living that are more fundamental even than colour,— but I don't know. I'm all mixed up. But evidently you don't feel that way, and you're just as likely to be right as me."

"Jinny!"

"My dear, I'm not trying to reproach you. I'm trying to look at things without sentiment. After all, in a negative way, merely by saying nothing, you're disclaiming your black blood in a country where it is an inconvenience,—oh! there's not a doubt about that. You may be proud of it, you may be perfectly satisfied with it—I am—but it certainly can shut you out of things. So why shouldn't you disclaim a living manifestation of that blood?"

Before this cool logic Angela was silent. Virginia looked at her sister, a maternal look oddly apparent on her young face. When she was middle-aged she would be the embodiment of motherhood. How her children would love her!

"Angela, you'll be careful!"

"Yes; darling. Oh if only I could make you understand what it's all about."

"Yes, well, perhaps another time. I've got to fly now." She hesitated, took Angela by the arms and gazed into her eyes. "About this grand white party that you were in the station with. Are you awfully in love with him?"

"I'm not in love with him at all."

"Oh, pshaw!" said innocent Virginia, "you've got nothing to worry about! Why, what's all the shooting for?"

PLUM BUN

Chapter I

A NGELA wanted to ride downtown with her sister. "Perhaps I might bring you luck." But on this theme Jinny was adamant. "You'd be much more likely to bring yourself bad luck. No, there's no sense in taking a chance. I'll take the elevated; my landlady said it would drop me very near the school where I'm taking the examination. You go some other way." Down in the hall Mrs. Gloucester was busy dusting, her short bustling figure alive with housewifely ardour. Virginia paused near her and held out her hand to Angela. "Good-bye, Miss Mory," she said wickedly, "it was very kind of you to give me so much time. If you can ever tear yourself away from your beloved Village, come up and I'll try to show you Harlem. I don't think it's going to take me long to learn it."

Obediently Angela let her go her way and walking over to Seventh Avenue mounted the 'bus, smarting a little under Jinny's generous precautions. But presently she began to realize their value, for at One Hundred and Fourteenth Street Anthony Cross entered. He sat down beside her. "I never expected to see you in my neighbourhood."

"Oh is this where you live? I've often wondered."

"As it happens I've just come here, but I've lived practically all over New York." He was thin, restless, unhappy. His eyes dwelt ceaselessly on her face. She said a little nervously:

"It seems to me I hardly ever see you any more. What do you do with yourself?"

"Nothing that you would be interested in."

She did not dare make the obvious reply and after all, though she did like him very much, she was not interested in his actions. For a long moment she sought for some phrase which would express just the right combination of friendliness and indifference.

"It's been a long time since we've had lunch together; come

546

and have it to-day with me. You be my guest." She thought
of Jinny and the possible sale of the house. "I've just found out
that I'm going to get a rather decent amount of money, certainly enough to stand us for lunch."

"Thank you, I have an engagement; besides I don't want to
lunch with you in public."

This was dangerous ground. Flurried, she replied unwisely:
"All right, come in some time for tea; every once in a while I
make a batch of cookies; I made some a week ago. Next time I
feel the mood coming on me I'll send you a card and you can
come and eat them, hot and hot."

"You know you've no intention of doing any such thing.
Besides you don't know my address."

"An inconvenience which can certainly be rectified," she
laughed at him.

But he was in no laughing mood. "I've no cards with me, but
they wouldn't have the address anyway." He tore a piece of
paper out of his notebook, scribbled on it. "Here it is. I have
to get off now." He gave her a last despairing look. "Oh, Angel,
you know you're never going to send for me!"

The bit of paper clutched firmly in one hand, she arrived finally at her little apartment. Naturally of an orderly turn of
mind she looked about for her address book in which to write
the street and number. But some unexplained impulse led her
to smooth the paper out and place it in a corner of her desk.
That done she took off her hat and gloves, sat down in the
comfortable chair and prepared to face her thoughts.

Yesterday! Even now at a distance of twenty-four hours she
had not recovered her equilibrium. She was still stunned, still
unable to realize the happening of the day. Only she knew that
she had reached a milestone in her life; a possible turning
point. If she did not withdraw from her acquaintanceship with
Roger now, even though she committed no overt act she would
never be the same; she could never again face herself with the
old, unshaken pride and self-confidence. She would never be
the same to herself. If she withdrew, then indeed, indeed she
would be the same old Angela Murray, the same girl save for a
little sophistication that she had been before she left Philadelphia, only she would have started on an adventure and would

not have seen it to its finish, she would have come to grips with life and would have laid down her arms at the first on-slaught. Would she be a coward or a wise, wise woman? She thought of two poems that she had read in "Hart's Class-Book", an old, old book of her father's,—one of them ran:

> 'He either fears his fate too much
> Or his deserts are small,
> Who dares not put it to the touch
> For fear of losing all.'

The other was an odd mixture of shrewdness and cow-ardice:

> 'He who fights and runs away
> Shall live to fight another day
> But he who is in battle slain
> Has fallen ne'er to rise again.'

Were her deserts small or should she run away and come back to fight another day when she was older, more experi-enced? More experienced! How was she to get that experience? Already she was infinitely wiser, she would, if occasion required it, exercise infinitely more wariness than she had yesterday with Roger. Yet it was precisely because of that experience that she would know how to meet, would even know when to expect similar conditions.

She thought that she knew which verse she would follow if she were Jinny, but, back once more in the assurance of her own rooms, she knew that she did not want to be Jinny, that she and Jinny were two vastly different persons. "But," she said to herself, "if Jinny were as fair as I and yet herself and placed in the same conditions as those in which I am placed her colour would save her. It's a safeguard for Jinny; it's always been a curse for me."

Roger had come for her in the blue car. There were a hamper and two folding chairs and a rug stored away in it. It was a gor-geous day. "If we can," he said, "we'll picnic." He was extremely handsome and extremely nervous. Angela was nervous too, though she did not show it except in the loss of her colour. She was rather plain to-day; to be so near the completion of her goal and yet to have to wait these last few agonizing moments, perhaps hours, was deadly. They were rather silent for a while, Roger intent on his driving. Traffic in New York is a desperate strain at all hours, at eleven in the morning it is deadly; the huge leviathan of a city is breaking into the last of its stride. For a few hours it will proceed at a measured though never leisurely pace and then burst again into the mad rush of the homeward bound.

But at last they were out of the city limits and could talk. For the first time since she had known him he began to speak of his possessions. "Anything, anything that money can buy, Angèle, I can get and I can give." His voice was charged with intention. They were going in the direction of Forest Hills; he had a cottage out there, perhaps she would like to see it. And there was a grove not far away. "We'll picnic there," he said, "and—and talk." He certainly was nervous, Angela thought, and liked him the better for it.

The cottage or rather the house in Forest Hills was beautiful, absolutely a gem. And it was completely furnished with taste and marked daintiness. "What do you keep it furnished for?" asked Angela wondering. Roger murmured that it had been empty for a long time but he had seen this equipment and it had struck him that it was just the thing for this house so he had bought it; thereby insensibly reminding his companion again that he could afford to gratify any whim. They drove away from the exquisite little place in silence. Angela was inclined to be amused; surely no one could have asked for a better opening than that afforded by the house. What would make him talk, she wondered, and what, oh what would he say? Something far, far more romantic than poor Matthew Henson could ever have dreamed of,—yes and far, far less romantic, something subconscious prompted her, than Anthony Cross had said. Anthony with his poverty and honour and desperate vows!

They had reached the grove, they had spread the rug and a tablecloth; Roger had covered it with dainties. He would not let her lift a finger, she was the guest and he her humble servant. She looked at him smiling, still forming vague contrasts with him and Matthew and Anthony.

Roger dropped his sandwich, came and sat behind her. He

put his arm around her and shifted his shoulder so that her head lay against it.

"Don't look at me that way Angèle, Angèle! I can't stand it."

So it was actually coming. "How do you want me to look at you?"

He bent his head down to hers and kissed her. "Like this, like this! Oh Angèle, did you like the house?"

"Like it? I loved it."

"Darling, I had it done for you, you know. I thought you'd like it."

It seemed a strange thing to have done without consulting her, and anyway she did not want to live in a suburb. Opal Street had been suburb enough for her. She wanted, required, the noise and tumult of cities.

"I don't care for suburbs, Roger." How strange for him to talk about a place to live in and never a word of love!

"My dear girl, you don't have to live in a suburb if you don't want to. I've got a place, an apartment in Seventy-second Street, seven rooms; that would be enough for you and your maid, wouldn't it? I could have this furniture moved over there, or if you think it too cottagey, you could have new stuff altogether."

Seven rooms for three people! Why she wanted a drawing-room and a studio and where would he put his things? This sudden stinginess was quite inexplicable.

"But Roger, seven rooms wouldn't be big enough."

He laughed indulgently, his face radiant with relief and triumph. "So she wants a palace, does she? Well, she shall have it. A whole *ménage* if you want it, a place on Riverside Drive, servants and a car. Only somehow I hadn't thought of you as caring about that kind of thing. After that little hole in the wall you've been living in on Jayne Street I'd have expected you to find the place in Seventy-Second Street as large as you'd care for!"

A little hurt, she replied: "But I was thinking of you too. There wouldn't be room for your things. And I thought you'd want to go on living in the style you'd been used to." A sudden welcome explanation dawned on her rising fear. "Are you keeping this a secret from your father? Is that what's the trouble?"

Under his thin, bright skin he flushed. "Keeping what a secret from my father? What are you talking about, Angèle?"

She countered with his own question. "What are *you* talking about, Roger?"

He tightened his arms about her, his voice stammered, his eyes were bright and watchful. "I'm asking you to live in my house, to live for me; to be my girl; to keep a love-nest where I and only I may come." He smiled shamefacedly over the cheap current phrase.

She pushed him away from her; her jaw fallen and slack but her figure taut. Yet under her stunned bewilderment her mind was racing. So this was her castle, her fortress of protection, her refuge. And what answer should she make? Should she strike him across his eager, half-shamed face, should she get up and walk away, forbidding him to follow? Or should she stay and hear it out? Stay and find out what this man was really like; what depths were in him and, she supposed, in other men. But especially in this man with his boyish, gallant air and his face as guileless and as innocent apparently as her own.

That was what she hated in herself, she told that self fiercely, shut up with her own thoughts the next afternoon in her room. She hated herself for staying and listening. It had given him courage to talk and talk. But what she most hated had been the shrewdness, the practicality which lay beneath that resolve to hear it out. She had thought of those bills; she had thought of her poverty, of her helplessness, and she had thought too of Martha Burden's dictum: "You must make him want you." Well here was a way to make him want her and to turn that wanting to account. "Don't," Martha said, "withhold too much. Give a little." Suppose she gave him just the encouragement of listening to him, of showing him that she did like him a little; while he meanwhile went on wanting, wanting—men paid a big price for their desires. Her price would be marriage. It was a game, she knew, which women played all over the world although it had never occurred to her to play it; a dangerous game at which some women burned their fingers. "Don't give too much," said Martha, "for then you lose yourself." Well, she would give nothing and she would not burn her fingers. Oh, it would be a great game.

Another element entered too. He had wounded her pride
and he should salve it. And the only unguent possible would
be a proposal of marriage. Oh if only she could be a girl in a
book and when he finally did ask her for her hand, she would
be able to tell him that she was going to marry someone else,
someone twice as eligible, twice as handsome, twice as wealthy.

Through all these racing thoughts penetrated the sound of
Roger's voice, pleading, persuasive, seductive. She was amazed
to find a certain shamefaced timidity creeping over her; yet it
was he who should have shown the shame. And she could not
understand either why she was unable to say plainly: "You say
you care for me, long for me so much, why don't you ask me
to come to you in the ordinary way?" But some pride either
unusually false or unusually fierce prevented her from doing
this. Undoubtedly Roger with his wealth, his looks and his
family connections had already been much sought after. He
knew he was an "eligible". Poor, unknown, stigmatized, if he
but knew it, as a member of the country's least recognized group
she could not bring herself to belong even in appearance to
that band of young women who so obviously seek a "good
match".

When he had paused a moment for breath she told him
sadly: "But, Roger, people don't do that kind of thing, not decent people."

"Angèle, you are such a child! This is exactly the kind of
thing people do do. And why not? Why must the world be let
in on the relationships of men and women? Some of the sweetest unions in history have been of this kind."

"For others perhaps, but not for me. Relationships of the
kind you describe don't exist among the people I know." She
was thinking of her parents, of the Hallowells, of the Hensons
whose lives were indeed like open books.

He looked at her curiously, "The people you know! Don't
tell me you haven't guessed about Paulette!"

She had forgotten about Paulette! "Yes I know about her.
She told me herself. I like her, she's been a mighty fine friend,
but, Roger, you surely don't want me to be like her."

"Of course I don't. It was precisely because you weren't like her that I became interested. You were such a babe in the woods. Anyone could see you'd had no experience with men."

This obvious lack of logic was too bewildering. She looked at him like the child which, in these matters, she really was. "But,—but Roger, mightn't that be a beginning of a life like Paulette's? What would become of me after we, you and I, had separated? Very often these things last only for a short time, don't they?"

"Not necessarily; certainly not between you and me. And I'd always take care of you, you'd be provided for." He could feel her gathering resentment. In desperation he played a cunning last card: "And besides who knows, something permanent may grow out of this. I'm not entirely my own master, Angèle."

Undoubtedly he was referring to his father whom he could not afford to offend. It never occurred to her that he might be lying, for why should he?

To all his arguments, all his half-promises and implications she returned a steady negative. As twilight came on she expressed a desire to go home; with the sunset her strength failed her; she felt beaten and weary. Her unsettled future, her hurt pride, her sudden set-to with the realities of the society in which she had been moving, bewildered and frightened her. Resentful, puzzled, introspective, she had no further words for Roger; it was impossible for him to persuade her to agree or to disagree with his arguments. During the long ride home she was resolutely mute.

Yet on the instant of entering Jayne Street she felt she could not endure spending the long evening hours by herself and she did not want to be alone with Roger. She communicated this distaste to him. While not dishevelled they were not presentable enough to invade the hotels farther uptown. But, anxious to please her, he told her they could go easily enough to one of the small cabarets in the Village. A few turns and windings and they were before a house in a dark side street knocking on its absurdly barred door, entering its black, mysterious portals. In a room with a highly polished floor, a few tables and chairs, some rather bizarre curtains, five or six couples were sitting, among them Paulette, Jack Hudson, a tall, rather big, extremely blonde girl whose name Angela learned was Carlotta Parks, and a slender, black-avised man whose name she failed to catch. Paulette hailed him uproariously; the blonde girl rose and precipitately threw her arms about Fielding's neck.

"Roger!"

"Don't," he said rather crossly. "Hello, Jack." He nodded to the dark man whom he seemed to know indifferently well. "What have they got to eat here, you fellows? Miss Mory and I are tired and hungry. We've been following the pike all day." Miss Parks turned and gave Angela a long, considering look.

"Sit here," said Paulette, "there's plenty of room. Jack, you order for them, the same things we've been having. You get good cooking here." She was radiant with happiness and content. Under the influence of the good, stimulating food Angela began to recover, to look around her.

Jack Hudson, a powerfully built bronze figure of a man, beamed on Paulette, saying nothing and in his silence saying everything. The dark man kept his eyes on Carlotta, who was oblivious to everyone but Roger, clearly her friend of long standing. She sat clasping one of his hands, her head almost upon his shoulder. "Roger it's so good to see you again! I've thought of you so often! I've been meaning to write to you; we're having a big house party this summer. You must come! Dad's asking up half of Washington; attachés, 'Prinzessen, Countessen and serene English Altessen'; he'll come up for week-ends."

A member of the *haut monde,* evidently she was well-connected, powerful, even rich. A girl of Roger's own set amusing herself in this curious company. Angela felt her heart contract with a sort of helpless jealousy.

The dark man, despairing of recapturing Carlotta's attention, suddenly asked Angèle if she would care to dance. He was a superb partner and for a moment or two, reinvigorated by the food and the snappy music, she became absorbed in the smooth, gliding motion and in her partner's pleasant conversation. Glancing over her shoulder she noted Carlotta still talking to Roger. The latter, however, was plainly paying the girl no attention. His eyes fixed on Angela, he was moodily following her every motion, almost straining, she thought, to catch her words. His eyes met hers and a long, long look passed between them so fraught, it seemed to her, with a secret understanding

and sympathy, that her heart shook with a moment's secret
wavering.

Her partner escorted her back to the table. Paulette, flushed
and radiant, with the mien of a dishevelled baby, was holding
forth while Hudson listened delightedly. As a *raconteuse* she
had a faint, delicious malice which usually made any recital of her
adventures absolutely irresistible. "Her name," she was saying loudly, regardless of possible listeners, "was Antoinette
Spewer, and it seems she had it in for me from the very first.
She told Sloane Corby she wanted to meet me and he invited
both of us to lunch. When we got to the restaurant she was
waiting for me in the lobby; Sloane introduced us and—she
pulled a lorgnette on me,—a lorgnette on *me*!" She said it very
much as a Westerner might speak of someone "pulling" a revolver. "But I fixed that. There were three or four people passing near us. I drew back until they were well within hearing
range, and then I said to her: 'I beg pardon but what did you
say your last name was?' Well, when a person's named Spewer
she can't shout it across a hotel lobby! Oh, she came climbing
down off her high horse; she respects me to this day, I tell
you."

Roger rose. "We must be going; I can't let Miss Mory get
too tired." He was all attention and courtesy. Miss Parks looked
at her again, narrowing her eyes.

In the car Roger put his arm about her. "Angèle, when you
were dancing with that fellow I couldn't stand it! And then
you looked at me,—oh such a look! You were thinking about
me, I felt it, I knew it."

Some treacherous barrier gave way within her "Yes, and I
could tell you were thinking about me."

"Of course you could! And without a word! Oh, darling,
darling, can't you see that's the way it would be? If you'd only
take happiness with me there we would be with a secret bond,
an invisible bond, existing for us alone and no one else in the
world the wiser. But we should know and it would be all the
sweeter for that secrecy."

Unwittingly he struck a responsive chord within her,—
stolen waters were the sweetest, she of all people knew that.

Aloud she said: "Here we are, Roger. Some of the day has
been wonderful; thank you for that."

"You can't go like this! You're going to let me see you again?

She knew she should have refused him, but again some treacherous impulse made her assent. He drove away, and, turning, she climbed the long, steep flights of stairs, bemused, thrilled, frightened, curious, the sense of adventure strong upon her. To-morrow she would see Jinny, her own sister, her own flesh and blood, one of her own people. Together they would thresh this thing out.

Chapter II

A CURIOUS period of duelling ensued. Roger was young, rich and idle. Nearly every wish he had ever known had been born within him only to be satisfied. He could not believe that he would fail in the pursuit of this baffling creature who had awakened within him an ardour and sincerity of feeling which surprised himself. The thought occurred to him more than once that it would have been a fine thing if this girl had been endowed with the name and standing and comparative wealth of—say Carlotta Parks,—but it never occurred to him to thwart in this matter the wishes of his father who would, he knew, insist immediately on a certified account of the pedigree, training and general fitness of any strange aspirant for his son's hand. Angela had had the good sense to be frank; she did not want to become immeshed in a tissue of lies whose relationship, whose sequence and interdependence she would be likely to forget. To Roger's few questions she had said quite truly that she was the daughter of "poor but proud parents";—they had laughed at the hackneyed phrase,—that her father had been a boss carpenter and that she had been educated in the ordinary public schools and for a time had been a school teacher. No one would ever try to substantiate these statements, for clearly the person to whom they applied would not be falsifying such a simple account. There would be no point in so doing. Her little deceits had all been negative, she had merely neglected to say that she had a brown sister and that her father had been black.

Roger found her unfathomable. His was the careless, unreasoned cynicism of the modern, worldly young man. He had truly, as he acknowledged, been attracted to Angela because of a certain incurious innocence of hers apparent in her observations and in her manner. He saw no reason why he should cherish that innocence. If questioned he would have answered: "She's got to learn about the world in which she lives sometime; she might just as well learn of it through me. And I'd always look out for her." In the back of his mind, for all his unassuming even simple attitude toward his wealth and power, lurked the conviction that that same wealth and power could heal any wound, atone for any loss. Still there were times when even he experienced a faint, inner qualm, when Angela would ask him: "But afterwards, what would become of me, Roger?" It was the only question he could not meet. Out of all his hosts of precedents from historical Antony and Cleopatra down to notorious affinities discovered through blatant newspaper "stories" he could find for this only a stammered "There's no need to worry about an afterwards, Angèle, for you and I would always be friends."

Their frequent meetings now were little more than a trial of strength. Young will and determination were pitted against young will and determination. On both the excitement of the chase was strong, but each was pursuing a different quarry. To all his protestations, arguments and demands, Angela returned an insistent: "What you are asking is impossible." Yet she either could not or would not drive him away, and gradually, though she had no intention of yielding to his wishes, her first attitude of shocked horror began to change.

For three months the conflict persisted. Roger interposed the discussion into every talk, on every occasion. Gradually it came to be the *raison d'être* of their constant comradeship. His arguments were varied and specious. "My dearest girl, think of a friendship in which two people would have every claim in the world upon each other and yet no claim. Think of giving all, not because you say to a minister 'I will', but from the generosity of a powerful affection. That is the very essence of free love. I give you my word that the happiest couples in the world are those who love without visible bonds. Such people are bound by the most durable ties. Theirs is a state of the closest because the freest, most elastic union in the world."

A singularly sweet and curious intimacy was growing up between them. Roger told Angela many anecdotes about his father and about his dead mother, whom he still loved, and for whom he even grieved in a pathetically boyish way. "She was so sweet to me, she loved me so. I'll never forget her. It's for her sake that I try to please my father, though Dad's some pumpkins on his own account." In turn she was falling into the habit of relating to him the little happenings of her every-day life, a life which she was beginning to realize must, in his eyes, mean the last word in the humdrum and the monotonous. And yet how full of adventure, of promise, even of mystery did it seem compared with Jinny's!

Roger had much intimate knowledge of people and told her many and dangerous secrets. "See how I trust you, Angèle; you might trust me a little!"

If his stories were true, certainly she might just as well trust him a great deal, for all her little world, judging it by the standards by which she was used to measuring people, was tumbling in ruins at her feet. If this were the way people lived then what availed any ideals? The world was made to take pleasure in; one gained nothing by exercising simple virtue, it was after all an extension of the old formula which she had thought out for herself many years ago. Roger spent most of his time with her, it seemed. Anything which she undertook to do delighted him. She would accept no money, no valuable presents. "And I can't keep going out with you to dinners and luncheons forever, Roger. It would be different if,—if we really meant anything to each other." He deliberately misunderstood her, "But nothing would give me more pleasure than for us to mean the world to one another." He sent her large hampers of fruit and even the more ordinary edibles; then he would tease her about being selfish. In order to get rid of the food she had asked him to lunch, to dinner, since nothing that she could say would make him desist from sending it.

Nothing gave her greater joy really than this playful housekeeping. She was very lonely; Jinny had her own happy interests; Anthony never came near her nor did she invite him to come; Martha Burden seemed engrossed in her own affairs, she was undergoing some secret strain that made her appear more remote, more strongly self-sufficient, more mysterious than ever. Paulette, making overt preparations to go to Russia with Hudson, was impossibly, hurtingly happy. Miss Powell,— but she could not get near her; the young coloured girl showed her the finest kind of courtesy, but it had about it a remote and frozen quality, unbreakable. However, Angela for the moment did not desire to break it; she must run no more risks with Roger, still she put Miss Powell on the list of those people whom she would some day aid,—when everything had turned out all right.

The result of this feeling of loneliness was, of course, to turn her more closely to Roger. He paid her the subtle compliment of appearing absolutely at home in her little apartment; he grew to like her plain, good cooking and the experiments which sometimes she made frankly for him. And afterwards as the fall closed in there were long, pleasant evenings before an open fire, or two or three last hours after a brisk spin in the park in the blue car. And gradually she had grown to accept and even inwardly to welcome his caresses. She perched with an air of great unconsciousness on the arm of the big chair in which he was sitting but the transition became constantly easier from the arm of the chair to his knee, to the steely embrace of his arm, to the sound of the hard beating of his heart, to his murmured: "This is where you belong, Angèle, Angèle." He seemed an anchor for her frail insecure bark of life.

It was at moments like these that he told her amazing things about their few common acquaintances. There was not much to say about Paulette. "I think," said Roger judicially, "that temperamentally she is a romantic adventurer. Something in her is constantly seeking a change but she will never be satisfied. She's a good sport, she takes as she gives, asking nothing permanent and promising nothing permanent." Angela thought it rather sad. But Roger dismissed the theme with the rather airy comment that there were women as there were men "like that". She wondered if he might not be a trifle callous.

More than once they had spoken of Martha Burden; Angela confessed herself tremendously intrigued by the latter, by that tense, brooding personality. She learned that Martha, made of the stuff which dies for causes, was constantly being torn between theory and practice.

"She's full," said Roger, "of the most high-falutin, advanced ideas. Oh I've known old Martha all my life, we were brought up together, it's through her really that I began to know the people in this part of town. She's always been a sort of sister. More than once I've had to yank her by the shoulders out of difficulties which she herself created. I made her marry Starr."

"Made her marry him,—didn't she want him?"

"Yes, she wanted him all right, but she doesn't believe in marriage. She's got the courage of her convictions, that girl. Why actually she lived with Starr two years while I was away doing

Europe. When I came back and found out what had happened I told Starr I'd beat him into pulp if he didn't turn around and make good."

"But why the violence? Didn't he want to?"

"Yes, only," he remembered suddenly his own hopes, "not every man is capable of appreciating a woman who breaks through the conventions for him. Some men mistake it for cheapness but others see it for what it is and love more deeply and gratefully." Softly, lingeringly he touched the soft hair shadowing her averted cheek. "I'm one of those others, Angèle."

She wanted to say: "But why shouldn't we marry? Why not make me safe as well as Martha?" But again her pride intervened. Instead she remarked that Martha did not seem always happy.

"No, well that's because she's got this fool idea of hers that now that they are bound the spontaneity is lacking. She wants to give without being obliged to give; to take because she chooses and not because she's supposed to. Oh she's as true as steel and the best fighter in a cause, but I've no doubt but that she leads old Starr a life with her temperament."

Angela thought that there were probably two sides to this possibility. A little breathlessly she asked Roger if he knew Anthony Cross.

"Cross, Cross! A sallow, rather thin fellow? I think I saw him once or twice at Paulette's. No, I don't really know him. A sullen, brooding sort of chap I should say. Frightfully self-absorbed and all that."

For some reason a little resentment sprang up in her. Anthony might brood, but his life had been lived on dark, troublesome lines that invited brooding; he had never known the broad, golden highway of Roger's existence. And anyway she did not believe, if Martha Burden had been Anthony's lifelong friend, almost his sister, that he would have told his sweetheart or his wife either of those difficult passages in her life. Well, she would have to teach Roger many things. Aloud she spoke of Carlotta Parks.

"She's an interesting type. Tell me about her."

But Roger said rather shortly that there was nothing to tell. "Just a good-hearted, high-spirited kid, that's all, who lets the whole world know her feelings."

*

According to Paulette there was more than this to be told about Miss Parks. "I don't know her myself, not being a member of that crowd. But I've always heard that she and Roger were childhood sweethearts, only they've just not pulled it off. Carlotta's family is as old as his. Her people have always been statesmen, her father's in the Senate. I don't think they have much money now. But the main thing is she pleases old man Fielding. Nothing would give him more pleasure than to see Carlotta Roger's wife. I may be mistaken, but I think nothing would give Carlotta more pleasure either."

"Doesn't he care for her?" Queer how her heart tightened, listening for the answer.

"Yes, but she likes him too much and shows it. So he thinks he doesn't want her. Roger will never want any woman who comes at his first call. Don't you hate that sort of man? They are really the easiest to catch; all you've got to do provided they're attracted at all, is to give one inviting glance and then keep steadily retreating. And they'll come—like Bo Peep's sheep. But I don't want a man like that; he'd cramp my style. His impudence, expecting a woman to repress or evoke her emotions just as he wants them! Hasn't a woman as much right to feel as a man and to feel first? Never mind, some woman is going to 'get' Roger yet. He doesn't think it possible because he has wealth and position. He'll be glad to come running to Carlotta then. I don't care very much for her,—she's a little too loud for me," objected the demure and conservative Miss Lister, "but I do think she likes Roger for himself and not for what he can give her!"

Undoubtedly this bit of knowledge lent a new aspect; the adventure began to take on fresh interest. Everything seemed to be playing into her hands. Roger's interest and longing were certainly undiminished. Martha Burden's advice, confirmed by Paulette's disclosure, was bound to bring results. She had only to "keep retreating".

But there was one enemy with whom she had never thought to reckon, she had never counted on the treachery of the forces of nature; she had never dreamed of the unaccountable weakening of those forces within. Her weapons were those furnished by the conventions but her fight was against conditions; impulses, yearnings which antedated both those weapons and the conventions which furnished them. Insensibly she began to see in Roger something more than a golden way out of her material difficulties; he was becoming more than a means through which she should be admitted to the elect of the world for whom all things are made. Before her eyes he was changing to the one individual who was kindest, most thoughtful of her, the one whose presence brought warmth and assurance. Furthermore, his constant attention, flatteries and caresses were producing their inevitable effect. She was naturally cold; unlike Paulette, she was a woman who would experience the grand passion only once, perhaps twice, in her life and she would always have to be kindled from without; in the last analysis her purity was a matter not of morals, nor of religion, nor of racial pride; it was a matter of fastidiousness. Bit by bit Roger had forced his way closer and closer into the affairs of her life, and his proximity had not offended that fastidiousness. Gradually his demands seemed to her to represent a very natural and beautiful impulse; his arguments and illustrations began to bear fruit; the conventions instead of showing in her eyes as the codified wisdom based on the experiences of countless generations of men and women, seemed to her prudish and unnecessary. Finally her attitude reduced itself to this: she would have none of the relationship which Roger urged so insistently, not because according to all the training which she had ever received, it was unlawful, but because viewed in the light of the great battle which she was waging for pleasure, protection and power, it was inexpedient.

The summer and the early fall had passed. A cold, rainy autumn was closing in; the disagreeable weather made motoring almost impossible. There were always the theatres and the cabarets, but Roger professed himself as happy nowhere else but at her fireside. And she loved to have him there, tall and strong and beautiful, sometimes radiant with hope, at others sulking with the assurance of defeat. He came in one day ostensibly to have tea with her; he had an important engagement for the evening but he could not let the day pass without seeing her. Angela was tired and a little dispirited. Jinny had sold the house and had sent her twelve hundred dollars as her share, but the original three thousand was almost dissipated. She must not touch this new gift from heaven; her goal was no nearer; the unwelcome possibility of teaching, on the contrary, was constantly before her. Moreover, she was at last realising the danger of this constant proximity, she was appalled by her thoughts and longings. Upon her a great fear was creeping not only of Roger but of herself.

Always watchful, he quickly divined her distrait mood, resolved to try its possibilities for himself. In a tense silence they drank their tea and sat gazing at the leaping, golden flames. The sullen night closed in. Angela reminded him presently that he must go but on he sat and on. At eight o'clock she reminded him again; he took out his watch and looked at it indifferently. "It's too late for me to keep it now, besides I don't want to go. Angèle be kind, don't send me away."

"But you've had no dinner."

"Nor you either. I'm like the beasts of the field keeping you like this. Shall we go out somewhere?" But she was languid; she did not want to stir from the warm hearth out into the chilly night.

"No, I don't want to go. But you go, Roger. I can find something here in the house for myself, but there's not a thing for you. I hate to be so inhospitable."

"Tell you what, suppose I go around to one of these *delicatessens* and get something. Too tired to fix up a picnic lunch?"

In half an hour he returned, soaked. "It's raining in torrents! Why I never saw such a night!" He shook himself, spattering rain-drops all over the tiny apartment.

"Roger! You'll have to take of your coat!"

He sat in his shirt-sleeves before the fire, his hair curling and damp, his head on his hand. He looked so like a little boy that her heart shook within her. Turning he caught the expression in her eyes, sprang towards her. "Angèle you know, you *know* you like me a little!"

"I like you a very great deal." He put his arm about her, kissed her; her very bones turned to water. She freed herself, finding an excuse to go into the kitchenette. But he came and stood towering over her in the doorway, his eyes on her every motion. They ate the meal, a good one, almost as silently as they had drunk the tea; a terrible awareness of each other's presence was upon them, the air was charged with passion. Outside the rain and wind beat and screamed.

"It's a terrible night," she said, but he made no reply. She said again, "Roger, it's getting late, you must go home." Very reluctantly then, his eyes still on hers, he rose to his feet, got into his overcoat and, hat in hand, stooped to kiss her good-night. His arm stole about her, holding her close against him. She could feel him trembling, she was trembling herself. Another second and the door had closed behind him.

Alone, she sat looking at the fire and thinking: "This is awful. I don't believe anything is going to come of this. I believe I'll send him a note to-morrow and tell him not to come any more."

Someone tapped on the door; astonished that a caller should appear at such an hour, but not afraid, she opened it. It was Roger. He came striding into the room, flinging off his wet coat, and yet almost simultaneously catching her up in his arms. "It's such a terrible night, Angèle; you can't send me out in it. Why should I go when the fire is here and you, so warm and soft and sweet!"

All her strength left her; she could not even struggle, could not speak. He swept her up in his arms, cradling her in them like a baby with her face beneath his own. "You know that we were meant for each other, that we belong to each other!"

A terrible lassitude enveloped her out of which she heard herself panting: "Roger, Roger let me go! Oh, Roger, must it be like this? Can't it be any other way?"

And from a great distance she heard his voice breaking, pleading, promising: "Everything will be all right, darling, darling. I swear it. Only trust me, trust me!"

Life rushed by on a great, surging tide. She could not tell whether she was utterly happy or utterly miserable. All that she could do was to feel; feel that she was Roger's totally. Her whole being turned toward him as a flower to the sun. Without him life meant nothing; with him it was everything. For the time being she was nothing but emotion; he was amazed himself at the depth of feeling which he had aroused in her.

Now for the first time she felt possessive; she found herself deeply interested in Roger's welfare because, she thought, he was hers and she could not endure having a possession whose qualities were unknown. She was not curious about his money nor his business affairs but she thirsted to know how his time away from her was spent, whom he saw, what other places he frequented. Not that she begrudged him a moment away from her side, but she must be able to account for that moment.

Yet if she felt possessive of him her feeling also recognized his complete absorption of her, so completely, so exhaustively did his life seem to envelop hers. For a while his wishes, his pleasure were the end and aim of her existence; she told herself with a slight tendency toward self-mockery that this was the explanation of being, of her being; that men had other aims, other uses but that the sole excuse for being a woman was to be just that,—a woman. Forgotten were her ideals about her Art; her ambition to hold a salon; her desire to help other people; even her intention of marrying in order to secure her future. Only something quite outside herself, something watchful, proud, remote from the passion and rapture which flamed within her, kept her free and independent. She would not accept money, she would not move to the apartment on Seventy-second Street; she still refused gifts so ornate that they were practically bribes. She made no explanations to Roger, but he knew and she knew too that her surrender was made out of the lavish fullness and generosity of her heart; there was no calculation back of it; if this were free love the freedom was the quality to be stressed rather than the emotion.

Sometimes, in her inchoate, wordless intensity of feeling which she took for happiness, she paused to take stock of that other life, those other lives which once she had known; that life which had been hers when she had first come to New York before she had gone to Cooper Union, in those days when she had patrolled Fourteenth Street and had sauntered through Union Square. And that other life which she knew in Opal Street, —æons ago, almost in another existence. She passed easily over those first few months in New York because even then she had been approaching a threshold, getting ready to enter on a new, undreamed of phase of being. But sometimes at night she lay for hours thinking over her restless, yearning childhood, her fruitless days at the Academy, the abortive wooing of Matthew Henson. The Hensons, the Hallowells, Hetty Daniels,—Jinny!

How far now she was beyond their pale! Before her rose the eager, starved face of Hetty Daniels; now she herself was cognizant of phases of life for which Hetty longed but so contemned. Angela could imagine the envy back of the tone in which Hetty, had she but known it, would have expressed her disapproval of her former charge's manner of living. "Mattie Murray's girl, Angela, has gone straight to the bad; she's living a life of sin with some man in New York." And then the final, blasting indictment. "He's a white man, too. Can you beat that?"

Chapter III

ROGER'S father, it appeared, had been greatly pleased with his son's management of the saw-mills in Georgia; as a result he was making more and more demands on his time. And the younger man half through pride, half through that steady determination never to offend his father, was always ready to do his bidding. Angela liked and appreciated her lover's filial attitude, but even in the period of her warmest interest she resented, secretly despised, this tendency to dependence. He was young, superbly trained; he had the gift of forming friendships whose strength rested on his own personality, yet he distrusted too much his own powers or else he was lazy—Angela could never determine which. During this phase of their acquaintanceship she was never sure that she loved him, but she was positive that if at this time he had been willing to fling aside his obsequious deference to his father's money and had said to her: "Angèle, if you'll help me, we'll build up a life, a fortune of our own," she would have adored him.

Her strong, independent nature, buffeted and sickened and strengthened by the constant attrition of colour prejudice, was unable to visualise or to pardon the frame of mind which kept Roger from joining battle with life when the odds were already so overwhelmingly in his favour. Alone, possessed of a handicap which if guessed at would have been as disabling as a game leg or an atrophied body, she had dared enter the lists. And she was well on the way to winning a victory. It was to cost her, she was beginning to realize, more than she had anticipated. But having entered she was not one to draw back,—unless indeed she changed her goal. Hers was a curious mixture of materialism and hedonism, and at this moment the latter quality was uppermost in her life. But she supposed that in some vague future she and Roger would marry. His ardour rendered her complacent.

But she was not conscious of any of these inner conflicts and criticisms; she was too happy. Now she was adopting a curious detachment toward life tempered by a faint cynicism,—a detachment which enabled her to say to herself: "Rules are for ordinary people but not for me." She remembered a verse from a poet, a coloured woman about whom she had often wondered. The lines ran:

> "The strong demand, contend, prevail.
>   The beggar is a fool!"

She would never be a beggar. She would ask no further counsel nor advice of anyone. She had been lucky thus far in seeking advice only from Paulette and Martha Burden, two people of markedly independent methods of thought and action. They had never held her back. Now she would no longer consult even them. She would live her life as an individualist, to suit herself without regard for the conventions and established ways of life. Her native fastidiousness, she was sure, would keep her from becoming an offence in her own eyes.

In spite of her increasing self-confidence and self-sufficiency Roger's frequent absences left her lonely. Almost then, without any conscious planning on her part, she began to work at her art with growing vigour and interest. She was gaining in assurance; her technique showed an increased mastery, above all she had gained in the power to compose, a certain sympathy, a breadth of comprehension, the manifestation of that ability to interpret which she had long suspected lay within her, lent themselves to her hand. Mr. Paget, the instructor, spoke of her paintings with increased respect; the attention of visitors was directed thereto. Martha Burden and even Paulette, in the intervals of her ecstatic preparations, admitted her to the freemasonry of their own assured standing. Anthony Cross reminded her of the possibilities for American students at Fontainebleau. But she only smiled wisely; she would have no need of such study, but she hoped with all her heart that Miss Powell would be the recipient of a prize which would enable her to attend there.

"If she isn't," she promised herself, "I'll make Roger give her her expenses. I'd be willing to take the money from him for that."

To her great surprise her other interest besides her painting lay in visiting Jinny. If anyone had asked her if she were satisfied with her own life, her reply would have been an instant affirmative. But she did not want such a life for her sister. For

Virginia there must be no risks, no secrets, no irregularities. Her efforts to find out how her sister spent her free hours amazed herself; their fruitlessness filled her with a constant irritation which Virginia showed no inclination to allay. The younger girl had passed her examination and had been appointed; she was a successful and enthusiastic teacher; this much Angela knew, but beyond this nothing. She gathered that Virginia spent a good deal of time with a happy, intelligent, rather independent group of young coloured men and women; there was talk occasionally of the theatre, of a dance, of small clubs, of hikes, of classes at Columbia or at New York City College. Angela even met a gay, laughing party, consisting of Virginia and her friends *en route* to Brooklyn, she had been later informed briefly. The girls were bright birds of paradise, the men, her artist's eye noted, were gay, vital fauns. In the subway beside the laughing, happy groups, white faces showed pale and bloodless, other coloured faces loomed dull and hopeless. Angela began tardily to recognize that her sister had made her way into that curious, limited, yet shifting class of the "best" coloured people; the old Philadelphia phrase came drifting back to her, "people that you know." She was amazed at some of the names which Virginia let drop from her lips in her infrequent and laconic descriptions of certain evenings which she had spent in the home of Van Meier, a great coloured American, a littérateur, a fearless and dauntless apostle of the rights of man; his name was known, Martha Burden had assured her, on both sides of the water.

Such information she picked up as best she might for Virginia vouchsafed nothing; nor did she, on the infrequent occasions on which she ran across her sister, even appear to know her. This Angela pointed out, was silly. "You might just as well speak," she told Jinny petulantly, remembering uncomfortably the occasion when she herself had cut her sister, an absolute stranger in New York. "Plenty of white and coloured people are getting to know each other and they always acknowledge the acquaintanceship. Why shouldn't we? No harm could come of it." But in Virginia's cool opinion no good could come of it either. Usually the younger girl preserved a discreet silence; whatever resolves she might have made with regard to the rupture between herself and her sister, she was certainly able to keep her own counsel. It was impossible to glean from her perfect, slightly distrait manner any glimpse of her inner life and her intentions. Frequently she showed an intense preoccupation from which she awakened to let fall a remark which revealed to Angela a young girl's normal reactions to the life about her, pleasant, uneventful and tinged with a cool, serene happiness totally different from the hot, heady, turgid rapture which at present was Angela's life.

The Jewish girl, Rachel Salting, who lived on the floor above, took to calling on Angela. "We're young and here by ourselves," she said smiling, "it's stupid for us not to get acquainted, don't you think so?" Hers was a charming smile and a charming manner. Indeed she was a very pretty girl, Angela thought critically. Her skin was very, very pale, almost pearly, her hair jet black and curling, her eyes large and almond-shaped. Her figure was straight and slender but bore none the less some faint hint of an exotic voluptuousness. Her interests, she informed her new friend, were all with the stage, her ideal being Raquel Meller.

Angela welcomed her friendliness. A strange apathy, an unusual experience for her, had invaded her being; her painting claimed, it is true, a great deal of time and concentration; her hours with Virginia, while not always satisfactory, were at least absorbing; but for the first time in her knowledge, her whole life was hanging on the words, the moods, the actions of some one else—Roger. Without him she was quite lost; not only was she unable to order her days without him in mind, she was even unable to go in quest of new adventures in living as was once her wont. Consequently she received with outstretched arms anything beyond the ordinary which might break the threatening monotony of her life.

Rachel Salting was like a fresh breeze, a curious mixture of Jewish conservatism and modernity. Hers was a keen, clear mind, well trained in the New York schools and colleges with many branching interests. She spoke of psychiatry, housing problems, Zionism, child welfare, with a knowledge and zest which astounded Angela, whose training had been rather superficial and who had begun to adopt Paulette's cleverness and Martha Burden's slightly professional, didactic attitude toward things in general as norms for herself. Rachel, except when dwelling on the Jewish problem, seemed to have no particular views to set forth. Her discussions, based on her wide reading, were purely academic, she had no desire to proselyte, she was no reformer. She was merely a "nice", rather jolly, healthy young woman, an onlooker at life which she had to get through with and which she was finding for the moment at any rate, extremely pleasant.

She was very happy; happy like Virginia with a happiness vastly different from what Angela was calling by that name; a breathless, constant, smiling happiness, palpable, transparent, for all the world to see. Within a few weeks after their acquaintanceship had started, Rachel with smiles and blushes revealed her great secret. She was going to be married.

"To the very best man in the world, Angèle."

"Yes, I'm sure of it."

"He's very good-looking, tall,——"

"As though I didn't know that."

"How could you know?"

"Darling child, haven't I seen him, at least the outline of him, often enough in the hall when I'd come in and turn on that wretched light? I didn't think you'd ever forgive me for it. It did seem as though I were doing it on purpose."

"Oh, I knew you weren't. Then you have seen him?"

"Yes, he's tall and blond. Quite a nice foil for your darkness. See, I'm always the artist."

"Yes," Rachel said slowly, "he is blond."

Angela thought she detected a faint undertone of worry in her hitherto triumphant voice but decided that that was unlikely.

But Rachel confirmed this impression by her next words: "If only everything will turn out all right."

Angel's rather material mind prompted her to ask: "What's the matter, is he very poor?"

Rachel stared. "Poor? As though that mattered. Yes, he's poor, but I don't care about that."

"Well, if you don't care about that, what's the trouble then? He's free, white and twenty-one, isn't he?"

"Yes, yes, it's only—oh you wouldn't understand, you lucky girl! It's nothing you'd ever have to bother about. You see we've

got to get our parents' consent first. We haven't spoken of it
yet. When we do, I'm afraid there'll be a row."

Some ritual inherent in her racial connections, Angela decided, and asked no further questions. Indeed, she had small
chance, for Rachel, once launched, had begun to expound her
gospel of marriage. It was an old, old story. Angela could have
closed her eyes and imagined her own mother rhapsodizing
over her future with Junius. They would be poor, very poor at
first but only at first, and they would not mind poverty a bit. It
would be fun together. There were little frame houses in the
Bronx that rented comparatively cheap. Perhaps Angela knew
of them.

Angela shuddering inwardly, acknowledged that she had
seen them, dull brown, high-shouldered affairs, perched perilously on stoops. The rooms would be small, square, ugly,——

Rachel would help her John in every way. They would economize. "I won't wash and iron, for that is heart-breaking work,
and I want to keep myself dainty and pretty for him, so that
when we do become better off he won't have to be ashamed of
me. And all the time even in our hardest days I'll be trying my
luck at play-writing." She spoke with the unquenchable ambition which was her racial dowry. "I'll be attending lectures and
sitting up in the galleries of theatres where they have the most
successful plays. And some day I'll land." Her fanciful imagination carried her years ahead. "On our First Night, Angela, you
must be in our box and I'll have an ermine coat. Won't it be
wonderful? But nothing will be more wonderful than those
first few years when we'll be absolutely dependent on each other;
I on what he makes, he on the way I run the home. That will
be heaven."

Confidences such as these left Angela unmoved but considerably shaken. There must be something in the life of sacrifice,
even drudgery which Rachel had depicted. Else why should so
many otherwise sensible girls take the risk? But there, it was
silly for her to dwell on such pictures and scenes. Such a life
would never come to her. It was impossible to conceive of such
a life with Roger. Yet there were times in her lonely room when
she pondered long and deeply, drawing pictures. The time
would be summer; she would be wearing a white dress, would
be standing in the doorway of a house in the suburbs very,

very near New York. There'd be the best possible dinner on
the table. She did love to cook. And a tall, strong figure would
be hurrying up the walk: "I had the best luck to-day, Angèle,
and I brought you a present." And presently after dinner she
would take him upstairs to her little work-room and she'd draw
aside the curtain and show him a portrait of a well-known society woman. "She's so pleased with it; and she's going to get me
lots of orders,———" Somehow she was absolutely sure that the
fanciful figure was not Roger.

Her lover, back from a three weeks' trip to Chicago, dissipated
that sureness. He was glad, overwhelmingly glad to be back
and to see Angèle. He came to her apartment directly from the
train, not stopping even to report to his father. "I can see him
to-morrow. To-night is absolutely yours. What shall we do,
Angèle? We can go out to dinner and the theatre or run out to
the Country Club or stay here. What do you say?"

"We'll have to stay here, Roger; I'll fix up a gorgeous dinner,
better than anything you've had to eat in any of your old
hotels. But directly after, I'll have to cut and run because I
promised Martha Burden faithfully to go to a lecture with her
tonight."

"I never knew you to be interested in a lecture before."

She was worried and showed it. "But this is a different sort
of lecture. You know how crazy Martha is about race and social
movements. Well, Van Meier is to speak to-night and Martha
is determined that a lot of her friends shall hear him. I'm to go
with her and Ladislas."

"What's to keep me from going?"

"Nothing, only he's coloured, you know."

"Well, I suppose it won't rub off. I've heard of him. They say
he really has brains. I've never seen a nigger with any yet; so
this bids fair to be interesting. And, anyway, you don't think
I'm going to let my girl run off from me the very moment I
come home, do you? Suppose I have Reynolds bring the big
car here and we'll take Martha and Ladislas along and anyone
else she chooses to bring."

The lecture was held in Harlem in East One Hundred and
Thirty-fifth Street. The hall was packed, teeming with suppressed excitement and a certain surcharged atmosphere. Angela

radiant, calmed with the nearness and devotion of Roger, looked about her with keen, observing eyes. And again she sensed that fullness, richness, even thickness of life which she had felt on her first visit to Harlem. The stream of living ran almost molten; little waves of feeling played out from groups within the audience and beat against her consciousness and against that of her friends, only the latter were without her secret powers of interpretation. The occasion was clearly one of moment. "I'd come any distance to hear Van Meier speak," said a thin-faced dark young man behind them. "He always has something to say and he doesn't talk down to you. To hear him is like reading a classic, clear and beautiful and true."

Angela, revelling in types and marshalling bits of information which she had got from Virginia, was able to divide the groups. There sat the most advanced coloured Americans, beautifully dressed, beautifully trained, whimsical, humorous, bitter, impatiently responsible, yet still responsible. In one section loomed the dark, eager faces of West Indians, the formation of their features so markedly different from that of the ordinary American as to give them a wild, slightly feral aspect. These had come not because they were disciples of Van Meier but because they were earnest seekers after truth. But unfortunately their earnestness was slightly marred by a stubbornness and an unwillingness to admit conviction. Three or four coloured Americans, tall, dark, sleek young men sat within earshot, speaking with a curious didactic precision. "They're quoting all the sociologists in the world," Ladislas Starr told his little group in astonishment.

Martha, with her usual thoroughness, knew all about them. They were the editors of a small magazine whose chief bid to fame lay in the articles which they directed monthly against Van Meier; articles written occasionally in a spirit of mean jealousy but usually in an effort to gain a sort of inverted glory by carrying that great name on its pages.

Here and there a sprinkling of white faces showed up plainly, startlingly distinct patterns against a back-ground of patient, softly stolid black faces; faces beaten and fashioned by life into a mold of steady, rock-like endurance, of unshakable, unconquered faith. Angela had seen such faces before in the churches in Philadelphia; they brought back old pictures to her mind.

"There he is!" exclaimed Martha triumphantly. "That's Van

Meier! Isn't he wonderful?" Angela saw a man, bronze, not very tall but built with a beautiful symmetrical completeness, cross the platform and sit in the tall, deep chair next to the table of the presiding officer. He sat with a curious immobility, gazing straight before him like a statue of an East Indian idol. And indeed there was about him some strange quality which made one think of the East; a completeness, a superb lack of self-consciousness, an odd, arresting beauty wrought by the perfection of his fine, straight nose and his broad, scholarly forehead. One look, however casual, gave the beholder the assurance that here indeed was a man, fearless, dauntless, the captain of his fate.

He began to speak on a clear, deep, bell-like note. Angela thought she had never heard its equal for beauty, for resonance, for culture. And as the young man had said he did not talk down. His English was the carefully sifted language of the savant, his periods polished, almost poetical. He was noted on two continents for his sociological and economic contributions, but his subject was racial sacrifice. He urged the deliberate introduction of beauty and pleasure into the difficult life of the American Negro. These objects should be theirs both as racial heritage and as compensation. Yet for a time, for a long time, there would have to be sacrifices, many sacrifices made for the good of the whole. "Our case is unique," the beautiful, cultured voice intoned; "those of us who have forged forward, who have gained the front ranks in money and training, will not, are not able as yet to go our separate ways apart from the unwashed, untutored herd. We must still look back and render service to our less fortunate, weaker brethren. And the first step toward making this a workable attitude is the acquisition not so much of a racial love as a racial pride. A pride that enables us to find our own beautiful and praiseworthy, an intense chauvinism that is content with its own types, that finds completeness within its own group; that loves its own as the French love their country, because it is their own. Such a pride can accomplish the impossible." He quoted:

> "It is not courage, no, nor hate
>   That lets us do the things we do;
>   It's pride that bids the heart be great,—"

He sat down to a surge of applause that shook the building. Dark, drooping faces took on an expression of ecstatic uplift, it was as though they suddenly saw themselves, transformed by racial pride as princes in a strange land in temporary serfdom, princes whose children would know freedom.

Martha Burden and Ladislas went up to speak to him; they were old friends. Angela, with Roger, visibly impressed, stood on one side and waited. Paulette and Hudson came pushing through the crowd, the former flushed and excited. Little groups of coloured people stood about, some deeply content with a sort of vicarious pride, some arguing; Angela caught sight of Virginia standing with three young men and two girls. They were for the most part gesticulating, lost in a great excitement. But Jinny seemed listless and aloof; her childish face looked thin and more forlornly young than ever. Anthony Cross and a tall man of undeniably Spanish type passed the little party and spoke to one of the men, received introductions. Presently Cross, swinging about, caught sight of Angela and Roger. He bowed hastily, flushing; caught his companion's arm and walked hurriedly from the hall, his head very straight, his slender figure always so upright, so *élancé*, more erect than ever.

Presently Martha's party was all out on the sidewalk; Roger in fine spirits invited Paulette and Hudson to ride down town in his car. Paulette was bubbling over with excited admiration of Van Meier. "He isn't a man, he's a god," she proclaimed. "Did you ever see such a superb personality? He's not a magnificent coloured man, he's not 'just as good as a white man'; he is a man, just that; colour, race, conditions in his case are pure accidents, he over-rides them all with his ego. Made me feel like a worm too; I gave him my prettiest smile, grand white lady making up to an 'exceptional Negro' and he simply didn't see me; took my hand,—I did my best to make my grasp a clinging one—and he passed me right along disengaging himself as cool as a cucumber and making room for a lady of colour." She finished reflectively, " I wonder what he would be like alone."

"None of your nonsense, Paulette," said Roger frowning.

Hudson smiled. "Paulette's a mighty attractive little piece, I'll admit, but I'd back Van Meier against her every time; she'd present no temptation to him; the man's not only a prophet and the son of a prophet; he's pride incarnate."

Roger said meditatively, "I wonder what proportion of white blood he has in his veins. Of course that's where he gets his ability."

"You make me tired," said Martha. "Of course he doesn't get it from his white blood; he gets it from all his bloods. It's the mixture that makes him what he is. Otherwise all white people would be gods. It's the mixture and the endurance which he has learned from being coloured in America and the determination to see life without bitterness,——"

"Oh help, help," exclaimed Roger. "No more lectures to-night. Look, you're boring Angèle to death."

"Nothing of the kind," said Angela, "on the contrary I never was more interested in my life." And reaching back she gave Martha's hand a hearty squeeze.

Sometimes as on that first day at the art class, the five of them, Miss Powell, Paulette, Cross, Martha and Angela met before hours. Miss Powell as always was silent—she came solely for her work—but the others enjoyed a little preliminary chat. A week or so after the Van Meier lecture all but Paulette were gathered thus on an afternoon when she too came rushing in, starry eyed, flushed, consumed with laughter.

"I've played the biggest joke on myself," she announced, I've been to see Van Meier."

Martha was instant attention. "A joke on Van Meier?"

"No, on myself, I tell you."

It appeared that she had got Miss Powell to introduce her to one of the clerks in the great leader's office. Paulettte then with deliberate intention had asked the girl to lunch and afterwards had returned with her to the office expressing a desire to meet her employer. Van Meier had received her cordially enough but with the warning that he was very busy.

"So I told him that I wouldn't sit down, thinking of course he'd urge me to. But he just raised his eyebrows in the most quiz-zical way and said, 'Well?'

"Of course I couldn't let matters rest like that so I sat down and began talking to him, nothing much you know, just telling him how wonderful he was and letting him see that I'd be glad

to know him better. You should have seen him looking at me
and not saying a word. Presently he reached out his hand and
touched a bell and Miss Thing-um-bob came in,—your friend,
you know, Miss Powell. He looked at her and nodding toward
me said: 'Take her away'. I never felt such small potatoes in my
life. I tell you he's a personage. Wasn't it great?"

Martha replied crossly that the whole thing seemed to her in
dreadfully poor taste, while Miss Powell, after one incredulous
stare at the first speaker, applied herself more sedulously to her
work. Even Anthony, shocked out of his habitual moroseness
pronounced the proceedings "a bit thick, Miss Lister". Angela
conscious of a swelling pride, stowed the incident away as a tit-
bit for Virginia.

Chapter IV

LIFE had somehow come to a standstill; gone was its quality of high adventure and yet with the sense of tameness came no compensating note of assurance, of permanence. Angela pondered much about this; with her usual instinct for clarity, for a complete understanding of her own emotional life, she took to probing her inner consciousness. The fault, she decided, was bound up in her relationship with Roger. At present in a certain sense she might be said to be living for him; at least his was the figure about which her life resolved, revolved. Yet she no longer had the old, heady desire to feel herself completely his, to claim him as completely hers, neither for his wealth nor for the sense of security which he could afford nor for himself. For some reason he had lost his charm for her, much, she suspected, in the same way in which girls in the position which was hers, often lost their charm for their lovers.

And this realization instead of bringing to her a sense of relief, brought a certain real if somewhat fantastic shame. If there was to be no permanence in the relationship, if laying aside the question of marriage, it was to lack the dignity, the graciousness of an affair of long standing, of sympathy, of mutual need, then indeed according to the code of her childhood, according to every code of every phase of her development, she had allowed herself to drift into an inexcusably vulgar predicament. Even when her material safety and security were at stake and she had dreamed vaguely of yielding to Roger's entreaties to ensure that safety and security, there might have been some excuse. Life, she considered, came before creed or code or convention. Or if she had loved and there had been no other way she might have argued for this as the supreme experience of her life. But she was no longer conscious of striving for marriage with Roger; and as for love—she had known a feeling of gratitude, intense interest, even intense possessiveness for him but she did not believe she had ever known love.

But because of this mingling of shame and reproach she found herself consciously striving to keep their relations on the highest plane possible in the circumstances. She wished now

not so much that she had never left Jinny and the security of
their common home-life, as that the necessity for it had never
arisen. Now suddenly she found herself lonely, she had been in
New York nearly three years but not even yet had she struck
down deep into the lode of genuine friendship. Paulette was
kind and generous; she desired, she said, a close woman friend
but Paulette was still the adventuress. She was as likely to
change her vocation and her place of dwelling as she was to
change her lover. Martha Burden, at once more stable and
more comprehending in the conduct of a friendship once she
had elected for it, was, on the other hand, much more conservative in the expenditure of that friendliness; besides she was
by her very nature as reserved as Paulette was expansive, and
her native intenseness made it difficult for her to dwell very
long on the needs of anyone whose problems did not centre
around her own extremely fixed ideas and principles.

As for Anthony Cross,—by some curious, utterly inexplicable
revulsion of feeling, Angela could not bring herself to dwell
long on the possibilities of a friendship with him. Somehow it
seemed to her sacrilegious in her present condition to bring
the memory of that far-off day in Van Cortlandt Park back to
mind. As soon as his image arose she dismissed it, though there
were moments when it was impossible for his vision to come
before her without its instantly bringing to mind Rachel
Salting's notions of love and self-sacrifice. Well, such dreams
were not for her, she told herself impatiently. For her own
soul's integrity she must make the most of this state in which
she now found herself. Either she must effect through it a marriage whose excuse should be that of safety, assurance and a
resulting usefulness; or she must resolve it by patience, steadfastness and affection into a very apotheosis of "free love." Of
all possible *affaires du coeur* this must in semblance at any rate,
be the ultimate image desideration, the finest flower of chivalry
and devotion.

To this end she began then devoting herself again to the renewal
of that sense of possessiveness in Roger and his affairs which
had once been so spontaneous within her. But to this Roger
presented unexpected barriers; he grew restive under such manifestations; he who had once fought so bitterly against her

indifference resented with equal bitterness any showing of possessive interest. He wanted no claims upon him, he acknowledged none. Gradually his absences, which at first were due to the business interests of his father, occurred for other reasons or for none at all. Angela could not grasp this all at once; it was impossible for her to conceive that kindness should create indifference; in spite of confirmatory stories which she had heard, of books which she had read, she could not make herself believe that devotion might sometimes beget ingratitude, loss of appreciation. For if that were so then a successful relationship between the sexes must depend wholly on the marriage tie without reference to compatibility of taste, training or ideals. This she could scarcely credit. In some way she must be at fault.

No young wife in the first ardour of marriage could have striven more than she to please Roger. She sought by reading and outside questions to inform herself along the lines of Roger's training—he was a mining engineer. His fondness for his father prompted her to numerous inquiries about the interest and pursuits of the older Fielding; she made suggestions for Roger's leisure hours. But no matter how disinterested her attitude and tone his response to all this was an increased sullenness, remoteness, wariness. Roger was experienced in the wiles of women; such interest could mean only one thing,—marriage. Well, Angela might just as well learn that he had no thought, had never had any thought, of marrying her or any other woman so far removed from his father's ideas and requirements.

Still Angela, intent on her ideals, could not comprehend. Things were not going well between them; affairs of this kind were often short-lived, that had been one of her first objections to the arrangement, but she had not dreamed that one withdrew when the other had committed no overt offence. She was as charming, as attractive, as pretty as she had ever been and far, far more kind and thoughtful. She had not changed, how could it be possible that he should be different?

A week had gone by and he had not dropped in to see her. Loneliness settled over her like a pall, frightening her seriously because she was realizing that this time she was not missing Roger so much as that a person for whom she had let slip the ideals engendered by her mother's early teaching, a man for whom she had betrayed and estranged her sister, was passing out of her ken. She had rarely called him on the telephone but suddenly she started to do so. For three days the suave voice of his man, Reynolds, told her that Mr. Fielding was "out, m'm."

"But did you give him my message? Did you ask him to call me as soon as he came in?"

"Yes, m'm."

"And did he?"

"That I couldn't tell you, m'm."

She could not carry on such a conversation with a servant.

On the fifth day Roger appeared. She sprang toward him. "Oh Roger, I'm so glad to see you. Did Reynolds tell you I called? Why have you been so long coming?"

"I'd have been still longer if you hadn't stopped 'phoning. Now see here, Angèle, this has got to stop. I can't have women calling me up all hours of the day, making me ridiculous in the eyes of my servants. I don't like it, it's got to stop. Do you understand me?"

Surprised, bewildered, she could only stammer: "But you call me whenever you feel like it."

"Of course I do, that's different. I'm a man." He added a cruel afterword. "Perhaps you notice that I don't call you up as often as I used."

Her pride was in arms. More than once she thought of writing him a brief note telling him that so far as she was concerned their "affair" was ended. But a great stubbornness possessed her; she was curious to see how this sort of thing could terminate; she was eager to learn if all the advice which older women pour into the ears of growing girls could be as true as it was trite. Was it a fact that the conventions were more important than the fundamental impulses of life, than generosity, kindness, unselfishness? For whatever her original motives, her actual relationship with Fielding had called out the most unselfish qualities in her. And she began to see the conventions, the rules that govern life, in a new light; she realized suddenly that for all their granite-like coldness and precision they also represented fundamental facts; a sort of concentrated compendium of the art of living and therefore as much to be observed and respected as warm, vital impulses.

Towards Roger she felt no rancour, only an apathy incapable

of being dispersed. The conversation about the telephone left an effect all out of proportion to its actual importance; it represented for her the apparently unbridgeable difference between the sexes; everything was for men, but even the slightest privilege was to be denied to a woman unless the man chose to grant it. At least there were men who felt like that; not all men, she felt sure, could tolerate such an obviously unjust status. Without intent to punish, with no set purpose in her mind, simply because she was no longer interested, she began to neglect Roger. She no longer let other engagements go for him; she made no attempt to be punctual in keeping such engagements as they had already made; in his presence she was often absorbed, absentminded, lost in thought. She ceased asking him questions about his affairs.

Long before their quarrel they had accepted an invitation from Martha Burden to a small party. Angela was surprised that Roger should remember the occasion, but clearly he did; he was on hand at the correct date and hour and the two of them fared forth. During the brief journey he was courteous, even politely cordial, but the difference between his attitude and that of former days was very apparent. The party was of a more frivolous type than Martha usually sponsored, she was giving it for a young, fun-loving cousin of Ladislas; there was no general conversation, some singing, much dancing, much pairing off in couples. Carlotta Parks was present with Ralph Ashley, the slender, dark man who had appeared with Carlotta when Angela first met her. As soon as Roger appeared Carlotta came rushing toward him.

"I've been waiting for you!" She dragged at his hand and not unwillingly he suffered himself to be led to a small sofa. They chatted a few minutes; then danced; Roger simply must look at Martha's new etchings. The pair was inseparable for the evening. Try as she might Angela could discover no feeling of jealousy but her dignity was hurt. She could not have received less attention from her former lover if they had never met. At first she thought she would make up to Ashley but something malicious in Carlotta's glance deterred her. No, she was sick of men and their babyish, faithless ways; she did not care enough about Roger to play a game for him. So she sat quietly in a deep chair, smoking, dipping into the scattered piles of books which lent the apartment its air of cheerful disorder. Occasionally she chatted; Ladislas Starr perched on the arm of her chair and beguiled her with gay tales of his university days in pre-war Vienna.

But she would never endure such an indignity again. On the way home she was silent. Roger glanced at her curiously, raised his eyebrows when she asked him to come in. She began quietly: "Roger I'll never endure again the treatment——"

But he was ready, even eager for a quarrel. "It looks to me as though you were willing to endure anything. No woman with an ounce of pride would have stood for what you've been standing lately."

She said evenly: "You mean this is the end? We're through?"

"Well, what do you think about it? You certainly didn't expect it to last for ever."

His tone was unbelievably insulting. Eyeing him speculatively she replied: "No, of course I didn't expect it to last for ever, but I didn't think it would end like this. I don't see yet why it should."

The knowledge of his unpardonable manner lay heavy upon him, drove him to fresh indignity. "I suppose you thought some day I'd kiss your hand and say 'You've been very nice to me; I'll always remember you with affection and gratitude. Good-bye.'"

"Well, why shouldn't you have said that? Certainly I'd expected that much sooner than a scene of this sort. I never dreamed of letting myself in for this kind of thing."

Some ugly devil held him in its grasp. "You knew perfectly well what you were letting yourself in for. Any woman would know it."

She could only stare at him, his words echoing in her ears: "You knew perfectly well what you were letting yourself in for."

The phrase had the quality of a cosmic echo; perhaps men had been saying it to women since the beginning of time. Doubtless their biblical equivalent were the last words uttered by Abraham to Hagar before she fared forth into the wilderness.

Chapter V

LONG after Roger had left her she sat staring into the dark shadows of the room. For a long time the end, she knew, had been imminent; she had been curious to see how it would arrive, but the thought had never crossed her mind that it would come with harsh words and with vulgarity. The departure of Roger himself—she shut her hand and opened it—meant nothing; she had never loved, never felt for him one-tenth of the devotion which her mother had known for her father, of the spontaneous affection which Virginia had offered Matthew Henson. Even in these latter weeks when she had consciously striven to show him every possible kindness and attention she had done so for the selfish preservation of her ideals. Now she looked back on those first days of delight when his emotions and her own had met at full tide; when she dreamed that she alone of all people in the world was exempt from ordinary law. How, she wondered futilely, could she ever have suffered herself to be persuaded to tamper with the sacred mysteries of life? If she had held in her hand the golden key,—love! But to throw aside the fundamental laws of civilization for passion, for the hot-headed wilfulness of youth and to have it end like this, drably, vulgarly, almost in a brawl! How could she endure herself? And Roger and his promises of esteem and golden memories!

For a moment she hated him for his fine words and phrases, hated him for tricking her. No matter what she had said, how she had acted, he should have let her go. Better a wound to her passion than later this terrible gash in her proud assurance, this hurt in the core of herself. "God!" she said, raging in her tiny apartment as a tiger in a menagerie rages in its inadequate cage, "God, isn't there any place where man's responsibility to woman begins?"

But she had grown too much into the habit of deliberately ordering her life, of hewing her own path, of removing the difficulties that beset that path, to let herself be sickened, utterly prostrated by what had befallen her. Roger, her companion, had gone; she had been caught up in an inexcusably needless affair without the pretext of love. Thank God she had taken nothing from Roger; she had not sold herself; only bestowed that self foolishly, unworthily. However upset and harassed her mind might be it could not dwell too long on this loss of a lover. There were other problems to consider; for Roger's passing meant the vanishing of the last hope of the successful marriage which once she had so greatly craved. And even though she had not actively considered this for some time, yet as a remote possibility it had afforded a sense of security. Now that mirage was dispelled; she was brought with a sudden shock back to reality. No longer was it enough for her to plan how she could win to a pleasant and happy means of existence, she must be on the *qui vive* for the maintenance of that very existence itself. New York had literally swallowed her original three thousand dollars; part of Virginia's gift was also dissipated. Less than a thousand dollars stood between her and absolute penury. She could not envisage turning to Jinny; life which had seemed so promising, so golden, had failed to supply her with a single friend to whom she could turn in an hour of extremity.

Such thoughts as these left her panic-stricken, cold with fear. The spectre of possible want filled her dreams, haunted her waking hours, thrust aside the devastating shame of her affair with Roger to replace it with dread and apprehension. In her despair she turned more ardently than ever to her painting; already she was capable of doing outstanding work in portraiture, but she lacked *cachet*; she was absolutely unknown.

This condition of her mind affected her appearance; she began to husband her clothes, sadly conscious that she could not tell where others would come from. Her face lost its roundness, the white warmness of her skin remained but there were violet shadows under her eyes; her forehead showed faint lines; she was slightly shabby. Gradually the triumphant vividness so characteristic of Angèle Mory left her, she was like any one of a thousand other pitiful, frightened girls thronging New York. Miss Powell glanced at her and thought: "she looks unhappy, but how can she be when she has a chance at everything in the world just because she's white?"

Anthony marked her fading brightness; he would have liked to question her, comfort her, but where this girl was concerned the rôle of comforter was not for him. Only the instructor, Mr. Paget guessed at her extremity. He had seen too many students not to recognize the signs of poverty, of disaster in love, of despair at the tardy flowering of dexterity that had been mistaken for talent. Once after class he stopped Angela and asked her if she knew of anyone willing to furnish designs for a well-known journal of fashion.

"Not very stimulating work, but the pay is good and the firm reliable. Their last artist was with them eight years. If you know of anyone,——"

She interrupted: "I know of myself. Do you think they'd take me on?"

"I could recommend you. They applied to me, you see. Doubtless they'd take my suggestions into account."

He was very kind; made all the necessary arrangements. The firm received Angela gladly, offering her a fair salary for work that was a trifle narrow, a bit stultifying. But it opened up possibilities; there were new people to be met; perhaps she would make new friends, form ties which might be lasting.

"Oh," she said hopefully to herself, "life is wonderful! It's giving me a new deal and I'll begin all over again. I'm young and now I'm sophisticated; the world is wide, somewhere there's happiness and peace and a place for me. I'll find it."

But her hope, her sanguineness, were a little forced, her superb self-confidence perceptibly diminished. The radiance which once had so bathed every moment of her existence was fading gently, inexorably into the "light of common day".

HOME AGAIN

Chapter I

Nᴇᴡ Yᴏʀᴋ, it appeared, had two visages. It could offer an aspect radiant with promise or a countenance lowering and forbidding. With its flattering possibilities it could elevate to the seventh heaven, or lower to the depths of hell with its crushing negations. And loneliness! Loneliness such as that offered by the great, noisy city could never be imagined. To realize it one would have to experience it. Coming home from work Angela used to study the people on the trains, trying to divine what cause had engraved a given expression on their faces, particularly on the faces of young women. She picked out for herself four types, the happy, the indifferent, the preoccupied, the lonely. Doubtless her classification was imperfect, but she never failed, she thought, to recognize the signs of loneliness, a vacancy of expression, a listlessness, a faintly pervading despair. She remembered the people in Union Square on whom she had spied so blithely when she had first come to New York. Then she had thought of them as being "down and out", mere idlers, good for nothing. It had not occurred to her that their chief disaster might be loneliness. Her office was on Twenty-third Street and often at the noon-hour she walked down to the dingy Square and looked again in on the sprawling, half-recumbent, dejected figures. And between them and herself she was able to detect a terrifying relationship. She still carried her notebook, made sketches, sitting watching them and jotting down a line now and then when their vacant, staring eyes were not fixed upon her. Once she would not have cared if they had caught her; she would have said with a shrug: "Oh they wouldn't mind, they're too far gone for that." But since then her sympathy and knowledge had waxed. How fiercely she would have rebelled had anyone from a superior social plane taken her for copy!

In the evenings she worked at the idea of a picture which

she intended for a masterpiece. It was summer and the classes
at Cooper Union had been suspended. But she meant to return
in the fall, perhaps she would enter the scholarship contest and
if successful, go abroad. But the urge to wander was no longer
in the ascendant. The prospect of Europe did not seem as alluring now as the prospect of New York had appeared when
she lived in Philadelphia. It would be nice to stay put, rooted;
to have friends, experiences, memories.

Paulette, triumphant to the last, had left with Hudson for Russia. Martha and Ladislas were spending the summer with Martha's people on Long Island. Roger had dropped into the void,
but she could not make herself miss him; to her he was the
symbol of all that was most futile in her existence, she could
forgive neither him nor herself for their year of madness. If the
experience, she told herself, had ended—so-be-it—everything
ends. If it had faded into a golden glow with a wealth of memories, the promise of a friendship, she would have had no qualms;
but as matters had turned out it was an offence in her nostrils,
a great blot on the escutcheon of her fastidiousness.

She wished that Martha had asked her to spend week-ends
with her but the idea had apparently never crossed the latter's
mind. "Good-bye until fall," she had said gaily, "do you know,
I'm awfully glad to go home this time. I always have my old
room; it's like begining life all over again. Of course I wouldn't
give up New York but life seems so much more real and durable
down there. After all it's where my roots are."

Her roots! Angela echoed the expression to herself on a note
that was wholly envious. How marvellous to go back to parents,
relatives, friends with whom one had never lost touch! The
peace, the security, the companionableness of it! This was a
relationship which she had forfeited with everyone, even with
Jinny. And as for her other acquaintances in Philadelphia,
Henson, Butler, Kate and Agnes Hallowell, so completely, so
casually, without even a ripple had she dropped out of their
lives that it would have been impossible for her to re-establish
their old, easy footing even had she so desired.

Virginia, without making an effort, seemed overwhelmed,
almost swamped by friendships, pleasant intimacies, a thousand
charming interests. She and Sara Penton, another teacher, had

taken an apartment together, a three room affair on the top floor of a house on 139th Street, in "Striver's Row", explained Jinny. Whether or not the nickname was deserved, it seemed to Angela well worth an effort to live in this beautiful block with its tree-bordered pavements, its spacious houses, its gracious neighbourliness. A doctor and his wife occupied the first two floors; they were elderly, rather lonely people, for their two children had married and gone to other cities. They had practically adopted Virginia and Sara; nursing them when they had colds, indulgently advising them as to their callers. Mrs. Bradley, the doctor's wife, occasionally pressed a dress for them; on stormy days the doctor drove them in his car around to "Public School 89" where they both taught. Already the two girls were as full of intimacies, joyous reminiscences, common plans as though they had lived together for years. Secrets, nicknames, allusions, filled the atmosphere. Angela grew sick of the phrases: "Of course you don't understand that; just some nonsense and it would take too long to explain it. Besides you wouldn't know any of the people." Even so, unwelcome as the expression was, she did not hear it very often, for Jinny did not encourage her visits to the apartment even as much as to the boarding house.

"Sara will think it strange if you come too often."

"We might tell her," Angela rejoined, "and ask her to keep it a secret."

But Jinny opined coolly that that would never do; it was bad to entrust people with one's secrets. "If you can't keep them yourself, why should they?" she asked sagely. Her attitude showed no malice, only the complete acceptance of the stand which her sister had adopted years ago.

In her sequestered rooms in the Village lying in the summer heat unkempt and shorn of its glamour Angela pondered long and often on her present mode of living. Her life, she was pretty sure, could not go on indefinitely as it did now. Even if she herself made no effort it was unlikely that the loneliness could persist. Jinny, she shrewdly suspected, had known something of this horrible condition when she, the older sister had left her so ruthlessly to go off and play at adventure. This loneliness and her unfortunate affair with Henson had doubtless

proved too much for her, and she had deliberately sought
change and distraction elsewhere. There were depths upon
depths of strength in Jinny and as much purpose and resource
as one might require. Now here she was established in New
York with friends, occupation, security, leading an utterly open
life, no secrets, no subterfuges, no goals to be reached by devious ways.

Jinny had changed her life and been successful. Angela had
changed hers and had found pain and unhappiness. Where did
the fault lie? Not, certainly, in her determination to pass from
one race to another. Her native good sense assured her that it
would have been silly for her to keep on living as she had in
Philadelphia, constantly, through no fault of her own, being
placed in impossible positions, eternally being accused and
hounded because she had failed to placard herself, forfeiting
old friendships, driven fearfully to the establishing of new ones.
No, the fault was not there. Perhaps it lay in her attitude toward her friends. Had she been too coldly deliberate in her use
of them? Certainly she had planned to utilize her connection
with Roger, but on this point she had no qualms; he had been
paid in full for any advantages which she had meant to gain.
She had not always been kind to Miss Powell, "but," she murmured to herself, "I was always as kind to her as I dared be in
the circumstances and far, far more attentive than any of the
others." As for Anthony, Paulette, and Martha, her slate was
clear on their score. She was struck at this point to realize that
during her stay of nearly three years these five were the only
people to whom she could apply the term friends. Of these
Roger had dropped out; Miss Powell was negative; Paulette
had gone to Russia. There remained only Martha and Anthony.
Martha was too intensely interested in the conduct of her own
life in connection with Ladislas to make a friend, a satisfying,
comfortable, intimate friend such as Sara Penton seemed to be
with Virginia. There remained then only Anthony—yes, and
her new acquaintance, Rachel Salting.

She began then in her loneliness to approach Rachel seeking
for nothing other than those almost sisterly intimacies which
spring up between solitary women cut off in big cities from their
homes and from all the natural resources which add so much

to the beauty and graciousness of young womanhood. "If anything comes out of this friendship to advance me in any way," she told herself solemnly, "it will happen just because it happens but I shall go into this with clean hands and a pure heart —merely because I like Rachel."

After the fever and fret of her acquaintanceship with Roger, the slight unwholesomeness attendant on Paulette, the didactic quality lurking in Martha's household, it was charming, even delicious to enter on a friendship with this simple, intelligent, enthusiastic girl. Rachel, for all her native endowment, her wide reading and her broad scholastic contacts, had the straightforward utter sincerity and simplicity of a child; at times Angela felt quite sophisticated, even blasé beside her. But in reality they were two children together; Angela's brief episode with Roger had left no trace on her moral nature; she was ashamed now of the affair with a healthy shame at its unworthiness; but beyond that she suffered from no morbidness. Her sum total of the knowledge of life had been increased; she saw men with a different eye, was able to differentiate between the attitudes underlying the pleasantries of the half dozen young men in her office; listening, laughing, weighing all their attentions, accepting none. In truth she had lost to a degree her taste for the current type of flirtations. She might marry some day but all that was still in the dim future. Meanwhile the present beckoned; materially she was once more secure, her itching ambition was temporarily lulled; she had a friend. It was just as well to let time slide by for a while.

The two girls spent their evenings together. Rachel's fiancé, John Adams, was a travelling salesman and nearly always out of town. When he was home Angela was careful to have an engagement, though Rachel assured her, laughing and sparkling, that the two were already so used to each other that a third person need not feel *de trop*. Occasionally the three of them went during the hot summer nights to Coney Island or Far Rockaway. But this jaunt took on the proportions more of an ordeal than a pleasure trip; so packed were the cars with helpless humanity, so crowded the beaches, so nightmarish the trip home. Fortunately Angela came face to face one day with Ralph Ashley, Carlotta's former friend. Low-spirited, lonely, distrait, he asked Angela eagerly to allow him to call occasionally. He seemed a rather bookish, serious young man who had failed to discover the possibilities of his inner resources. Without an acquaintance or a book he was helpless. Angela's self-reliance and cleverness seemed to offer a temporary harbour. Apparently with Carlotta out of town, he was at loose ends. By some tacit understanding he was taken into the little group and as he possessed a car which he was willing and eager to share the arrangement was a very happy one.

These were pleasant days. Long afterwards, Angela, looking back recalled them as among the happiest she had known in New York. In particular she liked the hours when she and Rachel were together busied with domestic, homely affairs. They advised each other on the subject of dress; Angela tried out new recipes. In the late evenings she worked on the sketches, recalling them from her note-book while Rachel, sitting side-wise in the big chair, her legs dangling comfortably over its arm, offered comments and suggestions. She had had "courses in art", and on a trip to France and Italy at the age of eighteen had visited the Louvre, the Pitti and Uffizi Galleries. All this lent a certain pithiness and authority to the criticisms which she poured forth for her friend's edification; her remarks rarely produced any effect on Angela, but both girls felt that Rachel's knowledge gave a certain effect of "atmosphere".

Usually Rachel's talk was on John and their approaching marriage, their unparalleled courtship. Many years later Angela could have related all the details of that simple, almost sylvan wooing, the growing awareness of the two lovers, their mutual fears and hopes, their questionings, assurances and their bliss-ful engagement. She knew to a penny what John made each week, how much he put by, the amount which thrifty Rachel felt must be in hand before they could marry. Once this recital, so unvarying, so persistent, would have bored her, but she was more sympathetic in these days; sometimes she found herself making suggestions, saving the house-wifely clippings culled from newspapers, proposing decorations for the interior of one of the ugly little houses on which Rachel had so inexplicably set her heart. She was a little older than her friend, she had had experience in keeping house and in shopping with her mother in those far-off days; she ventured occasionally to advise Rachel in her rare purchases very much as though the latter were her own sister instead of a chance acquaintance whom she had known less than a year.

It was a placid, almost ideal existence. Only one thread of worry ran through its fabric, the thought that Rachel and John would soon be marrying and again Angela would be left on the search for a new friend. With one of them in the Bronx and the other Greenwich Village, frequent communication would be physically impossible. But, curiously enough, whenever Angela lamented over this to her friend, a deep sombreness would descend on the latter; she would remark gloomily: "Time enough to worry about that; after all we might not get married. You never can tell." This was too enigmatic for Angela and finally she grew to look on it as a jest, a rather poor one but still a jest.

Chapter II

INTO the midst of this serenity came a bolt from the blue. Rachel, a librarian, was offered the position of head librarian in a far suburb of Brooklyn. Furthermore a wealthy woman from Butte, Montana, desiring to stay in New York for a few months and taking a fancy to the dinginess of Jayne Street and to the inconveniences of Rachel's apartment found she must live there and not otherwhere. No other location in the whole great city would do; she was willing to sublet at any figure. Unwillingly Rachel named a price which she secretly considered in the nature of highway robbery, but none of this mattered to Mrs. Denver, who was used to paying for what she wanted. And Rachel could not refuse, for both offers meant a substantial increase in the nest-egg which was to furnish the little brown house in the Bronx. In reality it meant to her extraordinary, unhoped for luck whose only flaw consisted in the enforced separation from her new friend. But to Angela it brought the awfulness of a catastrophe, though not for one moment would she let her deep dismay be suspected. After her first involuntary exclamation of consternation she never faltered in her complete acquiescence in the plan. But at heart she was sick.

The sudden flitting entailed much work and bustle. Rachel was as untidy as Angela was neat; everything she possessed had to be collected separately; there were no stacks of carefully folded clothing to be lifted wholesale and placed in gaping trunks. To begin with the trunks themselves were filled with dubious odds and ends which required to be sorted, given or even thrown away. There was no question of abandoning the *débris*, for the apartment must be left habitable for Mrs. Denver.

A nightmare then of feverish packing ensued; hasty meals, general house-cleaning. In order to assuage the sinking of her heart Angela plunged into it with great ardour. But at night, weary as she would be from the extra activity of the day, she could not fight off the sick dismay which overflowed her in great, submerging waves. It seemed to her she could not again endure loneliness; she could never summon the strength to seek out new friends, to establish fresh intimacies. She was twenty-six years old and the fact that after having lived all those years she was still solitary appalled her. Perhaps some curse such as one reads of in mediæval legends had fallen upon her. "Perhaps I'm not meant to have friends," she told herself lying face downwards in her pillows on the sweltering June nights. And a great nostalgia for something real and permanent swept upon her; she wished she were either very, very young, safe and contented once more in the protection of her father's household or failing that, very, very old.

A nature as strong, as self-reliant as hers could not remain long submerged; she had seen too many bad beginnings convert themselves into good endings. One of her most valuable native endowments lay in her ability to set herself and her difficulties objectively before her own eyes; in this way she had solved more than one problem. On the long ride in the subway back from Brooklyn whither she had accompanied Rachel on the night of the latter's departure she resolved to pursue this course that very night. Mercifully the terrible heat had abated, a little breeze came sifting in her open windows, moving the white sash curtains, even agitating some papers on the table. Soberly she set about the business of getting supper. Once she thought of running up to Rachel's former apartment and proffering some hospitality to Mrs. Denver. Even if the rich new tenant should not accept she'd be pleased doubtless; sooner or later she would be offering a return of courtesies, a new friendship would spring up. Again there would be possibilities. But something in her rebelled against such a procedure; these intimacies based on the sliding foundation of chance sickened her; she would not lend herself to them—not ever again. From this day on she'd devote herself to the establishing of permanencies.

Supper over, the dishes cleared away, she sat down and prepared to think. Callers were unlikely; indeed there was no one to call, since Ashley was out of town for the week-end, but the pathos of this fact left her untouched. To-night she courted loneliness.

An oft heard remark of her mother's kept running through her mind: "You get so taken up with the problem of living, with just life itself, that by and by being coloured or not is just one thing more or less that you have to contend with." It had been a long time since she had thought about colour; at one time it had seemed to complicate her life immensely, now it seemed to her that it might be of very little importance. But her thoughts skirted the subject warily for she knew how immensely difficult living could be made by this matter of race. But that should take a secondary place; at present life, a method of living was the main thing, she must get that problem adjusted and first she must see what she wanted. Companionship was her chief demand. No more loneliness, not even if that were the road that led to the fulfilment of vast ambition, to the realization of the loftiest hopes. And for this she was willing to make sacrifices, let go if need be of her cherished independence, lead a double life, move among two sets of acquaintances.

For deep in her heart she realized the longing to cast in her lot once more with Virginia, her little sister whom she should never have left. Virginia, it is true, showed no particular longing for her; indeed she seemed hardly cognizant of her existence; but this attitude might be a forced one. She thought, "I didn't want her, the darling, and so she just made herself put me out of her life." Angela was well aware of the pluck, the indomitableness that lay beneath Jinny's babyish exterior, but there was a still deeper stratum of tenderness and love and loyalty which was the real Virginia. To this Angela would make her appeal; she would acknowledge her foolishness, her selfishness; she would bare her heart and crave her sister's forgiveness. And then they would live together, Jinny and she and Sara Penton if need be; what a joke it would all be on Sara! And once again she would know the bliss and happiness of a home and the stabilities of friendships culled from a certain definite class of people, not friendships resulting from mere chance. There would be blessed Sunday mornings and breakfasts, long walks; lovely evenings in the autumn to be filled with reminiscences drawn from these days of separation. How Virginia would open her eyes at her tales of Paulette and Martha! She would never mention Roger. And as for colour; when it seemed best to be coloured she would be coloured; when it was best to be white she would be that. The main thing was, she would know once more the joys of ordinary living, home, companionship, loyalty, security, the bliss of possessing and being possessed. And to think it was all possible and waiting for her; it was only a matter of a few hours, a few miles.

A great sense of peace, of exaltation descended upon her. Almost she could have said: "I will arise and go unto my father".

On Sunday accordingly she betook herself to her sister's apartment in 139th Street. Miss Penton, she thought, would be out; she had gathered from the girls' conversation many pointed references to Sara's great fondness, of late, for church, exceeded only by her interest in the choir. This interest in the choir was ardently encouraged by a member of that body who occasionally walked home with Sara in order more fully to discuss the art of music. Virginia no longer went to church; Sunday had become her "pick-up day", the one period in the week which she devoted to her correspondence, her clothes and to such mysterious rites of beautifying and revitalizing as lay back of her healthy, blooming exquisiteness. This would be the first time in many months that the sisters would have been alone together and it was with high hopes that Angela, mounting the brown stone steps and ringing the bell, asked for Virginia.

Her sister was in, but so was Sara, so was a third girl, a Miss Louise Andrews. The room was full of the atmosphere of the lightness, of the badinage, of the laughter which belong to the condition either of youth or of extreme happiness. In the middle of the room stood a large trunk from whose yawning interior Jinny lifted a glowing, smiling face. Angela was almost startled at the bright ecstasy which radiated from it. Sara Penton was engaged rather negligently in folding clothes; Miss Andrews perched in magnificent ease on the daybed, struck an occasional tune from a ukelele and issued commands which nobody heeded.

"Hello," said Virginia carelessly. "Can you get in? I was thinking of writing to you."

"Oh," Angela's hopes fluttered, fell, perished. "You're not going away?" Her heart echoed Jinny's old cry: "And leave me—when I'm all ready to come back to you, when I need you so terribly!"

But of all this Virginia was, of course, unaware. "Nothing

different," she said briskly. "I'm going away this very afternoon to Philadelphia, Merion, points south and west, going to stay with Eda Brown."

Angela was aghast. "I wanted to see you about something rather important, Virginia—at least," she added humbly, "important to me." Rather impatiently she glanced at the two girls hoping they would take the hint and leave them, but they had not even heard her, so engrossed were they in discussing the relative merits of one- and two-piece sports clothes.

Her sister was kind but not curious. "Unless it's got something to do with your soul's salvation I'm afraid it'll have to wait a bit," she said gaily. "I'm getting a two o'clock train and I must finish this trunk—Sara's such a poor packer or I'd leave it for her. As it is she's going to send it after me. Aren't you, darling?" Already Angela's request was forgotten. "After I finish this," the gay voice went on, "I've got some 'phoning to do and—oh a million things."

"Let me help you," said Angela suddenly inspired, "then we'll call a taxi and we can go down to the station together and we'll have a long talk so I can explain things."

Virginia was only half-attentive. "Miss Mory wants to go to the station with me," she said throwing a droll look at her friends. "Shall I take her along?" She vanished into the bedroom, Louise Andrews at her heels, both of them overwhelmed with laughter bubbling from some secret spring.

Cut and humiliated, Angela stood silent. Sara Penton who had been looking after the vanishing figures turned and caught her expression. "Don't mind her craziness. She's not responsible to-day."

She came closer. "For heaven's sake don't let on I told you; she's engaged."

This was news. "Engaged? To whom?"

"Oh somebody she's always been crazy about." The inevitable phrase followed: "You wouldn't know who he was."

Not know who he was, not know Matthew! She began to say "Why I knew him before Virginia," but remembering her rôle, a stupid and silly one now, caught herself, stood expectantly.

"So you see," Sara went on mysteriously, one eye on the bedroom, "you mustn't insist on going to the station with her; he's going to take her down."

"Why, is he here?"

"Came yesterday. We've been threatening all morning to butt in. That's the reason she spoke as she did about your going down. She expressed herself to us, you bet, but she probably wouldn't feel like doing that to you."

"Probably not," said Angela, her heart cold. Her little sister was engaged and she was learning of it from strangers. It was all she could do to hold back the tears. "But you've only yourself to blame," she reminded herself valiantly.

The two girls came back; Virginia still laughing but underneath the merriment Angela was able to detect a flurry of nervousness. After all, Jinny was just a child. And she was so happy, it would never do to mar that happiness by the introduction of the slightest gloom or discomfort. Her caller rose to her feet. "I guess I'll be going."

Virginia made no effort to detain her, but the glance which she turned on her sister was suddenly very sweet and friendly. "Here, I'll run down to the door with you. Sara, be a darling and pick out the best of those stockings for me, put in lots. You know how hard I am on them."

Out in the hall she flung an impulsive arm about her sister. "Oh, Angela, I'm so happy, so happy. I'm going to write you about it right away, you'll be so surprised." Astonishingly she gave the older girl a great hug, kissed her again and again.

"Oh," said Angela, the tears welling from her eyes, "Oh Jinny, you do forgive me, you do, you do? I'm so sorry about it all. I've been wretched for a long time. I thought I had lost you, Virginia."

"I know," said Jinny, "I'm a hard-hearted little wretch." She giggled through her own tears, wiped them away with the back of her childish bronze hand. "I was just putting you through; I knew you'd get sick of Miss Anne's folks and come back to me. Oh Angela, I've wanted you so. But it's all right now. I won't be back for ten weeks, but then we will talk! I've got the most marvellous plans for both of us—for all of us." She looked like a wise baby. "You'll get a letter from me in a few days telling you all about it. Angela, I'm so happy, but I must fly. Good-bye, darling."

They clung for a moment in the cool, dim depths of the wide hall.

＊

Angela could have danced in the street. As it was she walked gaily down Seventh Avenue to 110th Street and into the bosky reaches of the park. Jinny had forgiven her. Jinny longed for her, needed her; she had known all along that Angela was suffering, had deliberately punished her. Well, she was right, everything was right this glorious memorable day. She was to have a sister again, some one of her own, she would know the joy of sharing her little triumphs, her petty woes. Wise Jinny, wonderful Jinny!

And beautiful Jinny, too, she thought. How lovely, how dainty, how fresh and innocent her little sister seemed. This brought her mind to Matthew and his great good fortune. "I'd like to see him again," she mused, smiling mischievously. "Doubtless he's forgotten me. It would be great fun to make him remember." Only, of course, now he was Jinny's and she would never get in the way of that darling. "Not even if he were some one I really wanted with all my heart and soul. But I'd never want Matthew." It would be fun, she thought, to see him again. He would make a nice brother, so sturdy and kind and reliable. She must be careful never to presume on that old youthful admiration of his. Smiling and happy she reached her house, actually skipped up the steps to her rooms. Her apartment no longer seemed lonely; it was not beautiful and bright like Jinny's but it was snug and dainty. It would be fun to have Virginia and Sara down; yes, and that new girl, that Miss Andrews, too. She didn't care what the other people in the house thought. And the girls themselves, how astonished they would be to learn the true state of affairs! Suddenly remembering Mrs. Denver, she ran up to see her; that lady, in spite of her wealth and means for self-indulgence, was palpably lonely. Angela cheered her up with mirthful accounts of her own first days in New York; she'd been lonely too, she assured her despondent hostess, sparkling and fascinating.

"I don't see how anybody with a disposition like yours could ever be lonely," said Mrs. Denver enviously. She'd been perilously near tears all day.

Gone, gone was all the awful melancholy, the blueness that had hung about her like a palpable cloud. She was young, fascinating; she was going to be happy,—again. *Again!* She caught her breath at that. Oh, God was good! This feeling of lightness, of exaltation had been unknown to her so long; not since the days when she had first begun to go about with Roger had she felt so free, bird-like. In the evening Ralph Ashley came with his car and drove her halfway across Long Island, or so it seemed. They stopped at a gorgeous hotel and had a marvellous supper. Ashley was swept off his feet by her gay vitalness. In the doorway of the Jayne Street house she gave him her hand and a bewitching smile. "You can't imagine how much I've enjoyed myself. I'll always remember it." And she spoke sincerely, for soon this sort of thing would be far behind her.

"You're a witch," said Ashley, his voice shaking a little. "You can have this sort of thing whenever you want it and you know it. Be kind to me, Angèle. I'm not a bad fellow." Frightened, she pushed him away, ran in and slammed the door. No, no, no, her heart pounded. Roger had taught her an unforgettable lesson. Soon she'd be with Jinny and Matthew, safe, sheltered.

Chapter III

IN the middle of the night she found herself sitting up in bed. A moment before she had been asleep, but a sudden thought had pierced her consciousness so sharply that the effect was that of an icy hand laid suddenly on her shoulder. Jinny and Matthew marry—why, that meant—why, of course it meant that they would have to live in Philadelphia. How stupid she had been! And she couldn't go back there—never, never. Not because of the difficulties which she had experienced as a child; she was perfectly willing to cast in her lot again with coloured people in New York. But that was different; there were signal injustices here, too—oh, many, many of them—but there were also signal opportunities. But Philadelphia with its traditions of liberty and its actual economic and social slavery, its iniquitous school system, its prejudiced theatres, its limited offering of occupation! A great, searing hatred arose in her for the huge, slumbering leviathan of a city which had hardly moved a muscle in the last fifty years. So hide-bound were its habits that deliberate insult could be offered to coloured people without causing the smallest ripple of condemnation or even consternation in the complacent commonwealth. Virginia in one of her expansive moments had told her of a letter received from Agnes Hallowell, now a graduate of the Women's Medical College. Agnes was as fair as Angela, but she had talked frankly, even with pride, of her racial connections. "I had nothing to be ashamed of," Angela could imagine her saying, her cheeks flushing, her black eyes snapping. On her graduation she had applied for an internship at a great hospital for the insane; a position greatly craved by ardent medical graduates because of the unusually large turnover of pathological cases. But the man in charge of such appointments, looking Agnes hard in the eye told her suavely that such a position would never be given to her "not if you passed ahead of a thousand white candidates."

As for Angela, here was the old problem of possible loneliness back on her hands. Virginia, it was true, would hardly marry at once, perhaps they would have a few happy months together. But afterwards. . . . She lay there, wide awake now, very still, very straight in her narrow bed, watching the thick blackness grow thinner, less opaque. And suddenly as on a former occasion, she thought of marriage. Well, why not? She had thought of it once before as a source of relief from poverty, as a final barrier between herself and the wolves of prejudice; why not now as a means of avoiding loneliness? "I must look around me," her thoughts sped on, and she blushed and smiled in the darkness at the cold-bloodedness of such an idea. But, after all, that was what men said—and did. How often had she heard the expression—"he's ready to settle down, so he's looking around for a wife". If that were the procedure of men it should certainly be much more so the procedure of women since their fate was so much more deeply involved. The room was growing lighter; she could see the pictures a deeper blur against the faint blur of the wall. Her passing shame suddenly spent itself, for, after all, she knew practically no men. There was Ashley— but she was through with men of his type. The men in her office were nearly all impossible, but there were three, she told herself, coldly, unenthusiastic, who were not such terrible pills.

"But no," she said out loud. "I'd rather stay single and lonely, too, all my life than worry along with one of them. There must be someone else." And at once she thought of Anthony Cross. Of course there was Anthony. "I believe I've always had him in the back of my mind," she spoke again to the glimmering greyness. And turning on her pillow she fell, smiling, asleep.

Monday was a busy day; copy must be prepared for the engraver; proofs of the current edition of the magazine had to be checked up; some important French fashion plates for which she was responsible had temporarily disappeared and must be unearthed. At four-thirty she was free to take tea with Mrs. Denver, who immediately thereafter bore her off to a "movie" and dinner. Not until nine o'clock was she able to pursue her new train of thought. And even when she was at liberty to indulge in her habit of introspection she found herself experiencing a certain reluctance, an unexpected shyness. Time was needed to brood on this secret with its promise of happiness;

this means of salvation from the problems of loneliness and weakness which beset her. For since the departure of Roger she frequently felt herself less assured; it would be a relief to have some one on whom to lean; some one who would be glad to shield and advise her,—and love her! This last thought seemed to her marvellous. She said to herself again and again: "Anthony loves me, I know it. Think of it, he loves me!" Her face and neck were covered with blushes; she was like a young girl on the eve of falling in love, and indeed she herself was entering on that experience for the first time. From the very beginning she had liked Anthony, liked him as she had never liked Roger—for himself, for his sincerity, for his fierce pride, for his poverty, for his honest, frantic love. "And now," she said solemnly, "I believe I'm going to love him; I believe I love him already."

There were many things to be considered. His poverty,—but she no longer cared about that; insensibly her association with Rachel Salting, her knowledge of Rachel's plans and her high flouting of poverty had worked their influence. It would be fun, fun to begin at the beginning, to save and scrape and mend. Like Rachel she would do no washing and ironing, she would keep herself dainty and unworn, but everything else, everything else she would do. Cook—and she could cook; she had her blessed mother to thank for that. For a moment she was home again on Opal Street, getting Monday dinner, laughing with Virginia about Mrs. Henrietta Jones. There they were at the table, her pretty mother, her father with his fine, black face—his black face, she had forgotten that.

Colour,—here the old problem came up again. Restlessly she paced the room, a smouldering cigarette in her fingers. She rarely smoked but sometimes the insensate little cylinder gave her a sense of companionship. Colour, colour, she had forgotten it. Now what should she do,—tell Anthony? He was Spanish, she remembered, or no,—since he came from Brazil he was probably Portuguese, a member of a race devoid, notoriously devoid of prejudice against black blood. But Anthony had lived in America long enough to become inoculated; had he ever spoken about coloured people, had the subject ever come up? Wait a minute, there was Miss Powell; she remembered now that his conduct towards the young coloured woman had always been conspicuously correct; he had placed chairs for her, opened doors, set up easels; once the three of them had walked out of Cooper Union together and Anthony had carefully helped Miss Powell on a car, removing his hat with that slightly foreign gesture which she admired so much. And so far as she knew he had never used any of Roger's cruelly slighting expressions; the terms "coon", "nigger", "darky" had never crossed his lips. Clearly he had no conscious feeling against her people—"my people" she repeated, smiling, and wondered herself which people she meant, for she belonged to two races, and to one far more conspicuously than the other. Why, Anthony had even attended the Van Meier lecture. And she wondered what Van Meier would say if she presented her problem to him. He had no brief, she knew, against intermarriage, though, because of the high social forfeit levied, he did not advocate its practice in America. For a moment she considered going to him and asking his advice. But she was afraid that he would speak to her about racial pride and she did not want to think of that. Life, life was what she was struggling for, the right to live and be happy. And once more her mother's dictum flashed into her mind. "Life is more important than colour." This, she told herself, was an omen, her mother was watching over her, guiding her. And, burying her face in her hands, she fell on her knees and wept and prayed.

Virginia sent a gay missive: "As soon as you left that wretch of a Sara told me that she had let you in on the great news. I wish I'd known it, I'd have spoken to you about it there in the hall; only there was so much to explain. But now you know the main facts, and I can wait until I see you to tell you the rest. But isn't it all wonderful? Angela, I do believe I'm almost the happiest girl alive!

"It's too lovely here. Edna is very kind and you know I always did like Pennsylvania country. Matthew is out almost every day. He tells me it renews his youth to come and talk about old times,—anyone to hear us reminiscing, starting every other sentence with 'do you remember——?' would think that we averaged at least ninety years apiece. It won't pique your vanity, will it, if I tell you that he seems to have recovered entirely from his old crush on you? Maybe he was just in love with the family and didn't know it.

"We go into Philadelphia every day or two. The city has changed amazingly. But after the hit or miss method of New York society there is something very restful and safe about this tight organization of 'old Philadelphians'. In the short time I've been here I've met loads of first families, people whose names we only knew when we were children. But they all seem to remember father and mother; they all begin: 'My dear, I remember when Junius Murray——' I meet all these people, old and young, through Matthew, who seems to have become quite the beau here and goes everywhere. He really is different. Even his hair in some mysterious way is changed. Not that I ever minded; only he's so awfully nice that I just would like all the nice things of the world added unto him. We were talking the other day about the wedding, and I was thinking what a really distinguished appearance he would make. Dear old Matt, I'm glad I put off marriage until he could cut a fine figure. Write me, darling, if you feel like it, but don't expect to hear much from me. I'm so happy I can't keep still long enough to write. The minute I get back to New York though we'll have such a talk as never was."

Mrs. Denver was growing happier; New York was redeeming itself and revealing all the riches which she had suspected lay hidden in its warehouses. Through one letter of introduction forced into her unwilling hands by an officious acquaintance on her departure from Butte she had gained an *entrée* into that kindest and happiest of New York's varied groups, the band of writers, columnists, publishers and critics. The lady from the middle West had no literary pretensions herself, but she liked people who had them and lived up to them; she kept abreast of literary gossip, read *Vanity Fair*, the *New Yorker*, and *Mercury*. As she was fairly young, dainty, wealthy and generous and no grinder of axes, she was caught up and whirled right along into the galaxy of teas, luncheons, theatre parties and "barbecues" which formed the relaxations of this joyous crowd. Soon she was overwhelmed, with more invitations than she could accept; to those which she did consider she always couched her acceptance in the same terms. "Yes I'll come if I may bring my young friend, Angèle Mory, along with me. She's a painter whom you'll all be glad to know some day." Angela's chance kindness to her in her days of loneliness and boredom had not fallen on barren ground.

Now indeed Angela was far removed from the atmosphere which she had known in Greenwich Village; the slight bohemianism which she had there encountered was here replaced by a somewhat bourgeois but satisfying sophistication. These people saw the "Village" for what it was, a network of badly laid off streets with, for the most part, uncomfortable, not to say inconvenient dwellings inhabited by a handful of artists in the midst of a thousand *poseurs*. Her new friends were frankly interested in the goods of this world. They found money an imperative, the pre-eminent, concomitant of life; once obtained, they spent it on fine apartments, beautiful raiment, delicate viands, and trips to Paris and Vienna. Conversation with them was something more than an exchange of words; "quips and jests" passed among them, and, though flavoured with allusions to stage and book, so that Angela was at times hard put to it to follow the trend of the talk, she half suspected that she was in this company assisting more nearly at the restoration of a lost art than in any other circles in the world save in the corresponding society of London.

Once again her free hours could be filled to overflowing with attention, with gaiety, with intellectual excitement; it came to her one day that this was the atmosphere of which she once had dreamed. But she was not quite happy, her economic condition interfered here. Constantly she was receiving every conceivable manifestation of an uncalculating generosity at the hands not only of Mrs. Denver but of her new acquaintances. And she could make no adequate return; her little apartment had turned too shabby for her to have guests of this calibre, even in to tea. Her rich friend, making short shrift of such furniture as Rachel Salting had left behind, had transformed her dwelling into a marvel of luxury and elegance; tiny but beautiful. Mrs. Denver was the soul of real and delicate kindness but Angela could not accept favours indefinitely; besides she was afraid to become too used to this constant tide from a horn of plenty on which she had absolutely no claim. If there were any one thing which the harsh experiences of these last three years had taught her it was the impermanence of relationships; she must, she felt, lay down and follow a method of living for herself which could never betray her when the attention of the rich and great should be withdrawn. Gradually she ceased accepting Mrs. Denver's invitations; she pleaded the necessity of outside work along the lines of her employment; she was busy, too, on the portrait of her mother, stimulating her vivid memory with an old faded photograph. Her intention was to have it as a surprise for Virginia upon the latter's return.

But before withdrawing completely she made the acquaintance of a young married woman and her husband, a couple so gifted, so genuine and sincere that she was unable to keep to the letter her spartan promise of cutting herself entirely adrift from this fascinating cross-section of New York society. The husband, Walter Sandburg, was a playwright; his name was a household word; the title of one or another of his dramas glittered on Broadway every night. His wife, Elizabeth, reviewed books for one of the great New York weeklies. Their charming apartment in Fifty-fifth Street was the centre for many clever and captivating people. Between these two and Angela something of a real friendship awakened; she was not ashamed to have them see the shabbiness of her apartment. The luncheons to which she treated Elizabeth in the Village tearooms and in apartment stores brought as great satisfaction as the more elaborate meals at the Algonquin, the favourite rendezvous of many of these busy, happy, contented workers.

Ashley, too, had returned to a town still devoid of Carlotta, and in his loneliness was again constantly seeking Angela. His attitude was perfect; never by word or look did he revive the unpleasant impression which he had once made; indeed, in a sober, disillusioned sort of way, she was growing to like him very much. He was shy, sensitive, sympathetic and miserably lonely. It was not likely that his possessions were as fabulously great as Roger's but it was certain that he belonged to Roger's social group with all that such a ranking implies. But in spite of this he was curiously diffident; lacking in pep, the girls in his "set" coldly classified him, and let him alone. Outside his group ambitious Amazons daubed him "easy" and made a mad rush for him and his fabled millions. The two verdicts left him ashamed and frightened; annually he withdrew farther and farther into his shell, emerging only in response to Carlotta's careless and occasional beckoning or to Angela's genuine and pre-occupied indifference.

But this was not her world; for years she had craved such a *milieu*, only to find herself, when once launched into it, outwardly perfectly at ease, inwardly perturbed and dismayed. Although she rarely thought of colour still she was conscious of living in an atmosphere of falseness, of tangled implications. She spoke often of Martha Burden and her husband; Walter Sandburg the playwright, knew Ladislas Starr; Elizabeth had met Paulette Lister in some field of newspaper activity, and Ashley of course had seen Roger in Angela's company. Behind these three or four names and the background which familiarity with them implied, she did not dare venture and in her gayest moments she was aware of the constant stirring within of a longing for someone real and permanent with whom she could share her life. She would, of course make up with Jinny, but Jinny was going to live in Philadelphia, where she herself would never sojourn again. That aftermath was the real consideration.

Her thoughts went constantly winging to Anthony; her determination became static. Saving only this invisible mixture of dark blood in her veins they, too, could meet on a par. They were both young, both gifted, ambitious, blessedly poor. Together they would climb to happier, sunnier heights. To be poor with Anthony; to struggle with him; to help him keep his secret vow; to win his surprised and generous approbation; finally to reach the point where she, too, could open her home to poor, unknown, struggling geniuses,—life could hold nothing more pleasing than these possibilities. And how kind she would be to these strangers! How much she hoped that among them there would be some girl struggling past the limitations of her heritage even as she herself had done. Through some secret, subtle bond of sympathy she would, she was sure, be able to recognize such a girl; and how she would help her and spur her on! To her communings she said humbly, "I am sure that this course will work out all right for me for see, I am planning chiefly for Anthony and for helpless, harassed people; hardly anything for myself but protection and love. I am willing to work for success and happiness." And even as she spoke she knew that the summit of her bliss would be reached in the days while she and Anthony were still poor and struggling and when she would be giving of her best to make things so.

Elizabeth Sandburg reminiscing about the early married days of herself and Walter gave a fillip to her thought. Said Elizabeth: "Walt and I were just as poor as we could be, we only made twenty dollars a week, and half of that went for a room in cheap hotel. Meals even at the punkest places were awfully expensive, and half the time I used to cook things over the gas-jet. I didn't know much about cooking, and I imagine the stuff was atrocious, but we didn't mind. There were we with no one to interfere with us; we had each other and we didn't give a damn."

Smiling, glowing, she gave Angela a commission to paint hers and her Walter's portraits. "We'll leave the price to you and if you really put the job over I'll get you a lot of other sitters. No, don't thank me. What are friends for? That's what I always say."

Chapter IV

SOMETIMES this thought confronted her: "Perhaps Anthony no longer needs me; has forgotten me." And at the bare idea her heart would contract with an actual, palpable movement. For by now he was representing not only surcease from loneliness but peace and security; a place not merely in society but in the world at large. Marriage appeared, too, in a different light. Until she had met Roger she had not thought much about the institution except as an adventure in romance or as a means to an end; in her case the method of achieving the kind of existence which once had been her ideal. But now she saw it as an end in itself; for women certainly; the only, the most desirable and natural end. From this state a gifted, an ambitious woman might reach forth and acquit herself well in any activity. But marriage must be there first, the foundation, the substratum. Of course there were undoubtedly women who, like men, took love and marriage as the sauce of existence and their intellectual interests as the main dish. Witness for instance, Paulette. Now that she came to think of it, Paulette might vary her lovers but she never varied in the manifestation of her restless, clever mental energy. At no time did she allow her "love-life", as the psycho-analyst termed it, to interfere with her mental interests. Indeed she made no scruple of furthering these same interests by her unusual and pervasive sex charm. But this was Paulette, a remarkable personage, a woman apart. But for most women there must be the safety, the assurance of relationship that marriage affords. Indeed, most women must be able to say as did men, "You are mine," not merely, "I am yours."

A certain scorching humility thrust itself upon her. In all her manifestations of human relationships, how selfish she had been! She had left Virginia, she had taken up with Roger to further her own interests. For a brief interval she had perhaps loved Roger with the tumultuous, heady passion of hot, untried youth. But again when, this subsiding, she had tried to introduce a note of idealism, it had been with the thought of saving her own soul. She thought of her day in the park with Anthony, his uncomplaining acceptance of her verdict; his wistfully grateful: "I almost touched happiness". How easily she might have made him happy if she had turned her thoughts to his needs. But she had never thought of that; she had been too intent always on happiness for herself. Her father, her mother and Jinny had always given and she had always taken. Why was that? Jinny had sighed: "Perhaps you *have* more white blood than Negro in your veins." Perhaps this selfishness was what the possession of white blood meant; the ultimate definition of Nordic Supremacy.

Then she remembered that Anthony was white and, bewildered, she ceased trying to cogitate, to unravel, decipher, evaluate. She was lonely, she loved. She meant to find a companion; she meant to be beloved.

She must act.

None of her new friends was acquainted with Anthony. Ralph Ashley in response to a tentative question could not recall ever having seen him. The time was August, consequently he could not be at the school. Telephone books revealed nothing. "Lost in a great city!" she told herself and smiled at the cheap novel flavour of the phrase. She sent her thoughts fluttering back to the last time she had really seen Anthony, to their last intimate conversation. They had met that day after she had cut Jinny; she remembered, smiling now in her superior knowledge, the slight panic which she had experienced at his finding her in a 'bus in Harlem. There had been some chaffing about tea and he had given her his address and she had put it,—where? It was not in her address book. A feverish search through her little desk revealed it in the pages of her prayer book, the one which she had used as a child. This she considered a good omen. The bit of paper was crinkled and blurred but she was able to make out an address on One Hundred and Fourteenth Street. Suppose he were no longer there! She could not brook the thought of another night of uncertainty; it was ten o'clock but she mounted a 'bus, rode up to One Hundred and Fourteenth and Seventh Avenue. Her heart beat so loudly as she turned the corner,—it seemed as though the inhabitants of the rather shabby block hearing that human dynamo would throng their windows. The street, like many others in New York, possessed the pseudo elegance and impressiveness which comes from an equipment of brown stone houses with their massive fronts, their ostentatious regularity and simplicity, but a second glance revealed its down-at-heel condition; gaping windows disclosed the pitiful smallness of the rooms that crouched behind the pretentious outsides. There was something faintly humorous, ironical, about being cooped up in these deceptive palaces; according to one's temperament one might laugh or weep at the thought of how these structures, the product of human energy could yet cramp, imprison, even ruin the very activity which had created them.

Angela found her number, mounted the steps, sought in the dim, square hall feverishly among the names in the bells. Sullivan, Brown, Hendrickson, Sanchez,—and underneath the name of Sanchez on the same card, five small, neat characters in Anthony's inimitably clear printing—Cross. She almost fainted with the relief of it. Her fingers stole to the bell,—perhaps her onetime fellow-student was up in his room now,—how strange that this bit of gutta percha and its attendant wires should bridge all the extent of time and space that had so long lain between them! But she could not push it; Anthony, she was sure, was real enough, close enough to the heart of living to refuse to be shocked by any mere breach of the conventionalities. Even so, however, to seek at eleven o'clock at night and without preliminary warning admission to the rooms of a man whom one has not noticed for a year, was, as he himself would have put it, "a bit thick".

The little note which she sent was a model of demureness and propriety. "Dear Anthony," it read, "Do you remember my promising to ask you in for tea the next time I made a batch of cookies? Well, to-morrow at 5.30 will be the next time. Do come!"

He had changed; her interested, searching eyes descried it in a moment. Always grave, always austere, always responsible, there was now in his manner an imponderable yet perceptible increment of each quality. But this was not all; his old familiar tortured look had left him; a peace, a quality of poise hovered about him, the composure which is achieved either by the attainment or by the relinquishment of the heart's desire. There is really very little difference, since each implies the cessation of effort.

All this passed rapidly through Angela's mind. Aloud she said: "How do, Anthony? you're really looking awfully well. It's nice to see you again."

"It's nice to see you," he replied. Certainly there was nothing remarkable about their conversation. After the bantering, the jests and allusions which she had been used to hearing at the Sandburgs,—compared with the snappy jargon of Mrs. Denver's "crowd" this was trivial, not to say banal. She burst out laughing. Anthony raised his eyebrows.

"What's so funny? Is it a secret joke?"

"No,—only I've been thinking hard about you for a long time." She made a daring stroke. "Presumably you've thought occasionally about me. Yet when we meet we sit up like a dandy and a dowager with white kid gloves on and exchange comments on our appearances. I suppose the next step in order would be to talk about the weather. Have you had much rain up in One Hundred and Fourteenth Street, Mr. Cross?"

Some of his poise forsook him. The pervasive peacefulness that sat so palpably upon him deserted him like a rended veil. "You've been thinking about me for a long time? Just how long?"

"I couldn't tell you when it began." She ventured another bold stroke. "But you've been in the back of my mind,—oh for ages, ages."

The poise, the composure, the peace were all fled now. Hastily, recklessly he set down his glass of tea, came and towered over her. She bit her lips to hide their trembling. Oh he was dear, dearer than she had ever imagined, so transparent, so honest. Who was she to deserve him?

His face quivered. He should never have come near this girl! As suddenly as he had left his chair he returned to it, settled himself comfortably and picked up his glass. "I've been away from you so long I had forgotten."

"Forgotten what?"

"Forgotten how dangerous you are. Forgotten how a woman like you plays with poor fools like me. Why did you send for me? To set me dancing once more to your tune?"

His bitterness surprised and frightened her. "Anthony, Anthony don't talk like that! I sent for you because I wanted to see you, wanted to talk to my old friend."

Appeased, he lounged back in the famous and unique easy chair, lit a cigarette. She brought out some of her sketches, displayed her note-book. He was especially interested in the "Fourteenth Street Types", was pleased with the portrait of her mother. "She doesn't look like you, though I can see you probably have her hair and that pearly tint of her skin. But you must have got your nose from your father. You know all the rest of your face," he dwelt on her features dreamily, "your lips, your eyes, your curly lashes are so deliciously feminine. But that straight nose of yours betokens strength." The faded, yet striking photograph lay within reach. He picked it up, studying it thoughtfully. "What a beautiful woman;—all woman I should say. Did she have much effect on your life?"

"N-no, I can't say she did." She remembered those Saturday excursions and their adventures in "passing", so harmless, yet so far-reaching. "Oh yes, in one respect she influenced me greatly, changed my whole life."

He nodded, gazing moodily at the picture. "My mother certainly affected me."

Angela started to say glibly, "She made you what you are to-day"; but a glance at his brooding countenance made her think better of it.

"What's this?" He had turned again to the sketch book and was poring upon a mass of lightly indicated figures passing apparently in review before the tall, cloaked form of a woman, thin to emaciation, her hands on her bony hips, slightly bent forward, laughing uproariously yet with a certain chilling malevolence. "I can't make it out."

With something shamefaced in her manner she took it from him. "I'm not sure yet whether I'll develop it. I,—it's an idea that has slowly taken possession of me since I've been in New York. The tall woman is Life and the idea is that she laughs at us; laughs at the poor people who fall into the traps which she sets for us."

Sorrow set its seal on his face as perceptibly as though it had been stamped there. He came closer. "You've found that out too? If I could have managed it you would never have known it. I wanted so to keep it from you." His manner suddenly changed. "I must go. This afternoon has been perfect; I can't thank you enough,—but I'm not coming again."

"Not coming again! What nonsense! Why, why ever not? Now, Anthony, don't begin that vow business. To-day has been perfect, marvellous. You don't suppose I'm going to let my friend go when I'm really just discovering him!"

Weakly he murmured that it was foolish for them to take up each other's time; he was going away.

"All the more reason, then, why we should be seeing each other."

His glance fell on the formless sketch. "If I could only get one laugh on life. . . . When are you going to let me see you again? I'm my own man just now; my time is at your disposal."

The next afternoon they met outside her office building and dined together. On Friday they sailed to the Atlantic Highlands. Saturday, Sunday, Monday, Tuesday flashed by, meaning nothing to either except for the few hours which they spent in each other's company. Thursday was a slack day; she arranged her work so as to be free for the afternoon, and they passed the hurrying, glamorous hours in Van Cortlandt Park, laughing, jesting, relating old dreams, relapsing into silences more intimate than talk, blissfully aware of each other's presence, still more throbbingly aware of a conversation held in this very Park years ago. Back again in the little hall on Jayne Street he took her in his arms and kissed her slowly, with rapture, with adoration and she returned his kisses. For a long time he held her close against his pounding heart; she opened her languid eyes to meet his burning gaze which she could feel rather than see. Slowly he took her arms from his neck, let them drop.

"Angel, Angel, I shall love you always. Life cannot rob me of that. Good-bye, my sweetest."

He was lost in the shadowy night.

The next day passed and the next. A week sped. Absolute silence. No sign of him by either word or line.

At the end of ten days, on a never to be forgotten Sunday afternoon, she went to see him. Without conscious volition on her part she was one moment in her apartment on Jayne Street;

and at the end of an hour she was pressing a button above the name Cross in a hall on One Hundred and Fourteenth Street, hearing the door click, mounting the black well of a stair-way, tapping on a door bearing the legend "Studio".

A listless voice said "Come in."

Presently the rather tall, slender young man sitting in his shirt sleeves, his back toward her, staring dejectedly but earnestly at a picture on the table before him asked: "What can I do for you?"

The long and narrow room boasted a rather good parquet floor and a clean plain wall paper covered with unframed pictures and sketches. In one corner stood an easel; the furniture for the most part was plain but serviceable and comfortable, with the exception of an old-fashioned horse-hair sofa which Angela thought she had never seen equalled for its black shininess and its promise of stark discomfort.

On entering the apartment she had felt perturbed, but as soon as she saw Anthony and realized that the picture at which he was gazing was an unfinished sketch of herself, her worry fled. He had asked his question without turning, so she addressed his back:

"You can tell me where you found that terrible sofa; I had no idea there were any in existence. Thought they had died out with the Dodo."

The sound of her voice brought him to her side. "Angèle, tell me what are you doing here?"

She tried to keep the light touch: "Not until you have told me about the sofa." But his dark, tormented face and the strain under which she had been suffering for the past week broke down her defence. Swaying, she caught at his hand. "Anthony, Anthony, how could you?"

He put his arm about her and led her to the despised sofa; looked at her moodily. "Why did you come to see me, Angèle?"

Ordinarily she would have fenced, indulged in some fancy skirmishing; but this was no ordinary occasion; indeed in ordinary circumstances she would not have been here. She spoke gravely and proudly.

"Because I love you. Because I think you love me." A sudden terrible fear assailed her. "Oh, Anthony, don't tell me you were only playing!"

"With you? So little was I playing that the moment I began to suspect you cared,—and I never dreamed of it until that last day in the park,—I ran away from you. I knew you had so many resources; men will always adore you, want you, that I thought you'd soon forget; turn to someone else just as you had turned for a sudden whim to me from God knows how many admirers."

She shook her head, but she was frightened; some nameless fear knocking at her heart. "I turned to you from no one, Anthony. I've had only one 'admirer' as you call it in New York and I had long, long since ceased thinking of him. No, Anthony, I came to you because I needed you; you of all men in New York. I think in the world. And I thought you needed me."

They sat in silence on the terrible sofa. He seized her hand and covered it with kisses; started to take her in his arms, then let them fall in a hopeless gesture.

"It's no good, Angel; there's no use trying to buck fate. Life has caught us again. What you're talking about is absolutely impossible."

"What do you mean, impossible?" The little mute fear that had lain within her for a long time as a result of an earlier confidence of his bestirred itself, spoke.

"Anthony, those men, those enemies that killed your father, —did you kill one of them?" She had her arms about him. "You know it's nothing to me. Don't even tell me about it. Your past belongs to you; it's your future I'm interested in, that I want."

He pushed her from him, finally, even roughly. "No, I've never killed a man. Though I've wanted to. But I was a little boy when it all happened and afterwards I wouldn't go back because of my mother." He went over to a drawer and took out a revolver. "I've half a mind to kill myself now, now before I go mad thinking how I've broken my promise, broken it after all these years." He looked at her wistfully, yet implacably. "I wish that I had died long before it was given to me to see that beautiful, loving look on your face change into one of hatred and dread and anger."

She thought he must be raving; she tried to sooth him. "Never mind, Anthony; I don't care a rap about what you've done.

Only tell me why do you say everything's impossible for us? Why can't we mean everything to each other, be married——"

"Because I'm coloured." In her bewildered relief she fell away from him.

"Yes, that's right, you damned American! I'm not fit for you to touch now, am I? It was all right as long as you thought I was a murderer, a card sharp, a criminal, but the black blood in me is a bit too much, isn't it?" Beside himself he rushed to the windows, looked on the placid Sunday groups festooning the front steps of the brown stone houses. "What are you going to do, alarm the neighbourhood? Well, let me tell you, my girl, before they can get up here I'll be dead." His glance strayed to the revolver. "They'll never catch me as they did my father."

It was on the point of her tongue to tell him her great secret. Her heart within her bubbled with laughter to think how quickly she could put an end to this hysteria, how she could calm this black madness which so seethed within him, poisoning the very spring of his life. But his last words turned her thoughts to something else, to another need. How he must have suffered, loving a girl who he felt sure would betray him; yet scorning to keep up the subterfuge.

She said to him gently: "Anthony, did you think I would do that?"

His answer revealed the unspeakable depths of his acquaintance with prejudice; his incurable cynicism. "You're a white American. I know there's nothing too dastardly for them to attempt where colour is involved."

A fantastic notion seized her. Of course she would tell him that she was coloured, that she was willing to live with coloured people. And if he needed assurance of her love, how much more fully would he believe in her when he realized that not even for the sake of the conveniences to be had by passing would she keep her association with white people secret from him. But first she must try to restore his faith in human goodness. She said to him gently: "Tell me about it, Anthony."

And sitting there in the ugly, tidy room in the sunshot duskiness of the early summer evening, the half-subdued noises of the street mounting up to them, he told her his story. An old story it was, but in its new setting, coupled with the fact that

Angela for years had closed her mind to the penalty which men sometimes pay for being "different", it sounded like some unbelievable tale from the Inquisition.

His father, John Hall, of Georgia, had been a sailor and rover, but John's father was a well-known and capable farmer who had stayed in his little town and slowly amassed what seemed a fortune to the poor and mostly ignorant whites by whom he was surrounded. In the course of John's wanderings he had landed at Rio de Janeiro and he had met Maria Cruz, a Brazilian with the blood of many races in her veins. She herself was apparently white, but she looked with favour on the brown, stalwart sailor, thinking nothing of his colour, which was very much the same as that of her own father. The two married and went to many countries. But finally John, wearying of his aimless life, returned to his father, arriving a month before it was time to receive the old man's blessing and his property. Thence all his troubles. Certain white men in the neighbourhood had had their eyes turned greedily on old Anthony Hall's possessions. His son had been a wanderer for many years; doubtless he was dead. Certainly it was not expected that he would return after all these years to his native soil; most niggers leaving the South left for ever. They knew better than to return with their uppity ways.

Added to the signal injustice of John Hall's return and the disappointment caused thereby, was the iniquity of his marriage to a beautiful and apparently white wife. Little Anthony could remember his father's constant admonition to her never to leave the house; the latter had, in his sudden zeal for home, forgotten what a sojourn in Georgia could mean. But his memory was soon refreshed and he was making every effort to dispose of his new possessions without total loss. This required time and patience, but he hoped that only a few months need elapse before they might shake off the dust of this cursed hole for ever.

"Just a little patience, Maria," he told his lovely wife.

But she could not understand. True, she never ventured into the town, but an infrequent visit to the little store was imperative and she did not mind an occasional admiring glance. Indeed she attributed her husband's admonitions to his not unwelcome jealousy. Anthony, always a grave child, constituted himself her constant guardian; his father, he knew, had to be away in neighbouring townships where he was trying to put through his deal, so the little boy accompanied his silly trusting mother everywhere. When they passed a group of staring, mouthing men he contrived to hurt his finger or stub his toe so as to divert his mother's attention. In spite of his childish subterfuges, indeed because of them, his mother attracted the notice of Tom Haley, son of the magistrate. Anthony apparently had injured his hand and his beautiful mother, bending over it with great solicitude, made a picture too charming, too challenging to be overlooked. Haley stepped forward, actually touched his cap. "Can I do anything to help you, ma'am?" She looked at him with her lovely, melting eyes, spoke in her foreign liquid voice. He was sure he had made a conquest. Afterwards, chagrined by the gibes of the bystanders who jeered at him for his courtesy to a nigger wench "for that's all she is, John Hall's wife", he ground his heel in the red dust; he would show her a thing or two.

In the hot afternoon, awakened from her siesta by a sudden knock, she came to the door, greeted her admirer of the early morning. She was not quite pleased with the look in his eyes, but she could not suspect evil. Haley, who had done some wandering on his own account and had picked up a few words of Spanish, let fall an insulting phrase or two. Amazed and angry she struck him across his face. The boy, Anthony, uneasily watching, screamed; there was a sudden tumult of voices and Haley fled, forgetting for the moment that these were Negro voices and so need not be dreaded. An old coloured man, mumbling and groaning "Gawd forgive you, Honey; we'se done fer now" guided the child and the panic-stricken mother into the swamp. And lying there hidden at night they could see the sparks and flames rising from the house and buildings, which represented the labour of Anthony Hall's sixty years. In a sudden lull they caught the sounds of the pistol shots which riddled John Hall's body.

"Someone warned my father," said Anthony Cross wearily, "but he would go home. Besides, once back in town he would have been taken anyway, perhaps mobbed and burned in the public square. They let him get into his house; he washed and dressed himself for death. Before nightfall the mob came to teach this man their opinion of a nigger who hadn't taught his wife her duty toward white men. First they set fire to the house, then called him to the window. He stepped out on a little veranda; Haley opened fire. The body fell over the railing dead before it could touch the ground, murdered by the bullets from twenty pistols. Souvenir hunters cut off fingers, toes, his ears, —a friend of my grandfather found the body at night and buried it. They said it was unlike anything they had ever seen before, totally dehumanized. After I heard that story I was unable to sleep for nights on end. As for my mother,——' "

Angela pressed his head close against her shoulder. There were no words for a thing like this, only warm human contact.

He went on wanly. "As for my mother, she was like a madwoman. She has gone all the rest of her life haunted by a terrible fear."

"Of white people," Angela supplemented softly. "Yes, I can see how she would."

He glanced at her sombrely. "No, of coloured people. She believes that we, particularly the dark ones, are cursed, otherwise, why should we be so abused, so hounded. Two years after my father's death she married a white man, not an American— that was spared me,—but a German who, I believe, treats her very kindly. I was still a little boy but I begged and pleaded with her to leave the whole race alone; I told her she owed it to the memory of my father. But she only said women were poor, weak creatures; they must take protection where they could get it."

Horrified, mute with the tragedy of it all, she could only stare at him white-lipped.

"Don't ask me how I came up. Angèle, for a time I was nothing, worthless, only I have never denied my colour; I have always taken up with coloured causes. When I've had a special point to make I've allowed the world to think of me as it would but always before severing my connections I told of the black blood that was in my veins. And then it came to me that for my father's sake I would try to make something of myself. So I sloughed off my evil ways, they had been assumed only in bravado,—and came to New York where I've been living quietly, I hope usefully, keeping my bitterness within myself where it could harm no one but me.

"I made one vow and kept it,—never by any chance to allow myself to become entangled with white people; never to listen to their blandishments; always to hate them with a perfect hate. Then I met you and loved you and somehow healing began. I thought, if she loves me she'll be willing to hear me through. And if after she hears me she is willing to take me, black blood and all,—but mind," he interrupted himself fiercely, "I'm not ashamed of my blood. Sometimes I think it's the leaven that will purify this Nordic people of their cruelty and their savage lust of power."

She ignored this. "So you were always going to tell me."

"Tell you? Of course I would have told you. Oh, I'm a man, Angel, with a man's record. When I was a sailor,—there're some pages in my life I couldn't let your fingers touch. But *that* I'd have told you, it was too vital, too important. Not that I think it really means this mixture of blood, as life goes, as God meant the world to go. But here in America it could make or mar life. Of course I'd have told you."

Here was honour, here was a man! So would her father have been. Having found this comparison her mind sought no further.

A deep silence descended upon them; in his case the silence of exhaustion. But Angela was thinking of his tragic life and of how completely, how surprisingly she could change it. Smiling, she spoke to him of happiness, of the glorious future. "I've something amazing to tell you, but I won't spring it on you all at once. Can't we go out to Van Cortlandt Park to-morrow evening?"

He caught her hand. "No matter what in the goodness of your heart you may be planning, there is no future, none, none, Angel, for you and me. Don't deceive yourself,—nor me. When I'm with you I forget sometimes. But this afternoon has brought it all back to me. I'll never forget myself and my vow again."

A bell shrilled three, four times.

He looked about frowning. "That's Sanchez; he's forgotten his key again. My dear girl, my Angel, you must go,—and you must not, must not come back. Hurry, hurry! I don't want him to see you here." He guided her towards the door, stemming her protestations. "I'll write you at once, but you must go. God bless and keep you."

In another moment she was out in the dim hall, passing a dark, hurrying figure on the stairs. The heavy door swung silently behind her, thrusting her inexorably out into the engulfing summer night; the shabby pretentious house was again between her and Anthony with his tragic, searing past.

Chapter V

ALL the next day and the next she dwelt on Anthony's story; she tried to put herself in his place, to force herself into a dim realization of the dark chamber of torture in which his mind and thoughts had dwelt for so many years. And she had added her modicum of pain, had been so unsympathetic, so unyielding; in the midst of the dull suffering, the sickness of life to which perhaps his nerves had become accustomed she had managed to inject an extra pinprick of poignancy. Oh, she would reward him for that; she would brim his loveless, cheated existence with joy and sweetness; she would cajole him into forgetting that terrible past. Some day he should say to her: "You have brought me not merely new life, but life itself." Those former years should mean no more to him than its pre-natal existence means to a baby.

Her fancy dwelt on, toyed with all the sweet offices of love; the delicate bondage that could knit together two persons absolutely *en rapport*. At the cost of every ambition which she had ever known she would make him happy. After the manner of most men his work would probably be the greatest thing in the world to him. And he should be the greatest thing in the world to her. He should be her task, her "job", the fulfilment of her ambition. A phrase from the writings of Anatole France came drifting into her mind. "There is a technique of love." She would discover it, employ it, not go drifting haphazardly, carelessly into this relationship. And suddenly she saw her affair with Roger in a new light; she could forgive him, she could forgive herself for that hitherto unpardonable union if through it she had come one iota nearer to the understanding and the need of Anthony.

His silence—for although the middle of the week had passed she had received no letter,—worried her not one whit. In the course of time he would come to her, remembering her perfect sympathy of the Sunday before and thinking that this woman was the atonement for what he considered her race. And then she would surprise him, she would tell him the truth, she would make herself inexpressibly dearer and nearer to him when he came to know that her sympathy and her tenderness were real, fixed and lasting, because they were based and rooted in the same blood, the same experiences, the same comprehension of this far-reaching, stupid, terrible race problem. How inexpressibly happy, relieved and overwhelmed he would be! She would live with him in Harlem, in Africa, anywhere, any place. She would label herself, if he asked it; she would tell every member of her little coterie of white friends about her mixed blood; she would help him keep his vow and would glory in that keeping. No sacrifice of the comforts which came to her from "passing", of the assurance, even of the safety which the mere physical fact of whiteness in America brings, would be too great for her. She would withdraw where he withdrew, hate where he hated.

His letter which came on Thursday interrupted her thoughts, her fine dreams of self-immolation which women so adore. It was brief and stern, and read:

> "Angèle, don't think for one moment that I do not thank you for Sunday. . . . My heart is at your feet for what you revealed to me then. But you and I have nothing in common, have never had, and now can never have. More than race divides us. I think I shall go away. Meanwhile you are to forget me; amuse yourself, beautiful, charming, magnetic Angel with the men of your own race and leave me to my own.
>
> "ANTHONY."

It was such a strange letter; its coldness and finality struck a chill to her heart. She looked at the lonely signature, "Anthony", —just that, no word of love or affection. And the phrase: "More than race divides us." Its hidden significance held a menace.

The letter was awaiting her return from work. She had come in all glowing with the promise of the future as she conceived it. And then here were these cold words killing her high hopes as an icy blast kills the too trusting blossoms of early spring. . . . Holding the letter she let her supper go untasted, unregarded, while she evolved some plan whereby she could see Anthony, talk to him. The tone of his letter did not sound as though he would yield to ordinary persuasion. And again in the midst of her bewilderment and suffering she was struck afresh with the difficulties inherent in womanhood in conducting the most ordinary and most vital affairs of life. She was still a little bruised in spirit that she had taken it upon herself to go to Anthony's rooms Sunday; it was a step she felt conventionally, whose justification lay only in its success. As long as she had considered it successful, she had been able to relegate it to the uttermost limbo of her self-consciousness. But now that it seemed to avail nothing it loomed up before her in all its social significance. She was that creature whom men, in their selfish fear, have contrived to paint as the least attractive of human kind,—"a girl who runs after men." It seemed to her that she could not stand the application of the phrase, no matter how unjustly, how inaptly used in her own case.

Looking for a word of encouragement she re-read the note. The expression "My heart is at your feet" brought some reassurance; she remembered, too, his very real emotion of Sunday, only a few days before. Men, real men, men like Anthony, do not change. No, she could not let him go without one last effort. She would go to Harlem once more to his house, she would see him, reassure him, allay his fears, quench his silly apprehensions of non-compatability. As soon as he knew that they were both coloured, he'd succumb. Now he was overwrought. It had never occurred to her before that she might be glad to be coloured. . . . She put on her hat, walked slowly out the door, said to herself with a strange foreboding: "When I see this room again, I'll either be very happy, or very, very sad. . . ." Her courage rose, braced her, but she was sick of being courageous, she wanted to be a beloved woman, dependent, fragile, sought for, feminine; after this last ordeal she would be "womanly" to the point of ineptitude. . . .

During the long ride her spirits rose a little. After all, his attitude was almost inevitable. He thought she belonged to a race which to him stood for treachery and cruelty; he had seen her with Roger, Roger, the rich, the gay; he saw her as caring only for wealth and pleasure. Of course in his eyes she was separated from him by race and by more than race.

For long years she was unable to reconstruct that scene; her mind was always too tired, too sore to re-enact it.

As in a dream she saw Anthony's set, stern face, heard his

firm, stern voice: "Angel-girl,—Angèle I told you not to come back. I told you it was all impossible."

She found herself clutching at his arm, blurting out the truth, forgetting all her elaborate plans, her carefully pre-concerted drama. "But, Anthony, Anthony, listen, everything's all right. I'm coloured; I've suffered too; nothing has to come between us."

For a moment off his guard he wavered. "Angèle, I didn't think you'd lie to me."

She was in tears, desperate. "I'm not lying, Anthony. It's perfectly true."

"I saw that picture of your mother, a white woman if I ever saw one,——"

"Yes, but a white coloured woman. My father was black, perfectly black and I have a sister, she's brown. My mother and I used to 'pass' sometimes just for the fun of it; she didn't mind being coloured. But I minded it terribly,—until very recently. So I left my home,—in Philadelphia,—and came here to live,—oh, going for white makes life so much easier. You know it, Anthony." His face wan and terrible frightened her. "It doesn't make you angry, does it? You've passed yourself, you told me you had. Oh Anthony, Anthony, don't look at me like that! What is it?"

She caught at his hand, following him as he withdrew to the shiny couch where they both sat breathless for a moment. "God!" he said suddenly; he raised his arms, beating the void like a madman. "You in your foolishness, I in my carelessness, 'passing, passing' and life sitting back laughing, splitting her sides at the joke of it. Oh, it was all right for you,—but I didn't care whether people thought I was white or coloured,—if we'd only known,——"

"What on earth are you talking about? It's all right now."

"It isn't all right; it's worse than ever." He caught her wrist. "Angel, you're sure you're not fooling me?"

"Of course I'm not. I have proof, I've a sister right here in New York; she's away just now. But when she comes back, I'll have you meet her. She is brown and lovely,—you'll want to paint her—don't you believe me, Anthony?"

"Oh yes, I believe you," he raised his arms again in a beautiful,

fluid gesture, let them fall. "Oh, damn life, damn it, I say
. . . isn't there any end to pain!"

Frightened, she got on her knees beside him. "Anthony, what's
the matter? Everything's going to be all right; we're going to
be happy."

"You may be. I'll never be happy. You were the woman I
wanted,—I thought you were white. For my father's sake I
couldn't marry a white girl. So I gave you up."

"And I wouldn't stay given up. See, here I am back again.
You'll never be able to send me away." Laughing but shame-
faced, she tried to thrust herself into his arms.

"No, Angel, no! You don't understand. There's, there's somebody else——"

She couldn't take it in. "Somebody else. You mean,—you're
married? Oh Anthony, you don't mean you're married!"

"No, of course not, of course not! But I'm engaged."

"Engaged, engaged and not to me,—to another girl? And
you kissed me, went around with me? I knew other men did
that, but I never thought that of you! I thought you were like
my father!" And she began to cry like a little girl.

Shame-faced, he looked on, jamming his hands tightly into
his pockets. "I never meant to harm you; I never thought until
that day in the park that you would care. And I cared so terribly! Think, I had given you up, Angèle,—I suppose that isn't your
name really, is it?—all of a sudden, you came walking back into
my life and I said, 'I'll have the laugh on this dammed mess
after all. I'll spend a few days with her, love her a little, just a
little. She'll never know, and I'll have a golden memory!' Oh, I
had it coming to me, Angel! But the minute I saw you were
beginning to care I broke off short."

A line from an old text was running through her head, rendering her speechless, inattentive. She was a little girl back in
the church again in Philadelphia; the minister was intoning
"All we like sheep have gone astray". He used to put the emphasis on the first word and Jinny and she would look at each
other and exchange meaning smiles; he was a West Indian and
West Indians had a way of misplacing the emphasis. The line
sounded so funny: "*All* we like sheep,——" but perhaps it
wasn't so funny after all; perhaps he had read it like that not

because he was a West Indian but because he knew life and human nature. Certainly *she* had gone astray,—with Roger. And now here was Anthony, Anthony who had always loved her so well. Yet in his background there was a girl and he was engaged.

This brought her to a consideration of the unknown fiancée, —her rival. Deliberately she chose the word, for she was not through yet. This unknown, unguessed at woman who had stolen in like a thief in the night. . . .

"Have you known her long?" she asked him sharply.

"Who? Oh my,—my friend. No, not as long as I've known you."

A newcomer, an upstart. Well at least she, Angela, had the advantage of precedence.

"She's coloured, of course?"

"Of course."

They sat in a weary silence. Suddenly he caught her in his arms and buried his head in her neck. A quick pang penetrated to the very core of her being. He must have been an adorable baby. . . . Anthony and babies!

"Now God, Life, whatever it is that has power, this time you must help me!" cried her heart. She spoke to him gently.

"Anthony, you know I love you. Do you still love me?"

"Always, always, Angel."

"Do you—Oh, Anthony, I don't deserve it, but do you by any chance worship me?"

"Yes, that's it, that's just it, I worship you. I adore you. You are God to me. Oh, Angèle, if you'd only let me know. But it's too late now."

"No, no don't say that, perhaps it isn't too late. It all depends on this. Do you worship *her*, Anthony?" He lifted his haggard face.

"No—but she worships *me*. I'm God to her do you see? If I fail her she won't say anything, she'll just fall back like a little weak kitten, like a lost sheep, like a baby. She'll die." He said as though unaware of his listener. "She's such a little thing. And sweet."

Angela said gently: "Tell me about her. Isn't it all very sudden? You said you hadn't known her long."

He began obediently. "It was not long after I—I lost you.

She came to me out of nowhere, came walking to me into my room by mistake; she didn't see me. And she put her head down on her hands and began to cry terribly. I had been crying too—in my heart, you understand,—and for a moment I thought she might be the echo of that cry, might be the cry itself. You see, I'd been drinking a little,—you were so far removed, white and all that sort of thing. I couldn't marry a white woman, you know, not a white American. I owed that to my father.

"But at last I saw it was a girl, a real girl and I went over to her and put my hand on her shoulder and said: 'Little girl, what's the matter?'

"And she lifted her head, still hidden in the crook of her arm, you know the way a child does and said: 'I've lost my sister'. At first I thought she meant lost in the street and I said "Well, come with me to the police station, I'll go with you, we'll give them a description and you'll find her again. People don't stay lost in this day and time'. I got her head on my shoulder, I almost took her on my knee, Angèle, she was so simple and forlorn. And presently she said: 'No, I don't mean lost that way; I mean she's left me, she doesn't want me any more. She wants other people'. And I've never been able to get anything else out of her. The next morning I called her up and somehow I got to seeing her, for her sake, you know. But afterwards when she grew happier,—she was so blithe, so lovely, so healing and blessed like the sun or a flower,—then I saw she was getting fond of me and I stayed away.

"Well, I ran across you and that Fielding fellow that night at the Van Meier lecture. And you were so happy and radiant, and Fielding so possessive,—damn him!—damn him!—he—you didn't let him hurt you Angèle?"

As though anything that had ever happened in her life could hurt her like this! She had never known what pain was before. White-lipped, she shook her head. "No, he didn't hurt me."

"Well, I went to see her the next day. She came into the room like a shadow,—I realized she was getting thin. She was kind and sweet and far-off; impalpable, tenuous and yet there. I could see she was dying for me. And all of a sudden it came to me how wonderful it would be to have someone care like that. I went to her; I took her in my arms and I said: 'Child,

child, I'm not bringing you a whole heart but could you love me?' You see I couldn't let her go after that."

"No," Angela's voice was dull, lifeless. "You couldn't. She'd die."

"Yes, that's it; that's just it. And I know you won't die, Angel."

"No, you're quite right. I won't die."

An icy hand was on her heart. At his first words: "She came walking into my room,——" an icy echo stirred a memory deep, deep within her inner consciousness. She heard Jinny saying: "I went walking into his room,——"

Something stricken, mortally stricken in her face fixed his attention. "Don't look like that, my girl, my dear Angel. . . . There are three of us in this terrible plight,—if I had only known. . . . I don't deserve the love of either of you but if one of you two must suffer it might as well be she as you. Come, we'll go away; even unhappiness, even remorse will mean something to us as long as we're together."

She shook her head. "No, that's impossible,—if it were someone else, I don't know, perhaps—I'm so sick of unhappiness, —maybe I'd take a chance. But in her case it's impossible."

He looked at her curiously. "What do you mean 'in her case'?"

"Isn't her name Virginia Murray?"

"Yes, yes! How did you guess it? Do you know her?"

"She's my sister. Angèle Mory,—Angela Murray, don't you see. It's the same name. And it's all my fault. I pushed her, sent her deliberately into your arms."

He could only stare.

"I'm the unkind sister who didn't want her. Oh, can't you understand? That night she came walking into your room by mistake it was because I had gone to the station to meet her and Roger Fielding came along. I didn't want him to know that I was coloured and I,—I didn't acknowledge her, I cut her."

"Oh," he said surprised and inadequate. "I don't see how you could have done that to a little girl like Virginia. Did she know New York?"

"No." She drooped visibly. Even the loss of him was nothing compared to this rebuke. There seemed nothing further to be said.

Presently he put his arm about her. "Poor Angèle. As though

you could foresee! It's what life does to us, leads us into pitfalls apparently so shallow, so harmless and when we turn around there we are, caught, fettered,——"

Her miserable eyes sought his. "I was sorry right away, Anthony. I tried my best to get in touch with her that very evening. But I couldn't find her;—already you see, life was getting even with me, she had strayed into your room."

He nodded. "Yes, I remember it all so plainly. I was getting ready to go out, was all prepared as a matter of fact. Indeed I moved that very night. But I loitered on and on, thinking of you.

"The worst of it is I'll always be thinking of you. Oh Angèle, what does it matter, what does anything matter if we just have each other? This damned business of colour, is it going to ruin all chances of happiness? I've known trouble, pain, terrible devastating pain all my life. You've suffered too. Together perhaps we could find peace. We'd go to your sister and explain. She is kind and sweet; surely she'd understand."

He put his arms about her and the two clung to each other, solemnly, desperately, like children.

"I'm sick of pain, too, Anthony, sick of longing and loneliness. You can't imagine how I've suffered from loneliness."

"Yes, yes I can. I guessed it. I used to watch you. I thought you were probably lonely inside, you were so different from Miss Lister and Mrs. Starr. Come away with me and we'll share our loneliness together, somewhere where we'll forget——"

"And Virginia? You said yourself she'd die,——"

"She's so young, she—she could get over it." But his tone was doubtful, wavering.

She tore herself from him. "No, I took her sister away from her; I won't take her lover. Kiss me good-bye, Anthony."

They sat on the hard sofa. "To think we should find one another only to lose each other! To think that everything, every single thing was all right for us but that we were kept apart by the stupidity of fate. I'd almost rather we'd never learned the truth. Put your dear arms about me closer, Angel, Angel. I want the warmth, the sweetness of you to penetrate into my heart. I want to keep it there forever. Darling, how can I let you go?"

She clung to him weeping, weeping with the heart-broken abandonment of a child.

A bell shrilled four times.

He jumped up. "It's Sanchez, he's forgotten his key; thank God he did forget it. My darling, you must go. But wait for me. I'll meet you,—we'll go to your house, we'll find a way. We can't part like this!" His breath was coming in short gasps; she could see little white lines deepening about his mouth, his nostrils. Fearfully she caught at her hat.

"God bless you; good-bye Anthony. I won't see you again."

Halfway down the black staircase she met the heedless Sanchez, tall, sallow, thin, glancing at her curiously with a slightly amused smile. Politely he stood aside to let her pass, one hand resting lightly against his hip. Something in his attitude made her think of her unfinished sketch of Life. Hysterical, beside herself, she rushed down the remaining steps afraid to look around lest she should see the thin dark figure in pursuit, lest her ears should catch the expansion of that faint meaning smile into a guffaw, uproarious, menacing.

Chapter VI

ONCE long ago in the old days in the house on Opal Street she had been taken mysteriously ill. As a matter of fact she had been coming down with that inglorious disease, the mumps. The expense of having a doctor was a consideration, and so for twenty-four hours she was the object of anxious solicitude for the whole house. Her mother had watched over her all night; her father came home twice in the day to see how she felt; Jinny had with some reluctance bestowed on her an oft-coveted, oft-refused doll. In the midst of all her childish pain and suffering she had realized that at least her agony was shared, that her tribulation was understood. But now she was ill with a sickness of the soul and there was no one with whom she could share her anguish.

For two days she lay in her little room; Mrs. Denver, happening in, showered upon her every attention. There was nothing, nothing that Angela could suggest, the little fluttering lady said sincerely, which she might not have. Angela wished that she would go away and leave her alone, but her experiences had rendered her highly sensitive to the needs of others; Mrs. Denver, for all her money, her lack of responsibility, her almost childish appetite for pleasure, was lonely too; waiting on the younger, less fortunate woman gave her a sense of being needed; she was pathetically glad when the girl expressed a desire for anything no matter how expensive or how trivial. Angela could not deprive her entirely of those doubtful pleasures. Still there were moments, of course, when even Mrs. Denver for all her kindly officiousness had to betake herself elsewhere and leave her willing patient to herself and her thoughts.

Minutely, bit by bit, in the long forty-eight hours she went over her life; was there anything, any over tact, any crime which she had committed and for which she might atone? She had been selfish, yes; but, said her reasoning and unwearied mind, "Everybody who survives at all is selfish, it is one of the prerequisites of survival." In "passing" from one race to the other she had done no harm to anyone. Indeed she had been forced to take this action. But she should not have forsaken Virginia.

Here at this point her brain, so clear and active along all other lines, invariably failed her. She could not tell what stand to take; so far as leaving Philadelphia was concerned she had left it to seek her fortune under more agreeable circumstances; if she had been a boy and had left home no one would have had a word of blame, it would have been the proper thing, to be expected and condoned. There remained then only the particular incident of her cutting Jinny on that memorable night in the station. That was the one really cruel and unjust action of her whole life.

"Granted," said something within her rooted either in extreme hard common sense or else in a vast sophistry, "granted, but does that carry with it as penalty the shattering of a whole life, or even the suffering of years? Certainly the punishment is far in excess of the crime." And it was then that she would lie back exhausted, hopeless, bewildered, unable to cope further with the myterious and apparently meaningless ferocity of life. For if this were a just penalty for one serious misdemeanour, what compensation should there not be for the years in which she had been a dutiful daughter, a loving sister? And suddenly she found herself envying people possessed of a blind religious faith, of the people who could bow the head submissively and whisper: "Thy will be done." For herself she could see how beaten and harried, one might subside into a sort of blind passivity, an acceptance of things as they are, but she would never be able to understand a force which gave one the imagination to paint a great desire, the tenacity to cling to it, the emotionalism to spend on its possible realization but which would then with a careless sweep of the hand wipe out the picture which the creature of its own endowment had created.

More than once the thought came to her of dying. But she hated to give up; something innate, something of the spirit stronger than her bodily will, set up a dogged fight, and she was too bruised and sore to combat it. "All right," she said to herself wearily, "I'll keep on living." She thought then of black people, of the race of her parents and of all the odds against living which a cruel, relentless fate had called on them to endure. And she saw them as a people powerfully, almost overwhelmingly endowed with the essence of life. They had to persist, had to survive because they did not know how to die.

*

Not because she felt like it, but because some day she must begin once more to take up the motions of life, she moved on the third day from her bed to the easy chair, sat there listless and motionless. To-morrow she would return to work,—to work and the sick agony of forcing her mind back from its dolorous, painful, vital thoughts to some consideration of the dull, uninteresting task in hand. God, how she hated that! She remembered studying her lessons as a girl; the intense absorption with which she used to concentrate. Sometimes she used to wonder: "Oh what will it be like when I am grown up; when I won't be studying lessons . . ." Well, this was what it was like. Or no, she was still studying with the same old absorption,—an absorption terribly, painfully concentrated,—the lessons set down by life. It was useless to revolve in her head the causes for her suffering, they were so trivial, so silly. She said to herself, "There is no sorrow in the world like my sorrow", and knew even as she said it that some one else, perhaps only in the next block, in the next house, was saying the same thing.

Mrs. Denver tapped lightly, opened the door, came in closing it mysteriously behind her.

"I've a great surprise for you." She went on with an old childish formula: "Will you have it now, or wait till you get it?"

Angela's features twisted into a wan smile. "I believe I'd better have it now. I'm beginning to think I don't care for surprises."

"You'll like this one." She went to the door and ushered in Rachel Salting.

"I know you two want to talk," Mrs. Denver called over her shoulder. "Cheer her up, Rachel, and I'll bring you both a fine spread in an hour or so." She closed the door carefully behind her.

Angela said, "What's the matter, Rachel?" She almost added, "I hardly knew you." For her friend's face was white and wan with grief and hopelessness; gone was all her dainty freshness, her pretty colour; indeed her eyes, dark, sunken, set in great pools of blackness, were the only note,—a terrible note,—of relief against that awful whiteness.

Angela felt her strength leaving her; she rose and tottered

back to the grateful security of her bed, lay down with an over-whelming sense of thankfulness for the asylum afforded her sudden faintness. In a moment, partly recovered, she motioned to Rachel to sit beside her.

"Oh," said Rachel, "you've been ill,—Mrs. Denver told me. I ought not to come bothering you with my worries. Oh, Angèle, I'm so wretched! Whatever shall I do?"

Her friend, watching her, was very gentle. "There're lots of awful things that can happen. I know that, Rachel. Maybe your trouble isn't so bad that it can't be helped. Have you told John about it?" But even as she spoke she sensed that the difficulty in some way concerned John. Her heart contracted at the thought of the pain and suffering to be endured.

"Yes, John knows,—it's about him. Angèle, we can't marry."

"Can't marry. Why, is he,—it can't be that he's—involved with some one else!"

A momentary indignation flashed into Rachel's face bring-ing back life and colour. For a small space she was the Rachel Salting of the old happy days. "Involved with some one else!" The indignation was replaced by utter despair. "How I wish he were! That at least could be arranged. But this can never be al-tered. He,—I, our parents are dead set against it. Hadn't you ever noticed, Angèle? He's a Gentile and I'm a Jew."

"But lots of Jews and Gentiles marry."

"Yes, I know. Only—he's a Catholic. But my parents are orthodox—they will never consent to my marriage. My father says he'd rather see me dead and my mother just sits and moans. I kept it from her as long as I could,—I used to pray about it, I thought God must let it turn out all right, John and I love each other so. But I went up to Utica the other day, John went with me, and we told them. My father drove him out of the house; he said if I married him he'd curse me. I am afraid of that curse. I can't go against them. Oh, Angèle, I wish I'd never been born."

It was a delicate situation; Angela had to feel her way; she could think of nothing but the trite and obvious. "After all, Rachel, your parents have lived their lives; they have no busi-ness trying to live yours. Personally I think all this pother about race and creed and colour, tommyrot. In your place I should certainly follow my own wishes; John seems to be the man for you."

But Rachel weeping, imbued with the spirit of filial piety, thought it would be selfish.

"Certainly no more selfish than their attempt to regulate your life for you."

"But I'm afraid," said Rachel shivering, "of my father's curse." It was difficult for Angela to sympathize with an attitude so archaic; she was surprised to find it lurking at the bottom of her friend's well-trained intelligence.

"Love," she said musing to herself rather than to her friend, "is supposed to be the greatest thing in the world but look how we smother and confine it. Jews mustn't marry Catholics; white people mustn't marry coloured——"

"Oh well, of course not," Rachel interrupted in innocent surprise. "I wouldn't marry a nigger in any circumstances. Why, would you?"

But Angela's only answer was to turn and, burying her head in her pillow, to burst into unrestrained and bitter laughter. Rachel went flying to call Mrs. Denver.

"Oh come quick, come quick! Angèle's in hyterics. I haven't the ghost of an idea what to do for her!"

Once more the period of readjustment. Once more the determination to take life as she found it; bitter dose after sweet, bitter after sweet. But it seemed to her now that both sweetness and bitterness together with her high spirit for adventure lay behind her. How now was she to pass through the tepid, tasteless days of her future? She was not quite twenty-seven, and she found herself wondering what life would be like in ten, five, even one year's time. Changes did flow in upon one, she knew, but in her own case she had been so used herself to give the impetus to these changes. Now she could not envisage herself as making a move in any direction. With the new sullenness which seemed to be creeping upon her daily, she said "Whatever move I make is always wrong. Let life take care of itself." And she saw life, even her own life, as an entity quite outside her own ken and her own directing. She did not care greatly what happened; she would not, it was true, take her own life, but she would not care if she should die. Once if her mind had harboured such thoughts she would have felt an instant self-pity. "What a shame that I so young, so gifted, with spirits so high should meet with death!" But now her senses were blunting; so much pain and confusion had brought about their inevitable attrition. "I might just as well be unhappy, or meet death as anyone else," she told herself still with that mounting sullenness.

Mrs. Denver, the Sandburgs and Ashley were the only people who saw her. It did seem to Mrs. Denver that the girl's ready, merry manner was a little dimmed; if her own happy, sunny vocabulary had known the term she would have daubed her cynical. The quasi-intellectual atmosphere at the Sandburgs suited her to perfection; the faint bitterness which so constantly marred her speech was taken for sophistication, her frequent silences for profoundness; in a small way, aided by her extraordinary good looks and the slight mystery which always hung about her, she became quite a personage in their entourage; the Sandburgs considered her a splendid find and plumed themselves on having "brought her out".

The long golden summer, so beautiful with its promise of happiness, so sickening with its actuality of pain ripened into early, exquisite September. Virginia was home again; slightly more golden, very, very faintly plumper, like a ripening fruit perfected; brimming with happiness, excitement and the most complete content, Angela thought, that she had ever seen in her life.

Jinny sent for the older girl and the two sat on a Sunday morning, away from Sara Penton and the other too insistent friends, over on Riverside Drive looking out at the river winding purple and alluring in the soft autumn haze.

"Weren't you surprised?" asked Jinny. Laconically, Angela admitted to no slight amazement. She still loved her sister but more humbly, less achingly than before. Their lives, she thought now would never, could never touch and she was quite reconciled. Moreover, in some of Virginia's remarks there was the hint of the acceptance of such a condition. Something had brought an irrevocable separation. They would always view each other from the two sides of an abyss, narrow but deep, deep.

The younger girl prattled on. "I don't know whether Sara told you his name,—Anthony Cross? Isn't it a dear name?"

"Yes, it's a nice name, a beautiful name," said Angela heartily; when she had learned it was of no consequence. She added without enthusiasm that she knew him already; he had been a member of her class at Cooper Union.

"You don't talk as though you were very much taken with him," said Jinny, making a face. "But never mind, he suits me, no matter whom he doesn't suit." There was that in her countenance which made Angela realize and marvel again at the resoluteness of that firm young mind. No curse of parents could have kept Virginia from Anthony's arms. As long as Anthony loved her, was satisfied to have her love, no one could come between them. Only if he should fail her would she shrivel up and die.

On the heels of this thought Virginia made an astounding remark: "You know it's just perfect that I met Anthony; he's really been a rock in a weary land. Next to Matthew Henson he will, I'm sure, make me happier than any man in the world." Dreamily she added an afterthought: "And I'll make him happy too, but, oh, Angela, Angela, I always wanted to marry Matthew!"

The irony of that sent Angela home. Virginia wanting Matthew and marrying Anthony; Anthony wanting Angela and marrying Virginia. Herself wanting Anthony and marrying, wanting, no other; unable to think of, even to dream of another lover. The irony of it was so palpable, so ridiculously palpable that it put her in a better mood; life was bitter but it was amusingly bitter; if she could laugh at it she might be able to outwit it yet. The thought brought Anthony to mind: "If I could only get a laugh on life, Angèle!"

Sobered, she walked from the 'bus stop to Jayne Street. Halfway up the narrow, tortuous stair case she caught sight of a man climbing, climbing. He stopped outside her door. "Anthony?" she said to herself while her heart twisted with pain. "If it is Anthony,——" she breathed, and stopped. But something within her, vital, cruel, persistent, completed her thought. "If it is Anthony,—after what Virginia said this morning,—if he knew that he was not the first, that even as there had been one other there might still be others; that Virginia in her bright, hard, shallow youthfulness would not die any more than she had died over Matthew,—would console herself for the loss of Anthony even as she had consoled herself for the loss of Matthew!" But no, what Jinny had told her was in confidence, a confidence from sister to sister. She would never break faith with Jinny again; nor with herself.

"But Anthony," she said to herself in the few remaining seconds left on the staircase, "you were my first love and I think I was yours."

However, the man at the door was not Anthony; on the contrary he was, she thought, a complete stranger. But as he turned at her footsteps, she found herself looking into the blue eyes of Roger. Completely astounded, she greeted him, "You don't mean it's you, Roger?"

"Yes," he said humbly, shamefacedly, "aren't you going to let me in, Angèle?"

"Oh yes, of course, of course"; she found herself hoping that he would not stay long. She wanted to think and she would like to paint; that idea must have been in the back of her head ever since she had left Jinny. Hard on this thought came another. "Here's Roger. I never expected to see him in these rooms again; perhaps some day Anthony will come back. Oh, God, be kind!"

But she must tear her thoughts away from Anthony. She looked at Roger curiously, searchingly; in books the man who had treated his sweetheart unkindly often returned beaten, dejected, even poverty-stricken, but Roger, except for a slight hesitation in his manner, seemed as jaunty, as fortunate, as handsome as ever. He was even a trifle stouter.

Contrasting him with Anthony's hard-bitten leanness, she addressed him half absently. "I believe you're actually getting fat!"

His quick high flush revealed his instant sensitiveness to her criticism. But he was humble. "That's all right, Angèle. I deserve anything you choose to say if you'll just say it."

She was impervious to his mood, utterly indifferent, so indifferent that she was herself unaware of her manner. "Heavens,

I've sort of forgotten, but I don't remember your ever having been so eager for criticism heretofore!"

He caught at one phrase. "Forgotten! You don't mean to say you've forgotten the past and all that was once so dear to us?"

Impatience overwhelmed her. She wished he would go and leave her to her thoughts and to her picture; such a splendid idea had come to her; it was the first time for weeks that she had felt like working. Aware of the blessed narcotic value of interesting occupation, she looked forward to his departure with a sense of relief; even hoped with her next words to precipitate it.

"Roger, you don't mean to say that you called on me on a hot September Sunday just to talk to me in that theatrical manner? I don't mind telling you I've a million things to do this afternoon; let's get down to bed rock so we can both be up and doing."

She had been sitting, almost lolling at ease in the big chair, not regarding him, absently twisting a scarf in her fingers. Now she glanced up and something in the hot blueness of his eyes brought her to an upright position, alert, attentive.

"Angèle, you've got to take me back."

"Back! I don't know what you're talking about. Between you and me there is no past, so don't mention it. If you've nothing better to say than that, you might as well get out."

He tried to possess himself of her hands but she shook him off, impatiently, angrily, with no pretence at feeling. "Go away, Roger. I don't want to be bothered with you!" This pinchbeck emotionalism after the reality of her feeling for Anthony, the sincerity of his feeling for her! "I won't have this sort of thing; if you won't go I will." She started for the door but he barred her way, suddenly straight and serious.

"No listen, Angèle, you must listen. I'm in earnest this time. You must forgive me for the past, for the things I said. Oh, I was unspeakable! But I had it in my head,—you don't know the things a man has borne in on him about designing women,—if he's got anything, family, money,——" she could see him striving to hide his knowledge of his vast eligibility. "I thought you were trying to 'get' me, it made me suspicious, angry. I knew you were poor,——"

"And nobody! Oh say it, say it!"

"Well, I will say it. According to my father's standards, nobody. And when you began to take an interest in me, in my affairs,——"

"You thought I was trying to marry you. Well, at first I was. I was poor, I was nobody! I wanted to be rich, to be able to see the world, to help people. And then when you and I came so near to each other I didn't care about marriage at all—just about living! Oh, I suppose my attitude was perfectly pagan. I hadn't meant to drift into such a life, all my training was against it, you can't imagine how completely my training was against it. And then for a time I was happy. I'm afraid I didn't love you really, Roger, indeed I know now that in a sense I didn't love you, but somehow life seemed to focus into an absolute perfection. Then you became petulant, ugly, suspicious, afraid of my interest, of my tenderness. And I thought, 'I can't let this all end in a flame of ugliness; it must be possible for people to have been lovers and yet remain friends.' I tried so hard to keep things so that it would at least remain a pleasant memory. But you resented my efforts. What I can't understand is—why shouldn't I, if I wanted to, either try to marry you or to make an ideal thing of our relationship? Why is it that men like you resent an effort on our part to make our commerce decent? Well, it's all over now. . . . Theoretically 'free love' or whatever you choose to call it, is all right. Actually, it's all wrong. I don't want any such relationship with you or with any other man in this world. Marriage was good enough for my mother, it's good enough for me."

"There's nothing good enough for you, Angèle; but marriage is the best thing that I have to offer and I'm offering you just that. And it's precisely because you were honest and frank and decent and tried to keep our former relationship from deteriorating into sordidness that I am back."

Clearly she was staggered. Marriage with Roger meant protection, position, untold wealth, unlimited opportunities for doing good. Once how she would have leapt to such an offer!

"What's become of Carlotta?" she asked bluntly.

"She's on the eve of marrying Tom Estes, a fellow who was in college with me. He has heaps more money than I. Carlotta thought she'd better take him on."

"I see." She looked at him thoughtfully, then the remembrance of her great secret came to her, a secret which she could never share with Roger. No! No more complications and their consequent disaster! "No, no, we won't talk about it any more. What you want is impossible; you can't guess how completely impossible."

He strode toward her, seized her hands. "I'm in earnest, Angèle; you've no idea how tired I am of loneliness and uncertainty and,—and of seeking women; I want someone whom I can love and trust, whom I can teach to love me,—we could get married to-morrow. There's not an obstacle in our way."

His sincerity left her unmoved. "What would your father say?"

"Oh, we wouldn't be able to tell him yet; he'd never consent! Of course we'd have to keep things quiet, just ourselves and one or two friends, Martha and Ladislas perhaps, would be in the know."

More secrets! She pulled her hands away from him. "Oh Roger, Roger! I wouldn't consider it. No, when I marry I want a man, a man, a real one, someone not afraid to go on his own!" She actually pushed him toward the door. "Some people might revive dead ashes, but not you and I. . . . I'd never be able to trust you again and I'm sick of secrets and playing games with human relationships. I'm going to take my friendships straight hereafter. Please go. I've had a hard summer and I'm very tired. Besides I want to work."

Baffled, he looked at her, surprise and indignation struggling in his face. "Angèle, are you sure you know what you're doing? I've no intention of coming back, so you'd better take me now."

"Of course you're not coming back! I'm sure I wouldn't want you to; my decision is final." Not unsympathetically she laughed up into his doleful face, actually touched his cheek. "If you only knew how much you look like a cross baby!"

Her newly developed sympathy and understanding made her think of Ashley. Doubtless Carlotta's defection would hit him very hard. Her conjecture was correct although the effect of the blow was different from what she had anticipated. Ashley was not so perturbed over the actual loss of the girl as confirmed in his opinion that he was never going to be able to form and keep a lasting friendship. In spite of his wealth, his native timidity had always made him distrustful of himself with women of his own class; a veritable Tony Hardcastle, he spent a great deal of time with women whom he did not actually admire, whom indeed he disliked, because, he said to Angela wistfully, they were the only ones who took him seriously.

"No one but you and Carlotta have ever given me any consideration, have ever liked me for myself, Angèle."

They were seeing a great deal of each other; in a quiet, unemotional way they were developing a real friendship. Angela had taken up her painting again. She had re-entered the classes at Cooper Union and was working with great zest and absorption on a subject which she meant to enter in the competition for scholarships at the school at Fontainebleau. Ashley, who wrote some good verse in the recondite, falsely free style of the present day, fell into the habit of bringing his work down to her little living room, and in the long tender autumn evenings the two worked seriously, with concentration. Ashley had travelled widely and had seen a great deal of life, though usually from the sidelines; Angela for all her lack of wandering, "had lived deeply", he used to tell her, pondering on some bit of philosophy which she let fall based on the experiences of her difficult life.

"You know, in your way you're quite a wonder, Angèle; there's a mystery hanging about you; for all your good spirits, your sense of humour, you're like the Duse, you seem to move in an aura of suffering, of the pain which comes from too great sensitivity. And yet how can that be so? You're not old enough, you've had too few contacts to know how unspeakable life can be, how damnably she can get you in wrong,——"

An enigmatic smile settled on her face. "I don't know about life, Ralph? How do you think I got the idea for this masterpiece of mine?" She pointed to the painting on which she was then engaged.

"That's true, that's true. I've wondered often about that composition; lots of times I've meant to ask you how you came to evolve it. But keep your mystery to yourself, child; it adds to your charm."

About this she had her own ideas. Mystery might add to the charm of personality but it certainly could not be said to add to the charm of living. Once she thought that stolen waters were sweetest, but now it was the unwinding road and the open book that most intrigued.

Ashley, she found, for all his shyness, possessed very definite ideas and convictions of his own, was absolutely unfettered in his mode of thought, and quite unmoved by social traditions and standards. An aristocrat if ever there were one, he believed none the less in the essential quality of man and deplored the economic conditions which so often tended to set up superficial and unreal barriers which make as well as separate the classes.

With some trepidation Angela got him on the subject of colour. He considered prejudice the greatest blot on America's shield. "We're wrong, all wrong about those people; after all they did to make America habitable! Some day we're going to wake up to our shame. I hope it won't be too late."

"But you wouldn't want your sister to marry a nigger!"

"I'm amazed, Angèle, at your using such a word as an exclusive term. I've known some fine coloured people. There're hardly any of unmixed blood in the United States, so the term Negro is usually a misnomer. I haven't a sister; if I had I'd advise her against marriage with an American coloured man because the social pressure here would probably be too great, but that would be absolutely the only ground on which I'd object to it. And I can tell you this; I wouldn't care to marry a woman from the Congo but if I met a coloured woman of my own nationality, well-bred, beautiful, sympathetic, I wouldn't let the fact of her mixed blood stand in my way, I can tell you."

A sort of secondary interest in living was creeping into to her perspective. The high lights, the high peaks had faded from her sight. She would never, she suspected, know such spontaneity of feeling and attitude again as she had felt toward both Roger and Anthony. Nor would she again approach the experiences of existence with the same naïve expectation, the same desire to see how things would turn out. Young as she was she felt like a battle-scarred veteran who, worn out from his own strenuous activities, was quite content to sit on the side-lines gazing at all phases of warfare with an equal eye.

Although she no longer intended to cast in her lot with Virginia, she made no further effort to set up barriers between herself and coloured people. Let the world take her as it would. If she were in Harlem, in company with Virginia and Sara Penton she went out to dinner, to the noisy, crowded, friendly "Y" dining-room, to "Gert's" tearoom, to the clean, inviting drug-store for rich "sundaes". Often, too, she went shopping with her sister and to the theatre; she had her meet Ashley and Martha. But she was careful in this company to avoid contact with people whose attitude on the race question was unknown, or definitely antagonistic.

Harlem intrigued her; it was a wonderful city; it represented, she felt, the last word in racial pride, integrity and even self-sacrifice. Here were people of a very high intellectual type, exponents of the realest and most essential refinement living cheek by jowl with coarse or ill-bred or even criminal, certainly indifferent, members of their race. Of course some of this propinquity was due to outer pressure, but there was present, too, a hidden consciousness of race-duty, a something which if translated said: "Perhaps you do pull me down a little from the height to which I have climbed. But on the other hand, perhaps, I'm helping you to rise."

There was a hair-dresser's establishment on 136th Street where Virginia used to have her beautiful hair treated; where Sara Penton, whose locks were of the same variety as Matthew's, used to repair to have their unruliness "pressed". Here on Saturdays Angela would accompany the girls and sit through the long process just to overhear the conversations, grave and gallant and gay, of these people whose blood she shared but whose disabilities by a lucky fluke she had been able to avoid. For, while she had been willing for the sake of Anthony to re-enlist in the struggles of this life, she had never closed her eyes to its disadvantages; to its limitedness! What a wealth of courage it took for these people to live! What high degree of humour, determination, steadfastness, undauntedness were not needed,—and poured forth! Maude, the proprietress of the business, for whom the establishment was laconically called "Maude's", was a slight, sweet-faced woman with a velvety seal-brown skin, a charming voice and an air of real refinement. She was from Texas, but had come to New York to seek her fortune, had travelled as ladies' maid in London and Paris, and was as thoroughly conversant with the arts of her calling as any hairdresser in the vicinity of the Rue de la Paix or on Fifth Avenue. A rare quality of hospitality emanated from her presence; her little shop was always full not only of patrons but of callers, visitors from "down home", actresses from the current coloured "show", flitting in like radiant birds of paradise with their rich brown skins, their exotic eyes and the gaily coloured clothing which an unconscious style had evolved just for them.

In this atmosphere, while there was no coarseness, there was no restriction; life in busy Harlem stopped here and yawned for a delicious moment before going on with its pressure and problems. A girl from Texas, visiting "the big town" for a few weeks took one last glance at her shapely, marvellously "treated" head, poised for a second before the glass and said simply, "Well, good-bye, Maude; I'm off for the backwoods, but I'll never forget Harlem." She passed out with the sinuous elegant carriage acquired in her few weeks' sojourn on Seventh Avenue.

A dark girl, immaculate in white from head to foot, asked: "What's she going back South for? Ain't she had enough of Texas *yet?*"

Maude replied that she had gone back there because of her property. "Her daddy owns most of the little town where they live."

"Child, ain't you learned that you don't *never* own no property in Texas as long as those white folks are down there too? Just let those Ku Kluxers get it into their heads that you've got something they want. She might just as well leave there first as last; she's bound to have to some day. I know it's more'n a notion to pull up stakes and start all over again in a strange town and a strange climate, but it's the difference between life and death. I know I done it and I don't expect ever to go back."

She was a frail woman, daintily dressed and shod. Her voice was soft and drawling. But Angela saw her sharply as the epitome of the iron and blood in a race which did not know how to let go of life.

MARKET IS DONE

Chapter I

THE eternal routine of life went on,—meals, slumber, talk, work—and all of it meaning nothing; a void starting nowhere and leading nowhither; a "getting through" with the days. Gradually however two points fixed themselves in her horizon, and about these her life revolved. One was her work, —her art. Every week found her spending three or four of its nights at her easel. She was feverishly anxious to win one of the prizes in the contest which would be held in May; if successful she would send in her application for registration in the Fountainebleau School of Fine Arts which was financed by Americans and established, so read the circular, "as a summer school for American architects, painters and sculptors". If she were successful in winning this, she would leave the United States for a year or two, thus assuring herself beyond question of a new deal of the cards. The tenacity with which she held to this plan frightened her a little until she found out that there were also possible funds from which she could, with the proper recommendation, borrow enough money to enable her to go abroad with the understanding that the refund was to be made by slow and easy payments. Ashley discovered this saving information, thus relieving her of the almost paralyzing fear which beset her from time to time. It both amused and saddened her to realize that her talent which she had once used as a blind to shield her real motives for breaking loose and coming to New York had now become the greatest, most real force in her life.

Miss Powell, with whom Angela in her new mood had arranged a successful truce, knew of her ambition, indeed shared it. If she herself should win a prize, that money, combined with some small savings of her own and used in connection with the special terms offered by the American Committee, would mean the fruition of her dearest dreams. All this she confided to Angela on two Sunday mornings which the latter spent with her in her rather compressed quarters up in 134th Street. A dwelling house nearby had been converted into a place of worship for one of the special divisions of religious creed so dear to coloured people's heart. Most of the service seemed to consist of singing, and so the several hours spent by the two girls in earnest talk were punctuated by the outbursts of song issuing from the brazen-coated throats of the faithful.

The other point about which her thoughts centred was her anomalous position. Yet that clear mind of hers warned her again and again that there was nothing inherently wrong or mean or shameful in the stand which she had taken. The method thereof might come in perhaps for a little censure. But otherwise her harshest critics, if unbiased, could only say that instead of sharing the burdens of her own group she had elected to stray along a path where she personally could find the greatest ease, comfort and expansion. She had long since given up the search for happiness. But there were moments when a chance discussion about coloured people couched in the peculiarly brutal terms which white America affects in the discussion of this problem made her blood boil, and she longed to confound her *vis-à-vis* and his tacit assumption that she, being presumably a white woman, would hold the same views as he, with the remark: "I'm one of them,—do you find me worthless or dishonest or offensive in any way?" Such a *dénouement* would have, she felt, been a fine gesture. But life she knew had a way of allowing grand gestures to go unremarked and unrewarded. Would it be worth while to throw away the benefits of casual whiteness in America when no great issue was at stake? Would it indeed be worth while to forfeit them when a great issue was involved? Remembering the material age in which she lived and the material nation of which she was a member, she was doubtful. Her mother's old dictum recurred: "Life is more important than colour."

The years slipped by. Virginia seemed in no haste to marry. Anthony whom Angela saw occasionally at the Art School shared apparently in this cool deliberateness. Yet there was nothing in his action or manner to make her feel that he was anticipating a change. Rather, if she judged him correctly he,

like herself, tired of the snarl into which the three of them had
been drawn, had settled down to a resigned acceptance of fate.
If conceivable, he was quieter, more reserved than ever, yet ra-
diating a strange restfulness and the peace which comes from
surrender.

In May the prizes for the contest were announced. Angela
received the John T. Stewart Prize for her "Fourteenth Street
Types"; her extreme satisfaction was doubled by the knowledge that the Nehemiah Sloan Prize, of equal value, had been
awarded Miss Powell for her picture entitled "A Street in Harlem". The coloured girl was still difficult and reserved, but under
Angela's persistent efforts at friendship her frank and sympathetic interest and comprehension of her class-mate's difficulties, the latter had finally begun to thaw a little. They were not
planning to live together in France, their tastes were not sufficiently common for that closeness, but both were looking
forward to a year of pleasure, of inspiring work, to a life that
would be "different". Angela was relieved, but Miss Powell was
triumphant; not unpleasantly, she gave the impression of having
justified not only her calling but herself and, in a lesser degree,
her race. The self-consciousness of colour, racial responsibility,
lay, Angela had discovered, deep upon her.

The passage money to France was paid. Through the terms
offered by the committee of the School for Americans at
Fontainebleau, an appreciable saving had been effected. The girls
were to sail in June. As the time drew nearer Angela felt herself
becoming more and more enthusiastic. She had at first looked
upon her sojourn abroad as a heaven-sent break in the montony
and difficulties of her own personal problems, but lately, with
the involuntary reaction of youth, she was beginning to recover
her sense of embarking on a great adventure. Her spirits mounted
steadily.

One evening she went around to Martha Burden's to discuss
the trip; she wanted information about money, clothes, possible
tips.

"Everything you can think of, Martha," she said with something of her former vital manner. "This is an old story to you,
—you've been abroad so many times you ought to write an
encyclopædia on "What to take to Europe". I mean to follow

your advice blindly and the next time I see Miss Powell I'll pass it along to her."

"No need to," said Martha laconically and sombrely. "She isn't going."

"Not going! Why she was going two weeks ago."

"Yes, but she's not going this week nor any other week I'm afraid; at least not through the good offices of the American Committee for the Fontainebleau School of Fine Arts. They've returned her passage money. Didn't you know it? I thought everybody had heard of it."

Angela fought against a momentary nausea. "No, I didn't know it. I haven't seen her for ages. I'm so busy getting myself together. Martha, what's it all about? Is it because she's coloured? You don't mean it's because she's coloured?"

"Well, it is. They said they themselves were without prejudice, but that they were sure the enforced contact on the boat would be unpleasant to many of the students, garnered as they would be from all parts of the United States. Furthermore they couldn't help but think that such contact would be embarrassing to Miss Powell too. Oh, there's no end to the ridiculous piffle which they've written and said. I've had a little committee of students and instructors going about, trying to stir up public sentiment. Mr. Cross has been helping and Paget too. I wish Paulette were here; she'd get some yellow journal publicity. Van Meier has come out with some biting editorials; he's shown up a lot of their silly old letters. I shouldn't be surprised but what if we kept at it long enough we'd get somewhere."

She reflected a moment. "Funny thing is we're having such a hard time in making Miss Powell show any fight. I don't understand that girl."

Angela murmured that perhaps she had no hope of making an impression on prejudice. "It's so unreasonable and far-reaching. Maybe she doesn't want to sacrifice her peace of mind for what she considers a futile struggle."

"That's what Mr. Cross said. He's been wonderful to her and an indefatigable worker. Of course you'll be leaving soon since none of this touches you, but come into a committee meeting or two, won't you? We're meeting here. I'll give you a ring."

"Well," said Angela to herself that night after she had regained her room. "I wonder what I ought to do now?" Even yet she was receiving an occasional reporter; the pleasant little stir of publicity attendant on her prize had not yet died away. Suppose she sent for one of them and announced her unwillingness to accept the terms of the American Committee inasmuch as they had withdrawn their aid from Miss Powell. Suppose she should finish calmly: "I, too, am a Negro". What would happen? The withdrawal of the assistance without which her trip abroad, its hoped for healing, its broadening horizons would be impossible. Evidently, there was no end to the problems into which this matter of colour could involve one, some of them merely superficial, as in this instance, some of them gravely physical. Her head ached with the futility of trying to find a solution to these interminable puzzles.

As a child she and Jinny had been forbidden to read the five and ten cent literature of their day. But somehow a copy of a mystery story entitled "Who killed Dr. Cronlin?" found its way into their hands, a gruesome story all full of bearded men, hands preserved in alcohol, shadows on window curtains. Shivering with fascination, they had devoured it after midnight or early in the morning while their trusting parents still slumbered. Every page they hoped would disclose the mystery. But their patience went unrewarded for the last sentence of the last page still read: "Who killed Dr. Cronlin?"

Angela thought of it now, and smiled and sighed. "Just what is or is not ethical in this matter of colour?" she asked herself. And indeed it was a nice question. Study at Fontainebleau would have undoubtedly changed Miss Powell's attitude toward life forever. If she had received the just reward for her painstaking study, she would have reasoned that right does triumph in essentials. Moreover the inspiration might have brought out latent talent, new possibilities. Furthermore, granted that Miss Powell had lost out by a stroke of ill-fortune, did that necessarily call for Angela's loss? If so, to what end?

Unable to answer she fell asleep.

Absorbed in preparations she allowed two weeks to pass by, then, remembering Martha's invitation, she went again to the Starr household on an evening when the self-appointed committee was expected to meet. She found Anthony, Mr. Paget,

Ladislas and Martha present. The last was more perturbed than ever. Indeed an air of sombre discouragement lay over the whole company.

"Well," asked the newcomer, determined to appear at ease in spite of Anthony's propinquity, "how are things progressing?"

"Not at all," replied Mr. Paget. "Indeed we're about to give up the whole fight."

Ladislas with a sort of provoked amusement explained then that Miss Powell herself had thrown up the sponge. "She's not only withdrawn but she sends us word to-night that while she appreciates the fight we're making she'd rather we'd leave her name out of it."

"Did you ever hear anything to equal that?" snapped Martha crossly. I wonder if coloured people aren't natural born quitters. Sometimes I think I'll never raise another finger for them."

"You don't know what you're talking about," said Anthony hotly. "If you knew the ceaseless warfare which most coloured people wage, you'd understand that sometimes they have to stop their fight for the trimmings of life in order to hang on to the essentials which they've got to have and for which they must contend too every day just as hard as they did the first day. No, they're not quitters, they've merely learned to let go so they can conserve their strength for another bad day. I'm coloured and I know."

There was a moment's tense silence while the three white people stared speechless with surprise. Then Martha said in a still shocked voice: "Coloured! Why, I can't believe it. Why, you never told us you were coloured."

"Which is precisely why I'm telling you now," said Anthony, coldly rude. "So you won't be making off-hand judgments about us." He started toward the door. "Since the object for which this meeting has been called has become null and void I take it that we are automatically dismissed. Goodnight."

Martha hastened after him. "Oh, Mr. Cross, don't go like that. As though it made any difference! Why should this affect our very real regard for each other?"

"Why should it indeed?" he asked a trifle enigmatically. "I'm sure I hope it won't. But I must go." He left the room, Paget and Ladislas both hastening on his heels.

Martha stared helplessly after him. "I suppose I haven't said

the right thing. But what could I do? I was so surprised!" She
turned to Angela: "And I really can't get over his being coloured, can you?"

"No," said Angela solemnly, "I can't . . ." and surprised
herself and Martha by bursting into a flood of tears.

For some reason the incident steadied her determination. Perhaps Anthony was the vicarious sacrifice, she told herself and
knew even as she said it that the supposition was pure bunk.
Anthony did not consider that he was making a sacrifice; his
confession or rather his statement with regard to his blood had
the significance of the action of a person who clears his room
of rubbish. Anthony did not want his mental chamber strewn
with the chaff of deception and confusion. He did not label himself, but on the other hand he indulged every now and then in
a general house-cleaning because he would not have the actions of his life bemused and befuddled.

As for Angela she asked for nothing better than to put all
the problems of colour and their attendant difficulties behind
her. She could not meet those problems in their present form
in Europe; literally in every sense she would begin life all over.
In France or Italy she would speak of her strain of Negro blood
and abide by whatever consequences such exposition would
entail. But the consequences could not engender the pain and
difficulties attendant upon them here.

Somewhat diffidently she began to consider the idea of
going to see Miss Powell. The horns of her dilemma resolved
themselves into an unwillingness to parade her own good fortune before her disappointed classmate and an equal unwillingness to depart for France, leaving behind only the cold sympathy
of words on paper. And, too, something stronger, more insistent than the mere consideration of courtesy urged her on.
After all, this girl was one of her own. A whim of fate had set
their paths far apart but just the same they were more than
"sisters under the skin." They were really closely connected
in blood, in racial condition, in common suffering. Once again
she thought of herself as she had years ago when she had seen
the coloured girl refused service in the restaurant: "It might so
easily have been Virginia."

Without announcement then she betook herself up town to

Harlem and found herself asking at the door of the girl's apartment if she might see Miss Powell. The mother whom Angela had last seen so proud and happy received her with a note of sullen bafflement which to the white girl's consciousness connoted: "Easy enough for you, all safe and sound, high and dry, to come and sympathize with my poor child." There was no trace of gratitude or of appreciation of the spirit which had inspired Angela to pay the visit.

To her inquiry Mrs. Powell rejoined: "Yes, I guess you c'n see her. There're three or four other people in there now pesterin' her to death. I guess one mo' won't make no diffunce."

Down a long narrow hall she led her, past two rooms whose dark interiors seemed Stygian in contrast with the bright sunlight which the visitor had just left. But the end of the hall opened into a rather large, light, plain but comfortable diningroom where Miss Powell sat entertaining, to Angela's astonishment, three or four people, all of them white. Her astonishment, however, lessened when she perceived among them John Banky, one of the reporters who had come rather often to interview herself and her plans for France. All of them, she judged angrily, were of his profession, hoping to wring their half column out of Miss Powell's disappointment and embarrassment.

Angela thought she had never seen the girl one half so attractive and exotic. She was wearing a thin silk dress, plainly made but of a flaming red from which the satin blackness of her neck rose, a straight column topped by her squarish, somewhat massive head. Her thin, rather flat dark lips brought into sharp contrast the dazzling perfection of her teeth; her high cheek bones showed a touch of red. To anyone whose ideals of beauty were not already set and sharply limited, she must have made a breathtaking appeal. As long as she sat quiescent in her rather sulky reticence she made a marvellous figure of repose; focussing all the attention of the little assemblage even as her dark skin and hair drew into themselves and retained the brightness which the sun, streaming through three windows, showered upon her.

As soon as she spoke she lost, however, a little of this perfection. For though a quiet dignity persisted, there were pain and bewilderment in her voice and the flat sombreness of utter despair. Clearly she did not know how to get rid of the intrud-ers, but she managed to maintain a poise and aloofness which kept them at their distance. Surely, Angela thought, listening to the stupid, almost impertinent questions put, these things can mean nothing to them. But they kept on with their baiting rather as a small boy keeps on tormenting a lonely and dispir-ited animal at the Zoo.

"We were having something of an academic discussion with Miss Powell here," said Banky, turning to Angela. "This," he informed his co-workers, "is Miss Mory, one of the prizewin-ners of the Art Exhibit and a classmate of Miss Powell. I believe Miss Powell was to cross with you,—as—er—your room-mate did you say?"

"No," said Angela, flushing a little for Miss Powell, for she thought she understood the double meaning of the question, "we weren't intending to be room-mates. Though so far as I am concerned," she heard herself, to her great surprise, saying: "I'd have been very glad to share Miss Powell's state-room if she had been willing." She wanted to get away from this aspect. "What's this about an academic discussion?"

Miss Powell's husky, rather mutinous voice interrupted: "There isn't any discussion, Miss Mory, academic or otherwise. It seems Mr. Paget told these gentlemen and Miss Tilden here, that I had withdrawn definitely from the fight to induce the Com-mittee for the American Art School abroad to allow me to take advantage of their arrangements. So they came up here to get me to make a statement and I said I had none to make other than that I was sick and tired of the whole business and I'd be glad to let it drop."

"And I," said Miss Tilden, a rangy young lady wearing an unbecoming grey dress and a peculiarly straight and hideous bob, "asked her if she weren't really giving up the matter because in her heart she knew she hadn't a leg to stand on."

Angela felt herself growing hot. Something within her urged caution, but she answered defiantly: "What do you mean she hasn't a leg to stand on?"

"Well, of course, this is awfully plain speaking and I hope Miss Powell won't be offended," resumed Miss Tilden, show-ing only too plainly that she didn't care whether Miss Powell were offended or not, "but after all we do know that a great many people find the—er—Negroes objectionable and so of course no self-respecting one of them would go where she wasn't wanted."

Miss Powell's mother hovering indefinitely in the background, addressing no one in particular, opined that she did not know that "that there committee owned the boat. If her daughter could only afford it she'd show them how quickly she'd go where she wanted and not ask no one no favours either."

"Ah, but," said Miss Tilden judicially, "there's the fallacy. Something else is involved here. There's a social side to this matter, inherent if not expressed. And that *is* the question." She shook a thin bloodless finger at Miss Powell. "Back of most of the efforts which you people make to get into schools and clubs and restaurants and so on, isn't there really this desire for social equality? Come now, Miss Powell, be frank and tell me."

With such sharpness as to draw the attention of everyone in the room Angela said: "Come, Miss Tilden, that's unpardonable and you know it. Miss Powell hadn't a thought in mind about social equality. All she wanted was to get to France and to get there as cheaply as possible."

Banky, talking in a rather affected drawl, confirmed the last speaker. "I think, too, that's a bit too much, Miss Tilden. We've no right to interpret Miss Powell's ideas for her."

A short, red-faced young man intervened: "But just the same *isn't* that the question involved? Doesn't the whole matter resolve itself into this: Has Miss Powell or any other young coloured woman knowing conditions in America the right to thrust her company on a group of people with whom she could have nothing in common except her art? If she stops to think she must realize that not one of the prospective group of students who would be accompanying her on that ship would really welcome her presence. Here's Miss Mory, for instance, a fellow student. What more natural under other circumstances than that she should have made arrangements to travel with Miss Powell? She knows she has to share her cabin with some one. But no; such a thought apparently never entered her head. Why? The answer is obvious. Very well then. If she, knowing Miss Powell, feels this way, how much more would it be the feeling of total strangers?"

A sort of shocked silence fell upon the room. It was an

impossible situation. How, thought Angela desperately, knowing the two sides, could she ever explain to these smug, complacent people Miss Powell's ambition, her chilly pride, the
remoteness with which she had treated her fellow-students,
her only too obvious endeavour to share their training and not
their friendship? Hastily, almost crudely, she tried to get something of this over, ashamed for herself, ashamed for Miss Powell
whose anguished gaze begged for her silence.

At last the coloured girl spoke. "It's wonderful of you to
take my part in this way, Miss Mory. I had no idea you understood so perfectly. But don't you see there's no use in trying to
explain it? It's a thing which one either does see or doesn't
see." She left her soft, full, dark gaze rest for a second on her
auditors. "I'm afraid it is not in the power of these persons to
grasp what you mean."

The stocky young man grew a little redder. "I think we do
understand, Miss Powell. All that Miss Mory says simply con-
firms my first idea. For otherwise, understanding and sympa-
thizing with you as she does, why has she, for instance, never
made any very noticeable attempt to become your friend? Why
shouldn't she have asked you to be her side-partner on this trip
which I understand you're taking together? There would have
been an unanswerable refutation for the committee's arguments. But no, she does nothing even though it means the
thwarting for you of a life-time's ambition. Mind, I'm not
blaming you, Miss Mory. You are acting in accordance with a
natural law. I'm just trying to show Miss Powell here how inevitable the workings of such a law are."

It was foolish reasoning and fallacious, yet containing enough
truth to make it sting. Some icy crust which had formed over
Angela's heart shifted, wavered, broke and melted. Suddenly it
seemed as though nothing in the world were so important as
to allay the poignancy of Miss Powell's situation; for this, she
determined quixotically, no price would be too dear. She said
icily in tones which she had never heard herself use before:
"It's true I've never taken any stand hitherto for Miss Powell for
I never thought she needed it. But now that the question has
come up I want to say that I'd be perfectly willing to share my
stateroom with her and to give her as much of my company as
she could stand. However, that's all out of the question now

because Miss Powell isn't going to France on the American Committee Fund and I'm not going either." She stopped a second and added quietly: "And for the same reason."

Someone said in bewilderment: "What do you mean when you say you're not going? And for the same reason?"

"I mean that if Miss Powell isn't wanted, I'm not wanted either. You imply that she's not wanted because she's coloured. Well, I'm coloured too."

One of the men said under his breath, "God, what a scoop!" and reached for his hat. But Banky, his face set and white, held him back.

"I don't believe you know what you're saying, Miss Mory. But anyway, whether it's true or untrue, for God's sake take it back!"

His tone of horror added the last touch. Angela laughed in his face. "Take it back!" She could hardly contain herself. "Do you really think that being coloured is as awful as all that? Can't you see that to my way of thinking it's a great deal better to be coloured and to miss—oh—scholarships and honours and pre-ferments, than to be the contemptible things which you've all shown yourselves to be this morning? Coming here baiting this poor girl and her mother, thrusting your self-assurance down their throats, branding yourselves literally dogs in the manger?" She turned to the coloured girl's mother. "Mrs. Powell, you surely don't want these people here any longer. Have I your permission to show them out?" Crossing the room su-perbly she opened the door. "This way, please, and don't come back any more. You can rest assured we'll find a way to keep you out."

Silently the little line filed out. Only Miss Tilden, laying her hand on Angela's arm paused to say avidly: "You'll let me come to see you, surely? I can give you some fine publicity, only I must have more data. How about an exclusive interview?"

Angela said stonily: "Mrs. Powell will show you the front door." Then she and her former class-mate stood regarding each other. The dark girl crossed the room and caught her hands and kissed them. "Oh," she said, "it was magnificent—I never guessed it,—but you shouldn't have done it. It's all so unjust, so—silly—and so tiresome. You, of course, only get it when you bring it upon yourself. But I'm black and I've had it all my life. You don't know the prizes within my grasp that have been snatched away from me again because of colour." She turned as her mother entered the room. "Mother, wasn't she magnificent?"

"She was a fool," Mrs. Powell replied shortly.

Her words brought the exalted Angela back to earth. "Yes," she said, smiling whimsically, "I am just that, a fool. I don't know what possessed me. I'm poor, I was in distress; I wanted a new deal. Now I don't know which way to turn for it. That story will be all over New York by to-morrow morning." She burst out laughing. "Think of my choosing four reporters before whom to make my great confession!" Her hand sought Miss Powell's. "Good-bye, both of you. Don't worry about me. I never dreamed that anything like this could happen, but the mere fact that is has shows that the truth was likely to come out any day. So don't blame yourselves for it. Goodbye."

Banky was waiting for her in the vestibule downstairs. "I'm so sorry about the whole damned business, Miss Mory," he said decently. "It's a damned shame. If there's anything I can do——"

Rather shortly she said there was nothing. "And you don't need to worry. As I told you upstairs, being coloured isn't as awful as all that. I'll get along." Ignoring his hand she passed by him into the street. It was Saturday afternoon so there was a chance of her finding Jinny at home.

"And if she isn't there I can wait," she told herself; and thanked God in her heart for the stability implied in sisterhood.

Jinny was home, mulling happily over the small affairs which kept her a little girl. Her sister, looking at the serene loveliness of her face, said irrelevantly: "You make me feel like an old woman."

"Well," replied Jinny, "you certainly have the art of concealing time's ravages, for you not only look young but you have the manner of someone who's just found a million dollars. Come in and tell me about it."

"Found a million dollars! H'm, lost it I should say!" But a sudden wave of relief and contentment broke over her. "Oh, Jinny, tell me, have I been an utter fool! I've thrown away

every chance I've ever had in the world,—just for a whim."
Suddenly close in the full tide of sisterliness, they sat facing
each other on the comfortable couch while Angela told her story.
"I hadn't the faintest idea in the world of telling it. I was thinking only the other day how lucky I was compared to Miss
Powell, and the first thing I knew there it all came tripping off
my tongue. But I had to do it. If you could just have seen
those pigs of reporters and Miss Powell's face under their relentless probing. And old Mrs. Powell, helpless and grunting
and sweating and thinking me a fool; she told me so, you
know. . . . Why, Jinny, darling, you're not ever crying! Darling, there's nothing to cry about; what's the matter, Honey!"

"It's because you *are* a fool that I am crying," said Jinny
sobbing and sniffling, her fingers in her eyes. "You're a fool
and the darlingest girl that ever lived, and my own precious,
lovely, wonderful sister back again. Oh, Angela, I'm so happy.
Tell them to send you your passage money back; say you don't
want anything from them that they don't want to give; let
them go, let them all go except the ones who like you for
yourself. And dearest, if you don't mind having to skimp a bit
for a year or two and not spreading yourself as you planned,
we'll get you off to Europe after all. You know I've got all my
money from the house. I've never touched it. You can have as
much of that as you want and pay me back later or not at all."

Laughing and crying, Angela told her that she couldn't think
of it. "Keep your money for your marriage, Jinny. It'll be some
time before—Anthony will make any real money, I imagine.
But I will take your advice and go to Europe after all. All this
stuff will be in the paper to-morrow, I suppose, so I'll write the
American Committee people to-night. As for the prize money,
if they want that back they can have it. But I don't think they
will; nothing was said about Miss Powell's. That's a thousand
dollars. I'll take that and go to Paris and live as long as I can. If
I can't have the thousand I'll use the few hundreds that I have
left and go anyway. And when I come back I'll go back to my
old job or—go into the schools. But all that's a long way off
and we don't know what might turn up."

There were one or two matters for immediate consideration.
The encounter with the reporters had left Angela a little more
shaken than was at first apparent. "I don't want to run into

them again," she said ruefully. Her lease on the little apartment in Jayne Street had still a month to run. She would go down this very evening, get together her things, and return to Jinny, with whom she would live quietly until it was time for her to sail. Her mail she could leave with the janitor to be called for. Fortunately the furniture was not hers; there were only a few pictures to be removed. After all, she had very few friends to consider,—just the Sandburgs, Martha Burden, Mrs. Denver, Ralph Ashley and Rachel Salting.

"And I don't know what to do about them," she said, pondering. "After all, you can't write to people and say: 'Dear friend:—You've always thought I was white. But I'm not really. I'm coloured and I'm going back to my own folks to live.' Now can you? Oh, Jinny, Jinny, isn't it a great old world?"

In the end, after the story appeared, as it assuredly did, in the next morning's paper, she cut out and sent to each of her former friends copies of Miss Tilden's story whose headlines read: "Socially Ambitious Negress Confesses to Long Hoax."

With the exception of Banky's all the accounts took the unkindest attitude possible. The young Hungarian played up the element of self-sacrifice and the theory that blood after all was thicker than water. Angela guessed rightly that if he could have he would have preferred omitting it, and that he had only written it up to offset as far as possible the other accounts. Of the three other meanly insinuating stories Miss Tilden's was the silliest and most dangerous. She spoke of mixed blood as the curse of the country, a curse whose "insidiously concealed influence constantly threatens the wells of national race purity. Such incidents as these make one halt before he condemns the efforts of the Ku Klux Klan and its unceasing fight for 100 per cent. Americanism."

The immediate effect of this publicity was one which neither of the sisters had foreseen. When Angela reported for work on the following Monday morning she found a note on her desk asking her immediate appearance in the office. The president returning her good-morning with scant courtesy, showed her a clipping and asked if she were the Miss Mory of the story. Upon her assurance that she was none other, he handed her a month's salary in lieu of notice and asked her to consider her connection with the firm at an end.

"We have no place for deceit in an institution such as this," he said augustly.

The incident shook both girls to a degree. Virginia, particularly was rendered breathless by its cruel immediacy. Never before had she come so close to the special variation of prejudice manifested to people in Angela's position. That the president of the concern should attribute the girl's reticence on this subject to deceit seemed to her the last ounce of injustice. Angela herself was far less perturbed.

"I've seen too much of this sort of thing to feel it as you do, Virginia. Of course, as you see, there are all kinds of absurdities involved. In your case, showing colour as you do, you'd have been refused the job at the very outset. Perhaps they would have said that they had found coloured people incompetent or that other girls had a strong natural aversion toward working beside one of us. Now here I land the position, hold it long enough to prove ability and the girls work beside me and remain untainted. So evidently there's no blind inherent disgust to be overcome. Looking just the same as I've ever looked I let the fact of my Negro ancestry be known. Mind, I haven't changed the least bit, but immediately there's all this holding up of hands and the cry of deceit is raised. Some logic, that! It really would be awfully funny, you see, Jinny, if it couldn't be fraught with such disastrous consequences for people like, say, Miss Powell."

"Don't mention her," said Jinny vehemently. "If it hadn't been for her you wouldn't have been in all this trouble."

Angela smiled. "If it hadn't been for her, you and I probably never would have really found each other again. But you mustn't blame her. Sooner or later I'd have been admitting,— 'confessing', as the papers say,—my black blood. Not that I myself think it of such tremendous importance; in spite of my efforts to break away I really don't, Virginia. But because this country of ours makes it so important, against my own conviction I was beginning to feel as though I were laden down with a great secret. Yet when I begin to delve into it, the matter of blood seems nothing compared with individuality, character, living. The truth of the matter is, the whole business was just making me fagged to death."

She sat lost intently in thought. "All of the complications of these last few years,—and you can't guess what complications there have been, darling child,—have been based on this business of 'passing'. I understand why Miss Powell gave up the uneven fight about her passage. Of course, in a way it would have been a fine thing if she could have held on, but she was perfectly justified in letting go so she could avoid still greater bitterness and disappointment and so she could have something left in her to devote to her art. You can't fight and create at the same time. And I understand, too, why your Anthony bestirs himself every little while and makes *his* confession; simply so he won't have to be bothered with the trappings of pretence and watchfulness. I suppose he told you about that night down at Martha Burden's?"

"Yes," said Jinny, sighing, "he has terrible ideals. There's something awfully lofty about Anthony. I wish he were more like Matthew, comfortable and homey. Matt's got some ideals, too, but he doesn't work them overtime. Anthony's a darling, two darlings, but he's awfully, awfully what-do-you-call-it, ascetic. I shouldn't be at all surprised but what he had a secret canker eating at his heart."

Angela said rather sternly, "Look here, Jinny, I don't believe you love him after all, do you?"

"Well now, when I get right down to it sometimes I think I do. Sometimes I think I don't. Of course the truth of the matter is, I'd hardly have thought about Anthony or marriage either just now, if I hadn't been so darn lonely. You know I'm not like you, Angela. When we were children I was the one who was going to have a career, and you were always going to have a good time. Actually it's the other way round; you're the one who's bound to have a career. You just gravitate to adventure. There's something so forceful and so strong about you that you can't keep out of the battle. But, Angela, I want a home,—with you if you could just stand still long enough, or failing that, a home with husband and children and all that goes with it. Of course I don't mind admitting that at any time I'd have given up even you for Matthew. But next to being his wife I'd rather live with you, and next to that I'd like to marry

Anthony. I don't like to be alone; for though I can fend for myself I don't want to."

Angela felt herself paling with the necessity of hiding her emotion. "So poor Anthony's only third in your life?"

"Yes, I'm afraid he is . . . Darling, what do you say to scallops for dinner? I feel like cooking to-day. Guess I'll hie me to market."

She left the room, and her sister turned to the large photograph of Cross which Virginia kept on the mantel. She put her fingers on the slight youthful hollows of his pictured cheeks, touched his pictured brow. "Oh Anthony, Anthony, is Life cheating you again? You'll always be first in my life, dearest."

Perhaps Virginia's diagnosis of her character was correct. At any rate she welcomed the present combination of difficulties through which she was now passing. Otherwise this last confession of Jinny's would have plunged her into fresh unhappiness. But she had many adjustments to make and to face. First of all there was her new status in the tiny circle in which she had moved. When at the end of two weeks she went down to her old apartment in Jayne Street to ask for her mail, she was, in spite of herself amazed and hurt to discover a chilled bewilderment, an aloofness, in the manner of Mrs. Denver, with whom she had a brief encounter. On the other hand there were a note and a calling card from Martha Burden, and some half dozen letters from Elizabeth and Walter Sandburg.

Martha's note ran: "Undoubtedly you and Mr. Cross are very fine people. But I don't believe I could stand another such shock very soon. Of course it was magnificent of you to act as you did. But oh, my dear, how quixotic. And after all *à quoi bon?* Will you come to see me as soon you get this, or send me word how I may see you? And Angèle, if you let all this nonsense interfere with your going to Europe I'll never forgive you. Ladislas and I have several thousand dollars stored away just begging to be put out at interest."

Elizabeth Sandburg said nothing about the matter, but Angela was able to read her knowledge between the lines. The kind-hearted couple could not sufficiently urge upon her their unchanging regard and friendship. "Why on earth don't you come and see us?" Elizabeth queried in her immense, wandering chirography, five words to a page. "You can't imagine how we miss you. Walter's actually getting off his feed. Do take a moment from whatever masterpiece you're composing and give us a week-end."

But from Rachel Salting and from Ashley not one single word!

Chapter II

MORE than ever her determination to sail became fixed. "Some people," she said to Jinny, "might think it the thing to stay here and fight things out. Martha, for instance, is keenly disappointed because I won't let the committee which had been working for Miss Powell take up my case. I suspect she thinks we're all quitters. But I know when I've had enough. I told her I wanted to spend my life doing something besides fighting. Moreover, the Committee, like myself, is pretty sick of the whole affair, though not for the same reason, and I think there'd be even less chance for a readjustment in my case than there was in Miss Powell's."

An interview with Clarke Otter, Chairman of the Advisory Board of the American Committee, had given her this impression. Mr. Otter's attitude betokened a curious admixture of resentment at what he seemed to consider her deceit in "passing" and exasperation at her having been quixotic enough to give the show away. "We think you are quite right in expressing your determination not to take advantage of the Committee's arrangements. It evidences a delicacy of feeling quite unusual in the circumstances." Angela was boiling with anger when she left.

A letter to the donor of the prize brought back the laconic answer that the writer was interested "not in Ethnology but in Art."

"I'd like to see that party," said Angela, reverting to the jargon of her youth. "I'll bet he's nowhere near as stodgy as he sounds. I shouldn't wonder but what he was just bubbling over with mirth at the silliness of it all."

Certainly she herself was bubbling over with mirth or with what served for that quality. Virginia could not remember ever having seen her in such high spirits, not since the days when they used to serve Monday's dinner for their mother and play at the *rôles* in which Mrs. Henrietta Jones had figured so largely. But Angela herself knew the shallowness of that mirth whose reality, Anthony, unable to remain for any length of time in her presence and yet somehow unable to stay away, sometimes suspected.

Her savings, alas! including the prize money, amounted roughly to 1,400 dollars. Anthony had urged her to make the passage second class on one of the large, comfortable boats. Then, if she proved herself a good sailor, she might come back third class.

"And anyway don't put by any more than enough for that," said Jinny maternally, "and if you need any extra money write to me and I'll send you all you want."

From stories told by former foreign students who had sometimes visited the Union it seemed as though she might stretch her remaining hundreds over a period of eight or nine months. "And by that time I'll have learned enough to know whether I'm to be an honest-to-God artist or a plain drawing teacher."

"I almost hope it will be the latter," said Jinny with a touching selfishness, "so you'll have to come back and live with us. Don't you hope so, Anthony?"

Angela could see him wince under the strain of her sister's artlessness. "Eight or nine months abroad ought to make a great difference in her life," he said with no particular relevance. "Indeed in the lives of all of us." Both he and Angela had only one thought these days, that the time for departure would have to arrive. Neither of them had envisaged the awfulness of this pull on their self-control.

Now there were only five days before her departure on Monday. She divided them among the Sandburgs, Anthony and Jinny who was coming down with a summer cold. On Saturday the thought came to her that she would like to see Philadelphia again; it was a thought so persistent that by nine o'clock she was in the train and by 11.15 she was preparing for bed in a small side-room in the Hotel Walton in the city of her birth. Smiling, she fell asleep vaguely soothed by the thought of being so close to all that had been once the scene of her steady, unchecked life.

The propinquity was to shake her more than she could dream.

In the morning she breakfasted in her room, then coming downstairs stood in the portico of the hotel drawing on her gloves as she had done so many years before when she had been a girl shopping with her mother. A flood of memories rushed over her, among them the memory of that day when her father and Virginia had passed them on the street and they had not spoken. How trivial the reason for not speaking seemed now! In later years she had cut Jinny for a reason equally trivial.

She walked up toward Sixteenth Street. It was Sunday and the beautiful melancholy of the day was settling on the quiet city. There was a freshness and a solemnity in the air as though even the atmosphere had been rarified and soothed. A sense of loneliness invaded her; this was the city of her birth, of her childhood and of most of her life. Yet there was no one, she felt, to whom she could turn this beautiful day for a welcome; old acquaintances might be mildly pleased, faintly curious at seeing her, but none of them would show any heart-warming gladness. She had left them so abruptly, so completely. Well, she must not think on these things. After all, in New York she had been lonely too.

The Sixteenth Street car set her down at Jefferson Street and slowly she traversed the three long blocks. Always quiet, always respectable, they were doubly so in the sanctity of Sunday morning. What a terrible day Sunday could be without friends, ties, home, family. Only five years ago, less than five years, she had had all the simple, stable fixtures of family life, the appetizing breakfast, the music, the church with its interesting, paintable types, long afternoons and evenings with visitors and discussions beating in the void. And Matthew Henson, would he, she wondered, give her welcome? But she thought that still she did not want to see him. She was not happy, but she was not through adventuring, through tasting life. And she knew that a life spent with Matthew Henson would mean a cessation of that. After all, was he, with his steadiness, his uprightness, his gift for responsibility any happier than she? She doubted it.

Oh, she hoped Sundays in Paris would be gay!

Opal Street came into her vision, a line, a mere shadow of a street falling upon the steadfastness of Jefferson. Her heart quickened, tears came into her eyes as she turned that corner which she had turned so often, that corner which she had once left behind her forever in order to taste and know life. In the hot July sun the street lay almost deserted. A young coloured man, immaculate in white shirt sleeves, slim and straight, bending in his doorway to pick up the bulky Sunday paper, straightened up to watch her advancing toward him. Just this side of

him stood her former home,—how tiny it was and yet how full
of secrets, of knowledge of joy, despair, suffering, futility—in
brief Life! She stood a few moments in front of it, just gazing,
but presently she went up and put her hand on the red brick,
wondering blindly if in some way the insensate thing might
not communicate with her through touch. A coloured woman
sitting in the window watching her rather sharply, came out
then and asked her suspiciously what she wanted.

"Nothing," Angela replied dully. "I just wanted to look at
the house."

"It isn't for sale, you know."

"No, no, of course not. I just wanted to look at it again. I
used to live here, you see. I wondered——" Even if she did get
permission to go inside, could she endure it? If she could just
stand once in that little back room and cry and cry—perhaps
her tears would flood away all that mass of regret and confusion and futile memories, and she could begin life all over with
a blank page. Thank God she was young! Suddenly it seemed
to her that entering the house once more, standing in that room
would be a complete panacea. Raising her eyes expectantly to
the woman's face she began: "Would you be so kind——?"

But the woman, throwing her a last suspicious look and
muttering that she was "nothing but poor white trash," turned
and, slamming the door behind her, entered the little square
parlour and pulled down the blinds.

The slim young man came running down the steet toward her.
Closer inspection revealed his ownership of a pleasant brown
freckled face topped by thick, soft, rather closely cropped dark-
red hair.

"Angela," he said timidly, and then with more assurance: "It
is Angela Murray."

She turned her stricken face toward him. "She wouldn't let
me in, Matthew. I'm going to France to-morrow and I thought
I'd like to see the old house. But she wouldn't let me look at it.
She called me,"—her voice broke with the injustice of it,—
"poor white trash."

"I know," he nodded gravely. "She'd do that kind of thing;
she doesn't understand, you see." He was leading her gently
toward his house. "I think you'd better come inside and rest a

moment. My father and mother have gone off for their annual trip to Bridgeton; mother was born there, you know. But you won't mind coming into the house of an old and tried friend."

"No," she said, conscious of an overwhelming fatigue and general sense of let-downness, "I should say I wouldn't." As they crossed the threshold she tried faintly to smile but the effort was too much for her and she burst into a flood of choking, strangling, noisy tears.

Matthew removed her hat and fanned her; brought her icewater and a large soft handkerchief to replace her own sodden wisp. Through her tears she smiled at him, understanding as she did so, the reason for Virginia's insistence on his general niceness. He was still Matthew Henson, still freckled and brown, still capped with that thatch of thick bad hair. But care and hair-dressings and improved toilet methods and above all the emanation of a fine and generous spirit had metamorphosed him into someone still the old Matthew Henson and yet someone somehow translated into a quintessence of kindliness and gravity and comprehending.

She drank the water gratefully, took out her powder puff.

"I don't need to ask you how you are," he said, uttering a prayer of thanks for averted hysterics. "When a lady begins to powder her nose, she's bucking up all right. Want to tell me all about it?"

"There's nothing to tell. Only I wanted to see the house and suddenly found myself unexpectedly homesick, lonely, misunderstood. And when that woman refused me so cruelly, it was just too much." Her gaze wavered, her eyes filled again.

"Oh," he said in terror, "for God's sake don't cry again! I'll go over and give her a piece of my mind; I'll make her turn the whole house over to you. I'll bring you her head on a charger. Only 'dry those tears'." He took her handkerchief and dried them himself very, very gently.

She caught his hand. "Matthew, you're a dear."

He shrugged negligently, "You haven't always thought that."

This turn of affairs would never do. "What were you planning to do when I barged in? Getting ready to read your paper and be all homey and comfortable?"

"Yes, but I don't want to do that now. Tell you what, Angela, let's have a lark. Suppose we have dinner here? You get it.

Remember how it used to make me happy as a king in the old days if you'd just hand me a glass of water? You said you were sailing to-morrow; you must be all packed. What time do you have to be back? I'll put you on the train."

The idea enchanted her. "I'd love it! Matthew, what fun!" They found an apron of his mother's, and in the ice-box, cold roast beef, lettuce which Philadelphians call salad, beets and corn. "I'll make muffins," said Angela joyously, "and you take a dish after dinner and go out and get some ice-cream. Oh, Matthew, how it's all coming back to me! Do you still shop up here in the market?"

They ate the meal in the little dark cool dining-room, the counterpart of the dining-room in Junius Murray's one-time house across the way. But somehow its smallness was no longer irksome; rather it seemed a tiny island of protection reared out of and against an encroaching sea of troubles. In fancy she saw her father and mother almost a quarter of a century ago coming proudly to such a home, their little redoubt of refuge against the world. How beautiful such a life could be, shared with some one beloved,—with Anthony! Involuntarily she sighed.

Matthew studying her thoughtfully said: "You're dreaming, Angela. Tell me what it's all about."

"I was thinking what a little haven a house like this could be; what it must have meant to my mother. Funny how I almost pounded down the walls once upon a time trying to get away. Now I can't think of anything more marvellous than having such a place as this, here, there, anywhere, to return to."

Startled, he told her of his surprise at hearing such words from her. "If Virginia had said them I should think it perfectly natural; but I hadn't thought of you as being interested in home. How, by the way, is Virginia?"

"Perfect."

With a wistfulness which barely registered with her absorption, he queried: "I suppose she's tremendously happy?"

"Happy enough."

"A great girl, little Virginia." In his turn he fell to musing, roused himself. "You haven't told me of your adventures and your flight into the great world."

"There's not much to tell, Matthew. All I've seen and experienced has been the common fate of most people, a little sharpened, perhaps, a little vivified. Briefly, I've had a lot of fun and a measure of trouble. I've been stimulated by adventure; I've known suffering and love and pain."

"You're still surprising me. I didn't suppose a girl like you could know the meaning of pain." He gave her a twisted smile. "Though you certainly know how to cause it. Even yet I can get a pang which no other thought produces if I let my mind go back to those first few desperate days after you left me. Heavens, can't you suffer when you're young!"

She nodded, laid her hand on his. "Terribly. Remember, I was suffering too, Matthew, though for different causes. I was so pushed, so goaded . . . well, we won't talk about that any more . . . I hope you've got over all that feeling. Indeed, indeed I wasn't worth it. Do tell me you haven't let it harass you all these years."

His hand clasped hers lightly, then withdrew. "No I haven't. . . . The suddenness, the inevitableness of your departure checked me, pulled me up short. I suffered, oh damnably, but it was suffering with my eyes open. I knew then you weren't for me; that fundamentally we were too far apart. And eventually I got over it. Those days!" He smiled again wryly, recalling a memory. "But I went on suffering just the same, only in another way. I fell in love with Jinny."

Her heart in her breast stopped beating. "Matthew, you didn't! Why on earth didn't you ever say so?"

"I couldn't. She was such a child, you see; she made it so plain all the time that she looked on me as her sister's beau and therefore a kind of dependable brother. After you went I used to go to see her, take her about. Why she'd swing on my arm and hold up her face for a good-night kiss! Once, I remember, we had been out and she became car-sick,—poor little weak thing! She was so ashamed! Like a baby, you know, playing at being grown-up and then ashamed for reverting to babyhood. I went to see her the next day and she was so little and frail and confiding! I stayed away then for a long time and the next thing I knew she was going to New York. I misjudged you awfully then, Angela. You must forgive me. I thought you had

pulled her away. I learned later that I was wrong, that you and
she rarely saw each other in New York. Do you know why she
left?"

There was her sister's pride to shield but her own need to
succour; who could have dreamed of such a dilemma? "I can't
betray Jinny," she said to herself and told him that while she
personally had not influenced her sister the latter had had a
very good reason for leaving Philadelphia.

"I suppose so. Certainly she left. But she'd write me, occasionally, letters just like her dear self, so frank and girlish and
ingenuous and making it so damnably plain that any demon-
stration of love on my part was out of the question. I said to
myself: 'I'm not going to wreck my whole life over those Murray girls'. And I let our friendship drift off into a nothingness.
. . . Then she came to visit Edna Brown this summer. I fairly
leaped out to Merion to see her. The moment I laid eyes on
her I realized that she had developed, had become a woman.
She was as always, kind and sweet, prettier, more alluring than
ever. I thought I'd try my luck . . . and Edna told me she
was engaged. What's the fellow like, Angela?

"Very nice, very fine."

"Wild about her, I suppose?"

Desperately she looked at him. "He's a rather undemonstra-
tive sort. I suppose he's wild enough. Only,—well they talk as
though they had no intention of marrying for years and years
and they both seem perfectly content with that arrangement."

He frowned incredulously. "What! If I thought they weren't
in earnest!"

Impulsively she broke out: "Oh, Matthew, don't you know,
—there's so much pain, such suffering in the world,—a man
should never leave any stone unturned to achieve his ultimate
happiness. Why don't you—write to Jinny, go to New York to
see her?"

Under his freckles his brown skin paled. "You think there's a
chance?"

"My dear, I wouldn't dare say. I know she likes you very,
very much. And I don't think she regards you as a brother."

"Angela, you wouldn't fool me?"

"Why should I do that? And remember after all I'm giving
you no assurance. I'm merely saying it's worth taking a chance.

Now let's see, we'll straighten up this place and then we must fly."

At the station she kissed him good-bye. "Anyway you're always a brother to me. Think of what I've told you, Matthew; act on it."

"I shall. Oh, Angela, suppose it should be that God sent you down here to-day?"

"Perhaps He did." They parted solemnly.

Three hours later found her entering her sister's apartment. Jinny, her cold raging, her eyes inflamed and weeping, greeted her plaintively. "Look at me, Angela. And you leaving tomorrow! I'll never be able to make that boat!" The telephone rang. "It's been ringing steadily for the last hour, somebody calling for you. Do answer it."

The message was from Ashley. He had been away in New Orleans. "And I came back and found that clipping. I knew you sent it. Girl, the way I've pursued you this day! Finally I caught up with Martha Burden, she told me where you were staying. May I come up? Be there in half an hour."

"Not to-night, Ralph. Would you like to come to the boat to-morrow?"

"So you're going anyhow? Bully! But not before I've seen you! Suppose I take you to the boat?"

"Awfully nice of you, but I'm going with my sister."

Here Jinny in a voice full of misplaced consonants told her she was going to do nothing of the sort. "With this cold!"

Angela spoke into the receiver again. "My sister says she isn't going, so I will fall back on you if I may." She hung up.

Virginia wanted to hear of the trip. The two sisters sat talking far into the night, but Angela said no word about Matthew.

Monday was a day of surprises. Martha and Ladislas Starr, unable to be on hand for the sailing of the boat, came up to the house to drive down town with the departing traveller. Secretly Angela was delighted with this arrangement, but it brought a scowl to Ashley's face.

Virginia, miserable with the wretchedness attendant on a summer cold, bore up bravely. "I don't mind letting you go like this from the house; but I couldn't stand the ship! Angela, you're not to worry about me one bit. Only come back to

me,—happy. I know you will. Oh how different this is from
that parting years ago in Philadelphia!"

"Yes," said Angela soberly. "Then I was to be physically
ninety miles away from you, but we were really seas apart. Now
—darling, three thousand miles are nothing when there is love
and trust and understanding. And Jinny, listen! Life is full of
surprises. If a chance for real happiness comes your way don't
be afraid to grasp at it."

"Cryptic," wheezed Jinny, laughing. "I don't know what
you're talking about, but I'll do my best to land any happiness
that comes drifting toward me." They kissed each other gravely,
almost coldly, without tears. But neither could trust herself to
say the actual good-bye.

Angela was silent almost all the way down to the dock, answering her friends only in monosyllables. There, another surprise awaited her in the shape of Mrs. Denver, who remained,
however, only for a few moments. "I couldn't stand having
you go," she said pitifully, "without seeing you for one last
time." And, folding the girl in a close embrace, she broke down
and murmured sadly of a lost daughter who would have been
"perhaps like you, dear, had she lived."

Elizabeth Sandburg, the gay, the complacent, the beloved of
life, clung to her, weeping, "I can't bear to lose you, Angèle."
Walter put his arm about her. "Kiss me, old girl. And mind, if
you need anything, *anything*, you're to call on us. If you get
sick we'll come over after you,—am I right, Lizzie?"

"Yes, of course, of course . . . and don't call me Lizzie.
. . . Come away, can't you, and leave them a moment together. Don't you see Ashley glaring at you?"

They withdrew to a good point of vantage on the dock.

Angela, surprised and weeping, remembering both Mrs.
Denver's words and the manifestations of kindness in her state-
room said: "They really did love me after all, didn't they?"

"Yes," said Ashley earnestly, "we all love you. I'm coming
over to see you by and by, Angèle, may I? You know we've a
lot of things to talk about, some things which you perhaps
think mean a great deal to me but which in reality mean nothing. Then on the other hand there are some matters which actually do mean something to me but whose value to you I'm
not sure of."

"Oh," she said, wiping her eyes and remembering her former secret. "You aren't coming over to ask me to marry you, are you? You don't have to do that. And anyway 'it is not now as it hath been before'. There's no longer a mystery about me, you know. So the real attraction's gone. Remember, I'm not expecting a thing of you, so please, please don't ask it. Ralph, I can't placard myself, and I suppose there will be lots of times when in spite of myself I'll be 'passing'. But I want you to know that from now on, so far as sides are concerned, I am on the coloured side. And I don't want you to come over on that side." She shook her head finally. "Too many complications even for you."

For though she knew he believed in his brave words, she was too sadly experienced to ask an American to put them to the test.

"All right," he said, smiling at her naïve assumptions. "I won't ask you to marry me,—at least not yet. But I'm coming over just the same. I don't suppose you've got a lien on Paris."

"Of course I haven't," she giggled a little. "You know perfectly well I want you to come." Her face suddenly became grave. "But if you do come you won't come to make love without meaning anything either, will you? I'd hate that between you and me."

"No," he said gently, instantly comprehending. "I won't do that either."

"You'll come as a friend?"

"Yes, as a friend."

A deck hand came up then and said civilly that in a few minutes they would be casting off and all visitors must go ashore.

Chapter III

A	MONG her steamer-letters was a brief note from Anthony:
"Angela, my angel, my dear girl, good-bye. These last few weeks have heaven and hell. I couldn't bear to see you go,—so I've taken myself off for a few hours . . . don't think I'll neglect Jinny. I'll never do that. Am I right in supposing that you still care a little? Oh Angela, try to forget me,—but don't do it! I shall never forget you!"

There were letters and flowers from the Burdens, gifts of all sorts from Ashley and Mrs. Denver, a set of notes for each day out from Virginia. She read letters, examined her gifts and laid them aside. But all day long Anthony's note reposed on her heart; it lay at night beneath her head.

Paris at first charmed and wooed her. For a while it seemed to her that her old sense of joy in living for living's sake had returned to her. It was like those first few days which she had spent in exploring New York. She rode delightedly in the motor-buses on and on to the unknown, unpredictable terminus; she followed the winding Seine; crossing and re-crossing the bridges each with its distinctive characteristics. Back of the Panthéon, near the church of St. Geneviève she discovered a Russian restaurant where strange, exotic dishes were served by tall blond waiters in white, stiff Russian blouses. One day, wandering up the Boulevard du Mont Parnasse, she found at its juncture with the Boulevard Raspail the Café Dome, a student restaurant of which many returned students had spoken in the Art School in New York. On entering she was recognized almost immediately by Edith Martin, a girl who had studied with her in Philadelphia.

Miss Martin had lived in Paris two years; knew all the gossip and the characters of the Quarter; could give Angela points on pensions, cafés, tips and the Gallic disposition. On all these topics she poured out perpetually a flood of information, presented her friends, summoned the new comer constantly to her studio or camped uninvited in the other girl's tiny quarters at the Pension Franciana. There was no chance for actual physical loneliness, yet Angela thought after a few weeks of persistent comradeship that she had never felt so lonely in her life. For the first time in her adventuresome existence she was caught up in a tide of homesickness.

Then this passed too with the summer, and she found herself by the end of September engrossed in her work. She went to the Academy twice a day, immersed herself in the atmosphere of the Louvre and the gallery of the Luxembourg. It was hard work, but gradually she schooled herself to remember that this was her life, and that her aim, her one ambition, was to become an acknowledged, a significant painter of portraits. The instructor, renowned son of a still more renowned father, almost invariably praised her efforts.

With the coming of the fall the sense of adventure left her. Paris, so beautiful in the summer, so gay with its thronging thousands, its hosts bent on pleasure, took on another garb in the sullen greyness of late autumn. The tourists disappeared and the hard steady grind of labour, the intent application to the business of living, so noticeable in the French, took the place of a transient, careless freedom. Angela felt herself falling into line; but it was good discipline as she herself realized. Once or twice, in periods of utter loneliness or boredom, she let her mind dwell on her curiously thwarted and twisted life. But the ability for self-pity had vanished. She had known too many others whose lives lay equally remote from goals which had at first seemed so certain. For a period she had watched feverishly for the incoming of foreign mail, sure that some word must come from Virginia about Matthew, but the months crept sullenly by and Jinny's letters remained the same artless missives prattling of school-work, Anthony, Sara Penton, the movies and visits to Maude the inimitable.

"Of course not everything can come right," she told herself. Matthew evidently had, on second thought, deemed it wisest to consult the evidence of his own senses rather than be guided by the hints which in the nature of things she could offer only vaguely.

Within those six months she lost forever the blind optimism of youth. She did not write Anthony nor did she hear from him.

*

Christmas Eve day dawned or rather drifted greyly into the beholder's perception out of the black mistiness of the murky night. In spite of herself her spirits sank steadily. Virginia had promised her a present,—"I've looked all over this whole town," she wrote, "to find you something good enough, something absolutely perfect. Anthony's been helping me. And at last I've found it. We've taken every possible precaution against the interference of wind or rain or weather, and unless something absolutely unpredictable intervenes, it will be there for you Christmas Eve or possibly the day before. But remember, don't open until Christmas."

But it was now six o'clock on Christmas Eve and no present had come, no letter, no remembrance of any kind. "Oh," she said to herself "what a fool I was to come so far away from home!" For a moment she envisaged the possibility of throwing herself on the bed and sobbing her heart out. Instead she remembered Edith Martin's invitation to make a night of it over at her place, a night which was to include dancing and chaffing, a trip just before midnight to hear Mass at St. Sulpice, and a return to the studio for doubtless more dancing and jesting and laughter, and possibly drunkenness on the part of the American male.

At ten o'clock as she stood in her tiny room rather sullenly putting the last touches to her costume, the maid, Héloïse, brought her a cable. It was a long message from Ashley wishing her health, happiness and offering to come over at a week's notice. Somehow the bit of blue paper cheered her, easing her taut nerves. "Of course they're thinking about me. I'll hear from Jinny any moment; it's not her fault that the delivery is late. I wonder what she sent me."

Returning at three o'clock Christmas morning from the party she put her hand cautiously in the door to switch on the light for fear that a package lay near the threshold, but there was no package there. "Well, even if it were there I couldn't open it," she murmured, "for I'm too sleepy." And indeed she had drugged herself with dancing and gaiety into an overwhelming drowsiness. Barely able to toss aside her pretty dress, she tumbled luxuriously into bed, grateful in the midst of her somnolence for the fatigue which would make her forget. . . .

In what seemed to her less than an hour, she heard a tremendous knocking at the door.

"*Entrez,*" she called sleepily and relapsed immediately into slumber. The door, as it happened, was unlocked; she had been too fatigued to think of it the night before. Heloise stuck in a tousled head. "My God," she told the cook afterwards, "such a time as I had to wake her! There she was asleep on both ears and the gentleman downstairs waiting!"

Angela finally opened bewildered eyes. "A gentleman," reiterated Héloise in her staccato tongue. "He awaits you below. He says he has a present which he must put into your own hands. Will Mademoiselle then descend or shall I tell him to come back?"

"Tell him to come back," she murmured, then opened her heavy eyes. "Is it really Christmas, Héloise? Where is the gentleman?"

"As though I had him there in my pocket," said Héloise later in her faithful report to the cook.

But finally the message penetrated. Grasping a robe and slippers, she half leaped, half fell down the little staircase and plunged into the five foot square drawing-room. Anthony sitting on the tremendously disproportionate tan and maroon sofa rose to meet her.

His eyes on her astonished countenance, he began searching about in his pockets, slapping his vest, pulling out keys and handkerchiefs. "There ought to be a tag on me somewhere," he remarked apologetically, "but anyhow Virginia and Matthew sent me with their love."

THE BLACKER THE BERRY

A NOVEL OF NEGRO LIFE

Wallace Thurman

To Ma Jack

The blacker the berry
The sweeter the juice . . .

—Negro folk saying

My color shrouds me in . . . .

—Countee Cullen

Contents

PART I

Emma Lou

M ORE acutely than ever before Emma Lou began to feel
that her luscious black complexion was somewhat of a
liability, and that her marked color variation from the other
people in her environment was a decided curse. Not that she
minded being black, being a Negro necessitated having a colored skin, but she did mind being too black. She couldn't understand why such should be the case, couldn't comprehend
the cruelty of the natal attenders who had allowed her to be
dipped, as it were, in indigo ink when there were so many
more pleasing colors on nature's palette. Biologically, it wasn't
necessary either; her mother was quite fair, so was her mother's
mother, and her mother's brother, and her mother's brother's
son; but then none of them had had a black man for a father.
Why *had* her mother married a black man? Surely there had
been some eligible brown-skin men around. She didn't particularly desire to have had a "high yaller" father, but for her sake
certainly some more happy medium could have been found.

She wasn't the only person who regretted her darkness either. It was an acquired family characteristic, this moaning and
grieving over the color of her skin. Everything possible had
been done to alleviate the unhappy condition, every suggested
agent had been employed, but her skin, despite bleachings,
scourgings, and powderings, had remained black—fast black—
as nature had planned and effected.

She should have been born a boy, then color of skin wouldn't
have mattered so much, for wasn't her mother always saying
that a black boy could get along, but that a black girl would
never know anything but sorrow and disappointment? But she
wasn't a boy; she was a girl, and color did matter, mattered so
much that she would rather have missed receiving her high
school diploma than have to sit as she now sat, the only odd
and conspicuous figure on the auditorium platform of the
Boise high school. Why had she allowed them to place her in

693

the center of the first row, and why had they insisted upon her dressing entirely in white so that surrounded as she was by similarly attired pale-faced fellow graduates she resembled, not at all remotely, that comic picture her Uncle Joe had hung in his bedroom? The picture wherein the black, kinky head of a little red-lipped pickaninny lay like a fly in a pan of milk amid a white expanse of bedclothes.

But of course she couldn't have worn blue or black when the call was for the wearing of white, even if white was not complementary to her complexion. She would have been odd-looking anyway no matter what she wore and she would also have been conspicuous, for not only was she the only dark-skinned person on the platform, she was also the only Negro pupil in the entire school, and had been for the past four years. Well, thank goodness, the principal would soon be through with his monotonous farewell address, and she and the other members of her class would advance to the platform center as their names were called and receive the documents which would signify their unconditional release from public school.

As she thought of these things, Emma Lou glanced at those who sat to the right and to the left of her. She envied them their obvious elation, yet felt a strange sense of superiority because of her immunity for the moment from an ephemeral mob emotion. Get a diploma?—What did it mean to her? College?—Perhaps. A job?—Perhaps again. She was going to have a high school diploma, but it would mean nothing to her whatsoever. The tragedy of her life was that she was too black. Her face and not a slender roll of ribbon-bound parchment was to be her future identification tag in society. High school diploma indeed! What she needed was an efficient bleaching agent, a magic cream that would remove this unwelcome black mask from her face and make her more like her fellow men.

"Emma Lou Morgan."

She came to with a start. The principal had called her name and stood smiling down at her benevolently. Some one—she knew it was her Cousin Buddie, stupid imp—applauded, very faintly, very provokingly. Some one else snickered.

"Emma Lou Morgan."

The principal had called her name again, more sharply than before and his smile was less benevolent. The girl who sat to the left of her nudged her. There was nothing else for her to do but to get out of that anchoring chair and march forward to receive her diploma. But why did the people in the audience have to stare so? Didn't they all know that Emma Lou Morgan was Boise high school's only nigger student? Didn't they all know—but what was the use. She had to go get that diploma, so summoning her most insouciant manner, she advanced to the platform center, brought every muscle of her lithe limbs into play, haughtily extended her shiny black arm to receive the proffered diploma, bowed a chilly thanks, then holding her arms stiffly at her sides, insolently returned to her seat in that forboding white line, insolently returned once more to splotch its pale purity and to mock it with her dark, outlandish difference.

Emma Lou had been born in a semi-white world, totally surrounded by an all-white one, and those few dark elements that had forced their way in had either been shooed away or else greeted with derisive laughter. It was the custom always of those with whom she came into most frequent contact to ridicule or revile any black person or object. A black cat was a harbinger of bad luck, black crape was the insignia of mourning, and black people were either evil niggers with poisonous blue gums or else typical vaudeville darkies. It seemed as if the people in her world never went half-way in their recognition or reception of things black, for these things seemed always to call forth only the most extreme emotional reactions. They never provoked mere smiles or mere melancholy, rather they were the signal either for boisterous guffaws or pain-induced and tear-attended grief.

Emma Lou had been becoming increasingly aware of this for a long time, but her immature mind had never completely grasped its full, and to her, tragic significance. First there had been the case of her father, old black Jim Morgan they called him, and Emma Lou had often wondered why it was that he of all the people she heard discussed by her family should always be referred to as if his very blackness condemned him to receive no respect from his fellow men.

She had also began to wonder if it was because of his blackness that he had never been in evidence as far as she knew.

Inquiries netted very unsatisfactory answers. "Your father is no good." "He left your mother, deserted her shortly after you were born." And these statements were always prefixed or followed by some epithet such as "dirty black no-gooder" or "durn his onery black hide." There was in fact only one member of the family who did not speak of her father in this manner, and that was her Uncle Joe, who was also the only person in the family to whom she really felt akin, because he alone never seemed to regret, to bemoan, or to ridicule her blackness of skin. It was her grandmother who did all the regretting, her mother who did the bemoaning, her Cousin Buddie and her playmates, both white and colored, who did the ridiculing.

Emma Lou's maternal grandparents, Samuel and Maria Lightfoot, were both mulatto products of slave-day promiscuity between male masters and female chattel. Neither had been slaves, their own parents having been granted their freedom because of their rather close connections with the white branch of the family tree. These freedmen had migrated into Kansas with their children, and when these children had grown up they in turn had joined the westward-ho parade of that current era, and finally settled in Boise, Idaho.

Samuel and Maria, like many others of their kind and antecedents, had had only one compelling desire, which motivated their every activity and dictated their every thought. They wished to put as much physical and mental space between them and the former home of their parents as was possible. That was why they had left Kansas, for in Kansas there were too many reminders of that which their parents had escaped and from which they wished to flee. Kansas was too near the former slave belt, too accessible to disgruntled southerners, who, deprived of their slaves, were inculcated with an easily communicable virus, nigger hatred. Then, too, in Kansas all Negroes were considered as belonging to one class. It didn't matter if you and your parents had been freedmen before the Emancipation Proclamation, nor did it matter that you were almost three-quarters white. You were, nevertheless, classed with those hordes of hungry, ragged, ignorant black folk arriving from the South in such great numbers, packed like so many stampeding cattle in dirty, manure-littered box cars.

From all of this these maternal grandparents of Emma Lou

fled, fled to the Rocky Mountain states which were too far away for the recently freed slaves to reach, especially since most of them believed that the world ended just a few miles north of the Mason-Dixon line. Then, too, not only were the Rocky Mountain states beyond the reach of this raucous and smelly rabble of recently freed cotton pickers and plantation hands, but they were also peopled by pioneers, sturdy land and gold seekers from the East, marching westward, always westward in search of El Dorado, and being too busy in this respect to be violently aroused by problems of race unless economic factors precipitated matters.

So Samuel and Maria went into the fast farness of a little known Rocky Mountain territory and settled in Boise, at the time nothing more than a trading station for the Indians and whites, and a red light center for the cowboys and sheepherders and miners in the neighboring vicinity. Samuel went into the saloon business and grew prosperous. Maria raised a family and began to mother nuclear elements for a future select Negro social group.

There was of course in such a small and haphazardly populated community some social intermixture between whites and blacks. White and black gamblers rolled the dice together, played tricks on one another while dealing faro, and became allies in their attempts to outfigure the roulette wheel. White and black men amicably frequented the saloons and dancehalls together. White and black women leaned out of the doorways and windows of the jerry-built frame houses and log cabins of "Whore Row." White and black housewives gossiped over back fences and lent one another needed household commodities. But there was little social intercourse on a higher scale. Slue-foot Sal, the most popular high yaller on "Whore Row," might be a buddy to Irish Peg and Blond Liz, but Mrs. Amos James, whose husband owned the town's only drygoods store, could certainly not become too familiar with Mrs. Samuel Lightfoot, colored, whose husband owned a saloon. And it was not a matter of the difference in their respective husbands' businesses. Mrs. Amos James did associate with Mrs. Arthur Emory, white, whose husband also owned a saloon. It was purely a matter of color.

Emma Lou's grandmother then, holding herself aloof from

the inmates of "Whore Row," and not wishing to associate with such as old Mammy Lewis' daughters, who did most of the town wash, and others of their ilk, was forced to choose her social equals slowly and carefully. This was hard, for there were so few Negroes in Boise anyway that there wasn't much cream to skim off. But as the years passed, others, who, like Maria and her husband, were mulatto offsprings of mulatto freedmen seeking a freer land, moved in, and were soon initiated into what was later to be known as the blue vein circle, so named because all of its members were fair-skinned enough for their blood to be seen pulsing purple through the veins of their wrists.

Emma Lou's grandmother was the founder and the acknowledged leader of Boise's blue veins, and she guarded its exclusiveness passionately and jealously. Were they not a superior class? Were they not a very high type of Negro, comparable to the persons of color group in the West Indies? And were they not entitled, ipso facto, to more respect and opportunity and social acceptance than the more pure blooded Negroes? In their veins was some of the best blood of the South. They were closely akin to the only true aristocrats in the United States. Even the slave masters had been aware of and acknowledged in some measure their superiority. Having some of Marse George's blood in their veins set them apart from ordinary Negroes at birth. These mulattoes as a rule were not ordered to work in the fields beneath the broiling sun at the urge of a Simon Legree lash. They were saved and trained for the more gentle jobs, saved and trained to be ladies' maids and butlers. Therefore, let them continue this natural division of Negro society. Let them also guard against unwelcome and degenerating encroachments. Their motto must be "Whiter and whiter every generation," until the grandchildren of the blue veins could easily go over into the white race and become assimilated so that problems of race would plague them no more.

Maria had preached this doctrine to her two children, Jane and Joe, throughout their apprentice years, and can therefore be forgiven for having a physical collapse when they both, first Joe, then Emma Lou's mother, married not mulattoes, but a copper brown and a blue black. This had been somewhat of a necessity, for, when the mating call had made itself heard to them, there had been no eligible blue veins around. Most of their youthful companions had been sent away to school or else to seek careers in eastern cities, and those few who had remained had already found their chosen life's companions. Maria had sensed that something of the kind might happen and had urged Samuel to send Jane and Joe away to some eastern boarding school, but Samuel had very stubbornly refused. He had his own notions of the sort of things one's children learned in boarding school, and of the greater opportunities they had to apply that learning. True, they might acquire the same knowledge in the public schools of Boise, but then there would be some limit to the extent to which they could apply this knowledge, seeing that they lived at home and perforce must submit to some parental supervision. A cot in the attic at home was to Samuel a much safer place for a growing child to sleep than an iron four poster in a boarding school dormitory.

So Samuel had remained adamant and the two carefully reared scions of Boise's first blue vein family had of necessity sought their mates among the lower orders. However, Joe's wife was not as undesirable as Emma Lou's father, for she was almost three-quarters Indian, and there was scant possibility that her children would have revolting dark skins, thick lips, spreading nostrils, and kinky hair. But in the case of Emma Lou's father, there were no such extenuating characteristics, for his physical properties undeniably stamped him as a full blooded Negro. In fact, it seemed as if he had come from one of the few families originally from Africa, who could not boast of having been seduced by some member of the southern aristocracy, or befriended by some member of a strolling band of Indians.

No one could understand why Emma Lou's mother had married Jim Morgan, least of all Jane herself. In fact she hadn't thought much about it until Emma Lou had been born. She had first met Jim at a church picnic, given in a woodlawn meadow on the outskirts of the city, and almost before she had realized what was happening she had found herself slipping away from home, night after night, to stroll down a well shaded street, known as Lover's Lane, with the man her mother had forbidden her to see. And it hadn't been long before they had decided that an elopement would be the only thing to assure themselves the pleasure of being together without worrying about Mama Lightfoot's wrath, talkative neighbors, prying town marshals, and grass stains.

Despite the rancor of her mother and the whispering of her mother's friends, Jane hadn't really found anything to regret in her choice of a husband until Emma Lou had been born. Then all the fears her mother had instilled in her about the penalties inflicted by society upon black Negroes, especially upon black Negro girls, came to the fore. She was abysmally stunned by the color of her child, for she had been certain that since she herself was so fair that her child could not possibly be as dark as its father. She had been certain that it would be a luscious admixture, a golden brown with all its mother's desirable facial features and its mother's hair. But she hadn't reckoned with nature's perversity, nor had she taken under consideration the inescapable fact that some of her ancestors too had been black, and that some of their color chromosomes were still imbedded within her. Emma Lou had been fortunate enough to have hair like her mother's, a thick, curly black mass of hair, rich and easily controlled, but she had also been unfortunate enough to have a face as black as her father's, and a nose which, while not exactly flat, was as distinctly negroid as her too thick lips.

Her birth had served no good purpose. It had driven her mother back to seek the confidence and aid of Maria, and it had given Maria the chance she had been seeking to break up the undesirable union of her daughter with what she termed an ordinary black nigger. But Jim's departure hadn't solved matters at all, rather it had complicated them, for although he was gone, his child remained, a tragic mistake which could not be stamped out or eradicated even after Jane, by getting a divorce from Jim and marrying a red-haired Irish Negro, had been accepted back into blue vein grace.

Emma Lou had always been the alien member of the family and of the family's social circle. Her grandmother, now a widow, made her feel it. Her mother made her feel it. And her Cousin Buddie made her feel it, to say nothing of the way she was regarded by outsiders. As early as she could remember, people had been saying to her mother, "What an extraordinarily black child! Where did you adopt it?" or else, "Such lovely unniggerish hair on such a niggerish-looking child." Some had even been facetious and made suggestions like, "Try some lye, Jane, it may eat it out. She can't look any worse."

Then her mother's re-marriage had brought another person into her life, a person destined to give her, while still a young child, much pain and unhappiness. Aloysius McNamara was his name. He was the bastard son of an Irish politician and a Negro washerwoman, and until he had been sent East to a parochial school, Aloysius, so named because that was his father's middle name, had always been known as Aloysius Washington, and the identity of his own father had never been revealed to him by his proud and humble mother. But since his father had been prevailed upon to pay for his education, Aloysius' mother thought it the proper time to tell her son his true origin and to let him assume his real name. She had hopes that away from his home town he might be able to pass for white and march unhindered by bars of color to fame and fortune.

But such was not to be the case, for Emma Lou's prospective stepfather was so conscious of the Negro blood in his veins and so bitter because of it, that he used up whatever talents he had groaning inwardly at capricious fate, and planning revenge upon the world at large, especially the black world. For it was Negroes and not whites whom he blamed for his own, to him, life's tragedy. He was not fair enough of skin, despite his mother's and his own hopes, to pass for white. There was a brownness in his skin, inherited from his mother, which immediately marked him out for what he was, despite the red hair and the Irish blue eyes. And his facial features had been modeled too generously. He was not thin lipped, nor were his nostrils as delicately chiseled as they might have been. He was a Negro. There was no getting around it, although he tried in every possible way to do so.

Finishing school, he had returned West for the express purpose of making his father accept him publicly and personally advance his career. He had wanted to be a lawyer and figured that his father's political pull was sufficiently strong to draw him beyond race barriers and set him as one apart. His father had not been entirely cold to these plans and proposals, but his father's wife had been. She didn't mind her husband giving this nigger bastard of his money, and receiving him in his home on rare and private occasions. She was trying to be liberal, but she wasn't going to have people point to her and say, "That's Boss McNamara's wife. Wonder if that nigger son is his'n or hers. They do say. . . ." So Aloysius had found himself shunted back into the black world he so despised. He couldn't be made to realize that being a Negro did not necessarily indicate that one must also be a ne'er-do-well. Had he been white, or so he said, he would have been a successful criminal lawyer, but being considered black it was impossible for him ever to be anything more advanced than a pullman car porter or a dining car waiter, and acting upon this premise, he hadn't tried to be anything else.

His only satisfaction in life was the pleasure he derived from insulting and ignoring the real blacks. Persons of color, mulattoes, were all right, but he couldn't stand detestable black Negroes. Unfortunately, Emma Lou fell into this latter class, and suffered at his hands accordingly, until he finally ran away from his wife, Emma Lou, Boise, Negroes, and all, ran away to Canada with Diamond Lil of "Whore Row."

Summer vacation was nearly over and it had not yet been decided what to do with Emma Lou now that she had graduated from high school. She herself gave no help nor offered any suggestions. As it was, she really did not care what became of her. After all it didn't seem to matter. There was no place in the world for a girl as black as she anyway. Her grandmother had assured her that she would never find a husband worth a dime, and her mother had said again and again, "Oh, if you had only been a boy!" until Emma Lou had often wondered why it was that people were not able to effect a change of sex or at least a change of complexion.

It was her Uncle Joe who finally prevailed upon her mother to send her to the University of Southern California in Los Angeles. There, he reasoned, she would find a larger and more intelligent social circle. In a city the size of Los Angeles there were Negroes of every class, color, and social position. Let Emma Lou go there where she would not be as far away from home as if she were to go to some eastern college.

Jane and Maria, while not agreeing entirely with what Joe

said, were nevertheless glad that at last something which seemed adequate and sensible could be done for Emma Lou. She was to take the four year college course, receive a bachelor degree in education, then go South to teach. That, they thought, was a promising future, and for once in the eighteen years of Emma Lou's life every one was satisfied in some measure. Even Emma Lou grew elated over the prospects of the trip. Her Uncle Joe's insistence upon the differences of social contacts in larger cities intrigued her. Perhaps he was right after all in continually reasserting to them that as long as one was a Negro, one's specific color had little to do with one's life. Salvation depended upon the individual. And he also told Emma Lou, during one of their usual private talks, that it was only in small cities one encountered stupid color prejudice such as she had encountered among the blue vein circle in her home town.

"People in large cities," he had said, "are broad. They do not have time to think of petty things. The people in Boise are fifty years behind the times, but you will find that Los Angeles is one of the world's greatest and most modern cities, and you will be happy there."

On arriving in Los Angeles, Emma Lou was so busy observing the colored inhabitants that she had little time to pay attention to other things. Palm trees and wild geraniums were pleasant to behold, and such strange phenomena as pepper trees and century plants had to be admired. They were very obvious and they were also strange and beautiful, but they impinged upon only a small corner of Emma Lou's consciousness. She was minutely aware of them, necessarily took them in while passing, viewing the totality without pondering over or lingering to praise their stylistic details. They were, in this instance, exquisite theatrical props, rendered insignificant by a more strange and a more beautiful human pageant. For to Emma Lou, who, in all her life, had never seen over five hundred Negroes, the spectacle presented by a community containing over fifty thousand, was sufficient to make relatively commonplace many more important and charming things than the far famed natural scenery of Southern California.

She had arrived in Los Angeles a week before registration day at the university, and had spent her time in being shown and seeing the city. But whenever these sightseeing excursions took her away from the sections where Negroes lived, she immediately lost all interest in what she was being shown. The Pacific Ocean in itself did not cause her heart beat to quicken, nor did the roaring of its waves find an emotional echo within her. But on coming upon Bruce's Beach for colored people near Redondo, or the little strip of sandied shore they had appropriated for themselves at Santa Monica, the Pacific Ocean became an intriguing something to contemplate as a background for their activities. Everything was interesting as it was patronized, reflected through, or acquired by Negroes.

Her Uncle Joe had been right. Here, in the colored social circles of Los Angeles, Emma Lou was certain that she would find many suitable companions, intelligent, broad-minded people of all complexions, intermixing and being too occupied otherwise to worry about either their own skin color or the skin color of those around them. Her Uncle Joe had said that Negroes were Negroes whether they happened to be yellow, brown, or black, and a conscious effort to eliminate the darker elements would neither prove or solve anything. There was nothing quite so silly as the creed of the blue veins: "Whiter and whiter, every generation. The nearer white you are the more white people will respect you. Therefore all light Negroes marry light Negroes. Continue to do so generation after generation, and eventually white people will accept this racially, bastard aristocracy, thus enabling those Negroes who really matter to escape the social and economic inferiority of the American Negro."

Such had been the credo of her grandmother and of her mother and of their small circle of friends in Boise. But Boise was a provincial town, given to the molding of provincial people with provincial minds. Boise was a backwoods town out of the main stream of modern thought and progress. Its people were cramped and narrow, their intellectual concepts stereotyped and static. Los Angeles was a happy contrast in all respects.

On registration day, Emma Lou rushed out to the campus of the University of Southern California one hour before the registrar's office was scheduled to open. She spent the time roaming around, familiarizing herself with the layout of the campus and learning the names of the various buildings, some old and vineclad, others new and shiny in the sun, and watching the crowds of laughing students, rushing to and fro, greeting one another and talking over their plans for the coming school year. But her main reason for such an early arrival on the campus had been to find some of her fellow Negro students. She had heard that there were to be quite a number enrolled, but in all her hour's stroll she saw not one, and finally somewhat disheartened she got into the line stretched out in front of the registrar's office, and, for the moment, became engrossed in becoming a college freshman.

All the while, though, she kept searching for a colored face, but it was not until she had been duly signed up as a student and sent in search of her advisor that she saw one. Then three colored girls had sauntered into the room where she was having a conference with her advisor, sauntered in, arms interlocked, greeted her advisor, then sauntered out again. Emma Lou had wanted to rush after them—to introduce herself, but of course it had been impossible under the circumstances. She had immediately taken a liking to all three, each of whom was what is known in the parlance of the black belt as high brown, with modishly-shingled bobbed hair and well formed bodies, fashionably attired in flashy sport garments. From then on Emma Lou paid little attention to the business of choosing subjects and class hours, so little attention in fact that the advisor thought her exceptionally tractable and somewhat dumb. But she liked students to come that way. It made the task of being advisor easy. One just made out the program to suit oneself, and had no tedious explanations to make as to why the student could not have such and such a subject at such and such an hour, and why such and such a professor's class was already full.

After her program had been made out, Emma Lou was directed to the bursar's office to pay her fees. While going down the stairs she almost bumped into two dark-brown-skinned boys, obviously brothers if not twins, arguing as to where they should go next. One insisted that they should go back to the registrar's office. The other was being equally insistent that they should go to the gymnasium and make an appointment for their required physical examination. Emma Lou boldly stopped when she saw them, hoping they would speak, but they merely glanced up at her and continued their argument, bringing cards and pamphlets out of their pockets for reference and guidance. Emma Lou wanted to introduce herself to them, but she was too bashful to do so. She wasn't yet used to going to school with other Negro students, and she wasn't exactly certain how one went about becoming acquainted. But she finally decided that she had better let the advances come from the others, especially if they were men. There was nothing forward about her, and since she was a stranger it was no more than right that the old-timers should make her welcome. Still, if these had been girls . . . , but they weren't, so she continued her way down the stairs.

In the bursar's office, she was somewhat overjoyed at first to find that she had fallen into line behind another colored girl who turned around immediately, and, after saying hello, announced in a loud, harsh voice:

"My feet are sure some tired!"

Emma Lou was so taken aback that she couldn't answer. People in college didn't talk that way. But meanwhile the girl was continuing:

"Ain't this registration a mess?"

Two white girls who had fallen into line behind Emma Lou snickered. Emma Lou answered by shaking her head. The girl continued:

"I've been standin' in line and climbin' stairs and talkin' and a-signin' till I'm just 'bout done for."

"It is tiresome," Emma Lou returned softly, hoping the girl would take a hint and lower her own strident voice. But she didn't.

"Tiresome ain't no name for it," she declared more loudly than ever before, then, "Is you a new student?"

"I am," answered Emma Lou, putting much emphasis on the "I am."

She wanted the white people who were listening to know that she knew her grammar if this other person didn't. "Is you," indeed! If this girl was a specimen of the Negro students with whom she was to associate, she most certainly did not want to meet another one. But it couldn't be possible that all of them—those three girls and those two boys for instance—

were like this girl. Emma Lou was unable to imagine how such a person had ever gotten out of high school. Where on earth could she have gone to high school? Surely not in the North. Then she must be a southerner. That's what she was, a southerner—Emma Lou curled her lips a little—no wonder the colored people in Boise spoke as they did about southern Negroes and wished that they would stay South. Imagine any one preparing to enter college saying "Is you," and, to make it worse, right before all these white people, these staring white people, so eager and ready to laugh. Emma Lou's face burned.

"Two mo', then I goes in my sock."

Emma Lou was almost at the place where she was ready to take even this statement literally, and was on the verge of leaving the line. Supposing this creature did "go in her sock!" God forbid!

"Wonder where all the spades keep themselves? I ain't seen but two 'sides you."

"I really do not know," Emma Lou returned precisely and chillily. She had no intentions of becoming friendly with this sort of person. Why she would be ashamed even to be seen on the street with her, dressed as she was in a red-striped sport suit, a white hat, and white shoes and stockings. Didn't she know that black people had to be careful about the colors they affected?

The girl had finally reached the bursar's window and was paying her fees, and loudly differing with the cashier about the total amount due.

"I tell you it ain't that much," she shouted through the window bars. "I figured it up myself before I left home."

The cashier obligingly turned to her adding machine and once more obtained the same total. When shown this, the girl merely grinned, examined the list closely, and said:

"I'm gonna' pay it, but I still think you're wrong."

Finally she moved away from the window, but not before she had turned to Emma Lou and said,

"You're next," and then proceeded to wait until Emma Lou had finished.

Emma Lou vainly sought some way to escape, but was unable to do so, and had no choice but to walk with the girl to the registrar's office where they had their cards stamped in return for the bursar's receipt. This done, they went onto the campus together. Hazel Mason was the girl's name. Emma Lou had fully expected it to be either Hyacinth or Geranium. Hazel was from Texas, Prairie Valley, Texas, and she told Emma Lou that her father, having become quite wealthy when oil had been found on his farm lands, had been enabled to realize two life ambitions—obtain a Packard touring car and send his only daughter to a "fust-class" white school.

Emma Lou had planned to loiter around the campus. She was still eager to become acquainted with the colored members of the student body, and this encounter with the crass and vulgar Hazel Mason had only made her the more eager. She resented being approached by any one so flagrantly inferior, any one so noticeably a typical southern darky, who had no business obtruding into the more refined scheme of things. Emma Lou planned to lose her unwelcome companion somewhere on the campus so that she could continue unhindered her quest for agreeable acquaintances.

But Hazel was as anxious to meet some one as was Emma Lou, and having found her was not going to let her get away without a struggle. She, too, was new to this environment and in a way was more lonely and eager for the companionship of her own kind than Emma Lou, for never before had she come into such close contact with so many whites. Her life had been spent only among Negroes. Her fellow pupils and teachers in school had always been colored, and as she confessed to Emma Lou, she couldn't get used "to all these white folks."

"Honey, I was just achin' to see a black face," she had said, and, though Emma Lou was experiencing the same ache, she found herself unable to sympathize with the other girl, for Emma Lou classified Hazel as a barbarian who had most certainly not come from a family of best people. No doubt her mother had been a washerwoman. No doubt she had innumerable relatives and friends all as ignorant and as ugly as she. There was no sense in any one having a face as ugly as Hazel's, and Emma Lou thanked her stars that though she was black, her skin was not rough and pimply, nor was her hair kinky, nor were her nostrils completely flattened out until they seemed to spread all over her face. No wonder people were prejudiced against dark skinned people when they were so ugly, so haphazard in their dress, and so boisterously mannered as was this present specimen. She herself was black, but nevertheless she had come from a good family, and she could easily take her place in a society of the right sort of people.

The two strolled along the lawn-bordered gravel path which led to a vine-covered building at the end of the campus. Hazel never ceased talking. She kept shouting at Emma Lou, shouting all sorts of personal intimacies as if she were desirous of the whole world hearing them. There was no necessity for her to talk so loudly, no necessity for her to afford every one on the crowded campus the chance to stare and laugh at them as they passed. Emma Lou had never before been so humiliated and so embarrassed. She felt that she must get away from her offensive companion. What did she care if she had to hurt her feelings to do so. The more insulting she could be now, the less friendly she would have to be in the future.

"Good-by," she said abruptly, "I must go home." With which she turned away and walked rapidly in the opposite direction. She had only gone a few steps when she was aware of the fact that the girl was following her. She quickened her pace, but the girl caught up with her and grabbing hold of Emma Lou's arm, shouted,

"Whoa there, Sally."

It seemed to Emma Lou as if every one on the campus was viewing and enjoying this minstrel-like performance. Angrily she tried to jerk away, but the girl held fast.

"Gal, you sure walk fast. I'm going your way. Come on, let me drive you home in my buggy."

And still holding on to Emma Lou's arm, she led the way to the side street where the students parked their cars. Emma Lou was powerless to resist. The girl didn't give her a chance, for she held tight, then immediately resumed the monologue which Emma Lou's attempted leave-taking had interrupted. They reached the street, Hazel still talking loudly, and making elaborate gestures with her free hand.

"Here we are," she shouted, and releasing Emma Lou's arm, salaamed before a sport model Stutz roadster. "Oscar," she continued, "meet the new girl friend. Pleased to meetcha, says he. Climb aboard."

And Emma Lou had climbed aboard, perplexed, chagrined,

thoroughly angry, and disgusted. What was this little black fool doing with a Stutz roadster? And of course, it would be painted red—Negroes always bedecked themselves and their belongings in ridiculously unbecoming colors and ornaments. It seemed to be a part of their primitive heritage which they did not seem to have sense enough to forget and deny. Black girl—white hat—red and white striped sport suit—white shoes and stockings—red roadster. The picture was complete. All Hazel needed to complete her circus-like appearance, thought Emma Lou, was to have some purple feathers stuck in her hat.

Still talking, the girl unlocked and proceeded to start the car. As she was backing it out of the narrow parking space, Emma Lou heard a chorus of semi-suppressed giggles from a neighboring automobile. In her anger she had failed to notice that there were people in the car parked next to the Stutz. But as Hazel expertly swung her machine around, Emma Lou caught a glimpse of them. They were all colored and they were all staring at her and at Hazel. She thought she recognized one of the girls as being one of the group she had seen earlier that morning, and she did recognize the two brothers she had passed on the stairs. And as the roadster sped away, their laughter echoed in her ears, although she hadn't actually heard it. But she had seen the strain in their faces, and she knew that as soon as she and Hazel were out of sight, they would give free rein to their suppressed mirth.

Although Emma Lou had finished registering, she returned to the university campus on the following morning in order to continue her quest for collegiate companions without the alarming and unwelcome presence of Hazel Mason. She didn't know whether to be sorry for the girl and try to help her or to be disgusted and avoid her. She didn't want to be intimately associated with any such vulgar person. It would damage her own position, cause her to be classified with some one who was in a class by herself, for Emma Lou was certain that there was not, and could not be, any one else in the university just like Hazel. But despite her vulgarity, the girl was not all bad. Her good nature was infectious, and Emma Lou had surmised from her monologue on the day before how utterly unselfish a person she could be and was. All of her store of the world's goods were at hand to be used and enjoyed by her friends. There was not, as she had said, "a selfish bone in her body." But even that did not alter the disgusting fact that she was not one who would be welcome by the "right sort of people." Her flamboyant style of dress, her loud voice, her raucous laughter, and her flagrant disregard or ignorance of English grammar seemed inexcusable to Emma Lou, who was unable to understand how such a person could stray so far from the environment in which she rightfully belonged to enter a first class university. Now Hazel, according to Emma Lou, was the type of Negro who should go to a Negro college. There were plenty of them in the South whose standard of scholarship was not beyond her ability. And then, in one of those schools, her darky-like clownishness would not have to be paraded in front of white people, thereby causing discomfort and embarrassment to others of her race, more civilized and circumspect than she.

The problem irritated Emma Lou. She didn't see why it had to be. She had looked forward so anxiously, and so happily to her introductory days on the campus, and now her first experience with one of her fellow colored students had been an unpleasant one. But she didn't intend to let that make her unhappy. She was determined to return to the campus alone, seek out other companions, see whether they accepted or ignored the offending Hazel, and govern herself accordingly.

It was early and there were few people on the campus. The grass was still wet from a heavy overnight dew, and the sun had not yet dispelled the coolness of the early morning. Emma Lou's dress was of thin material and she shivered as she walked or stood in the shade. She had no school business to attend to; there was nothing for her to do but to walk aimlessly about the campus.

In another hour, Emma Lou was pleased to see that the campus walks were becoming crowded, and that the side streets surrounding the campus were now heavy with student traffic. Things were beginning to awaken. Emma Lou became jubilant and walked with jaunty step from path to path, from building to building. It then occurred to her that she had been told that there were more Negro students enrolled in the School of Pharmacy than in any other department of the university, so finding the Pharmacy building she began to wander through its crowded hallways.

Almost immediately, she saw a group of five Negro students, three boys and two girls, standing near a water fountain. She was both excited and perplexed, excited over the fact that she was so close to those she wished to find, and perplexed because she did not know how to approach them. Had there been only one person standing there, the matter would have been comparatively easy. She could have approached with a smile and said, "Good morning." The person would have returned her greeting, and it would then have been a simple matter to get acquainted.

But five people in one bunch, all known to one another and all chatting intimately together!—it would seem too much like an intrusion to go bursting into their gathering—too forward and too vulgar. Then, there was nothing she could say after having said "good morning." One just didn't break into a group of five and say, "I'm Emma Lou Morgan, a new student, and I want to make friends with you." No, she couldn't do that. She would just smile as she passed, smile graciously and friendly. They would know that she was a stranger, and her smile would assure them that she was anxious to make friends, anxious to become a welcome addition to their group.

One of the group of five had sighted Emma Lou as soon as she had sighted them:

"Who's this?" queried Helen Wheaton, a senior in the College of Law.

"Some new 'pick,' I guess," answered Bob Armstrong, who was Helen's fiance and a senior in the School of Architecture.

"I bet she's going to take Pharmacy," whispered Amos Blaine.

"She's hottentot enough to take something," mumbled Tommy Brown. "Thank God, she won't be in any of our classes, eh Amos?"

Emma Lou was almost abreast of them now. They lowered their voices, and made a pretense of mumbled conversation among themselves. Only Verne Davis looked directly at her and it was she alone who returned Emma Lou's smile.

"Whatcha grinnin' at?" Bob chided Verne as Emma Lou passed out of earshot.

"At the little frosh, of course. She grinned at me. I couldn't stare at her without returning it."

"I don't see how anybody could even look at her without grinning."

"Oh, she's not so bad," said Verne.

"Well, she's bad enough."

"That makes two of them."

"Two of what, Amos?"

"Hottentots, Bob."

"Good grief," exclaimed Tommy, "why don't you recruit some good-looking co-eds out here?"

"We don't choose them," Helen returned.

"I'm going out to the Southern Branch where the sight of my fellow female students won't give me dyspepsia."

"Ta-ta, Amos," said Verne, "and you needn't bother to sit in my car any more if you think us so terrible." She and Helen walked away, leaving the boys to discuss the sad days which had fallen upon the campus.

Emma Lou, of course, knew nothing of all this. She had gone her way rejoicing. One of the students had noticed her, had returned her smile. This getting acquainted was going to be an easy matter after all. It was just necessary that she exercise a little patience. One couldn't expect people to fall all over one without some preliminary advances. True, she was a stranger, but she would show them in good time that she was worthy of their attention, that she was a good fellow and a well-bred individual quite prepared to be accepted by the best people.

She strolled out on to the campus again trying to find more prospective acquaintances. The sun was warm now, the grass dry, and the campus overcrowded. There was an infectious germ of youth and gladness abroad to which Emma Lou could not remain immune. Already she was certain that she felt the presence of that vague something known as "college spirit." It seemed to enter into her, to make her jubilant and set her every nerve tingling. This was no time for sobriety. It was the time for youth's blood to run hot, the time for love and sport and wholesome fun.

Then Emma Lou saw a solitary Negro girl seated on a stone bench. It did not take her a second to decide what to do. Here was her chance. She would make friends with this girl and should she happen to be a new student, they could become friends and together find their way into the inner circle of those colored students who really mattered.

Emma Lou was essentially a snob. She had absorbed this trait from the very people who had sought to exclude her from their presence. All of her life she had heard talk of "right sort of people," and of "the people who really mattered," and from these phrases she had formed a mental image of those to whom they applied. Hazel Mason most certainly could not be included in either of these categories. Hazel was just a vulgar little nigger from down South. It was her kind, who, when they came North, made it hard for the colored people already resident there. It was her kind who knew nothing of the social niceties or the polite conventions. In their own home they had been used only to coarse work and coarser manners. And they had been forbidden the chance to have intimate contact in schools and in public with white people from whom they might absorb some semblance of culture. When they did come North and get a chance to go to white schools, white theaters, and white libraries, they were too unused to them to appreciate what they were getting, and could be expected to continue their old way of life in an environment where such a way was decidedly out of place.

Emma Lou was determined to become associated only with those people who really mattered, northerners like herself or superior southerners, if there were any, who were different from whites only in so far as skin color was concerned. This girl, to whom she was now about to introduce herself, was the type she had in mind, genteel, well and tastily dressed, and not ugly.

"Good morning."

Alma Martin looked up from the book she was reading, gulped in surprise, then answered, "Good morning."

Emma Lou sat down on the bench. She was congeniality itself. "Are you a new student?" she inquired of the astonished Alma, who wasn't used to this sort of thing.

"No, I'm a 'soph'," then realizing she was expected to say more, "you're new, aren't you?"

"Oh yes," replied Emma Lou, her voice buoyant and glad. "This will be my first year."

"Do you think you will like it?"

"I'm just crazy about it already. You know," she advanced confidentially, "I've never gone to school with any colored people before."

"No?"

"No, and I am just dying to get acquainted with the colored students. Oh, my name's Emma Lou Morgan."

"And mine is Alma Martin."

They both laughed. There was a moment of silence. Alma looked at her wrist watch, then got up from the bench.

"I'm glad to have met you. I've got to see my advisor at ten-thirty. Good-by." And she moved away gracefully.

Emma Lou was having difficulty in keeping from clapping her hands. At last she had made some headway. She had met a second-year student, one who, from all appearances, was in the know, and, who, as they met from time to time, would see that she met others. In a short time Emma Lou felt that she would be in the whirl of things collegiate. She must write to her Uncle Joe immediately and let him know how well things were going. He had been right. This was the place for her to be. There had been no one in Boise worth considering. Here she was coming into contact with really superior people, intelligent, genteel, college-bred, all trying to advance themselves and their race, unconscious of intra-racial schisms, caused by differences in skin color.

She mustn't stop upon meeting one person. She must find others, so once more she began her quest and almost immediately met Verne and Helen strolling down one of the campus paths. She remembered Verne as the girl who had smiled at her. She observed her more closely, and admired her pleasant dark brown face, made doubly attractive by two evenly placed dimples and a pair of large, heavily-lidded, pitch black eyes. Emma Lou thought her to be much more attractive than the anemic-looking yellow girl with whom she was strolling. There was something about this second girl which made Emma Lou feel that she was not easy to approach.

"Good morning." Emma Lou had evolved a formula.

"Good morning," the two girls spoke in unison. Helen was about to walk on but Verne stopped.

"New student?" she asked.

"Yes, I am."

"So am I. I'm Verne Davis."

"I'm Emma Lou Morgan."

"And this is Helen Wheaton."

"Pleased to meet you, Miss Morgan."

"And I'm pleased to meet you, too, both of you," gushed Emma Lou. "You see, I'm from Boise, Idaho, and all through high school I was the only colored student."

"Is that so?" Helen inquired listlessly. Then turning to Verne said, "Better come on Verne if you are going to drive us out to the 'Branch'."

"All right. We've got to run along now. We'll see you again, Miss Morgan. Good-by."

"Good-by," said Emma Lou and stood watching them as they went on their way. Yes, college life was going to be the thing to bring her out, the turning point in her life. She would show the people back in Boise that she did not have to be a "no-gooder" as they claimed her father had been, just because she was black. She would show all of them that a dark skin girl could go as far in life as a fair skin one, and that she could have as much opportunity and as much happiness. What did the color of one's skin have to do with one's mentality or native ability? Nothing whatsoever. If a black boy could get along in the world, so could a black girl, and it would take her, Emma Lou Morgan, to prove it.

With which she set out to make still more acquaintances.

Two weeks of school had left Emma Lou's mind in a chaotic state. She was unable to draw any coherent conclusions from the jumble of new things she had experienced. In addition to her own social strivings, there had been the academic routine to which she had had to adapt herself. She had found it all bewildering and overpowering. The university was a huge business proposition and every one in it had jobs to perform. Its bigness awed her. Its blatant reality shocked her. There was nothing romantic about going to college. It was, indeed, a serious business. One went there with a purpose and had several other purposes inculcated into one after school began. This getting an education was stern and serious, regulated and systematized, dull and unemotional.

Besides being disappointed at the drabness and lack of romance in college routine, Emma Lou was also depressed by her inability to make much headway in the matter of becoming intimately associated with her colored campus mates. They were all polite enough. They all acknowledged their introductions to her and would speak whenever they passed her, but seldom did any of them stop for a chat, and when she joined the various groups which gathered on the campus lawn between classes, she always felt excluded and out of things because she found herself unable to participate in the general conversation. They talked of things about which she knew nothing, of parties and dances, and of people she did not know. They seemed to live a life off the campus to which she was not privy, and into which they did not seem particularly anxious to introduce her.

She wondered why she never knew of the parties they talked about, and why she never received invitations to any of their affairs. Perhaps it was because she was still new and comparatively unknown to them. She felt that she must not forget that most of them had known one another for a long period of time and that it was necessary for people who "belonged" to be wary of strangers. That was it. She was still a stranger, had only been among them for about two weeks. What did she expect? Why was she so impatient?

The thought of the color question presented itself to her time and time again, but she would always dismiss it from her mind. Verne Davis was dark and she was not excluded from the sacred inner circle. In fact, she was one of the most popular colored girls on the campus. The only thing that perplexed Emma Lou was that although Verne too was new to the group, had just recently moved into the city, and was also just beginning her first year at the University, she had not been kept at a distance or excluded from any of the major extra-collegiate activities. Emma Lou could not understand why there should be this difference in their social acceptance. She was certainly as good as Verne.

In time Emma Lou became certain that it was because of her intimacy with Hazel that the people on the campus she really wished to be friendly with paid her so little attention. Hazel was a veritable clown. She went scooting about the campus, cutting capers, playing the darky for the amused white students. Any time Hazel asked or answered a question in any of the lecture halls, there was certain to be laughter. She had a way of phrasing what she wished to say in a manner which was invariably laugh provoking. The very tone and quality of her voice designated her as a minstrel type. In the gymnasium she would do buck and wing dances and play low-down blues on the piano. She was a pariah among her own people because she did not seem to know, as they knew, that Negroes could not afford to be funny in front of white people even if that was their natural inclination. Negroes must always be sober and serious in order to impress white people with their adaptability and non-difference in all salient characteristics save skin color. All of the Negro students on the campus, except Emma Lou, laughed at her openly and called her Topsy. Emma Lou felt sorry for her although she, too, regretted her comic propensities and wished that she would be less the vaudevillian and more the college student.

Besides Hazel, there was only one other person on the campus who was friendly with Emma Lou. This was Grace Giles, also a black girl, who was registered in the School of Music. The building in which she had her classes was located some distance away, and Grace did not get over to the main campus grounds very often, but when she did, she always looked for Emma Lou and made welcome overtures of friendship. It was her second year in the university, and yet, she too seemed to be on the outside of things. She didn't seem to be invited to the parties and dances, nor was she a member of the Greek letter sorority which the colored girls had organized. Emma Lou asked her why.

"Have they pledged you?" was Grace Giles' answer.

"Why no."

"And they won't either."

"Why?" Emma Lou asked surprised.

"Because you are not a high brown or half-white."

Emma Lou had thought this too, but she had been loathe to believe it.

"You're silly, Grace. Why—Verne belongs."

"Yeah," Grace had sneered, "Verne, a bishop's daughter with plenty of coin and a big Buick. Why shouldn't they ask her?"

Emma Lou did not know what to make of this. She did not want to believe that the same color prejudice which existed among the blue veins in Boise also existed among the colored college students. Grace Giles was just hypersensitive. She wasn't taking into consideration the fact that she was not on the campus regularly and thus could not expect to be treated as if she were. Emma Lou fully believed that had Grace been a regularly enrolled student like herself, she would have found things different, and she was also certain that both she and Grace would be asked to join the sorority in due time.

But they weren't. Nor did an entire term in the school change things one whit. The Christmas holidays had come and gone and Emma Lou had not been invited to one of the many parties. She and Grace and Hazel bound themselves together and sought their extra-collegiate pleasures among people not on the campus. Hazel began to associate with a group of housemaids and mature youths who worked only when they had to, and played the pool rooms and the housemaids as long as they proved profitable. Hazel was a welcome addition to this particular group what with her car and her full pocket-book. She had never been proficient in her studies, had always found it impossible to keep pace with the other students, and, finally realizing that she did not belong and perhaps never would, had decided to "go to the devil," and be done with it.

It was not long before Hazel was absent from the campus more often than she was present. Going to cabarets and parties, and taking long drunken midnight drives made her more and more unwilling and unable to undertake the scholastic grind on the next morning. Just before the mid-term examinations, she was advised by the faculty to drop out of school until the next year, and to put herself in the hands of a tutor during the intervening period. It was evident that her background was not all that it should be; her preparatory work had not been sufficiently complete to enable her to continue in college. As it was, they told her, she was wasting her time. So Hazel disappeared from the campus and was said to have gone back to Texas. "Serves her right, glad she's gone," was the verdict of her colored campus fellows.

The Christmas holidays for Emma Lou were dull and uneventful. The people she lived with were rheumatic and not much given to yuletide festivities. It didn't seem like Christmas to Emma Lou anyway. There was no snow on the ground, and the sun was shining as brightly and as warmly as it had shone during the late summer and early autumn months. The wild geraniums still flourished, the orange trees were blossoming, and the whole southland seemed to be preparing for the annual New Year's Day Tournament of Roses parade in Pasadena.

Emma Lou received a few presents from home, and a Christmas greeting card from Grace Giles. That was all. On Christmas Day she and Grace attended church in the morning, and spent the afternoon at the home of one of Grace's friends. Emma Lou never liked the people to whom Grace introduced her. They were a dull, commonplace lot for the most part, people from Georgia, Grace's former home, untutored people who didn't really matter. Emma Lou borrowed a word from her grandmother and classified them as "fuddlers," because they seemed to fuddle everything—their language, their clothes, their attempts at politeness, and their efforts to appear more intelligent than they really were.

The holidays over, Emma Lou returned to school a little reluctantly. She wasn't particularly interested in her studies, but having nothing else to do kept up in them and made high grades. Meanwhile she had been introduced to a number of young men and gone out with them occasionally. They too were friends of Grace's and of the same caliber as Grace's other friends. There were no college boys among them except Joe Lane who was flunking out in the School of Dentistry. He did not interest Emma Lou. As it was with Joe, so it was with all the other boys. She invariably picked them to pieces when they took her out, and remained so impassive to their emotional advances that they were soon glad to be on their way and let her be. Emma Lou was determined not to go out of her class, determined either to associate with the "right sort of people" or else to remain to herself.

Had any one asked Emma Lou what she meant by the "right sort of people" she would have found herself at a loss for a comprehensive answer. She really didn't know. She had a vague idea that those people on the campus who practically ignored her were the only people with whom she should associate. These people, for the most part, were children of fairly well-to-do families from Louisiana, Texas and Georgia, who, having made nest eggs, had journeyed to the West for the same reasons that her grandparents at an earlier date had also journeyed West. They wanted to live where they would have greater freedom and greater opportunity for both their children and themselves. Then, too, the World War had given impetus to this westward movement. There was more industry in the West and thus more chances for money to be made, and more opportunities to invest this money profitably in property and progeny.

The greater number of them were either mulattoes or light brown in color. In their southern homes they had segregated themselves from their darker skinned brethren and they continued this practice in the North. They went to the Episcopal, Presbyterian, or Catholic churches, and though they were not as frankly organized into a blue vein society as were the Negroes of Boise, they nevertheless kept more or less to themselves. They were not insistent that their children get "whiter and whiter every generation", but they did want to keep their children and grandchildren from having dark complexions. A light brown was the favored color; it was therefore found expedient to exercise caution when it came to mating.

The people who, in Emma Lou's phrase, really mattered, the business men, the doctors, the lawyers, the dentists, the more moneyed pullman porters, hotel waiters, bank janitors, and majordomos, in fact all of the Negro leaders and members of the Negro upper class, were either light skinned themselves or else had light skinned wives. A wife of dark complexion was considered a handicap unless she was particularly charming, wealthy, or beautiful. An ordinary looking dark woman was no suitable mate for a Negro man of prominence. The college youths on whom the future of the race depended practiced this precept of their elders religiously. It was not the girls in the school who were prejudiced—they had no reason to be, but they knew full well that the boys with whom they wished to associate, their future husbands, would not tolerate a dark girl unless she had, like Verne, many things to compensate for her dark skin. Thus they did not encourage a friendship with some one whom they knew didn't belong. Thus they did not even pledge girls like Grace, Emma Lou, and Hazel into their sorority, for they knew that it would make them the more miserable to attain the threshold only to have the door shut in their faces.

Summer vacation time came and Emma Lou went back to Boise. She was thoroughly discouraged and depressed. She had been led to expect so much pleasure from her first year in college and in Los Angeles; but she had found that the people in large cities were after all no different from people in small cities. Her Uncle Joe had been wrong—her mother and grandmother had been right. There was no place in the world for a dark girl.

Being at home depressed her all the more. There was absolutely nothing for her to do nor any place for her to go. For a month or more she just lingered around the house, bored by her mother's constant and difficult attempts to be maternal, and irritated by her Cousin Buddy's freshness. Adolescent boys were such a nuisance. The only bright spot on the horizon was the Sunday School Union picnic scheduled to be held during the latter part of July. It was always the crowning social event of the summer season among the colored citizens of Boise. Both the Methodists and Baptists missions cooperated in this affair and had their numbers augmented by all the denominationally unattached members of the community. It was always a gala, democratic affair designed to provide a pleasant day in the out-of-doors. It was, besides the annual dance fostered by the local chapters of the Masons and the Elks, the only big community gathering to which the entire colored population of Boise looked forward.

Picnic day came, and Emma Lou accompanied her mother, her uncle, and her cousin to Bedney's Meadow, a green, heavily forested acre of park land, which lay on the outskirts of the city, surrounded on three sides by verdant foothills. The day went by pleasantly enough. There were the usually heavily laden wooden tables, to which all adjourned in the late afternoon, and there were foot races, games, and canoeing.

Emma Lou took part in all these activities and was surprised to find that she was having a good time. The company was congenial, and she found that since she had gone away to college she had become somewhat of a personage. Every one seemed to be going out of his way to be congenial to her. The blue veins did not rule this affair. They were, in fact, only a minority element, and, for one of the few times of the year, mingled freely and unostentatiously with their lower caste brethren.

All during the day, Emma Lou found herself paired off with a chap by the name of Weldon Taylor. In the evening they went for a stroll up the precipitous footpaths in the hills which grew up from the meadow. Weldon Taylor was a newcomer in the West trying to earn sufficient money to re-enter an eastern school and finish his medical education. Emma Lou rather liked him. She admired his tall, slender body, the deep burnish of his bronze colored skin, and his mass of black curly hair. Here, thought Emma Lou, is the type of man I like. Only she did wish that his skin had been colored light brown instead of dark brown. It was better if she was to marry that she did not get a dark skin mate. Her children must not suffer as she had and would suffer.

The two talked of commonplace things as they walked along, comparing notes on their school experiences, and talking of their professors and their courses of study. It was dusk now and the sun had disappeared behind the snow capped mountains. The sky was a colorful haze, a master artist's canvas on which the colors of day were slowly being dominated by the colors of night. Weldon drew Emma Lou off the little path they had been following, and led her to a huge bowlder which jutted out, elbow like, from the side of a hill, and which was hidden from the meadow below by clumps of bushes. They sat down, his arm slipped around her waist, and, as the darkness of night more and more conquered the evanescent light of day, their lips met, and Emma Lou grew lax in Weldon's arms. . . .

When they finally returned to the picnic grounds all had left save a few stragglers like themselves who had sauntered away from the main party. These made up a laughing, half-embarrassed group, who collected their baskets and reluctantly withdrew from the meadow to begin the long walk back to their homes. Emma Lou and Weldon soon managed to fall at the end of the procession, walking along slowly, his arm around her waist. Emma Lou felt an ecstasy surging through her at this moment greater than she had ever known before. This had been her first intimate sexual contact, her first awareness of the physical and emotional pleasures able to be enjoyed by two human beings, a woman and a man. She felt some magnetic force drawing her to this man walking by her side, which made her long to feel the pleasure of his body against hers, made her want to know once more the pleasure which had attended the union of their lips, the touching of their tongues. It was with a great effort that she walked along apparently calm, for inside she was seething. Her body had become a kennel for clashing, screaming compelling urges and desires. She loved this man. She had submitted herself to him, had gladly suffered momentary physical pain in order to be introduced into a new and incomparably satisfying paradise.

Not for one moment did Emma Lou consider regretting the loss of her virtue, not once did any of her mother's and grandmother's warnings and solicitations revive themselves and cause her conscience to plague her. She had finally found herself a mate; she had finally come to know the man she should love, some inescapable force had drawn them together, had made them feel from the first moment of their introduction that they belonged to one another, and that they were destined to explore nature's mysteries together. Life was not so cruel after all. There were some compensatory moments. Emma Lou believed that at last she had found happiness, that at last she had found her man.

Of course, she wasn't going back to school. She was going to stay in Boise, marry Weldon, and work with him until they should have sufficient money to go East, where he could re-enter medical school, and she could keep a home for him and spur him on. A glorious panorama of the future unrolled itself in her mind. There were no black spots in it, no shadows, nothing but luminous landscapes, ethereal in substance.

It was the way of Emma Lou always to create her worlds within her own mind without taking under consideration the fact that other people and other elements, not contained within herself, would also have to aid in their molding. She had lived to herself for so long, had been shut out from the stream of things in which she was interested for such a long period during the formative years of her life, that she considered her own imaginative powers omniscient. Thus she constructed a future world of love on one isolated experience, never thinking for the moment that the other party concerned might not be of the same mind. She had been lifted into a superlatively perfect emotional and physical state. It was unthinkable, incongruous, that Weldon, too, had not been similarly lifted. He had for the moment shared her ecstasy, therefore, according to Emma Lou's line of reasoning, he would as effectively share what she imagined would be the fruits of that ecstatic moment.

The next two weeks passed quickly and happily. Weldon called on her almost every night, took her for long walks, and thrilled her with his presence and his love making. Never before in her life had Emma Lou been so happy. She forgot all the sad past. Forgot what she had hitherto considered the tragedy of her birth, forgot the social isolation of her childhood and of her college days. What did being black, what did the antagonistic mental attitudes of the people who really mattered mean when she was in love? Her mother and her Uncle Joe were so amazed at the change in her that they became afraid, sensed danger, and began to be on the look-out for some untoward development; for hitherto Emma Lou had always been sullen and morose and impertinent to all around the house. She had always been the anti-social creature they had caused her to feel she was and, since she was made to feel that she was a misfit, she had encroached upon their family life and sociabilities only to the extent that being in the house made necessary. But now she was changed—she had become a vibrant, joyful being. There was always a smile on her face, always a note of joy in her voice as she spoke or sang. She even made herself agreeable to her Cousin Buddy, who in the past she had either ignored or else barely tolerated.

"She must be in love, Joe," her mother half whined.

"That's good," he answered laconically. "It probably won't last long. It will serve to take her mind off herself."

"But suppose she gets foolish?" Jane had insisted, remembering no doubt her own foolishness, during a like period of her own life, with Emma Lou's father.

"She'll take care of herself," Joe had returned with an assurance he did not feel. He, too, was worried, but he was also pleased at the change in Emma Lou. His only fear was that perhaps in the end she would make herself more miserable than she had ever been before. He did not know much about this Weldon fellow, who seemed to be a reliable enough chap, but no one had any way of discerning whether or no his intentions were entirely honorable. It was best, thought Joe, not to worry about such things. If, for the present, Emma Lou was more happy than she had ever been before, there would be time enough to worry about the future when its problems materialized.

"Don't you worry about Emma Lou. She's got sense."

"But, Joe, suppose she does forget herself with this man? He is studying to be a doctor and he may not want a wife, especially when. . . ."

"Damn it, Jane!" her brother snapped at her. "Do you think every one is like you? The boy seems to like her."

"Men like any one they can use, but you know as well as I that no professional man is going to marry a woman dark as Emma Lou."

"Men marry any one they love, just as you and I did."

"But I was foolish."

"Well?"

"That's right—Be unconcerned. That's right—Let her go to the devil. There's no hope for her anyway. Oh—why—why did I marry Jim Morgan?" and she had gone into the usual crying fit which inevitably followed this self-put question.

Then, without any warning, as if to put an end to all problems, Weldon decided to become a Pullman porter. He explained to Emma Lou that he could make more money on the railroad than he could as a hotel waiter in Boise. It was necessary for his future that he make as much money as possible in as short a time as possible. Emma Lou saw the logic of this and agreed that it was the best possible scheme, until she realized that it meant his going away from Boise, perhaps forever. Oakland, California, was to be his headquarters, and he, being a new man, would not have a regular run. It was possible that he might be sent to different sections of the country each and every time he made a trip. There was no way of his knowing before he reported for duty just where he might be sent. It might be Boise or Palm Beach or Albany or New Orleans. One never knew. That was the life of the road, and one had to accept it in order to make money.

It made Emma Lou shiver to hear him talk so dispassionately about the matter. There didn't seem to be the least note of regret in his voice, the least suggestion that he hated to leave her or that he would miss her, and, for the first time since the night of their physical union, Emma Lou began to realize that perhaps after all he did not feel toward her as she did toward him. He couldn't possibly love her as much as she loved him, and, at the same time, remain so unconcerned about having to part from her. There was something radically wrong here, something conclusive and unexpected which was going to hurt her, going to plunge her back into unhappiness once more. Then she realized that not once had he ever spoken of marriage or even hinted that their relationship would continue indefinitely. He had said that he loved her, he had treated her kindly, and had seemed as thrilled as she over their physical contacts. But now it seemed that since he was no longer going to be near her, no longer going to need her body, he had forgotten that he loved her. It was then that all the old preachments of her mother and grandmother were resurrected and began to swirl through her mind. Hadn't she been warned that men didn't marry black girls? Hadn't she been told that they would only use her for their sexual convenience? That was the case with Weldon! He hadn't cared about her in the first place. He had taken up with her only because he was a stranger in the town and lonesome for a companion, and she, like a damn fool, had submitted herself to him! And now that he was about to better his condition, about to go some place where he would have a wider circle of acquaintances, she was to be discarded and forgotten.

Thus Emma Lou reasoned to herself and grew bitter. It never occurred to her that the matter of her color had never once entered the mind of Weldon. Not once did she consider that he was acting toward her as he would have acted toward any girl under similar circumstances, whether her face had been white, yellow, brown, or black. Emma Lou did not understand that Weldon was just a selfish normal man and not a color prejudiced one, at least not while he was resident in a community where the girls were few, and there were none of his college friends about to tease him for liking "dark meat." She did not know that for over a year he had been traveling about from town to town, always seeking a place where money was more plentiful and more easily saved, and that in every town he had managed to find a girl, or girls, who made it possible for him to continue his grind without being totally deprived of pleasurable moments. To Emma Lou there could only be one reason for his not having loved her as she had loved him. She was a black girl and no professional man could afford to present such a wife in the best society. It was the tragic feature of her life once more asserting itself. There could be no happiness in life for any woman whose face was as black as hers.

Believing this more intensely than ever before Emma Lou yet felt that she must manage in some way to escape both home and school. That she must find happiness somewhere else. The idea her Uncle Joe had given her about the provinciality of people in small towns re-entered her mind. After all Los Angeles, too, was a small town mentally, peopled by mentally small southern Negroes. It was no better than Boise. She was now determined to go East where life was more cosmopolitan and people were more civilized. To this end she begged her mother and uncle to send her East to school.

"Can't you ever be satisfied?"

"Now Jane," Joe as usual was trying to keep the peace——

"Now Jane, nothing! I never saw such an ungrateful child."

"I'm not ungrateful. I'm just unhappy. I don't like that school. I don't want to go there any more."

"Well, you'll either go there or else stay home." Thus Jane ended the discussion and could not be persuaded to reopen it.

And rather than remain home Emma Lou returned to Los Angeles and spent another long miserable, uneventful year in the University of Southern California, drawing more and more within herself and becoming more and more bitter. When vacation time came again she got herself a job as maid in a theater, rather than return home, and studied stenography during her spare hours. School began again and Emma Lou re-entered with more determination than ever to escape should the chance present itself. It did, and once more Emma Lou fled into an unknown town to escape the haunting chimera of intra-racial color prejudice.

PART II

Harlem

EMMA LOU turned her face away from the wall, and quizzically squinted her dark, pea-like eyes at the recently closed door. Then, sitting upright, she strained her ears, trying to hear the familiar squeak of the impudent floor boards, as John tiptoed down the narrow hallway toward the outside door. Finally, after she had heard the closing click of the double-barrelled police lock, she climbed out of the bed, picked up a brush from the bureau and attempted to smooth the sensuous disorder of her hair. She had just recently had it bobbed, boyishly bobbed, because she thought this style narrowed and enhanced the fulsome lines of her facial features. She was always trying to emphasize those things about her that seemed, somehow, to atone for her despised darkness, and she never faced the mirror without speculating upon how good-looking she might have been had she not been so black.

Mechanically, she continued the brushing of her hair, stopping every once in a while to give it an affectionate caress. She was intensely in love with her hair, in love with its electric vibrancy and its unruly buoyance. Yet, this morning, she was irritated because it seemed so determined to remain disordered, so determined to remain a stubborn and unnecessary reminder of the night before. Why, she wondered, should one's physical properties always insist upon appearing awry after a night of stolen or forbidden pleasure? But not being anxious to find an answer, she dismissed the question from her mind, put on a stocking-cap, and jumped back into the bed.

She began to think about John, poor John who felt so hurt because she had told him that he could not spend any more days or nights with her. She wondered if she should pity him, for she was certain that he would miss the nights more than he would the days. Yet, she must not be too harsh in her conclusions, for, after all, there had only been two nights, which, she smiled to herself, was a pretty good record for a newcomer to

Harlem. She had been in New York now for five weeks, and it seemed like, well, just a few days. Five weeks—thirty-five days and thirty-five nights, and of these nights John had had two. And now he sulked because she would not promise him another; because she had, in fact, boldly told him that there could be no more between them. Mischievously, she wished now that she could have seen the expression on his face, when, after seeming moments of mutual ecstasy, she had made this cold, manifesto-like announcement. But the room had been dark, and so was John. Ugh!

She had only written home twice. This, of course, seemed quite all right to her. She was not concerned about any one there except her Uncle Joe, and she reasoned that since he was preparing to marry again, he would be far too busy to think much about her. All that worried her was the pitiful spectacle of her mother, her uncle, and her cousin trying to make up lies to tell inquiring friends. Well, she would write today, that is, if she did not start to work, and she must get up at eight o'clock—was the alarm set?—and hie herself to an employment agency. She had only thirty-five dollars left in the bank, and, unless it was replenished, she might have to rescind her avowals to John in order to get her room rent paid.

She must go to sleep for another hour, for she wished to look "pert" when she applied for a job, especially the kind of job she wanted, and she must get the kind of job she wanted in order to show those people in Boise and Los Angeles that she had been perfectly justified in leaving school, home, and all, to come to New York. They all wondered why she had come. So did she, now that she was here. But at the moment of leaving she would have gone any place to escape having to remain in that hateful Southern California college, or having to face the more dreaded alternative of returning home. Home? It had never been a home.

It did seem strange, this being in Harlem when only a few weeks before she had been over three thousand miles away. Time and distance—strange things, immutable, yet conquerable. But was time conquerable? Hadn't she read or heard somewhere that all things were subject to time, even God? Yet, once she was there and now she was here. But even at that she hadn't conquered time. What was that line in Cullen's verse, "I run, but Time's abreast with me?" She had only traversed space and defied distance. This suggested a more banal, if a less arduous thought tangent. She had defied more than distance, she had defied parental restraint—still there hadn't been much of that —friendly concern—there had been still less of that, and malicious, meddlesome gossip, of which there had been plenty. And she still found herself unable to understand why two sets of people in two entirely different communities should seemingly become almost hysterically excited because she, a woman of twenty-one, with three years' college training and ample sophistication in the ways of sex and self-support, had decided to take a job as an actress' maid in order to get to New York. They had never seemed interested in her before.

Now she wondered why had she been so painfully anxious to come to New York. She had given as a consoling reason to inquisitive friends and relatives, school. But she knew too well that she had no intentions of ever re-entering school. She had had enough of *that* school in Los Angeles, and her experiences there, more than anything else, had caused this foolhardy hegira to Harlem. She had been desperately driven to escape, and had she not escaped in this manner she might have done something else much more mad.

Emma Lou closed her eyes once more, and tried to sublimate her mental reverie into a sleep-inducing lullaby. Most of all, she wanted to sleep. One had to look "pert" when one sought a job, and she wondered if eight o'clock would find her looking any more "pert" than she did at this present moment. What had caused her to urge John to spend what she knew would be his last night with her when she was so determined to be at her best the following morning! O, what the hell was the use? She was going to sleep.

The alarm had not yet rung, but Emma Lou was awakened gradually by the sizzling and smell of fried and warmed-over breakfast, by the raucous early morning wranglings and window to window greetings, and by the almost constant squeak of those impudent hall floor boards as the various people in her apartment raced one another to the kitchen or to the bathroom or to the front door. How could Harlem be so happily busy, so alive and merry at eight o'clock. Eight o'clock? The alarm rang. Emma Lou scuttled out of the bed and put on her clothes.

An hour later, looking as "pert" as possible, she entered the first employment agency she came to on 135th Street, between Lenox and Seventh Avenues. It was her first visit to such an establishment and she was particularly eager to experience this phase of a working girl's life. Her first four weeks in Harlem had convinced her that jobs were easy to find, for she had noticed that there were three or four employment agencies to every block in business Harlem. Assuring herself in this way that she would experience little difficulty in obtaining a permanent and tasty position, Emma Lou had abruptly informed Mazelle Lindsay that she was leaving her employ.

"But, child," her employer had objected, "I feel responsible for you. Your—your mother! Don't be preposterous. How can you remain in New York alone?"

Emma Lou had smiled, asked for her money once more, closed her ears to all protest, bid the chagrined woman good-bye, and joyously loafed for a week.

Now, with only thirty-five dollars left in the bank, she thought that she had best find a job—find a job and then finish seeing New York. Of course she had seen much already. She had seen John—and he—oh, damn John, she wanted a job.

"What can I do for you?" the harassed woman at the desk was trying to be polite.

"I—I want a job." R-r-ring. The telephone insistently petitioned for attention, giving Emma Lou a moment of respite, while the machine-like woman wearily shouted monosyllabic answers into the instrument, and, at the same time, tried to hush the many loud-mouthed men and women in the room, all, it seemed, trying to out-talk one another. While waiting, Emma Lou surveyed her fellow job-seekers. Seedy lot, was her verdict. Perhaps I should have gone to a more high-toned place. Well, this will do for the moment.

"What kinda job d'ye want?"

"I prefer," Emma Lou had rehearsed these lines for a week, "a stenographic position in some colored business or professional office."

" 'Ny experience?"

"No, but I took two courses in business college, during school vacations. I have a certificate of competency."

" 'Ny reference?"

"No New York ones."

"Where'd ya work before?"

"I—I just came to the city."

"Where'd ya come . . . ?" R-r-ring. The telephone mercifully reiterated its insistent blare, and, for a moment, kept that pesky woman from droning out more insulting queries.

"Now," she had finished again, "where'd ya come from?"

"Los Angeles."

"Ummm. What other kind of work would ya take?"

"Anything congenial."

"Waal, what is that, dishwashing, day work, nurse girl?"

Didn't this damn woman know what congenial meant? And why should a Jewish woman be in charge of a Negro employment agency in Harlem?

"Waal, girlie, others waiting."

"I'll consider anything you may have on hand, if stenographic work is not available."

"Wanta work part-time?"

"I'd rather not."

"Awright. Sit down. I'll call you in a moment."

"What can I do for you, young man?" Emma Lou was dismissed.

She looked for a place to sit down, and, finding none, walked across the narrow room to the window, hoping to get a breath of fresh air, and at the same time an advantageous position from which to watch the drama of some one else playing the rôle of a job-seeker.

R-r-ring.

"Whadda want? Wait a minute. Oh, Sadie."

A heavy set, dark-brown-skinned woman, with full, flopping breasts, and extra wide buttocks, squirmed off a too narrow chair, and bashfully wobbled up to the desk.

"Wanta' go to a place on West End Avenue? Part-time cleaning, fifty cents an hour, nine rooms, yeah? All right? Hello, gotta girl on the way. 'Bye. Two and a half, Sadie. Here's the address. Run along now, don't idle."

R-r-ring. "'Lo, yes. What? Come down to the office. I can't sell jobs over the wire."

Emma Lou began to see the humor in this sordid situation, began to see something extremely comic in all these plaintive, pitiful-appearing colored folk, some greasy, some neat, some fat, some slim, some brown, some black (why was there only one mulatto in this crowd?), boys and men, girls and women, all single-filing up to the desk, laconically answering laconic questions, impertinently put, showing thanks or sorrow or indifference, as their cases warranted, paying off promptly, or else seeking credit, the while the Jewish overseer of the dirty, dingy office asserted and reasserted her superiority.

Some one on the outside pushed hard on the warped door. Protestingly it came open, and the small stuffy room was filled with the odor and presence of a stout, black lady dressed in a greasy gingham housedress, still damp in the front from splashing dishwater. On her head was a tight turban, too round for the rather long outlines of her head. Beneath this turban could be seen short and wiry strands of recently straightened hair. And her face! Emma Lou sought to observe it more closely, sought to fathom how so much grease could gather on one woman's face. But her head reeled. The room was vile with noise and heat and body-smells, and this woman——

"Hy, Rosie, yer late. Got a job for ya."

The greasy-faced black woman grinned broadly, licked her pork chop lips and, with a flourish, sat down in an empty chair beside the desk. Emma Lou stumbled over three pairs of number ten shoes, pulled open the door and fled into the street.

She walked hurriedly for about twenty-five yards, then slowed down and tried to collect her wits. Telephone bells echoed in her ears. Sour smells infested her nostrils. She looked up and discovered that she had paused in front of two garbage cans, waiting on the curbstone for the scavenger's truck.

Irritated, she turned around and retraced her steps. There were few people on the street. The early morning work crowds had already been swallowed by the subway kiosks on Lenox Avenue, and it was too early for the afternoon idlers. Yet there was much activity, much passing to and fro. One Hundred and Thirty-Fifth Street, Emma Lou mumbled to herself as she strolled along. How she had longed to see it, and what a different thoroughfare she had imagined it to be! Her eyes sought the opposite side of the street and blinked at a line of monotonously regular fire-escape-decorated tenement buildings. She thanked whoever might be responsible for the architectural difference of the Y.M.C.A., for the streaming bit of Seventh Avenue near by, and for the arresting corner of the newly constructed teachers' college building, which dominated the hill three blocks away, and cast its shadows on the verdure of the terraced park beneath.

But she was looking for a job. Sour smells assailed her nostrils once more. Rasping voices. Pleading voices. Tired voices. Domineering voices. And the insistent ring of the telephone bell all re-echoed in her head and beat against her eardrums. She must have staggered, for a passing youth eyed her curiously, and shouted to no one in particular, "oh, *no*, now." Some one else laughed. They thought she was drunk. Tears blurred her eyes. She wanted to run, but resolutely she kept her steady, slow pace, lifted her head a little higher, and, seeing another employment agency, faltered for a moment, then went in.

This agency, like the first, occupied the ground floor front of a tenement house, three-quarters of the way between Lenox and Seventh Avenue. It was cagey and crowded, and there was a great conversational hubbub as Emma Lou entered. In the rear of the room was a door marked "private," to the left of this door was a desk, littered with papers and index cards, before which was a swivel chair. The rest of the room was lined with a miscellaneous assortment of chairs, three rows of them, tied together and trying to be precise despite their varying sizes and shapes. A single window looked out upon the street, and the Y.M.C.A. building opposite.

All of the chairs were occupied and three people stood lined up by the desk. Emma Lou fell in at the end of this line. There was nothing else to do. In fact, it was all she could do after entering. Not another person could have been squeezed into that room from the outside. This office too was noisy and hot and pregnant with clashing body smells. The buzzing electric fan, in a corner over the desk, with all its whirring, could not stir up a breeze.

The rear door opened. A slender, light-brown-skinned boy,

his high cheekbones decorated with blackheads, his slender form accentuated by a tight fitting jazz suit of the high-waist-line, one-button coat, bell-bottom trouser variety, emerged smiling broadly, cap in one hand, a slip of pink paper in the other. He elbowed his way to the outside door and was gone.

"Musta got a job," somebody commented. "It's about time," came from some one else, "he said he'd been sittin' here a week."

The rear door opened again and a lady with a youthful brown face and iron-gray hair sauntered in and sat down in the swivel chair before the desk. Immediately all talk in the outer office ceased. An air of anticipation seemed to pervade the room. All eyes were turned toward her.

For a moment she fingered a pack of red index cards, then, as if remembering something, turned around in her chair and called out:

"Mrs. Blake says for all elevator men to stick around."

There was a shuffling of feet and a settling back into chairs. Noticing this, Emma Lou counted six elevator men and wondered if she was right. Again the brown aristocrat with the tired voice spoke up:

"Day workers come back at one-thirty. Won't be nothing doin' 'til then."

Four women, all carrying newspaper packages, got out of their chairs, and edged their way toward the door, murmuring to one another as they went, "I ain't fixin' to come back."

"Ah, she keeps you hyar."

They were gone.

Two of the people standing in line sat down, the third approached the desk, Emma Lou close behind.

"I wantsa—"

"What kind of job do you want?"

Couldn't people ever finish what they had to say?

"Porter or dishwashing, lady."

"Are you registered with us?"

"No'm."

"Have a seat. I'll call you in a moment."

The boy looked frightened, but he found a seat and slid into it gratefully. Emma Lou approached the desk. The woman's cold eyes appraised her. She must have been pleased with what she saw for her eyes softened and her smile reappeared. Emma Lou smiled, too. Maybe she was "pert" after all. The tailored blue suit——

"What can I do for you?"

The voice with the smile wins. Emma Lou was encouraged.

"I would like stenographic work."

"Experienced?"

"Yes." It was so much easier to say than "no."

"Good."

Emma Lou held tightly to her under-arm bag.

"We have something that would just about suit you. Just a minute, and I'll let you see Mrs. Blake."

The chair squeaked and was eased of its burden. Emma Lou thought she heard a telephone ringing somewhere in the distance, or perhaps it was the clang of the street car that had just passed, heading for Seventh Avenue. The people in the room began talking again.

"Dat last job." "Boy, she was dressed right down to the bricks."

"And I told him. . . ." "Yeah, we went to see 'Flesh and the Devil'." "Some parteee." "I just been here a week."

Emma Lou's mind became jumbled with incoherent wisps of thought. Her left foot beat a nervous tattoo upon a sagging floor board. The door opened. The gray-haired lady with the smile in her voice beckoned, and Emma Lou walked into the private office of Mrs. Blake.

Four people in the room. The only window facing a brick wall on the outside. Two telephones, both busy. A good-looking young man, fingering papers in a filing cabinet, while he talked over one of the telephones. The lady from the outer office. Another lady, short and brown, like butterscotch, talking over a desk telephone and motioning for Emma Lou to sit down. Blur of high powered electric lights, brighter than daylight. The butterscotch lady hanging up the receiver.

"I'm through with you young man." Crisp tones. Metal, warm in spite of itself.

"Well, I ain't through with you." The fourth person was speaking. Emma Lou had hardly noticed him before. Sullen face. Dull black eyes in watery sockets. The nose flat, the lips thick and pouting. One hand clutching a derby, the other clenched, bearing down on the corner of the desk.

"I have no intention of arguing with you. I've said my say. Go on outside. When a cook's job comes in, you can have it. That's all I can do."

"No, it ain't all you can do."

"Well, I'm not going to give you your fee back."

The lady from the outside office returns to her post. The good-looking young man is at the telephone again.

"Why not, I'm entitled to it."

"No, you're not. I send you on a job, the man asks you to do something, you walk out, Mister Big I-am. Then, show up here two days later and want your fee back. No siree."

"I didn't walk out."

"The man says you did."

"Aw, sure, he'd say anything. I told him I came there to be a cook, not a waiter. I——"

"It was your place to do as he said, then, if not satisfied, to come here and tell me so."

"I am here."

"All right now. I'm tired of this. Take either of two courses— go on outside and wait until a job comes in or else go down to the license bureau and tell them your story. They'll investigate. If I'm right——"

"You know you ain't right."

"Not according to you, no, but by law, yes. That's all."

Telephone ringing. Warm metal whipping words into it. The good-looking young man yawning. He looks like a Y.M.C.A. secretary. The butterscotch woman speaking to Emma Lou:

"You're a stenographer?"

"Yes."

"I have a job in a real estate office, nice firm, nice people. Fill out this card. Here's a pen."

"Mrs. Blake, you know you ain't doin' right."

Why didn't this man either shut up or get out?

"I told you what to do. Now please do one or the other. You've taken up enough of my time. The license bureau——"

"You know I ain't goin' down there. I'd rather you keep the fee, if you think it will do you any good."

"I only keep what belongs to me. I've found out that's the best policy."

Why should they want three people for reference? Where had she worked before? Lies. Los Angeles was far away.

"Then, if a job comes in you'll give it to me?"

"That's what I've been trying to tell you."

"Awright." And finally he went out.

Mrs. Blake grinned across the desk at Emma Lou. "Your folks won't do, honey."

"Do you have many like that?"

The card was made out. Mrs. Blake had it in her hand. Telephones ringing, both at once. Loud talking in the outer office. Lies. Los Angeles was far away. I can bluff. Mrs. Blake had finished reading over the card.

"Just came to New York, eh?"

"Yes."

"Like it better than Los Angeles?"

The good-looking young man turned around and stared at her coldly. Now he did resemble a Y.M.C.A. secretary. The lady from the outer office came in again. There was a triple criss-cross conversation carried on. It ended. The short bob-haired butterscotch boss gave Emma Lou instructions and information about her prospective position. She was half heard. Sixteen dollars a week. Is that all? Work from nine to five. Address on card. Corner of 139th Street, left side of the avenue. Dismissal. Smiles and good luck. Pay the lady outside five dollars. Awkward, flustered moments. Then the entrance door and 135th Street once more. Emma Lou was on her way to get a job.

She walked briskly to the corner, crossed the street and turned north on Seventh Avenue. Her hopes were high, her mind a medley of pleasing mental images. She visualized herself trim and pert in her blue tailored suit being secretary to some well-groomed Negro business man. There had not been many such in the West, and she was eager to know and admire one. There would be other girls in the office, too, girls who, like herself, were college trained and reared in cultured homes, and through these fellow workers she would meet still other girls and men, get in with the right sort of people.

She continued day-dreaming as she went her way, being practical only at such fleeting moments when she would wonder,—would she be able to take dictation at the required rate of speed?—would her fingers be nimble enough on the keyboard of the typewriter? Oh, bother. It wouldn't take her over one day to adapt herself to her new job.

A street crossing. Traffic delayed her and she was conscious of a man, a blurred tan image, speaking to her. He was ignored. Everything was to be ignored save the address digits on the buildings. Everything was secondary to the business at hand. Let traffic pass, let men aching for flirtations speak, let Seventh Avenue be spangled with forenoon sunshine and shadow, and polka-dotted with still or moving human forms. She was going to have a job. The rest of the world could go to hell.

Emma Lou turned into a four-story brick building and sped up one flight of stairs. The rooms were not numbered and directing signs in the hallway only served to confuse. But Emma Lou was not to be delayed. She rushed back and forth from door to door on the first floor, then to the second, until she finally found the office she was looking for.

Angus and Brown were an old Harlem real estate firm. They had begun business during the first decade of the century, handling property for a while in New York's far-famed San Juan Hill district. When the Negro population had begun to need more and better homes, Angus and Brown had led the way in buying real estate in what was to be Negro Harlem. They had been fighters, unscrupulous and canny. They had revealed a perverse delight in seeing white people rush pell-mell from the neighborhood in which they obtained homes for their colored clients. They had bought three six-story tenement buildings on 140th Street, and, when the white tenants had been slow in moving, had personally dispossessed them, and, in addition, had helped their incoming Negro tenants fight fistic battles in the streets and hallways, and legal battles in the court.

Now they were a substantial firm, grown fat and satisfied. Junior real estate men got their business for them. They held the whip. Their activities were many and varied. Politics and fraternal activities occupied more of their time than did real estate. They had had their hectic days. Now they sat back and took it easy.

Emma Lou opened the door to their office, consisting of one

medium-sized outer room overlooking 139th Street and two cubby holes overlooking Seventh Avenue. There were two girls in the outer office. One was busy at a typewriter; the other was gazing over her desk through a window into the aristocratic tree-lined city lane of 139th Street. Both looked up expectantly. Emma Lou noticed the powdered smoothness of their fair skins and the marcelled waviness of their shingled brown hair. Were they sisters? Hardly, for their features were in no way similar. Yet that skin color and that brown hair——.

"Can I do something for you?" The idle one spoke, and the other ceased her peck-peck-pecking on the typewriter keys. Emma Lou was buoyant.

"I'm from Mrs. Blake's employment agency."

"Oh," from both. And they exchanged glances. Emma Lou thought she saw a quickly suppressed smile from the fairer of the two as she hastily resumed her typing. Then——

"Sit down a moment, won't you, please? Mr. Angus is out, but I'll inform Mr. Brown that you are here." She picked a powder puff from an open side drawer in her desk, patted her nose and cheeks, then got up and crossed the office to enter cubby hole number one. Emma Lou observed that she, too, looked "pert" in a trim, blue suit and high-heeled patent leather oxfords——

"Mr. Brown?" She had opened the door.

"Come in Grace. What is it?" The door was closed.

Emma Lou felt nervous. Something in the pit of her stomach seemed to flutter. Her pulse raced. Her eyes gleamed and a smile of anticipation spread over her face, despite her efforts to appear dignified and suave. The typist continued her work. From the cubby hole came a murmur of voices, one feminine and affected, the other masculine and coarse. Through the open window came direct sounds and vagrant echoes of traffic noises from Seventh Avenue. Now the two in the cubby hole were laughing, and the girl at the typewriter seemed to be smiling to herself as she worked.

What did this mean? Nothing, silly. Don't be so sensitive. Emma Lou's eyes sought the pictures on the wall. There was an early twentieth century photographic bust-portrait, encased in a bevelled glass frame, of a heavy-set good-looking, brown-skinned man. She admired his mustache. Men didn't seem to take pride in such hirsute embellishments now. Mustaches these days were abbreviated and limp. They no longer were virile enough to dominate and make a man's face appear more strong. Rather, they were only insignificant patches weakly keeping the nostrils from merging with the upper lip.

Emma Lou wondered if that was Mr. Brown. He had a brown face and wore a brown suit. No, maybe that was Mr. Angus, and perhaps that was Mr. Brown on the other side of the room, in the square, enlarged kodak print, a slender yellow man, standing beside a motor car, looking as if he wished to say, "Yeah, this is me and this is my car." She hoped he was Mr. Angus. She didn't like his name and since she was to see Mr. Brown first, she hoped he was the more flatteringly portrayed.

The door to the cubby hole opened and the girl Mr. Brown had called Grace, came out. The expression on her face was too business-like to be natural. It seemed as if it had been placed there for a purpose.

She walked toward Emma Lou, who got up and stood like a child, waiting for punishment and hoping all the while that it will dissipate itself in threats. The typewriter was stilled and Emma Lou could feel an extra pair of eyes looking at her. The girl drew close then spoke:

"I'm sorry, Miss. Mr. Brown says he has some one else in view for the job. We'll call the agency. Thank you for coming in."

Thank her for coming in? What could she say? What should she say? The girl was smiling at her, but Emma Lou noticed that her fair skin was flushed and that her eyes danced nervously. Could she be hoping that Emma Lou would hurry and depart? The door was near. It opened easily. The steps were steep. One went down slowly. Seventh Avenue was still spangled with forenoon sunshine and shadow. Its pavement was hard and hot. The windows in the buildings facing it, gleaming reflectors of the mounting sun.

Emma Lou returned to the employment agency. It was still crowded and more stuffy than ever. The sun had advanced high into the sky and it seemed to be centering its rays on that solitary defenseless window. There was still much conversation. There were still people crowded around the desk, still people in all the chairs, people and talk and heat and smells.

"Mrs. Blake is waiting for you," the gray-haired lady with the young face was unflustered and cool. Emma Lou went into the inner office. Mrs. Blake looked up quickly and forced a smile. The good-looking young man, more than ever resembling a Y.M.C.A. secretary, turned his back and fumbled with the card files. Mrs. Blake suggested that he leave the room. He did, beaming benevolently at Emma Lou as he went.

"I'm sorry," Mrs. Blake was very kind and womanly. "Mr. Brown called me. I didn't know he had some one else in mind. He hadn't told me."

"That's all right," replied Emma Lou briskly. "Have you something else?"

"Not now. Er-er. Have you had luncheon? It's early yet, I know, but I generally go about this time. Come along, won't you, I'd like to talk to you. I'll be ready in about thirty minutes if you don't mind the wait."

Emma Lou warmed to the idea. At that moment, she would have warmed toward any suggestion of friendliness. Here, perhaps, was a chance to make a welcome contact. She was lonesome and disappointed, so she readily assented and felt elated and superior as she walked out of the office with the "boss."

They went to Eddie's for luncheon. Eddie's was an elbow-shaped combination lunch-counter and dining room that embraced a United Cigar Store on the northeast corner of 135th Street and Seventh Avenue. Following Mrs. Blake's lead, Emma Lou ordered a full noontime dinner, and, flattered by Mrs. Blake's interest and congeniality, began to talk about herself. She told of her birthplace and her home life. She told of her high school days, spoke proudly of the fact that she had been the only Negro student and how she had graduated cum laude. Asked about her college years, she talked less freely. Mrs. Blake sensed a cue.

"Didn't you like college?"

"For a little while, yes."

"What made you dislike it? Surely not the studies?"

"No." She didn't care to discuss this. "I was lonesome, I guess."

"Weren't there any other colored boys and girls? I thought. . . ."

Emma Lou spoke curtly. "Oh, yes, quite a number, but I suppose I didn't mix well."

The waiter came to take the order for dessert, and Emma Lou seized upon the fact that Mrs. Blake ordered sliced oranges to talk about California's orange groves, California's sunshine—anything but the California college she had attended and from which she had fled. In vain did Mrs. Blake try to maneuver the conversation back to Emma Lou's college experiences. She would have none of it and Mrs. Blake was finally forced to give it up.

When they were finished, Mrs. Blake insisted upon taking the check. This done, she began to talk about jobs.

"You know, Miss Morgan, good jobs are rare. It is seldom I have anything to offer outside of the domestic field. Most Negro business offices are family affairs. They either get their help from within their own family group or from among their friends. Then, too," Emma Lou noticed that Mrs. Blake did not look directly at her, "lots of our Negro business men have a definite type of girl in mind and will not hire any other."

Emma Lou wondered what it was Mrs. Blake seemed to be holding back. She began again:

"My advice to you is that you enter Teachers' College and if you *will* stay in New York, get a job in the public school system. You can easily take a light job of some kind to support you through your course. Maybe with three years' college you won't need to go to training school. Why don't you find out about that? Now, if I were you. . . ." Mrs. Blake talked on, putting much emphasis on every "If I were you."

Emma Lou grew listless and antagonistic. She didn't like this little sawed-off woman as she was now, being business like and giving advice. She was glad when they finally left Eddie's, and more than glad to escape after having been admonished not to oversleep, "But be in my office, and I'll see what I can do for you, dearie, early in the morning. There's sure to be something."

Left to herself, Emma Lou strolled south on the west side of Seventh Avenue to 134th Street, then crossed over to the east side and turned north. She didn't know what to do. It was too late to consider visiting another employment agency, and, furthermore, she didn't have enough money left to pay another fee. Let jobs go until tomorrow, then she would return to Mrs. Blake's, ask for a return of her fee, and find some other employment agency, a more imposing one, if possible. She had had enough of those on 135th Street.

She didn't want to go home, either. Her room had no outside vista. If she sat in the solitary chair by the solitary window, all she could see were other windows and brick walls and people either mysteriously or brazenly moving about in the apartments across the court. There was no privacy there, little fresh air, and no natural light after the sun began its downward course. Then the apartment always smelled of frying fish or of boiling cabbage. Her landlady seemed to alternate daily between these two foods. Fish smells and cabbage smells pervaded the long, dark hallway, swirled into the room when the door was opened and perfumed one's clothes disagreeably. Moreover, urinal and foecal smells surged upward from the garbage-littered bottom of the court which her window faced.

If she went home, the landlady would eye her suspiciously and ask, "Ain't you got a job yet?" then move away, shaking her head and dipping into her snuff box. Occasionally, in moments of excitement, she spat on the floor. And the little fat man who had the room next to Emma Lou's could be heard coughing suggestively—tapping on the wall, and talking to himself in terms of her. He had seen her slip John in last night. He might be more bold now. He might even try—oh no he wouldn't.

She was crossing 137th Street. She remembered this corner. John had told her that he could always be found there after work any spring or summer evening.

Emma Lou had met John on her first day in New York. He was employed as a porter in the theatre where Mazelle Lindsay was scheduled to perform, and, seeing a new maid on the premises, had decided to "make" her. He had. Emma Lou had not liked him particularly, but he had seemed New Yorkish and genial. It was John who had found her her room. It was John who had taught her how to find her way up and down town on the subway and on the elevated. He had also conducted her on a Cook's tour of Harlem, had strolled up and down Seventh Avenue with her evenings after they had come uptown from the theater. He had pointed out for her the Y.W.C.A. with its imposing annex, the Emma Ranson House, and suggested that she get a room there later on. He had taken her on a Sunday

to several of the Harlem motion picture and vaudeville theaters, and he had been as painstaking in pointing out the
churches as he had been lax in pointing out the cabarets.
Moreover, as they strolled Seventh Avenue, he had attempted
to give her all the "inside dope" on Harlem, had told her of
the "rent parties," of the "numbers," of "hot" men, of "sweetbacks," and other local phenomena.

Emma Lou was now passing a barber shop near 140th
Street. A group of men were standing there beneath a huge
white and black sign announcing, "Bobbing's, fifty cents; hair-
cuts, twenty-five cents." They were whistling at three school
girls, about fourteen or fifteen years of age, who were passing,
doing much switching and giggling. Emma Lou curled her
lips. Harlem streets presented many such scenes. She looked at
the men significantly, forgetting for the moment that it was
none of her business what they or the girls did. But they didn't
notice her. They were too busy having fun with those fresh little
chippies.

Emma Lou experienced a feeling of resentment, then, realizing how ridiculous it all was, smiled it away and began to
think of John once more. She wondered why she had submitted herself to him. Was it cold-blooded payment for his kind
chaperoning? Something like that. John wasn't her type. He
was too pudgy and dark, too obviously an ex-cotton-picker
from Georgia. He was unlettered and she couldn't stand for
that, for she liked intelligent-looking, slender, light-brown-
skinned men, like, well . . . like the one who was just passing.
She admired him boldly. He looked at her, then over her, and
passed on.

Seventh Avenue was becoming more crowded now. School
children were out for their lunch hour, corner loafers and pool-
hall loiterers were beginning to collect on their chosen spots.
Knots of people, of no particular designation, also stood around
talking, or just looking, and there were many pedestrians,
either impressing one as being in a great hurry, or else seeming
to have no place at all to go. Emma Lou was in this latter class.
By now she had reached 142nd Street and had decided to cross
over to the opposite side and walk south once more. Seventh
Avenue was a wide, well-paved, busy thoroughfare, with a long,
narrow, iron fenced-in parkway dividing the east side from the

west. Emma Lou liked Seventh Avenue. It was so active and alive, so different from Central Avenue, the dingy main street of the black belt of Los Angeles. At night it was glorious! Where else could one see so many different types of Negroes? Where else would one view such a heterogeneous ensemble of mellow colors, glorified by the night?

People passing by. Children playing. Dogs on leashes. Stray cats crouching by the sides of buildings. Men standing in groups or alone. Black men. Yellow men. Brown men. Emma Lou eyed them. They eyed her. There were a few remarks passed. She thought she got their import even though she could not hear what they were saying. She quickened her step and held her head higher. Be yourself, Emma Lou. Do you want to start picking men up off of the street?

The heat became more intense. Brisk walking made her perspire. Her underclothes grew sticky. Harlem heat was so muggy. She could feel the shine on her nose and it made her self-conscious. She remembered how the "Grace" in the office of Angus and Brown had so carefully powdered her skin before confronting her employer, and, as she remembered this, she looked up, and sure enough, here she was in front of the building she had sought so eagerly earlier that morning. Emma Lou drew closer to the building. She must get that shine off of her nose. It was bad enough to be black, too black, without having a shiny face to boot. She stopped in front of the tailor shop directly beneath the office of Angus and Brown, and, turning her back to the street, proceeded to powder her shiny member. Three noisy lads passed by. They saw Emma Lou and her reflection in the sunlit show window. The one closest to her cleared his throat and crooned out, loud enough for her to hear, "There's a girl for you, 'Fats.'" "Fats" was the one in the middle. He had a rotund form and a coffee-colored face. He was in his shirt sleeves and carried his coat on his arm. Bell bottom trousers hid all save the tips of his shiny tan shoes. "Fats" was looking at Emma Lou, too, but as he passed, he turned his eyes from her and broadcast a withering look at the lad who had spoken:

"Man, you know I don't haul no coal." There was loud laughter and the trio merrily clicked their metal-cornered heels on the sun-baked pavement as they moved away.

PART III

Alva

IT WAS nine o'clock. The alarm rang. Alva's roommate awoke cursing.

"Why the hell don't you turn off that alarm?"

There was no response. The alarm continued to ring.

"Alva!" Braxton yelled into his sleeping roommate's ear, "Turn off that clock. Wake up," he began shaking him, "Wake up, damn you . . . ya dead?"

Alva slowly emerged from his stupor. Almost mechanically he reached for the clock, dancing merrily on a chair close to the bed, and, finding it, pushed the guilty lever back into the silent zone. Braxton watched him disgustedly:

"Watcha gettin' up so early for? Don'tcha know this is Monday?"

"Shure, I know it's Monday, but I gotta go to Uncle's. The landlord'll be here before eleven o'clock."

"Watcha gonna pawn?"

"My brown suit. I won't need it 'til next Sunday. You got your rent?"

"I got four dollars," Braxton advanced slowly.

"Cantcha get the other two?"

Braxton grew apologetic and explanatory, "Not today . . . ya . . . see. . . ."

"Aw, man, you make me sick."

Disgust overcoming his languor, Alva got out of the bed. This was getting to be a regular Monday morning occurrence. Braxton was always one, two or three dollars short of having his required half of the rent, and Alva, who had rented the room, always had to make it up. Luckily for Alva, both he and the landlord were Elks. Fraternal brothers must stick together. Thus it was an easy matter to pay the rent in installments. The only difficulty being that it was happening rather frequently. There is liable to be a limit even to a brother Elk's patience, especially where money is concerned.

748

Alva put on his dressing gown, and his house shoes, then went into the little alcove which was curtained off in the rear from the rest of the room. Jumbled together on the marble topped stationary washstand were a half dozen empty gin bottles bearing a pre-prohibition Gordon label, a similar number of empty ginger ale bottles, a cocktail shaker, and a medley of assorted cocktail, water, jelly and whiskey glasses, filled and surrounded by squeezed orange and lemon rinds. The little two-burner gas plate atop a wooden dry goods box was covered with dirty dishes, frying pan, egg shells, bacon rinds, and a dominating though lopsided tea kettle. Even Alva's trunk, which occupied half the entrance space between the alcove and the room, littered as it was with paper bags, cracker boxes and greasy paper plates, bore evidence of the orgy which the occupants of the room staged over every weekend.

Alva surveyed this rather intimate and familiar disorder, faltered a moment, started to call Braxton, then remembering previous Monday mornings set about his task alone. It was Braxton's custom never to arise before noon. Alva who worked as a presser in a costume house was forced to get up at seven o'clock on every week day save Monday when he was not required to report for work until twelve o'clock. His employers thus managed to accumulate several baskets of clothes from the sewing room before their pressers arrived. It was better to have them remain at home until this was done. Then you didn't have to pay them so much, and having let the sewing room get head start, there was never any chance for the pressing room to slow down.

Alva's mother had been an American mulatto, his father a Filipino. Alva himself was small in stature as his father had been, small and well developed with broad shoulders, narrow hips and firm well modeled limbs. His face was oval shaped and his features more oriental than Negroid. His skin was neither yellow nor brown but something in between, something warm, arresting and mellow with the faintest suggestion of a parchment tinge beneath, lending it individuality. His eyes were small, deep and slanting. His forehead high, hair sparse and finely textured.

The alcove finally straightened up, Alva dressed rather

hurriedly, and, taking a brown suit from the closet, made his regular Monday morning trip to the pawn shop.

Emma Lou finished rinsing out some silk stockings and sat down in a chair to reread a letter she had received from home that morning. It was about the third time she had gone over it. Her mother wanted her to come home. Evidently the home-town gossips were busy. No doubt they were saying, "Strange mother to let that gal stay in New York alone. She ain't goin' to school, either. Wonder what she's doin'?" Emma Lou read all this between the lines of what her mother had written. Jane Morgan was being tearful as usual. She loved to suffer, and being tearful seemed the easiest way to let the world know that one was suffering. Sob stuff, thought Emma Lou, and, tearing the letter up, threw it into the waste paper basket.

Emma Lou was now maid to Arline Strange, who was play-ing for the moment the part of a mulatto Carmen in an alleged melodrama of Negro life in Harlem. Having tried, for two weeks to locate what she termed "congenial work," Emma Lou had given up the idea and meekly returned to Mazelle Lindsay. She had found her old job satisfactorily filled, but Mazelle had been sympathetic and had arranged to place her with Arline Strange. Now her mother wanted her to come home. Let her want. She was of age, and supporting herself. Moreover, she felt that if it had not been for gossip her mother would never have thought of asking her to come home.

"Stop your mooning, dearie." Arline Strange had returned to her dressing room. Act One was over. The Negro Carmen had become the mistress of a wealthy European. She would now shed her gingham dress for an evening gown.

Mechanically, Emma Lou assisted Arline in making the change. She was unusually silent. It was noticed.

"'Smatter, Louie. In love or something?"

Emma Lou smiled, "Only with myself."

"Then snap out of it. Remember, you're going cabareting with us tonight. This brother of mine from Chicago insists upon going to Harlem to check up on my performance. He'll enjoy himself more if you act as guide. Ever been to Small's?" Emma Lou shook her head. "I haven't been to any of the cabarets."

"What?" Arline was genuinely surprised. "You in Harlem and never been to a cabaret? Why I thought all colored people went."

Emma Lou bristled. White people were so stupid. "No," she said firmly. "All colored people don't go. Fact is, I've heard that most of the places are patronized almost solely by whites."

"Oh, yes, I knew that, I've been to Small's and Barron's and the Cotton Club, but I thought there were other places." She stopped talking, and spent the next few moments deepening the artificial duskiness of her skin. The gingham dress was now on its hanger. The evening gown clung glamorously to her voluptuous figure. "For God's sake, don't let on to my brother you ain't been to Small's before. Act like you know all about it. I'll see that he gives you a big tip." The call bell rang. Arline said "Damn," gave one last look into the mirror, then hurried back to the stage so that the curtain could go up on the cabaret scene in Act Two.

Emma Lou laid out the negligee outfit Arline would be killed in at the end of Act Three, and went downstairs to stand in the stage wings, a makeup box beneath her arm. She never tired of watching the so-called dramatic antics on the stage. She wondered if there were any Negroes of the type portrayed by Arline and her fellow performers. Perhaps there were, since there were any number of minor parts being played by real Negroes who acted much different from any Negroes she had ever known or seen. It all seemed to her like a mad caricature.

She watched for about the thirtieth time Arline acting the part of a Negro cabaret entertainer, and also for about the thirtieth time, came to the conclusion that Arline was being herself rather than the character she was supposed to be playing. From where she was standing in the wings she could see a small portion of the audience, and she watched their reaction. Their interest seemed genuine. Arline did have pep and personality, and the alleged Negro background was strident and kaleidoscopic, all of which no doubt made up for the inane plot and vulgar dialogue.

They entered Small's Paradise, Emma Lou, Arline and Arline's brother from Chicago. All the way uptown he had plied Emma Lou with questions concerning New York's Black Belt. He had reciprocated by relating how well he knew the Negro

section of Chicago. Quite a personage around the Black and
Tan cabarets there, it seemed. "But I never," he concluded as
the taxi drew up to the curb in front of Small's, "have seen any
black gal in Chicago act like Arline acts. She claims she is presenting a Harlem specie. So I am going to see for myself." And
he chuckled all the time he was helping them out of the taxi
and paying the fare. While they were checking their wraps in
the foyer, the orchestra began playing. Through the open entrance way Emma Lou could see a hazy, dim-lighted room,
walls and ceiling colorfully decorated, floor space jammed with
tables and chairs and people. A heavy set mulatto in tuxedo,
after asking how many were in their party, led them through a
lane of tables around the squared off dance platform to a ring-
side seat on the far side of the cabaret.

Immediately they were seated, a waiter came to take their
order.

"Three bottles of White Rock." The waiter nodded, twirled
his tray on the tip of his fingers and skated away.

Emma Lou watched the dancers, and noticed immediately
that in all that insensate crowd of dancing couples there were
only a few Negroes.

"My God, such music. Let's dance, Arline," and off they
went, leaving Emma Lou sitting alone. Somehow or other she
felt frightened. Most of the tables around her were deserted,
their tops littered with liquid-filled glasses, and bottles of ginger ale and White Rock. There was no liquor in sight, yet Emma
Lou was aware of pungent alcoholic odors. Then she noticed a
heavy-jowled white man with a flashlight walking among the
empty tables and looking beneath them. He didn't seem to be
finding anything. The music soon stopped. Arline and her
brother returned to the table. He was feigning anxiety because
he had not seen the type of character Arline claimed to be por-
traying, and loudly declared that he was disappointed.

"Why there ain't nothing here but white people. Is it always
like this?"

Emma Lou said it was and turned to watch their waiter, who
with two others had come dancing across the floor, holding
aloft his tray, filled with bottles and glasses. Deftly, he maneuvered away from the other two and slid to their table, put
down a bottle of White Rock and an ice-filled glass before each

one, then, after flicking a stub check on to the table, rejoined his companions in a return trip across the dance floor.

Arline's brother produced a hip flask, and before Emma Lou could demur mixed her a highball. She didn't want to drink. She hadn't drunk before, but. . . .

"Here come the entertainers!" Emma Lou followed Arline's turn of the head to see two women, one light brown skin and slim, the other chocolate colored and fat, walking to the center of the dance floor.

The orchestra played the introduction and vamp to "Muddy Waters." The two entertainers swung their legs and arms in rhythmic unison, smiling broadly and rolling their eyes, first to the left and then to the right. Then they began to sing. Their voices were husky and strident, neither alto nor soprano. They muddled their words and seemed to impregnate the syncopated melody with physical content.

As they sang the chorus, they glided out among the tables, stopping at one, then at another, and another, singing all the time, their bodies undulating and provocative, occasionally giving just a promise of an obscene hip movement, while their arms waved and their fingers held tight to the dollar bills and silver coins placed in their palms by enthusiastic onlookers.

Emma Lou, all of her, watched and listened. As they approached her table, she sat as one mesmerized. Something in her seemed to be trying to give way. Her insides were stirred, and tingled. The two entertainers circled their table; Arline's brother held out a dollar bill. The fat, chocolate colored girl leaned over the table, her hand touched his, she exercised the muscles of her stomach, muttered a guttural "thank you" in between notes and moved away, moaning "Muddy Waters," rolling her eyes, shaking her hips.

Emma Lou had turned completely around in her chair, watching the progress of that wah-wahing, jello-like chocolate hulk, and her slim light brown skin companion. Finally they completed their rounds of the tables and returned to the dance floor. Red and blue spotlights played upon their dissimilar figures, the orchestra increased the tempo and lessened the intensity of its playing. The swaying entertainers pulled up their dresses, exposing lace trimmed stepins and an island of flesh. Their stockings were rolled down below their knees, their stepins discreetly short and delicate. Finally, they ceased their swaying and began to dance. They shimmied and whirled, charlestoned and black-bottomed. Their terpsichorean ensemble was melodramatic and absurd. Their execution easy and emphatic. Emma Lou forgot herself. She gaped, giggled and applauded like the rest of the audience, and only as they let their legs separate, preparatory to doing one final split to the floor, did Emma Lou come to herself long enough to wonder if the fat one could achieve it without seriously endangering those ever tightening stepins.

"Dam' good, I'll say," a slender white youth at the next table asseverated, as he lifted an amber filled glass to his lips.

Arline sighed. Her brother had begun to razz her. Emma Lou blinked guiltily as the lights were turned up. She had been immersed in something disturbingly pleasant. Idiot, she berated herself, just because you've had one drink and seen your first cabaret entertainer, must your mind and body feel all aflame?

Arline's brother was mixing another highball. All around, people were laughing. There was much more laughter than there was talk, much more gesticulating and ogling than the usual means of expression called for. Everything seemed unrestrained, abandoned. Yet, Emma Lou was conscious of a note of artificiality, the same as she felt when she watched Arline and her fellow performers cavorting on the stage in "Cabaret Gal." This entire scene seemed staged, they were in a theater, only the proscenium arch had been obliterated. At last the audience and the actors were as one.

A call to order on the snare drum. A brutal sliding trumpet call on the trombone, a running minor scale by the clarinet and piano, an umpah, umpah by the bass horn, a combination four measure moan and strum by the saxophone and banjo, then a melodic ensemble, and the orchestra was playing another dance tune. Masses of people jumbled up the three entrances to the dance square and with difficulty, singled out their mates and became closely allied partners. Inadvertently, Emma Lou looked at Arline's brother. He blushed, and appeared uncomfortable. She realized immediately what was on his mind. He didn't know whether or not to ask her to dance with him. The ethics of the case were complex. She was a Negro and hired maid. But was she a hired maid after hours, and in this environment? Emma Lou had difficulty in suppressing a smile, then she decided to end the suspense.

"Why don't you two dance. No need of letting the music go to waste."

Both Arline and her brother were obviously relieved, but as they got up Arline said, "Ain't much fun cuddling up to your own brother when there's music like this." But off they went, leaving Emma Lou alone and disturbed. John ought to be here, slipped out before she remembered that she didn't want John any more. Then she began to wish that John had introduced her to some more men. But he didn't know the kind of men she was interested in knowing. He only knew men and boys like himself, porters and janitors and chauffeurs and bootblacks. Imagine her, a college trained person, even if she hadn't finished her senior year, being satisfied with the company of such unintelligent servitors. How had she stood John so long with his constant of defense, "I ain't got much education, but I got mother wit." Mother wit! Creation of the unlettered, satisfying illusion to the dumb, ludicrous prop to the mentally unfit. Yes, he had mother wit all right.

Emma Lou looked around and noticed at a near-by table three young colored men, all in tuxedos, gazing at her and talking. She averted her glance and turned to watch the dancers. She thought she heard a burst of ribald laughter from the young men at the table. Then some one touched her on the shoulder, and she looked up into a smiling oriental-like face, neither brown nor yellow in color, but warm and pleasing beneath the soft lights, and, because of the smile, showing a gleaming row of small, even teeth, set off by a solitary gold incisor. The voice was persuasive and apologetic, "Would you care to dance with me?" The music had stopped, but there was promise of an encore. Emma Lou was confused, her mind blankly chaotic. She was expected to push back her chair and get up. She did. And, without saying a word, allowed herself to be maneuvered to the dance floor.

In a moment they were swallowed up in the jazz whirlpool. Long strides were impossible. There were too many other legs striding for free motion in that over populated area. He held her close to him; the contours of her body fitting his. The two highballs had made her giddy. She seemed to be glowing inside.

The soft lights and the music suggested abandon and intrigue. They said nothing to one another. She noticed that her partner's face seemed alive with some inner ecstasy. It must be the music, thought Emma Lou. Then she got a whiff of his liquor-laden breath.

After three encores, the clarinet shrilled out a combination of notes that seemed to say regretfully, "That's all." Brighter lights were switched on, and the milling couples merged into a struggling mass of individuals, laughing, talking, over-animated individuals, all trying to go in different directions, and getting a great deal of fun out of the resulting confusion. Emma Lou's partner held tightly to her arm, and pushed her through the insensate crowd to her table. Then he muttered a polite "thank you" and turned away. Emma Lou sat down. Arline and her brother looked at her and laughed. "Got a dance, eh Louie?" Emma Lou wondered if Arline was being malicious, and for an answer she only nodded her head and smiled, hoping all the while that her smile was properly enigmatic.

Arline's brother spoke up. "Whadda say we go. I've seen enough of this to know that Arline and her stage director are all wet." Their waiter was called, the check was paid, and they were on their way out. In spite of herself, Emma Lou glanced back to the table where her dancing partner was sitting. To her confusion, she noticed that he and his two friends were staring at her. One of them said something and made a wry face. Then they all laughed, uproariously and cruelly.

Alva had overslept. Braxton, who had stayed out the entire night, came in about eight o'clock, and excitedly interrupted his drunken slumber.

"Ain't you goin' to work?"

"Work?" Alva was alarmed. "What time is it?"

" 'Bout eight. Didn't you set the clock?"

"Sure, I did." Alva picked up the clock from the floor and examined the alarm dial. It had been set for ten o'clock instead of for six. He sulked for a moment, then attempted to shake off the impending mood of regretfulness and disgust for self.

"Aw, hell, what's the dif'. Call 'em up and tell 'em I'm sick.

There's a nickel somewhere in that change on the dresser."
Braxton had taken off his tuxedo coat and vest.

"If you're not goin' to work ever, you might as well quit. I
don't see no sense in working two days and laying off three."

"I'm goin' to quit the damn job anyway. I been working
steady now since last fall."

"I thought it was about time you quit." Braxton had stripped
off his white full dress shirt, put on his bathrobe, and started
out of the room, to go downstairs to the telephone. Alva
reached across the bed and pulled up the shade, blinked at the
inpouring daylight and lay himself back down, one arm thrown
across his forehead. He had slipped off into a state of semi-
consciousness again when Braxton returned.

"The girl said she'd tell the boss. Asked who I was as usual."
He went into the alcove to finish undressing, and put on his
pajamas. Alva looked up.

"You goin' to bed?"

"Yes, don't you think I want some sleep?"

"Thought you was goin' to look for a job?"

"I was, but I hadn't figured on staying out all night."

"Always some damn excuse. Where'd you go?"

"Down to Flo's."

"Who in the hell is Flo?"

"That little yaller broad I picked up at the cabaret last night."

"I thought she had a nigger with her."

"She did, but I jived her along, so she ditched him, and gave
me her address. I met her there later."

Braxton was now ready to get into the bed. All this time he
had been preparing himself in his usual bedtime manner. His
face had been cold-creamed, his hair greased and tightly covered by a silken stocking cap. This done, he climbed over Alva
and lay on top of the covers. They were silent for a moment,
then Braxton laughed softly to himself.

"Where'd *you* go last night?"

"Where'd I go?" Alva seemed surprised. "Why I came home,
where'd ya think I went?" Braxton laughed again.

"Oh, I thought maybe you'd really made a date with that
coal scuttle blond you danced with."

"Ya musta thought it."

"Well, ya seemed pretty sweet on her."

"Whaddaya mean, sweet? Just because I danced with her once. I took pity on her, cause she looked so lonesome with those ofays. Wonder who they was?"

"Oh, she probably works for them. It's good you danced with her. Nobody else would."

"I didn't see nothing wrong with her. She might have been a little dark."

"Little dark is right, and you know when they comes blacker'n me, they ain't got no go." Braxton was a reddish brown aristocrat, with clear-cut features and curly hair. His paternal grandfather had been an Iroquois Indian.

Emma Lou was very lonesome. She still knew no one save John, two or three of the Negro actors who worked on the stage with Arline, and a West Indian woman who lived in the same apartment with her. Occasionally John met her when she left the theater at night and escorted her to her apartment door. He repeatedly importuned her to be nice to him once more. Her only answer was a sigh or a smile.

The West Indian woman was employed as a stenographer in the office of a Harlem political sheet. She was shy and retiring, and not much given to making friends with American Negroes. So many of them had snubbed and pained her when she was newly emigrant from her home in Barbadoes, that she lumped them all together, just as they seemed to do her people. She would not take under consideration that Emma Lou was new to Harlem, and not even aware of the prejudice American-born Harlemites nursed for foreign-born ones. She remembered too vividly how, on ringing the bell of a house where there had been a vacancy sign in the window, a little girl had come to the door, and, in answer to a voice in the back asking, "Who is it, Cora?" had replied, "monkey chaser wants to see the room you got to rent." Jasmine Griffith was wary of all contact with American Negroes, for that had been only one of the many embittering incidents she had experienced.

Emma Lou liked Jasmine, but was conscious of the fact that she could never penetrate her stolid reserve. They often talked to one another when they met in the hallway, and sometimes they stopped in one another's rooms, but there was never any talk of going places together, never any informal revelations or intimacies.

The Negro actors in "Cabaret Gal" all felt themselves superior to Emma Lou, and she in turn felt superior to them. She was just a maid. They were just common stage folk. Once she had had an inspiration. She had heard that "Cabaret Gal" was liable to run for two years or more on Broadway before road shows were sent out. Without saying anything to Arline she had approached the stage director and asked him, in all secrecy, what her chances were of getting into the cabaret ensemble. She knew they paid well, and she speculated that two or three years in "Cabaret Gal" might lay the foundations for a future stage career.

"What the hell would Arline do," he laughed, "if she didn't have you to change her complexion before every performance?"

Emma Lou had smiled away this bit of persiflage and had re-iterated her request in such a way that there was no mistaking her seriousness.

Sensing this, the director changed his mood, and admitted that even then two of the girls were dropping out of "Cabaret Gal" to sail for Europe with another show, booked for a season on the continent. But he hastened to tell her, as he saw her eyes brighten with anticipation:

"Well, you see, we worked out a color scheme that would be a complement to Arline's makeup. You've noticed, no doubt, that all of the girls are about one color, and. . . ."

Unable to stammer any more, he had hastened away, embarrassed.

Emma Lou hadn't noticed that all the girls were one color. In fact, she was certain they were not. She hastened to stand in the stage wings among them between scenes and observe their skin coloring. Despite many layers of liquid powder she could see that they were not all one color, but that they were either mulatto or light-brown skin. Their makeup and the lights gave them an appearance of sameness. She noticed that there were several black men in the ensemble, but that none of the women were dark. Then the breach between Emma Lou and the show people widened.

Emma Lou had had another inspiration. She had decided to move. Perhaps if she were to live with a homey type of family they could introduce her to "the right sort of people." She blamed her enforced isolation on the fact that she had made no worthwhile contacts. Mrs. Blake was a disagreeable remembrance. Since she came to think about it, Mrs. Blake had been distinctly patronizing like . . . like . . . her high school principal, or like Doris Garrett, the head of the only Negro sorority in the Southern California college she had attended. Doris Garrett had been very nice to all her colored schoolmates, but had seen to it that only those girls who were of a mulatto type were pledged for membership in the Greek letter society of which she was the head.

Emma Lou reasoned that she couldn't go on as she was, being alone and aching for congenial companionship. True, her job didn't allow her much spare time. She had to be at Arline's apartment at eleven every morning, but except on the two matinee days, she was free from two until seven-thirty P.M., when she had to be at the theater, and by eleven-thirty every night, she was in Harlem. Then she had all day Sunday to herself. Arline paid her a good salary, and she made tips from the first and second leads in the show, who used her spare moments. She had been working for six weeks now, and had saved one hundred dollars. She practically lived on her tips. Her salary was twenty-five dollars per week. Dinner was the only meal she had to pay for, and Arline gave her many clothes.

So Emma Lou began to think seriously of getting another room. She wanted more space and more air and more freedom from fish and cabbage smells. She had been in Harlem now for about fourteen weeks. Only fourteen weeks? The count stunned her. It seemed much longer. It was this rut she was in. Well, she would get out of it. Finding a room, a new room, would be the first step.

Emma Lou asked Jasmine how one went about it. Jasmine was noncommittal, and said she didn't know, but she had heard that *The Amsterdam News*, a Harlem Negro weekly, carried a large "Furnished rooms for rent" section. Emma Lou bought a copy of this paper, and, though attracted, did not stop to read the news columns under the streaming headlines to the effect "Headless Man Found In Trunk"; "Number Runner Given Sentence"; "Benefit Ball Huge Success"; but turned immediately to the advertising section.

There were many rooms advertised for rent, rooms of all sizes and for all prices, with all sorts of conveniences and inconveniences. Emma Lou was more bewildered than ever. Then, remembering that John had said that all the "dictys" lived between Seventh and Edgecombe Avenues on 136th, 137th, 138th and 139th Streets, decided to check off the places in these streets. John had also told her that "dictys" lived in the imposing apartment houses on Edgecombe, Bradhurst and St. Nicholas Avenues. "Dictys" were Harlem's high-toned people, folk listed in the local social register, as it were. But Emma Lou did not care to live in another apartment building. She preferred, or thought she would prefer, living in a private house where there would be fewer people and more privacy.

The first place Emma Lou approached had a double room for two girls, two men, or a couple. They thought their advertisement had said as much. It hadn't, but Emma Lou apologized, and left. The next three places were nice but exorbitant. Front rooms with two windows and a kitchenette, renting for twelve, fourteen and sixteen dollars a week. Emma Lou had planned to spend not more than eight or nine dollars at the most. The next place smelled far worse than her present home. The room was smaller and the rent higher. Emma Lou began to lose hope, then rallying, had gone to the last place on her list from *The Amsterdam News*. The landlady was the spinster type, garrulous and friendly. She had a high forehead, keen intellectual eyes, and a sharp profile. The room she showed to Emma Lou was both spacious and clean, and she only asked eight dollars and fifty cents per week for it.

After showing her the room, the landlady had invited Emma Lou downstairs to her parlor. Emma Lou found a place to sit down on a damask covered divan. There were many other seats in the room, but the landlady, *Miss* Carrington, as she had introduced herself, insisted upon sitting down beside her. They talked for about a half an hour, and in that time, being a successful "pumper," *Miss* Carrington had learned the history of Emma Lou's experiences in Harlem. Satisfied of her ground, she grew more familiar, placed her hand on Emma Lou's knee, then finally put her arm around her waist. Emma Lou felt uncomfortable. This sudden and unexpected intimacy disturbed her. The room was close and hot. Damask coverings seemed to be everywhere. Damask coverings and dull red draperies and mauve walls.

"Don't worry any more, dearie, I'll take care of you from now on," and she had tightened her arm around Emma Lou's waist, who, feeling more uncomfortable than ever, looked at her wrist watch.

"I must be going."

"Do you want the room?" There was a note of anxiety in her voice. "There are lots of nice girls living here. We call this the 'Old Maid's Home.' We have parties among ourselves, and just have a grand time. Talk about fun! I know you'd be happy here."

Emma Lou knew she would too, and said as much. Then hastily, she gave *Miss* Carrington a three dollar deposit on the room, and left . . . to continue her search for a new place to live.

There were no more places on her *Amsterdam News* list, so noticing "Vacancy" signs in windows along the various streets, Emma Lou decided to walk along and blindly choose a house. None of the houses in 137th Street impressed her, they were all too cold looking, and she was through with 136th Street. *Miss* Carrington lived there. She sauntered down the "L" trestled Eighth Avenue to 138th Street. Then she turned toward Seventh Avenue and strolled along slowly on the south side of the street. She chose the south side because she preferred the appearance of the red brick houses there to the green brick ones on the north side. After she had passed by three "Vacancy" signs, she decided to enter the very next house where such a sign was displayed.

Seeing one, she climbed the terraced stone stairs, rang the doorbell and waited expectantly. There was a long pause. She rang the bell again, and just as she relieved her pressure, the door was opened by a bedizened yellow woman with sand colored hair and deep set corn colored eyes. Emma Lou noted the incongruous thickness of her lips.

"How do you do. I . . . I . . . would like to see one of your rooms."

The woman eyed Emma Lou curiously and looked as if she were about to snort. Then slowly she began to close the door in the astonished girl's face. Emma Lou opened her mouth and tried to speak, but the woman forestalled her, saying testily in broken English:

"We have nothing here."

Persons of color didn't associate with blacks in the Caribbean Island she had come from.

From then on Emma Lou intensified her suffering, mulling over and magnifying each malignant experience. They grew within her and were nourished by constant introspection and livid reminiscences. Again, she stood upon the platform in the auditorium of the Boise high school. Again that first moment of realization and its attendant strictures were disinterred and revivified. She was black, too black, there was no getting around it. Her mother had thought so, and had often wished that she had been a boy. Black boys can make a go of it, but black girls. . . .

No one liked black anyway. . . .

Wanted: light colored girl to work as waitress in tearoom. . . .

Wanted: Nurse girl, light colored preferred (children are afraid of black folks). . . .

"I don' haul no coal. . . ."

"It's like this, Emma Lou, they don't want no dark girls in their sorority. They ain't pledged us, and we're the only two they ain't, and we're both black."

The ineluctability of raw experience! The muddy mirroring of life's perplexities. . . . Seeing everything in terms of self. . . . The spreading sensitiveness of an adder's sting.

"Mr. Brown has some one else in mind. . . ."

"We have nothing here. . . ."

She should have been a boy. A black boy could get along, but a black girl. . . .

Arline was leaving the cast of "Cabaret Gal" for two weeks. Her mother had died in Chicago. The Negro Carmen must be played by an understudy, a real mulatto this time, who, lacking Arline's poise and personality, nevertheless brought down the house because of the crude vividity of her performance. Emma Lou was asked to act as her maid while Arline was away. Indignantly, she had taken the alternative of a two weeks' vacation. Imagine her being maid for a *Negro* woman! It was unthinkable.

Left entirely to herself, she proceeded to make herself more miserable. Lying in bed late every morning, semi-conscious, body burning, mind disturbed by thoughts of sex. Never before had she experienced such physical longing. She often thought of John and at times was almost driven to slip him into her room once more. But John couldn't satisfy her. She felt that she wanted something more than just the mere physical relationship with some one whose body and body coloring were distasteful to her.

When she did decide to get up, she would spend an hour before her dresser mirror, playing with her hair, parting it on the right side, then on the left, then in the middle, brushing it straight back, or else teasing it with the comb, inducing it to crackle with electric energy. Then she would cover it with a cap, pin a towel around her shoulders, and begin to experiment with her complexion.

She had decided to bleach her skin as much as possible. She had bought many creams and skin preparations, and had tried to remember the various bleaching aids she had heard of throughout her life. She remembered having heard her grandmother speak of that "old fool, Carrie Campbell," who, already a fair mulatto, had wished to pass for white. To accomplish this she had taken arsenic wafers, which were guaranteed to increase the pallor of one's skin.

Emma Lou had obtained some of these arsenic wafers and eaten them, but they had only served to give her pains in the pit of her stomach. Next she determined upon a peroxide solution in addition to something which was known as Black and White Ointment. After she had been using these for about a month she thought that she could notice some change. But in reality the only effects were an increase in blackheads, irritating rashes, and a burning skin.

Meanwhile she found her thoughts straying often to the chap she had danced with in the cabaret. She was certain he lived in Harlem, and she was determined to find him. She took it for granted that he would remember her. So day after day, she strolled up and down Seventh Avenue from 125th to 145th Street, then crossed to Lenox Avenue and traversed the same distance.

He was her ideal. He looked like a college person. He dressed well. His skin was such a warm and different color, and she had been tantalized by the mysterious slant and deepness of his oriental-like eyes.

After walking the streets like this the first few days of her vacation, she became aware of the futility of her task. She saw many men on the street, many well dressed, seemingly cultured, pleasingly colored men and boys. They seemed to congregate in certain places, and stand there all the day. She found herself wondering when and where they worked, and how they could afford to dress so well. She began to admire their well formed bodies and gloried in the way their trousers fit their shapely limbs, and in the way they walked, bringing their heels down so firmly and so noisily on the pavement. Rubber heels were out of fashion. Hard heels, with metal heel plates were the mode of the day. These corner loafers were so care-free, always smiling, eyes always bright. She loved to hear them laugh, and loved to watch them, when, without any seeming provocation, they would cut a few dance steps or do a jig. It seemed as if they either did this from sheer exuberance or else simply to relieve the monotony of standing still.

Of course, they noticed her as she passed and repassed day after day. She eyed them boldly enough, but she was still too self-conscious to broadcast an inviting look. She was too afraid of public ridicule or a mass mocking. Ofttimes men spoke to her, and tried to make advances, but they were never the kind she preferred. She didn't like black men, and the others seemed to keep their distance.

One day, tired of walking, she went into a motion picture theater on the avenue. She had seen the feature picture before, but was too lethargic and too uninterested in other things to go some place else. In truth, there was no place else for her to go. So she sat in the darkened theater, squirmed around in her seat, and began to wonder just how many thousands of Negroes there were in Harlem. This theater was practically full, even in mid-afternoon. The streets were crowded, other theaters were crowded, and then there must be many more at home and at work. Emma Lou wondered what the population of Negro Harlem was. She should have read that Harlem number of the Survey Graphic issued two or three years ago.

But Harlem hadn't interested her then for she had had no idea at the time that she would ever come to Harlem.

Some one sat down beside her. She was too occupied with herself to notice who the person was. The feature picture was over and a comedy was being flashed on the screen. Emma Lou found herself laughing, and, finding something on the screen to interest her, squared herself in her seat. Then she felt a pressure on one of her legs, the warm fleshy pressure of another leg. Her first impulse was to change her position. Perhaps she had touched the person next to her. Perhaps it was an accident. She moved her leg a little, but she still felt the pressure. Maybe it wasn't an accident. Her heart beat fast, her limbs began to quiver. The leg which was pressed against hers had such a pleasant, warm, fleshy feeling. She stole a glance at the person who had sat down next to her. He smiled . . . an impudent boyish smile and pressed her leg the harder.

"Funny cuss, that guy," he was speaking to her.

Slap him in the face. Change your seat. Don't be an idiot. He has a nice smile. Look at him again.

"Did you see him in 'Long Pants'?"

He was leaning closer now, and Emma Lou took note of a teakwood tan hand resting on her knee. She took another look at him, and saw that he had curly hair. He leaned toward her, and she leaned toward him. Their shoulders touched, his hand reached for hers and stole it from her lap. She wished that the theater wasn't so dark. But if it hadn't been so dark this couldn't have happened. She wondered if his hair and eyes were brown or jet black.

The feature picture was being reeled off again. They were too busy talking to notice that. When it was half over, they left their seats together. Before they reached the street, Emma Lou handed him three dollars, and, leaving the theater, they went to an apartment house on 140th Street, off Lenox Avenue. Emma Lou waited downstairs in the dirty marble hallway where she was stifled by urinal smells and stared at by passing people, waited for about ten minutes, then, in answer to his call, climbed one flight of stairs, and was led into a well furnished, though dark, apartment.

His name was Jasper Crane. He was from Virginia. Living in Harlem with his brother, so he said. He had only been in New

York a month. Didn't have a job yet. His brother wasn't very nice to him. . . wanted to kick him out because he was jealous of him, thought his wife was more attentive than a sister-in-law should be. He asked Emma Lou to lend him five dollars. He said he wanted to buy a job. She did. And when he left her, he kissed her passionately and promised to meet her on the next day and to telephone her within an hour.

But he didn't telephone nor did Emma Lou ever see him again. The following day she waited for an hour and a half in the vicinity of that hallway where they were supposed to meet again. Then she went to the motion picture theater where they had met, and sat in the same seat in the same row so that he could find her. She sat there through two shows, then came back on the next day, and on the next. Meanwhile several other men approached her, a panting fat Jew, whom she reported to the usher, a hunchback, whom she pitied and then admired as he "made" the girl sitting on the other side of him; and there were several not very clean, trampy-looking men, but no Jasper.

He had asked her if she ever went to the Renaissance Casino, a public hall, where dances were held every night, so Emma Lou decided to go there on a Saturday, hoping to see him. She drew twenty-five dollars from the bank in order to buy a new dress, a very fine elaborate dress, which she got from a "hot" man, who had been recommended to her by Jasmine. "Hot" men sold supposedly stolen goods, thus enabling Harlem folk to dress well but cheaply. Then she spent the entire afternoon and evening preparing herself for the night, had her hair washed and marcelled, and her fingernails manicured.

Before putting on her dress she stood in front of her mirror for over an hour, fixing her face, drenching it with a peroxide solution, plastering it with a mudpack, massaging it with a bleaching ointment, and then, as a final touch, using much vanishing cream and powder. She even ate an arsenic wafer. The only visible effect of all this on her complexion was to give it an ugly purple tinge, but Emma Lou was certain that it made her skin less dark.

She hailed a taxi and went to the Renaissance Casino. She did feel foolish, going there without an escort, but the doorman didn't seem to notice. Perhaps it was all right. Perhaps it was customary for Harlem girls to go about unaccompanied.

She checked her wraps and wandered along the promenade that bordered the dance floor. It was early yet, just ten-thirty, and only a few couples were dancing. She found a chair, and tried to look as if she were waiting for some one. The orchestra stopped playing, people crowded past her. She liked the dance hall, liked its draped walls and ceilings, its harmonic color design and soft lights.

The music began again. She didn't see Jasper. A spindly legged yellow boy, awkward and bashful, asked her to dance with him. She did. The boy danced badly, but dancing with him was better than sitting there alone, looking foolish. She did wish that he would assume a more upright position and stop scrunching his shoulders. It seemed as if he were trying to bend both their backs to the breaking point. As they danced they talked about the music. He asked her did she have an escort. She said yes, and hurried to the ladies' room when the dance was over.

She didn't particularly like the looks of the crowd. It was well-behaved enough, but . . . well . . . one could see that they didn't belong to the cultured classes. They weren't the right sort of people. Maybe nice people didn't come here. Jasper hadn't been so nice. She wished she could see him, wouldn't she give him a piece of her mind?—And for the first time she really sensed the baseness of the trick he had played on her.

She walked out of the ladies' room and found herself again on the promenade. For a moment she stood there, watching the dancers. The floor was more crowded now, the dancers more numerous and gay. She watched them swirl and glide around the dance floor, and an intense longing for Jasper or John or any one welled up within her. It was terrible to be so alone, terrible to stand here and see other girls contentedly curled up in men's arms. She had been foolish to come, Jasper probably never came here. In truth he was no doubt far away from New York by now. What sense was there in her being here. She wasn't going to stay. She was going home, but before starting toward the check room, she took one more glance at the dancers and saw her cabaret dancing partner.

He was dancing with a slender brown-skin girl, his smile as ecstatic and intense as before. Emma Lou noted the pleasing lines of his body encased in a form-fitting blue suit. Why didn't he look her way?

"May I have this dance?" A well modulated deep voice. A slender stripling, arrayed in brown, with a dark brown face. He had dimples. They danced. Emma Lou was having difficulty in keeping track of Alva. He seemed to be consciously striving to elude her. He seemed to be deliberately darting in among clusters of couples, where he would remain hidden for some time, only to reappear far ahead or behind her.

Her partner was congenial. He introduced himself, but she did not hear his name, for at that moment, Alva and his partner glided close by. Emma Lou actually shoved the supple, slender boy she was dancing with in Alva's direction. She mustn't lose him this time. She must speak. They veered close to one another. They almost collided. Alva looked into her face. She smiled and spoke. He acknowledged her salute, but stared at her, frankly perplexed, and there was no recognition in his face as he moved away, bending his head close to that of his partner, the better to hear something she was asking him.

The slender brown boy clung to Emma Lou's arm, treated her to a soda, and, at her request, piloted her around the promenade. She saw Alva sitting in a box in the balcony, and suggested to her companion that they parade around the balcony for a while. He assented. He was lonesome too. First summer in New York. Just graduated from Virginia Union University. Going to Columbia School of Law next year. Nice boy, but no appeal. Too—supple.

They passed by Alva's box. He wasn't there. Two other couples and the girl he had been dancing with were. Emma Lou and her companion walked the length of the balcony, then retraced their steps just in time to see Alva coming around the corner carrying a cup of water. She watched the rhythmic swing of his legs, like symmetrical pendulums, perfectly shaped; and she admired once more the intriguing lines of his body and pleasing foreignness of his face. As they met, she smiled at him. He was certain he did not know her but he stopped and was polite, feeling that he must find out who she was and where he had met her.

"How do you do?" Emma Lou held out her hand. He

shifted the cup of water from his right hand to his left. "I'm glad to see you again." They shook hands. His clasp was warm, his palm soft and sweaty. The supple lad stepped to one side. "I—I," Emma Lou was speaking now, "have often wondered if we would meet again." Alva wanted to laugh. He could not imagine who this girl with the purple-powdered skin was. Where had he seen her? She must be mistaking him for some one else. Well, he was game. He spoke sincerely:

"And I, too, have wanted to see you."

Emma Lou couldn't blush, but she almost blubbered with joy.

"Perhaps we'll have a dance together."

"My God," thought Alva, "she's a quick worker."

"Oh, certainly, where can I find you?"

"Downstairs on the promenade, near the center boxes."

"The one after this?" This seemed to be the easiest way out. He could easily dodge her later.

"Yes," and she moved away, the supple lad clinging to her arm again.

"Who's the 'spade,' Alva?" Geraldine had seen him stop to talk to her.

"Damned if I know."

"Aw, sure you know who she is. You danced with her at Small's." Braxton hadn't forgotten.

"Well, I never. Is that *it*?" Laughter all around as he told about their first meeting. But he didn't dodge her, for Geraldine and Braxton riled him with their pertinacious badinage. He felt that they were making more fun of him than of her, and to show them just how little he minded their kidding he stalked off to find her. She was waiting, the slim, brown stripling swaying beside her, importuning her not to wait longer. He didn't want to lose her. She didn't want to lose Alva, and was glad when they danced off together.

"Who's your boy friend?" Alva had fortified himself with gin. His breath smelled familiar.

"Just an acquaintance." She couldn't let him know she had come here unescorted. "I didn't think you'd remember me."

"Of course, I did; how could I forget you?" Smooth tongue, phrases with a double meaning.

"I didn't forget *you*." Emma Lou was being coy. "I have often looked for you."

Looked for him where? My God, what an impression he must have made! He wondered what he had said to her before. Plunge in boy, plunge! The blacker the berry—he chuckled to himself.

Orchestra playing "Blue Skies," as an especial favor to her. Alva telling her his name and giving her his card, and asking her to 'phone him some day. Alva close to her and being nice, his arms tightening about her. She would call him tomorrow. Ecstasy ended too soon. The music stopped. He thanked her for the dance and left her standing on the promenade by the side of the waiting slender stripling. She danced with him twice more, then let him take her home.

At ten the next morning Emma Lou called Alva. Braxton came to the telephone.

"Alva's gone to work; who is it?" People should have more sense than to call that early in the morning. He never got up until noon. Emma Lou was being apologetic.

"Could you tell me what time he will be in?"

"'Bout six-thirty. Who shall I say called? This is his room-mate."

"Just . . . Oh . . . I'll call him later. Thank you."

Braxton swore. "Why in the hell does Alva give so many damn women his 'phone number?"

Six-thirty-five. His roommate had said about six-thirty. She called again. *He* came to the 'phone. She thought his voice was more harsh than usual.

"Oh, I'm all right, only tired."

"Did you work hard?"

"I always work hard."

"I . . . I . . . just thought I'd call."

"Glad you did, call me again some time. Good-bye"—said too quickly. No chance to say "When will I see you again?"

She went home, got into the bed and cried herself to sleep.

Arline returned two days ahead of schedule. Things settled back into routine. The brown stripling had taken Emma Lou out twice, but upon her refusal to submit herself to him, had gone away in a huff, and had not returned. She surmised that it was the first time he had made such a request of any one. He did it so ineptly. Work. Home. Walks. Theaters downtown during the afternoon, and thoughts of Alva. Finally, she just had to call him again. He came to the 'phone:

"Hello. Who? Emma Lou? Where have you been? I've been wondering where you were?"

She was shy, afraid she might be too bold. But Alva had had his usual three glasses of before-dinner gin. He helped her out.

"When can I see you, Sugar?"

Sugar! He had called her "sugar." She told him where she worked. He was to meet her after the theater that very night.

"How many nights a week you gonna have that little inkspitter up here?"

"Listen here, Brax, you have who you want up here, don't you?"

"That ain't it. I just don't like to see you tied up with a broad like that."

"Why not? She's just as good as the rest, and you know what they say, 'The blacker the berry, the sweeter the juice.'"

"The only thing a black woman is good for is to make money for a brown-skin papa."

"I guess I don't know that."

"Well," Braxton was satisfied now, "if that's the case. . . ."

He had faith in Alva's wisdom.

PART IV

Rent Party

SATURDAY evening. Alva had urged her to hurry uptown from work. He was going to take her on a party with some friends of his. This was the first time he had ever asked her to go to any sort of social affair with him. She had never met any of his friends save Braxton, who scarcely spoke to her, and never before had Alva suggested taking her to any sort of social gathering either public or semipublic. He often took her to various motion picture theaters, both downtown and in Harlem, and at least three nights a week he would call for her at the theater and escort her to Harlem. On these occasions they often went to Chinese restaurants or to ice cream parlors before going home. But usually they would go to City College Park, find an empty bench in a dark corner where they could sit and spoon before retiring either to her room or to Alva's.

Emma Lou had, long before this, suggested going to a dance or to a party, but Alva had always countered that he never attended such affairs during the summer months, that he stayed away from them for precisely the same reason that he stayed away from work, namely, because it was too hot. Dancing, said he, was a matter of calisthenics, and calisthenics were work. Therefore it, like any sort of physical exercise, was taboo during hot weather.

Alva sensed that sooner or later Emma Lou would become aware of his real reason for not taking her out among his friends. He realized that one as color-conscious as she appeared to be would, at some not so distant date, jump to what for him would be uncomfortable conclusions. He did not wish to risk losing her before the end of summer, but neither could he risk taking her out among his friends, for he knew too well that he would be derided for his unseemly preference for "dark meat," and told publicly without regard for her feelings, that "black cats must go."

Furthermore he always took Geraldine to parties and dances.

Geraldine with her olive colored skin and straight black hair. Geraldine, who of all the people he pretended to love, really inspired him emotionally as well as physically, the one person he conquested without thought of monetary gain. Yet he had to do something with Emma Lou, and release from the quandary presented itself from most unexpected quarters.

Quite accidentally, as things of the sort happen in Harlem with its complex but interdependable social structure, he had become acquainted with a young Negro writer, who had asked him to escort a group of young writers and artists to a house-rent party. Though they had heard much of this phenomenon, none had been on the inside of one, and because of their rather polished manners and exteriors, were afraid that they might not be admitted. Proletarian Negroes are as suspicious of their more sophisticated brethren as they are of white men, and resent as keenly their intrusions into their social world. Alva had consented to act as cicerone, and, realizing that these people would be more or less free from the color prejudice exhibited by his other friends, had decided to take Emma Lou along too. He was also aware of her intellectual pretensions, and felt that she would be especially pleased to meet recognized talents and outstanding personalities. She did not have to know that these were not his regular companions, and from then on she would have no reason to feel that he was ashamed to have her meet his friends.

Emma Lou could hardly attend to Arline's change of complexion and clothes between acts and scenes, so anxious was she to get to Alva's house and to the promised party. Her happiness was complete. She was certain now that Alva loved her, certain that he was not ashamed or even aware of her dusky complexion. She had felt from the first that he was superior to such inane truck, now she knew it. Alva loved her for herself alone, and loved her so much that he didn't mind her being a coal scuttle blond.

Sensing something unusual, Arline told Emma Lou that she would remove her own make-up after the performance, and let her have time to get dressed for the party. This she proceeded to do all through the evening, spending much time in front of the mirror at Arline's dressing table, manicuring her nails, marcelling her hair, and applying various creams and cosmetics to her face in order to make her despised darkness less obvious. Finally, she put on one of Arline's less pretentious afternoon frocks, and set out for Alva's house.

As she approached his room door, she heard much talk and laughter, moving her to halt and speculate whether or not she should go in. Even her unusual and high-tensioned jubilance was not powerful enough to overcome immediately her shyness and fears. Suppose these friends of Alva's would not take kindly to her? Suppose they were like Braxton, who invariably curled his lip when he saw her, and seldom spoke even as much as a word of greeting? Suppose they were like the people who used to attend her mother's and grandmother's teas, club meetings and receptions, dismissing her with—"It beats me how this child of yours looks so unlike the rest of you . . . Are you sure it isn't adopted." Or suppose they were like the college youth she had known in Southern California? No, that couldn't be. Alva would never invite her where she would not be welcome. These were his friends. And so was Braxton, but Alva said he was peculiar. There was no danger. Alva had invited her. She was here. Anyway she wasn't so black. Hadn't she artificially lightened her skin about four or five shades until she was almost brown? Certainly it was all right. She needn't be a foolish ninny all her life. Thus, reassured, she knocked on the door, and felt herself trembling with excitement and internal uncertainty as Alva let her in, took her hat and coat, and proceeded to introduce her to the people in the room.

"Miss Morgan, meet Mr. Tony Crews. You've probably seen his book of poems. He's the little jazz boy, you know."

Emma Lou bashfully touched the extended hand of the curly-headed poet. She had not seen or read his book, but she had often noticed his name in the newspapers and magazines. He was all that she had expected him to be except that he had pimples on his face. These didn't fit in with her mental picture.

"Miss Morgan, this is Cora Thurston. Maybe I should'a introduced you ladies first."

"I'm no lady, and I hope you're not either, Miss Morgan." She smiled, shook Emma Lou's hand, then turned away to continue her interrupted conversation with Tony Crews.

"Miss Morgan, meet . . . ," he paused, and addressed a tall, dark yellow youth stretched out on the floor, "What name you going by now?"

The boy looked up and smiled.

"Why, Paul, of course."

"All right then, Miss Morgan, this is Mr. Paul, he changes his name every season."

Emma Lou sought to observe this person more closely, and was shocked to see that his shirt was open at the neck and that he was sadly in need of a haircut and shave.

"Miss Morgan, meet Mr. Walter." A small slender dark youth with an infectious smile and small features. His face was familiar. Where had she seen him before?

"Now that you've met every one, sit down on the bed there beside Truman and have a drink. Go on with your talk folks," he urged as he went over to the dresser to fill a glass with a milk colored liquid. Cora Thurston spoke up in answer to Alva's adjuration:

"Guess there ain't much more to say. Makes me mad to discuss it anyhow."

"No need of getting mad at people like that," said Tony Crews simply and softly. "I think one should laugh at such stupidity."

"And ridicule it, too," came from the luxurious person sprawled over the floor, for he did impress Emma Lou as being luxurious, despite the fact that his suit was unpressed, and that he wore neither socks nor necktie. She noticed the many graceful gestures he made with his hands, but wondered why he kept twisting his lips to one side when he talked. Perhaps he was trying to mask the size of his mouth.

Truman was speaking now, "Ridicule will do no good, nor mere laughing at them. I admit those weapons are about the only ones an intelligent person would use, but one must also admit that they are rather futile."

"Why futile?" Paul queried indolently.

"They are futile," Truman continued, "because, well, those people cannot help being like they are—their environment has made them that way."

Miss Thurston muttered something. It sounded like "hooey," then held out an empty glass. "Give me some more firewater,

Alva." Alva hastened across the room and refilled her glass. Emma Lou wondered what they were talking about. Again Cora broke the silence, "You can't tell me they can't help it. They kick about white people, then commit the same crime."

There was a knock on the door, interrupting something Tony Crews was about to say. Alva went to the door.

"Hello, Ray." A tall, blond, fair-skinned youth entered. Emma Lou gasped, and was more bewildered than ever. All of this silly talk and drinking, and now—here was a white man!

"Hy, everybody. Jusas Chraust, I hope you saved me some liquor." Tony Crews held out his empty glass and said quietly, "We've had about umpteen already, so I doubt if there's any more left."

"You can't kid me, bo. I know Alva would save me a dram or two." Having taken off his hat and coat he squatted down on the floor beside Paul.

Truman turned to Emma Lou. "Oh, Ray, meet Miss Morgan. Mr. Jorgenson, Miss Morgan."

"Glad to know you; pardon my not getting up, won't you?" Emma Lou didn't know what to say, and couldn't think of anything appropriate, but since he was smiling, she tried to smile too, and nodded her head.

"What's the big powwow?" he asked. "All of you look so serious. Haven't you had enough liquor, or are you just trying to settle the ills of the universe?"

"Neither," said Paul. "They're just damning our 'pink niggers'."

Emma Lou was aghast. Such extraordinary people—saying "nigger" in front of a white man! Didn't they have any race pride or proper bringing up? Didn't they have any common sense?

"What've they done now?" Ray asked, reaching out to accept the glass Alva was handing him.

"No more than they've always done," Tony Crews answered. "Cora here just felt like being indignant, because she heard of a forthcoming wedding in Brooklyn to which the prospective bride and groom have announced they will *not* invite any dark people."

"Seriously now," Truman began. Ray interrupted him.

"Who in the hell wants to be serious?"

"As I was saying," Truman continued, "you can't blame light Negroes for being prejudiced against dark ones. All of you know that white is the symbol of everything pure and good, whether that everything be concrete or abstract. Ivory Soap is advertised as being ninety-nine and some fraction per cent pure, and Ivory Soap is white. Moreover, virtue and virginity are always represented as being clothed in white garments. Then, too, the God we, or rather most Negroes worship is a patriarchal white man, seated on a white throne, in a spotless white Heaven, radiant with white streets and white-apparelled angels eating white honey and drinking white milk."

"Listen to the boy rave. Give him another drink," Ray shouted, but Truman ignored him and went on, becoming more and more animated.

"We are all living in a totally white world, where all standards are the standards of the white man, and where almost invariably what the white man does is right, and what the black man does is wrong, unless it is precedented by something a white man has done."

"Which," Cora added scornfully, "makes it all right for light Negroes to discriminate against dark ones?"

"Not at all," Truman objected. "It merely explains, not justifies, the evil—or rather, the fact of intra-racial segregation. Mulattoes have always been accorded more consideration by white people than their darker brethren. They were made to feel superior even during slave days . . . made to feel proud, as Bud Fisher would say, that they were bastards. It was for the mulatto offspring of white masters and Negro slaves that the first schools for Negroes were organized, and say what you will, it is generally the Negro with a quantity of mixed blood in his veins who finds adaptation to a Nordic environment more easy than one of pure blood, which, of course, you will admit, is, to an American Negro, convenient if not virtuous."

"Does that justify their snobbishness and self-evaluated superiority?"

"No, Cora, it doesn't," returned Truman. "I'm not trying to excuse them. I'm merely trying to give what I believe to be an explanation of this thing. I have never been to Washington and only know what Paul and you have told me about conditions there, but they seem to be just about the same as conditions in

Los Angeles, Omaha, Chicago, and other cities in which I have lived or visited. You see, people have to feel superior to something, and there is scant satisfaction in feeling superior to domestic animals or steel machines that one can train or utilize. It is much more pleasing to pick out some individual or some group of individuals on the same plane to feel superior to. This is almost necessary when one is a member of a supposedly despised, mistreated minority group. Then consider that the mulatto is much nearer white than he is black, and is therefore more liable to act like a white man than like a black one, although I cannot say that I see a great deal of difference in any of their actions. They are human beings first and only white or black incidentally."

Ray pursed up his lips and whistled.

"But you seem to forget," Tony Crews insisted, "that because a man is dark, it doesn't necessarily mean he is not of mixed blood. Now look at. . . ."

"Yeah, let him look at you or at himself or at Cora," Paul interrupted. "There ain't no unmixed Negroes."

"But I haven't forgotten that," Truman said, ignoring the note of finality in Paul's voice. "I merely took it for granted that we were talking only about those Negroes who were lightskinned."

"But all light-skinned Negroes aren't color struck or color prejudiced," interjected Alva, who, up to this time, like Emma Lou, had remained silent. This was, he thought, a strategic moment for him to say something. He hoped Emma Lou would get the full significance of this statement.

"True enough," Truman began again. "But I also took it for granted that we were only talking about those who were. As I said before, Negroes are, after all, human beings, and they are subject to be influenced and controlled by the same forces and factors that influence and control other human beings. In an environment where there are so many color-prejudiced whites, there are bound to be a number of color-prejudiced blacks. Color prejudice and religion are akin in one respect. Some folks have it and some don't, and the kernel that is responsible for it is present in us all, which is to say, that potentially we are all color-prejudiced as long as we remain in this environment. For, as you know, prejudices are always caused by differences, and the majority group sets the standard. Then, too, since black is the favorite color of vaudeville comedians and jokesters, and, conversely, as intimately associated with tragedy, it is no wonder that even the blackest individual will seek out some one more black than himself to laugh at."

"So saith the Lord," Tony answered soberly.

"And the Holy Ghost saith, let's have another drink."

"Happy thought, Ray," returned Cora. "Give us some more ice cream and gin, Alva."

Alva went into the alcove to prepare another concoction. Tony started the victrola. Truman turned to Emma Lou, who, all this while, had been sitting there with Alva's arm around her, every muscle in her body feeling as if it wanted to twitch, not knowing whether to be sad or to be angry. She couldn't comprehend all of this talk. She couldn't see how these people could sit down and so dispassionately discuss something that seemed particularly tragic to her. This fellow Truman, whom she was certain she knew, with all his hi-faluting talk, disgusted her immeasurably. She wasn't sure that they weren't all poking fun at her. Truman was speaking:

"Miss Morgan, didn't you attend school in Southern California?" Emma Lou at last realized where she had seen him before. So *this* was Truman Walter, the little "cock o' the walk," as they had called him on the campus. She answered him with difficulty, for there was a sob in her throat. "Yes, I did." Before Truman could say more to her, Ray called to him:

"Say, Bozo, what time are we going to the party? It's almost one o'clock now."

"Is it?" Alva seemed surprised. "But Aaron and Alta aren't here yet."

"They've been married just long enough to be late to everything."

"What do you say we go by and ring their bell?" Tony suggested, ignoring Paul's Greenwich Village wit.

"'Sall right with me." Truman lifted his glass to his lips. "Then on to the house-rent party . . . on to the bawdy bowels of Beale Street!"

They drained their glasses and prepared to leave.

*

"Ahhhh, sock it." . . . "Ummmm" . . . Piano playing—slow, loud, and discordant, accompanied by the rhythmic sound of shuffling feet. Down a long, dark hallway to an inside room, lit by a solitary red bulb. "Oh, play it you dirty no-gooder." . . . A room full of dancing couples, scarcely moving their feet, arms completely encircling one another's bodies . . . cheeks being warmed by one another's breath . . . eyes closed . . . animal ecstasy agitating their perspiring faces. There was much panting, much hip movement, much shaking of the buttocks. . . . "Do it twice in the same place." . . . "Git off that dime." Now somebody was singing, "I ask you very confidentially. . . ." "Sing it man, sing it." . . . Piano treble moaning, bass rumbling like thunder. A swarm of people, motivating their bodies to express in suggestive movements the ultimate consummation of desire.

The music stopped, the room was suffocatingly hot, and Emma Lou was disturbingly dizzy. She clung fast to Alva, and let the room and its occupants whirl around her. Bodies and faces glided by. Leering faces and lewd bodies. Anxious faces and angular bodies. Sad faces and obese bodies. All mixed up together. She began to wonder how such a small room could hold so many people. "Oh, play it again . . ." She saw the pianist now, silhouetted against the dark mahogany piano, saw him bend his long, slick-haired head, until it hung low on his chest, then lift his hands high in the air, and as quickly let them descend upon the keyboard. There was one moment of cacophony, then the long, supple fingers evolved a slow, tantalizing melody out of the deafening chaos.

Every one began to dance again. Body called to body, and cemented themselves together, limbs lewdly intertwined. A couple there kissing, another couple dipping to the floor, and slowly shimmying, belly to belly, as they came back to an upright position. A slender dark girl with wild eyes and wilder hair stood in the center of the room, supported by the strong, lithe arms of a longshoreman. She bent her trunk backward, until her head hung below her waistline, and all the while she kept the lower portion of her body quivering like jello.

"She whips it to a jelly," the piano player was singing now, and banging on the keys with such might that an empty gin bottle on top of the piano seemed to be seized with the ague. "Oh, play it Mr. Charlie." Emma Lou grew limp in Alva's arms.

"What's the matter, honey, drunk?" She couldn't answer. The music augmented by the general atmosphere of the room and the liquor she had drunk had presumably created another person in her stead. She felt like flying into an emotional frenzy —felt like flinging her arms and legs in insane unison. She had become very fluid, very elastic, and all the while she was giving in more and more to the music and to the liquor and to the physical madness of the moment.

When the music finally stopped, Alva led Emma Lou to a settee by the window which his crowd had appropriated. Every one was exceedingly animated, but they all talked in hushed, almost reverential tones.

"Isn't this marvelous?" Truman's eyes were ablaze with interest and excitement. Even Tony Crews seemed unusually alert.

"It's the greatest I've seen yet," he exclaimed.

Alva seemed the most unemotional one in the crowd. Paul the most detached. "Look at 'em all watching Ray."

"Remember, Bo," Truman counselled him. "Tonight you're 'passing.' Here's a new wrinkle, white man 'passes' for Negro."

"Why not? Enough of you pass for white." They all laughed, then transferred their interest back to the party. Cora was speaking:

"Didya see that little girl in pink—the one with the scar on her face—dancing with that tall, lanky, one-armed man? Wasn't she throwing it up to him?"

"Yeah," Tony admitted, "but she didn't have anything on that little Mexican-looking girl. She musta been born in Cairo."

"Saay, but isn't that one bad looking darkey over there, two chairs to the left; is he gonna smother that woman?" Truman asked excitedly.

"I'd say she kinda liked it," Paul answered, then lit another cigarette.

"Do you know they have corn liquor in the kitchen? They serve it from a coffee pot." Aaron seemed proud of his discovery.

"Yes," said Alva, "and they got hoppin'-john out there too."

"What the hell is hoppin'-john?"

"Ray, I'm ashamed of you. Here you are passing for colored and don't know what hoppin'-john is!"

"Tell him, Cora, I don't know either."

"Another one of these foreigners." Cora looked at Truman disdainfully. "Hoppin'-john is black-eyed peas and rice. Didn't they ever have any out in Salt Lake City?"

"Have they any chitterlings?" Alta asked eagerly.

"No, Alta," Alva replied, dryly. "This isn't Kansas. They have got pig's feet though."

"Lead me to 'em," Aaron and Alta shouted in unison, and led the way to the kitchen. Emma Lou clung to Alva's arm and tried to remain behind. "Alva, I'm afraid."

"Afraid of what? Come on, snap out of it! You need another drink." He pulled her up from the settee and led her through the crowded room down the long narrow dark hallway to the more crowded kitchen.

When they returned to the room, the pianist was just preparing to play again. He was tall and slender, with extra long legs and arms, giving him the appearance of a scarecrow. His pants were tight in the waist and full in the legs. He wore no coat, and a blue silk shirt hung damply to his body. He acted as if he were king of the occasion, ruling all from his piano stool throne. He talked familiarly to every one in the room, called women from other men's arms, demanded drinks from any bottle he happened to see being passed around, laughed uproariously, and made many grotesque and ofttimes obscene gestures.

There were sounds of a scuffle in an adjoining room, and an excited voice exclaimed, "You goddam son-of-a-bitch, don't you catch my dice no more." The piano player banged on the keys and drowned out the reply, if there was one.

Emma Lou could not keep her eyes off the piano player. He was acting like a maniac, occasionally turning completely around on his stool, grimacing like a witch doctor, and letting his hands dawdle over the keyboard of the piano with an agonizing indolence, when compared to the extreme exertion to which he put the rest of his body. He was improvising. The melody of the piece he had started to play was merely a base for more bawdy variations. His left foot thumped on the floor in time with the music, while his right punished the piano's loud-pedal. Beads of perspiration gathered grease from his slicked-down hair, and rolled oleagenously down his face and neck, spotting the already damp baby-blue shirt, and streaking his already greasy black face with more shiny lanes.

A sailor lad suddenly ceased his impassioned hip movement and strode out of the room, pulling his partner behind him, pushing people out of the way as he went. The spontaneous moans and slangy ejaculations of the piano player and of the more articulate dancers became more regular, more like a chanted obligato to the music. This lasted for a couple of hours interrupted only by hectic intermissions. Then the dancers grew less violent in their movements, and though the piano player seemed never to tire there were fewer couples on the floor, and those left seemed less loathe to move their legs.

Eventually, the music stopped for a long interval, and there was a more concerted drive on the kitchen's corn liquor supply. Most of the private flasks and bottles were empty. There were more calls for food, too, and the crap game in the side room annexed more players and more kibitzers. Various men and women had disappeared altogether. Those who remained seemed worn and tired. There was much petty person to person badinage and many whispered consultations in corners. There was an argument in the hallway between the landlord and two couples, who wished to share one room without paying him more than the regulation three dollars required of one couple. Finally, Alva suggested that they leave. Emma Lou had drifted off into a state of semi-consciousness and was too near asleep or drunk to distinguish people or voices. All she knew was that she was being led out of that dreadful place, that the perturbing "pilgrimage to the proletariat's parlor social," as Truman had called it, was ended, and that she was in a taxicab, cuddled up in Alva's arms.

Emma Lou awoke with a headache. Some one was knocking at her door, but when she first awakened it had seemed as if the knocking was inside of her head. She pressed her fingers to her throbbing temples, and tried to become more conscious. The knock persisted and she finally realized that it was at her door rather than in her head. She called out, "Who is it?"

"It's me." Emma Lou was not far enough out of the fog to recognize who "me" was. It didn't seem important anyway, so without any more thought or action, she allowed herself to doze off again. Whoever was on the outside of the door banged the louder, and finally Emma Lou distinguished the voice of her landlady, calling, "Let me in, Miss Morgan, let me in." The voice grew more sharp . . . "Let me in," and then in an undertone, "Must have some one in there." This last served to awaken Emma Lou more fully, and though every muscle in her body protested, she finally got out of the bed and went to the door. The lady entered precipitously, and pushing Emma Lou aside sniffed the air and looked around as if she expected to surprise some one, either squeezing under the bed or leaping through the window. After she had satisfied herself that there was no one else in the room, she turned on Emma Lou furiously:

"Miss Morgan, I wish to talk to you." Emma Lou closed the door and wearily sat down upon the bed. The wrinkled faced old woman glared at her and shifted the position of her snuff so she could talk more easily. "I won't have it, I tell you, I won't have it." Emma Lou tried hard to realize what it was she wouldn't have, and failing, she said nothing, just screwed up her eyes and tried to look sober.

"Do you hear me?" Emma Lou nodded. "I won't have it. When you moved in here I thought I made it clear that I was a respectable woman and that I kept a respectable house. Do you understand that now?" Emma Lou nodded again. There didn't seem to be anything else to do. "I'm glad you do. Then it won't be necessary for me to explain why I want my room."

Emma Lou unscrewed her eyes and opened her mouth. What was this woman talking about? "I don't think I understand."

The old lady was quick with her answer. "There ain't nothin' for you to understand, but that I want you to get out of my house. I don't have no such carryings-on around here. A drunken woman in my house at all hours in the morning, being carried in by a man! Well, you coulda knocked me over with a feather."

At last Emma Lou began to understand. Evidently the landlady had seen her when she had come in, no doubt had seen Alva carry her to her room, and perhaps had listened outside the door. She was talking again:

"You must get out. Your week is up Wednesday. That gives

you three days to find another room, and I want you to act like a lady the rest of that time, too. The idea!" she sputtered, and stalked out of the room.

This is a pretty mess, thought Emma Lou. Yet she found herself unable to think or do anything about it. Her lethargic state worried her. Here she was about to be dispossessed by an irate landlady, and all she could do about it was sit on the side of her bed and think—maybe I ought to take a dose of salts. Momentarily, she had forgotten it was Sunday, and began to wonder how near time it was for her to go to work. She was surprised to discover that it was still early in the forenoon. She couldn't possibly have gone to bed before four-thirty or five, yet it seemed as if she had slept for hours. She felt like some one who had been under the influence of some sinister potion for a long period of time. Had she been drugged? Her head still throbbed, her insides burned, her tongue was swollen, her lips chapped and feverish. She began to deplore her physical condition, and even to berate herself and Alva for last night's debauchery.

Funny people, his friends. Come to think of it they were all very much different from any one else she had ever known. They were all so, so—she sought for a descriptive word, but could think of nothing save that revolting, "Oh, sock it," she had heard on first entering the apartment where the house-rent party had been held.

Then she began to wonder about her landlady's charges. There was no need arguing about the matter. She had wanted to move anyway. Maybe now she could go ahead and find a decent place in which to live. She had never had the nerve to begin another room hunting expedition after the last one. She shuddered as she thought about it, then climbed back into the bed. She could see no need in staying up so long as her head ached as it did. She wondered if Alva had made much noise in bringing her in, wondered how long he had stayed, and if he had had any trouble manipulating the double-barrelled police lock on the outside door. Harlem people were so careful about barricading themselves in. They all seemed to fortify themselves, not only against strangers, but against neighbors and friends as well.

And Alva? She had to admit that she was a trifle disappointed in him and in his friends. They certainly weren't what she could have called either intellectuals or respectable people. Whoever heard of decent folk attending such a lascivious festival? She remembered their enthusiastic comments and tried to comprehend just what it was that had intrigued and interested them. Looking for material, they had said. More than likely they were looking for liquor and a chance to be licentious.

Alva himself worried her a bit. She couldn't understand why gin seemed so indispensable to him. He always insisted that he had to have at least three drinks a day. Once she had urged him not to follow this program. Unprotestingly, he had come to her the following evening without the usual juniper berry smell on his breath, but he had been so disagreeable and had seemed so much like a worn out and dissipated person that she had never again suggested that he not have his usual quota of drinks. Then, too, she had discovered that he was much too lovable after having had his "evening drams" to be discouraged from taking them. Emma Lou had never met any one in her life who was as loving and kind to her as Alva. He seemed to anticipate her every mood and desire, and he was the most soothing and satisfying person with whom she had ever come into contact. He seldom riled her—seldom ruffled her feelings. He seemed to give in to her on every occasion, and was the most chivalrous escort imaginable. He was always courteous, polite and thoughtful of her comfort.

As yet she had been unable to become angry with him. Alva never argued or protested unduly. Although Emma Lou didn't realize it, he used more subtle methods. His means of remaining master of all situations were both tactful and sophisticated; for example, Emma Lou never realized just how she had first begun giving him money. Surely he hadn't asked her for it. It had just seemed the natural thing to do after a while, and she had done it, willingly and without question. The ethical side of their relationship never worried her. She was content and she was happy—at least she was in possession of something that seemed to bring her happiness. She seldom worried about Alva not being true to her, and if she questioned him about such matters, he would pretend not to hear her and change the conversation. The only visible physical reaction would be a slight narrowing of the eyes, as if he were trying not to wince from the pain of some inner hurt.

Once she had suggested marriage, and had been shocked when Alva told her that to him the marriage ceremony seemed a waste of time. He had already been married twice, and he hadn't even bothered to obtain a divorce from his first wife before acquiring number two. On hearing this, Emma Lou had urged him to tell her more about these marital experiments, and after a little coaxing, he had done so, very impassively and very sketchily, as if he were relating the experiences of another. He told her that he had really loved his first wife, but that she was such an essential polygamous female that he had been forced to abdicate and hand her over to the multitudes. According to Alva, she had been as vain as Braxton, and as fundamentally dependent upon flattery. She could do without three square meals a day, but she couldn't do without her contingent of mealy-mouthed admirers, all eager to outdo one another in the matter of compliments. One man could never have satisfied her, not that she was a nymphomaniac with abnormal physical appetites, but because she wanted attention, and the more men she had around her, the more attention she could receive. She hadn't been able to convince Alva, though, that her battalion of admirers were all of the platonic variety. "I know niggers too well," Alva had summed it up to Emma Lou, "so I told her she just must go, and she went."

"But," Emma Lou had queried when he had started to talk about something else, "what about your second wife?"

"Oh," he laughed, "well, I married her when I was drunk. She was an old woman about fifty. She kept me drunk from Sunday to Sunday. When I finally got sober she showed me the marriage license and I well nigh passed out again."

"But where is she?" Emma Lou had asked, "and how did they let you get married while you were drunk and already had a wife?"

Alva had shrugged his shoulders. "I don't know where she is. I ain't seen her since I left her room that day. I sent Braxton up there to talk to her. Seems like she'd been drunk too. So, it really didn't matter. And as for a divorce, I know plenty spades right here in Harlem get married any time they want to. Who in the hell's gonna take the trouble getting a divorce, when, if you must marry and already have a wife, you can get another without going through all that red tape?"

Emma Lou had had to admit that this sounded logical, if illegal. Yet she hadn't been convinced. "But," she had insisted, "don't they look you up and convict you of bigamy?"

"Hell, no. The only thing the law bothers niggers about is for stealing, murdering, or chasing white women, and as long as they don't steal from or murder ofays, the law ain't none too particular about bothering them. The only time they act about bigamy is when one of the wives squawk, and they hardly ever do that. They're only too glad to see the old man get married again—then they can do likewise, without spending lots of time on lawyers and courthouse red tape."

This, and other things which Emma Lou had elicited from Alva, had convinced her that he was undoubtedly the most interesting person she had ever met. What added to this was the strange fact that he seemed somewhat cultured despite his admitted unorganized and haphazard early training. On being questioned, he advanced the theory that perhaps this was due to his long period of service as waiter and valet to socially prominent white people. Many Negroes, he had explained, even of the "dicty" variety, had obtained their *savoir faire* and knowledge of the social niceties in this manner.

Emma Lou lay abed, remembering the many different conversations they had had together, most of which had taken place on a bench in City College Park, or in Alva's room. With enough gin for stimulation, Alva could tell many tales of his life and hold her spellbound with vivid descriptions of the various situations he had found himself in. He loved to reminisce, when he found a good listener, and Emma Lou loved to listen when she found a good talker. Alva often said that he wished some one would write a story of his life. Maybe that was why he cultivated an acquaintance with these writer people. . . . Then it seemed as if this one-sided conversational communion strengthened their physical bond. It made Emma Lou more palatable to Alva, and it made Alva a more glamorous figure to Emma Lou.

But here she was day dreaming, when she should be wondering where she was going to move. She couldn't possibly remain in this place, even if the old lady relented and decided to give her another chance to be respectable. Somehow or other she felt that she had been insulted, and for the first time, began to feel angry with the old snuff-chewing termagant.

Her head ached no longer, but her body was still lethargic. Alva, Alva, Alva. Could she think of nothing else? Supposing— she sat upright in the bed—supposing she and Alva were to live together. They might get a small apartment and be with one another entirely. Immediately she was all activity. The head-ache was forgotten. Out of bed, into her bathrobe, and down the hall to the bathroom. Even the quick shower seemed to be a slow, tedious process, and she was in such a hurry to hasten into the street and telephone Alva, in order to tell him of her new plans, that she almost forgot to make the very necessary and very customary application of bleaching cream to her face. As it was, she forgot to rinse her face and hands in lemon juice.

Alva had lost all patience with Braxton, and profanely told him so. No matter what his condition, Braxton would not work. He seemed to believe that because he was handsome, and be-cause he was Braxton, he shouldn't have to work. He graced the world with his presence. Therefore, it should pay him. "A thing of beauty is joy forever," and should be sustained by a communal larder. Alva tried to show him that such a larder didn't exist, that one either worked or hustled.

But as Alva had explained to Emma Lou, Braxton wouldn't work, and as a hustler he was a distinct failure. He couldn't gamble successfully, he never had a chance to steal, and he al-ways allowed his egotism to defeat his own ends when he tried to get money from women. He assumed that at a word from him, anybody's pocketbook should be at his disposal, and that his handsomeness and personality were a combination none could withstand. It is a platitude among sundry sects and indi-viduals that as a person thinketh, so he is, but it was not within the power of Braxton's mortal body to become the being his imagination sought to create. He insisted, for instance, that he was a golden brown replica of Rudolph Valentino. Every pic-ture he could find of the late lamented cinema sheik he pasted either on the wall or on some of his belongings. The only rea-son that likenesses of his idol did not decorate all the wall space was because Alva objected to this flapperish ritual. Braxton emulated his silver screen mentor in every way, watched his every gesture on the screen, then would stand in front of his mirror at home and practice Rudy's poses and facial expressions. Strange as it may seem, there was a certain likeness between the two, especially at such moments when Braxton would suddenly stand in the center of the floor and give a spontaneous impersonation of his Rudy making love or conquering enemies. Then, at all times, Braxton held his head as Rudy held his, and had even learned how to smile and how to use his eyes in the same captivating manner. But his charms were too obviously cultivated, and his technique too clumsy. He would attract almost any one to him, but they were sure to bolt away as suddenly as they had come. He could have, but he could not hold.

Now, as Alva told Emma Lou, this was a distinct handicap to one who wished to be a hustler, and live by one's wits off the bounty of others. And the competition was too keen in a place like Harlem, where the adaptability to city ways sometimes took strange and devious turns, for a bungler to have much success. Alva realized this, if Braxton didn't, and tried to tell him so, but Braxton wouldn't listen. He felt that Alva was merely being envious—the fact that Alva had more suits than he, and that Alva always had clean shirts, liquor money and room rent, and that Alva could continue to have these things, despite the fact that he had decided to quit work during the hot weather, meant nothing to Braxton at all. He had facial and physical perfection, a magnetic body and much sex appeal. Ergo, he was a master.

However, lean days were upon him. His mother and aunt had unexpectedly come to New York to help him celebrate the closing day of his freshman year at Columbia. His surprise at seeing them was nothing in comparison to their surprise in finding that their darling had not even started his freshman year. The aunt was stoic—"What could you expect of a child with all that wild Indian blood in him? Now, our people. . . ." She hadn't liked Braxton's father. His mother simply could not comprehend his duplicity. Such an unnecessarily cruel and deceptive performance was beyond her understanding. Had she been told that he was guilty of thievery, murder, or rape, she

could have borne up and smiled through her tears in true maternal fashion, but that he could so completely fool her for
nine months—incredible; preposterous! it just couldn't be!

She and her sister returned to Boston, telling every one there
what a successful year their darling had had at Columbia, and
telling Braxton before they left that he could not have another
cent of their money that summer, that if he didn't enter Columbia in the fall . . . well, he was not yet of age. They made
many vague threats; none so alarming, however, as the threat
of a temporary, if not permanent, suspension of his allowance.

By pawning some of his suits, his watch, and diamond ring,
he amassed a small stake and took to gambling. Unlucky at
love, he should, so Alva said, have been lucky at cards, and was.
But even a lucky man will suffer from lack of skill and foolhar-
diness. Braxton would gamble only with mature men who
gathered in the police-protected clubs, rather than with young
chaps like himself, who gathered in private places. He couldn't
classify himself with the cheap or the lowly. If he was to gamble,
he must gamble in a professional manner, with professional
men. As in all other affairs, he had luck, but no skill and little
sense. His little gambling stake lasted but a moment, flitted
from him feverishly, and left him holding an empty purse.

Then he took to playing the "numbers," placing quarters and
half dollars on a number compounded of three digits and anxiously perusing the daily clearing house reports to see whether
or not he had chosen correctly. Alva, too, played the numbers
consistently and somehow or other, managed to remain ahead
of the game, but Braxton, as was to be expected, "hit" two or
three times, then grew excited over his winnings and began to
play two or three or even five dollars daily on one number.
Such plunging, unattended by scientific observation or close
calculation, put him so far behind the game that his winnings
were soon dissipated and he had to stop playing altogether.

Alva had quit work for the summer. He contended that it
was far too hot to stand over a steam pressing machine during
the sultry summer months, and there was no other congenial
work available. Being a bellhop in one of the few New York
hotels where colored boys were used, called for too long hours
and broken shifts. Then they didn't pay much money and he
hated to work for tips. He certainly would not take an elevator

job, paying only sixty or sixty-five dollars a month at the most, and making it necessary for him to work nights one week from six to eight, and days the next week, vice versa. Being an elevator operator in a loft building required too much skill, patience, and muscular activity. The same could be said of the shipping clerk positions, open in the various wholesale houses. He couldn't, of course, be expected to be a porter, and swing a mop. Bootblacking was not even to be considered. There was nothing left. He was unskilled, save as a presser. Once he had been apprenticed to a journeyman tailor, but he preferred to forget that.

No, there was nothing he could do, and there was no sense in working in the summer. He never had done it; at least, not since he had been living in New York—so he didn't see why he should do it now. Furthermore, his salary hardly paid his saloon bill, and since his board and room and laundry and clothes came from other sources, why not quit work altogether and develop these sources to their capacity output? Things looked much brighter this year than ever before. He had more clothes, he had "hit" the numbers more than ever, he had won a baseball pool of no mean value, and, in addition to Emma Lou, he had made many other profitable contacts during the spring and winter months. It was safe for him to loaf, but he couldn't carry Braxton, or rather, he wouldn't. Yet he liked him well enough not to kick him into the streets. Something, he told Emma Lou, should be done for him first, so Alva started doing things.

First, he got him a girl, or rather steered him in the direction of one who seemed to be a good bet. She was. And as usual, Braxton had little trouble in attracting her to him. She was a simple-minded over-sexed little being from a small town in Central Virginia, new to Harlem, and had hitherto always lived in her home town where she had been employed since her twelfth year as maid-of-all-work to a wealthy white family. For four years, she had been her master's concubine, and probably would have continued in that capacity for an unspecified length of time, had not the mistress of the house decided that after all it might not be good for her two adolescent sons to become aware of their father's philandering. She had had to accept it. Most of the women of her generation and in her circle had done likewise. But these were the post world war days of modernity . . . and, well, it just wasn't being done, what with the growing intelligence of the "darkies," and the increased sophistication of the children.

So Anise Hamilton had been surreptitiously shipped away to New York, and a new maid-of-all-work had mysteriously appeared in her place. The mistress had seen to it that this new maid was not as desirable as Anise, but a habit is a habit, and the master of the house was not the sort to substitute one habit for another. If anything, his wife had made herself more miserable by the change, since the last girl loved much better than she worked, while Anise had proved competent on both scores, thereby pleasing both master and mistress.

Anise had come to Harlem and deposited the money her former mistress had supplied her with in the postal savings. She wouldn't hear to placing it in any other depository. Banks had a curious and discomforting habit of closing their doors without warning, and without the foresight to provide their patrons with another nest egg. If banks in Virginia went broke, those in wicked New York would surely do so. Now, Uncle Sam had the whole country behind him, and everybody knew that the United States was the most wealthy of the world's nations. Therefore, what safer place than the post office for one's bank account?

Anise got a job, too, almost immediately. Her former mistress had given her a letter to a friend of hers on Park Avenue, and this friend had another friend who had a sister who wanted a stock girl in her exclusive modiste shop. Anise was the type to grace such an establishment as this person owned, just the right size to create a smart uniform for, and shapely enough to allow the creator of the uniform ample latitude for bizarre experimentation. Most important of all, her skin, the color of beaten brass with copper overtones, synchronized with the gray plaster walls, dark hardwood furniture and powder blue rugs on the Maison Quantrelle.

Anise soon had any number of "boy friends," with whom she had varying relations. But she willingly dropped them all for Braxton, and, simple village girl that she was, expected him to do likewise with his "girl friends." She had heard much about the "two-timing sugar daddies" in Harlem, and while she was well versed in the art herself, having never been particularly true to her male employer, she did think that this sort of thing was different, and that any time she was willing to play fair, her consort should do likewise.

Alva was proud of himself when he noticed how rapidly things progressed between Anise and Braxton. They were together constantly, and Anise, not unused to giving her home town "boy friends" some of "Mister Bossman's bounty," was soon slipping Braxton spare change to live on. Then she undertook to pay his half of the room rent, and finally, within three weeks, was, as Alva phrased it, "treating Braxton royally."

But as ever, he was insistent upon being perverse. His old swank and swagger was much in evidence. With most of his clothing out of the pawnshop, he attempted to dazzle the Avenue when he paraded its length, the alluring Anise, attired in clothes borrowed from her employer's stockroom, beside him. The bronze replica of Rudolph Valentino was, in the argot of Harlem's pool hall Johnnies, "out the barrel." The world was his. He had in it a bottle, and he need only make it secure by corking. But Braxton was never the person to make anything secure. He might manage to capture the entire universe, but he could never keep it pent up, for he would soon let it alone to look for two more like it. It was to be expected, then, that Braxton would lose his head. He did, deliberately and diabolically. Because Anise was so madly in love with him, he imagined that all other women should do as she had done, and how much more delightful and profitable it would be to have two or three Anises instead of one. So he began a crusade, spending much of Anise's money for campaign funds. Alva quarrelled, and Anise threatened, but Braxton continued to explore and expend.

Anise finally revolted when Braxton took another girl to a dance on her money. He had done this many times before, but she hadn't known about it. She wouldn't have known about it this time if he hadn't told her. He often did things like that. Thought it made him more desirable. Despite her simplemindedness, Anise had spunk. She didn't like to quarrel, but she wasn't going to let any one make a fool out of her, so, the next week after the heartbreaking incident, she had moved and left no forwarding address. It was presumed that she had gone downtown to live in the apartment of the woman for whom she worked. Braxton seemed unconcerned about her disappearance, and continued his peacock-like march for some time, with feathers unruffled, even by frequent trips to the pawnshop. But a peacock can hardly preen an unplumaged body, and, though Braxton continued to strut, in a few weeks after the break, he was only a sad semblance of his former self.

Alva nagged at him continually. "Damned if I'm going to carry you." Braxton would remain silent. "You're the most no-count nigger I know. If you can't do anything else, why in the hell don't you get a job?" "I don't see you working," Braxton would answer.

"And you don't see me starving, either," would be the come-back.

"Oh, jost 'cause you got that little black wench . . ."

"That's all right about the little black wench. She's forty with me, and I know how to treat her. I bet you couldn't get five cents out of her."

"I wouldn't try."

"Hell, if you tried it wouldn't make no difference. There's a gal ready to pay to have a man, and there are lots more like her. You couldn't even keep a good-looking gold mine like Anise. Wish I could find her."

Braxton would sulk a while, thinking that his silence would discourage Alva, but Alva was not to be shut up. He was truly outraged. He felt that he was being imposed upon, being used by some one who thought himself superior to him. He would admit that he wasn't as handsome as Braxton, but he certainly had more common sense. The next Monday Braxton moved.

Alva was to take Emma Lou to the midnight show at the La-fayette Theater. He met her as she left work and they had taken the subway uptown. On the train they began to talk, shouting into one another's ears, trying to make their voices heard above the roar of the underground tube.

"Do you like your new home?" Alva shouted. He hadn't seen her since she had moved two days before.

"It's nice," she admitted loudly, "but it would be nicer if I had you there with me."

He patted her hand and held it regardless of the onlooking crowd.

"Maybe so, sugar, but you wouldn't like me if you had to live with me all the time."

Emma Lou was aggrieved: "I don't see how you can say that. How do you know? That's what made me mad last Sunday."

Alva saw that Emma Lou was ready for argument and he had no intention of favoring her, or of discomfiting himself. He was even sorry that he said as much as he had when she had first broached the "living together" matter over the telephone on Sunday, calling him out of bed before noon while Geraldine was there too, looking, but not asking, for information. He smiled at her indulgently:

"If you say another word about it, I'll kiss you right here in the subway."

Emma Lou didn't put it beyond him so she could do nothing but smile and shut up. She rather liked him to talk to her that way. Alva was shouting into her ear again, telling her a scandalous tale he claimed to have heard while playing poker with some of the boys. He thus contrived to keep her entertained until they reached the 135th Street station where they finally emerged from beneath the pavement to mingle with the frowsy crowds of Harlem's Bowery, Lenox Avenue.

They made their way to the Lafayette, the Jew's gift of entertainment to Harlem colored folk. Each week the management of this theater presents a new musical revue of the three a day variety with motion pictures—all guaranteed to be from three to ten years old—sandwiched in between. On Friday nights there is a special midnight performance lasting from twelve o'clock until four or four-thirty the next morning, according to the stamina of the actors. The audience does not matter. It would as soon sit until noon the next day if the "high yaller" chorus girls would continue to undress, and the black face comedians would continue to tell stale jokes, just so long as there was a raucous blues singer thrown in every once in a while for vulgar variety.

Before Emma Lou and Alva could reach the entrance door, they had to struggle through a crowd of well dressed young men and boys, congregated on the sidewalk in front of the theater.

The midnight show at the Lafayette on Friday is quite a social event among certain classes of Harlem folk, and, if one is a sweetback or a man about town, one must be seen standing in front of the theater, if not inside. It costs nothing to obstruct the entrance way, and it adds much to one's prestige. Why, no one knows.

Without untoward incident Emma Lou and Alva found the seats he had reserved. There was much noise in the theater, much passing to and fro, much stumbling down dark aisles. People were always leaving their seats, admonishing their companions to hold them, and some one else was always taking them despite the curt and sometimes belligerent, "This seat is taken." Then, when the original occupant would return there would be still another argument. This happened so frequently that there seemed to be a continual wrangling automatically staged in different parts of the auditorium. Then people were always looking for some one or for something, always peering into the darkness, emitting code whistles, and calling to Jane or Jim or Pete or Bill. At the head of each aisle, both upstairs and down, people were packed in a solid mass, a grumbling, garrulous mass, elbowing their neighbors, cursing the management, and standing on tiptoe trying to find an empty, intact seat—intact because every other seat in the theater seemed to be broken. Hawkers went up and down the aisle shouting, "Ice cream, peanuts, chewing gum or candy." People hissed at them and ordered what they wanted. A sadly inadequate crew of ushers inefficiently led people up one aisle and down another trying to find their supposedly reserved seats; a lone fireman strove valiantly to keep the aisles clear as the fire laws stipulated. It was a most chaotic and confusing scene.

First, a movie was shown while the organ played mournful jazz. About one o'clock the midnight revue went on. The curtain went up on the customary chorus ensemble singing the customary, "Hello, we're glad to be here, we're going to please you" opening song. This was followed by the usual song and dance team, a blues singer, a lady Charleston dancer, and two black faced comedians. Each would have his turn, then begin all over again, aided frequently by the energetic and noisy chorus, which somehow managed to appear upon the stage almost naked in the first scene, and keep getting more and more naked as the evening progressed.

Emma Lou had been to the Lafayette before with John and had been shocked by the scantily clad women and obscene skits. The only difference that she could see in this particular revue was that the performers were more bawdy and more boisterous. And she had never been in or seen such an audience. There was as much, if not more, activity in the orchestra and box seats than there was on the stage. It was hard to tell whether the cast was before or behind the proscenium arch. There seemed to be a veritable contest going on between the paid performers and their paying audience, and Emma Lou found the spontaneous monkey shines and utterances of those around her much more amusing than the stereotyped antics of the hired performers on the stage.

She was surprised to find that she was actually enjoying herself, yet she supposed that after the house-rent party she could stand anything. Imagine people opening their flats to the public and charging any one who had the price to pay twenty-five cents to enter? Imagine people going to such bedlam Bacchanals?

A new scene on the stage attracted her attention. A very colorfully dressed group of people had gathered for a party. Emma Lou immediately noticed that all the men were dark, and that all the women were either a very light brown or "high yaller." She turned to Alva:

"Don't they ever have anything else but fair chorus girls?"

Alva made a pretense of being very occupied with the business on the stage. Happily, at that moment, one of a pair of black faced comedians had set the audience in an uproar with a suggestive joke. After a moment Emma Lou found herself laughing too. The two comedians were funny, no matter how prejudiced one might be against unoriginality. There must be other potent elements to humor besides surprise. Then a very Topsy-like girl skated onto the stage to the tune of "Ireland must be heaven because my mother came from there." Besides being corked until her skin was jet black, the girl had on a wig of kinky hair. Her lips were painted red—their thickness exaggerated by the paint. Her coming created a stir. Every one concerned was indignant that something like her should crash their party. She attempted to attach herself to certain men in the crowd. The straight men spurned her merely by turning away. The comedians made a great fuss about it, pushing her from one to the other, and finally getting into a riotous argument because each accused the other of having invited her. It ended by them agreeing to toss her bodily off the stage to the orchestral accompaniment of "Bye, Bye, Blackbird," while the entire party loudly proclaimed that "Black cats must go."

Then followed the usual rigamarole carried on weekly at the Lafayette concerning the undesirability of black girls. Every one, that is, all the males, let it be known that high browns and "high yallers" were "forty" with them, but that. . . . They were interrupted by the re-entry of the little black girl riding a mule and singing mournfully as she was being thus transported across the stage:

> A yellow gal rides in a limousine,
> A brown-skin rides a Ford,
> A black gal rides an old jackass
> But she gets there, yes my Lord.

Emma Lou was burning up with indignation. So color-conscious had she become that any time some one mentioned or joked about skin color, she immediately imagined that they were referring to her. Now she even felt that all the people near by were looking at her and that their laughs were at her expense. She remained silent throughout the rest of the performance, averting her eyes from the stage and trying hard not to say anything to Alva before they left the theater. After what seemed an eternity, the finale screamed its good-bye at the audience, and Alva escorted her out into Seventh Avenue.

Alva was tired and thirsty. He had been up all night the night before at a party to which he had taken Geraldine, and he had had to get up unusually early on Friday morning in order to go after his laundry. Of course when he had arrived at Bobby's apartment where his laundry was being done, he found that his shirts were not yet ironed, so he had gone to bed there, with the result that he hadn't been able to go to sleep, nor had the shirts been ironed, but that was another matter.

"First time I ever went to a midnight show without something on my hip," he complained to Emma Lou as they crossed the taxi-infested street in order to escape the crowds leaving the theater and idling in front of it, even at four A.M. in the morning.

"Well," Emma Lou returned vehemently, "it's the last time I'll ever go to that place any kind of way."

Alva hadn't expected this. "What's the matter with you?"

"You're always taking me some place, or placing me in some position where I'll be insulted."

"Insulted?" This was far beyond Alva. Who on earth had insulted her and when. "But," he paused, then advanced cautiously, "Sugar, I don't know what you mean."

Emma Lou was ready for a quarrel. In fact she had been trying to pick one with him ever since the night she had gone to that house-rent party, and the landlady had asked her to move on the following day. Alva's curt refusal of her proposal that they live together had hurt her far more than he had imagined. Somehow or other he didn't think she could be so serious about the matter, especially upon such short notice. But Emma Lou had been so certain that he would be as excited over the suggestion as she had been that she hadn't considered meeting a definite refusal. Then the finding of a room had been irritating to contemplate. She couldn't have called it irritating of accomplishment because Alva had done that for her. She had told him on Sunday morning that she had to move and by Sunday night he had found a place for her. She had to admit that he had found an exceptionally nice place too. It was just two blocks from him, on 138th Street between Eighth Avenue and Edgecombe. It was near the elevated station, near the park, and cost only ten dollars and fifty cents per week for the room, kitchenette and private bath.

On top of his refusal to live with her, Alva had broken two dates with Emma Lou, claiming that he was playing poker. On one of these nights, after leaving work, Emma Lou had decided to walk past his house. Even at a distance she could see that there was a light in his room, and when she finally passed the house, she recognized Geraldine, the girl with whom she had seen Alva dancing at the Renaissance Casino, seated in the window. Angrily, she had gone home, determined to break with Alva on the morrow, and on reaching home had found a letter from her mother which had disturbed her even more. For a long time now her mother had been urging her to come home, and her Uncle Joe had even sent her word that he meant to forward a ticket at an early date. But Emma Lou had no intentions of going home. She was so obsessed with the idea that her mother didn't want her, and she was so incensed at the people with whom she knew she would be forced to associate, that she could consider her mother's hysterically-put request only as an insult. Thus, presuming, she had answered in kind, giving vent to her feelings about the matter. This disturbing letter was in answer to her own spleenic epistle, and what hurt her most was, not the sharp counsellings and verbose lamentations therein, but the concluding phrase, which read, "I don't see how the Lord could have given me such an evil, black hussy for a daughter."

The following morning she had telephoned Alva, determined to break with him, or at least make him believe she was about to break with him, but Alva had merely yawned and asked her not to be a goose. Could he help it if Braxton's girl chose to sit in his window? It was as much Braxton's room as it was his. True, Braxton wouldn't be there long, but while he was, he certainly should have full privileges. That had quieted Emma Lou then, but there was nothing that could quiet her now. She continued arguing as they walked toward 135th Street.

"You don't want to know what I mean."

"No, I guess not," Alva assented wearily, then quickened his pace. He didn't want to have a public scene with this black wench. But Emma Lou was not to be appeased.

"Well, you will know what I mean. First you take me out with a bunch of your supposedly high-toned friends, and sit silently by while they poke fun at me. Then you take me to a theater, where you know I'll have my feelings hurt." She stopped for breath. Alva filled in the gap.

"If you ask me," he said wearily, "I think you're full of stuff. Let's take a taxi. I'm too tired to walk." He hailed a taxi, pushed her into it, and gave the driver the address. Then he turned to Emma Lou, saying something which he regretted having said a moment later.

"How did my friends insult you?"

"You know how they insulted me, sitting up there making fun of me 'cause I'm black."

Alva laughed, something he also regretted later.

"That's right, laugh, and I suppose you laughed with them then, behind my back, and planned all that talk before I arrived."

Alva didn't answer and Emma Lou cried all the rest of the way home. Once there he tried to soothe her.

"Come on, Sugar, let Alva put you to bed."

But Emma Lou was not to be sugared so easily. She continued to cry. Alva sat down on the bed beside her.

"Snap out of it, won't you, Honey? You're just tired. Go to bed and get some sleep. You'll be all right tomorrow."

Emma Lou stopped her crying.

"I may be all right, but I'll never forget the way you've allowed me to be insulted in your presence."

This was beginning to get on Alva's nerves but he smiled at her indulgently:

"I suppose I should have gone down on the stage and biffed one of the comedians in the jaw?"

"No," snapped Emma Lou, realizing she was being ridiculous, "but you could've stopped your friends from poking fun at me."

"But, Sugar," this was growing tiresome. "How can you say they were making fun of you. It's beyond me."

"It wasn't beyond you when it started. I bet you told them about me before I came in, told them I was black. . . ."

"Nonsense, weren't some of them dark? I'm afraid," he advanced slowly, "that you are a trifle too color-conscious," he was glad he remembered that phrase.

Emma Lou flared up: "Color-conscious . . . who wouldn't be color-conscious when everywhere you go people are always talking about color. If it didn't make any difference they wouldn't talk about it, they wouldn't always be poking fun, and laughing and making jokes. . . ."

Alva interrupted her tirade. "You're being silly, Emma Lou. About three-quarters of the people at the Lafayette tonight were either dark brown or black, and here you are crying and fuming like a ninny over some reference made on the stage to a black person." He was disgusted now. He got up from the bed. Emma Lou looked up.

"But, Alva, you don't know."

"I do know," he spoke sharply for the first time, "that you're a damn fool. It's always color, color, color. If I speak to any of my friends on the street you always make some reference to their color and keep plaguing me with—'Don't you know nothing else but light-skinned people?' And you're always beefing about being black. Seems like to me you'd be proud of it. You're not the only black person in this world. There are gangs of them right here in Harlem, and I don't see them going around a-moanin' 'cause they ain't half white."

"I'm not moaning."

"Oh, yes you are. And a person like you is far worse than a hinkty yellow nigger. It's your kind helps make other people color-prejudiced."

"That's just what I'm saying; it's because of my color. . . ."

"Oh, go to hell!" And Alva rushed out of the room, slamming the door behind him.

Braxton had been gone a week. Alva, who had been out with Marie, the creole Lesbian, came home late, and, turning on the light, found Geraldine asleep in his bed. He was so surprised that he could do nothing for a moment but stand in the center of the room and look—first at Geraldine and then at her toilet articles spread over his dresser. He twisted his lips in a wry smile, muttered something to himself, then walked over to the bed and shook her.

"Geraldine, Geraldine," he called. She awoke quickly and smiled at him.

"Hello. What time is it?"

"Oh," he returned guardedly, "somewhere after three."

"Where've you been?"

"Playing poker."

"With whom?"

"Oh, the same gang. But what's the idea?"

Geraldine wrinkled her brow.

"The idea of what?"

"Of sorta taking possession?"

"Oh," she seemed enlightened, "I've moved to New York."

It was Alva's cue to register surprise.

"What's the matter? You and the old lady fall out?"

"Not at all."

"Does she know where you are?"

"She knows I'm in New York."

"You know what I mean. Does she know you're going to stay?"

"Certainly."

"But where are you going to live?"

"Here."

"Here?"

"Yes."

"But . . . but . . . well, what is this all about, anyhow?"

She sat up in the bed and regarded him for a moment, a light smile playing around her lips. Before she spoke she yawned; then in a cool, even tone of voice, announced "I'm going to have a baby."

"But," he began after a moment, "can't you—can't you . . . ?"

"I've tried everything and now it's too late. There's nothing to do but have it."

PART V

Pyrrhic Victory

IT was two years later. "Cabaret Gal," which had been on the road for one year, had returned to New York and the company had been disbanded. Arline was preparing to go to Europe and had decided not to take a maid with her. However, she determined to get Emma Lou another job before she left. She inquired among her friends, but none of the active performers she knew seemed to be in the market for help, and it was only on the eve of sailing that she was able to place Emma Lou with Clere Sloane, a former stage beauty, who had married a famous American writer and retired from public life.

Emma Lou soon learned to like her new place. She was Clere's personal maid, and found it much less tiresome than being in the theater with Arline. Clere was less temperamental and less hurried. She led a rather leisurely life, and treated Emma Lou more as a companion than as a servant. Clere's husband, Campbell Kitchen, was very congenial and kind too, although Emma Lou, at first, seldom came into contact with him, for he and his wife practically led separate existences, meeting only at meals, or when they had guests, or when they both happened to arise at the same hour for breakfast. Occasionally, they attended the theater or a party together, and sometimes entertained, but usually they followed their own individual paths.

Campbell Kitchen, like many other white artists and intellectuals, had become interested in Harlem. The Negro and all things negroid had become a fad, and Harlem had become a shrine to which feverish pilgrimages were in order. Campbell Kitchen, along with Carl Van Vechten, was one of the leading spirits in this "Explore Harlem; Know the Negro" crusade. He, unlike many others, was quite sincere in his desire to exploit those things in Negro life which he presumed would eventually win for the Negro a more comfortable position in American life. It was he who first began the agitation in the higher places of journalism which gave impetus to the spiritual craze. It was he who ferreted out and gave publicity to many unknown blues singers. It was he who sponsored most of the younger Negro writers, personally carrying their work to publishers and editors. It wasn't his fault entirely that most of them were published before they had anything to say or before they knew how to say it. Rather it was the fault of the faddistic American public which followed the band wagon and kept clamoring for additional performances, not because of any manifested excellence, but rather because of their sensationalism and pseudo-barbaric *decor*.

Emma Lou had heard much of his activity, and had been surprised to find herself in his household. Recently he had written a book concerning Negro life in Harlem, a book calculated by its author to be a sincere presentation of those aspects of life in Harlem which had interested him. Campbell Kitchen belonged to the sophisticated school of modern American writers. His novels were more or less fantastic bits of realism, skipping lightly over the surfaces of life, and managing somehow to mirror depths through superficialities. His novel on Harlem had been a literary failure because the author presumed that its subject matter demanded serious treatment. Hence, he disregarded the traditions he had set up for himself in his other works, and produced an energetic and entertaining hodgepodge, where the bizarre was strangled by the sentimental, and the erotic clashed with the commonplace.

Negroes had not liked Campbell Kitchen's delineation of their life in the world's greatest colored city. They contended that, like "Nigger Heaven" by Carl Van Vechten, the book gave white people a wrong impression of Negroes, thus lessening their prospects of doing away with prejudice and race discrimination. From what she had heard, Emma Lou had expected to meet a sneering, obscene cynic, intent upon ravaging every Negro woman and insulting every Negro man, but he proved to be such an ordinary, harmless individual that she was won over to his side almost immediately.

Whenever they happened to meet, he would talk to her about her life in particular and Negro life in general. She had to admit that he knew much more about such matters than she or any other Negro she had ever met. And it was because of one of these chance talks that she finally decided to follow Mrs. Blake's advice and take the public school teachers' examination.

Two years had wrought little change in Emma Lou, although much had happened to her. After that tearful night, when Alva had sworn at her and stalked out of her room, she had somewhat taken stock of herself. She wondered if Alva had been right in his allegations. Was she supersensitive about her color? Did she encourage color prejudice among her own people, simply by being so expectant of it? She tried hard to place the blame on herself, but she couldn't seem to do it. She knew she hadn't been color-conscious during her early childhood days; that is, until she had had it called to her attention by her mother or some of her mother's friends, who had all seemed to take delight in marvelling, "What an extraordinarily black child!" or "Such beautiful hair on such a black baby!"

Her mother had even hidden her away on occasions when she was to have company, and her grandmother had been cruel in always assailing Emma Lou's father, whose only crime seemed to be that he had had a blue black skin. Then there had been her childhood days when she had ventured forth into the streets to play. All of her colored playmates had been mulattoes, and her white playmates had never ceased calling public attention to her crow-like complexion. Consequently, she had grown sensitive and had soon been driven to play by herself, avoiding contact with other children as much as possible. Her mother encouraged her in this, had even suggested that she not attend certain parties because she might not have a good time.

Then there had been the searing psychological effect of that dreadful graduation night, and the lonely embittering three years at college, all of which had tended to make her color more and more a paramount issue and ill. It was neither fashionable nor good for a girl to be as dark as she, and to be, at the same time, as untalented and undistinguished. Dark girls could get along if they were exceptionally talented or handsome or wealthy, but she had nothing to recommend her, save a beautiful head of hair. Despite the fact that she had managed to lead her classes in school, she had to admit that mentally she was merely mediocre and average. Now, had she been as intelligent as Mamie Olds Bates, head of a Negro school in Florida, and president of a huge national association of colored women's clubs, her darkness would not have mattered. Or had she been as wealthy as Lillian Saunders, who had inherited the millions her mother had made producing hair straightening commodities, things might have been different; but here she was, commonplace and poor, ugly and undistinguished.

Emma Lou recalled all these things, while trying to fasten the blame for her extreme color-consciousness on herself as Alva had done, but she was unable to make a good case of it. Surely, it had not been her color-consciousness which had excluded her from the only Negro sorority in her college, nor had it been her color-consciousness that had caused her to spend such an isolated three years in Southern California. The people she naturally felt at home with had, somehow or other, managed to keep her at a distance. It was no fun going to social affairs and being neglected throughout the entire evening. There was no need in forcing one's self into a certain milieu only to be frozen out. Hence, she had stayed to herself, had had very few friends, and had become more and more resentful of her blackness of skin.

She had thought Harlem would be different, but things had seemed against her from the beginning, and she had continued to go down, down, down, until she had little respect left for herself.

She had been glad when the road show of "Cabaret Gal" had gone into the provinces. Maybe a year of travel would set her aright. She would return to Harlem with considerable money saved, move into the Y.W.C.A., try to obtain a more congenial position, and set about becoming respectable once more, set about coming into contact with the "right sort of people." She was certain that there were many colored boys and girls in Harlem with whom she could associate and become content. She didn't wish to chance herself again with a Jasper Crane or an Alva.

Yet, she still loved Alva, no matter how much she regretted it, loved him enough to keep trying to win him back, even after his disgust had driven him away from her. She sadly recalled how she had telephoned him repeatedly, and how he had hung up the receiver with the brief, cruel "I don't care to talk to you," and she recalled how, swallowing her pride, she had gone to his house the day before she had left New York. Alva had greeted her coolly, then politely informed her that he couldn't let her in, as he had other company.

This had made her ill, and for three days after "Cabaret Gal" opened in Philadelphia, she had confined herself to her hotel room and cried hysterically. When it was all over, she had felt much better. The outlet of tears had been good for her, but she had never ceased to long for Alva. He had been the only completely satisfying thing in her life, and it didn't seem possible for one who had pretended to love her as much as he, suddenly to become so completely indifferent. She measured everything by her own moods and reactions, translated everything into the language of Emma Lou, and variations bewildered her to the extent that she could not believe in their reality.

So, when the company had passed through New York on its way from Philadelphia to Boston, she had approached Alva's door once more. It had never occurred to her that any one save Alva would answer her knock, and the sight of Geraldine in a negligee had stunned her. She had hastened to apologize for knocking on the wrong door, and had turned completely away without asking for Alva, only to halt as if thunderstruck when she heard his voice, as Geraldine was closing the door, asking, "Who was it, Sugar?"

For a while, Alva had been content. He really loved Geraldine, or so he thought. To him she seemed eminently desirable in every respect, and now that she was about to bear him a child, well . . . he didn't yet know what they would do with it, but everything would work out as it should. He didn't even mind having to return to work, nor, for the moment, mind having to give less attention to the rest of his harem.

Of course, Geraldine's attachment of herself to him ruled Emma Lou out more definitely than it did any of his other "paying off" people. He had been thoroughly disgusted with her and had intended to relent only after she had been forced to chase him for a considerable length of time. But Geraldine's coming had changed things altogether. Alva knew when not to attempt something, and he knew very well that he could not toy with Emma Lou and live with Geraldine at the same time. Some of the others were different. He could explain Geraldine to them, and they would help him keep themselves secreted from her. But Emma Lou, never! She would be certain to take it all wrong.

The months passed; the baby was born. Both of the parents were bitterly disappointed by this sickly, little "ball of tainted suet," as Alva called it. It had a shrunken left arm and a deformed left foot. The doctor ordered oil massages. There was a chance that the infant's limbs could be shaped into some semblance of normality. Alva declared that it looked like an idiot. Geraldine had a struggle with herself, trying to keep from smothering it. She couldn't see why such a monstrosity should live. Perhaps as the years passed it would change. At any rate, she had lost her respect for Alva. There was no denying to her that had she mated with some one else, she might have given birth to a normal child. The pain she had experienced had shaken her. One sight of the baby and continual living with it and Alva in that one, now frowsy and odoriferous room, had completed her disillusionment. For one of the very few times in her life, she felt like doing something drastic.

Alva hardly ever came home. He had quit work once more and started running around as before, only he didn't tell her about it. He lied to her or else ignored her altogether. The baby now a year old was assuredly an idiot. It neither talked nor walked. Its head had grown out of all proportion to its body, and Geraldine felt that she could have stood its shrivelled arm and deformed foot, had it not been for its insanely large and vacant eyes which seemed never to close, and for the thick grinning lips, which always remained half open and through which came no translatable sounds.

Geraldine's mother was a pious woman, and, of course, denounced the parents for the condition of the child. Had they not lived in sin, this would not be. Had they married and lived respectably, God would not have punished them in this manner. According to her, the mere possession of a marriage license and an official religious sanction of their mating would have assured them a bouncing, healthy, normal child. She refused to take the infant. Her pastor had advised her not to, saying that the parents should be made to bear the burden they had brought upon themselves.

For once, neither Geraldine nor Alva knew what to do. They

couldn't keep on as they were now. Alva was drinking more and more. He was also becoming less interested in looking well. He didn't bother about his clothes as much as before, his almond shaped eyes became more narrow, and the gray parchment conquered the yellow in his skin and gave him a deathlike pallor. He hated that silent, staring idiot infant of his, and he had begun to hate its mother. He couldn't go into the room sober. Yet his drinking provided no escape. And though he was often tempted, he felt that he could not run away and leave Geraldine alone with the baby.

Then he began to need money. Geraldine couldn't work because some one had to look after the child. Alva wouldn't work now, and made no effort to come into contact with new "paying off" people. The old ones were not as numerous or as generous as formerly. Those who hadn't drifted away didn't care enough about the Alva of today to help support him, his wife and child. Luckily, though, about this time, he "hit" the numbers twice in one month, and both he and Geraldine borrowed some money on their insurance policies. They accrued almost a thousand dollars from these sources, but that wouldn't last forever, and the problem of what they were going to do with the child still remained unsolved.

Both wanted to kill it, and neither had the courage to mention the word "murder" to the other. Had they been able to discuss this thing frankly with one another, they could have seen to it that the child smothered itself or fell from the crib sometime during the night. No one would have questioned the accidental death of an idiot child. But they did not trust one another, and neither dared to do the deed alone. Then Geraldine became obsessed with the fear that Alva was planning to run away from her. She knew what this would mean and she had no idea of letting him do it. She realized that should she be left alone with the child it would mean that she would be burdened throughout the years it lived, forced to struggle and support herself and her charge. But were she to leave Alva, some more sensible plan would undoubtedly present itself. No one expected a father to tie himself to an infant, and if that infant happened to be ill and an idiot . . . well, there were any number of social agencies which would care for it. Assuredly, then she must get away first. But where to go?

She was stumped again and forced to linger, fearing all the while that Alva would fail to return home once he left. She tried desperately to reintroduce a note of intimacy into their relationship, tried repeatedly to make herself less repellent to him, and, at the same time, discipline her own self so that she would not communicate her apprehensions to him. She hired the little girl who lived in the next room to take charge of the child, bought it a store of toys and went out to find a job. This being done, she insisted that Alva begin taking her out once again. He acquiesced. He wasn't interested one way or the other as long as he could go to bed drunk every night and keep a bottle of gin by his bedside.

Neither, though, seemed interested in what they were doing. Both were feverishly apprehensive at all times. They quarrelled frequently, but would hasten to make amends to one another, so afraid were they that the first one to become angry might make a bolt for freedom. Alva drank more and more. Geraldine worked, saved and schemed, always planning and praying that she would be able to get away first.

Then Alva was taken ill. His liquor-burned stomach refused to retain food. The doctor ordered him not to drink any more bootleg beverages. Alva shrugged his shoulders, left the doctor's office and sought out his favorite speakeasy.

Emma Lou was busy, and being busy, had had less time to think about herself than ever before. Thus, she was less distraught and much less dissatisfied with herself and with life. She was taking some courses in education in the afternoon classes at City College, preparatory to taking the next public school teacher's examination. She still had her position in the household of Campbell Kitchen, a position she had begun to enjoy and appreciate more and more as the master of the house evinced an interest in her and became her counsellor and friend. He encouraged her to read and opened his library to her. Ofttimes he gave her tickets to musical concerts or to the theater, and suggested means of meeting what she called "the right sort of people."

She had moved meanwhile into the Y.W.C.A. There she had met many young girls like herself, alone and unattached in New York, and she had soon found herself moving in a different world altogether. She even had a pal, Gwendolyn Johnson, a likable, light-brown-skinned girl, who had the room next to hers. Gwendolyn had been in New York only a few months. She had just recently graduated from Howard University, and was also planning to teach school in New York City. She and Emma Lou became fast friends and went everywhere together. It was with Gwendolyn that Emma Lou shared the tickets Campbell Kitchen gave her. Then on Sundays they would attend church. At first they attended a different church every Sunday, but finally took to attending St. Marks A.M.E. Church on St. Nicholas Avenue regularly.

This was one of the largest and most high-toned churches in Harlem. Emma Lou liked to go there, and both she and Gwendolyn enjoyed sitting in the congregation, observing the fine clothes and triumphal entries of its members. Then, too, they soon became interested in the various organizations which the church sponsored for young people. They attended the meetings of a literary society every Thursday evening, and joined the young people's bible class which met every Tuesday evening. In this way, they came into contact with many young folk, and were often invited to parties and dances.

Gwendolyn helped Emma Lou with her courses in education and the two obtained and studied copies of questions which had been asked in previous examinations. Gwendolyn sympathized with Emma Lou's color hyper-sensitivity and tried hard to make her forget it. In order to gain her point, she thought it necessary to down light people, and with this in mind, ofttimes told Emma Lou many derogatory tales about the mulattoes in the social and scholastic life at Howard University in Washington, D.C. The color question had never been of much moment to Gwendolyn. Being the color she was, she had never suffered. In Charleston, the mulattoes had their own churches and their own social life and mingled with darker Negroes only when the jim crow law or racial discrimination left them no other alternative. Gwendolyn's mother had belonged to one of these "persons of color" families, but she hadn't seen much in it all. What if she was better than the little black girl who lived around the corner? Didn't they both have to attend the same colored school, and didn't they both have to ride in the same section of the street car, and were not they both subject to be called nigger by the poor white trash who lived in the adjacent block?

She had thought her relatives and associates all a little silly, especially when they had objected to her marrying a man just two or three shades darker than herself. She felt that this was carrying things too far even in ancient Charleston where customs, houses and people all seemed antique and far removed from the present. Stubbornly she had married the man of her choice, and had exulted when her daughter had been nearer the richer color of her father than the washed-out color of herself. Gwendolyn's father had died while she was in college, and her mother had begun teaching in a South Carolina Negro industrial school, but she insisted that Gwendolyn must finish her education and seek her career in the North.

Gwendolyn's mother had always preached for complete tolerance in matters of skin color. So afraid was she that her daughter would develop a "pink" complex that she wilfully discouraged her associating with light people and persistently encouraged her to choose her friends from among the darker elements of the race. And she insisted that Gwendolyn must marry a dark brown man so that her children would be real Negroes. So thoroughly had this become inculcated into her, that Gwendolyn often snubbed light people, and invariably, in accordance with her mother's sermonisings, chose dark-skinned friends and beaux. Like her mother, Gwendolyn, was very exercised over the matter of intra-racial segregation and attempted to combat it verbally as well as actively.

When she and Emma Lou began going around together, trying to find a church to attend regularly, she had immediately black-balled the Episcopal Church, for she knew that most of its members were "pinks," and despite the fact that a number of dark-skinned West Indians, former members of the Church of England, had forced their way in, Gwendolyn knew that the Episcopal Church in Harlem, as in most Negro communities, was dedicated primarily to the salvation of light-skinned Negroes.

But Gwendolyn was a poor psychologist. She didn't realize that Emma Lou was possessed of a perverse bitterness and that she idolized the thing one would naturally expect her to hate. Gwendolyn was certain that Emma Lou hated "yaller" niggers as she called them. She didn't appreciate the fact that Emma Lou hated her own color and envied the more mellow complexions. Gwendolyn's continual damnation of "pinks" only irritated Emma Lou and made her more impatient with her own blackness, for, in damning them, Gwendolyn also enshrined them for Emma Lou, who wasn't the least bit anxious to be classified with persons who needed a champion.

However, for the time being, Emma Lou was more free than ever from tortuous periods of self-pity and hatred. In her present field of activity, the question of color seldom introduced itself except as Gwendolyn introduced it, which she did continually, even to the extent of giving lectures on race purity and the superiority of unmixed racial types. Emma Lou would listen attentively, but all the while she was observing Gwendolyn's light-brown skin, and wishing to herself that it were possible for her and Gwendolyn to effect a change in complexions, since Gwendolyn considered a black skin so desirable.

They both had beaux, young men whom they had met at the various church meetings and socials. Gwendolyn insisted that they snub the "high yallers" and continually was going into ecstasies over the browns and blacks they conquested. Emma Lou couldn't get excited over any of them. They all seemed so young and so pallid. Their air of being all-wise amused her, their affected church purity and wholesomeness, largely a verbal matter, tired her. Their world was so small—church, school, home, mother, father, parties, future. She invariably compared them to Alva and made herself laugh by classifying them as a litter of sick puppies. Alva was a bulldog and a healthy one at that. Yet these sick puppies, as she called them, were the next generation of Negro leaders, the next generation of respectable society folk. They had a future; Alva merely lived for no purpose whatsoever except for the pleasure he could squeeze out of each living moment. He didn't construct anything; the litter of pups would, or at least they would be credited with constructing something whether they did or not. She found herself strangely uninterested in anything they might construct. She didn't see that it would make much difference in the world whether they did or did not. Months of sophisticated reading under Campbell Kitchen's tutelage had cultivated the seeds of pessimism experience had sown. Life was all a bad dream recurrent in essentials. Every dog had his day and every dog died. These priggish little respectable persons she now knew and associated with seemed infinitely inferior to her. They were all hypocritical and colorless. They committed what they called sin in the same colorless way they served God, family, and race. None of them had the fire and gusto of Alva, nor his light-heartedness. At last she had met the "right sort of people" and found them to be quite wrong.

However, she quelled her growing dissatisfaction and immersed herself in her work. Campbell Kitchen had told her again and again that economic independence was the solution to almost any problem. When she found herself a well-paying position she need not worry more. Everything else would follow and she would find herself among the pursued instead of among the pursuers. This was the gospel she now adhered to and placed faith in. She studied hard, finished her courses at Teachers College, took and passed the school board examination, and mechanically followed Gwendolyn about, pretending to share her enthusiasms and hatreds. All would soon come to the desired end. Her doctrine of pessimism was weakened by the optimism the future seemed to promise. She had even become somewhat interested in one of the young men she had met at St. Mark's. Gwendolyn discouraged this interest. "Why, Emma Lou, he's one of them yaller niggers; you don't want to get mixed up with him."

Though meaning well, she did not know that it was precisely because he was one of those "yaller niggers" that Emma Lou liked him.

Emma Lou and her new "yaller nigger," Benson Brown, were returning from church on a Tuesday evening where they had attended a Young People's Bible Class. It was a beautiful early fall night, warm and moonlit, and they had left the church early, intent upon slipping away from Gwendolyn, and taking a walk before they parted for the night. Emma Lou had no reason for liking Benson save that she was flattered that a man as light as he should find himself attracted to her. It always gave her a thrill to stroll into church or down Seventh Avenue with him. And she loved to show him off in the reception room of the Y.W.C.A. True, he was almost as colorless and uninteresting to her as the rest of the crowd with whom she now associated, but he had a fair skin and he didn't seem to mind her darkness. Then, it did her good to show Gwendolyn that she, Emma Lou, could get a yellow-skinned man. She always felt that the reason Gwendolyn insisted upon her going with a dark-skinned man was because she secretly considered it unlikely for her to get a light one.

Benson was a negative personality. His father was an ex-preacher turned Pullman porter because, since prohibition times, he could make more money on the Pullman cars than he could in the pulpit. His mother was an active church worker and club woman, "one of the pillars of the community," the current pastor at their church had called her. Benson himself was in college, studying business methods and administration. It had taken him six years to finish high school, and it promised to take him much longer to finish college. He had a placid, ineffectual dirty yellow face, topped by red mariney hair, and studded with gray eyes. He was as ugly as he was stupid, and he had been as glad to have Emma Lou interested in him as she had been glad to attract him. She actually seemed to take him seriously, while every one else more or less laughed at him. Already he was planning to quit school, go to work, and marry her; and Emma Lou, while not anticipating any such sudden consummation, remained blind to everything save his color and the attention he paid to her.

Benson had suggested their walk and Emma Lou had chosen Seventh Avenue in preference to some of the more quiet side streets. She still loved to promenade up and down Harlem's main thoroughfare. As usual on a warm night, it was crowded. Street speakers and their audiences monopolized the corners. Pedestrians and loiterers monopolized all of the remaining sidewalk space. The street was jammed with traffic. Emma Lou was more convinced than ever that there was nothing like it anywhere. She tried to formulate some of her impressions and attempted to convey them to Benson, but he couldn't see anything unusual or novel or interesting in a "lot of niggers hanging out here to be seen." Then, Seventh Avenue wasn't so much. What about Broadway or Fifth Avenue downtown where the white folks gathered and strolled. Now those were the streets, Seventh Avenue, Harlem's Seventh Avenue, didn't enter into it.

Emma Lou didn't feel like arguing. She walked along in silence, holding tightly to Benson's arm and wondering whether or not Alva was somewhere on Seventh Avenue. Strange she had never seen him. Perhaps he had gone away. Benson wished to stop in order to listen to one of the street speakers who, he informed Emma Lou, was mighty smart. It seemed that he was the self-styled mayor of Harlem, and his spiel nightly was concerning the fact that Harlem Negroes depended upon white people for most of their commodities instead of opening food and dress commissaries of their own. He lamented the fact that there were no Negro store owners, and regretted that wealthy Negroes did not invest their money in first class butcher shops, grocery stores, et cetera. Then, he perorated, the Jews, who now grew rich off their Negro trade, would be forced out, and the money Negroes spent would benefit Negroes alone.

Emma Lou knew that this was just the sort of thing that Benson liked to hear. She had to tug hard on his arm to make him remain on the edge of the crowd, so that she could see the passing crowds rather than center her attention on the speaker. In watching, Emma Lou saw a familiar figure approach, a very trim, well garbed figure, alert and swaggering. It was Braxton. She didn't know whether to speak to him or not. She wasn't sure that he would acknowledge her salute should she address him, yet here was her chance to get news of Alva, and she felt that she might risk being snubbed. It would be worth it. He drew near. He was alone, and, as he passed, she reached out her arm and touched him on the sleeve. He stopped, looked down at her and frowned.

"Braxton," she spoke quickly, "pardon me for stopping you, but I thought you might tell me where Alva is."

"I guess he's at the same place," he answered curtly, then moved away. Emma Lou bowed her head shamefacedly as Benson turned toward her long enough to ask who it was she had spoken to. She mumbled something about an old friend, then suggested that they go home. She was tired. Benson agreed reluctantly and they turned toward the Y.W.C.A.

A taxi driver had brought Alva home from a saloon where he had collapsed from cramps in the stomach. That had been on a Monday. The doctor had come and diagnosed his case. He was in a serious condition, his stomach lining was practically eaten away and his entire body wrecked from physical excess. Unless he took a complete rest and abstained from drinking liquor and all other forms of dissipation, there could be no hope of recovery. This hadn't worried Alva very much. He chafed at having to remain in bed, but the possibility of death didn't worry him. Life owed him very little, he told Geraldine. He was content to let the devil take his due. But Geraldine was quite worried about the whole matter. Should Alva die or even be an invalid for any lengthy period, it would mean that she alone would have the burden of their misshapen child. She didn't want that burden. In fact, she was determined not to have it. And neither did she intend to nurse Alva.

On the Friday morning after the Monday Alva had been taken ill, Geraldine left for work as was her custom. But she did not come back that night. Every morning during that week she had taken away a bundle of this and a bundle of that until she had managed to get away most of her clothes. She had saved enough money out of her earnings to pay her fare to Chicago. She had chosen Chicago because a man who was interested in her lived there. She had written to him. He had been glad to hear from her. He ran a buffet flat. He needed some one like her to act as hostess. Leaving her little bundles at a girl friend's day after day and packing them away in a second hand trunk, she had planned to leave the moment she received her pay on Saturday. She had intended going home on Friday night, but at the last moment she had faltered and reasoned that as long as she was away and only had twenty-four hours more in New York she might as well make her disappearance then. If she went back she might betray herself or else become soft-hearted and remain.

Alva was not very surprised when she failed to return home from work that Friday. The woman in the next room kept coming in at fifteen-minute intervals after five-thirty inquiring: "Hasn't your wife come in yet?" She wanted to get rid of the child which was left in her care daily. She had her own work to do, her own husband and child's dinner to prepare; and, furthermore, she wasn't being paid to keep the child both day and night. People shouldn't have children unless they intended taking care of them. Finally Alva told her to bring the baby

back to his room . . . his wife would be in soon. But he knew
full well that Geraldine was not coming back. Hell of a mess.
He was unable to work, would probably have to remain in bed
another week, perhaps two. His money was about gone, and
now Geraldine was not there to pay the rent out of her earnings. Damn. What to do . . . what to do? He couldn't keep
the child. If he put it in a home they would expect him to contribute to its support. It was too bad that he didn't know some
one to leave this child of his with as his mother had done in his
case. He began to wish for a drink.

Hours passed. Finally the lady came into the room again to
see if he or the baby wanted anything. She knew Geraldine had
not come in yet. The partition between the two rooms was so
thin that the people in one were privy to everything the people
in the other did or said. Alva told her his wife must have gone
to see her sick mother in Long Island. He asked her to take
care of the baby for him. He would pay her for her extra trouble. The whole situation offered her much pleasure. She went
away radiant, eager to tell the other lodgers in the house her
version of what had happened.

Alva got up and paced the room. He felt that he could no
longer remain flat on his back. His stomach ached, but it also
craved for alcoholic stimulant. So did his brain and nervous
system in general. Inadvertently, in one of his trips across the
room, he looked into the dresser mirror. What he saw there
halted his pacing. Surely that wan, dissipated, bloated face did
not belong to him. Perhaps he needed a shave. He set about
ridding himself of a week's growth of beard, but being shaved
only made his face look more like the face of a corpse. It was liquor he needed. He wished to hell some one would come
along and get him some. But no one came. He went back to
bed, his eyes fixed on the clock, watching its hands approach
midnight. Five minutes to go. . . . There was a knock on the
door. Eagerly he sat up in the bed and shouted, "Come in."

But he was by no means expecting or prepared to see Emma
Lou.

Emma Lou's room in the Y.W.C.A. at three o'clock that same
morning. Emma Lou busy packing her clothes. Gwendolyn in
negligee, hair disarrayed, eyes sleepy, yet angry:

"You mean you're going over there to live with that man?"

"Why not? I love him."

Gwendolyn stared hard at Emma Lou. "But don't you understand he's just tryin' to find some one to take care of that brat of his? Don't be silly, Emma Lou. He doesn't really care for you. If he did, he never would have deserted you as you once told me he did, or have subjected you to all those insults. And . . . he isn't your type of man. Why, he's nothing but a . . ."

"Will you mind tending to your own business, Gwendolyn," her purple powdered skin was streaked with tears.

"But what about your appointment?"

"I shall take it."

"What!" She forgot her weariness. "You mean to say you're going to teach school and live with that man, too? Ain't you got no regard for your reputation? I wouldn't ruin myself for no yaller nigger. Here you're doing just what folks say a black gal always does. Where is your intelligence and pride? I'm through with you, Emma Lou. There's probably something in this stuff about black people being different and more low than other colored people. You're just a common ordinary nigger! God, how I despise you!" And she had rushed out of the room, leaving Emma Lou dazed by the suddenness and wrath of her tirade.

Emma Lou was busier than she had ever been before in her life. She had finally received her appointment and was teaching in one of the public schools in Harlem. Doing this in addition to nursing Alva and Alva Junior, and keeping house for them in Alva's same old room. Within six months she had managed to make little Alva Junior take on some of the physical aspects of a normal child. His little legs were in braces, being straightened. Twice a week she took him to the clinic where he had violet ray sun baths and oil massages. His little body had begun to fill out and simultaneously it seemed as if his head was decreasing in size. There was only one feature which remained unchanged; his abnormally large eyes still retained their insane stare. They appeared frozen and terrified as if their owner was gazing upon some horrible, yet fascinating object or occurrence. The doctor said that this would disappear in time.

During those six months there had been a steady change in Alva Senior, too. At first he had been as loving and kind to Emma Lou as he had been during the first days of their relationship. Then, as he got better and began living his old life again, he more and more relegated her to the position of a hired nurse girl. He was scarcely civil to her. He seldom came home except to eat and get some pocket change. When he did come home nights, he was usually drunk, so drunk that his companions would have to bring him home, and she would have to undress him and put him to bed. Since his illness, he could not stand as much liquor as before. His stomach refused to retain it, and his legs refused to remain steady.

Emma Lou began to loathe him, yet ached for his physical nearness. She was lonesome again, cooped up in that solitary room with only Alva Junior for company. She had lost track of all her old friends, and, despite her new field of endeavor, she had made no intimate contacts. Her fellow colored teachers were congenial enough, but they didn't seem any more inclined to accept her socially than did her fellow white teachers. There seemed to be some question about her antecedents. She didn't belong to any of the collegiate groups around Harlem. She didn't seem to be identified with any one who mattered. They wondered how she had managed to get into the school system.

Of course Emma Lou made little effort to make friends among them. She didn't know how. She was too shy to make an approach and too suspicious to thaw out immediately when some one approached her. The first thing she noticed was that most of the colored teachers who taught in her school were lighter colored than she. The darkest was a pleasing brown. And she had noticed them putting their heads together when she first came around. She imagined that they were discussing her. And several times upon passing groups of them, she imagined that she was being pointed out. In most cases what she thought was true, but she was being discussed and pointed out, not because of her dark skin, but because of the obvious traces of an excess of rouge and powder which she insisted upon using.

It had been suggested, in a private council among the Negro members of the teaching staff, that some one speak to Emma Lou about this rather ludicrous habit of making up. But no one had the nerve. She appeared so distant and so ready to take offense at the slightest suggestion even of friendship that they were wary of her. But after she began to be a standard joke among the pupils and among the white teachers, they finally decided to send her an anonymous note, suggesting that she use fewer aids to the complexion. Emma Lou, on receiving the note, at first thought that it was the work of some practical joker. It never occurred to her that the note told the truth and that she looked twice as bad with paint and powder as she would without it. She interpreted it as being a means of making fun of her because she was darker than any one of the other colored girls. She grew more haughty, more acid, and more distant than ever. She never spoke to any one except as a matter of business. Then she discovered that her pupils had nicknamed her . . . "Blacker'n me."

What made her still more miserable was the gossip and comments of the woman in the next room. Lying in bed nights or else sitting at her table preparing her lesson plans, she could hear her telling every one who chanced in——

"You know that fellow in the next room? Well, let me tell you. His wife left him, yes-sireee, left him flat on his back in the bed, him and the baby, too. Yes, she did. Walked out of here just as big as you please to go to work one morning and she ain't come back yet. Then up comes this little black wench. I heard her when she knocked on the door that very night his wife left. At first he was mighty s'prised to see her, then started laying it on, kissed her and hugged her, a-tellin' her how much he loved her, and she crying like a fool all the time. I never heard the likes of it in my life. The next morning in she moves an' she's been here ever since. And you oughter see how she carries on over that child, just as loving, like as if she was his own mother. An' now that she's here an' workin' an' that nigger's well again, what does he do but go out an' get drunk worse than he uster with his wife. Would you believe it? Stays away three and four nights a week, while she hustles out of here an' makes time every morning. . . ."

On hearing this for about the twentieth time, Emma Lou determined to herself that she was not going to hear it again. (She had also planned to ask for a transfer to a new school, one on the east side in the Italian section where she would not have to associate with so many other colored teachers.) Alva hadn't been home for four nights. She picked Alva Junior from out his crib and pulled off his nightgown, letting him lie naked in her lap. She loved to fondle his warm, mellow-colored body, loved to caress his little crooked limbs after the braces had been removed. She wondered what would become of him. Obviously she couldn't remain living with Alva, and she certainly couldn't keep Alva Junior forever. Suppose those evil school teachers should find out how she was living and report it to the school authorities? Was she morally fit to be teaching youth? She remembered her last conversation with Gwendolyn.

For the first time now she also saw how Alva had used her during both periods of their relationship. She also realized that she had been nothing more than a commercial proposition to him at all times. He didn't care for dark women either. He had never taken her among his friends, never given any signs to the public that she was his girl. And now when he came home with some of his boy friends, he always introduced her as Alva Junior's mammy. That's what she was, Alva Junior's mammy, and a typical black mammy at that.

Campbell Kitchen had told her that when she found economic independence, everything else would come. Well now that she had economic independence she found herself more enslaved and more miserable than ever. She wondered what he thought of her. She had never tried to get in touch with him since she had left the Y.W.C.A., and had never let him know of her whereabouts, had just quit communicating with him as unceremoniously as she had quit the Y.W.C.A. No doubt Gwendolyn had told him the whole sordid tale. She could never face him again unless she had made some effort to reclaim herself. Well, that's what she was going to do. Reclaim herself. She didn't care what became of Alva Junior. Let Alva and that yellow slut of a wife of his worry about their own piece of tainted suet.

She was leaving. She was going back to the Y.W.C.A., back to St. Mark's A.M.E. Church, back to Gwendolyn, back to Benson. She wouldn't stay here and have that child grow up to call her "black mammy." Just because she was black was no reason why she was going to let some yellow nigger use her. At once she was all activity. Putting Alva Jr.'s nightgown on, she laid him back into his crib and left him there crying while she packed her trunk and suitcase. Then, asking the woman in the next room to watch him until she returned, she put on her hat and coat and started for the Y.W.C.A., making plans for the future as she went.

Halfway there she decided to telephone Benson. It had been seven months now since she had seen him, seven months since, without a word of warning or without leaving a message, she had disappeared, telling only Gwendolyn where she was going. While waiting for the operator to establish connections, she recalled the conversation she and Gwendolyn had had at the time, recalled Gwendolyn's horror and disgust on hearing what Emma Lou planned doing, recalled . . . some one was answering the 'phone. She asked for Benson, and in a moment heard his familiar:

"Hello."

"Hello, Benson, this is Emma Lou." There was complete silence for a moment, then:

"Emma Lou?" he dinned into her ear. "Well, where have you been. Gwennie and I have been trying to find you."

This warmed her heart; coming back was not going to be so difficult after all.

"You did?"

"Why, yes. We wanted to invite you to our wedding."

The receiver fell from her hand. For a moment she stood like one stunned, unable to move. She could hear Benson on the other end of the wire clicking the receiver and shouting "Hello, Hello," then the final clicking of the receiver as he hung up, followed by a deadened . . . "operator" . . . "operator" from central.

Somehow or other she managed to get hold of the receiver and replace it in the hook. Then she left the telephone booth and made her way out of the drugstore into the street. Seventh Avenue as usual was alive and crowded. It was an early spring evening and far too warm for people to remain cooped up in stuffy apartments. Seventh Avenue was the gorge into which Harlem cliff dwellers crowded to promenade. It was heavy laden, full of life and color, vibrant and leisurely. But for the first time since her arrival in Harlem, Emma Lou was impervious to all this. For the moment she hardly realized where she was. Only the constant jostling and the raucous ensemble of street noises served to bring her out of her daze.

Gwendolyn and Benson married. "What do you want to waste your time with that yaller nigger for? I wouldn't marry a yaller nigger."

"Blacker'n me" . . . "Why don't you take a hint and stop plastering your face with so much rouge and powder."

Emma Lou stumbled down Seventh Avenue, not knowing where she was going. She noted that she was at 135th Street. It was easy to tell this particular corner. It was called the campus. All the college boys hung out there when the weather permitted, obstructing the traffic and eyeing the passersby professionally. She turned west on 135th Street. She wanted quiet. Seventh Avenue was too noisy and too alive and too happy. How could the world be happy when she felt like she did? There was no place for her in the world. She was too black, black is a portent of evil, black is a sign of bad luck.

> "A yaller gal rides in a limousine
> A brown-skin does the same;
> A black gal rides in a rickety Ford,
> But she gets there, yes, my Lord."

"Alva Jr's black mammy." "Low down common nigger." "Jes' crazy 'bout that little yaller brat."

She looked up and saw a Western Union office sign shining above a lighted doorway. For a moment she stood still, repeating over and over to herself Western Union, Western Union, as if to understand its meaning. People turned to stare at her as they passed. They even stopped and looked up into the air trying to see what was attracting her attention, and, seeing nothing, would shrug their shoulders and continue on their way. The Western Union sign suggested only one thing to Emma Lou and that was home. For the moment she was ready to rush into the office and send a wire to her Uncle Joe, asking for a ticket, and thus be able to escape the whole damn mess. But she immediately saw that going home would mean beginning her life all over again, mean flying from one degree of unhappiness into another probably much more intense and tragic than the present one. She had once fled to Los Angeles to escape Boise, then fled to Harlem to escape Los Angeles, but these mere geographical flights had not solved her problems in the past, and a further flight back to where her life had begun, although facile of accomplishment, was too futile to merit consideration.

Rationalizing thus, she moved away from in front of the Western Union office and started toward the park two blocks away. She felt that it was necessary that she do something about herself and her life and do it immediately. Campbell Kitchen had said that every one must find salvation within one's self, that no one in life need be a total misfit, and that there was some niche for every peg, whether that peg be round or square. If this were true then surely she could find hers even at this late date. But then hadn't she exhausted all possibilities? Hadn't she explored every province of life and everywhere met the same problem? It was easy for Campbell Kitchen or for Gwendolyn to say what they would do had they been she, for they were looking at her problem in the abstract, while to her it was an empirical reality. What could they know of the adjustment proceedings necessary to make her life more full and more happy? What could they know of her heartaches?

She trudged on, absolutely oblivious to the people she passed or to the noise and bustle of the street. For the first time in her life she felt that she must definitely come to some conclusion about her life and govern herself accordingly. After all she wasn't the only black girl alive. There were thousands on thousands, who, like her, were plain, untalented, ordinary, and who, unlike herself, seemed to live in some degree of comfort. Was she alone to blame for her unhappiness? Although this had been suggested to her by others, she had been too obtuse to accept it. She had ever been eager to shift the entire blame on others when no doubt she herself was the major criminal.

But having arrived at this—what did it solve or promise for the future? After all it was not the abstractions of her case which at the present moment most needed elucidation. She could strive for a change of mental attitudes later. What she needed to do now was to accept her black skin as being real and unchangeable, to realize that certain things were, had been, and would be, and with this in mind begin life anew, always fighting, not so much for acceptance by other people, but for acceptance of herself by herself. In the future she would be eminently selfish. If people came into her life—well and good. If they didn't—she would live anyway, seeking to find herself and achieving meanwhile economic and mental independence. Then possibly, as Campbell Kitchen had said, life would open up for her, for it seemed as if its doors yielded more easily to the casual, self-centered individual than to the ranting, praying pilgrim. After all it was the end that mattered, and one only wasted time and strength seeking facile open-sesame means instead of pushing along a more difficult and direct path.

By now Emma Lou had reached St. Nicholas Avenue and was about to cross over into the park when she heard the chimes of a clock and was reminded of the hour. It was growing late—too late for her to wander in the park alone where she knew she would be approached either by some persistent male or an insulting park policeman. Wearily she started towards home, realizing that it was necessary for her to get some rest in order to be able to be in her class room on the next morning. She mustn't jeopardize her job, for it was partially through the money she was earning from it that she would be able to find her place in life. She was tired of running up blind alleys all of which seemed to converge and lead her ultimately to the same blank wall. Her motto from now on would be "find —not seek." All things were at one's finger-tips. Life was most kind to those who were judicious in their selections, and she, weakling that she now realized she was, had not been a connoisseur.

As she drew nearer home she felt certain that should she attempt to spend another night with Alva and his child, she would surely smother to death during the night. And even though she felt this, she also knew within herself that no matter how much at the present moment she pretended to hate Alva that he had only to make the proper advances in order to win her to him again. Yet she also knew that she must leave him if she was to make her self-proposed adjustment—leave him now even if she should be weak enough to return at some not so distant date. She was determined to fight against Alva's influence over her, fight even though she lost, for she reasoned that even in losing she would win a pyrrhic victory and thus make her life less difficult in the future, for having learned to fight future battles would be easy.

She tried to convince herself that it would not be necessary for her to have any more Jasper Cranes or Alvas in her life. To assure herself of this she intended to look John up on the morrow and if he were willing let him re-enter her life. It was clear to her now what a complete fool she had been. It was clear to her at last that she had exercised the same discrimination against her men and the people she wished for friends that they had exercised against her—and with less reason. It served her right that Jasper Crane had fooled her as he did. It served her right that Alva had used her once for the money she could give him and again as a black mammy for his child. That was the price she had had to pay for getting what she thought she wanted. But now she intended to balance things. Life after all was a give and take affair. Why should she give important things and receive nothing in return?

She was in front of the house now and looking up saw that all the lights in her room were lit. And as she climbed the stairs she could hear a drunken chorus of raucous masculine laughter. Alva had come home meanwhile, drunk of course and accompanied by the usual drunken crowd. Emma Lou started to turn back, to flee into the street—anywhere to escape being precipitated into another sordid situation, but remembering that this was to be her last night there, and that the new day would find her beginning a new life, she subdued her flight impulse and without knocking threw open the door and walked into the room. She saw the usual and expected sight: Alva, face a death mask, sitting on the bed embracing an effeminate boy whom she knew as Bobbie, and who drew hurriedly away from Alva as he saw her. There were four other boys in the room, all in varied states of drunkenness—all laughing boisterously at some obscene witticism. Emma Lou suppressed a shudder and calmly said "Hello Alva"—The room grew silent. They all seemed shocked and surprised by her sudden appearance. Alva did not answer her greeting but instead turned to Bobbie and asked him for another drink. Bobbie fumbled nervously at his hip pocket and finally produced a flask which he handed to Alva. Emma Lou stood at the door and watched Alva drink the liquor Bobbie had given him. Every one else in the room watched her. For the moment she did not know what to say or what to do. Obviously she couldn't continue standing there by the door nor could she leave and let them feel that she had been completely put to rout.

Alva handed the flask back to Bobbie, who got up from the bed and said something about leaving. The others in the room also got up and began staggering around looking for their hats. Emma Lou thought for a moment that she was going to win without any further struggle, but she had not reckoned with Alva who, meanwhile, had sufficiently emerged from his stupor to realize that his friends were about to go.

"What the hell's the matter with you," he shouted up at Bobbie, and without waiting for an answer reached out for Bobbie's arm and jerked him back down on the bed.

"Now stay there till I tell you to get up."

The others in the room had now found their hats and started toward the door, eager to escape. Emma Lou crossed the room to where Alva was sitting and said, "You might make less noise, the baby's asleep."

The four boys had by this time opened the door and staggered out into the hallway. Bobbie edged nervously away from Alva, who leered up at Emma Lou and snarled "If you don't like it—"

For the moment Emma Lou did not know what to do. Her first impulse was to strike him, but she was restrained because underneath the loathsome beast that he now was, she saw the Alva who had first attracted her to him, the Alva she had always loved. She suddenly felt an immense compassion for him and had difficulty in stifling an unwelcome urge to take him into her arms. Tears came into her eyes, and for a moment it seemed as if all her rationalization would go for naught. Then once more she saw Alva, not as he had been, but as he was now, a drunken, drooling libertine, struggling to keep the embarrassed Bobbie in a vile embrace. Something snapped within her. The tears in her eyes receded, her features grew set, and she felt herself hardening inside. Then, without saying a word, she resolutely turned away, went into the alcove, pulled her suitcases down from the shelf in the clothes-closet, and, to the blasphemous accompaniment of Alva berating Bobbie for wishing to leave, finished packing her clothes, not stopping even when Alva Junior's cries deafened her, and caused the people in the next room to stir uneasily.

CHRONOLOGY

BIOGRAPHICAL NOTES

NOTE ON THE TEXTS

NOTES

Chronology

1919   February 17: Returning veterans of the Fifteenth Regiment of New York's National Guard march triumphally through Harlem. February 19–21: While the Paris Peace Conference is taking place, W.E.B. Du Bois organizes Pan-African Conference in Paris, attended by fifty-seven delegates from the United States, the West Indies, Europe, and Africa; conference calls for acknowledgment and protection of the rights of Africans under colonial rule. March: Release of *The Homesteader*, directed and produced by self-published novelist and entrepreneur Oscar Micheaux, first feature-length film by an African American. May: Hair-care entrepreneur Madam C. J. Walker dies at her estate in Irvington, New York; her daughter A'Lelia Walker assumes control of the Madam C.J. Walker Manufacturing Company. May–October: In what becomes known as "the Red Summer," racial conflicts boil over in the wake of the return of African American veterans; incidents of racial violence erupt across the United States, including outbreaks in Charleston, South Carolina; Longview, Texas; Omaha; Washington, D.C.; Chicago; Knoxville; and Elaine, Arkansas. June: Marcus Garvey establishes his Black Star Line (the shipping concern will operate until 1922). July: Claude McKay's poem "If We Must Die," written in response to the summer of violence, appears in Max Eastman's magazine *The Liberator*. September: Jessie Redmon Fauset joins staff of *The Crisis*, the literary magazine of the NAACP founded in 1910, as literary editor.

1920   January: *The Brownie's Book*, a magazine for African American children, founded by W.E.B. Du Bois with Jessie Redmon Fauset and Augustus Dill, begins its run of twenty-four issues. Oscar Micheaux releases the anti-lynching film, *Within Our Gates*, an answer both to D. W. Griffith's inflammatory *The Birth of a Nation* (1915) and the Red Summer of 1919. April: In an article in *The Crisis*, W.E.B. Du Bois writes: "A renaissance of American Negro literature is due." August: The Universal Negro Improvement Association (UNIA), founded by Jamaican immigrant and Pan-Africanist Marcus Garvey, holds its first convention at Madison Square Garden

in New York City, attended by some 25,000 delegates.
November: James Weldon Johnson becomes executive sec-
retary (and first black officer) of the NAACP. Mamie Smith's
"Crazy Blues" is released by Okeh Records. Eugene O'Neill's
The Emperor Jones, starring Charles Gilpin, opens at the
Provincetown Playhouse in Greenwich Village.

Books
W.E.B. Du Bois: *Darkwater: Voices from Within the Veil* (Har-
    court, Brace & Howe)
Claude McKay: *Spring in New Hampshire and Other Poems*
    (Grant Richards)

1921   February: Max Eastman invites Claude McKay, just returned from England, to become associate editor of *The
Liberator*. March: Harry Pace forms Black Swan Phonograph Company, one of the first black-owned record com-
panies in Harlem; its most successful recording artist is Ethel
Waters. May: *Shuffle Along*, a pioneering all–African American production, with book by Flournoy Miller and Aubrey
Lyles and music and lyrics by Eubie Blake and Noble Sissle,
opens on Broadway and becomes a hit. It showcases such
stars as Florence Mills and Josephine Baker. June: Langston
Hughes publishes his poem "The Negro Speaks of Rivers"
in *The Crisis*. August–September: Exhibit of African American art at the 135th Street branch of the New York Public
Library, including work by Henry Ossawa Tanner, Meta
Fuller, and Laura Wheeler Waring. December: René Maran,
a native of Martinique, becomes the first black recipient of
the Prix Goncourt, for his novel *Batouala*; soon translated
into English, it will be widely discussed in the African
American press.

1922   January: The Dyer Anti-Lynching Bill is passed by the
House of Representatives; it is subsequently blocked in the
Senate. Spring: *Birthright*, novel of African American life
by the white novelist T. S. Stribling, is published by Century Publications. (Oscar Micheaux will make two films
based on the book, in 1924 and 1938.) White real estate
magnate William E. Harmon establishes the Harmon
Foundation to advance African American achievements.

Books
Georgia Douglas Johnson: *Bronze* (B. J. Brimmer)
James Weldon Johnson, editor: *The Book of American Ne-
    gro Poetry* (Harcourt, Brace)

Claude McKay: *Harlem Shadows* (Harcourt, Brace; expanded version of *Spring in New Hampshire*)
T. S. Stribling: *Birthright* (Century)

1923   January: *Opportunity: A Journal of Negro Life*, published by the National Urban League and edited by sociologist Charles S. Johnson, is founded. Claude McKay addresses the Fourth Congress of the Third International in Moscow. February: Bessie Smith's "Downhearted Blues" (written and originally recorded by Alberta Hunter) is released by Columbia Records and sells nearly a million copies within six months. May: Willis Richardson's *The Chip Woman*, produced by the National Ethiopian Art Players, becomes the first serious play by an African American playwright to open on Broadway. June: Marcus Garvey receives a five-year sentence for mail fraud. December: Tenor Roland Hayes, having won acclaim in London as a singer of classical music, gives a concert of lieder and spirituals at Town Hall in New York. *The Messenger*, founded in 1917 by Asa Philip Randolph and Chandler Owen as a black trade unionist magazine with socialist sympathies, begins publishing more literary material under editorial guidance of George S. Schuyler and Theophilus Lewis.

Books
Marcus Garvey: *Philosophy and Opinion of Marcus Garvey* (Universal Publishing House)
Jean Toomer: *Cane* (Boni & Liveright)

1924   March: The Civic Club dinner, held in honor of Jessie Redmon Fauset on publishing her first novel *There Is Confusion*, is sponsored by *Opportunity* and Charles S. Johnson. Those in attendance include Alain Locke, W.E.B. Du Bois, Countee Cullen, Eric Walrond, Gwendolyn Bennett, and such representatives of the New York publishing world as Alfred A. Knopf and Horace Liveright. (In retrospect the occasion is often taken to mark the beginning of the Harlem Renaissance.) May: W.E.B. Du Bois attacks Marcus Garvey in *The Crisis* article "A Lunatic or a Traitor." Eugene O'Neill's play *All God's Chillun Got Wings*, starring Paul Robeson and controversial for its theme of miscegenation, opens. Autumn: Countee Cullen is the first recipient of Witter Bynner Poetry Competition. September: René Maran publishes poems by Countee Cullen, Langston Hughes, Claude McKay, and Jean Toomer in his Paris newspaper, *Les Continents.* Louis Armstrong comes to New York from Chicago to join Fletcher Henderson's band at the Roseland Ballroom.

Books

W.E.B. Du Bois: *The Gift of Black Folk: The Negroes in the Making of America* (Stratford)

Jessie Redmon Fauset: *There Is Confusion* (Boni & Liveright)

Walter White: *The Fire in the Flint* (Knopf)

1925   February: After his appeals are denied, Marcus Garvey begins serving his sentence for mail fraud at Atlanta Federal Penitentiary. March: Howard Philosophy Professor Alain Locke edits a special issue of *The Survey Graphic* titled "Harlem: Mecca of the New Negro"; in November *The New Negro,* an expanded book version, is published by Albert and Charles Boni. The volume features six pages of painter Aaron Douglas's African-inspired illustrations, and includes writing by Jean Toomer, Rudolph Fisher, Zora Neale Hurston, Eric Walrond, Countee Cullen, James Weldon Johnson, Langston Hughes, Georgia Douglas Johnson, Richard Bruce Nugent, Anne Spencer, Claude McKay, Jessie Redmon Fauset, Arthur Schomburg, Charles S. Johnson, W.E.B. Du Bois, and E. Franklin Frazier. May: *Opportunity* holds its first awards dinner, recognizing, among others, Langston Hughes ("The Weary Blues," first prize), Countee Cullen, Zora Neale Hurston, Eric Walrond, and Sterling Brown. Paul Robeson appears at Greenwich Village Theatre in a concert entirely devoted to spirituals, accompanied by Lawrence Brown. August: A. Phillip Randolph organizes the Brotherhood of Sleeping Car Porters. October: The American Negro Labor Congress is founded in Chicago. November: First prize of *The Crisis* awards goes to poet Countee Cullen. Paul Robeson stars in Oscar Micheaux's film *Body and Soul.* December: Marita Bonner publishes essay "On Being Young—A Woman—And Colored" in *The Crisis,* about the predicament and possibilities of the educated black woman.

Books

Countee Cullen: *Color* (Harper)

James Weldon Johnson and J. Rosamond Johnson, editors: *The Book of American Negro Spirituals* (Viking Press)

Alain Locke, editor: *The New Negro: An Interpretation* (Albert and Charles Boni)

1926 January: The Harmon Foundation announces its first awards for artistic achievement by African Americans. Palmer Hayden, a World War I veteran and menial laborer, wins the gold medal for painting. February: Jessie Redmon Fauset steps down as editor of *The Crisis*. The play *Lulu Belle*, starring Lenore Ulric in blackface as well as the African American actress Edna Thomas, opens to great success on Broadway; it helps create a vogue of whites frequenting Harlem nightspots. March: The Savoy Ballroom opens on Lenox Avenue between 140th and 141st Streets. June: Successive issues of *The Nation* feature Langston Hughes's "The Negro Artist and the Racial Mountain" and George S. Schuyler's "The Negro-Art Hokum." July: W.E.B. Du Bois founds Krigwa Players, Harlem theater group devoted to plays depicting African American life. August: Carl Van Vechten, white novelist and close friend to many Negro Renaissance figures, publishes his roman à clef, *Nigger Heaven*, with Knopf. Although many of his friends—including James Weldon Johnson, Nella Larsen, and Langston Hughes—are supportive, the book is widely disliked by African American readers, and notably condemned by W.E.B. Du Bois. October: Arthur Schomburg's collection of thousands of books, manuscripts, and artworks is purchased for the New York Public Library by the Carnegie Corporation; it will form the basis of what will become the Schomburg Center for Research in Black Culture. November: *Fire!!*, a journal edited by Wallace Thurman, makes its sole appearance. Contributors include Langston Hughes, Zora Neale Hurston, and Gwendolyn Bennett, among others. "Smoke, Lilies and Jade," a short story by Richard Bruce Nugent published in *Fire!!*, shocks many by its delineation of a homosexual liaison as well as by Nugent's suggestive line drawings. Most copies are accidentally destroyed in a fire. December: Countee Cullen begins contributing a column, "The Dark Tower," to *Opportunity*. (It will run until September 1928.)

Books

W. C. Handy, editor: *Blues: An Anthology* (Boni & Boni)
Langston Hughes: *The Weary Blues* (Knopf)
Alain Locke, editor: *Four Negro Poets* (Simon & Schuster)

Carl Van Vechten: *Nigger Heaven* (Knopf)
Eric Walrond: *Tropic Death* (Boni & Liveright; story collection)
Walter White: *Flight* (Knopf)

1927   July: Ethel Waters stars on Broadway in the revue *Africana*.
        August: Rudolph Fisher's essay "The Caucasian Storms
        Harlem" is published in *The American Mercury*. September:
        James Weldon Johnson's *The Autobiography of an Ex-Colored
        Man*, first published anonymously in 1912, is republished
        by Knopf. October: A'Lelia Walker, cosmetics heiress and
        Harlem socialite, opens The Dark Tower, a tearoom in-
        tended as a cultural gathering place, at her home on West
        130th Street: "We dedicate this tower to the aesthetes.
        That cultural group of young Negro writers, sculptors,
        painters, music artists, composers, and their friends." The
        Theatre Guild production of DuBose Heyward's play
        Porgy, with an African American cast, opens to great suc-
        cess. December: Marcus Garvey, pardoned by Calvin
        Coolidge after serving more than half of five-year sentence
        for mail fraud, is deported. Duke Ellington and his orches-
        tra begin what will prove a years-long engagement at the
        Cotton Club of Harlem.

        Books
        Countee Cullen: *Copper Sun* (Harper)
        Countee Cullen, editor: *Caroling Dusk: An Anthology of
            Verse by Negro Poets* (Harper)
        Langston Hughes: *Fine Clothes to the Jew* (Knopf)
        Charles S. Johnson, editor: *Ebony and Topaz* (Journal of
            Negro Life/National Urban League)
        James Weldon Johnson: *God's Trombones: Seven Negro Ser-
            mons in Verse* (Knopf)
        Alain Locke and Montgomery Gregory, editors: *Plays of
            Negro Life* (Harper)

1928   January: The first Harmon Foundation art exhibition opens
        at New York's International House. April 9: Countee Cul-
        len marries Nina Yolande, daughter of W.E.B. Du Bois;
        the wedding is a major social event, attended by thousands
        of people. (The marriage breaks up several months later.)
        May: Bill "Bojangles" Robinson appears on Broadway in
        the revue *Blackbirds of 1928*. June: *The Messenger* ceases
        publication when the Brotherhood of Sleeping Car Porters
        can no longer financially support the journal. November:

Wallace Thurman publishes the first and only issue of the magazine *Harlem: A Forum of Negro Life*.

Books

W.E.B. Du Bois: *Dark Princess: A Romance* (Harcourt, Brace)

Jessie Redmon Fauset: *Plum Bun* (Frederick Stokes)

Rudolph Fisher: *The Walls of Jericho* (Knopf)

Georgia Douglas Johnson: *An Autumn Love Cycle* (Harold Vinal)

Nella Larsen: *Quicksand* (Knopf)

Claude McKay: *Home to Harlem* (Harper)

1929   February: *Harlem*, co-authored by Wallace Thurman and William Rapp, opens on Broadway to mixed reviews. Archibald Motley, Jr. wins gold medal for painting from the Harmon Foundation. October 29: The New York stock market plunges, eliminating much of the funding powering "New Negro" literature and arts.

Books

Countee Cullen: *The Black Christ and Other Poems* (Harper)

Nella Larsen: *Passing* (Knopf)

Claude McKay: *Banjo: A Story Without a Plot* (Harper)

Wallace Thurman: *The Blacker the Berry* (Macaulay)

Walter White: *Rope and Faggot: A Biography of Judge Lynch* (Knopf)

1930   February: *The Green Pastures*, a play by Marc Connelly, based on Roark Bradford's *Ol' Man Adam an' His Chillun* (1928), opens on Broadway with an all-black cast; it will be one of the most successful plays of its era. July: The Nation of Islam, colloquially known as the Black Muslims, founded by W. D. Fard in Detroit at the Islam Temple. Dancer and anthropology student Katharine Dunham founds Ballet Nègre in Chicago. James Weldon Johnson publishes a limited edition of "Saint Peter Relates an Incident of the Resurrection Day," a poem protesting the insulting treatment accorded to African American Gold Star Mothers visiting American cemeteries in Europe.

Books

Langston Hughes: *Not Without Laughter* (Macmillan)

Charles S. Johnson: *The Negro in American Civilization: A Study of Negro Life and Race Relations* (Henry Holt)

James Weldon Johnson: *Black Manhattan* (Knopf)

James Weldon Johnson: *Saint Peter Relates an Incident of the Resurrection Day* (Viking Press)

1931   April–July: The "Scottsboro Boys," a group of young African American men accused of raping two white women, are tried and convicted; a massive, lengthy, and only partly successful campaign to free them begins. Sculptor Augusta Savage, whose real-life rebuff by the white art establishment becomes part of the back story for *Plum Bun*, establishes the Savage Studio of Arts and Crafts in Harlem.

Books
Arna Bontemps: *God Sends Sunday* (Harcourt, Brace)
Sterling Brown: *Outline for the Study of Poetry of American Negroes* (Harcourt, Brace)
Countee Cullen: *One Way to Heaven* (Harper)
Jessie Redmon Fauset: *The Chinaberry Tree* (Frederick Stokes)
Langston Hughes: *Dear Lovely Death* (Troutbeck Press)
George S. Schuyler: *Black No More* (Macaulay)
Jean Toomer: *Essentials: Definitions and Aphorisms* (Lakeside Press)

1932   June: Langston Hughes, Dorothy West, Louise Thompson, and more than a dozen other African Americans travel to the Soviet Union to film *Black and White*, a movie about American racism. (Due to shifting Soviet policies, the movie will never be made.)

Books
Sterling Brown: *Southern Road* (Harcourt, Brace)
Rudolph Fisher: *The Conjure-Man Dies* (Covici-Friede)
Langston Hughes: *The Dream Keeper* (Knopf)
Claude McKay: *Gingertown* (Harper; story collection)
George S. Schuyler: *Slaves Today* (Brewer, Warren, and Putnam)
Wallace Thurman: *Infants of the Spring* (Macaulay)
Wallace Thurman and Abraham Furman: *Interne* (Macaulay)

1933   **Books**
Jessie Redmon Fauset: *Comedy: American Style* (Frederick A. Stokes)
James Weldon Johnson: *Along This Way* (Knopf)

Alain Locke: *The Negro in America* (American Library Association)

Claude McKay: *Banana Bottom* (Harper)

1934   January: The Apollo Theater opens. February: *Negro*, an anthology of work by and about African Americans, edited by Nancy Cunard, is published by Wishart in London. March: Dorothy West founds the magazine *Challenge*. May: W.E.B. Du Bois resigns from the NAACP; he is replaced as editor of *The Crisis* by Roy Wilkins. November: Aaron Douglas completes *Aspects of Negro Life*, four murals commissioned by the New York Public Library. December: Wallace Thurman and Rudolph Fisher die within days of one another. Richard Wright writes the initial draft of his first novel, *Lawd Today*, published posthumously in 1963. M. B. Tolson completes sequence of poems *A Gallery of Harlem Portraits*, published posthumously in 1979.

Books

Langston Hughes: *The Ways of White Folks* (Knopf; story collection)

Zora Neale Hurston: *Jonah's Gourd Vine* (Lippincott)

James Weldon Johnson: *Negro Americans, What Now?* (Viking Press)

1935   March 19: A riot sparked by rumors of white violence against a Puerto Rican youth results in three African American deaths and millions of dollars in damage to white-owned properties. April: In "Harlem Runs Wild," published in *The Nation*, Claude McKay asserts that the riot is "the gesture of despair of a bewildered, baffled, and disillusioned people." The Works Progress Administration (WPA) established by U.S. President Franklin Delano Roosevelt; writers and artists who will eventually find employment under its aegis include Richard Wright, Ralph Ellison, Dorothy West, Margaret Walker, Augusta Savage, Romare Bearden, and Jacob Lawrence. October: Langston Hughes's play *Mulatto* and George Gershwin's opera *Porgy and Bess* open on Broadway.

Books

Countee Cullen: *The Medea and Some Poems* (Harper)

Frank Marshall Davis: *Black Man's Verse* (Black Cat Press)

W.E.B. Du Bois: *Black Reconstruction in America, 1860–1880* (Harcourt, Brace)

Zora Neale Hurston: *Mules and Men* (Lippincott)

James Weldon Johnson: *Saint Peter Relates an Incident: Selected Poems* (Viking Press)

1936   February: The National Negro Congress, representing some 600 organizations, holds its first meeting in Chicago. June: Mary McLeod Bethune is appointed Director of the Division of Negro Affairs of the National Youth Administration, becoming the highest-ranking African American official of the Roosevelt administration.

Books

Arna Bontemps: *Black Thunder* (Macmillan)

Alain Locke: *Negro Art—Past and Present* (Associates in Negro Folk Education)

Alain Locke: *The Negro and His Music* (Associates in Negro Folk Education)

Biographical Notes

Jean Toomer   Born Nathan Pinchback Toomer on December 26, 1899, in Washington, D.C., the only son of Nathan Eugene Toomer, a Georgia planter who had been born into slavery, and Nina Pinchback, the daughter of P.B.S. Pinchback, a Louisiana politician who during Reconstruction served as the state's lieutenant governor (and briefly as acting governor) and was elected to the U.S. Senate in 1873 but did not serve owing to the contestation of his election. Toomer's parents were of mixed race and, like Toomer, very light-skinned. His parents separated when he was very young; he grew up in the household of his maternal grandfather. Most, if not all, of his early years were spent in Washington, D.C.; he later commented that he did not really live in an African American neighborhood until he was a teenager. Following a short residence in upstate New York with his mother and her second husband, Toomer returned to Washington following her death in 1909 and graduated in 1914 from the elite all-black M Street School (renamed Paul Laurence Dunbar High School in 1916). Toomer enrolled in classes at a variety of schools, including the University of Wisconsin, the Massachusetts College of Agriculture, the American College of Physical Training (Chicago), the University of Chicago, the City College of New York, and New York University, but did not earn an undergraduate degree. He changed his name to Jean Toomer and in his early twenties lived in Greenwich Village where he met writers including Van Wyck Brooks and Witter Bynner, and formed a close friendship with Waldo Frank. In the fall of 1921 he took a temporary teaching job at an agricultural school in Sparta, Georgia, an experience that became the basis for much of *Cane*, a fusion of fiction, poetry, and drama that was published by Boni and Liveright in 1923. His poetry and prose appeared in magazines such as *Broom*, *The Liberator*, *Nomad*, and *The Little Review*, and *Cane* upon publication received wide critical acclaim. Toomer became interested in the mystical ideas of George Ivanovich Gurdjieff; in January 1924 in New York he met A. R. Orage, an English disciple of Gurdjieff, and spent that summer at Gurdjieff's Institute for the Harmonious Development of Man at Fontainebleau, France. Returning to America, he conducted Gurdjieff workshops in New York, Chicago, and Portage, Wisconsin. He married the writer Margery Latimer in 1931, and their marriage led to a national anti-miscegenation scandal when reported on by *Time*. (At the time of the marriage Toomer issued a statement in which he wrote: "There is a new race in America. I am a member of this new race. It is neither white nor black nor in-between. It is the American race [. . .]." Latimer died the following year as a result of giving birth to their daughter Margery. Toomer married Marjorie Content in 1934, and thereafter settled permanently in Doylestown, Pennsylvania. After the appearance of *Cane* he continued to publish poems and prose pieces in magazines, but did not widely circulate much of the writing—including novels, stories, poetry, and plays—composed during that period. *Essentials: Definitions and Aphorisms* and *A Fiction and Some Facts*, small privately printed volumes, appeared in 1931, and the long poem "The Blue Horizon," a meditation on a raceless America on which he had begun work in the early 1920s, was published in the poetry anthology *The New Caravan* in 1936. He traveled to India in 1939. He joined the Religious Society of Friends (Quakers) in 1940. In later years he published *An Interpretation of Friends Worship* (1947) and *The Flavor of Man* (1949). His writings were collected posthumously in *The Wayward and the Seeking: A Collection of Writings by Jean Toomer* (1980) and *The Collected Poems of Jean Toomer* (1988). Toomer was in poor health in his last decades; he died March 30, 1967, in Doylestown.

Claude McKay   Born Festus Claudius McKay on September 15, 1889, in Sunny Ville, Jamaica, last of eleven children of the relatively prosperous farmers Thomas Francis McKay and Hannah Ann Edwards McKay. Around 1897 he went to live with his eldest brother, Uriah Theodore (U'Theo), a teacher, who was entrusted with his education. During a brief period of apprenticeship to a local craftsman, McKay met Walter Jekyll, an English scholar and folklorist resident in Jamaica who encouraged his literary ambitions. In 1911 McKay joined the Jamaican constabulary, leaving the force after a year. His first two books, *Songs of Jamaica* and *Constab Ballads*, collections of poetry mostly written in local Jamaican vernacular, were published in 1912. McKay moved to the United States in the summer of 1912 to attend the Tuskegee Institute in Alabama; he transferred to Kansas State University, where he studied for nearly two years but did not complete a degree. (Of his first encounter with white American racial attitudes he later wrote: "I had heard of prejudice in America but never dreamed of it being so intensely bitter.") After moving to New York City in 1914, McKay was briefly married to Eulalie Imelda Edwards, whom he had known in Jamaica, and for a short time he ran a restaurant in Brooklyn. His wife returned to Jamaica after six months; there she gave birth to their daughter Ruth, who never met her father. McKay never remarried and is thought to have been romantically involved with both men and women. On his move to Harlem, which was his base from 1917 to 1919, he later wrote: "Harlem was my first positive reaction to American life . . . After two years in the blue-sky-law desert of Kansas, it was like entering a paradise of my own people." He worked initially at a variety of jobs before settling into longer-term employment as a dining-car waiter on the Pennsylvania Railroad. His poetry appeared in *Seven Arts* in 1917 and (following a friendly meeting with editor Frank Harris) in *Pearson's Magazine* in 1918. He became involved in radical political circles, forming a friendship with the black socialist leader Hubert H. Harrison and joining the IWW (International Workers of the World), as well as Cyril Briggs's semi-secret radical organization the African Blood Brotherhood, in 1919. (Within the next few years, in all likelihood, he joined the American Communist Party, then functioning as an illegal underground organization.) After publishing a poem in *The Liberator* he became friendly with the magazine's editor Max Eastman and his sister Crystal Eastman; in July 1919 *The Liberator* published a spread of seven poems by McKay, including the sonnet "If We Must Die," written in response to the racial violence of the Red Summer of 1919. With the help of some British admirers, he traveled to London, where he lived from the fall of 1919 to the end of 1920. He became involved with Sylvia Pankurst's Workers' Socialist Federation and eventually became a staff member of her magazine *The Workers' Dreadnought*. The critic C. K. Ogden published a large selection of McKay's poetry in *Cambridge Magazine* and arranged for the publication of the poetry collection *Spring in New Hampshire*. Disillusioned by what he considered the problematic racial attitudes of many on the English left, and embroiled in the internal politics of the WSF, McKay decided to return to New York. Upon his return he was invited by Max Eastman to become associate editor of *The Liberator* along with Floyd Dell and Robert Minor; subsequently Dell and Minor were replaced by Michael Gold. Internal tensions at the magazine led McKay to resign his editorship in August 1922, leaving Gold, a more orthodox Communist, as sole editor. *Harlem Shadows*, a poetry collection incorporating all the poems from *Spring in New Hampshire* along with much other work, appeared in 1922. With the help of a fund-raising campaign, McKay traveled to the Soviet Union in September 1922. Working as a stoker on his way across the Atlantic, he stopped in London and Berlin before traveling to Moscow, where he attended the Fourth Congress of the Third International despite initial opposition from a dominant faction in the American Communist Party. In a speech before the Congress, McKay was critical of unexamined racial prejudice on the part of white American radicals; during the conference he also met with Leon Trotsky. He remained in Russia for another six months, meeting a number of literary figures including Boris Pilnyak, Yevgeny Zamyatin, and Vladimir

Mayakovsky and publishing articles in the Soviet press which he reworked into the study *The Negroes in America*, published in Russian in 1923. Afterward he settled mostly in France, spending a great deal of time in Marseilles and Toulon, and with periods of residence in Spain and Morocco. He destroyed his novel "Color Scheme" after it was rejected by a number of publishers. His first published novel, *Home to Harlem* (1928), was a commercial success, although it met with much negative criticism in the African American press. McKay subsequently published a second novel describing the port life of Marseilles, *Banjo: A Story Without a Plot* (1929), *Gingertown* (1932), a collection of stories, and *Banana Bottom* (1933), a novel set in Jamaica; another novel, "The Jungle and the Bottoms" (later retitled "Romance in Marseilles") remained unpublished. He left France in 1930 and began a three-year residence in Morocco. His essay "A Negro Writer to His Critics" appeared in the New York *Herald Tribune* in 1932. He returned to the United States in January 1934, settling in Harlem. He began publishing journalism in *The Nation*, including "Harlem Runs Wild," an account of the Harlem riots of March 19, 1935; found employment with the Federal Writers' Project; and published a memoir, *A Long Way from Home* (1937), and the study *Harlem: Negro Metropolis* (1940). His attempts to establish a Negro Authors' Guild ended in failure. Having suffered from ill health for years, he suffered a major collapse in 1942, followed by a debilitating stroke the next year, and received assistance from Friendship House, a Catholic lay organization. He published no further books, although his essays and poetry continued to appear in *The New Leader*, *The Nation*, *The Amsterdam News*, and other periodicals. McKay converted to Catholicism a few years before his death in Chicago, where he worked for the National Catholic Youth Organization. He died on May 22, 1948.

Nella Larsen   Born Nellie Walker in Chicago on April 13, 1891, the daughter of Peter Walker, a cook from the Danish West Indies (now U.S. Virgin Islands), and Mary Hansen, a Danish immigrant. (There are no documents to establish whether her parents were legally married.) Her father apparently died or left the family when she was very young, and her mother married Peter Larsen, also of Scandinavian ancestry, and had a daughter, Anna, with him. Anna was considered white, and Nella would subsequently feel alienated from the family as the one dark daughter. For several years in her childhood (probably between 1895 and 1898) Larsen lived in Denmark with her mother and half-sister. On returning to the United States, Larsen attended Fisk University's high school in Nashville. After leaving Fisk—she may have been expelled as a result of her protest against Fisk's dress code—she traveled again to Denmark, remaining there until 1912 and by her own account auditing courses at the University of Copenhagen. Subsequently Larsen studied nursing in New York City at Lincoln Hospital and later worked at Tuskegee Hospital and for the New York City Health Department. Larsen married physicist Elmer S. Imes in May 1919 and within three years had left nursing and begun a brief career as a librarian in the New York Public Library system, including the Children's Room at the 135th Street branch. Larsen's first publication, an article on Danish children's games, appeared in *The Brownie's Book*, a magazine for African American children published under the auspices of the NAACP's *The Crisis*. With her husband Larsen led an active social life in New York, where her friends in cultural and literary circles included Walter White and James Weldon Johnson; she became particularly close to Carl Van Vechten. Her novels *Quicksand* (1928) and *Passing* (1929) were published by Alfred A. Knopf and attracted considerable praise, including laudatory reviews by W.E.B. Du Bois; she became the first black woman to win the Guggenheim Fellowship (1930). She was accused of plagiarism when resemblances were detected between her short story "Sanctuary" (1930) and an earlier story by the English writer Sheila Kaye-Smith. Her husband joined the faculty of Fisk, where he began an affair with Edith Gilbert, the school's white director of publicity and finances. Larsen traveled alone to Europe on her Guggenheim Fellowship, staying in Spain and France and completing a novel ("Mirage"), which was rejected by Knopf. (This and other unpublished work by Larsen does not survive in manuscript.) After returning to America she lived for a time with her husband at Fisk, although the two led separate lives; they were divorced in 1933. In later life Larsen distanced herself from most of her friends, some of whom later suggested she may have battled problems with alcohol or drugs. She returned to professional nursing in 1944, working at Gouverneur Hospital on New York's Lower East Side. In 1961 Larsen began working as night supervisor in the psychiatric ward of Metropolitan Hospital, where she remained employed until her death on March 30, 1964.

Jessie Redmon Fauset   Born Jessie Redmon Fauset in Camden County, New Jersey, near Philadelphia, on April 27, 1882, the seventh child of African Methodist Episcopal minister Redmon Fauset and Annie Seamon Fauset, who died when Fauset was still a young girl. After her father's remarriage to Bella Huff, Fauset moved to Philadelphia, where she attended the predominantly white Philadelphia High School for Girls. Having been denied admission to Bryn Mawr on the basis of race, she attended Cornell University, 1901–05, and received an undergraduate degree in classical languages; she was also the first African American female Phi Beta Kappa key holder. She began corresponding with W.E.B. Du Bois in 1903, and with his help secured a summer teaching position at Fisk University in 1904. After graduating from Cornell, and unable to find employment in Philadelphia's segregated high school system, she taught for fourteen years at M Street High School (renamed Paul Laurence Dunbar High School in 1916) in Washington, D.C., the educational home of the District of Columbia's black elite. Fauset earned a master's degree in French at the University of Pennsylvania in 1919. That same year Du Bois offered her the opportunity to move to New York City as literary editor of the NAACP publication *The Crisis*, to which she had been contributing articles, stories, and poems since 1912. As editor she encouraged the work of Jean Toomer, Claude McKay, Langston Hughes, Nella Larsen, Countee Cullen, George S. Schuyler, and other emerging African American writers. With fellow *Crisis* staff member Augustus Granville Dill, Fauset edited the NAACP's children's publication, *The Brownie's Book*, 1920–21. She continued to contribute prolifically to *The Crisis*; her essay "The Gift of Laughter" was included in Alain Locke's anthology *The New Negro* (1925); and her Sunday teas and literary soirées became gathering places for writers and intellectuals. (Langston Hughes would comment about these occasions: "A good time was shared by talking literature and reading poetry aloud and perhaps enjoying some conversation in French. White people were seldom present unless they were very distinguished white people, because Jessie Fauset did not feel like opening her home to mere sightseers, or faddists momentarily in love with Negro life.") In 1921 she attended the Second Pan-African Congress in Brussels as a delegate of the Delta Sigma Theta sorority. The publication of her first novel, *There Is Confusion*, by Boni and Liveright was celebrated by a dinner at the Civic Club on March 21, 1924, widely attended by African American writers and by representatives of mainstream publishing houses, and was afterward taken as an inaugural event of the Harlem Renaissance. She traveled again in Europe, 1924–25. A second novel, *Plum Bun* (1928), was followed by *The Chinaberry Tree* (1931) and *Comedy: American Style* (1933), all published by Frederick A. Stokes. Fauset left *The Crisis* in 1927 and returned to teaching at New York City's De Witt Clinton High School (where she may have taught the young James Baldwin). In 1929 she married Herbert Harris, an insurance agent. She gave up teaching in 1944 and moved with her husband to Montclair, New Jersey; she had little involvement in literary circles in her later years. After her husband's death in 1958 she moved to Philadelphia, where she died on April 30, 1961.

Wallace Thurman   Born August 16, 1902, in Salt Lake City, Utah, the son of Beulah Jackson and Oscar Thurman, and raised by his mother and grandmother in Utah, his parents having divorced in the year of Thurman's birth. His mother was married at least six times; his father he scarcely knew in his adult years except for an encounter in 1929. His maternal grandmother, Emma Jackson ("Ma Jack"), kept a tavern and engaged in bootlegging activities at various times. A voracious reader at an early age, Thurman briefly attended high school in Omaha, Nebraska, where he had gone with his mother, before returning to Salt Lake City where he graduated from West Salt Lake High School. He spent two years as a pre-med student at the University of Utah; after a hiatus, he enrolled in 1922 in the journalism program at the University of Southern California, apparently dropping out after a semester. After leaving school he was employed as associate editor at the Los Angeles newspaper *The Pacific Defender*. He also worked as a postal clerk, forming a friendship with fellow postal worker Arna Bontemps. Thurman founded *The Outlet*, described by him as "the first western Negro literary magazine," of which he published six issues (no copies are known to have survived). After the failure of the magazine he moved to New York, arriving in Harlem in the fall of 1925 and renewing his friendship with Bontemps, who found him a room in the same boarding house where he was staying. Plagued by ill health, Thurman supported himself with difficulty. (In a 1928 letter to Claude McKay, he wrote: "I came to Harlem knowing one individual. Since then I have struggled and starved and had a hell of a good time generally.") Along with Nella Larsen, Aaron Douglas, and other Harlem writers and artists he attended Jean Toomer's workshop on Gurdjieff's teachings. Theophilus Lewis, for whose short-lived magazine *The Looking Glass* Thurman had worked as writer and editorial assistant, found Thurman an editorial position at *The Messenger*, to which he also contributed articles and reviews. He played the leading role in editing the literary journal *Fire!!* (1926), whose other editors were Langston Hughes, Zora Neale Hurston, Richard Bruce Nugent, Gwendolyn Bennett, John P. Davis, and Aaron Douglas. Only one issue appeared, in November 1926; it was controversial, due in part to the sexual frankness of Nugent's "Smoke, Lilies and Jade" and Thurman's story "Cordelia the Crude." The print run was almost completely destroyed in an apartment fire, and Thurman bore most of the burden of the magazine's considerable financial losses. Also in November 1926 Thurman moved into an apartment at 267 West 136th Street (nicknamed "Niggeratti Manor"), which he shared with the artist and writer Richard Bruce Nugent and which became a social center frequented by Hughes, Hurston, Dorothy West, and others. Another journal launched by Thurman in 1928, *Harlem: A Journal of Negro Life*, published only a single issue. His article "Negro Life in New York's Harlem" was published in the Haldeman-Julius Little

Blue Book series in 1928. In August 1928 he married Louise Thompson but the marriage broke up within months (or perhaps weeks); Thompson would later remark of Thurman that "he took nothing seriously. He laughed about everything. He would often threaten to commit suicide but you knew he would never try it. And he would never admit he was a homosexual." He worked as an editor at Macfadden Publishers and contributed stories to *True Story* under pseudonyms. His novel *The Blacker the Berry* was published by the Macaulay Company in February 1929. The same month, his play *Harlem: A Melodrama of Negro Life in Harlem*, written in collaboration with the white playwright William Jourdan Rapp and based on Thurman's story "Cordelia the Crude," opened on Broadway and ran for ninety-three performances. Thurman began to spend much time outside of New York City, returning to Salt Lake City and later staying in Los Angeles and the Long Island home of Theophilus Lewis. He finished a collection of essays, "Aunt Hagar's Children," which was not published in his lifetime. A second novel, *Infants of the Spring*, containing thinly veiled portraits of himself and many of his artistic colleagues, was published by Macaulay in 1932. He was hired as a reader and subsequently as editor at Macaulay. *The Interne*, a novel based on a play by Thurman and co-written with Abraham Furman, was published in 1932. Furman subsequently introduced Thurman to the independent film producer Brian Foy; Thurman went to Hollywood in February 1934 and wrote the stories for two low-budget films, *Tomorrow's Children* and *High School Girl*. He returned to New York in poor health, exacerbated by heavy drinking, and following a diagnosis of acute tuberculosis entered City Hospital on Welfare Island. He died there on December 22, 1934.

Note on the Texts

This volume collects five novels—*Cane* (1923), by Jean Toomer; *Home to Harlem* (1928), by Claude McKay; *Quicksand* (1928), by Nella Larsen; *Plum Bun* (1928), by Jessie Redmon Fauset; and *The Blacker the Berry* (1929), by Wallace Thurman—associated with what has come to be known as the Harlem Renaissance, a period of great creativity and change in African American cultural life, with its epicenter in New York's Harlem neighborhood. A companion volume in The Library of America series, *Harlem Renaissance: Four Novels of the 1930s*, includes four later novels: *Not Without Laughter* (1930), by Langston Hughes; *Black No More* (1931), by George S. Schuyler; *The Conjure-Man Dies* (1932), by Rudolph Fisher; and *Black Thunder* (1936), by Arna Bontemps. The texts of all of these novels have been taken from the first printings of the first editions.

Cane. By Jean Toomer's own account in *The Wayward and the Seeking* (1980), his posthumously published autobiographical writings, he began the poems, sketches, and short stories later gathered in *Cane* at the end of November 1921, "on the train coming north" after a stint during the fall as temporary principal of a school in rural Sparta, Georgia. He had in fact already written one story subsequently adapted in *Cane*, "Georgia Night," sending it to *The Liberator* while still in Sparta. But back in Washington, D.C., Toomer intensified his literary efforts. By March 24, 1922, he was able to report, in a letter to Waldo Frank: "I have thrown my energies into writing. I have written any number of poems, several sketches in play form, and one long piece which I call a Play in Three Acts." Frank—the established writer of the pair, whom Toomer had met in 1920—encouraged Toomer to send his work, and having read it responded with enthusiasm. He immediately suggested that Toomer submit "some of the shorter things" to the *Dial* and *Broom*, and he followed up on April 25, 1922, with a detailed critical evaluation of Toomer's manuscripts. He faulted "Natalie Mann," a play Toomer did not ultimately include in *Cane*, and praised "Kabnis" in particular, while suggesting changes: "I wonder if you would not have done better in a freer form of narrative, in which your dialog, which has no kinship with the theatric, might have thrived more successfully." Toomer accepted almost all of Frank's advice and began revising. He also announced a plan for a book in a letter to Frank on July 19: "I've had the impulse to collect my sketches and poems under the title perhaps of CANE. Such pieces as Karintha, Carma, Avey, and Kabnis (revised) coming under the sub head of Cane Stalks and Choruses. Poems under the sub head of Leaves and Syrup Songs. And my vignettes, of which I have any number, under Leaf Traceries in Washington." The two corresponded extensively about each other's work in July and August, and in September and October they traveled together to Spartanburg, South Carolina, where Frank, then working on his novel *Holiday* (1923), hoped to get a firsthand sense of the South. Returning from Spartanburg, Toomer wrote "Box Seat," "Theater," and "Blood-Burning Moon"; on December 12, he sent Frank a completed draft of *Cane*. Boni & Liveright, to whom Frank had already recommended the book, decided to accept *Cane* for publication around the end of the year. Frank reread Toomer's manuscript before meeting with Horace Liveright on January 8, 1923, and suggested further revisions. He hoped Toomer might cut several poems ("Something Is Melting Down in Washington," "Tell Me," "Glaciers of Dusk," and "Prayer") and revise the story "Box Seat." Toomer argued that "Prayer" was important to the integrity of his work but he yielded on the other poems and sent Frank additional ones, giving him the authority to choose which, if any, to add. He rearranged the book's parts and revised "Box Seat," about which the two had especially corresponded. Toomer sent his revised manuscript to Horace Liveright on February 27. Both Toomer and Frank read proofs (Frank arguing, for one, for the retention of Toomer's irregular two- and three-dot ellipses). *Cane* was published by Boni & Liveright in September 1923.

Many of the poems, sketches, and stories gathered in *Cane* were published in magazines between April 1922 and September 1923. The following is a list of these periodical appearances, in the order in which Toomer's works were ultimately published in *Cane*:

Karintha: *Broom*, January 1923
November Cotton Flower: *The Nomad*, Summer 1923
Becky: *The Liberator*, October 1922
Face: *Modern Review*, January 1923 (with "Conversion" and "Portrait in Georgia," one of three "Georgia Portraits")
Carma: *The Liberator*, September 1922
Song of the Son: *The Crisis*, April 1922
Georgia Dusk: *The Liberator*, September 1922
Fern: *The Little Review*, Autumn 1922
Esther: *Modern Review*, January 1923
Conversion: *Modern Review*, January 1923
Portrait in Georgia: *Modern Review*, January 1923
Blood-Burning Moon: *Prairie*, March–April 1923
Seventh Street: *Broom*, December 1922

Storm Ending: *Double Dealer*, September 1922
Her Lips Are Copper Wire: *S4N*, May–August 1923
Calling Jesus: *Double Dealer*, September 1922 (as "Nora")
Harvest Song: *Double Dealer*, December 1922
Kabnis: *Broom*, August 1923 (section I); *Broom*, September 1923
    (section V)

To varying degrees, Toomer revised most of these individual works
before he gathered them in *Cane*, and (along with Frank) he retained
considerable control over the form in which they finally appeared.
Boni & Liveright reprinted *Cane* once, in 1927, without altering the
text; another reprint (New York: University Place Press) was published
in 1951. The present volume prints the text of the 1923 Boni & Liveright first printing.

Home to Harlem. Claude McKay began his first novel, *Home to
Harlem*, on the suggestion of William Aspinwall Bradley, an American
literary agent based in Paris. Toward the end of 1926, Bradley visited
McKay in Cap d'Antibes, where McKay was staying with his friend
Max Eastman. Bradley conveyed the good news that Harper &
Brothers in New York would be willing to publish a collection of sto-
ries that McKay had recently completed. But a novel, they felt—as
McKay recalled in his 1937 memoir *A Long Way from Home*—would
bring him "more prestige and remuneration than a book of short sto-
ries." McKay and Bradley agreed that "Home to Harlem," a story
McKay had written in 1925, would work well at greater length, and
McKay quickly began expanding it. In February 1927, he told Bradley
that he had finished two chapters: "I am having a picnic doing it.
Everything is clear and I see through the whole story to the end."
Bradley, in the meantime, retrieved a copy of the story "Home to
Harlem" from the magazine *Opportunity*, to which McKay had sent it
for a 1926 competition and which he feared might publish it. McKay
finished the novel by May and sent Bradley the final chapters. By early
December, having "fled to Marseilles," he was correcting proofs.
    During the writing of *Home to Harlem* McKay had expressed a de-
sire to avoid any confrontation over potentially objectionable content
and a willingness to be edited, but in the end he was happy, he wrote
Bradley, that Harper & Brothers had not "chopped it up" as he feared
they might. Eugene Saxton, his editor at the firm, had changed only
occasional words and phrases, McKay reported. No manuscripts or
other prepublication versions of the novel are now known to be extant, so further detail about Saxton's revisions is unavailable. Harper
& Brothers published the novel in early March 1928; in April, McKay
wrote Bradley: "I see *Home to Harlem* like an impudent dog has

[moved] right in among the best sellers in New York." The firm reprinted the novel at least eleven times in 1928 and 1929, without altering the text; it was not subsequently republished until after McKay's death. The present volume prints the text of the 1928 Harper & Brothers first printing.

Quicksand. In early drafts, Nella Larsen's *Quicksand* was titled "Cloudy Amber." In July 1926, when she had half-completed the novel, she discussed potential publishers with her friend Carl Van Vechten; at Van Vechten's suggestion, she decided it ought to go first to Alfred A. Knopf rather than to Albert and Charles Boni, a less prestigious firm then advertising a $1000 prize for the best novel "about Negro life and written by a Negro." In November 1926, as she was finishing "Cloudy Amber," Larsen met Walter White—novelist and then assistant secretary of the NAACP—at a party hosted by Knopf senior editor Harry Block. White offered the assistance of his secretary, Carrie Overton, in typing Larsen's manuscript. Larsen gave Van Vechten a copy of "Cloudy Amber" on December 4, 1926; "read this after dinner & find it in many ways remarkable," he noted in his daybook. Van Vechten responded promptly and in detail, suggesting that she lengthen the novel and change its title and offering to take the novel personally to Knopf (his own publisher, with whom he had considerable influence). Larsen took Van Vechten's advice. In March 1927, Knopf accepted her revised *Quicksand* and returned an edited manuscript. She made final revisions and sent the manuscript back to Knopf to be typeset, receiving her first copies of the book about a year later. *Quicksand* was officially published on March 31, 1928 and was not reprinted during her lifetime. The present volume prints the text of the first Knopf edition.

Plum Bun. Jessie Redmon Fauset began her second novel, *Plum Bun*, during the summer of 1924, just a few months after Boni & Liveright had published her first, *There Is Confusion*. On October 8 she wrote to Langston Hughes from Paris: "I like the stuff of my next novel—I have a good title for it too—but I am troubled as I have never been before with form. Somehow I've never thought much about form except for verse. But now I think I am over zealous—I write and destroy and smoke and get nervous." By the next fall she had finished a draft of the novel, titled "Market." She shared this version with W.E.B. Du Bois, whose unpublished response was dated September 10, 1925, and submitted her manuscript to Boni & Liveright. On October 21, 1925, she wrote to Carl Van Vechten in the hope that he might help her to find a new publisher for "Market": "Mr. Liveright has rejected the book and it is now being read by the Viking Press. I know that you are acquainted with members of that firm and

if you can help me in this case I should certainly appreciate it." But
Viking, too, decided not to publish the book. It would be three years
before the novel finally appeared in print, under the title *Plum Bun*.
No manuscript versions of the novel are known to be extant, and the
extent to which Fauset may have revised "Market" in the interim is
uncertain. Her agent, Brandt & Brandt, finally placed the novel with
the London firm of Elkin Mathews & Marrot, which published it in
October 1928. Early the next year the novel was released in the United
States by the New York firm of Frederick A. Stokes, in the form of the
British sheets with the Stokes imprint on the title page. Stokes subsequently had the text reset, and by April 1929 the publisher was able to
call its current printing the "third"; but this American setting, which
repeats the British spellings, introduced new errors into the text and
contains no changes that can be considered authorial. *Plum Bun* did
not appear in print again during Fauset's lifetime. The text in the
present volume follows the 1928 Elkin Mathews & Marrot edition.

The Blacker the Berry. Relatively little evidence has survived about
the composition and textual history of *The Blacker the Berry*, Wallace
Thurman's first novel. On April 22, 1927, Thurman's friend Harold
Jackman reported in a letter to Countee Cullen that Thurman had
finished a novel; about a month later, in an undated letter to Langston
Hughes, Thurman wrote that he had sent the novel to Doubleday. In
another undated letter to Hughes (January 1928?) Thurman gave an
update: "The novel is about re-written." By April 22, 1928, he had
shown the novel to Jackman (who called it "very good" in a letter to
Claude McKay). Doubleday evidently decided not to accept the
novel; instead, it was published by the Macaulay Company in New
York on February 1, 1929. *The Blacker the Berry* was not reprinted
during Thurman's lifetime. The text in the present volume has been
taken from the 1929 Macaulay first edition.

This volume presents the texts of the editions chosen for inclusion
here but does not attempt to reproduce every feature of their typo-
graphic design. The texts are reprinted without change, except for the
correction of typographical errors. Spelling, punctuation, and capital-
ization are often expressive features, and they are not altered, even
when inconsistent or irregular. The following is a list of typographical
errors corrected, cited by page and line number: 36.18, at thought;
51.6, overhead; 87.22, me.'; 6 104.13, home.'; 107.35, Otherwise. . .";
123.21, do think; 127.21, her She; 151.17, cabarets a; 176.17, dearie.';
201.14, and was; 204.22, burninshed; 209.23, hynotize; 236.8, News,;
246.16–17, on shopping; 247.27, with powder; 267.28, overwhem;
275.32, Telli me; 281.30, exhibtion; 301.37, mouth;; 308.27, compli-

cated.; 310.13, Money,; 312.6, enentirely; 316.6, twenty odd; 330.5, She; 330.16, a well; 347.10, she was; 350.17, as welfare; 363.13, Fisher,; 370.25, Kirkplads; 373.2–3, Amielenborg; 377.21, "Helios"; 381.29, Konigen's; 416.35–36, dusting mending; 428.14, Huh! she; 452.32, fimly; 466.7, profession.; 475.28, argue;; 484.19, "Look; 484.20, means!"; 485.27–28, Angela trim; 488.23, Hotel She; 506.11, whch; 511.37, tabulating; 514.12, on your; 516.9, he did; 518.21, filled; 519.25, her car; 525.1, happiness would; 530.37–38, again again; 563.3, conventions,; 575.23, married; 578.36, 'Well'?"; 586.29, herself "God!"; 590.15, sobeit; 608.36, glaxy; 614.11–12, bewildered; she; 616.20, Mr Cross; 617.23, glibly;; 618.26, ago Back; 620.32, revolver "I've; 623.31, swamp And; 631.12, understand There's; 631.28, memory! Oh; 640.4, her.'; 641.30, years'; 642.11–12, sunny, vocabulary; 644.8, herself,; 651.17, week's; 653.22–23, presumbably; 662.7, herself ashamed; 674.23, nothing with; 675.40, Let's; 675.40, you; 683.31, Movies; 707.21, redstripped; 713.11, good-loking; 734.24, Yer; 735.3, fire-escape decorated; 750.27, one; 751.4, "No" she; 753.15, inpregnate; 759.3, Gal,"; 770.13, "She's; 790.7, Supposing she; 820.6, but possibility; 821.38, Geraldine; 822.3, Geraldine; 822.30, Junior,; 823.15, Junior,.

Notes

In the notes below, the reference numbers denote page and line of the present volume; the line count includes titles and headings but not blank lines. No note is made for material found in standard desk-reference works. For additional information and references to other studies, see Wayne F. Cooper, *Claude McKay: Rebel Sojourner in the Harlem Renaissance* (Baton Rouge: Louisiana State University Press, 1987); Thadious M. Davis, *Nella Larsen, Novelist of the Harlem Renaissance: A Woman's Life Unveiled* (Baton Rouge: Louisiana State University Press, 1994); Geneviève Fabre and Michel Feith, eds., *Jean Toomer and the Harlem Renaissance* (New Brunswick, New Jersey: Rutgers University Press, 2001); Brent Hayes Edwards, *The Practice of Diaspora: Literature, Translation, and the Rise of Black Internationalism* (Cambridge, Massachusetts: Harvard University Press, 2003); Nathan Irvin Huggins, *Harlem Renaissance* (New York: Oxford University Press, 1971); George Hutchinson, *In Search of Nella Larsen: A Biography of the Color Line* (Cambridge, Massachusetts: Harvard University Press, 2006); George Hutchinson, ed., *The Cambridge Companion to the Harlem Renaissance* (Cambridge, United Kingdom: Cambridge University Press, 2007); David Levering Lewis, *When Harlem Was in Vogue* (New York: Alfred A. Knopf, 1980); Nellie Y. McKay, *Jean Toomer, Artist: A Study of His Literary Life and Work, 1894–1936* (Chapel Hill: University of North Carolina Press, 1984); Jacquelyn Y. McLendon, *The Politics of Color in the Fiction of Jessie Fauset and Nella Larsen* (Charlottesville: University Press of Virginia, 1995); Eleonore van Notten, *Wallace Thurman's Harlem Renaissance* (Amsterdam: Rodopi, 1994); Kathleen Pfeiffer, ed., *Brother Mine: The Correspondence of Jean Toomer and Waldo Frank* (Champaign: University of Illinois Press, 2010); Charles Scruggs and Lee Vandemarr, *Jean Toomer and the Terrors of American History* (Philadelphia: University of Pennsylvania Press, 1998); Amritjit Singh and Daniel M. Scott III, eds., *The Collected Writings of Wallace Thurman: A Harlem Renaissance Reader* (New Brunswick, New Jersey: Rutgers University Press, 2003); Carolyn Wedin Sylvander, *Jessie Redmon Fauset, Black American Writer* (Troy, New York: Whitston Publishing, 1981); and Steven Watson, *The Harlem Renaissance: Hub of African-American Culture, 1920–1930* (New York: Pantheon, 1995).

CANE

1.1   CANE]   The first edition of *Cane* included the following foreword by
Waldo Frank (1889–1967), author of *Our America* (1919), *City Block* (1922),
and many other works, with whom Toomer had collaborated closely while
writing the novel:

> Reading this book, I had the vision of a land, heretofore sunk in the
> mists of muteness, suddenly rising up into the eminence of song. Innu-
> merable books have been written about the South; some good books
> have been written in the South. This book *is* the South. I do not mean
> that *Cane* covers the South or is the South's full voice. Merely this: a
> poet has arisen among our American youth who has known how to
> turn the essences and materials of his Southland into the essences and
> materials of literature. A poet has arisen in that land who writes, not as
> a Southerner, not as a rebel against Southerners, not as a Negro, not as
> apologist or priest or critic: who writes as a *poet*. The fashioning of
> beauty is ever foremost in his inspiration: not forcedly but simply, and
> because these ultimate aspects of his world are to him more real than
> all its specific problems. He has made songs and lovely stories of his
> land . . . not of its yesterday, but of its immediate life. And that has
> been enough.
>
> How rare this is will be clear to those who have followed with con-
> cern the struggle of the South toward literary expression, and the par-
> ticular trial of that portion of its folk whose skin is dark. The gifted
> Negro has been too often thwarted from becoming a poet because his
> world was forever forcing him to recollect that he was a Negro. The
> artist must lose such lesser identities in the great well of life. The En-
> glish poet is not forever protesting and recalling that he is English. It is
> so natural and easy for him to be English that he can sing as a man. The
> French novelist is not forever noting: "This is French." It is so atmo-
> spheric for him to be French, that he can devote himself to saying:
> "This is human." This is an imperative condition for the creating of
> deep art. The whole will and mind of the creator must go below the
> surfaces of race. And this has been an almost impossible condition for
> the American Negro to achieve, forced every moment of his life into a
> specific and superficial plane of consciousness.
>
> The first negative significance of *Cane* is that this so natural and re-
> strictive state of mind is completely lacking. For Toomer, the Southland
> is not a problem to be solved; it is a field of loveliness to be sung: the
> Georgia Negro is not a downtrodden soul to be uplifted; he is material
> for gorgeous painting: the segregated self-conscious brown belt of
> Washington is not a topic to be discussed and exposed; it is a subject of
> beauty and of drama, worthy of creation in literary form.
>
> It seems to me, therefore, that this is a first book in more ways than
> one. It is a harbinger of the South's literary maturity: of its emergence
> from the obsession put upon its minds by the unending racial crisis—an

obsession from which writers have made their indirect escape through sentimentalism, exoticism, polemic, "problem" fiction, and moral melodrama. It marks the dawn of direct and unafraid creation. And, as the initial work of a man of twenty-seven, it is the harbinger of a literary force of whose incalculable future I believe no reader of this book will be in doubt.

How typical is *Cane* of the South's still virgin soil and of its pressing seeds! and the book's chaos of verse, tale, drama, its rhythmic rolling shift from lyrism to narrative, from mystery to intimate pathos! But read the book through and you will see a complex and significant form take substance from its chaos. Part One is the primitive and evanescent black world of Georgia. Part Two is the threshing and suffering brown world of Washington, lifted by opportunity and contact into the anguish of self-conscious struggle. Part Three is Georgia again . . . the invasion into this black womb of the ferment seed: the neurotic, educated, spiritually stirring Negro. As a broad form this is superb, and the very looseness and unexpected waves of the book's parts make *Cane* still more *South*, still more of an æsthetic equivalent of the land.

What a land it is! What an Æschylean beauty to its fateful problem! Those of you who love our South will find here some of your love. Those of you who know it not will perhaps begin to understand what a warm splendor is at last at dawn.

> A feast of moon and men and barking hounds,
> An orgy for some genius of the South
> With bloodshot eyes and cane-lipped scented mouth
> Surprised in making folk-songs. . . .

So, in his still sometimes clumsy stride (for Toomer is finally a poet in prose) the author gives you an inkling of his revelation. An individual force, wise enough to drink humbly at this great spring of his land . . . such is the first impression of Jean Toomer. But beyond this wisdom and this power (which shows itself perhaps most splendidly in his complete freedom from the sense of persecution), there rises a figure more significant: the artist, hard, self-immolating, the artist who is not interested in races, whose domain is Life. The book's final Part is no longer "promise"; it is achievement. It is no mere dawn: it is a bit of the full morning. These materials . . . the ancient black man, mute, inaccessible, and yet so mystically close to the new tumultuous members of his race, the simple slave Past, the shredding Negro Present, the iridescent passionate dream of the To-morrow . . . are made and measured by a craftsman into an unforgettable music. The notes of his counterpoint are particular, the themes are of intimate connection with us Americans. But the result is that abstract and absolute thing called Art.

4.1   ⌒]   The curved lines reproduced here and on pages 45 and 92 have been taken from the first edition of *Cane* (1923). Toomer himself suggested they be added. "Between each of the three sections, a curve," he wrote Waldo Frank in a letter of December 12, 1922, having just sent a completed draft of the book. "These, to vaguely indicate the design." His letter begins:

> My brother!
> CANE is on its way to you!
> For two weeks I have worked steadily at it. The book is done. From three angles, CANE'S design is a circle. Aesthetically, from simple forms to complex ones, and back to simple forms. Regionally, from the South up into the North, and back into the South again. From the point of view of the spiritual entity behind the work, the curve really starts with Bona and Paul (awakening), plunges into Kabnis, emerges in Karintha etc. swings upward into Theatre and Box Seat, and ends (pauses) in Harvest Song.
> Whew!

11.29   hant]   Haunt, ghost.

15.20   mazda]   Electric light bulbs. (From "Mazda," a trademark used as a generic term.)

53.9   normal school]   Teachers' college.

59.34   Dictie]   African American slang: snobbish, high class.

64.6   eoho]   Toomer's rendition of a call or exclamation.

92.2   Waldo Frank]   See note 1.1.

103.21   Mame Lamkins]   See Walter White, "The Work of the Mob," *The Crisis*, September 1918, and Stephen Graham, *Children of the Slaves* (London: Macmillan, 1920) on the lynching of Mary Turner, Toomer's source for the story of Mame Lamkins.

HOME TO HARLEM

136.2   *Louise Bryant*]   Bryant (1885–1936), American-born author of *Six Red Months in Russia* (1918) and *Mirrors of Moscow* (1923), had helped McKay financially, enabling him to travel to the south of France after a bout of influenza in 1923–24, and worked with him to find a publisher for a collection of short stories, one of which was expanded as *Home to Harlem*.

140.30–31   Bal Musette]   A dance hall, usually featuring accordion music.

141.25–26   Limehouse]   A port district of London.

148.5   *maisons closes.*]   Brothels.

148.6   apaches]   Ruffians or thugs (from the "Apaches," a turn-of-the-century Parisian street gang).

150.4   dickty]   See note 59.34.

152.2   sweetmen]   Ladies' men or pimps, who lived off women's money.

168.31   f.o.c.]   Free of charge.

169.5–6   Thomas Nelson Page's . . . Cohen's porter]   Page (1853–1922) was the author, among other works, of *In Ole Virginia* (1887), a collection of plantation stories in negro dialect; Cohen (1891–1959) published over 200 magazine stories featuring the "porter-philosopher" Epic Peters, some of them later collected in *Epic Peters, Pullman Porter* (1930).

170.17–19   Jack Johnson . . . Madame Walker.]   Jack Johnson (1878–1946), the first African American heavyweight boxing world champion; James Reese Europe (1881–1919), bandleader and composer; Ada Overton Walker (1880–1914), vaudeville performer; Charles "Buddy" Gilmore (fl. c. 1905–1925), drummer for dancers Vernon Castle (1887–1918) and Irene Castle (1893–1969), who introduced the "Castle Walk" around 1912; Madam C. J. Walker (1867–1919), wealthy hair-care entrepreneur.

170.28   Bert Williams and Walker]   Egbert Williams (1874–1922) and George Walker (1873–1911) performed together as Williams & Walker, a vaudeville comedy duo.

173.7   'Tickling Blues']   Probably the "Tickling Blues" (1928) by Julia Johnson (fl. 1920s).

180.31   coon-can]   Conquian, an early form of the card game Rummy.

181.9   Virginia Dare]   A popular brand of sweet white wine produced by Garrett and Company, originally from North Carolina scuppernong grapes and ater flavored California grapes. During Prohibition the wine was de-alcoholized.

181.12   White Rock]   A brand of soda water.

184.15   jippi-jappa hat]   A panama hat, woven from palm straw.

200.13   Code Napoleon]   The French civil code introduced in 1804 under Napoleon Bonaparte.

202.4   those wonderful pagan verses]   The Biblical Song of Songs, sometimes interpreted as an account of a relationship between King Solomon and the Queen of Sheba.

203.21   Dr. Frank Crane.]   Crane (1861–1928), a Presbyterian minister, columnist, public speaker, and advocate of positive thinking, was the author of the ten-volume *Four Minute Essays* (1919) and *Everyday Wisdom* (1927).

211.21   *Et l'âme . . . l'air.*]   From the poem "L'Ideal" (1865) by Sully Prudhomme (1839–1907).

245.1   Henri Barbusse's *Le Feu*]   *Under Fire* (1916), novel based on the World War I experiences of Henri Barbusse (1873–1935).

250.27   p-i.]   Pimp.

263.13   A.B.S.]   Able seaman, a rank in the merchant marine.

285.17–19   Bert Williams . . . Cole and Johnson.]   For Bert Williams
and George Walker, see note 170.28; for Aida Overton Walker (as she was
sometimes billed), see note 170.17–19. Anita Patti Brown (c. 1882–1950) was a
noted soprano; Robert Allen Cole (1868–1911), along with John Rosamond
Johnson (1873–1954) and his brother James Weldon Johnson (1871–1939), wrote
and performed as "Cole and Johnson" and "Cole and the Johnson Brothers."

QUICKSAND

298.1   *E. S. I.*]   Elmer S. Imes (1883–1941), Larsen's husband until 1933.

299.1–5   *My old man* . . . HUGHES]   From Langston Hughes' poem
"Cross," first published in *The Crisis* in 1925 and collected in *The Weary Blues*
(1926).

302.13   Marmaduke Pickthall's *Saïd the Fisherman.*]   A popular picaresque
novel (1903) set in London and the Levant.

303.12–13   hewers of wood . . . water]   See Joshua 9:21.

342.22   Duncan Phyfe]   Phyfe (1768–1854) was a noted early American
furniture designer.

346.33–34   Pavlova . . . Robeson.]   Anna Pavlova (1881–1931), a Russian
prima ballerina; Florence Mills (1896–1927), an African American singer and
dancer who starred in *Shuffle Along* (1921) and other revues; John McCormack
(1884–1945), an Irish tenor; Taylor Gordon (1893–1971), African American
tenor and vaudeville performer; Walter Hampden (1879–1955), a white actor
and theater manager; Paul Robeson (1898–1976), celebrated actor and
bass-baritone.

347.5–6   Ibsen's remark]   Larsen borrows from *Books in General* (1919), by
the English critic Sir John Collings Squire (1884–1958), writing under the
pseudonym Solomon Eagle: "As Ibsen used so often to remark, there is a great
deal wrong with the drains; but after all there are other parts of the edifice."

349.35–36   the Garvey movement.]   Jamaican-born Marcus Garvey (1887–
1940) founded the Universal Negro Improvement Association in 1914, the
newspaper *The Negro World* in 1918, and the Black Star Line, a shipping company, in 1919. A stirring orator, he encouraged racial pride and a return to African roots; his organization acquired a large following and spread to many
countries. In 1925, he was convicted of mail fraud and in 1927 he was deported
to Jamaica.

372.11   "The far-off interest of tears."]   From Tennyson's *In Memoriam
A.H.H.* (1850), canto 1.

377.19–20   Danish melodies of Gade and Heise.]   Niels Wilhelm Gade
(1817–1890) and Peter Heise (1830–1879).

377.21   Nielsen's 'Helios']   The *Helios Overture* (1903), a short orchestral work by Danish composer Carl August Nielsen (1865–1931).

379.28–29   "Everybody Gives Me Good Advice."]   A 1906 "comic coon song" with words by Alfred Bryan (1871–1958) and music by James Kendis (1883–1946) and Herman Paley (1879–1955).

381.29   Kongens Nytorv]   Kongens Nytorv (Danish: King's New Square), a central square in Copenhagen often used for exhibitions.

406.35–36   *Showers of . . . blessings*]   See Ezekiel 34:26 for the source of this text, on which several hymns have been based.

427.35–428.13   Anatole France . . . call him to mind."]   See "The Procurator of Judea," a story about early Christians, in *Mother of Pearl* (1908), by Anatole France (1844–1924).

431.13   Houbigant]   French perfume manufacturer, founded in 1775.

PLUM BUN

433.4–7   *"To Market . . . is done."*]   Traditional English nursery rhyme.

445.34   "bad hair"]   Hard-to-straighten, closely curled hair.

455.35   Lycidas]   Elegy by John Milton (1608–1674), first published in 1638.

463.20   and siller hae]   And silver have: see "The Siller Croun" (c. 1788) by Susanna Blamire (1747–1794), the "muse of Cumberland"; the poem was later set to music (c. 1800) by Joseph Haydn (1732–1809).

548.4–15   two poems . . . again.']   See John S. Hart's *Class Book of Poetry, Consisting of Selections from Distinguished English and American Poets*, first published in 1845. The first poem is from "I'll Never Love Thee More," an English song often attributed to and perhaps adapted by James Graham, 1st Marquess of Montrose (1612–1650); the second is from Oliver Goldsmith's 1762 revision, in an anthology titled *The Art of Poetry on a New Plan*, of Samuel Butler's *Hudibras* (1663–78).

569.1–5   a verse from a poet . . . fool!"]   See "The Suppliant," from the book *Bronze* (1922), by Georgia Douglas Johnson (c. 1880–1966).

571.18–19   Raquel Meller]   Meller (1888–1962), a Spanish singer and actress, performed in New York to considerable acclaim beginning in 1926.

576.37–39   "It is not courage . . . great,—"]   See "To Lucasta on Going to the War—for the Fourth Time," from *Fairies and Fusiliers* (1918), by Robert Graves (1895–1985), as misquoted in the opening editorial of *The Crisis*, March 1919.

648.3   Tony Hardcastle]   Tony Lumpkin, son of Mrs. Hardcastle in the play *She Stoops to Conquer* (1773), by Oliver Goldsmith (1728–1774).

648.25 the Duse] Eleonora Duse (1858–1924), Italian actress.

655.5–14 "Not going . . . because she's coloured?"] Fauset's account of Rachel Powell's career closely parallels the story of Augusta Savage (1892–1962), an African American sculpture student and a recent graduate of Cooper Union who, in a widely publicized incident in 1923, was denied the scholarship she had won to the Fontainebleau School of Fine Arts because of her race.

656.18 "Who killed Dr. Cronlin?"] See *Who Killed Dr. Cronin; or, At Work on the Great Chicago Mystery* (1889), by Old Cap Lee, number 341 in the New York Detective Library series, published in Chicago by Frank Tousey. "Old Cap Lee" was a house name used for many of the firm's detective and mystery stories.

THE BLACKER THE BERRY

688.1 *To Ma Jack*] Emma Ellen Jackson (1862–c. 1940), Thurman's maternal grandmother, with whom he lived for considerable periods during his childhood and adolescence.

689.4–5 My color . . . *Cullen*] See the opening lines of "The Shroud of Color" (1924), a poem by Countee Cullen (1903–1946).

698.27 Simon Legree] A cruel plantation master in the novel *Uncle Tom's Cabin* (1852), by Harriet Beecher Stowe (1811–1896).

730.40–731.1 that line in Cullen's . . . abreast with me?"] See "To You Who Read My Book," the opening poem in Countee Cullen's *Color* (1925).

737.21–22 'Flesh and the Devil'] Film (1926) directed by Clarence Brown, starring Greta Garbo, John Gilbert, and Lars Hanson.

740.23–24 San Juan Hill district.] A mainly African American neighborhood on Manhattan's West Side that has been described as a "proto-Harlem"; it was largely razed during the 1960s.

746.6–7 "hot" men, of "sweetbacks,"] "'Hot men' sell 'hot stuff,'" Thurman wrote in his 1927 essay "Negro Life in New York's Harlem"; "which when translated from Harlemese into English, means merchandise supposedly obtained illegally and sold on the q.t. far below par." A sweetback, as he defined the term in his 1929 glossary "Harlemese," is "a colored gigolo, or man who lived off women." See also note 152.2.

765.39–40 that Harlem . . . Survey Graphic] The March 1925 issue of *Survey Graphic*—published in book form as *The New Negro* (1925)—focused on "Harlem: Mecca of the New Negro." It included "Enter the New Negro," by Alain Locke, "The Making of Harlem," by James Weldon Johnson, "The South Lingers On," by Rudolph Fisher, and "The Black Man Brings His Gifts," by W.E.B. Du Bois, among other items.

766.20   'Long Pants']   1927 film directed by Frank Capra and starring comedian Harry Langdon.

771.7   "Blue Skies,"]   Popular 1926 song by Irving Berlin (1888–1989).

778.27   Bud Fisher]   The physician and novelist Rudolph Fisher (1897–1934), nicknamed "Bud."

799.35–36   "Ireland must be . . . there."]   Popular 1916 song with lyrics by Joseph McCarthy (1885–1943) and Howard Johnson (1887–1941), and music by Fred Fisher (1875–1942).

800.17–20   A yellow gal rides . . . my Lord.]   Thurman's version of a blues set piece. A similar lyric by Henry Thomas (1874–c. 1950) was recorded in 1929 as "Charmin' Betsy."

807.29   "Nigger Heaven" . . . Van Vechten]   Controversial roman à clef (1926) by white novelist Carl Van Vechten (1880–1964).

THE LIBRARY OF AMERICA SERIES

The Library of America fosters appreciation and pride in America's literary heritage by publishing, and keeping permanently in print, authoritative editions of America's best and most significant writing. An independent nonprofit organization, it was founded in 1979 with seed funding from the National Endowment for the Humanities and the Ford Foundation.

To subscribe to the series or to order individual copies, please visit www.loa.org or call (800) 964.5778.

This book is set in 10 point Linotron Galliard,
a face designed for photocomposition by Matthew Carter
and based on the sixteenth-century face Granjon. The paper
is acid-free lightweight opaque and meets the requirements
for permanence of the American National Standards Institute.
The binding material is Brillianta, a woven rayon cloth made
by Van Heek-Scholco Textielfabrieken, Holland. Compo-
sition by Dedicated Book Services. Printing by
Malloy Incorporated. Binding by Dekker Book-
binding. Designed by Bruce Campbell.